The Mammoth Book of

Literary Anecdotes

D0166605

The Mammoth Book of
Literary Anecdotes

EDITED BY PHILIP GOODEN

CARROLL & GRAF PUBLISHERS
New York

Carroll & Graf Publishers
An imprint of Avalon Publishing Group, Inc.
161 William Street
16th Floor
NY 10038-2607
www.carrollandgraf.com

First published in the UK by Robinson,
an imprint of Constable & Robinson Ltd, 2002

First Carroll & Graf edition 2002

ISBN 0–7867–1003–9

Printed and bound in the EU

Contents

Acknowledgments   vii
Introduction   ix

Abroad   1
Addiction   17
Animals   32
Boredom & Despair   45
Crime, Punishment & Mystery   59
Day Jobs   95
Death   103
Disciples & Fans   131
Forgeries & Frauds   140
Friendships & First Meetings   156
Illness & Disability   193
Inspiration   213
Jealousy, Rivalry & Malice   232
Kings, Queens & Presidents   241
Last Words   257
Law   261
Love, Sex & Marriage   272
Manuscripts   307
Mistakes   322
Money   330
Obsessions & Eccentricities   339
Parents & Children   354
Pastoral   368
Publishers, Patrons & Booksellers   374
Reading & Readers   381
Rejection   395
Religion   402

Reputation   411
School & University   430
Shakespeariana   435
Theatre & Film   452
Wars & Fights   461
Writing   477

Index of Writers   487

Acknowledgments

The editor and publishers are grateful to the following for permission to reproduce copyright material:

Peter Owen Ltd for an excerpt from *Agatha Christie and the Eleven Missing Days* by Jared Cade; Scott Ferris Associates for an excerpt from *Henry Miller: A Life* by Robert Fergusson; Weidenfeld & Nicolson and David Higham Associates for an excerpt from *Rebecca West: A Life* by Victoria Glendinning; Macmillan, London, UK for an excerpt from *Foreign Correspondent* by Peter Lennon; David Higham Associates for an excerpt from *The Infernal Grove* by Malcolm Muggeridge; Justin Wintle and Gillon Aitken Associates for an excerpt from *Furious Interiors: Wales, R.S.Thomas and God* by Justin Wintle.

All efforts have been made to contact the respective copyright holders. In some rare cases, it has not proven possible to ascertain the whereabouts of authors, agents or estates. They are welcome to write c/o the publishers if I have inadvertently made use of a story they control rights in.

Where no origin has been given for an anecdote, in most cases the story has been compiled, often from several sources, and retold by the editor.

Introduction

"Who would write, who had anything better to do?" said the poet George Gordon Byron. The stories about Lord Byron, and there are plenty of them, show that he did many other things apart from write. In his packed, hectic 36 years of life, Byron had time to scandalize London, seduce countless women, make extensive tours of the Continent and – in his final year – prepare to participate in the Greek War of Independence.

The lives of few writers even begin to approach Byron's for drama, yet a surprising number of them have got up to some surprising things when away from their desks, pens and typewriters. This is perhaps more true of earlier periods than the present. In the past, certainly into the nineteenth century, there was a much stronger feeling that writing was a by-product of other activities or at least that it didn't preclude them. A playwright might become a member of parliament (Richard Sheridan); a member of Charles II's court could dash down obscene verses (the Earl of Rochester); a great Victorian novelist took time out to invent the pillar box (Anthony Trollope). Now the writer is expected to be a professional, to earn a living, almost to keep office hours. Or perhaps, in an age when the state of an author's teeth can make the headlines, it's simply that they're duller than their predecessors.

This anthology of literary anecdotes is a selection of some of the oddest or most exciting or revealing incidents in writers' lives. Among over 350 entries you will find the story behind Agatha Christie's eleven-day disappearance as well as a real-life mystery solved by Arthur Conan Doyle; the first meeting of James Boswell and Doctor Johnson; the very different first meeting of Anais Nin and *Tropic of Cancer* author Henry Miller, and the bizarre encounter between W.E. Johns, the

man who created Biggles, and Lawrence of Arabia. Also included here is the story of how Elizabethan playwright Ben
Jonson escaped the gallows after killing a man in a duel – and
how Mark Twain tricked his way out of fighting a duel at all.
And so on . . .

The anecdotes are arranged by subject matter (from **Abroad**
to **Writing**) and the order inside each section is chronological.
Some names crop up much more than others. Byron is an
obvious example, as are Oscar Wilde and Mark Twain. Some
writers simply seem to generate material – they do things, or
things happen to them, more than with most people. A biographical portrait builds up across several anecdotes. We get a
kind of cumulative impression of the brilliantly shambolic poet
Samuel Taylor Coleridge; of the toughness of novelist Fanny
Burney; the comic eccentricities of poet and paper-boat-sailor
Percy Bysshe Shelley; the elusive behaviour of Graham Greene;
the grouchy stance of thriller writer Raymond Chandler.

This isn't really a reference book. Details like dates of birth
are accurate (an index of the principal authors appears at the
end of the anthology) and there is ample evidence for many of
the encounters and events recorded in these pages. But there are
also some stories which stretch belief. Even for those stories
which are more or less accurate, it's likely that a bit of embel-
lishment or polish has been applied. What Mark Twain says at
the end of one of his anecdotes – "Now, then, that is the tale.
Some of it is true." – could apply to most of the pieces here. So,
the criterion for selecting these anecdotes hasn't been their
reliability but whether they make entertaining tales or scenes or
whether they throw a bit of light on some literary figure.
Whether, in short, they provide a good read.

Philip Gooden

Abroad

Thomas Coryate was one of the earliest travel writers. In 1608 he began his explorations (of Europe) on foot and produced a narrative account called Coryats Crudities. *Later on he travelled to Asia and, as recounted in the following anecdote, died in Surat, India.*

In Surat being over-kindly used by some of the English, who gave him Sack★, which they had brought from England, he calling for, as soon as he first heard of it, and crying, *Sack, Sack, is there such a thing as Sack?* I pray give me some Sack, and drinking of it moderately, (for he was very temperate), it increased his flux which he had then upon him: and this caused him within a few days after his very tedious and troublesome travels, (for he went most on foot), at that place to come to his journey's end . . . For if one should go to the extremest part of the world East, another West, another North, and another South, they must all meet at last together in the Field of Bones, wherein our traveller hath now taken up his lodging.

(Anthony A. Wood, *Athenae Oxonienses*)

The 18th century poet Thomas Gray was invited to go on a European Grand Tour by the writer Horace Walpole. As they were crossing the Alps by carriage on the way to Geneva, disaster almost struck.

The sixth [day] we began to go up several of these mountains; and, as we were passing one, met with an odd accident enough. Mr Walpole had a little fat black spaniel, that he was very fond

★ Sack – a white wine from Spain

of, which he sometimes used to set down, and let it run by the chaise side. We were at that time in a very rough road, not two yards broad at most; on one side was a great wood of pines, and on the other a vast precipice; it was noon-day, and the sun shone bright, when all of a sudden, from the wood-side (which was as steep upwards, as the other part was downwards) out rushed a great wolf, came close to the head of the horses, seized the dog by the throat, and rushed up the hill again with him in his mouth. This was done in less than a quarter of a minute; we all saw it, and yet the servants had not time to draw their pistols, or do anything to save the dog. If he had not been there, and the creature had thought fit to lay hold of one of the horses, chaise, and we, and all must have inevitably tumbled above fifty fathom perpendicular down the precipice.

(Thomas Gray, *letter to his mother, November, 1739*)

Michael Kelly was an 18th-century singer and composer, a friend to playwright Richard Brinsley Sheridan and other literary figures of the day. As this excerpt from his memoirs shows, he was also a skilful, funny story-teller. Finding himself almost without money in Venice, Kelly remembered that he had been given a letter of introduction to a Signor Andrioli. Hungry and down to his last two coins, Kelly went in search of this gentleman, hoping for some relief to his troubles.

In the morning, I went to the Rialto coffee-house, to which I was directed by the address of the letter. Here I found the gentleman who was the object of my search; after reading my credentials very graciously, he smiled, and requested me to take a turn with him in the Piazza St Marc. He was a fine looking man, of about sixty years old. I remarked there was an aristo-cratic manner about him, and he wore a very large tie-wig, well powdered, with an immensely long tail. He addressed me with a benevolent and patronizing air, and told me that he should be delighted to be of service to me, and bade me from that moment consider myself under his protection. "A little business," said he, "calls me away at this moment, but if you will meet me here at two o'clock we will adjourn to my Casino [house], where, if you can dine on one dish, you will perhaps do me the favour to partake of a boiled capon and rice. I can only offer you that; perhaps a rice soup, for which my cook is famous; and, it may be, just one or two little things not worth mentioning."

A boiled capon – rice soup – other little things, thought I – manna in the wilderness! I strolled about, not to get an appetite, for that was ready, but to kill time. My excellent, hospitable, long-tailed friend was punctual to the moment; I joined him, and proceeded towards his residence.

As we were bending our steps thither, we happened to pass a Luganigera's (a ham-shop), where there was some ham ready dressed in the window. My powdered patron paused – it was an awful pause; he reconnoitred, examined, and at last said, "Do you know, Signor, I was thinking that some of that ham would eat deliciously with our capon: – I am known in this neighbourhood, and it would not do for *me* to be seen buying ham – but do you go in, my child, and get two or three pounds of it, and I will walk on, and wait for you."

I went in of course, and purchased three pounds of the ham, to pay for which, I was obliged to change one of my two zecchinos. I carefully folded up the precious viand, and rejoined my excellent patron, who eyed the relishing slices with the air of a gourmand; indeed, he was somewhat diffuse in his own dispraise for not having recollected to order his servant to get some before he left home. During this peripatetic lecture on gastronomy, we happened to pass a cantina – in plain English – a wine cellar. At the door he made another full stop.

"In that house," said he, "they sell the best Cyprus wine in Venice – peculiar wine – a sort of wine not to be had any where else; I should like you to taste it; but I do not like to be seen buying wine by retail to carry home; – go in yourself, buy a couple of flasks, and bring them to *my Casino*; nobody hereabouts knows you, and it won't signify in the least."

This last request was quite appalling; my pocket groaned to its very centre: however, recollecting that I was in the high road to preferment and that a patron, cost what he might, was still a patron, I made the plunge, and, issuing from the cantina, set forward for my venerable friend's Casino, with three pounds of ham in my pocket and a flask of wine under each arm, *sans six sous et sans souci!*

I continued walking with my excellent and long-tailed patron, expecting every moment to see an elegant, agreeable
residence, smiling in all the beauties of nature and art; when,
at last, in a dirty miserable lane, at the door of a tall dingy-
looking house, my Maecenas [patron] stopped, indicated that
we had reached our journey's end, and, marshalling me the way
that I should go, began to mount three flights of sickening
stairs, at the top of which I found his Casino – it was a little Cas,
and a deuce of a place to boot – in plain English, it was a garret.
The door was opened by a wretched old miscreant, who acted as
cook, and whose drapery, to use a gastronomic simile, was 'done
to rags'.

Upon a rickety apology for a table was placed a tattered
cloth, which once had been white, and two plates; and presently
in came a large bowl of boiled rice.

"Where's the capon?" said my patron to his man.

"Capon!" echoed the ghost of a servant – "The – "

"Has not the rascal sent it?" cried the master.

"Rascal!" repeated the man, apparently terrified.

"I knew he would not," exclaimed my patron, with an air of
exultation for which I saw no cause. "Well, well, never mind,
put down the ham and the wine; with those and the rice, I dare
say, young gentleman, you will be able to make it out. I ought to
apologize – but in fact it is all your own fault that there is not
more; if I had fallen in with you earlier, we should have had a
better dinner."

I confess I was surprised, disappointed, and amused; but, as
matters stood, there was no use in complaining, and accordingly
we fell to, neither of us wanting the best of all sauces – appetite.

I soon perceived that my promised patron had baited his trap
with a fowl to catch a fool; but as we ate and drank, all care
vanished, and, rogue as I suspected him to be, my long-tailed
friend was a clever witty fellow, and, besides telling me a
number of anecdotes, gave me some very good advice; amongst
other things to be avoided, he cautioned me against numbers of
people who, in Venice, lived only by duping the unwary. I
thought this counsel came very ill from him. "Above all," said
he, "keep up your spirits, and recollect the Venetian proverb,
Cento anni di malinconia non pagheranno un soldo dei debiti." –

"A hundred years of melancholy will not pay one farthing of debt."

After we had regaled ourselves upon my ham and wine, we separated; he desired me to meet him the following morning at the coffee-house, and told me he would give me a ticket for the private theatre of Count Pepoli, where I should see a comedy admirably acted by amateurs; and in justice to my long-tailed friend, I must say, he was punctual, and gave me the ticket, which, however, differed from a boiled capon in one respect — he got it gratis.

(Michael Kelly, *Reminiscences*)

Going abroad has always offered a good chance to get free of a moralistic atmosphere at home. In the 18th century any well-born young man on a European Grand Tour was more likely to be looking for some easy sex than looking at the cultural sights which were the pretext for going abroad in the first place. James Boswell, later famous as the friend and biographer of Dr Samuel Johnson, certainly fell into this category. (It's been calculated that he contracted nineteen separate venereal infections between the ages of 19 and 50.) Here he shows a typically no-nonsense attitude during a stay in Berlin in 1764.

I was quite drunk with brisk spirits, and about eight, in came a woman with a basket of chocolate to sell. I toyed with her and found she was with child. Oho! a safe piece. Into my closet. "Habs er ein Man?" "Ja, in den Gards bei Potsdam." ["You have a husband?" "Yes, in the Guards in Potsdam."] To bed directly. In a minute — over. I rose cool and astonished, half angry, half laughing. I sent her off.

(James Boswell, quoted in Ian Littlewood's *Sultry Climates*)

*Poet John Keats died in Rome, where he had travelled in a desperate attempt to delay the spread of the tuberculosis which finally killed him in February 1821 (see also **Death**). However he was robust enough in the early days to deal with some inferior foreign food, as reported in this story by his friend Joseph Severn.*

In our first Roman days we got very odd and bad dinners sent in, as the Roman custom is, from a Trattoria, or restaurant. This was the more intolerable as we paid a crown for each meal, and as each, for all their cunning disguises in sauces and spices, was more unpalatable than the other. We put up with this annoyance for more than a week, although we made daily complaints to the *padrona di casa*, but one day we both pronounced the dinner to be unfit to eat. Keats hit on an expedient by which we always got good dinners afterwards. He would not tell me what it was to be. When the porter came as usual with the basket, and was beginning to set out the dinner, Keats stepped forward, and smiling roguishly at me, with a, "Now, Severn, you'll see it," he opened the window, which was over the front steps, and taking up each dish one after the other he quietly emptied the contents out of the window and returned the plate to the basket – and thus disappeared a fowl, a rice pudding, cauliflower, a dish of macaroni, &c. This was all done to the amusement of the porter and the padrona. He then quietly but very decidedly pointed to the basket for the porter to take away, which he did without demur. "Now," said Keats, "you'll see, Severn, that we'll have a decent dinner." And sure enough in less than half an hour an excellent one came, and we continued to be similarly well treated every day. In the account, moreover, the padrona was discreet enough not to charge for the dinners thrown out of the window.

(Joseph Severn, *Recollections*)

William Makepeace Thackeray, author of Vanity Fair, *went on a lecture tour to America in 1852. He was welcomed by the poet and book-shop owner James T. Fields.*

Thackeray announced to me by letter in the early autumn of 1852 that he had determined to visit America, and would sail for Boston by the *Canada* on the 30th of October. All the necessary arrangements for his lecturing tour had been made without troubling him with any of the details. He arrived on a frosty November evening, and went directly to the Tremont House, where rooms had been engaged for him. I remember his delight in getting off the sea, and the enthusiasm with which he hailed the announcement that dinner would be ready shortly. A few friends were ready to sit down with him, and he seemed greatly to enjoy the novelty of an American repast. In London he had been very curious in his inquiries about American oysters, as marvellous stories, which he did not believe, had been told him of their great size. We apologized – although we had taken care that the largest specimens to be procured should startle his unwonted vision when he came to the table – for what we called the extreme *smallness* of the oysters, promising that we would do better next time. Six bloated Falstaffian bivalves lay before him in their shells. I noticed that he gazed at them anxiously with fork upraised; then he whispered to me, with a look of anguish, "How shall I do it?" I described to him the simple process by which the free-born citizens of America were accustomed to accomplish such a task. He seemed satisfied that the thing was feasible, selected the smallest one in the half-dozen (rejecting a large one, "because," he said, "it resembled the High Priest's servant's ear that Peter cut off"); and then bowed his head as if he were saying grace. All eyes were upon him to watch the effect of a new sensation in the person of a great British author. Opening his mouth very wide, he struggled for a moment, and then all was over. I shall never forget the comic look of despair he cast upon the other five over-occupied shells. I broke the perfect stillness by asking him how he felt. "Profoundly grateful," he gasped, "and as if I had swallowed a little baby."

(James T. Fields, *Yesterdays With Authors*)

On another of Thackeray's American visits, James T. Fields regretted taking Thackeray along to hear a boring scientific lecture.

During his second visit to Boston I was asked to invite him to attend an evening meeting of a scientific club, which was to be held at the house of a distinguished member. I was very reluctant to ask him to be present, for I knew he could be easily bored, and I was fearful that a prosy essay or geological speech might ensue, and I knew he would be exasperated with me, even although I were the innocent cause of his affliction.

My worst fears were realized. We had hardly got seated, before a dull, bilious-looking old gentleman rose, and applied his auger with such pertinacity that we were all bored nearly to distraction. I dared not look at Thackeray, but I felt that his eye was upon me. My distress may be imagined, when he got up quite deliberately from the prominent place where a chair had been set for him, and made his exit very noiselessly into a small anteroom leading into the larger room, and in which no one was sitting. The small apartment was dimly lighted, but he knew that I knew he was there. Then commenced a series of pantomimic feats impossible to describe adequately. He threw an imaginary person (myself, of course) upon the floor, and proceeded to stab him several times with a paper-folder, which he caught up for the purpose. After disposing of his victim in this way, he was not satisfied, for the dull lecture still went on in the other room, and he fired an imaginary revolver several times at an imaginary head. Still, the droning speaker proceeded with his frozen subject (it was something about the Arctic regions, if I remember rightly), and now began the greatest pantomimic scene of all, namely, murder by poison, after the manner in which the player king is disposed of in *Hamlet*. Thackeray had found a small vial on the mantel-shelf, and out of that he proceeded to pour the imaginary "juice of cursed hebenon" into the imaginary porches of somebody's ears. The whole thing was inimitably done, and I hoped nobody saw it but myself; but years afterwards, a ponderous, fat-witted young man put the question squarely to me: "What was the matter with Mr Thackeray, that night the club met at Mr —'s house?"

(James T. Fields, *Yesterdays With Authors*)

When he was on his home ground in London Thackeray could be a mischievous guide to foreign visitors.

Some years ago a famous and witty French critic was in London with whom I walked the streets. I am ashamed to say that I informed him (being in hopes that he was about to write some papers regarding the manners and customs of this country) that all the statues he saw represented the Duke of Wellington. That on the arch opposite Apsley House? The Duke in a cloak, and a cock-hat on horseback. That behind Apsley House in an airy fig-leaf of costume? The Duke again. That in Cockspur Street? The Duke with a pig-tail – and so on. I showed him an army of Dukes.

(W. M. Thackeray, *Roundabout Papers*)

Victorian novelist Anthony Trollope describes in his autobiography meeting Brigham Young, the leader of the Mormons, in Salt Lake City, Utah.

I came home across America from San Francisco to New York, visiting Utah and Brigham Young on the way. I did not achieve great intimacy with the great polygamist of the Salt Lake City. I called upon him, sending to him my card, apologizing for doing so without an introduction, and excusing myself by saying that I did not like to pass through the territory without seeing a man of whom I had heard so much. He received me in his doorway, not asking me to enter and inquired whether I were not a miner. When I told him that I was not a miner, he asked me whether I earned my bread. I told him I did. "I guess you're a miner," said he. I again assured him that I was not. "Then how do you earn your bread?" I told him that I did so by writing books. "I'm sure you're a miner," said he. Then he turned upon his heel, went back into the house, and closed the door. I was properly punished, as I was vain enough to conceive that he would have heard my name.

(Anthony Trollope, *An Autobiography*)

Oscar Wilde made a lecture tour of America when he was still in his twenties. The aesthete ended up in some surprising places – like Leadville in Colorado.

I was told that if I went there they would be sure to shoot me or my travelling manager. I wrote and told them that nothing they could do to my travelling manager would intimidate me. They are miners – men working in metals, so I lectured them on the Ethics of Art. I read them passages from the Autobiography of

Benvenuto Cellini, and they seemed most delighted. I was reproved by my hearers for not having brought him with me. I explained that he had been dead for some little time, which elicited the enquiry, "Who shot him?" They afterwards took me to a dancing saloon where I saw the only rational method of art criticism I have ever come across. Over the piano was printed a notice:

PLEASE DO NOT SHOOT THE PIANIST
HE IS DOING HIS BEST

The mortality among pianists in that place is marvellous. Then they asked me to supper, and having accepted, I had to descend a mine in a rickety bucket in which it was impossible to be graceful. Having got into the heart of the mountain I had supper, the first course being whisky, the second whisky and the third whisky. I went to the theatre to lecture and I was informed that just before I went there two men had been seized for committing a murder, and in that theatre they had been brought onto the stage at eight o'clock in the evening, and then and there tried and executed before a crowded audience.

But I found these miners very charming and not at all rough.

(Oscar Wilde, *Impressions of America*)

The idea of "Abroad" works both ways. Novelist Joseph Conrad was born Teodor Josef Konrad Korzeniowski in Poland in 1857. His early life was dominated by the desire to go to sea, and his maritime experiences formed the basis of many of his novels. Conrad had a highly romantic notion of England long before he reached the country, before he'd even heard any words of English spoken to him. In 1874 he was in Marseilles and it was from a Pilot boat off the coast of the French port that Conrad had his first encounter with a ship which hailed from what would become his adopted land.

Something not foreseen by me did happen, something which causes me to remember my last outing with the pilots. It was on this occasion that my hand touched, for the first time, the side of an English ship.

No fresh breeze had come with the dawn, only the steady little draught got a more keen edge on it as the eastern sky became bright and glassy with a clean, colourless light. It was while we were all ashore on the islet that a steamer was picked up by the telescope, a black speck like an insect posed on the hard edge of the offing. She emerged rapidly to her water-line and came on steadily, a slim hull with a long streak of smoke slanting away from the rising sun. We embarked in a hurry, and headed the boat out for our prey, but we hardly moved three miles an hour.

She was a big, high-class cargo-steamer of a type that is to be met on the sea no more, black hull, with low, white super-structures, powerfully rigged with three masts and a lot of yards on the fore; two hands at her enormous wheel – steam steering gear was not a matter of course in these days – and with them on the bridge three others, bulky in thick blue jackets, ruddy-faced, muffled up with peaked caps – I suppose all her officers. There are ships I have met more than once and known well by sight whose names I have forgotten; but the name of that ship seen once so many years ago in the clear flush of a cold pale sunrise I have not forgotten. How could I – the first English ship on whose side I ever laid my hand! The name – I read it letter by letter on the bow – was *James Westoll*. Not very romantic you will say. The name of a very considerable, well-known and universally respected North-country ship-owner, I believe. *James Westoll*! What better name could an honourable hard-working ship have ? To me the very grouping of the letters is alive with the romantic feeling of her reality as I saw her floating motionless, and borrowing an ideal grace from the austere purity of the light.

We were then very near her, and, on a sudden impulse, I volunteered to pull bow in the dinghy which shoved off at once to put the pilot on board while our boat, fanned by the faint air which had attended us all through the night, went on gliding gently past the black glistening length of the ship. A few strokes brought us alongside, and it was then that, for the very first time in my life, I heard myself addressed in English – the speech of my secret choice, of my future, of long friendships, of the deepest affections, of hours of toil and hours of ease, and of solitary hours too, of books read, of thoughts pursued, of remembered emotions – of my very dreams! And if (after being thus fashioned by it in that part of me which cannot decay) I dare not claim it aloud as my own, then, at any rate the speech of my children. Thus small events grow memorable by the passage of time. As to the quality of the address itself I cannot say it was very striking. Too short for eloquence and devoid of all charm of tone, it consisted precisely of the three words, "Look out there," growled out huskily above my head.

It proceeded from a big fat fellow – he had an obtrusive, hairy double chin – in a blue woollen shirt and roomy breeches pulled up very high, even to the level of his breast-bone, by a pair of braces quite exposed to public view. As where he stood there was no bulwark but only a rail and stanchions, I was able to take in at a glance the whole of his voluminous person from his feet to the high crown of his soft black hat, which sat like an absurd flanged cone on his big head. The grotesque and massive aspect of that deck hand (I suppose he was that – very likely the lamp-trimmer) surprised me very much. My course of reading, of dreaming and longing for the sea had not prepared me for a sea-brother of that sort . . .

The object of his concise address was to call my attention to a rope which he incontinently flung down for me to catch. I caught it, though it was not really necessary, the ship having no way on her by that time. Then everything went on very swiftly. The dinghy came with a slight bump against the steamer's side, the pilot, grabbing the rope ladder, had scrambled halfway up before I knew that our task of boarding was done; the harsh, muffled clanging of the engine-room telegraph struck my ear through the iron plate; my companion in the dinghy was urging me to "shove off – push hard"; and when I bore against the smooth flank of the first English ship I ever touched in my life, I felt it already throbbing under my open palm.

Her head swung a little to the west, pointing towards the miniature lighthouse of the Jolliette breakwater, far away there, hardly distinguishable against the land. The dinghy danced a squashy, splashy jig in the wash of the wake and turning in my seat I followed the *James Westoll*, with my eyes. Before she had gone in a quarter of a mile she hoisted her flag as the harbour regulations prescribe for arriving and departing ships. I saw it suddenly flicker and stream out on the flagstaff.

The Red Ensign! In the pellucid, colourless atmosphere bathing the drab and grey masses of that southern land, the livid islets, the sea of pale glassy blue under the pale glassy sky of that cold sunrise, it was as far as the eye could reach the only spot of ardent colour – flame-like, intense, and presently as minute as the tiny red spark the concentrated reflection of a great fire kindles in the clear heart of a globe of crystal. The Red Ensign – the symbolic, protecting warm bit of bunting flung wide upon the seas, and destined for so many years to be the only roof over my head.

(Joseph Conrad, *A Personal Record*)

Frederick Rolfe was a highly eccentric writer whose best-known work is Hadrian the Seventh *(1904), the wish-fulfilment story of an obscure Englishman who is elected Pope. Five years before his death in 1913 Rolfe moved to Venice where he lived in poverty. From there he wrote a series of letters to Charles Masson Fox, an English Quaker, who seems to have shared Rolfe's homosexual interests. In part, they are begging letters – "For God's sake send me five pounds," concludes the final letter – but they are also a record of Rolfe's (fantasy?) activities in Venice, where beautful young men were available for very little – or for nothing. Here Rolfe describes meeting "Amadeo Amadei" at the Venetian quayside.*

It was getting dusk and I was just in time to see his lissome muscular figure come dancing down the long plank from the ship with his last sack of dried lily-flowers silhouetted against the sunset. As he passed, I said, "Do me the pleasure to come and drink a little beaker of wine." "With the greatest possible respect to your valorous face," he answered, passing on. When he had delivered his load in the warehouse, he came out and joined me. While he was working he had on a pair of thin flannel trousers tightly tucked into his socks, canvas slippers, and a thin sleeveless shirt open from neck to navel. Over this, his day's work done, he wore a voluminous cloak of some thick dark stuff and a broad-brimmed hat. He flung one end of the cloak over his shoulder like a toga. I describe his attire thus particularly, for reasons which will appear later on. "Take me," I said, "to a quiet wine shop where we can have much private conversation." We went through a few back alleys to a little quay in a blind canal off the Rio Malcontent where there was a very decent wineshop kept by an apparent somnambulist. I called for a litre of New Red (very fresh and heady) at 6d. We sat at the back of the shop among the barrels, our two chairs being together on one side of the only table there. The counter with its sleepy proprietor was between us and the door; and no one else was present . . .

He assured me that he knew incredible tricks for amusing his patrons. "First, Sior, see my person," he said. And the vivacious creature did all which follows in about 30 seconds of time. Not more. I have said that we were sitting side by side at the little table. Moving, every inch of him, as swiftly and smoothly as a cat, he stood up, casting a quick glance into the shop to make sure that no one noticed. Only the sleepy proprietor slept there. He rolled his coat into a pillow and put it on my end of the table, ripped open his trousers, stripped them down to his feet, and sat barebottomed on the other end. He turned his shirt right up over his head, holding it in one hand, opened his arms wide and lay back along the little table with his shoulders on the pillow (so that his breast and belly and thighs formed one slightly slanting line unbroken by the arch of the ribs, as is the case with flat distention) and his beautiful throat and his rosy laughing face strained backwards while his widely open arms were an invitation. He was just one brilliant rosy series of muscles, smooth as satin, breasts and belly and groin and closely folded thighs with (in the midst of the black blossom of exuberant robustitude) a yard like a rose-tipped lance. And – the fragrance of his healthy youth and of the lily-flowers' dust was intoxicating. He crossed his ankles, ground his thighs together with a gently rippling motion, writhed his groin and hips once or twice and stiffened into the most inviting mass of fresh meat conceivable, laughing in my face as he made his offering of lively flesh. And the next instant he was up, his trousers buttoned, his shirt tucked in and his cloak folded around him. The litre of wine was gone. I called for another. "Sior," he said, "half a litre this time, with permission." So we made it half. Would I not like to take him to [a brothel at]

Padova from Saturday till Monday? Indeed I would. Nothing better. But because I see that you, my Amadeo (i.e., Love God, quite a Puritan name) are a most discreet youth as well as a very capable one, I shall tell you my secret; for, in fact, you shall know that I am no longer a rich English but a poor, having being ruined by certain traitors and obliged to deny myself luxuries. To hear that gave him affliction and much dolour. But he wished to say that he was all and entirely at my disposal simply for affection; because, feeling sure that he had the ability to provide me with an infinity of diversions, each different and far more exciting than its predecessor, he asked me as a favour, as a very great favour, that I should afterwards recommend him to nobles who were my friends.

(Frederick Corvo, letter, November, 1909)

Novelist Arnold Bennett was struck by one of the sights on a visit to New York.

At the centre of the first cross-roads, I saw a splendid and erect individual, flashing forth authority, gaiety, and utter smartness in the gloom. Impossible not to believe that he was the owner of all the adjacent ground, disguised as a cavalry officer on foot.

"What is that archduke?" I inquired.

"He's just a cop."

I knew then that I was in a great city.

(Arnold Bennett, Those United States)

Novelist Ernest Hemingway lived in Paris in the early 1920s, part of the expatriate artistic community, largely made up of American exiles. Money was tight, and Hemingway recounted how the pigeons in the Luxembourg Gardens often kept his young family from starvation. He used to wheel a pram and child through the gardens which were known "for the classiness of its pigeons". He would wait until the duty gendarme went across the street for a glass of wine before selecting a pigeon, preferably a plump one. Then he lured the bird across with corn, snatched it, wrung its neck, and hid it under the baby's blanket. He said later, "We got a little tired of pigeon that year, but they filled many a void."

There is a story that the Irish nationalist playwright Brendan Behan, in Paris in 1949, was offered cash by a café-owner (who spoke no English) to paint a sign that would draw in foreign tourists. Behan duly did as requested, pocketed the money and exited from the scene. The sign which he'd carefully painted and which the proprietor as carefully hung up in his window is supposed to have read:

> Come in, you Anglo-Saxon swine
> And drink of my Algerian wine.
> 'Twill turn you eyeballs black and blue,
> And damn well good enough for you.

Addiction

The 18th century was a hard-drinking period. This is a story about Jonathan Swift, author of Gulliver's Travels *and Dean of St Patrick's, Dublin.*

The last time I dined with Dean Swift, which was about three years before he fell into that distemper which totally deprived him of his understanding, I observed that he was affected by the wine which he drank, about a pint of claret. The next morning, as we were walking together in his garden, he complained much of his head, when I took the liberty to tell him (for I most sincerely loved him) that I was afraid he drank too much wine. He was a little startled, and answered, that as to his drinking, he had always looked on himself as a very temperate man, for he never exceeded the quantity which his physician had allowed and prescribed him. Now his physician never drank less than two bottles of claret after dinner.

(Edward King, *Anecdotes*)

This story about and by James Boswell, biographer of Dr Johnson, shows him in Edinburgh going one better, in fact several times better, than Swift's physician (see above).

I went to Fortune's; found nobody in the house but Captain James Gordon of Ellon. He and I drank five bottles of claret and were most profound politicians. He pressed me to take another; but my stomach was against it. I walked off very gravely though much intoxicated.

Ranged through the streets till, having run hard down the Advocates' Close, which is very steep, I found myself on a sudden bouncing down an almost perpendicular stone stair. I could not stop, but when I came to the bottom of it, fell with a good deal of violence, which sobered me much.

It was amazing that I was not killed or very much hurt; I only bruised my right heel severely.

(James Boswell, *Journal, November, 1774*)

George Crabbe, 18th-century poet and clergyman (as well as would-be surgeon in his youth), was prescribed opium for his health; as his son reports, the drug worked wonders.

My father, now about his forty-sixth year, was much more stout and healthy than when I first remember him. Soon after that early period, he became subject to vertigoes, which he thought indicative of a tendency to apoplexy; and was occasionally bled rather profusely, which only increased the symptoms. When he preached his first sermon at Muston, in the year 1789, my mother foreboded, as she afterwards told us, that he would preach very few more: but it was on one of his early journeys into Suffolk, in passing through Ipswich, that he had the most alarming attack. Having left my mother at the inn, he walked into the town alone, and suddenly staggered in the street, and fell. He was lifted up by the passengers [passers-by], and overheard some one say, significantly, "Let the gentleman alone, he will be better by and by," for his fall was attributed to the bottle. He was assisted to his room, and the late Dr Clubbe was sent for, who, after a little examination, saw through the case with great judgment. "There is nothing the matter with your head," he observed, "nor any apoplectic tendency; let the digestive organs bear the whole blame: you must take opiates." From that time his health began to amend rapidly, and his constitution was renovated; a rare effect of opium, for that drug almost always inflicts some partial injury, even when it is necessary; but to him it was only salutary, and to a constant but slightly increasing dose of it may be attributed his long and generally healthy life.

(from *The Life of George Crabbe* by his son)

Thomas de Quincey, whose most famous book is his Confessions of an
English Opium Eater, *remembers the first time that he took the drug.*

It is very long since I first took opium; so long, that if it had been a
trifling incident in my life, I might have forgotten its date: but
cardinal events are not to be forgotten; and, from circumstances
connected with it, I remember that this inauguration into the use
of opium must be referred to the spring or to the autumn of 1804;
during which seasons I was in London, having come thither for
the first time since my entrance at Oxford. And this event arose in
the following way: from an early age I had been accustomed to
wash my head in cold water at least once a day; being suddenly
seized with toothache, I attributed it to some relaxation caused by
a casual intermission of that practice; jumped out of bed, plunged
my head into a basin of cold water, and with hair thus wetted went
to sleep. The next morning, as I need hardly say, I awoke with
excruciating rheumatic pains of the head and face, from which I
had hardly any respite for about twenty days. On the twenty-first
day I think it was, and on a Sunday, that I went out into the
streets; rather to run away, if possible, from my torments, than
with any distinct purpose of relief. By accident, I met a college
acquaintance, who recommended opium. Opium! dread agent of
unimaginable pleasure and pain! I had heard of it as I had heard of
manna or of ambrosia, but no further. How unmeaning a sound
was opium at that time! what solemn chords does it now strike
upon my heart! what heart-quaking vibrations of sad and happy
remembrances! Reverting for a moment to these, I feel a mystic
importance attached to the minutest circumstances connected
with the place, and the time, and the man (if man he was), that first
laid open to me the paradise of opium-eaters. It was a Sunday
afternoon, wet and cheerless; and a duller spectacle this earth of
ours has not to show than a rainy Sunday in London. My road
homewards lay through Oxford Street; and near "the stately
Pantheon" (as Mr Wordsworth has obligingly called it) I saw a
druggist's shop. The druggist (unconscious minister of celestial
pleasures!), as if in sympathy with the rainy Sunday, looked dull
and stupid, just as any mortal druggist might be expected to look
on a rainy London Sunday; and when I asked for the tincture of
opium, he gave it to me as any other man might do; and,

furthermore, out of my shilling returned to me what seemed to be real copper halfpence, taken out of a real wooden drawer. Nevertheless, and notwithstanding all such indications of humanity, he has ever since figured in my mind as a beatific vision of an immortal druggist, sent down to earth on a special mission to myself. And it confirms me in this way of considering him, that when I next came up to London, I sought him near the stately Pantheon, and found him not; and thus to me, who knew not his name (if, indeed, he had one), he seemed rather to have vanished from Oxford Street, than to have fitted into any other locality, or (which some abominable man suggested) to have absconded from the rent. The reader may choose to think of him as, possibly, no more than a sublunary druggist; it may be so, but my faith is better. I believe him to have evanesced. So unwillingly would I connect any mortal remembrances with that hour, and place, and creature that first brought me acquainted with the celestial drug.

Arrived at my lodgings, it may be supposed that I lost not a moment in taking the quantity prescribed. I was necessarily ignorant of the whole art and mystery of opium-taking; and what I took, I took under every disadvantage. But I took it; and in an hour, O heavens! what a revulsion! what a resurrection, from its lowest depths, of the inner spirit! what an apocalypse of the world within me! That my pains had vanished, was now a trifle in my eyes; this negative effect was swallowed up in the immensity of those positive effects which had opened before me, in the abyss of divine enjoyment thus suddenly revealed. Here was a panacea . . . for all human woes; here was the secret of happiness, about which philosophers had disputed for so many ages, at once discovered; happiness might now be bought for a penny, and carried in the waist-coat-pocket; portable ecstasies might be corked up in a pint-bottle and peace of mind could be sent down by the mail.

(Thomas de Quincey, *Confessions of an English Opium Eater*)

In this story Thomas de Quincey, himself an expert on the drug (see above), describes the effects of opium addiction on the poet and philosopher Samuel Taylor Coleridge.

It was not long after this event that my own introduction to Coleridge occurred. At that time some negotiation was pending between him and the Royal Institution, which ended in their engaging him to deliver a course of lectures on Poetry and the Fine Arts, during the ensuing winter. For this series (twelve or sixteen, I think,) he received a sum of 100 guineas. And considering the slightness of the pains which he bestowed upon them, he was well remunerated. I fear that they did not increase his reputation; for never did any man treat his audience with less respect, or his task with less careful attention. I was in London for part of the time, and can report the circumstances, having made a point of attending duly at the appointed hours. Coleridge was at that time living uncomfortably enough at the *Courier* [newspaper] office, in the Strand. In such a situation, annoyed by the sound of feet passing his chamber-door continually to the printing rooms of this great establishment, and with no gentle ministrations of female hands to sustain his cheerfulness, naturally enough his spirits flagged; and he took more than ordinary doses of opium. I called upon him daily, and pitied his forlorn condition. There was no bell in the room, which for many months answered the double purpose of bed-room and sitting-room. Consequently, I often saw him, picturesquely enveloped in night caps, surmounted by handkerchiefs endorsed upon handkerchiefs, shouting from the attics of the *Courier* office, down three or four flights of stairs, to a certain "Mrs Brainbridge", his sole attendant, whose dwelling was in the subterranean regions of the house. There did I often see the philosopher, with a most lugubrious face, invoking with all his might this uncouth name of "Brainbridge", each syllable of which he intonated with long-drawn emphasis, in order to overpower the hostile hubbub coming downwards from the press, and the roar from the Strand, which entered at all the front windows. "Mrs Brainbridge! I say, Mrs Brainbridge!" was the perpetual cry, until I expected to hear the Strand, and distant Fleet Street, take up the echo of "Brainbridge!" Thus unhappily situated, he sank more than ever under the dominion of opium; so that, at two o'clock, when he should have been in attendance at the Royal Institution, he was too often unable to rise from bed. Then came dismissals of audience after audience with pleas of illness; and on many of his lecture days, I have seen all Albemarle Street closed by a "lock" of carriages filled with women of distinction, until the servants of the Institution or their own footmen advanced to the carriage doors with the intelligence that Mr Coleridge had been suddenly taken ill. This plea, which at first had been received with expressions of concern, repeated too often, began to rouse disgust. Some in anger, and some in real uncertainty whether it would not be trouble thrown away, ceased to attend. And we that were more constant, too often found reason to be disappointed with the quality of his lecture. His appearance was generally that of a person struggling with pain and overmastering illness. His lips were baked with feverish heat, and often black in colour, and in spite of the water which he continued drinking through the whole course of his lecture, he often seemed to labour under an almost paralytic inability to raise the upper jaw from the lower. In such a state it is clear that nothing could save the lecture itself from reflecting his own feebleness and exhaustion, except the advantage of having been precomposed in some happier mood. But that never happened: most unfortunately he relied upon his extempore ability to carry him through. Now, had he been in spirits, or had he gathered animation and kindled by his own motion, no written lecture could have been more effectual than one of his unpremeditated colloquial harangues. But either he was depressed originally below the point from which any re-ascent was possible, or else this reaction was intercepted by continual disgust, from looking back upon his own ill success; for assuredly he never once recovered that free and eloquent movement of thought which he could command at any time in private company.

(Thomas de Quincey, *Recollections of the Lakes and the Lake Poets*)

At times Samuel Taylor Coleridge would realize the damage opium was doing to him . He made great efforts to kick the habit, even paying someone to literally stand in his way and prevent him entering the "druggist's shop". Thomas de Quincey points out the contradiction in paying someone to stop you from doing what you want to do.

Coleridge did make prodigious efforts to deliver himself from this thraldom [to opium]; and he went so far at one time in Bristol, to my knowledge, as to hire a man for the express purpose, and armed with the power of resolutely interposing between himself and the door of any druggist's shop. It is true that an authority derived only from Coleridge's will could not be valid against Coleridge's counter-determination: he could resume as easily as he could delegate the power. But the scheme did not entirely fail; a man shrinks from exposing to another that infirmity of will which he might else have but a feeble motive for disguising to himself; and the delegated man, the external conscience, as it were of Coleridge, though destined – in the final resort, if matters came to absolute rupture, and to an obstinate duel, as it were, between himself and his principal – in that extremity to give way, yet might have long protracted the struggle . . . and in fact, I know, upon absolute proof, that before reaching that crisis, the man shewed fight; and faithful to his trust, and comprehending the reasons for it, he declared that if he must yield, he would "know the reason why."

(Thomas de Quincey, *Recollections
of the Lakes and the Lake Poets*)

*The poet Alfred Tennyson was addicted to the pleasures of tobacco,
according to his friend, the Anglo-German scholar F.Max Muller.*

Tennyson's pipe was almost indispensable to him, and I remember one time when I and several friends were staying at his house, the question of tobacco turned up. Some of his friends taunted Tennyson that he could never give up tobacco. "Anybody can do that," he said, "if he chooses to do it." When his friends still continued to doubt and tease him, "Well," he said, "I shall give up smoking from tonight." The very same evening I was told that he threw his tobacco and pipe out the window of his bedroom. The next day he became very moody and captious, the third day no one knew what to do with him. But after a disturbed night I was told that he got out of bed in the morning, went quietly into the garden, picked up one of his pipes, stuffed it with the remains of the tobacco scattered about, and then having had a few puffs came to breakfast all right again.

Like many 19th-century authors, Wilkie Collins, creator of the thrillers The Moonstone *and* The Woman in White, *depended on laudanum, a tincture of opium (i.e. the drug taken in a solution of alcohol). In the course of a lengthy conversation with the novelist Hall Caine he complained that his brain wasn't very clear. Collins then took a wine-glass and bottle from a cupboard, and poured himself a full glass of what appeared to be port. The dialogue went like this.*

"I am going to show you the secrets of my prison-house," said Collins. "Do you see that? It's laudanum."

He drank the whole glass straight off.

"Good heavens, Wilkie Collins! How long have you taken that drug?" asked Caine.

"Twenty years."

"More than once a day?"

"Oh, yes, much more. Don't be alarmed. Remember that De Quincey used to drink laudanum out of a jug."

"Why do you take it?"

"To stimulate the brain and steady the nerves."

"And you think it does that?"

"Undoubtedly."

Hall Caine asked whether laudanum had the same stimulating effect on other people as on Collins.

"It had on Bulwer Lytton [author of *The Last Days of Pompeii*]. He told me so himself."

When Hall Caine asked whether he should take the drug as an antidote to his own severe "nervous exhaustion'", he records how Wilkie Collins "paused, changed colour slightly, and then said quietly, 'No'."

(conversation quoted in
Alethea Hayter's *Opium and the Romantic Imagination*)

Hall Caine, the author who is the source of the dialogue with Wilkie Collins quoted above, seems to have a had a fairly extensive experience of

*writers and addiction. As a young man Caine was befriended by the poet
and painter Dante Gabriel Rossetti after he had given a lecture praising
Rossetti. The older man, who'd been critically savaged for some of his
work, was grateful for Caine's praise while the younger one – eager to get
a foothold in literary life – was ready to establish himself as Rossetti's
disciple. A short but intense friendship blossomed during the last months
of the poet's life. Caine later wrote about it in Recollections of Rossetti.
(See also Inspiration for the peculiar story of Rossetti's exhumation of
his wife's body.) Here he describes how he spent his first night in Rossetti's
large, gloomy house in Cheyne Walk on the Thames embankment. It
reads like an extract from a Gothic novel. More important, it was at this
moment that Caine first became aware of the poet's addiction to chloral, a
sedative drug. He had already been disturbed earlier in the evening by the
paranoid quality of Rossetti's conversation.*

We took candles from a table in the hall and went up a narrow
and tortuous staircase, which was otherwise dark, to a landing
from which many rooms seemed to open, so large was the house
in which Rossetti lived alone, except for a cook and two
maidservants.

"You are to sleep in Watts's room tonight," he said, and then
he suggested that before going to my own bedroom I should
take a look at his. I cheerfully assented, but walking through the
long corridor that led to the poet's room, we had to pass another
apartment, and after a moment's pause, Rossetti opened the
door and we went in. It was the drawing-room, a very large
chamber, barely illuminated by the candles in our hands, and
full of the musty odour of a place long shut up.

Suspended from the middle of the ceiling there hung a huge
Venetian candelabra, from whose facets the candlelight glittered.
On the walls were a number of small water-colour drawings in
plain oak frames. Rossetti drew me up to the pictures, and I
remember that they seemed to me rather crude in colour and in
drawing, but very touching in sentiment (one in particular,
representing a young girl parting from her lover on the threshold
of a convent, being deeply charged with feeling), and that I said:
"I should have thought that the man who painted these pictures
was rather a poet than a painter – who was it?"

Rossetti, who was standing before the drawing, as I see him

still, in the dark room, with the candle in his hand, said in a low voice: "It was my wife. She had great genius."

His own bedroom was entered from another and smaller room, which he told me he used as a breakfast-room. The outer room was made fairly bright by another glittering chandelier (the property at one time, he said, of David Garrick). By the rustle of the trees against the window-pane, one realized that it overlooked the garden. But the inner room was dark with heavy hangings around the walls as well as about the bed (a black four-poster) and thick velvet curtains before the windows, so that the candles we carried seemed unable to light it, and our voices to sound muffled and thick.

An enormous black oak chimney-piece of curious design, having an ivory crucifix on the largest of its ledges, covered a part of one side of the room, and reached to the ceiling. Cabinets, a hip-bath, and the usual furniture of a bedroom occupied places about the floor, and in the middle of it, before a little couch, there was a small table on which stood a wired lantern containing a candle, which Rossetti lit from the open one in his hand, another candle lying by its side. I remarked that he probably burnt a light all night, and he said that was so.

"My curse is insomnia," he added. "Two or three hours hence I shall get up and lie on the couch and, to pass away a weary hour, read this book" – a volume of Boswell's *Johnson* which he had taken out of the bookcase as we left the studio.

Then I saw that on the table were two small bottles, sealed and labelled, and beside them was a little measuring glass. Without looking further, but with a painful suspicion coming over me, I asked if that was his medicine.

"They say there's a skeleton in every cupboard," he said in a low voice. "That's mine; it's chloral."

When I reached the room I was to occupy for the rest of the night, I found it, like Rossetti's bedroom, heavy with hangings, and black with antique picture panels; having a ceiling so high as to be out of all reach and sight, and being so dark from various causes that the candle seemed only to glitter in it.

Presently, Rossetti, who had left me in my room, came back, for no purpose that I can remember, except to say that he had much enjoyed my visit. I replied that I should never forget it.

"If you desire to settle in London," he said, "I trust you'll come and live with me, and then many such evenings must remove the memory of this one."

I laughed, for what he so generously hinted at seemed to me the remotest contingency.

"I have just taken sixty grains of chloral," he said as he was going out. "In four hours I shall take sixty more, and in four hours after that yet another sixty."

"Doesn't the dose increase with you?" I asked.

"It has not done so perceptibly in recent years. I judge I've taken more chloral than any man whatever. Marshall" (his medical man) "says if I were put into a Turkish bath I should sweat it at every pore."

As he said this, standing half outside the threshold, there was something in his tone and laugh suggesting that he was even proud of the accomplishment. To me it was a frightful revelation, accounting largely, if not entirely, for what had puzzled and distressed me in the delusions I have referred to.

And so, after four in the morning, amid the odour of bygone ages, with thoughts of that big and almost empty house, of the three women servants somewhere out of all reach and sound, of Rossetti in his muffled room, of that wired lantern, and the two bottles of chloral, I fell asleep.

Rossetti's health continued to get worse and Hall Caine took him off to a remote cottage in Cumberland in the hope that a change of air would improve things. They were accompanied by a "nurse" (in fact, Rossetti's mistress, Fanny Cornforth). But the place was boring and, worse, Caine found himself in the position of having to dole out Rossetti's doses of chloral.

If Rossetti's days were now cheerless and heavy, what shall I say of the nights? At that time of the year the night closed in as early as seven o'clock, and then in that little house among the solitary hills, his disconsolate spirit would sometimes sink beyond solace into irreclaimable depths of depression. Night after night we sat up until eleven, twelve, one, and two o'clock, watching the long hours go by with heavy steps, waiting, waiting, waiting for the time at which he could take his first draught of chloral, drop back on his pillow, and snatch three or four hours of dreamless sleep . . .

I have said that on the night I first slept at Cheyne Walk, Rossetti, coming into my room at the last moment before going to bed, told me that he had just taken sixty grains of chloral, that in four hours he would take sixty more, and four later yet another sixty. Whether there was a conscious exaggeration, or whether (being incapable of affectation or untruthfulness) he was deceived by his doctors for the good purpose of operating to advantage on his all-potent imagination, I do not know; but I do know that when the chloral came under my own control I was strictly warned that one bottle at one dose was all that it was necessary or safe for Rossetti to take. This single bottle (by Dr Marshall's advice) I gave him on going to bed, and we made the hour of retiring as late as possible, so that when he awoke it might be day.

But the power of the dose was now decreasing rapidly, and hence it came to pass that towards four o'clock in the leaden light of early dawn Rossetti would come to my room and beg for more. Let those who never knew Rossetti censure me, if they think well, for yielding at last to his pathetic importunities. The low, pleading voice, the note of pain, the awful sense of a body craving rest and a brain praying for unconsciousness, they are with me even yet in my memories of the man sitting on the side of my bed and asking for my pity and my forgiveness.

These were among the moments when Rossetti was utterly irresistible, but to compromise with my conscience I would give him half a bottle more, and he would go off with an appearance of content. The result was disastrous enough, but in a way that might have been least expected.

I was already painfully aware of the corroding influence of the drug on Rossetti's better nature, and one morning, as I took out of its hiding-place the key that was to open the glass doors of the little cabinet which contained the chloral, I caught a look in his eyes which seemed to say that in future he would find it for himself. To meet the contingency, and at the same time to test a theory which I had begun to cherish, that the drug was only necessary to Rossetti because he believed it to be so, I decided to try an experiment, and so defeat by a trick the trick I expected.

The solution of chloral was hardly distinguishable at any time from pure water, and certainly not at all in the dead white light of dawn, so, with the connivance of the nurse, I opened a bottle, emptied it of the drug, filled it afresh with water, corked and covered it again, with its parchment cap tied about by a collar of red string, placed it in the cabinet, and then awaited results.

Next morning I awoke of myself exactly at the hour at which Rossetti had been accustomed to awaken me, and I heard him coming as noiselessly as he could down the corridor towards my room. He opened the door, leaned over me to satisfy himself that I was asleep, fumbled for and found the key to the cabinet, opened it, took away the bottle I had left ready for him, and then crept back to bed. After some ten minutes or more I rose and went to his room to see what had occurred; and there, sure enough, lay Rossetti, sleeping soundly, and my bottle standing empty on the table by his side.

In my ignorance I imagined I had solved the problem of Rossetti's insomnia (of nearly all insomnia), and found the remedy for half the troubles of his troubled life. He was indeed "Of imagination all compact", and if we could only continue to make him think he was consuming chloral while he was really drinking water, we should in good time conquer his baneful habit altogether.

What the result might have been of any consistent attempt to put my theory into practice it is not possible for me to say, for fate was stronger than good intentions, and my experiment was not to be repeated. While I was out walking the next morning the nurse, taking the liberty of an old friend, told the whole story of what I had done to Rossetti in a well-meant, but foolish, attempt to triumph over his melancholy, and then more mischief was done than the mischief I had tried to undo.

Besides the crushing humiliation that came to him, as to De Quincey, with the consciousness of the lowering of his moral nature from the use of the drug, and of our being so obviously aware of it, there was the fact that from that day forward he believed I was always deceiving him, and that what I gave him for chloral was mainly water. As if to establish my theory that Rossetti's body answered entirely to the mood of his mind, sleep, from that day forward, refused to come to him at all after the single bottle which the doctor had permitted me to give him . . .

I had tried to check the craving for chloral, but unwittingly I had done worse than not check it; and where the lifelong efforts of older friends had failed to eradicate a morbid, ruinous, and fatal thirst, it seemed presumptuous, if not ridiculous, to think that the task of conquering it could be compassed by a young fellow with heart and nerves of wax.

(Hall Caine, *Recollections of Rossetti*)

Mystery writer Raymond Chandler, creator of the archetypal private eye Philip Marlowe, had a severe drink problem. When he was working on the film The Blue Dahlia, *Chandler also had a problem over how to end the story. Chandler worked in Hollywood over several years, never very happily (see also* **Theatre & Film**). *The Blue Dahlia was his only original script, however, and it was this that made him despair of getting to the end. His producer John Houseman recalled the unique bargain which Raymond Chandler struck with him.*

The next morning, true to his promise, Chandler appeared in my office, looking less distraught but grimmer than the day before. He said that after a sleepless and tormented night he had come to the unalterable conclusion that he was incapable of finishing *The Blue Dahlia* script on time – or ever. This declaration was followed by a silence of several minutes during which we gazed at each other, more in sorrow than anger. Then, having finished his coffee and carefully put down his cup on the floor, Ray spoke again, softly and seriously. After some prefatory remarks about our common background and the esteem and affection in which he held me, he made the following astonishing proposal: I was certainly aware (or had heard it rumoured) that he had for some years been a serious drinker – to the point where he had gravely endangered his health. By an intense effort of will he had managed to overcome his addiction. This abstinence, he explained, had been all the more difficult to sustain, since alcohol gave him an energy and a self-assurance. This brought us to the crux of the matter; having repeated that he was unable and unwilling to continue working on *The Blue*

Dahlia at the studio sober, Ray assured me of his complete confidence to finish it, at home – drunk.

He did not minimize the hazards: he pointed out that his plan, if adopted, would call for deep faith on my part and supreme courage on his, since he would in effect be completing the script at the risk of his life. (It wasn't the drinking that was dangerous, he explained, since he had a doctor who gave him such massive injections of glucose that he could last for weeks with no solid food at all. It was the sobering up that was perilous; the terrible strain of his return to normal living.) That was why Cissy [Chandler's wife] had so long and so bitterly opposed his proposed scheme, till Ray had finally convinced her that honour came before safety, and that his was deeply engaged, through me, in *The Blue Dahlia* . . . [*Reluctantly, John Houseman agreed to Chandler's suggestion.*]

During those last eight days of shooting Chandler did not draw one sober breath, nor did one speck of solid food pass his lips. He was polite and cheerful when I appeared and his doctor came twice a day to give him intravenous injections. The rest of the time, except when he was asleep, with his black cat by his side, Ray was never without a glass in his hand. He did not drink much. Having reached the euphoria that he needed, he continued to consume just enough bourbon and water to maintain him in that condition. He worked about a third of the time. Between eight and ten every evening, he sat in Cissy's room and they listened together to the Gas Company's programme of classical music on the radio. The rest of the time was spent in a light sleep from which he woke in full possession of his faculties and picked up exactly where he had stopped with whichever of the rotating secretaries happened to be with him. He continued until he felt himself growing drowsy again, then dropped back comfortably into sleep while the girl went into the next room, typed the pages, and left them on the table beside him to be reread and corrected when he woke up. As his last line of the script, Ray wrote in pencil: "*Did somebody say something about a drink of bourbon?*" – and that's how we shot it.

(John Houseman, Lost Fortnight)

Animals

Henry Baker was a very minor 18th-century poet – but a pioneer in the use of microscopes.

The Duke of Montague was famous for his love to the whole animal creation, and for his being able to keep a very grave face when not in the most serious earnest. Mr Baker, a distinguished member of the Royal Society, had one day entertained this nobleman and several other persons with the sight of the peristaltic motion of the bowels in a louse, by the microscope. When the observation was over, he was going to throw the creature away; but the Duke, with a face that made him believe he was perfectly in earnest, told him it would be not only cruel, but ungrateful, in return for the entertainment that creature had given them, to destroy it. He ordered the boy to be brought in from whom it was procured, and after praising the smallness and delicacy of Mr Baker's fingers, persuaded him carefully to replace the animal in its former territories and to give the boy a shilling not to disturb it for a fortnight.

(anecdote quoted in Isaac Disraeli's
Calamities and Quarrels of Authors)

The 18th-century poet Alexander Pope was an early opponent of animal vivisection. In particular, he had a great affection for dogs and regretted the fact that Dr Hales, a clergyman who lived near Pope in Twickenham, did experiments on them, however good the amateur scientist's motives.

"I shall be very glad to see Dr Hales, and always love to see him; he is so worthy and good a man," [said Spence].

"Yes he is a very good man, only I'm sorry he has his hands imbrued with blood" [Pope replied].

"What, he cuts up rats?"

"Aye, and dogs too!" (And with what emphasis and concern he spoke it.) Indeed, he commits most of these barbarities with the thought of its being of use to man. But how do we know that we have a right to kill creatures that we are so little above as dogs, for our curiosity, or even for some use to us?

(Joseph Spence, *Anecdotes*)

Dr Johnson's biographer, James Boswell, talks about his friend's fondness for cats.

Nor would it be just under this head, to omit the fondness which he shewed for animals which he had taken under his protection. I never shall forget the indulgence with which he treated Hodge his cat: for whom he himself used to go out and buy oysters, lest the servants having that trouble should take a dislike to the poor creature. I am, unluckily, one of those who have an antipathy to a cat, so that I am uneasy when in the room with one; and I own, I frequently suffered a good deal from the presence of this same Hodge. I recollect him one day scrambling up Dr Johnson's breast, apparently with much satisfaction, while my friend, smiling, and half whistling, rubbed down his back, and pulled him by the tail; and, when I observed he was a fine cat, saying: "Why, yes, Sir; but I have had cats whom I liked better than this," and then, as if perceiving Hodge to be out of countenance, adding, "But he is a very fine cat, a very fine cat indeed."

This reminds me of the ludicrous account which he gave Mr Langton, of the despicable state of a young gentleman of good family. "Sir, when I heard of him last, he was running about town shooting cats." And then, in a sort of kindly reverie, he bethought himself of his own favourite cat, and said, "But Hodge shan't be shot: no, no, Hodge shall not be shot."

(James Boswell, *Life of Dr Johnson*)

*The 18th-century novelist Henry Fielding, sailing to Lisbon, witnesses
an accident at sea.*

A most tragical Incident fell out this day at Sea. While the Ship
was under Sail, but making, as will appear, no great Way, a Kitten,
one of four of the Feline Inhabitants of the Cabin, fell from the
Window into the Water: an Alarm was immediately given to the
Captain, who was then upon Deck, and received it with the utmost
Concern. He immediately gave Orders to the Steersman in favour
of the poor Thing, as he called it; the Sails were instantly
slackened, and all Hands, as the Phrase is, employed to recover
the poor Animal. I was, I own, extremely surprised at all this; less,
indeed, at the Captain's extreme Tenderness, than at his con-
ceiving any Possibility of Success; for, if Puss had had nine
thousand, instead of nine Lives, I concluded they had been all
lost. The Boatswain, however, had more sanguine Hopes; for,
having stript himself of his Jacket, Breeches, and Shirt, he leapt
boldly into the Water, and, to my great Astonishment, in a few
Minutes, returned to the Ship, bearing the motionless Animal in
his Mouth. Nor was this, I observed, a Matter of such great
Difficulty as it appeared to my Ignorance, and possibly may seem
to that of my Fresh-water Reader: the Kitten was now exposed to
Air and Sun on the Deck, where its Life, of which it retained no
Symptoms, was despaired of by all.

The Captain's humanity, if I may so call it, did not so totally
destroy his Philosophy, as to make him yield himself up to
affliction on this melancholy Occasion. Having felt his Loss like
a Man, he resolved to shew he could bear it like one; and, having
declared, he had rather have lost a Cask of Rum or Brandy, betook
himself to threshing at Backgammon with the Portuguese Friar,
in which innocent Amusement they passed their leisure hours.

But as I have, perhaps, a little too wantonly endeavoured to
raise the tender Passions of my Readers, in this Narrative, I
should think myself unpardonable if I concluded it, without
giving them the Satisfaction of hearing that the Kitten at last
recovered, to the great Joy of the good Captain.

(Henry Fielding, *Journal of a Voyage to Lisbon*)

The poet William Cowper, a gentle and depressive man, kept pet hares. In this letter he describes the escape of one.

The following occurrence ought not to be passed over in silence, in a place where so few notable ones are to be met with. Last Wednesday night, while we were at supper, between the hours of eight and nine, I heard an unusual noise in the back parlour, as if one of the hares was entangled, and endeavouring to disengage herself. I was just going to rise from table, when it ceased. In about five minutes, a voice on the outside of the parlour door inquired if one of my hares had got away. I immediately rushed into the next room, and found that my poor favourite Puss had made her escape.

She had gnawed in sunder the strings of a lattice work, with which I thought I had sufficiently secured the window, and which I preferred to any other sort of blind, because it admitted plenty of air.

From thence I hastened to the kitchen, where I saw the redoubtable Thomas Freeman, who told me that, having seen her, just after she had dropped into the street, he attempted to cover her with his hat, but she screamed out, and leaped directly over his head. I then desired him to pursue as fast as possible, and added Richard Coleman to the chace, as being nimbler, and carrying less weight than Thomas; not expecting to see her again, but desirous to learn, if possible, what became of her. In something less than an hour, Richard returned, almost breathless, with the following account: that soon after he began to run, he left Tom behind him, and came in sight of a most numerous hunt of men, women, children, and dogs; that he did his best to keep back the dogs, and presently outstripped the crowd, so that the race was at last disputed between himself and Puss; – she ran right through the town, and down the lane that leads to Dropshost. A little before she came to the house, he got the start and turned her; she pushed for the town again, and soon after she entered it, sought shelter in Mr Wagstaff's tanyard, adjoining to old Mr Drakets. Sturges' harvest men were at supper, and saw her from the opposite side of the way. There she encountered the tanpits full of water; and while she was struggling out of one pit, and plunging into another, and almost drowned, one of the men drew her out by the ears, and secured her. She was then well washed in a bucket to get the lime out of her coat, and brought home in a sack at ten o'clock.

This frolic cost us four shillings, but you may believe we did not grudge a farthing of it.

The poor creature received only a little hurt in one of her claws, and in one of her ears and is now almost as well as ever

(William Cowper, *letter to Rev. John Newton, August, 1780*)

The poet Percy Bysshe Shelley writes to the novelist Thomas Love Peacock from Ravenna where he is staying with Lord Byron.

Lord B's establishment consists, besides servants, of ten horses, eight enormous dogs, three monkeys, five cats, an eagle, a crow, and a falcon; and all these, except the horses, walk about the house, which every now and then resounds with their unarbitrated quarrels, as if they were the masters of it . . .

After I have sealed my letter, I find that my enumeration of the animals in this Circaean palace was defective, and that in a material point. I have just met on the grand stair-case five peacocks, two guinea hens, and an Egyptian crane. I wonder who all these animals were, before they were changed into these shapes.

(Shelley to Peacock, *Ravenna, August 1821*)

Another story about some dogs that belonged to Lord Byron shows the incredible attraction which anything belonging to the poet had for women.

Drury had some dogs (two, I believe) sent him that had belonged to Lord Byron. One day he was told that two ladies wished to see him, and he found their business was to ask, as a great favour, some relic of Lord Byron. Expecting to be asked for some of his handwriting, or a bit of his hair, he was amused to find that it was a bit of the hair of one of the dogs they wanted. The dog being brought forward the ladies observed a *clot* on his back, which had evidently resisted any efforts at ablution that might have been exerted on the animal, and immediately selected this as the most precious part to be cut off; "the probability," they said, "being that Lord B. might have patted that clot."

(Tome Moore, *Diary, June, 1827*)

Novelist Sir Walter's Scott's benevolent attitude towards his pet dog and cat is described by his early biographer John Gibson Lockhart.

I observed, during the first evening I spent with him in this sanctum [Scott's study], that while he talked, his hands were hardly ever idle; sometimes he folded letter-covers – sometimes he twisted paper into matches, performing both tasks with great mechanical expertness and nicety; and when there was no loose paper fit to be so dealt with, he snapped his fingers, and the noble Maida aroused himself from his lair on the hearthrug, and laid his head across his master's knees, to be caressed and fondled. The room had no space for pictures except one, a portrait of Claverhouse, which hung over the chimneypiece, with a Highland target on either side, and broadswords and dirks (each having its own story) disposed star-fashion round them. A few green tin boxes, such as solicitors keep title-deeds in, were piled over each other on one side of the window; and on the top of these lay a fox's tail, mounted on an antique silver handle, wherewith, as often as he had occasion to take down a book, he gently brushed the dust off the upper leaves before opening it. I think I have mentioned all the furniture of the room except a sort of ladder, low, broad, well carpeted, and strongly guarded with oaken rails, by which he helped himself to books from his higher shelves. On the top step of this convenience, Hinse of Hinsfeldt . . . a venerable tom-cat, fat and sleek, and no longer very locomotive, usually lay watching the proceedings of his master and Maida with an air of dignified equanimity; but when Maida chose to leave the party, he signified his inclinations by thumping the door with his huge paw, as violently as ever a fashionable footman handled a knocker in Grosvenor Square; the Sheriff rose and opened it for him with courteous alacrity –

and then Hinse came down purring from his perch, and mounted guard by the footstool, *vice* Maida absent upon furlough. Whatever discourse might be passing, was broken every now and then by some affectionate apostrophe to these four-footed friends. He said they understood everything he said to them – and I believe they did understand a great deal of it. But at all events, dogs and cats, like children, have some infallible tact for discovering at once who is, and who is not, really fond of their company; and I venture to say, Scott was never five minutes in any room before the little pets of the family, whether dumb or lisping, had found out his kindness for all their generation.

(John Gibson Lockhart, *Life of Sir Walter Scott*)

The poets Wordsworth and Coleridge show their lack of practical ability when it comes to geting a collar off a horse.

I led my horse to the stable, where a sad perplexity arose. I removed the harness without difficulty; but after many strenuous attempts I could not remove the collar. In despair I called for assistance, when Mr Wordsworth brought his ingenuity into exercise; but after several unsuccessful efforts, he relinquished the achievement as a thing altogether impracticable. Mr Coleridge now tried his hand, but showed no more skill than his predecessors; for, after twisting the poor horse's neck almost to strangulation and the great danger of his eyes, he gave up the useless task, pronouncing that the horse's head must have grown since the collar was put on; for he said, "It was a downright impossibility for such a huge *os frontis* to pass through so narrow an aperture." Just at this instant, a servant girl came near, and understanding the cause of the consternation, "Ha! master," said she, "you don't go about the work in the right way. You should do like this," when, turning the collar upside down, she slipped it off in a moment, to our great humilation and wonderment, each satisfied afresh that there were heights of knowledge in the world to which we had not yet attained.

(Joseph Cottle, *Early Recollections*)

Emily Bronte was devoted to animals and showed an instinctive affinity with them. It didn't stop her punishing her dog on one memorable occasion. The bulldog, called "Keeper" figures in her sister Charlotte's novel Shirley. *The romantic picture of the author of* Wuthering Heights *as a remote, dreamy figure is shattered by this story.*

The same tawny bull-dog (with his "strangled whistle"), called "Tartar" in *Shirley* was "Keeper" in Haworth parsonage; a gift to Emily. With the gift came a warning. Keeper was faithful to the depths of his nature as long as he was with friends; but he who struck him with a stick or whip, roused the relentless nature of the brute, who flew at his throat forthwith, and held him there till one or the other was at the point of death. Now Keeper's household fault was this. He loved to steal upstairs, and stretch his square, tawny limbs, on the comfortable beds, covered over with delicate white counterpanes. But the cleanliness of the parsonage arrangements was perfect; and this habit of Keeper's was so objectionable, that Emily, in reply to [the servant] Tabby's remonstrances, declared that, if he was found again transgressing, she herself, in defiance of warning and his well-known ferocity of nature, would beat him so severely that he would never offend again. In the gathering dusk of an autumn evening, Tabby came, half-triumphantly, half-tremblingly, but in great wrath, to tell Emily that Keeper was lying on the best bed, in drowsy voluptuousness. Charlotte saw Emily's whitening face, and set mouth, but dared not speak to interfere; no one dared when Emily's eyes glowed in that manner out of the paleness of her face, and when her lips were so compressed into stone. She went upstairs, and Tabby and Charlotte stood in the gloomy passage below, full of the dark shadows of coming night. Downstairs came Emily, dragging after her the unwilling Keeper, his hind legs set in a heavy attitude of resistance, held by the "scuft of his neck", but growling low and savagely all the time. The watchers would fain have spoken, but durst not, for fear of taking off Emily's attention, and causing her to avert her head for a moment from the enraged brute. She let him go, planted in a dark corner at the bottom of the stairs; no time was there to fetch stick or rod, for fear of the strangling clutch at her throat – her bare clenched fist struck against his red fierce eyes, before he had time to make his spring, and, in the language of the turf, she "punished him" till his eyes were swelled up, and the half-blind, stupified beast was led to his accustomed lair, to have his swollen head fomented and cared for by the very Emily herself. The generous dog owed her no grudge; he loved her dearly ever after; he walked first among the mourners to her funeral; he slept moaning for nights at the door of her empty room, and never, so to speak, rejoiced, dog-fashion, after her death. He, in his turn, was mourned over by the surviving sister. Let us somehow hope, in half Red Indian creed, that he follows Emily now; and, when he rests, sleeps on some soft white bed of dreams, unpunished when he awakens to the life of the land of shadows.

(Elizabeth Gaskell, *Life of Charlotte Bronte*)

The poet Elizabeth Barrett Browning was devoted to her spaniel Flush. Henriette Cockran, as a child, was introduced to the dog in Paris.

"Flush is a dear, devoted old dog. When I was very ill Flush never left my side, day and night. Every time I put my hand out of bed, I could always feel his curly head and cold nose."

Flush, on hearing his mistress mention his name, looked up in her face with intense love in his beautiful wistful eyes. We gave Flush some slices of bread and butter, which he accepted but instead of eating them, he disappeared under a big satin sofa; but when I presented him with a piece of plum cake he swallowed it there and then with gusto. I recollect that Mrs Barrett Browning whispered to me that if I looked under the divan I would find the bread and butter hidden there . . . that Flush was far too polite a dog to refuse anything offered to him, but from personal observation she knew he would not eat bread and butter when he saw any chance of getting plum-cake. Pen [Elizabeth Barrett Browning's young son] and I crept on all fours and looked under the divan; yes, there were all the slices of thin bread and butter in a row and untouched.

(Henriette Cockran, *Celebrities and I*)

This odd, half-believable story is told by Mark Twain in his auto-biography. It comes from an early stage in his writing life when he was working as a newspaper correspondent and had just signed a contract to write The Innocents Abroad. *Twain and a friend, William Clinton, had formed a two-man syndicate in Washington to supply stories to "obscure and poor" weekly magazines out in the West. The modest $24 a week they received for their work was constantly eaten into by Clinton's appetite for Scotch whisky. The day came when the money ran out, and as Twain tells it he came up with this bizarre scheme. Nelson A. Miles, who figures in the story, was a Civil War general who was evidently well-known.*

I remember a time when a shortage occurred; we had to have three dollars, and we had to have it before the close of the day. I don't know now how we happened to want all that money at one time; I only know we had to have it. Clinton told me to go out and find it – and he said he would also go out and see what he could do. He didn't seem to have any doubt that we would succeed, but I knew that that was his religion working in him; I hadn't the same confidence; I hadn't any idea where to turn to raise all that bullion, and I said so. I think he was ashamed of me, privately, because of my weak faith. He told me to give myself no uneasiness, no concern; and said in a simple, confident, and unquestioning way, "The Lord will provide." I saw that he fully believed the Lord would provide, but it seemed to me that if he had had my experience –

But never mind that; before he was done with me his strong faith had had its influence, and I went forth from the place almost convinced that the Lord really would provide.

I wandered around the streets for an hour, trying to think up some way to get that money, but nothing suggested itself. At last I lounged into the big lobby of the Ebbitt House, which was then a new hotel, and sat down. Presently a dog came loafing along. He paused, glanced up at me and said, with his eyes, "Are you friendly?" I answered, with my eyes, that I was. He gave his tail a grateful little wag and came forward and rested his jaw on my knee and lifted his brown eyes to my face in a winningly affectionate way. He was a lovely creature – as beautiful as a girl, and he was made all of silk and velvet. I stroked his smooth brown head and fondled his drooping ears, and we were a pair of lovers right away. Pretty soon Brigadier General Miles, the hero of the land, came strolling by in his blue and gold splendours, with everybody's admiring gaze upon him. He saw the dog and stopped, and there was a light in his eye which showed that he had a warm place in his heart for dogs, like this gracious creature; then he came forward and patted the dog and said, "He is very fine – he is a wonder; would you sell him?"

I was greatly moved; it seemed a marvellous thing to me, the way Clinton's prediction had come true. I said, "Yes."

The General said, "What do you ask for him?"

"Three dollars."

The General was manifestly surprised. He said, "Three dollars? Only three dollars? Why, that dog is a most uncommon dog; he can't possibly be worth less than fifty. If he were mine, I wouldn't take a hundred for him. I'm afraid you are not aware of his value. Reconsider your price if you like, I don't wish to wrong you."

But if he had known me he would have known that I was no more capable of wronging him than he was of wronging me. I responded with the same quiet decision as before, "No – three dollars. That is his price."

"Very well, since you insist upon it," said the General, and he gave me three dollars and led the dog away, and disappeared upstairs.

In about ten minutes a gentle-faced middle-aged gentleman came along, and began to look around here and there and under tables and everywhere, and I said to him, "Is it a dog you are looking for?"

His face was sad, before, and troubled; but it lit up gladly now, and he answered, "Yes – have you seen him?"

"Yes," I said, "he was here a minute ago, and I saw him follow a gentleman away. I think I could find him for you if you would like me to try."

I have seldom seen a person look so grateful – and there was gratitude in his voice, too, when he conceded that he would like me to try. I said I would do it with great pleasure, but that as it might take a little time I hoped he would not mind paying me something for my trouble. He said he would do it most gladly – repeating that phrase "most gladly" – and asked me how much. I said, "Three dollars."

He looked surprised, and said, "Dear me, it is nothing! I will pay you ten, quite willingly."

But I said, "No, three is the price" – and I started for the stairs without waiting for any further argument, for Clinton had said that that was the amount that the Lord would provide, and it seemed to me that it would be sacrilegious to take a penny more than was promised.

I got the number of the General's room from the office-clerk, as I passed by his wicket, and when I reached the room I found the General there caressing his dog, and quite happy. I said, "I am sorry, but I have to take the dog again."

He seemed very much surprised, and said, "Take him again? Why, he is my dog; you sold him to me, and at your own price."

"Yes," I said, " it is true – but I have to have him, because the man wants him again."

"What man?"

"The man that owns him; he wasn't my dog."

The General looked even more surprised than before, and for a moment he couldn't seem to find his voice; then he said, "Do you mean to tell me that you were selling another man's dog – and knew it?"

"Yes, I knew it wasn't my dog."

"Then why did you sell him?"

I said, "Well, that is a curious question to ask. I sold him because you wanted him. You offered to buy the dog; you can't deny that. I was not anxious to sell him – I had not even thought of selling him, but it seemed to me that if it could be any accommodation to you – "

He broke me off in the middle, and said, "*Accommodation* to me? It is the most extraordinary spirit of accommodation I have ever heard of – the idea of your selling a dog that didn't belong to you – "

I broke him off there, and said, "There is no relevancy about this kind of argument; you said yourself that the dog was probably worth a hundred dollars, I only asked you three; was there anything unfair about that? You offered to pay more, you know you did. I only asked you three; you can't deny it."

"Oh, what in the world has that to do with it! The crux of the matter is that you didn't own the dog – can't you see that? You seem to think that there is no impropriety in selling property that isn't yours provided you sell it cheap. Now, then – "

I said, "Please don't argue about it any more. You can't get around the fact that the price was perfectly fair, perfectly reasonable – considering that I didn't own the dog – and so arguing about it is only a waste of words. I have to have him back again because the man wants him; don't you see that I haven't any choice in the matter? Put yourself in my place. Suppose you had sold a dog that didn't belong to you; suppose you – "

"Oh," he said, "don't muddle my brains any more with your idiotic reasonings! Take him along, and give me a rest."

So I paid back the three dollars and led the dog downstairs and passed him over to his owner, and collected three for my trouble.

I went away then with a good conscience, because I had acted honourably; I never could have used the three that I sold the dog for, because it was not rightly my own, but the three I got for restoring him to his rightful owner was righteously and properly mine, because I had earned it. That man might never have gotten that dog back at all, if it hadn't been for me. My principles have remained to this day what they were then. I was always honest; I know I can never be otherwise. It is as I said in the beginning – I was never able to persuade myself to use money which I had acquired in questionable ways.

Now, then, that is the tale. Some of it is true.

(Mark Twain, *Chapters from my Autobiography*)

Boredom & Despair

Richard Cumberland, an 18th-century playwright who produced both comedies and tragedies, was obviously considered a thoroughly boring man and writer by his contemporaries. In these linked stories Michael Kelly, a singer and composer, describes how Cumberland threatened everybody with a recital of his own dramas.

. . . I got to Mr Cumberland's [in Tunbridge Wells] in time for dinner. The party consisted of myself, Bannister, Mrs Cumberland, an agreeable well-informed old lady, and our host, who by-the-by, during dinner called his wife, mamma. We passed a pleasant evening enough, but wine was scarce; however, what we had was excellent, and what was wanting in beverage, was amply supplied in converse sweet, and the delights of hearing the reading of a five-act comedy.

Five acts of a play, read by its author, after *tea*, are at any time opiates of the most determined nature, even if one has risen late and moved little; but with such a predisposition to somnolency as I found the drive, the dust, the sun, the air, the dinner, and a little sensible conversation had induced, what was to be expected? Long before the end of the second act I was fast as a church – a slight tendency to snoring, rendered this misfortune more appalling than it otherwise would have been; and the numberless kicks which I received under the table from Bannister, served only to vary, by fits and starts, the melody with which nature chose to accompany my slumbers.

When it is recollected, that our host and reader served Sheridan as a model for Sir Fretful [Plagiary, a character in Sheridan's play *The Critic*], it may be supposed that he was somewhat irritated by my inexcusable surrender of myself: but no; he closed his proceedings and his manuscript at the end of the second act, and we adjourned to a rational supper upon a cold mutton bone, and dissipated in two tumblers of weak red wine and water.

When the repast ended, the bard conducted us to our bed-rooms: the apartment in which I was to sleep, was his study; he paid me the compliment to say, he had a little tent-bed put up there, which he always appropriated to his favourite guest. "The bookcase at the side," he added, "was filled with his own writings."

I bowed, and said, "I dare say, Sir, I shall sleep very soundly."

"Ah! very good," said he; "I understand you – a hit, Sir, a palpable hit; you mean, being so close to my writings, they will act as a soporific. You are a good soul, Mr Kelly, but a very drowsy one – God bless you – you are a kind creature, to come into the country to listen to my nonsense – *buonas noches*! as we say in Spain – good night. I hope it will be fine weather for you to walk about in the morning; for I think, with Lord Falkland, who said he pitied unlearned gentlemen on a rainy day – umph – good night, God bless you – you are so kind."

I could plainly perceive, that the old gentlenman was not over-pleased, but I really had no intention of giving him offence. He was allowed, however, to be one of the most sensitive of men, when his own writings were spoken of; and, moreover, reckoned envious in the highest degree. He had an inveterate dislike to Mr Sheridan, and would not allow him the praise of a good dramatic writer; which, considering the ridicule Sheridan had heaped upon him in "The Critic", is not so surprising. – That piece was wormwood to him; he was also very sore at what Sheridan had said of him before he drew his portrait in that character.

This anecdote Mr Sheridan told me. When the "School for Scandal" came out, Cumberland's children prevailed upon their father to take them to see it; -they had the stage box – their father was seated behind them; and, as the story was told by a gentleman, a friend, of Sheridan's, who was close by, every time the children laughed at what was going on on the stage, he pinched them, and said,

"What are you laughing at, my dear little folks? You should

not laugh, my angels; there is nothing to laugh at." – And then, in an under tone, "Keep still, you little dunces."

Sheridan having been told of this, said, "It was very ungrateful in Cumberland to have been displeased with his poor children, for laughing at *my comedy*; for I went the other night to see *his tragedy*, and laughed at it from beginning to end."

But with all the irritability which so frequently belongs to dramatists, Mr Cumberland was a perfect gentleman in his manners, and a good classical scholar. I was walking with him on the pantiles one morning, and took the opportunity of telling him (which was the truth) that his dramatic works were in great request at Vienna; and that his "West Indian" and "Brothers", particularly, were first-rate favourites; this pleased the old man so much, that (I flattered myself) it made him forget my drowsy propensities . . .

A letter arrived the next morning, as we had planned, which called me to London; we informed our host, that we were obliged to quit his hospitable roof early the following day. "My children," said he, "I regret that you must leave your old bard, but business must be attended to; and as this is the last day I am to have the pleasure of your company, when you return from your evening's rambles on the pantiles, I will give you what I call a treat."

After dinner, Bannister and myself went to the library. "What," said I to Bannister, "can be the treat Cumberland has promised us tonight? I suppose he took notice of your saying at dinner, that our favourite meal was supper; and he intends, as we are going away tomorrow morning, to give us some little delicacies." Bannister professed entire ignorance, and some doubt; and on our return from our walk, we found Cumberland in his parlour, waiting for us. As I had anticipated, the cloth was laid for supper, and in the middle of the table was a large dish with a cover on it.

When we were seated, with appetites keen, and eyes fixed upon the mysterious dainty, our host, after some preparation, desired a servant to remove the cover, and on the dish lay another manuscript play. "There, my boys," said he, "there is the treat which I promised you; that, Sirs, is my 'Tiberius', in five acts; and after we have had our sandwich and wine and water, I will read you every word of it. I am not vain, but I do think it by far the best play I ever wrote, and I think you'll say so."

The threat itself was horrible; the Reading sauce was ill suited to the light supper, and neither poppy nor Mandragore, nor even the play of the preceding evening, would have been half so bad as his "Tiberius"; but will the reader believe that it was no joke, but all in earnest, and that he actually fulfilled his horrid promise, and read the three first acts? But seeing violent symptoms of our old complaint coming over us, he proposed that we should go to bed, and in the morning that he should treat us, before we started, by reading the fourth and fifth acts; but we saved him the trouble, for we were off before he was out of his bed. Such are the perils and hair-breadth 'scapes which attend the guests of dramatists who live in the country.

(Michael Kelly, *Reminiscences*)

The poet Thomas Chatterton's short and tragic life began in Bristol in 1752. While still in his early teens he created an imaginary medieval poet called Thomas Rowley, producing poems in an appropriate 15th-century style (see also **Forgeries & Frauds***). Brilliant but unstable, Chatterton decided to try his literary chances in London, hoping to make money not so much through poetry as by writing political articles for various magazines.*

[Chatterton] arrived in town on the 25th or 26th of April, 1770, at five in the evening. From his first letter to his mother we gather that he had several relations in London, one of whom, Mrs Ballance, lodged at the house of a Mr Walmsley, a plasterer, in Shoreditch. Chatterton himself obtained a room in the same house. The family was composed of the plasterer and his wife, a niece of the latter, who was a girl of about seventeen, and her brother, who was about three years younger . . .

That Chatterton soon began to experience the hardships and vicissitudes incident on a literary life is clear from his letters home, notwithstanding the boastful and confident terms in which they are expressed. He exaggerates and expatiates on the more attractive features of his daily life; on projected literary schemes; on his introductions to great people, and on the places of amusement he frequents, which, as he says, and truly enough for one whose employment obliged him to be conversant with current topics, were as necessary to him as food.

Mrs Ballance, when he had been in town two or three weeks, recommended him to get into some office, whereupon "he stormed about the room like a madman and frightened her not a little by telling her he hoped, with the blessing of God, very soon to be sent prisoner to the Tower, which would make his fortune . . . He frequently said he would settle the nation before he had done." He was, she says, "as proud as Lucifer". He very soon quarrelled with her for calling him "cousin Tommy", and asked if she ever heard of a poet's being called Tommy . . .

By this time, indeed, Chatterton must have been too well aware of the precarious nature of political writing, and, however abstemious in his habits, must have been brought face to face with absolute want. He took his meals with his relative and fellow-lodger Mrs Ballance; but his dinner consisted generally of only a tart and glass of water. Sometimes he was seen by the plasterer's nephew, who shared his bedroom, to pull out a sheep's tongue from his pocket and eat it, and this, we may believe, was the only animal food he ate. The small fund he had brought from Bristol had probably been exhausted, and as to his earnings for literary work, it is too certain that the men with whom he had to deal were taking advantage of the boy's inexperience and necessities.

Chatterton's hopes of getting by through political writing came to nothing. He earned 5 guineas by producing "a musical extravaganza", but by now his writing career was at an end. He was clutching at straws.

Thus, with no further means of disposing of his work, and unable to obtain payment for what he had already done, his situation had, by the middle of August, become almost desperate. One forlorn hope still remained. It will be remembered that when younger he had solicited Barrett to give him some instruction in surgery, and though the doctor did not consent,

Chatterton had probably gained from his books some little theoretical knowledge of the subject. At any rate, he considered it sufficient to enable him to give an opinion on medical subjects, and in one of his letters to his sister we find him giving some advice as to the treatment of a friend who was unwell, with all the confidence of a legitimate practitioner.

To go out to sea as a surgeon had no doubt early presented itself to his mind as a last resource, and in the letter just referred to, written little more than a month after his arrival in town, he says: "I might have a recommendation to Sir George Cole-brook, an East India Director, as qualified for an office in no ways despicable; but I shall not take a step to the sea whilst I can continue on land." The time had now come when it seemed impossible to do so any longer, and his last remaining hope was that Mr Barrett would give him a certificate testifying to his possessing the very scanty qualifications then required for a surgeon's mate. In the last letter preserved, which is addressed to George Catcott [a Bristol friend of Chatterton's], after much affected and forced talk about Bristol and other general matters, his real object appears in the concluding paragraph. "Mr. Barrett has it in his power to assist me greatly, by his giving me a physical character [i.e. a testimonial]. I hope he will."

This letter is dated 12 August. Barrett's refusal, which must have reached him in five or six days, left him without resource. For a few days longer he lingered on in gradually increasing destitution. Without any means of earning a subsistence, he was too proud to beg it, or even to accept it as an alms. Mr Cross, an apothecary in Brook Street with whom he had formed acquaintance, several times, it is said, pressed him to take a meal with him, but he continually declined. Once only was he induced to join him at supper, and he was then observed to eat "voraciously". A day or two later Mrs Angel his landlady noticed his evident want, and "as she knew he had not eaten anything for two or three days, she begged he would take some dinner with her on the 24th of August; but he was offended at her expressions, which seemed to hint he was in want, and assured her he was not hungry."

This day was his last. During the night of Friday the 24th of August, by means of arsenic in water, he put an end to his life.

His remains, distorted with the death struggle, were discovered when his door was broken open the next day. The floor of the room was strewn with the torn-up remnants of his latest work.

So perished, in destitution, obscurity, and despair, one whose name might under different circumstances have ranked amongst the first of his own generation. Overwhelmed by the neglect of his fellow-men, hopeless of any future career, unconscious even of the fame, which slowly though it has been accorded, was already laid in store for him, he deliberately and stoically resigned his life . . .

What remains of his story may be told in few words. An inquest was held on his body, and on the 28th of August it was consigned to a pauper's grave in the burial-ground of Shoe-Lane workhouse in the parish of St. Andrew's, Holborn, in which Brook Street is situated. His name is wrongly entered in the parish register as William Chatterton, to which a later hand has added the words "the poet". But there is good reason to believe that he did not find his last resting-place here. It is said that by the interest of some friends in London his mother was enabled to have the body conveyed to Bristol, and that Chatterton's uncle, Richard Philips, the sexton of St Mary's, who had always regarded his nephew with peculiar affection, buried it secretly in Redcliff churchyard. The story itself is by no means incredible, and is as well authenticated as many of the received facts of his life. It is at any rate a pleasing uncertainty which will allow us to hope that his grave is not with the nameless; that his body lies in the consecrated ground which had been the care of many generations of his forefathers, and within the shadow of that church which will ever form the noblest and most fitting monument to Chatterton's genius.

(Edward Bell, *Memoir of Thomas Chatterton*)

The poet Robert Southey went to extreme lengths to ensure that fellow-poet Percy Bysshe Shelley would have to sit through a reading of one of his "terrible" epic works.

Southey was addicted to reading his terrible epics – before they were printed – to any one who seemed to be a fit subject for the cruel experiment. He soon set his eyes on the new comer, and one day having effected the caption of Shelley, he immediately lodged him securely in the little study upstairs, carefully locking the door upon himself and prisoner and putting the key in his waistcoat pocket. There was a window in the room, it is true, but it was so high above the ground that Baron Trenck himself would not have attempted it.

"Now you shall be delighted," Southey said; "but sit down." Poor Bysshe sighed, and took his seat at the table. The author seated himself opposite, and placing his MS on the table before him, began to read slowly and distinctly. The poem, if I mistake not, was *The Curse of Kehamah.* Charmed with his own composition the admiring author read on, varying his voice occasionally, to point out the finer passages and invite applause. There was no commendation; no criticism; all was hushed. This was strange. Southey raised his eyes from the neatly-written MS; Shelley had disappeared. This was still more strange. Escape was impossible; every precaution had been taken, yet he had vanished. Shelley had glided noiselessly from his chair to the floor, and the insensible young Vandal lay buried in profound sleep underneath the table.

(Thomas Jefferson Hogg, *Life of Shelley*)

*Throughout his comparatively short life the poet Percy Bysshe Shelley (see above) had an obsession with water and drowning. He died in the way he had perhaps wished to: in a boating accident off Livorno in Italy (see **Death**). Shortly before this final and fatal voyage he went out to sea in a rowing boat with a friend, Jane Williams, and her young children. The apparent purpose of this expedition was to meet up with Jane's husband Edward, who was becalmed offshore. But when they were afloat Shelley was overtaken by one of his despairing moods – so despairing that he was evidently thinking of suicide there and then. In Edward Trelawny's account, as told to him by Jane Williams, quick thinking was required.*

On a calm sultry evening, Jane was sitting on the sands before the villa on the margin of the sea with her two infants watching for her husband – he was becalmed in the offing awaiting the sea breeze. Shelley came from the house dragging the skiff: after launching her he said to Jane,

"The sand and air are hot, let us float on the cool calm sea, there is room with careful stowage for us all in my barge."

His flashing eyes and vehement eager manner determined the instant execution of any project that took his fancy, however perilous. He overbore all opposition in those less self-willed than he was, and women are of a trusting nature and have faith in an earnest man. So Jane impulsively and promptly squatted in the bottom of the frail bark with her babies. The Poet, proud of his freight, triumphantly shoved off from the shore, and to exhibit his skill as a mariner rowed round a jutting promontory into deep blue water. The sea is very shallow for a considerable distance from the land in the bay, and Jane understood that Percy intended to float on the water near the shore, for the gunwale of the boat was only a hand's breadth out of the water; a puff of wind, a ripple on the water, or an incautious movement of the Poet, or herself or children, and the tub of a thing that could barely sustain the weight within it would cant over and fill and glide from under them. There was no eye watching them, no boat within a mile, the shore fast receding, the water deepening, and the Poet dreaming. As these dismal facts flashed on Jane's mind, her insane folly in trusting herself to a man of genius, but devoid of judgment, prudence, or skill, dismayed her.

After pulling out a long way, the Poet rested on his oars, unconscious of her fears and apparently of where he was, absorbed in a deep reverie, probably reviewing all he had gone through of suffering and wrong, with no present or future.

He was a brooding and silent man, feeling acutely, but never complaining – the wounds that bleed inwards are the most fatal. He took no heed of the occurrences of daily life, or men's selfish hopes or fears; his mind was so organized that it required a nice perception to know when and how to strike the chord that would excite his attention. Spellbound by terror, she kept her eyes on the awful boatman: sad and dejected, with his head leaning on his chest, his spirit seemed crushed; his hand had been for every man, and every man's hand against him. He was "the shorn lamb, but the wind was not tempered." At any other time or place Jane would have sympathized deeply with the lorn and despairing bard. She had made several remarks, but they met with no response. She saw death in his eyes. Suddenly he raised his head, his brow cleared and his face brightened as with a bright thought, and he exclaimed joyfully,

"Now let us together solve the great mystery."

An ordinary lady-kind would have screamed or got up to implore, to pray, or reason, and thus herself have accomplished what she most dreaded – the Poet's suggestion; but Jane, with a true woman's instinct – a safer guide in perilous emergencies than could be found in a senate of sages – knowing Shelley was unlike all other men, felt that to be silent or strike a discordant note to his feelings might make him stamp his foot, and the leaden waters would roll over and wrap round them as a winding-sheet; that her only chance was to distract his thoughts from his dismal past life to the less dreary present – to kindle hope. In answer to his kind and affectionate proposal of "solving the great mystery", suppressing her terror and assuming her usual cheerful voice, she answered promptly,

"No, thank you, not now; I should like my dinner first, and so would the children."

This gross material answer to his sublime proposition shocked the Poet, as showing his companion could not enter into the spirit of his idea.

"And look," she continued, "the sea breeze is coming in, the mist is clearing away, and Edward is coming on shore with Trelawny; they have been out since first light and must be famished, they took nothing with them, and tomorrow you are to have the boat-race to see if you can beat the *Bolivar*. I wish we were at shore; they'll be surprised at our being out at this time, and Edward says this boat is not safe."

"Safe!" said the Poet; "I'd go to Leghorn or anywhere in her."

Death's demon, always attending the Poet on the water, now spread his wings and vanished. Jane felt his thoughts were veering round and continued,

"You haven't written the words for the Indian air."

"Yes, I have," he answered, "long ago. I must write them out again, for I can't read what I compose and write out of doors.

You must play the air again and I'll try and make the thing better."

The weird boatman now paddled to where our boat had landed. Williams, not finding his wife in the house, came down to the beach in dismay, when I pointed her out to him in the skiff: the fisherman's boat that landed us had shoved off.

The Poet, deluded by the wiles of a woman into postponing his voyage to solve the great mystery, paddled his cockle shell of a boat into shallow water.

As soon as Jane saw the sandy bottom, she snatched up her babies and clambered out so hurriedly that the punt was capsized. Edward and I picked them up; the bard was underneath the boat and rose with it partly on his back, and was not unlike a turtle, or a hermit crab that houses itself in any empty shell it can find. Edward, surprised at his wife's lubberly way of getting out of the boat, said,

"We would have hauled the boat up, if you had waited a moment."

"No, thank you. Oh, I have escaped the most dreadful fate; never will I put my foot in that horrid coffin. Solve the great mystery? Why, he is the greatest of all mysteries. Who can predict what he will do? – and he casts a spell over everything. You can form some notion of what other people will do as they partake of our common nature – not what he will do. He is seeking after what we all avoid, death. I wish we were away, I shall always be in terror."

Leaving them to their cogitation, I went to make my toilet, the sea my washing-basin – there was no other. As usual we had a fish dinner. Jane ate nothing; the sight of the natives of the deep was enough. Condemned men can eat, but not the suddenly reprieved.

"You won't catch me in a boat with Shelley alone," said Jane.

(Edward Trelawny, *Records of Shelley, Byron and the Author*)

At the beginning of 1925 Evelyn Waugh was 22. He had finished his time at Oxford University – years which had been glittering in social terms but academically dismal – with gloomy views of what he described as "a completely hopeless future". After an abortive period at an art school, he fell into teaching at a preparatory school on the north Wales coast. The school, Arnold House in Denbighshire, was bleak and dull, matching Waugh's fortunes at this period. After a couple of terms he seemed to have found an escape-route when he obtained a job as a secretary to an English writer and translator in Pisa. Only after handing in his notice to the headmaster did Waugh discover that the offer of the secretary's job had all been a misunderstanding. This came on top of another blow, when Waugh received an unenthusiastic response from a friend to whom he had sent the draft of a novel. In fact, the reaction was so cool that Waugh recounts in his autobiography, *A Little Learning*, how he took the exercise books containing the draft chapters and threw them into the school boiler. He compared his own grim lot with the careers of his more fortunate friends. "I alone, it seemed, was rejected, at the end of my short tether."

One summer evening Evelyn Waugh went down to the beach, discarded his clothes and started swimming out to sea. As he tells the story, this was to be a final, dramatic gesture. To show it, he had deliberately not brought a towel (since this would be a one-way trip) and – on a more intellectual level – he left a note on the shore containing a quotation from the Greek tragic dramatist, Euripides. It was a calm, moonlit night and Waugh swam steadily out into deeper waters. Before he reached the point of no return, however, he was stung on the shoulder by a jellyfish and then stung again a few yards further on. The shock seems to have brought him back to his senses. He turned round and swam back to the sandy beach where the boys from the prep school had been playing that morning. He dressed himself again and tore up the piece of paper bearing the Greek quotation, leaving it to be carried away by the sea instead.

When Waugh grew old he suffered from a return of the boredom and melancholy which had never been far below the surface. In Selina Hastings' 1994 biography there is a poignant description of Waugh near the end of his life sitting in his library in his house in Combe Florey in Somerset. "He did no work, spending the day, he said, breathing on the library window, playing noughts and crosses, and drinking gin."

The novelist Graham Greene suffered all his life from boredom which sometimes approached despair. Although the following story has been doubted by some of his biographers, it has achieved mythical status as a piece of Greene-lore. According to his autobiography, *A Sort of Life*, he was in his late teens when he discovered a revolver and a boxful of bullets belonging to his elder brother. Instinctively, he claims, he pocketed the gun, walked to a secluded spot on the common near his family home, inserted a single bullet, spun the chamber, and fired the gun at his temple. Greene's version of Russian Roulette was far from being a suicidal act; rather, he intended it as a means of regaining enjoyment of the world "by risking its total loss". This desperate remedy worked – precisely because the gun did not. Only one shot away from the lethal chamber, Greene was left unscathed and with a sense of life's infinite possibilities. He repeated the experience a number of times later on, comparing it to shots of adrenalin, until the thrill started to wear thin. On another occasion, also related in *A Sort of Life*, Greene fought off boredom by having a perfectly good tooth taken out under gas because a "few minutes' unconsciousness was like a holiday from the world."

The Irish-born writer Samuel Beckett moved to Paris in his early twenties. There he formed a close friendship with his fellow Irish exile, James Joyce, and began to write novels and poems. But it was to be many years before the success of the play Waiting for Godot *(1953) turned him into an international literary figure. The comic desolation of this and other works was reflected in Beckett's own philosophy of life. The writer and journalist Peter Lennon struck up a friendship with the great playwright in the Paris of the 1960s.*

There is no disputing that Samuel Beckett was an anguished man and never attained consistent social ease. Late one night in the Falstaff [bar], he stopped paying attention to us; as was our way we left him to his silence. Then quite deliberately he raised his mug of beer and poured it slowly over his head. That seems like ammunition for another anecdote about Irish writers' buffoonery – but with someone you know you can tell the difference between clowning and private distress. It was a gesture of desperation. There was a quality in it, too, of spreading ashes on the head, or of dousing an intolerable pain. No one made any comment and, shortly after, we walked him part of the way home.

On another occasion after a performance of *Endgame* when we were having a drink in a terraced cafe by the Studio des Champs-Elysées, Pat Magee turned to Victor Herbert and in his grinding voice enquired: "Victor, why are you always so happy?"

"Because nothing ever troubles me," Victor said, not entirely truthfully.

"Did you hear that, Sam?" Magee said.

Beckett looked at them: "I have never," he said, "had a single untroubled moment in my entire life."

(Peter Lennon, Foreign Correspondent)

Crime, Punishment & Mystery

The playwright John Fletcher was contemporary with Shakespeare and wrote many plays in collaboration with Francis Beaumont.

John Fletcher, son of Richard Fletcher, doctor of divinity, was (as by proportion of time is collectible) born in this county [Northamptonshire], before his father was bishop of Bristol or London, and whilst as yet he was dean of Peterborough. He had an excellent wit, which the backfriends to stage-plays will say was neither idle, nor well employed. For he and Francis Beaumont esquire, like Castor and Pollux, (most happy when in conjunction) raised the English, to equal the Athenian and Roman theatre; Beaumont bringing the ballast of judgement, Fletcher the sail of fantasy, both compounding a poet to admiration.

Meeting once in a tavern, to contrive the rude draft of a tragedy, Fletcher undertook to kill the king therein, whose words being overheard by a listener (though his loyalty not to be blamed herein) he was accused of high treason, till the mistake soon appearing, that the plot was only against a dramatic and scenical king, all wound off in merriment.

(Thomas Fuller, *Fuller's Worthies*)

Playwright Ben Jonson had the misfortune to fall foul of King James I when he made some derogatory comments about the Scots (James was Scottish) in Eastward Ho, *a play which he had co-authored with two others.*

He was dilated [reported] by Sir James Murray to the King, for writting something against the Scots, in a play *Eastward Ho*, and voluntarily imprisoned himself with Chapman and Marston, who had written it amongst them. The report was, that they should then have had their ears cut and noses. After their delivery, he banqueted all his friends; there was Camden, Selden, and others; at the midst of the feast his old Mother dranke to him, and shew him a paper which she had (if the sentence had taken execution) to have mixed in the prisson among his drinke, which was full of lustie strong poison, and that she was no churle, she told, she minded first to have drunk of it herself.

(William Drummond, *Conversations with William Drummond of Hawthornden*)

This story is hard to believe but it has John Donne, 17th-century poet and Dean of St Paul's, working as an amateur detective. True or not, it's too good to miss.

When Doctor Donne, afterwards Dean of St Paul's, London, took possession of the first living he ever had, being a speculative man, he took a walk into the Churchyard, where the sexton was digging up a grave, and, throwing up a skull, the Doctor took it up, to contemplate thereon; and found a small sprigg, or headless nail, sticking in the temple, which he drew out secretly, and wrapped it up in the corner of his handkerchief; he then demanded of the gravedigger whether he knew whose skull it was. He said he did very well, declaring it was a man's who kept a brandy-shop, an honest drunken fellow, who, one night taking two quarts of that comfortable creature [i.e. brandy], was found dead in his bed the next morning. "Had he a wife?" said the Doctor. "Yes." "Is she living?" "Yes." "What character does she bear?" "A very good one; only indeed the neighbours reflected on her, because she married the day after her husband was buried; though, to be sure, she had no great reason to grieve after him." This was enough for the Doctor, who, under pretence of visiting all his parishioners, called on her: he asked her several questions; amongst others, what sickness her first husband had died of. She, giving him the same account he had before received, he suddenly opened the handkerchief and cried, in an authoritative voice: "Woman, do you know this nail?" She was struck with horror at the unexpected demand, and instantly owned the fact [confessed the crime] . . .The unhappy criminal was struck with horror at the demand and the sight, and instantly owned that she had been the perpetrator of the deed which had hurried her husband, in a state of intoxication, into the eternal world.

(Edwin Paxton, *The World of Anecdote*)

The diarist John Evelyn is a victim of a highway robbery in June, 1652.

The morning growing excessivly hot, I sent my footman some hours before, and so rode negligently, under favour of the shade, 'til being now come to within three miles of Bromely, at a place calld the procession Oake, started out two Cuttthroates, and striking with their long staves at the horse, taking hold of the reignes, threw me downe, and immediately tooke my sword, and haled me into a deepe Thickett, some quarter of a mile from the high-way, where they might securely rob me, as they soone did; what they got of mony was not considerable, but they tooke two rings, the one an Emrald with diamonds, an Onyx, and a pair of boucles set with rubies and diamonds which were of value, and after all, barbarously bound my hands behind me, and my feete, having before pull'd off my bootes: and then set me up against an Oake, with most bloudy threatnings to cutt my throat, if I offerd to crie out, or make any noise, for that they should be within hearing, I not being the person they looked for: I told them, if they had not basely surpriz'd me, they should not have made so easy a prize, and that it should teach me hereafter never to ride neere an hedge since had I ben in the mid way, they durst not have adventur'd on me, at which they cock'd their pistols, and told me they had long guns too, and were 14 companions, which all were lies: I begg'd for my Onyx and told them it being engraven with my armes, would betray them, but nothing prevaild: My horses bridle they slipt, and search'd the saddle which they likewise pull'd off, but let the horse alone to graze, and then turning againe bridld him, and tied him to a Tree, yet so as he might graze, and so left me bound: The reason they tooke not my horse, was I suppose, because he was mark'd, and cropt on both Eares and well known on that roade, and these rogues were lusty foote padders, as they are cald: Well, being left in this manner, grievously was I tormented with the flies, the ants, and the sunn, so as I sweate intollerably, nor little was my anxiety how I should get loose in that solitary place, where I could neither heare or see any creature but my poore horse and a few sheepe stragling in the Coppse; til after neere two houres attempting I got my hands to turne paulme to paulme, whereas before they were tied back to back, and then I stuck a greate while ere' I could slip the cord over my wrist to my thumb, which at last I did, and then being quite loose soone unbound my feete, and so sadling my horse, and roaming a while about, I at last perceiv'd a dust to rise, and soone after heard the rattling of a Cart, towards which I made, and by the help of two Country fellows that were driving it, got downe a steepe bank, into the highway againe; but could heare nothing of the Villains: So I rod to Colonel Blounts a greate justiciarie of the times, who sent out hugh and Crie immediately . . . The next morning weary and sore as I was at my wrists and armes, I went from Deptford to Lond, got 500 ticketts printed and dispers'd, by an officer of Gould Smiths-hall, describing what I had lost, and within two daies after had tidings of all I lost, except my Sword which was a silver hilt, and some other trifles: These rogues had paund my Rings etc for a trifle to a Goldsmiths Servant, before the tickets came to the shop, by which meanes they scap'd, the other ring was bought by a Victualer, who brought it to a Goldsmith, that having seene the ticket, seiz'd upon him; but whom I afterwards discharg'd upon the mediation of friends, and protestation of his inno-cency: Thus did God deliver me from these villains, and not onely so, but restor'd to me what they tooke, as twise before he had graciously don, both at sea and land, I meane, when I had ben rob'd by Pyrates and was in danger of a considerable losse at Amsterdam, for which and many, many signal preservations I am eternaly obligd to give thanks to God my Saviour.

10 July I had newes of the taking of one of the knaves who robbd me, and was summon'd to appeare against him . . . but not

being bound over (nor willing to hang the fellow) I did not appeare . . .

15 July . . . I received a letter from Sir Tho: Peyton, and a petition from the Prisoner (whose father I understood was an honest old fermor in Kent) to be favourable which I was; not withstanding, others comming in, about a Rape, and that he had ben in Goeile [gaol] before, he was condemn'd, but repriv'd by Sir Tho: I was told he was a bloudy rascal, and had murderd severall of his Majesties Subjects being a souldier in Ireland, and that had it not ben for his companion, a younger fellow, 'twas ten to one, but he had knock'd me on the head: This I came to know afterwards and that in the End, upon some other Crime, he being obstinate and not pleading, was press'd to death*: one thing I remember, that he was one of the worst look'd fellows I ever saw.

(John Evelyn, *Diary*)

In his life of the unlucky Richard Savage, Samuel Johnson describes how the poet and some friends nearly paid the supreme penalty under the law.

On the 20th of November, 1727, Mr Savage came from Richmond, where he then lodged, that he might pursue his studies with less interruption, with an intent to discharge another lodging which he had in Westminster; and accidentally meeting two gentlemen, his acquaintances, whose names were Merchant and Gregory, he went in with them to a neighbouring coffeehouse, and sat drinking till it was late, it being in no time of Mr Savage's life any part of his character to be the first of the company that desired to separate. He would willingly have gone to bed in the same house; but there was not room for the whole company and therefore they agreed to ramble about the streets, and divert themselves with such amusements as should offer themselves till morning.

---

* Press'd to death This punishment (the so-called "peine forte et dure") – in effect, a death sentence by torture – could be applied to an accused person who refused to plead either guilty or not guilty. It involved being pressed to death by heavy weights.

In this walk they happened unluckily to discover a light in Robinson's coffee-house, near Charing-Cross, and therefore went in. Merchant with some rudeness demanded a room, and was told that there was a good fire in the next parlour, which the company were about to leave, being then paying their reckoning. Merchant, not satisfied with this answer, rushed into the room, and was followed by his companions. He then petulantly placed himself between the company and the fire, and soon after kicked down the table. This produced a quarrel, swords were drawn on both sides, and one Mr James Sinclair was killed. Savage having likewise wounded a maid that held him, forced his way with Merchant out of the house, but being intimidated and confused, without resolution either to fly or stay, they were taken in a back court by one of the company and some soldiers, whom he had called to his assistance.

Being secured and guarded that night, they were in the morning carried before three justices, who committed them to the Gatehouse [at Westminster], from whence, upon the death of Mr Sinclair which happened the same day, they were removed in the night to Newgate, where they were however treated with some distinction, exempted from the ignominy of chains, and confined, not among the common criminals, but in the Press-yard.

When the day of trial came the court was crowded in a very unusual manner, and the public appeared to interest itself as in a cause of general concern. The witnesses against Mr Savage and his friends were the woman who kept the house, which was a house of ill fame, and her maid, the men who were in the room with Mr Sinclair, and a woman of the town, who had been drinking with them, and with whom one of them had been seen in bed. They swore in general that Merchant gave the provocation, which Savage and Gregory drew their swords to justify; that Savage drew first, and that he stabbed Sinclair when he was not in a posture of defence, or while Gregory commanded his sword; that after he had given the thrust he turned pale, and would have retired, but the maid clung round him, and one of the company endeavoured to detain him, from whom he broke, by cutting the maid on the head, but was afterwards taken in a court.

There was some difference in their depositions: one did not see Savage give the wound, another saw it given when Sinclair held his point towards the ground; and the woman of the town asserted that she did not see Sinclair's sword at all: this difference however was very far from amounting to inconsistency; but it was sufficient to show that the hurry of the dispute was such, that it was not easy to discover the truth with relation to particular circumstances, and that therefore some deductions were to be made from the credibility of the testimonies.

Sinclair had declared several times before his death that he received his wound from Savage; nor did Savage at his trial deny the fact, but endeavoured partly to extenuate it, by urging the suddenness of the whole action, and the impossibility of any design or premeditated malice, and partly to justify it by the necessity of self-defence, and the hazard of his own life, if he had lost that opportunity of giving the thrust: he observed that neither reason nor law obliged a man to wait for the blow which was threatened, and which, if he should suffer it, he might never be able to return; that it was always allowable to prevent an assault, and to preserve life by taking away that of the adversary by whom it was endangered.

With regard to the violence with which he endeavoured to escape, he declared that it was not his design to fly from justice, or decline a trial, but to avoid the expenses and severities of a prison; and that he intended to have appeared at the bar without compulsion.

This defence, which took up more than an hour, was heard by the multitude that thronged the court with the most attentive and respectful silence: those who thought he ought not to be acquitted, owned that applause could not be refused him; and those who before pitied his misfortunes, now reverenced his abilities.

The witnesses which appeared against him were proved to be persons of characters which did not entitle them to much credit; a common strumpet, a woman by whom strumpets were entertained, and a man by whom they were supported; and the character of Savage was by several persons of distinction asserted to be that of a modest, inoffensive man, not inclined to broils or to insolence, and who had, to that time, been only known for his misfortunes and his wit.

Had his audience been his judges, he had undoubtedly been acquitted; but Mr Page, who was then upon the bench, treated him with his usual insolence and severity, and when he had summed up the evidence, endeavoured to exasperate the jury, as Mr Savage used to relate it, with this eloquent harangue:

"Gentlemen of the jury, you are to consider that Mr Savage is a very great man, a much greater man than you or I, gentlemen of the jury; that he wears very fine clothes, much finer clothes than you or I, gentlemen of the jury; that he has abundance of money in his pocket, much more money than you or I, gentlemen of the jury; but, gentlemen of the jury, is it not a very hard case, gentlemen of the jury, that Mr Savage should therefore kill you or me, gentlemen of the jury?"

Mr Savage hearing his defence thus misrepresented, and the men who were to decide his fate incited against him by invidious comparisons, resolutely asserted that his cause was not candidly explained, and began to recapitulate what he had before said with regard to his condition, and the necessity of endeavouring to escape the expenses of imprisonment; but the judge having ordered him to be silent, and repeated his orders without effect, commanded that he should be taken from the bar by force.

The jury then heard the opinion of the judge that good characters were of no weight against positive evidence, though they might turn the scale where it was doubtful; and that though, when two men attack each other, the death of either is only manslaughter; but where one is the aggressor, as in the case before them, and, in pursuance of his first attack, kills the other, the law supposes the action, however sudden, to be malicious. They then deliberated upon their verdict, and determined that Mr Savage and Mr Gregory were guilty of murder; and Mr Merchant, who had no sword, only of manslaughter.

Thus ended this memorable trial, which lasted eight hours. Mr Savage and Mr Gregory were conducted back to prison, where they were more closely confined, and loaded with irons of fifty pounds weight: four days afterwards they were sent back to the court to receive sentence . . .

There were desperate attempts by Savage's friends to save him from the death penalty. Queen Caroline, wife of George II, was appealed to. Savage's life was made even more precarious by the bitter hostility of his mother who put about the story that her son had once tried to murder her (he was illegitimate and she had hated him since birth). Accordingly the queen at first refused to listen to the pleas for mercy.

Thus had Savage perished by the evidence of a bawd, a strumpet and his mother, had not justice and compassion procured him an advocate of rank too great to be rejected unheard, and of virtue too eminent to be heard without being believed. His merit and his calamities happened to reach the ear of the Countess of Hertford, who engaged in his support with all the tenderness that is excited by pity, and all the zeal which is kindled by generosity; and, demanding an audience of the Queen, laid before her the whole series of his mother's cruelty, exposed the improbability of an accusation by which he was charged with an intent to commit a murder [i.e. the murder of his mother] that could conduce no advantage, and soon convinced her how little his former conduct could deserve to be mentioned as a reason for extraordinary severity.

   The interposition of this lady was so successful that he was soon after admitted to bail, and, on the 9th of March, 1728, pleaded the King's pardon.

(Samuel Johnson, *Life of Savage*)

17th-century writer and diarist Horace Walpole describes in a letter how his coach was held up by a highwayman.

The night I had the honour of writing to your Ladyship last, I was robbed – and, as if I were a sovereign or a nation, have had a discussion ever since whether it was not a *neighbour* who robbed me and should it come to the ears of the newspapers, it might produce as ingenious a controversy amongst our anonymous wits as any of the noble topics I have been mentioning. *Voici le fait.* Lady Browne and I were, as usual, going to the

Duchess of Montrose at seven o'clock. The evening was very dark. In the close lane under her park-pale, and within twenty yards of the gate, a black figure on horseback pushed by between the chaise and the hedge on my side. I suspected it was a highwayman, and so I found did Lady Browne, for she was speaking and stopped. To divert her fears, I was just going to say, "Is not that the apothecary going to the Duchess?" when I heard a voice cry "Stop!" and the figure came back to the chaise. I had the presence of mind, before I let down the glass, to take out my watch and stuff it within my waistcoat under my arm. He said, "Your purse and watches!" I replied, "I have no watch." "Then your purse!" I gave it to him; it had nine guineas. It was so dark that I could not see his hand, but felt him take it. He then asked for Lady Browne's purse, and said, "Don't be frightened; I will not hurt you." I said, "No; you won't frighten the lady?" He replied, "No; I give you my word I will do you no hurt." Lady Browne gave him her purse, and was going to add her watch, but he said, "I am much obliged to you! I wish you good night!" pulled off his hat, and rode away. "Well?" said I, "Lady Browne, you will not be afraid of being robbed another time, for you see there is nothing in it." "Oh, but I am," said she, "and now I am in terrors lest he should return, for I have given him a purse with only bad money that I carry on purpose." "He certainly will not open it directly," said I, "and at worst he can only wait for us at our return; but I will send my servant back for a horse and a blunderbuss," which I did. The next distress was not to terrify the Duchess, who is so paralytic and nervous. I therefore made Lady Browne go into the parlour, and desired one of the Duchess's servants to get her a glass of water, while I went into the drawing-room to break it to the Duchess. "Well," said I, laughing to her and the rest of the company, "you won't get much from us tonight." "Why," said one of them, "have you been robbed?" "Yes, a little," said I. The Duchess trembled; but it went off. Her groom of the chambers said not a word, but slipped out, and Lady Margaret and Miss Howe having servants there on horseback, he gave them pistols and dispatched them different ways. This was exceedingly clever, for he knew the Duchess would not have suffered it, as lately he had detected a man who had robbed her garden, and she would not allow him to take up the fellow.

(Horace Walpole, *letter to the Countess of Upper Ossory, October 1781*)

William Cobbet was a radical journalist and writer who spent much of his life battling the authorities. He enlisted in the army in 1784 and was stationed in Canada. His tremendous energy and self-belief soon brought him recognition and promotion. Cobbett, however, was outraged by the casual acceptance of corruption among the officer class and resolved to expose the crime. He needed to gather evidence but had to do it in secret.

The object of my quitting the army, to which I was attached, was to bring certain officers to justice for having, in various ways, wronged both the public and the soldier. I was so situated as to save England thousands and thousands of pounds during the time that my regiment was stationed in New Brunswick. My vigilance was incessant; and I pursued the interest of the government at home, with as much zeal as if my life depended on the result . . .

If my officers had been men of manifest superiority of mind, I should, perhaps, not have so soon conceived the project of bringing them, or some of them, at least, to shame and punishment for the divers flagrant breaches of the law, committed by them. The circumstance which first disgusted me, and that finally made me resolve to tear myself from a service, to which my whole mind and heart were devoted, was, the abuses, the shocking abuses as to money matters, the peculation, in short, which I witnessed, and which I had, in vain, endeavoured to correct.

This project was conceived so early as the year 1787 when an affair happened, that first gave me a full insight into regimental justice. It was shortly this: that the Quarter-Master, who had the issuing of the men's provisions to them, kept about a fourth part of it to himself. This, the old sergeants told me, had been the case for many years; and, they were quite astonished and terrified at the idea of my complaining of it. This I did, however but, the reception I met with convinced me, that I must never make another complaint, till I got safe to England and safe out of the reach of that most curious of courts, a court-martial.

From this time forward, I began to collect material for an exposure, upon my return to England. I had ample opportunities for this, being the keeper of all the books of every sort, in the regiment, and knowing the whole of its affairs better than any other man. But, the winter previous to our return to England, I thought it necessary to make extracts from the books, lest the books themselves should be destroyed. In order to be able to prove that these extracts were correct, it was necessary that I should have a witness as to their being true copies. This was a very ticklish point. One foolish step here, could have sent me down to the ranks with a pair of bloody shoulders. I hesitated many months. At one time I had given the thing up. I dreamt twenty times, I daresay, of my papers being discovered, and of my being tried and flogged half to death. At last, however, some fresh act of injustice towards us made me set all danger at defiance. I opened my project to a corporal, whose name was William Bestland, who wrote in the office under me, and who was very much bound to me, for my goodness to him. To work we went, and during a long winter, while the rest were boozing and snoring, we gutted no small part of the regimental books, rolls, and other documents. Our way was this: to take a copy, sign it with our names, and clap the regimental seal to it, so that we might be able to swear to it, when produced in court.

All these papers were put into a little box, which I myself had made for the purpose. When we came to Portsmouth, there was a talk of searching all the boxes, etc., which gave us great alarm; and induced us to take all the papers, put them in a bag, and trust them to a custom-house officer, who conveyed them on shore to his own house, when I removed them in a few days after.

Thus prepared, I, after securing my discharge, went to London, and, on the 14th of January, 1792, I wrote to the then Secretary of War, Sir George Yonge, stating my situation, my business with him, and my intentions; enclosing him a letter or petition from myself to the King. I waited from the 14th to

the 24th of January, without receiving any answer at all, and
then all I heard was, that he wished to see me at the War
Office . . .

Sir George Yonge heard my story; and that was apparently all
he wanted of me. I was to hear from him again in a day or two;
and, after waiting for fifteen days, without hearing from him, or
anyone else, upon the subject, I wrote him again, reminding
him that I had, from the first, told him that I had no other
business in London; that my stock of money was necessarily
scanty; and that to detain me in London was to ruin me.

*Cobbett started to suspect that the authorities were interested not in
justice but in obstructing him. In particular, he was dismayed that any
court-martial of the accused officers was likely to be held in Portsmouth, a naval and garrison town. Eventually Cobbett wrote to the
Prime Minister, William Pitt.*

Plainly seeing what was going forward, I, on the 7th of March,
made, in a letter to Mr Pitt, a representation of the whole case.
This letter had the effect of changing the place of the court-
martial, which was now to be held in London; but, as to my
other great ground of complaint, the leaving of the regimental
books unsecured, it had no effect at all; and, it will be recollected, that without those books, there could be no proof
produced, without bringing forward Corporal Bestland, and
the danger of doing that will presently be seen. Without these
written documents nothing of importance could be proved,
unless the non-commissioned officers and men of the regiment
could get the better of their dread of the lash; and, even then,
they could only speak from memory. As the court-martial was
to assemble on the 24th of March, I went down to Portsmouth
on the 20th, in order to know for certain what was become of the
books; and, I found, that they had never been secured at all; that
they had been left in the hands of the accused from the 14th of
January to the very hour of trial.

There remained, then, nothing to rest upon with safety but
our extracts, confirmed by the evidence of Bestland, and this I
had solemnly engaged with him not to have recourse to, unless
he was first out of the army; that is to say, out of the reach of the

vindictive and bloody lash. There was a suspicion of his connection with me, and, therefore, they resolved to keep him.

I resolved not to appear at the court-martial, unless the
discharge of Bestland was first granted. Accordingly, on the
20th of March, I wrote from Fratton, a village near Portsmouth,
to the Judge-Advocate, stating over again all the obstacles that
had been thrown in my way, and concluding by demanding the
discharge of a man, whom I should name, as the only condition
upon which I would attend the court-martial. I requested him
to send me an answer by the next day, and told him, that, unless
such an answer was received, he and those to whom my repeated
applications had been made, might do what they pleased with
their court-martial; for, that I confidently trusted, that a few
days would place me beyond the scope of their power. No
answer came, and, as I had learned in the meanwhile, that there
was a design to prosecute me for sedition, that was an additional
motive to be quick in my movements.

As I was going down to Portsmouth, I met several of the
sergeants coming up, together with the music-master; and, as
they had none of them been in America, I wondered what they
could be going to London for; but, upon my return, I was told
by a Captain Lane, who had been in the regiment, that they had
been brought up to swear, that, at an entertainment given to
them by me, before my departure from the regiment, I had
drunk "the destruction of the House of Brunswick"*. This was
false; but, I knew that that was no reason why it should not be
sworn by such persons and in such a case. I had talked pretty
freely upon the occasion alluded to; but I had neither said, nor
thought anything against the King, and, as to the House of
Brunswick, I hardly knew what it meant. My head was filled
with the corruptions and baseness in the army. I knew nothing
at all about politics . . . I was told they would send me to Botany
Bay†; and, I now verily believe, that, if I had remained, I should
have furnished a pretty good example to those, who wished to
correct military abuses. I did not, however, leave England from
this motive. I could not obtain a chance of success, without

* House of Brunswick – the Royal House of George IV.
† Botany Bay – i.e. "transported" to Australia.

exposing the back of my poor faithful friend Bestland. It was useless to appear, until I could have tolerable fair play; and, besides, it seemed better to leave the whole set to do as they pleased, than to be made a mortified witness of what it was quite evident they had resolved to do.

(William Cobbett, *An Autobiography*)

Cobbett did give up the case and retreated first to France and then to America. Some years later, after he'd returned to England, he was imprisoned for two years for attacking the use of flogging in the army.

The poet and journalist Leigh Hunt received a 2-year jail sentence in 1813 for libelling the Prince Regent in the Examiner, *a newspaper which Hunt edited with his brother. He had referred to the prince as a "corpulent man of fifty . . . a violator of his word, a libertine". His imprisonment wasn't too bad in some respects; he had his own quarters, his family were allowed to be with him, and he could continue to work. In this excerpt from his autobiography Leigh Hunt describes how he was locked in on his first night by the wife of the gaoler, a tactful woman who was obviously aware that this new inmate was different from the ordinary run of prisoners.*

It was the business of this woman to lock me up in my garret; but she did it so softly the first night, that I knew nothing of the matter. The night following, I thought I heard a gentle tampering with the lock. I tried it, and found it fastened. She heard me as she was going downstairs, and said the next day, "Ah, sir I thought I should have turned the key so as for you not to hear it; but I found you did." The whole conduct of this couple towards us, from first to last, was a piece with this singular delicacy.

My bed was shortly put up, and I slept in my new room. It was on an upper story, and stood in a corner of the quadrangle, on the right hand as you enter the prison gate. The windows (which had now been accommodated with glass, in addition to their "excellent shutters") were high up, and barred; but the room was large and airy, and there was a fireplace. It was intended to be a common room for the prisoners on that story; but the cells were then empty. The cells were ranged on either side of the arcade, of which the story is formed, and the room opened at the end of it. At night-time the door was locked; then another on the top of the staircase, then another on the middle of the staircase, then a fourth at the bottom, a fifth that shut up the little yard belonging to that quarter, and how many more, before you got out of the gates, I forget: but I do not exaggerate when I say there were ten or eleven. The first night I slept there, I listened to them, one after the other, till the weaker part of my heart died within me. Every fresh turning of the key seemed a malignant insult to my love of liberty. I was alone, and away from my family; I, who to this day have never slept from home above a dozen weeks in my life. Furthermore, the reader will bear in mind that I was ill. With a great flow of natural spirits, I was subject to fits of nervousness, which had latterly taken a more continued shape. I felt one of them coming on, and having learned to anticipate and break the force of it by exercise, I took a stout walk by pacing backwards and forwards for the space of three hours. This threw me into a state in which rest, for rest's sake, became pleasant. I got hastily into bed, and slept without a dream till morning.

By the way, I never dreamt of prison but twice all the time I was there, and my dream was the same on both occasions. I fancied I was at the theatre, and the whole house looked at me in surprise, as much as to say, "How could he get out of prison?"

(Leigh Hunt, Autobiography)

The era of public executions provided the public with an opportunity for righteous voyeurism. Writers weren't immune. To his substantial bank of experience Lord Byron added a triple beheading which he witnessed in Italy.

The day before I left Rome I saw three robbers guillotined. The ceremony – including the masqued priests; the half-naked executioners; the bandaged criminals; the black Christ & his banner; the scaffold; the soldiery; the slow procession, & the quick rattle and heavy fall of the axe, the splash of the blood, & the ghastliness of the exposed heads – is altogether more

impressive than the vulgar and ungentlemanly "new drop" &
dog-like agony of infliction upon the sufferers of the English
sentence. Two of these men behaved calmly enough, but the
first of the three died with great terror and reluctance, which
was very horrible. He would not lie down; then his neck was too
large for the aperture, and the priest was obliged to drown his
exclamations by still louder exhortations. The head was off
before the eye could trace the blow; but from an attempt to draw
back the head, notwithstanding it was held forward by the hair,
the first head was cut off clean to the ears; the other two were
taken off more cleanly. It is better than the Oriental way & (I
should think) than the axe of our ancestors. The pain seems
little; & yet the effect to the spectator, & the preparation to the
criminal, is very striking & chilling. The first turned me quite
hot and thirsty, & made me shake so that I could hardly hold the
opera-glass (I was close but was determined to see, as one
should see everything, once, with attention) the second and
third (which shows how dreadfully soon things grow indifferent) I am ashamed to say had no effect on me as a horror though
I would have saved them if I could.

(Byron, *letter, Venice, May, 1817*)

*Sir Walter Scott reveals to Tom Moore, poet and diarist, the source of
a scene in his novel* Marmion.

Scott mentioned the contrast in the behaviour of two criminals,
whom he had himself seen: the one a woman, who had poisoned
her husband in some drink, which she gave him while he was ill;
the man not having the least suspicion, but leaning his head on
her lap, while she still mixed more poison in the drink, as he
became thirsty and asked for it. The other a man, who had made
a bargain to sell a subject (a young child) to a surgeon; his
bringing it at night in a bag; the surgeon's surprise at hearing it
cry out; the man then saying, "Oh, you wanted it dead, did
you?" and stepping behind a tree and killing it. The woman
(who was brought up to judgment with a child at her breast)
stood with the utmost calmness to hear her sentence; while the
man, on the contrary, yelled out, and showed the most dis-

gusting cowardice. Scott added, that this suggested to him the scene in *Marmion*.

(Tom Moore, *Diaries, October 22nd 1826*)

Edmund Gosse, the late Victorian writer, remembers discussing with his father – a profoundly and narrowly religious man – that favourite Victorian topic: murder.

Sometimes, in the course of this winter, my Father and I had long cosy talks together over the fire. Our favourite subject was murders. I wonder whether little boys of eight, soon to go upstairs alone at night, often discuss violent crime with a widower-papa? The practice, I cannot help thinking, is unusual; it was, however, consecutive with us. We tried other secular subjects, but we were sure to come round at last to "what do you suppose they really did with the body?" I was told, a thrilled listener, the adventure of Mrs Manning, who killed a gentleman on the stairs and buried him in quick-lime in the back-kitchen, and it was at this time that I learned the useful historical fact, which abides with me after half a century, that Mrs Manning was hanged in black satin, which thereupon went wholly out of fashion in England. I also heard about Burke and Hare [the body snatchers], whose story nearly froze me into stone with horror.

These were crimes which appear in the chronicles. But who will tell me what "the Carpet-bag Mystery" was, which my Father and I discussed evening after evening ? I have never come across a whisper of it since, and I suspect it of having been a hoax. As I recall the details, people in a boat, passing down the Thames, saw a carpet bag hung high in air, on one of the projections of a pier of Waterloo Bridge. Being with difficulty dragged down – or perhaps up – this bag was found to be full of human remains, dreadful butcher's business of joints and fragments. Persons were missed, were identified, were again denied – the whole is a vapour in my memory which shifts as I try to define it. But clear enough is the picture I hold of myself, in a high chair, on the left-hand side of the sitting-room fireplace, the leaping flames reflected in the glass-case of tropical insects on the opposite wall, and my Father, leaning anxiously forward, with uplifted finger, emphasizing to me the pros and cons of the horrible carpet-bag evidence.

I suppose that my interest in these discussions – and Heaven knows I was animated enough – amused and distracted my Father, whose idea of a suitable theme for childhood's ear now seems to me surprising. I soon found that these subjects were not welcome to everybody, for, starting the Carpet-bag Mystery one morning with Miss Marks, in the hope of delaying my arithmetic lesson, she fairly threw her apron over her ears, and told me, from that vantage, that if I did not desist at once, she should scream.

(Edmund Gosse, *Father and Son*)

This story again comes from Edmund Gosse, who was a friend of Robert Louis Stevenson and who tells this episode from the childhood of the author of Treasure Island.

He was still a rather little boy when, in the summer holidays, having been reading a number of "detective" novels of a bad kind, he was passing one Sunday afternoon along a road which led through one of the suburbs of Edinburgh, and saw a deserted house, left furnished, but without, apparently, a caretaker. It suddenly struck Stevenson that it would be a very gallant thing to break into this house. No one was in sight, and, stealing round, he found it possible to open a window at the back, and so climb in. It really was unoccupied, and he prowled from room to room, looking at the books and pictures, in a great excitement of spirit, until he heard, as he thought, a noise in the garden. This sent him immediately, in an instant collapse of courage, under a bed, and then terror seized him. He imagined himself pounced upon, charged with robbery, marched home with gyves [fetters] upon his wrists, and arriving just as the family were assembling to attend evening service. He burst out crying, and could not stop, and his sobs echoed in the empty house.

He crept out where he had crept in, having done no harm to anything except his little tender Scottish conscience. But the spirit of adventure, which was native to him, is exemplified in the story, and also a sort of solitude, as of a boy obliged to play by himself for want of other pirates and burglars to combine with.

(Edmund Gosse, *from an article in Chambers' Journal*)

Samuel Clemens (Mark Twain) had a burglar alarm installed at his house in Hartford, Connecticut. It was a complicated mechanism, wired up to every door and window in the house but, as he tells the story, it was completely useless – except on one occasion.

That burglar-alarm which Susy [Twain's daughter] mentions led a gay and careless life, and had no principles. It was generally out of order at one point or another; and there was plenty of opportunity, because all the windows and doors in the house, from the cellar up to the top floor, were connected with it. However, in its seasons of being out of order it could trouble us for only a very little while: we quickly found out that it was fooling us, and that it was buzzing its blood-curdling alarm merely for its own amusement. Then we would shut it off, and send to New York for the electrician – there not being one in all Hartford in those days. When the repairs were finished we would set the alarm again and re-establish our confidence in it. It never did any real business except upon one single occasion. All the rest of its expensive career was frivolous and without purpose. Just that one time it performed its duty, and its whole duty – gravely, seriously, admirably. It let fly about two o'clock one black and dreary March morning, and I turned out promptly, because I knew that it was not fooling, this time. The bath-room door was on my side of the bed. I stepped in there, turned up the gas, looked at the annunciator, and turned off the alarm – so far as the door indicated was concerned – thus stopping the racket. Then I came back to bed. Mrs Clemens opened the debate:

"What was it?"

"It was the cellar door."

"Was it a burglar, do you think?"

"Yes," I said, "of course it was. Did you suppose it was a Sunday-school superintendent?"

"No. What do you suppose he wants?"

"I suppose he wants jewellery, but he is not acquainted with the house and he thinks it is in the cellar. I don't like to disappoint a burglar whom I am not acquainted with, and who has done me no harm, but if he had had common sagacity enough to inquire I could have told him we kept nothing down there but coal and vegetables. Still, it may be that he is acquainted with the place and that what he really wants is coal and vegetables. On the whole, I think it is vegetables he is after."

"Are you going down to see?"

"No; I could not be of any assistance. Let him select for himself; I don't know where the things are."

Then she said, "But suppose he comes up to the ground floor!"

"That's all right. We shall know it the minute he opens a door on that floor. It will set off the alarm."

Just then the terrific buzzing broke out again. I said, "He has arrived. I told you he would. I know all about burglars and their ways. They are systematic people."

I went into the bath-room to see if I was right, and I was. I shut off the dining-room and stopped the buzzing, and came back to bed. My wife said,

"What do you suppose he is after now ?"

I said, "I think he has got all the vegetables he wants and is coming up for napkin-rings and odds and ends for the wife and children. They all have families – burglars have – and they are always thoughtful of them, always take a few necessaries of life for themselves, and fill out with tokens of remembrance for the family. In taking them they do not forget us: those very things represent tokens of his remembrance of us, and also of our remembrance of him. We never get them again; the memory of the attention remains embalmed in our hearts."

"Are you going down to see what it is he wants now?"

"No," I said, "I am no more interested than I was before. They are experienced people – burglars; *they* know what they want; I should be no help to him. I *think* he is after ceramics and bric-a-brac and such things. If he knows the house he knows that that is all that he can find on the dining-room floor."

She said, with a strong interest perceptible in her tone, "Suppose he comes up here!"

I said, "It is all right. He will give us notice."

"What shall we do then?"

"Climb out of the window."

She said, a little restively, "Well, what is the use of a burglar alarm for us?"

"You have seen, dear heart, that it has been useful up to the present moment, and I have explained to you how it will be continuously useful after he gets up here."

That was the end of it. He didn't ring any more alarms. Presently I said, "He is disappointed, I think. He has gone off with the vegetables and the bric-a-brac, and I think he is dissatisfied."

We went to sleep, and at a quarter before eight in the morning I was out, and hurrying, for I was to take the 8.29 train for New York. I found the gas burning brightly – full head – all over the first floor. My new overcoat was gone; my old umbrella was gone; my new patent-leather shoes, which I had never worn, were gone. The large window which opened into the *ombra* at the rear of the house was standing wide. I passed out through it and tracked the burglar down the hill through the trees; tracked him without difficulty, because he had blazed his progress with imitation silver napkin-rings, and my umbrella, and various other things which he had disapproved of; and I went back in triumph and proved to my wife that he was a disappointed burglar. I had suspected he would be, from the start, and from his not coming up to our floor to get human beings.

(Mark Twain, *Chapters from my Autobiography*)

*When Oscar Wilde was sentenced to prison (see also **Law** and* ***Mistakes****) the public acclaim and admiration he'd received turned vindictive and sour. There is a story that, after the verdict had been handed down at the Old Bailey, people literally danced for joy in the streets outside the court and prostitutes kicked up their skirts with delight. "'E'll 'ave his 'air cut regular now!" shouted one of them. When Wilde was being transferred from Wandsworth to Reading Gaol, he and his guards had to change trains at Clapham Junction. A*

*man who'd been staring at the handcuffed figure said loudly enough for
the bystanders to hear, "By God, that's Oscar Wilde." Then he
stepped up and spat in Wilde's face. This is Wilde's own account of
that terrible moment.*

On 13 November 1895 I was brought down here [Reading
Gaol] from London. From two o'clock till half-past two on that
day I had to stand on the centre platform of Clapham Junction
in convict dress and handcuffed, for the world to look at. I had
been taken out of the Hospital Ward without a moment's notice
being given to me. Of all possible objects I was the most
grotesque. When people saw me they laughed. Each train as
it came up swelled the audience. Nothing could exceed their
amusement. That was of course before they knew who I was. As
soon as they had been informed, they laughed still more. For
half an hour I stood there in the grey November rain surrounded by a jeering mob.

For a year after that was done to me I wept every day at the
same hour and for the same space of time.

(Oscar Wilde, *De Profundis*)

As Arthur Conan Doyle's fame as the creator of Sherlock
Holmes grew he found himself caught up in real-life mysteries.
Conan Doyle wasn't at all reluctant to be called on to investigate
such cases, particularly where he considered an injustice had
been done. He was a natural crusader.

Perhaps the oddest of these mysteries involved the discovery
in August 1903 of a mutilated pit-pony in a field outside the
mining village of Great Wyrley near Birmingham. This was the
latest in a string of animal mutilations and killings which had
shaken the area, the more so because they were accompanied by
Jack-the-Ripper-style anonymous letters, threatening to "do
twenty wenches like the horses before next March".

The local police already had a suspect in their sights. He was
George Edalji, the Anglo-Indian son of the local vicar, the
Reverend Shapurji Edalji and his English wife Charlotte. An
outsider – and therefore an oddity – George Edalji practised as a
solicitor in Birmingham. Years before the animal mutilations

his father had been the target of a hate campaign involving anonymous letters, graffiti, etc. The police considered George responsible even though there was no proof of his guilt. But the memory of these events together with George Edalji's local reputation for being a bit odd were enough to send a contingent of police to the vicarage, where George still lived with his parents. They found evidence (apparent bloodstains and horse-hairs on his coat, mud on his boots) strong enough to lead to the solicitor's arrest later that day at his Birmingham office.

The police bungled the evidence gathering and didn't put up a convincing case in court. Despite this and despite the fact that other incidents of horse mutilation occurred while George Edalji was locked up in custody, he was still sentenced to seven years in prison. Then, only three years into his sentence, Edalji was released – without explanation. But he wasn't pardoned, and he wasn't able to resume his solicitor's practice. In effect, he was still a guilty man. Arthur Conan Doyle first heard of the Edalji case through a magazine campaign and it at once seized his imagination. Convinced of the young man's innocence, he devoted several months to studying the case, paying all the expenses involved and in the end identifying the probable criminal. Holmes could not have done better.

As a first step Conan Doyle asked to meet George Edalji in a London hotel. Charles Higham, one of Doyle's biographers, describes the scene, showing how the creator of Sherlock Holmes at once started using his own powers of deduction. Doyle "saw the young man sitting in the lobby, reading a newspaper. A significant detail immediately caught his atten-tion. Edalji was peering at the paper painfully through thick pebble glasses, obviously only just able to make out the words. The mutilations had all taken place at night. Conan Doyle knew that Edalji could not have effectively overpowered large animals and aimed a razor precisely at the vulnerable points, even with the aid of a light, if he was almost blind. It was the oculist as well as the detective in Conan Doyle that made him observe this detail."

As he questioned Edalji, Doyle became even more convinced that the Anglo-Indian had been a victim of injustice. He carried his investigation into the field, following the supposed country route which Edalji had taken to mutilate the animals. He also examined the "evidence" which had helped to convict his friend, discovering among other things that the bloodstains came not from a horse but from undercooked meat which Edalji had eaten on the night of the crime.

Conan Doyle then turned to his most effective weapon, the pen. Among his many talents he was a fine campaigning journalist. He wrote an 18,000-word statement, *The Case of Mr George Edalji,* which was serialized in the *Daily Telegraph.* Doyle pointed out the weakness of the charges against Edalji and indicated that colour prejudice was at the root of his conviction. He accused the authorities of turning a blind eye to injustice – since Edalji had been freed but with a shadow still over his name – and finished with a ringing appeal: "Now we turn to the last tribunal of all, a tribunal which never errs when the facts are laid before them, and we ask the public of Great Britan whether this thing is to go on."

While he was investigating the case Conan Doyle had un-covered evidence which seemed to point to an individual called Rodney Sharp as being the guilty party behind the animal mutilations and killings, as well as some of the anonymous letters which had emerged over the years. Sharp had worked in a butcher's shop and on a cattle boat. More important, he had built up a grudge against George Edalji.

In the end George Edalji was not compensated for the time he'd spent in prison. But Conan Doyle's intervention high-lighted the injustice and brought some tangible benefits to the solicitor; he was readmitted to his practice by the Law Society, and a subscription fund was raised for him. Rather than these compensations it might have been Conan Doyle's friendship and advocacy that George Edalji valued most of all. When the great novelist married for the second time in 1907, Edalji attended the wedding reception. Doyle wrote later: "There was no guest whom I was prouder to see."

Thomas Hardy pasted this excerpt from a newspaper article in a scrapbook marked "Personal". Some of the details were wrong (he didn't know the hanged woman, for example) but he was obviously excited by the occasion; elsewhere he wrote of how the woman's "fine figure showed against the sky as she hung in the misty rain".

Mr Neil Munro tells a curious story of the origin of Mr Hardy's "Tess". When Hardy was a boy he used to come into Dorchester to school, and he made the acquaintance of a woman there who, with her husband, kept an inn. She was beautiful, good and kind, but married to a dissipated scoundrel who was unfaithful to her. One day she discovered her husband under circumstances which so roused her passion that she stabbed him with a knife and killed him. She was tried, convicted, and condemned to execution. Young Hardy, with another boy, came into Dorchester and witnessed the execution from a tree that overlooked the yard in which the gallows was placed. He never forgot the rustle of the thin black gown the woman was wearing as she was led forth by the warders. A penetrating rain was falling; the white cap was no sooner over the woman's head than it clung to her features, and the noose was put round the head of what looked like a marble statue. Hardy looked at the scene with the strange illusion of its being unreal, and was brought to his complete senses when the drop fell with a thud and his companion fell fainting on the ground. The tragedy haunted Hardy, and, at last, provided the emotional inspiration and some of the matter for "Tess of the D'Urbevilles".

(item in *The Sketch, November 1904*)

One of the oddest "literary" mysteries of the 20th century was the eleven-day disappearance of mystery's most famous practitioner, Agatha Christie, creator of Miss Marple and Hercule Poirot. Christie's vanishing trick seems to have been engineered to spite her husband Archie, whose on-going affair with his mistress Nancy Neele was deeply distressing the writer. There were other strains in the marriage too, not least the success and fame which Agatha was winning through her innovative detective novels. The story of how her abandoned car was discovered and the nation-wide hunt which followed reads like one of Christie's plots, as Jared Cade points out in this excerpt from his investigation into "the eleven missing days".

What no one could have predicted on the night of Agatha's disappearance from her home in Berkshire were the unprecedented steps the authorities would take to find her and the way the press would blow the incident up into a front-page sensation.

Agatha's absence was first noticed on the morning of Saturday 4 December 1926 through the discovery of her abandoned Morris Cowley near Newlands Corner, a local beauty spot frequented by motorists and tourists five miles from Guildford in the neighbouring county of Surrey. The car was three hundred yards below the plateau of Newlands Corner at the edge of a chalk pit by Water Lane, a rutted, twisting dirt track leading to the village of Albury in the gently sloping valley below. The situation was like a scene from one of Agatha's detective novels, and what was to follow in the next week and a half was more bizarre than anything she ever penned.

The headlights of the abandoned four-seater were first seen piercing the winter darkness around seven o'clock by a Chilworth cattleman, Harry Green, but as he was on his way to work he did nothing at the time. Almost an hour elapsed before Jack Best, a gypsy boy on his way to work for a shooting party, passed the spot and took a closer look. The person who actually brought the matter to the attention of the authorities, shortly after eight o'clock, was Frederick Dore, a car tester who worked in Thames Ditton, who subsequently recalled: "When I found the car the brakes were off, and it was in neutral gear. The running board and the under part of the carriage were resting on the bush. From its position it appeared to me that the car must have been given a push at the top of the hill and sent down deliberately. The lights were off and I found that the battery had run right down. The lamps had evidently been left on until the current became exhausted. If anyone had accidentally run off the road the car would have pulled up earlier. There was no sign that the brakes had been applied. I looked for skid marks on the soft ground but could find none."

A gypsy girl told Dore she had heard a car about midnight coming along the track on the top of the downs leading from Guildford. While there was no way of knowing whether the two incidents were connected the unusual discovery prompted Dore to take immediate action: "I went to Mr Alfred Luland, who looks after the refreshment kiosk on the other side of the road, and asked him to take charge of the car, while I informed the policeman at Merrow." Dore telephoned the police from the Newlands Corner Hotel, some five hundred yards away on the Clandon Road.

The first intimation Archie [Christie] had of Agatha's disappearance was when her secretary Charlotte rang the home of his hosts, Sam and Madge James, at Hurtmore Cottage near Godalming to tell him that a policeman had turned up at Styles that morning to announce that Mrs Christie appeared to be missing. Archie was none too pleased at having his weekend with Nancy interrupted. He had no sooner terminated the telephone call and announced he had to leave because his mother had been taken ill than a police officer set the tongues of the Jameses' servants wagging by turning up on the doorstep.

Archie was escorted back to Styles. He insisted that he was unable to shed any light on Agatha's whereabouts, saying he had last seen her on the Friday morning before departing for work. He gave every indication of being completely baffled, but after surreptitiously reading the letter that Agatha had left for him on the hall table the previous night he burned it without telling the police of its existence or contents. He adjured Charlotte, who knew of the letter, to silence by telling her it had been written before Agatha had changed her plans to go to Beverley for the weekend.

News of the discovery of the abandoned car was relayed to the Surrey County Police Headquarters in Woodbridge Road in Guildford, but it was not until 11 p.m. that the matter came to the attention of Deputy Chief Constable William Kenward. The 50-year-old recipient of the King's Police Medal had been involved two years earlier in the investigations which had led to the trial and conviction of the Frenchman Jean Vacquier in what was known as the Byfleet murder. The press had been riveted by the story, tailing the police twenty-four hours a day, often interviewing important witnesses before the police arrived. Deputy Chief Constable Kenward was not to know that the press would be even more enthralled by this new story.

He took a grim view of the affair from the very first: "The car was found in such a position as to indicate that some unusual proceeding had taken place, the car being found halfway down a grassy slope well off the main road with its bonnet buried in some bushes, as if it had got out of control. In the car was found a fur coat, a dressing case containing various articles of ladies' wearing apparel and a driving licence indicating that the owner was Mrs Agatha Christie of Sunningdale, Berkshire."

Several questions needed urgent answers. How, why and when had Agatha's car been abandoned? And why had her handbag, distinguished by its fashionable zip, been removed?

Another intriguing factor was the weather. On the night of the disappearance the temperature at six o'clock had been 41 degrees Fahrenheit, a quarter of the sky had been covered in cloud and there had been a westerly breeze. By midnight the temperature had fallen to 36 degrees, the sky had completely cleared of cloud cover and the breeze had swung round to the north-west. So why had Agatha's heavy fur coat been abandoned on the back seat?

Deputy Chief Constable Kenward's bewilderment was shared by his officers, including Tom Roberts, a 21-year-old probationary constable, who described the mysterious affair at Newlands Corner as "the most sensational event that occurred whilst I was at Headquarters . . . The bushes were crushed and broken from the impact of the car, but they had prevented it from falling into the chalk pit."

Curiously, there was very little damage to the car, which was found in an upright position with the glass windscreen intact. Furthermore, the folding canvas roof was still erect and the plastic side-screens in place, although the bonnet was slightly damaged, the speedometer cable was broken and one of the wings was a little bent. The car doors were closed, the brakes were off and the gears were in neutral. The spare tin of petrol, carried on the side step, appeared to have been knocked off when the car collided with the bushes and was found lying in the grass. By the time Deputy Chief Constable Kenward arrived on the scene the battery was flat, in accordance with Frederick Dore's observations.

The police officer's subsequent inquiries did not bode well: "I immediately instituted inquiries, and found that the lady had left her home at Sunningdale in the car, late the previous evening, under rather unusual circumstances. I also learned that Mrs Christie had been very depressed and that just before leaving in the car she had gone upstairs and kissed her daughter who was in bed asleep."

A pall of bewilderment and uncertainty hung over Styles. The police slowly gathered together the known details of Agatha's last week in the hope of finding a clue to her whereabouts.

Gradually, the pieces fell into place like a jigsaw – only Deputy Chief Constable Kenward discovered there were pieces missing. It transpired that on the Monday Agatha had played golf with her friend, Mrs da Silva. On Wednesday they had gone to London on a shopping expedition, and Agatha had stayed overnight at her club, the Forum, before meeting her literary agent on Thursday morning to discuss the impending publication of *The Big Four* and her difficulties over finishing her latest novel, *The Mystery of the Blue Train*. She had also been contracted to write six stories for a US magazine and had another two to complete. Agatha had returned to Styles on Thursday afternoon and later that night had gone dancing with her secretary at Ascot. Charlotte had last seen her employer on the morning of Friday the 3rd and said that Agatha had appeared in such good spirits, happily playing with [her daughter] Rosalind, that she had decided to take up her employer's offer of a day off and visit London.

But where exactly had Agatha driven to that morning before returning to Styles for lunch? If the police had thought to follow this up, the answer could have helped them find the missing writer, but they did not. The case's many other baffling features, along with other apparently promising leads, proved too distracting.

Charlotte had last communicated with Agatha when she had rung her employer shortly after six o'clock on the night of the disappearance to see if she was all right; Agatha had answered the telephone, sounding normal despite her earlier row with Archie, and had urged Charlotte to enjoy herself and return by the last train. The police were forced to ask themselves whether the writer's mood was of any special significance or whether she had merely been determined to keep her problems to herself.

After the ten-minute walk from Sunningdale Station Charlotte had arrived back at Styles at eleven o'clock. She told the police that she had been confronted by the parlour-maid and cook who expressed concern at the unusual manner in which Agatha had left the house at 9.45 that night. After leaving Rosalind's bedroom Agatha had come downstairs, kissed and patted [her dog] Peter, placed him on the front hall mat and then driven off without telling her staff where she was going.

It transpired that Agatha had left behind a letter addressed to Charlotte, which the servants gave her as soon as she returned home. The letter asked the secretary to cancel rooms that had been booked for Agatha in Beverley for the weekend. Agatha implied that she was in great trouble and would contact Charlotte the next day to let her know her plans. The secretary admitted she had felt so uneasy about the letter that she had wanted to contact the police that night, because it included such sentences as "My head is bursting. I cannot stay in this house", but she had not dared do so for fear of offending her employer. Early on Saturday morning, before news of the abandoned car had reached Styles, Charlotte had telephoned Ascot Post Office to arrange for a telegram to be sent to the boarding-house in Beverley: "Regret cannot come – Christie."

Agatha's disappearance led to increasing apprehension among her family and friends. They were apparently at a loss as to the missing woman's whereabouts. The police took Charlotte and Archie to Newlands Corner on Saturday afternoon. A number of interested bystanders were already there, eager to fmd out what the police were doing. The secretary and the Colonel were shown the car but said they were unable to explain what had happened.

What appeared to have been a casual night drive had turned into something disturbing and inexplicable. As the police became aware of the disharmony between husband and wife they realized the importance of locating the writer in case her life was in jeopardy. Wilfrid Morton, one of the Surrey probationary police officers on the case, told me his instructions were: "Find Mrs Agatha Christie as quickly as you can."

Deputy Chief Constable Kenward's inquiries established that Agatha did not carry out her intention to travel north to the boarding-house in Beverley. Her last known journey on the day of the disappearance was to her mother-in-law's home in Dorking for afternoon tea. It was revealed that Agatha had visited her wearing the knitted green outfit in which she had gone missing later that evening. Peg told the police that the only plan Agatha had mentioned was to go to Beverley that weekend.

The police investigation was complicated by the fact that it was impossible to tell whether Agatha had driven directly to Newlands Corner. It was not known how much petrol had been in the tank at the outset of the journey. Nearly two gallons remained, and the spare petrol can of two gallons had not been used. There was plenty of water in the radiator, and when the car was hauled up on to the main road on the afternoon of Saturday the 4th the police had no difficulty in starting it. Although there were no signs of blood in or around the car it was kept overnight at the Guildford Garage on the Epsom Road.

One of the less disturbing theories considered by the authorities during the initial stages of the investigation was the possibility that on the Friday night Agatha had wandered away from the car after abandoning it and had got herself lost in the thick undergrowth. On the Saturday afternoon, accompanied by seven or eight regular police officers and a number of special constables, Deputy Chief Constable Kenward initiated a search of the surrounding area. The special constables were a group of registered men living throughout Surrey whose voluntary services were available to the county in the event of an emergency, and they were directly accountable to the Surrey Constabulary through their leader Captain Tuckwell and his deputy Colonel Bethall.

Deputy Chief Constable Kenward's interest in the Silent Pool, a quarter of a mile away from Newlands Corner at the bottom of the hill on the left-hand side of the A25 Dorking Road, captured the imagination of many, since it was rumoured that two people had already died there in tragic circumstances. According to legend, in medieval times a naked young woman had been spied bathing there and she had retreated to the deepest part of the pool to avoid the lascivious advances of King John. Her brother had drowned trying to save her, and their bodies had never been recovered. (Nowadays a car-park has been built by the side of the A25 near the shallow basin known as Sherbourne Pond. This is sometimes mistaken for the Silent Pool, which is higher up on the incline, shielded by a copse and overlooked by a bird-watching hut.)

As the news of Agatha's absence spread, civilian volunteers were quick to offer their services to the police. A statement that Agatha had been seen driving through Shere, a village two miles from Newlands Corner, at four o'clock on Saturday morning by a cow-man moving a herd of cattle was subsequently disproved, since the informant stated after being questioned a second time that the car he had seen had a square radiator. Agatha's Morris Cowley, like all the older models of this car, had a round radiator; the distinctive square radiators appeared for the first time in 1926.

By Saturday night Archie was growing increasingly agitated. He was filled with dread at the possible consequences of Agatha's disappearance. A minor accident, in which she had wandered away from her car alive and well, seemed increasingly improbable to the Colonel, and he began to worry that he might have driven her to suicide by telling her that their trial reconciliation was over. The two letters Agatha had left behind at Styles had not given any clue as to her proposed movements, and Archie had reassured their daughter by telling her that Agatha had gone to Ashfield to do some writing. Inquiries by the Torquay police, however, had revealed that Ashfield was uninhabited. What concerned the Colonel most was the fact that the longer Agatha remained missing the more likely it was that his relationship with Nancy would come out into the open.

On Sunday the 5th Deputy Chief Constable Kenward mounted an all-day search around Newlands Corner, unaware that a third letter, written by Agatha before she left Styles on the Friday night, had since been delivered by post to the London workplace of Archie's brother, Campbell Christie, an instructor at the Royal Woolwich Military Academy. The letter had been posted in London on the morning her car had been found abandoned. Campbell did not immediately pass on the information because he had yet to learn that his sister-in-law was missing.

One of the civilian helpers during the search on Sunday was 18-year-old Jack Boxall, a local gardener in Guildford. He vividly recalls the feeling of community spirit that prompted him, together with his father and a number of friends, to walk several miles from his home to Newlands Corner. He told me the police search parties were working in the direction of the Silent Pool and the village of Shere in the south-east, while his own party undertook to search that area in the north-west between Newlands Corner and Merrow known as the Roughs. It was an area very familiar to his father, a house painter, who in his spare time played golf in the open spaces on the Roughs. Despite their diligent efforts to locate Agatha, there was no sign of the missing woman as dusk fell, and the group was forced to admit defeat. Jack Boxall recalls that this did not discourage a veritable posse of police officers from continuing the search by lamplight. On Sunday night the police visited the village of Albury on receiving a report from a hotel there that a woman had been seen who answered the description of the novelist. They searched the wood at the back of Albury but drew a blank. Later that evening a missing persons notice was circulated to the 50 police stations nearest the village:

Missing from her home, Styles, Sunningdale, Berkshire, Mrs Agatha Mary Clarissa Christie, age 35 [she was actually 36]; height 5 feet 7 inches; hair, red, shingled part grey; complexion, fair, build slight; dressed in grey stockinette skirt, green jumper, grey and dark grey cardigan and small velour hat; wearing a platinum ring with one pearl; no wedding ring; black handbag with purse containing perhaps £5 or £10. Left home by car at 9.45 p.m. Friday leaving note saying that she was going for a drive.

The failure of the police to locate Agatha, and the fact that they received no word from her by the end of the weekend, led to the forfeiting of her privacy. What might have remained a private incident in the life of an intensely private woman instead fell rapidly under the harsh glare of the media spotlight.

(Jared Cade, *Agatha Christie and the Eleven Missing Days*)

The search for Agatha Christie spread across the country. It excited genuine public interest and excitement, with many false sightings and dead-ends. Three famous mystery writers made their deductions public. Edgar Wallace wrote an article in the Daily Mail, *in which he came near the truth by saying that Christie's vanishing trick was essentially an act of "spite". Dorothy L. Sayers, creator of Lord Peter Wimsey, used aspects of the disappearance in her third detective novel, while an ageing Arthur Conan Doyle – by then well into his spiritualist last phase – gave a glove belonging to Agatha to a medium, who intuited that its owner was "half dazed . . . half purposeful". The story of Agatha Christie's disappearance has a happy ending, of sorts. She was tracked down to a hotel in Harrogate where she had registered under the name of Mrs Teresa Neele, using the surname of her husband Archie's mistress, Nancy. Husband and wife were reunited and a public explanation of "amnesia" was provided to account for the author's missing days. But if Christie's disappearance was a desperate attempt to save her marriage, it didn't work. Agatha and Archie were eventually divorced in 1928. She later married the archaeologist Max Mallowan.*

Before he became famous, playwright Joe Orton, author of the classic 1960s farces *Loot* and *What the Butler Saw*, served time in prison for the unusual crime of deliberately damaging library books. Together with his long-time lover Kenneth Halliwell, Orton set about systematically stealing books from their local library in the Islington district of London. The operation began in 1959 and finished when they were arrested in April 1962. Halliwell used a wartime gas-mask case and Orton a satchel to smuggle the books back to their nearby flat. There they practised some creative defacement on the covers and the contents by pasting images of monkeys or birds' heads onto human heads and other pictures. Titles were changed so that, for example, the playwright Emlyn Williams was revealed to be the author of *Knickers Must Fall* or *Fucked by Monty*. In particular Joe Orton enjoyed typing up blurbs for the detective novels of Dorothy L. Sayers since the book jackets had empty yellow flaps which seemed to invite comment. Orton, who must have enjoyed upsetting the rather refined world of a Sayers whodunnit, finished a typical blurb with the warning: "READ THIS BEHIND CLOSED DOORS. And have a good shit while you are reading!"

Orton and Halliwell would return the books and then often stand in corners to watch the reactions of other library users as they picked up the doctored volumes. The library staff had no success in trying to catch the two men red-handed, although they had suspicions about them, and resorted to a complicated scam to prove their guilt. Halliwell was provoked into writing a letter to Islington Borough Council, and it became obvious that the same typewriter had been used both for the letter and for the fake book blurbs. Orton and Halliwell were arrested, appeared before a magistrate and sentenced to six months in jail. The relatively severe sentence, Orton considered, was "because we were queers".

The prison sentence also seems to have been a crystallizing experience for both men. Within a couple of years Orton would produce his first real stage success, *Entertaining Mr Sloane*, and become one of the most representative figures of the "swinging sixties". For Halliwell, on the other hand, the prison sentence merely confirmed the downward slope of his life. As the playwright's fortunes went up and up, the relationship soured. In August 1967 Halliwell murdered Orton in the same small flat where they had creatively vandalized library books together. Halliwell bludgeoned Orton to death with a hammer before committing suicide with an overdose of Nembutal.

By a nice irony Islington Library now has an archive devoted to the author. It includes some of the books which Orton and Halliwell so carefully defaced.

Day Jobs

This is one of the many legends which circulates about Shakespeare's early life and the employment he might have had as a boy.

Mr William Shakespeare was borne at Stratford upon Avon in the County of Warwick. His father was a Butcher, and I have been told heretofore by some of the neighbours, that when he was a boy he exercised his Father's Trade, but when he kill'd a Calfe he would doe it in a high style, and make a Speech. There was at this time another Butcher's son in this Towne that was held not at all inferior to him for natural witt, his acquaintance and coetanean [someone the same age], but dyed young.

(John Aubrey, *Brief Lives*)

George Crabbe was already a published poet by the time he went to London in 1775 in the attempt to pick up a little "surgical knowledge". Crabbe had hopes of becoming a doctor but he wasn't really cut out for the job and his time in London was unhappy.

Among other distresses of this time, he had, soon after he reached London, a narrow escape from being carried before the Lord Mayor as a resurrectionist [body-snatcher]. His landlady, having discovered that he had a dead child in his closet, for the purpose of dissection, took it into her head that it was no other than an infant whom she had had the misfortune to lose the week before. "Dr Crabbe had dug up William; she was certain he had; and to the Mansion house he must go." Fortunately, the countenance of the child had not yet been touched with the knife. The "doctor" arrived when the tumult was at its height, and, opening the closet door, at once established his innocence of the charge.

(from *The Life of George Crabbe* by his son)

Robert Burns – Scotland's national poet – worked on his father's farm as ploughman and labourer. When he achieved literary success his "simple" background was part of his attraction. However, his finances remained shaky until in the 1790s he was able to give up the failing farm and take a post with the Excise, responsible for making sure that duty was paid on liquor. Burns's heart doesn't really seem to have been in the job, according to the following story (author unknown).

It may be readily guessed with what interest I heard, one Thornhill fair-day, that Burns was to visit the market. Boy as I then was, an interest was awakened in me respecting this extraordinary man, which was sufficient, in addition to the ordinary attraction of a village fair, to command my presence in the market. Burns actually entered the fair about twelve; and man, wife, and lass were all on the outlook for a peep of the Ayrshire ploughman. I carefully dogged him from stand to stand, and from door to door. An information had been lodged against a poor widow of the name of Kate Watson, who had ventured to serve a few of her old country friends with a draught of unlicenced ale, and a lacing of whisky, on this village jubilee. I saw him enter her door, and anticipated nothing short of an immediate seizure of a certain greybeard and barrel, which, to my personal knowledge, contained the contraband commodities our bard was in quest of. A nod, accompanied by a significant movement of the forefinger, brought Kate to the doorway or trance [passage], and I was near enough to hear the following words distinctly uttered: "Kate, are ye mad; D'ye no ken that the supervisor and I will be upon you in the course of forty minutes! Guid-bye t'ye at present." Burns was in the street and in the midst of the crowd in an instant, and I had reason to know that his friendly hint was not neglected. It saved a poor widow from a fine of several pounds.

(from the *Edinburgh Literary Journal*)

*Anthony Trollope spent most of his working life in the Post Office (he was responsible for the introduction of pillar boxes). He took his profession very seriously even though he was also, for much of the time, writing with clockwork regularity every morning before starting work (see also **Writing**). Early in his civil service career he was sent to Ireland and found himself dealing with customers' complaints.*

A gentleman in county Cavan had complained most bitterly of the injury done to him by some arrangement of the Post Office. The nature of his grievance has no present significance; but it was so unendurable that he had written many letters, couched in the strongest language. He was most irate, and indulged himself in that scorn which is so easy to an angry mind. The place was not in my district, but I was borrowed, being young and strong, that I might remember the edge of his personal wrath. It was midwinter, and I drove up to his house, a squire's country seat, in the middle of a snow-storm, just as it was becoming dark. I was on an open jaunting-car, and was on my way from one little town to another, the cause of his complaint having reference to some mail conveyance between the two. I was certainly very cold, and very wet, and very uncomfortable when I entered his house. I was admitted by a butler, but the gentleman himself hurried into the hall. I at once began to explain my business. "God bless me!" he said, "you are wet through. John, get Mr Trollope some brandy and water – very hot." I was beginning my story about the post again when he himself took off my greatcoat, and suggested that I should go up to my bedroom before I troubled myself with business. "Bedroom!" I exclaimed. Then he assured me that he would not turn a dog out on such a night as that, and into a bedroom I was shown, having first drank the brandy and water standing at the drawing-room fire. When I came down I was introduced to his daughter, and the three of us went into dinner. I shall never forget his righteous indignation when I again brought up the postal question on the departure of the young lady. Was I such a Goth as to contaminate wine with business? So I drank my wine, and then heard the young lady sing while her father slept in his armchair. I spent a very pleasant evening, but my host was too sleepy to hear anything about the Post Office that night.

It was absolutely necessary that I should go away the next morning after breakfast, and I explained that the matter must be discussed then. He shook his head and wrung his hands in unmistakable disgust – almost in despair. "But what am I to say in my report?" I asked. "Anything you please," he said. "Don't spare me, if you want an excuse for yourself. Here I sit all the day – with nothing to do; and I like writing letters." I did report that Mr — was now quite satisfied with the postal arrangement of his district; and I felt a soft regret that I should have robbed my friend of his occupation. Perhaps he was able to take up the Poor Law Board, or to attack the Excise. At the Post Office nothing more was heard from him.

(Anthony Trollope, *An Autobiography*)

Another story from Anthony Trollope's working life concerns this incident in his office.

On one occasion in the performance of my duty, I had to put a private letter containing bank-notes on the secretary's table – which letter I had duly opened, as it was not marked PRIVATE. The letter was seen by the Colonel, but had not been moved by him when he left the room. On his return it was gone. In the meantime I had returned to the room, again in the performance of some duty. When the letter was missed I was sent for, and there I found the Colonel much moved about his letter, and a certain chief clerk, who, with a long face, was making suggestions as to the probable fate of the money. "The letter has been taken," said the Colonel, "and, by G—! there has been nobody in the room but you and I." As he spoke, he thundered his fist down upon the table. "Then," said I, "by G—! you have taken it." And I also thundered my fist down – but, accidentally, not upon the table. There was there a standing movable desk, at which, I presume, it was the Colonel's habit to write, and on this movable desk was a large bottle full of ink. My fist unfortunately came on the desk, and the ink at once flew up, covering the Colonel's face and shirtfront. Then it was a sight to see that senior clerk, as he seized a quire of blotting-paper, and rushed to the aid of his superior officer, striving to mop up the ink; and a sight also to see the colonel, in his agony, hit right out through the blotting-paper at that senior clerk's unoffending stomach. At that moment there came the Colonel's private secretary, with the letter and the money, and I was desired to go back to my own room.

(Anthony Trollope, *An Autobiography*)

Like T. S. Eliot (see below), comic novelist P. G. Wodehouse began his working life in a bank, a branch of the Hong Kong and Shanghai in the City of London. Although Wodehouse had been writing all the time he was working in the bank he finally resigned in 1902 and began a freelance career. One event – in fact, the only event which seems to have happened during his two-year stint as a clerk – indicated he wasn't cut out for a business career. At his desk one day he opened a new ledger and absent-mindedly started writing a story on the first page. Realizing what he'd done, Wodehouse tore out the page. When the head cashier picked up the ledger he saw that the page was missing and promptly rang the printer to complain. Soon someone from the printer's arrived to confirm that the ledger had been delivered intact. The only alternative was that the first page had been taken out by someone working in the bank. And only an imbecile would remove the first page of a ledger. Was there an imbecile working for the bank? The chief cashier thought for a moment, then said, "Why, yes. Young Wodehouse."

In the same year (1917) that he produced his first volume of verse, T.S.Eliot began working as a clerk in a London branch of Lloyds bank. He remained there for eight years, well after the publication of "The Waste Land", arguably the most famous and influential poem of the 20th century. Eliot's fellow-poet Ezra Pound considered Eliot's bank employment to be "the worst waste in contemporary literature". There is an apocryphal story that Pound and the writer and artist Wyndham Lewis paid Eliot a visit at his place of work. While Pound and Lewis were waiting for their friend, they fell into conversation with the bank manager who asked if there was any truth in the rumour that Eliot wrote poetry. When they answered that he did, the manager is supposed to have responded, "I think it's good for a man to have a hobby – as long as it doesn't interfere with his work."

Like Anthony Trollope, the American novelist and Nobel Prize winner William Faulkner worked for the postal service. For almost three years he was postmaster at the University of Mississippi post office. While Trollope took his work very seriously, Faulkner seems to have been indifferent to the job, using his working hours to write or play cards. He eventually resigned, saying, "I reckon I'll be at the beck and call of folks with money all my life, but thank God I won't ever again have to be at the beck and call of every son of a bitch who's got two cents to buy a stamp."

Like a number of other writers, Evelyn Waugh worked for a brief period as a schoolmaster (others include W. H. Auden and Anthony Burgess). Waugh taught in a preparatory school on the north Wales coast (see also *Boredom & Despair*). Arnold House was a bleak and depressing place and Waugh, by his own account, was thoroughly miserable – although he did make good, comic use of the experience in his first novel, *Decline and Fall*. Waugh especially resented having to do any duties outside the classroom (or inside it, for that matter). When asked what he was writing during evening supervision sessions, he always replied, "A history of the Eskimos." Waugh also met some eccentric or shameless figures among the staff, useful raw material for a would-be comic novelist. In particular, one master was noted for his constant drunkenness as well as having been forced to leave three schools "through his being taken in sodomy". "And yet," Waugh recorded in his diary, "he goes on getting better and better jobs."

After an unpaid apprenticeship on the *Nottingham Journal* Graham Greene found (paid) work on the London *Times*. In his autobiography *A Sort of Life* Greene says that he "can think of no better career for a young novelist than to be for some years a sub-editor on a rather conservative newspaper." The office hours, from four till midnight, gave plenty of time for him to write in the morning when he was fresh – while the newspaper was actually employing him "during his hours of fatigue". Greene found other skills useful to his prospective career as a novelist: taking clichés out of news stories, compressing the material so that every word counted. He was happy at *The Times* but continued to write. Two novels went unpublished and Greene embarked on a third, telling himself that if this one didn't succeed he would abandon the ambition to write altogether. This ultimatum to himself worked, as sometimes happens. The publishers Heinemann accepted *The Man Within* in 1928 and Greene was launched on his remarkable career.

Julian Maclaren-Ross was a maverick figure who haunted Soho in the 1940s and 50s. His *Memoirs of the Forties* is a very funny book and (for better or worse) something of a cult one now. Maclaren-Ross was perpetually short of money. Before World War Two, he had worked as a vacuum-cleaner salesman in the seaside resort of Bognor Regis. When he told Graham Greene what he was doing, the novelist was interested. (Years later he made the central character in his satirical spy novel *Our Man in Havana* a vacuum-cleaner salesman.) But when Greene – never anything other than a ruthlessly professional writer – asked the question, "Are you doing it to get material?" Maclaren-Ross's reply was straightforward enough: "No, I'm doing it because I wouldn't have any money otherwise."

Advertising copywriting seems to be a natural activity for authors. At least three were associated early in their writing lives with the firm of Ogilvy & Mather. In Britain Salman Rushdie, author of *The Satanic Verses*, occasionally wrote copy for them, as did novelist Fay Weldon who is credited with creating the punning slogan "Go to Work on an Egg" for the Egg Marketing Board back in the 1960s. Reclusive US author

Don Delillo worked for Ogilvy & Mather but departed at the age of 28 to finish his first novel. Unusually for an author, Delillo didn't leave with any high-sounding aspirations: "I quit my job just to quit. I didn't quit my job to write fiction. I just didn't want to work any more." Joseph Heller, author of the famous anti-war satire *Catch-22*, was working as a copywriter in a New York advertising agency when he began the novel in 1953. In the eight years which it took to complete Heller went on to work for two famous magazines, *Time* and *McCall's*.

Death

The death of Christopher Marlowe, author of the Elizabethan dramas
The Jew of Malta *and* Dr Faustus, *was quick and violent. Spec-*
ulation has been rife ever since that this was no simple, spontaneous
killing in a tavern but a plot. Marlowe was a known atheist (when it
was not safe to be one) and supposedly a spy. Ingram Frizar and at
least one of the other men round the table were connected to the
Elizabethan secret service – and Frizar was pardoned only a month
after this killing took place.

It so happened that at Detford, a little village about three miles
distant from London, as he [Marlowe] went to stab with his
ponyard [dagger] one named Ingram, that had invited him thither
to a feast, and was then playing at tables, he quickly perceyving it,
so avoyded the thrust, that withal drawing out his dagger for his
defence hee stabd this Marlowe into the eye, in such sort, that his
braines comming out at the daggers point, hee shortly after dyed.

(William Vaughan, *Golden Grove*)

Sir Walter Raleigh, traveller, poet, courtier, historian, was executed
at the Tower of London in 1618 on a charge of treason. Even his
enemies had to concede that he died with style and grace.

The last night of his existence was occupied by what the letter-
writer calls "a remembrancer to be left with his lady", to
acquaint the world with his sentiments, should he be denied
their delivery from the scaffold, as he had been at the bar of the
King's Bench. His lady visited him that night, and amidst her
tears acquainted him that she had obtained the favour of
disposing of his body; to which he answered smiling, "It is

well, Bess, that thou mayst dispose of that dead, thou hadst not always the disposing of when it was alive." At midnight he intreated her to leave him. It must have been then that, with unshaken fortitude, Raleigh sat down to compose those verses on his death, which being short, the most appropriate may be repeated.

> Even such is Time, that takes on trust
> Our youth, our joys, our all we have,
> And pays us but with age and dust;
> Who in the dark and silent grave,
> When we have wandered all our ways,
> Shuts up the story of our days. . . .

On the morning of his death he smoked, as usual, his favourite tobacco, and when they brought him a cup of excellent sack, being asked how he liked it, Raleigh answered, "As the fellow, that, drinking of St Giles's bowl, as he went to Tyburn, said, 'that was good drink if a man might tarry by it.' " The day before, in passing from Westminster-hall to the Gate-house his eye had caught Sir Hugh Beeston in the throng and calling on him, requested that he would see him die tomorrow. Sir Hugh, to secure himself a seat on the scaffold, had provided himself with a letter to the sheriff, which was not read at the time, and Sir Walter found his friend thrust by, lamenting that he could not get there. "Farewell!" exclaimed Raleigh, "I know not what shift you will make, but I am sure to have a place."

In going from the prison to the scaffold, among others who were pressing hard to see him, one old man, whose head was bald, came very forward, insomuch that Raleigh noticed him, and asked, "Whether he would have aught of him?" The old man answered, "Nothing but to see him, and to pray to God for him." Raleigh replied, "I thank thee, good friend, and I am sorry I have no better thing to return thee for thy good will." Observing his bald head, he continued, "but take this night-cap, (which was a very rich wrought one that he wore) for thou hast more need of it now than I . . ."

He ascended the scaffold with the same cheerfulness he had passed to it, and observing the lords seated at a distance, some at windows, he requested they would approach him, as he wished what he had to say they should all witness. This request was complied with by several. His speech is well known; but some copies contain matters not in others. When he finished, he requested Lord Arundel that the king would not suffer any libels to defame him after death – "And now I have a long journey to go, and must take my leave."

"He embraced all the lords and other friends with such courtly compliments, as if he had met them at some feast," says a letter-writer. Having taken off his gown, he called to the headsman to show him the axe, which not being instantly done, he repeated, "I prithee let me see it. Dost thou think that I am afraid of it?" He passed the edge lightly over his finger, and smiling, observed to the sheriff, "This is a sharp medicine, but a sound cure for all diseases," and, kissing it, laid it down. Another writer has, "This is that, that will cure all sorrows." After this he went to three several corners of the scaffold, and kneeling down, desired all the people to pray for him, and recited a long prayer to himself. When he began to fit himself for the block he first laid himself down to try how the block fitted him; after rising up, the executioner kneeled down to ask his forgiveness, which Raleigh with an embrace did, but entreated him not to strike till he gave a token by lifting up his hand, "*and then, fear not, but strike home!*" When he laid his head down to receive the stroke, the executioner desired him to lay his face towards the east. "It was no great matter which way a man's head stood, so the heart lay right," said Raleigh, but these were not his last words. He was once more to speak in this world with the same intrepidity he had lived in it – for, having lain some minutes on the block in prayer, he gave the signal, but the executioner, either unmindful, or in fear, failed to strike, and Raleigh, after once or twice putting forth his hands, was compelled to ask him, "Why dost thou not strike? Strike, man!" In two blows he was beheaded but from the first, his body never shrunk from the spot, by any discomposure of his posture, which, like his mind, was unmoveable.

(Isaac Disraeli, *Curiosities of Literature*)

The poet John Donne was appointed Dean of St Paul's in 1621. Some ten years later he prepared to give his last sermon.

Before that month ended, he was appointed to preach upon his old constant day, the first Friday in Lent; he had notice of it, and had in his sickness so prepared for that employment, that as he had long thirsted for it: so he resolved his weakness should not hinder his journey; he came therefore to London, some few days before his appointed day of preaching. At his coming thither, many of his friends (who with sorrow saw his sickness had left him but so much flesh as did only cover his bones) doubted his strength to perform that task; and did therefore dissuade him from undertaking it, assuring him however, it was like to shorten his life; but he passionately denied their requests; saying, he would not doubt that that God who in so many weaknesses had assisted him with an unexpected strength, would now withdraw it in his last employment; professing an holy ambition to perform that sacred work. And, when to the amazement of some beholders he appeared in the pulpit, many of them thought he presented himself not to preach mortifica-tion by a living voice: but, mortality by a decayed body and a dying face. And doubtless, many did secretly ask that question in *Ezekiel*: "Do these bones live? Or, can that soul organize that tongue, to speak so long time as the sand in that glass will move towards its centre, and measure out an hour of this dying man's unspent life?" Doubtless it cannot; and yet, after some faint pauses in his zealous prayer, his strong desires enabled his weak body to discharge his memory of his preconceived meditations, which were of dying: the text being, "To God the Lord belong the issues from death." Many that then saw his tears, and heard his faint and hollow voice, professing they thought the Text prophetically chosen, and that Dr Donne had preached his own funeral sermon . . .

   . . . Dr Donne, by the persuasion of Dr Fox, easily yielded at this very time to have a monument made for him; but Dr Fox undertook not to persuade him how, or what monument it should be; that was left to Dr Donne himself.

A monument being resolved upon, Dr Donne sent for a carver to make for him in wood the figure of an urn, giving him directions for the compass and height of it; and to bring with it a board of the just height of his body. These being got: then without delay a choice painter was got to be in a readiness to draw his picture, which was taken as followeth. Several charcoal fires being first made in his large study, he brought with him into that place his winding sheet in his hand, and, having put off all his clothes, had this sheet put on him, and so tied with knots at his head and feet, and his hands so placed, as dead bodies are usually fitted to be shrouded and put into their coffin, or grave. Upon this urn he thus stood with his eyes shut, and with so much of the sheet turned aside as might show his lean, pale, and death-like face, which was purposely turned toward the east, from whence he expected the second coming of his and our Saviour Jesus. In this posture he was drawn at his just height; and when the picture was fully finished, he caused it to be set by his bed-side, where it continued, and became his hourly object till his death: and, was then given to his dearest friend and executor, Doctor Henry King, then chief Residentiary of St. Pauls, who caused him to be thus carved in one entire piece of white marble, as it now stands in that church.

(Izaak Walton, *Life of John Donne*)

Francis Bacon was an Elizabethan statesman and philosopher, author of An Advancement of Learning *among other works. The theory that Bacon was the "real" author of Shakespeare's plays seems to have originated in the 18th-century. The graph of Bacon's public life, however, rose much higher – and fell more dramatically – than Shakespeare's. One of the odder features of it was the manner of his death in 1626.*

Mr Hobbs told me that the cause of his Lordship's death was trying an Experiment; viz. as he was taking the aire in a Coach with Dr Witherborne (a Scotchman, Physitian to the King) towards High-gate, snow lay on the ground, and it came into my Lord's thoughts, why flesh might not be preserved in snow, as in Salt. They were resolved they would try the Experiment presently. They alighted out of the Coach and went into a poore woman's house at the bottom of Highgate hill, and bought a

Hen and made the woman exenterate [gut] it, and then stuffed
the body with Snow, and my Lord did help to doe it himselfe.
The Snow so chilled him that he immediately fell so extremely
ill, that he could not returne to his Lodging (I suppose then at
Gray's Inne) but went to the Earle of Arundel's house at
Highgate, where they putt him into a good bed warmed with
a Panne, but it was a damp bed that had not been layn-in in
about a yeare before, which gave him such a colde that in 2 or 3
dayes as I remember Mr Hobbes told me, he dyed of Suffoca-
tion.

(John Aubrey, *Brief Lives*)

Sir John Suckling was a minor poet of the early 17th-century and a
royalist supporter of Charles I. This story of how he died is almost
certainly untrue – but still worth repeating.

Sir John was a man of great vivacity and spirit. He died about
the beginning of the Civil War, and his death was occasioned by
a very uncommon accident. He entered warmly into the King's
interests and was sent over by him into France with some letters
of great consequence to the Queen. He arrived late at Calais,
and in the night his servant ran away with his portmanteau, in
which was his money and papers. When he was told of this in
the morning he immediately inquired which way his servant
had taken, and ordered horses to be got ready instantly. In
pulling on his boots he found one of them extremely uneasy to
him, but as the horses were at the door he leaped into his saddle
and forgot his pain. He pursued his servant so eagerly that he
overtook him two or three posts off, recovered his portmanteau,
and soon after complained of a vast pain in one of his feet, and
fainted away with it. When they came to pull off his boots to
fling him into bed, they found one of them full of blood. It
seems his servant (who knew his master's temper well and was
sure he would pursue him as soon as his villainy should be
discovered) had driven a nail up into one of his boots in hopes of
disabling him from pursuing him. Sir John's impetuosity made
him regard the pain only just at first, and his pursuit hurried
him from the thoughts of it for some time after. However, the

wound was so bad and so much inflamed that it flung him into a violent fever which ended his life in a very few days. This incident, as strange as it may seem, might be proved from some original letters in Lord Oxford's collection.

(Joseph Spence, *Anecdotes*)

Another story has Sir John Suckling committing suicide because of his poverty in Paris. In this version he "tooke poyson, which killed him miserably with vomiting."

Dr William Harvey was a 17th-century physician and the author of the first treatise on the circulation of the blood.

Dr Harvey was ever afraid of becoming blind: early one morning, for he always rose early, his housekeeper coming into his chamber to call him, opened the window shutters, told him the hour, and asked him if he would not rise. Upon which he asked if she had opened the shutters; she replied yes – then shut them again – she did so – then opened them again. But still the effect was the same to him, for he had awakened stone blind. Upon which he told her to fetch him a bottle (which she herself had observed to stand on a shelf in his chamber for a long time), out of which he drank a large draught and it being a strong poison, which it is supposed he had long before prepared and set there for this purpose, he expired within three hours after.

(Edward Hasted, *The History and Topographical Survey of the County of Kent*)

Dr Samuel Johnson in his life of the 17th-century poet John Dryden tells a peculiar story about the undignified farce of Dryden's funeral. Johnson didn't give much credence to the story; he called it "wild". Even so he thought it worth printing in full. Here it is, with the speech marks and the closing comment which enabled Johnson to put a distance between himself and the anecdote.

"Mr Dryden dying on the Wednesday morning, Dr Thomas Sprat, then bishop of Rochester and dean of Westminster, sent

the next day to the lady Elizabeth Howard, Mr Dryden's
widow, that he would make a present of the ground, which
was forty pounds, with all the other Abbey fees. The lord
Halifax likewise sent to the lady Elizabeth and Mr Charles
Dryden her son, that, if they would give him leave to bury Mr
Dryden, he would inter him with a gentleman's private funeral,
and afterwards bestow five hundred pounds on a monument in
the Abbey; which, as they had no reason to refuse they accepted.
On the Saturday following the company came: the corpse was
put into a velvet hearse, and eighteen mourning coaches, filled
with company, attended. When they were just ready to move,
the lord Jefferies, son of the lord chancellor Jefferies, with some
of his rakish companions coming by, asked whose funeral it was:
and being told Mr Dryden's, he said, 'What shall Dryden, the
greatest honour and ornament of the nation, be buried after this
private manner! No, gentlemen, let all that loved Mr Dryden,
and honour his memory, alight and join with me in gaining my
lady's consent to let me have the honour of his interment, which
shall be after another manner than this; and I will bestow a
thousand pounds on a monument in the Abbey for him.' The
gentlemen in the coaches, not knowing of the bishop of Rochester's favour, nor of the lord Halifax's generous design (they
both having, out of respect to the family, enjoined the lady
Elizabeth and her son to keep their favour concealed to the
world, and let it pass for their own expence) readily came out of
the coaches, and attended lord Jefferies up to the lady's bedside,
who was then sick; he repeated the purport of what he had
before said; but she absolutely refusing, he fell on his knees,
vowing never to rise till his request was granted. The rest of the
company by his desire kneeled also; and the lady, being under a
sudden surprise, fainted away. As soon as she recovered her
speech, she cried, *No, no.* Enough, gentlemen, replied he; my
lady is very good, she says, *Go, go.* She repeated her former
words with all her strength, but in vain; for her feeble voice was
lost in their acclamations of joy; and the lord Jefferies ordered
the hearsemen to carry the corpse to Mr Russell's, an undertaker's in Cheapside, and leave it there till he should send orders
for the embalment, which, he added, should be after the royal
manner. His directions were obeyed, the company dispersed,

and lady Elizabeth and her son remained inconsolable. The next day Mr Charles Dryden waited on the lord Halifax and the bishop, to excuse his mother and himself, by relating the real truth. But neither his lordship nor the bishop would admit of any plea; especially the latter, who had the Abbey lighted, the ground opened, the choir attending, an anthem ready set, and himself waiting for some time without any corpse to bury. The undertaker, after three days' expectance of orders for embalment without receiving any, waited on the lord Jefferies; who pretending ignorance of the matter, turned it off with an ill-natured jest, saying, That those who observed the orders of a drunken frolick deserved no better; that he remembered nothing at all of it; and that he might do what he pleased with the corpse. Upon this, the undertaker waited upon the lady Elizabeth and her son, and threatened to bring the corpse home, and set it before the door. They desired a day's respite, which was granted. Mr Charles Dryden wrote a handsome letter to the lord Jefferies, who returned it with this cool answer, 'That he knew nothing of the matter, and would be troubled no more about it.' He then addressed the lord Halifax and the bishop of Rochester, who absolutely refused to do anything in it. In this distress Dr Garth sent for the corpse to the College of Physicians, and proposed a funeral by subscription, to which himself set a most noble example. At last a day, about three weeks after Mr Dryden's decease, was appointed for the interment: Dr Garth pronounced a fine Latin oration, at the College, over the corpse; which was attended to the Abbey by a numerous train of coaches. When the funeral was over, Mr Charles Dryden sent a challenge to the lord Jefferies, who refusing to answer it, he sent several others, and went often himself; but could neither get a letter delivered, nor admittance to speak to him: which so incensed him, that he resolved, since his lordship refused to answer him like a gentleman, that he would watch an opportunity to meet and fight off-hand, though with all the rules of honour; which his lordship hearing, left the town: and Mr Charles Dryden could never have the satisfaction of meeting him, though he sought it till his death with the utmost application."

This story I once intended to omit, as it appears with no great evidence; nor have I met with any confirmation, but in a letter of Farquhar, and he only relates that the funeral of Dryden was tumultuary and confused.

(Samuel Johnson, *Life of Dryden*)

The poet Alexander Pope described his own life as a "long disease". He suffered from a curvature of the spine and stunted growth. Nevertheless he lived a comparatively long life for the period, dying at the age of 56.

In May 1744 his death was approaching; on the 6th, he was all day delirious, which he mentioned four days afterwards as a sufficient humiliation of the vanity of man; he afterwards complained of seeing things as through a curtain and in false colours, and one day, in the presence of Dodsley, asked what arm it was that came out from the wall. He said that his greatest inconvenience was inability to think.

Pope expressed undoubting confidence of a future state . . . after the priest had given him the last sacraments, he said, "There is nothing that is meritorious but virtue and friendship; and indeed friendship itself is only a part of virtue."

He died in the evening of the 30th day of May 1744, so placidly, that his attendants did not discern the exact time of his expiration. He was buried at Twickenham, near his father and mother . . .

(Samuel Johnson, *Life of Pope*)

Dr Johnson, the author of the stories about Pope and Dryden quoted above, belonged to a Literary Society which occasionally met for dinner. Among its members were Oliver Goldsmith and Sir Joshua Reynolds – and a Dr Nugent.

. . . this was, I believe, in the year 1775 or 1776. It was a supper meeting then, and I fancy Dr Nugent ordered an omelet sometimes on a Friday or Saturday night; for I remember Mr Johnson felt very painful sensations at the sight of that dish soon after his death, and cried, "Ah, my poor dear friend! I shall never eat omelet with thee again!" quite in an agony. The truth is, nobody suffered more from pungent sorrow at a friend's death than Johnson, though he would suffer no one else to complain of their losses in the same way; "for (says he) we must either outlive our friends you know, or our friends must outlive us; and I see no man that would hesitate about the choice."

(Hesther Lynch Piozzi, *Anecdotes of Samuel Johnson*)

Dr Johnson was preoccupied with death, as these little stories show.

Knowing the state of Mr Johnson's nerves, and how easily they were affected, I forbore reading in a new Magazine one day, the death of a Samuel Johnson who expired that month; but my companion snatching up the book, saw it himself, and contrary to my expectations – "Oh (said he)! I hope Death will now be glutted with Sam. Johnsons, and let me alone for some time to come: I read of another namesake's departure last week."

(Hesther Lynch Piozzi, *Anecdotes of Samuel Johnson*)

Johnson's friend, the actor David Garrick, gives him a tour of his new house.

Soon after Garrick's purchase at Hampton Court he was showing Dr Johnson over the grounds, the house, Shakespeare's temple, &c. and concluded by asking him, "Well, Doctor, how do you like all this?" "Why, it is pleasant enough," growled the Doctor, "for the present; but all these things, David, make death very terrible."

(William Cooke, *Life of Samuel Foote*)

Novelist Sir Walter Scott describes the death of the 18th-century author Laurence Sterne.

In February 1768 Laurence Sterne, his frame exhausted by long debilitating illness, expired at his lodgings at Bond Street, London. There was something in the manner of his death singularly resembling the particulars detailed by Mrs Quickly, as attending that of Falstaff, the compeer of Yorick for infinite jest, however unlike in other particulars. As he lay on his bed totally exhausted, he complained that his feet were cold, and requested the female attendant to chafe them. She did so, and it seemed to relieve him. He complained that the cold came up higher; and whilst the assistant was in the act of chafing his ankles and legs, he expired without a groan. It was also remarkable that his death took place much in the manner which he himself had wished; and that the last offices were rendered him, not in his own house, or by the hand of kindred affection, but in an inn and by strangers.

(Sir Walter Scott, *Lives of the Novelists*)

There's a tradition that Laurence Sterne's body was dug up or "resurrected" after his death and sold to a Professor of Anatomy at Cambridge for dissection. There it was recognized by a friend, who fainted on the spot.

The "easy" death of Edward Gibbon, the 18th-century author of the Decline and Fall of the Roman Empire, *is told by Lytton Strachey.*

At every period of his life Gibbon is a pleasant thing to contemplate, but perhaps most pleasant of all in the closing weeks of it, during his last visit to England. He had hurried home from Lausanne to join his friend Lord Sheffield, whose wife had died suddenly, and who, he felt, was in need of his company. The journey was no small proof of his affectionate nature; old age was approaching; he was corpulent, gouty, and accustomed to every comfort; and the war of the French Revolution was raging in the districts through which he had to pass. But he did not hesitate, and after skirting the belligerent armies in his chaise, arrived safely in England. After visiting Lord Sheffield he proceeded to Bath, to stay with his step-mother. The amazing little figure, now almost spherical, bowled along the Bath Road in the highest state of exhilaration . . . Mrs Gibbon, a very old lady, but still full of vitality, worshipped her stepson, and the two spent ten days together, talking, almost always tête-à-tête, for ten hours a day. Then the historian went off to Althorpe, where he spent a happy morning with Lord Spencer, looking at a early editions of Cicero. And so back to London. In London a little trouble arose. A protuberance* in the lower part of his person, which, owing to years of characteristic *insouciance*, had grown to extraordinary proportions, required attention; an operation was necessary; but it went off well, and there seemed to be no danger. Once more Mr Gibbon dined out. Once more he was seen, in his accustomed attitude, with advanced forefinger, addressing the company, and rapping his snuff box at the close of each particularly pointed phrase. But illness came on again – nothing very serious. The great man lay in bed discussing how much longer he would live – he was 56 – 10 years, 12 years, or perhaps 20. He ate some chicken and drank three glasses of madeira. Life seemed almost as charming as usual. Next morning, getting out of bed for a necessary moment, "*Je suis plus adroit*," he said with his odd smile to his French valet. Back in bed again, he muttered something more, a little incoherently, lay back among the pillows, dozed, half-woke, dozed again, and became unconscious – for ever.

(Lytton Strachey *Portraits in Miniature*)

Poet John Keats travelled to Rome in the hope that a better climate would delay the advancing tuberculosis which eventually killed him in 1821. He was accompanied by his friend Joseph Severne who recalls his final days.

At times during his last days he made me go to see the place where he was to be buried, and he expressed pleasure at my description of the locality of the Pyramid of Caius Cestius, about the grass and the many flowers, particularly the innumerable violets, also about a flock of goats and sheep and a young shepherd – all these intensely interested him. Violets

* Protuberance – This was in fact a swelling on his left testicle which Gibbon himself described "almost as big as a small child". During one operation 4 quarts of liquid were drained from it. He died because the liquid, gathering there again, turned septic.

were his favourite flowers, and he joyed to hear how they overspread the graves. He assured me that he already seemed to feel the flowers growing over him . . .

Again and again, while warning me that his death was fast approaching, he besought me to take all care of myself, telling me I was not to look at him in his dying gasp nor breathe his passing breath, not even breathe upon him. From time to time he gave me all his directions as to what he wanted done after his death. It was in the same sad hour when he told me with greater agitation than he had shown on any other subject, to put the letter which had just come from Miss Brawne* (which he was unable to bring himself to read, or even to open), with any other that should arrive too late to reach him in life, inside his winding-sheet on his heart – it was then, also, that he asked that I should see cut upon his gravestone as sole inscription, not his name, but simply "Here lies one whose name is writ in water."

(Joseph Severn, *Recollections*)

Edward Trelawny recalls his last sight of Shelley as the poet sailed with his friend Edward Williams for Leghorn on the Italian coast.

On Monday, the 8th of July, 1822, I went with Shelley to his bankers, and then to a store. It was past one p.m. when we went on board our respective boats – Shelley and Williams to return to their home in the Gulf of Spezzia; I in the *Bolivar*, to accompany them into the offing. When we were under weigh, the guard-boat boarded us to overhaul our papers. I had not got my port clearance, the captain of the port having refused to give it to the mate, as I had often gone out without. The officer of the Health Office consequently threatened me with fourteen days' quarantine. It was hopeless to think of detaining my friends. Williams had been for days fretting and fuming to be off; they had no time to spare, it was past two o'clock, and there was very little wind.

Sullenly and reluctantly I reanchored, furled my sails, and

* Miss Brawne – Keats was probably engaged to Fanny Brawne. She wore mourning for him for several years after his death.

with a ship's glass watched the progress of my friends' boat. My Genoese mate observed – "They should have sailed this morning at three or four a.m., instead of three p.m. They are standing too much in shore; the current will set them there."

I said, "They will soon have the land-breeze."

"Maybe," continued the mate, "she will soon have too much breeze; that gaff topsail is foolish in a boat with no deck and sailor on board." Then, pointing to the S.W., "Look at those black lines and the dirty rags hanging on them out of the sky – they are a warning; look at the smoke on the water; the devil is brewing mischief."

There was a sea-fog, in which Shelley's boat was soon after enveloped, and we saw nothing more of her.

Although the sun was obscured by mists, it was oppressively sultry. There was not a breath of air in the harbour. The heaviness of the atmosphere and an unwonted stillness benumbed my senses. I went down into the cabin and sank into a slumber. I was roused up by a noise overhead and went on deck. The men were getting up a chain cable to let go another anchor. There was a general stir amongst the shipping; shifting berths, getting down yards and masts, veering out cables, hauling in of hawsers, letting go anchors, hailing from the ships and quays, boats sculling rapidly to and fro. It was almost dark, although only half-past six o'clock. The sea was of the colour, and looked as solid and smooth as a sheet of lead, and covered with an oily scum. Gusts of wind swept over without ruffling it, and big drops of rain fell on its surface, rebounding, as if they could not penetrate it. There a commotion in the air, made up of many threatening sounds, coming upon us from the sea. Fishing-craft and coasting vessels under bare poles rushed by us in shoals, running foul of the ships in the harbour. As yet the din and hubbub was that made by men, but their shrill pipings were suddenly silenced by the crashing voice of a thunder squall that burst right over our heads. For some time no other sounds were to be heard than the thunder, wind, and rain. When the fury of the storm, which did not last for more than twenty minutes, had abated, and the horizon was in some degree cleared, I looked to seaward anxiously, in the hope of descrying Shelley's boat amongst the many small craft scattered about. I watched every

speck that loomed on the horizon, thinking that they would
have borne up on their return to the port, as all the other boats
that had gone out in the same direction had done.

I sent our Genoese mate on board some of the returning craft
to make inquiries, but they all professed not to have seen the
English boat. So remorselessly are the quarantine laws enforced
in Italy, that, when at sea, if you render assistance to a vessel in
distress, or rescue a drowning stranger, on returning to port you
are condemned to a long and rigorous quarantine of fourteen or
more days. The consequence is, should one vessel see another in
peril, or even run it down by accident, she hastens on her
course, and by general accord, not a word is said or reported on
the subject. But to resume my tale. I did not leave the *Bolivar*
until dark. During the night it was gusty and showery, and the
lightning flashed along the coast: at daylight I returned on
board, and resumed my examinations of the crews of the various
boats which had returned to the port during the night. They
either knew nothing, or would say nothing. My Genoese, with
the quick eye of a sailor, pointed out, on board a fishing-boat, an
English-made oar that he thought he had seen in Shelley's boat,
but the entire crew swore by all the saints in the calendar that
this was not so. Another day was passed in horrid suspense. On
the morning of the third day I rode to Pisa. Byron had returned
to the Lanfranchi Palace. I hoped to find a letter from the Villa
Magni: there was none. I told my fears to Hunt, and then went
upstairs to Byron. When I told him, his lip quivered, and his
voice faltered as he questioned me. I sent a courier to Leghorn
to despatch the *Bolivar* to cruise along the coast, whilst I
mounted my horse and rode in the same direction. I also
despatched a courier along the coast to go as far as Nice. On
my arrival at Via Reggio, I heard that a punt, a water keg, and
some bottles had been found on the beach. These things I
recognized as having been in Shelley's boat when he left Leghorn. Nothing more was found for seven or eight days, during
which time of painful suspense I patrolled the coast with the
coast-guard, stimulating them to keep a good look-out by the
promise of a reward. It was not until many days after this that
my worst fears were confirmed. Two bodies were found on the
shore – one near Via Reggio, which I went and examined. The

face and hands, and parts of the body not protected by the dress, were fleshless. The tall slight figure, the jacket, the volume of Aeschylus in one pocket, and Keats's poems in the other, doubled back, as if the reader, in the act of reading, had hastily thrust it away, were all too familiar to me to leave a doubt on my mind that this mutilated corpse was any other than Shelley's. The other body was washed on shore three miles distant from Shelley's, near the tower of Migliarino, at the Bocca Lericcio. I went there at once. This corpse was much more mutilated; it had no other covering than – the shreds of a shirt, and that partly drawn over the head as if the wearer had been in the act of taking it off, – a black silk handkerchief, tied sailor-fashion round the neck – socks, and one boot, indicating also that he had attempted to strip. The flesh, sinews, and muscles hung about in rags, like the shirt, exposing the ribs and bones. I had brought with me from Shelley's house a boot of Williams', and this exactly matched the one the corpse had on. That, and the handkerchief, satisfied me that it was the body of Shelley's comrade. Williams was the only one of the three who could swim, and it is probable he was the last survivor. It is likewise possible, as he had a watch and money, and was better dressed than the others, that his body might have been plundered when found. Shelley always declared that in case of wreck he would vanish instantly, and not imperil valuable lives by permitting others to aid in saving his, which he looked upon as valueless. It was not until three weeks after that a third body was found – four miles from the other two. This I concluded to be that of the sailor boy, Charles Vivian, although it was a mere skeleton, and impossible to be identified. It was buried in the sand, above the reach of the waves. I mounted my horse, and rode to the Gulf of Spezzia, put up my horse and walked until I caught sight of the lone house on the seashore in which Shelley and Williams had dwelt, and where their widows still lived. Hitherto in my frequent visits – in the absence of direct evidence to the contrary – I had buoyed up their spirits by maintaining that it was not impossible but that the friends still lived; now I had to extinguish the last hope of these forlorn women. I had ridden fast, to prevent any ruder messenger from bursting in upon them. As I stood on the threshold of their house, the bearer, or rather confirmer, of news which would rack every fibre of their quivering frames to the utmost, I paused, and, looking at the sea, my memory reverted to our joyous parting only a few days before.

The two families then had all been in the verandah, over-hanging a sea so clear and calm that every star was reflected on the water, as if it had been a mirror; the young mothers singing some merry tune, with the accompaniment of a guitar. Shelley's shrill laugh – I heard it still – rang in my ears, with Williams's friendly hail, the general *buona notte* of all the joyous party, and the earnest entreaty to me to return as soon as possible, and not to forget the commissions they had severally given me. I was in a small boat beneath them, slowly rowing myself on board the *Bolivar*, at anchor in the bay, loth to part from what I verily believed to have been at that time the most united, and happiest, set of human beings in the whole world. And now by the blow of an idle puff of wind the scene was changed. Such is human happiness.

Trelawny took the lead in making funeral arrangements for Williams and Shelley, who were cremated in that order on successive days. The bodies had been buried on the shore where they had been washed up so it was necessary to first dig them up before they could be ceremonially burnt.

I got a furnace made at Leghorn, of iron-bars and strong sheet-iron, supported on a stand, and laid in a stock of fuel, and such things as were said to be used by Shelley's much loved Hellenes on their funeral pyres.

On the 13th of August, 1822, I went on board the *Bolivar*, with an English acquaintance, having written to Byron and Hunt to say I would send them word when everything was ready, as they wished to be present. I had previously engaged two large feluccas, with drags and tackling, to go before, and endeavour to find the place where Shelley's boat had foundered; the captain of one of the feluccas having asserted that he was out in the fatal squall, and had seen Shelley's boat go down off Via Reggio, with all sail set. With light and fitful breezes we were eleven hours reaching our destination – the tower of Migliarino, at the Bocca Lericcio, in the Tuscan States. There was a village there, and about two miles from that place Williams was buried. So I anchored, landed, called on the officer in command, a major, and told him my object in coming, of which he was already apprised by his own government. He assured me I should have every aid from him. As it was too late in the day to commence operations, we went to the only inn in the place, and I wrote to Byron to be with us the next day at noon. The major sent my letter to Pisa by a dragoon, and made arrangements for the next day. In the morning he was with us early, and gave me a note from Byron, to say he would join us as near noon as he could. At ten we went on board the commandant's boat, with a squad of soldiers in working dresses, armed with mattocks and spades, an officer of quarantine service, and some of his crew. They had their peculiar tools, so fashioned as to do their work without coming into personal contact with things that might be infectious – long-handled tongs, nippers, poles with iron hooks and spikes, and divers others that gave one a lively idea of the implements of torture devised by the holy inquisitors. Thus freighted, we started, my own boat following with the furnace, and the things I had brought from Leghorn. We pulled along the shore for some distance, and landed at a line of strong posts and railings which projected into the sea – forming the boundary dividing the Tuscan and Lucchese States. We walked along the shore to the grave, where Byron and Hunt soon joined us; they, too, had an officer and soldiers from the tower of Migliarino, an officer of the Health Office, and some dismounted dragoons, so we were surrounded by soldiers; but they kept the ground clear, and readily lent their aid. There was a considerable gathering of spectators from the neighbourhood, and many ladies richly dressed were amongst them. The spot where the body lay was marked by the gnarled root of a pine tree.

A rude hut, built of young pine-tree stems, and wattled with their branches, to keep the sun and rain out, and thatched with reeds, stood on the beach to shelter the look-out man on duty. A few yards from this was the grave, which we commenced opening – the Gulf of Spezzia and Leghorn at equal distances of 22 miles from us. As to fuel I might have saved myself the trouble of bringing any, for there was an ample supply of broken spars and planks cast on the shore from wrecks, besides the fallen and decaying timber in a stunted pine forest close at hand. The soldiers collected fuel whilst I erected the furnace, and then the men of the Health Office set to work, shovelling away the sand which covered the body, while we gathered round, watching anxiously. The first indication of their having found the body was the appearance of the end of a black silk handkerchief – I grubbed this out with a stick, for we were not allowed to touch anything with our hands – then some shreds of linen were met with, and a boot with the bone of the leg and the foot in it. On the removal of a layer of brushwood, all that now remained of my lost friend was exposed – a shapeless mass of bones and flesh. The limbs separated from the trunk on being touched.

"Is that a human body?" exclaimed Byron; "why, it's more like the carcass of a sheep, or any other animal than a man: this is a satire on our pride and folly."

I pointed to the letters E. E. W. on the black silk handkerchief.

Byron, looking on, muttered, "The entrails of a worm hold together longer than the potter's clay of which man is made. Hold! let me see the jaw," he added, as they were removing the skull, "I can recognize any one by the teeth, with whom I have talked. I always watch the lips and mouth: they tell what the tongue and eyes try to conceal."

I had a boot of Williams' with me; it exactly corresponded with the one found in the grave. The remains were removed piecemeal into the furnace.

"Don't repeat this with me," said Byron; "let my carcass rot where it falls."

The funereal pyre was now ready; I applied the fire, and the materials being dry and resinous the pine-wood burnt furiously, and drove us back. It was hot enough before, there was no breath of air, and the loose sand scorched our feet. As soon as the flames became clear, and allowed us to approach, we threw frankincense and salt into the furnace, and poured a flask of wine and oil over the body. The Greek oration was omitted, for we had lost our Hellenic bard. It was now so insufferably hot that the officers and soldiers were all seeking shade.

"Let us try the strength of these waters that drowned our friends," said Byron, with his usual audacity. "How far out do you think they were when their boat sank?"

"If you don't wish to be put into the furnace, you had better not try; you are not in condition."

He stripped, and went into the water, and so did I and my companion. Before we got a mile out, Byron was sick, and persuaded to return to the shore. My companion, too, was seized with cramp, and reached the land by my aid. At four o'clock the funereal pyre burnt low, and when we uncovered the furnace, nothing remained in it but dark-coloured ashes, with fragments of the larger bones. Poles were now put under the red-hot furnace, and it was gradually cooled in the sea. I gathered together the human ashes, and placed them in a small oak box, bearing an inscription on a brass plate, screwed it down, and placed it in Byron's carriage. He returned with Hunt to Pisa, promising to be with us on the following day at Via Reggio. I returned with my party in the same way we came, and supped and slept at the inn. On the following morning we went on board the same boats, with the same things and party, and rowed down the little river near Via Reggio to the sea, pulled along the coast towards Massa, then landed, and began our preparations as before.

Three white wands had been stuck in the sand to mark the Poet's grave, but as they were at some distance from each other, we had to cut a trench thirty yards in length, in the line of the sticks, to ascertain the exact spot, and it was nearly an hour before we came upon the grave.

In the meantime Byron and Leigh Hunt arrived in the carriage, attended by soldiers, and the Health Officer, as before. The lonely and grand scenery that surrounded us so exactly harmonized with Shelley's genius, that I could imagine his spirit soaring over us. The sea, with the islands of Gorgona, Capraja, and Elba, was before us; old battlemented watch-towers stretched along the coast, backed by the marble-crested Apennines glistening in the sun, picturesque from their diversified outlines, and not a human dwelling was in sight. As I thought of the delight Shelley felt in such scenes of loneliness and grandeur whilst living, I felt we were no better than a herd of wolves or a pack of wild dogs, in tearing out his battered and naked body from the pure yellow sand that lay so lightly over it, to drag him back to the light of day; but the dead have no voice, nor had I power to check the sacrilege – the work went on silently in the deep and unresisting sand, not a word was spoken, for the Italians have a touch of sentiment, and their feelings are easily excited into sympathy. Byron was silent and thoughtful. We were startled and drawn together by a dull hollow sound that followed the blow of a mattock; the iron had struck a skull, and the body was soon uncovered. Lime had been strewn on it; this, or decomposition, had the effect of staining it of a dark and indigo colour. Byron asked me to preserve the skull for him but remembering that he had formerly used one as a drinking cup, I was determined Shelley's should not be so profaned. The limbs did not separate from the trunk, as in the case of Williams' body, so that the corpse was removed entire into the furnace. I had taken the precaution of having more and larger pieces of timber, in consequence of my experience of the day before of the difficulty of consuming a corpse in the open air with our apparatus. After the fire was well kindled we repeated the ceremony of the previous day; and more wine was poured over Shelley's dead body than he had consumed during his life. This with the oil and salt made the yellow flames glisten and quiver. The heat from the sun and fire was so intense that the atmosphere was tremulous and wavy. The corpse fell open and the heart was laid bare. The frontal bone of the skull, where it had been struck with the mattock, fell off; and, as the back of the head rested on the red-hot bottom bars of the furnace, the brains literally seethed, bubbled and boiled as in a cauldron, for a very long time.

Byron could not face this scene, he withdrew to the beach and swam off to the *Bolivar*. Leigh Hunt remained in the carriage. The fire was so fierce as to produce a white heat on the iron and to reduce its contents to grey ashes. The only portions that were not consumed were some fragments of bones, the jaw, and the skull; but what surprised us all was that the heart remained entire. In snatching this relic from the fiery furnace, my hand was severely burnt; and had any one seen me do the act I should have been put into quarantine.

After cooling the iron machine in the sea, I collected the human ashes and placed them in a box, which I took on board the *Bolivar*. Byron and Hunt retraced their steps to their home, and the officers and soldiers returned to their quarters. I liberally rewarded the men for the admirable manner in which they behaved during the two days they had been with us.

Edward Trelawny also saw to the disposal of Shelley's ashes in Rome.

When I arrived at Leghorn, as I could not immediately go on to Rome, I consigned Shelley's ashes to our Consul at Rome, Mr Freeborn, requesting him to keep them in his custody until my arrival. When I reached Rome, Freeborn told me that to quiet the authorities there, he had been obliged to inter the ashes with the usual ceremonies in the Protestant burying-place. When I came to examine the ground with the man who had the custody of it, I found Shelley's grave amidst a cluster of others. The old Roman wall partly enclosed the place, and there was a niche in the wall formed by two buttresses – immediately under an ancient pyramid, said to be the tomb of Caius Cestius. There were no graves near it at that time. This suited my taste, so I purchased the recess, and sufficient space for planting a row of the Italian upright cypresses . . . Without more ado, masons were hired, and two tombs built in the recess. In one of these, when completed, I deposited the box, with Shelley's ashes, and covered it in with solid stone, inscribed with a Latin epitaph, written by Leigh Hunt . . .

To the first inscription . . . I added two lines from Shelley's favourite play, "The Tempest".

> Nothing of him that doth fade,
> But doth suffer a sea change
> Into something rich and strange.

The other tomb, built merely to fill up the recess, was likewise covered in in the same way – but blank without as within. I planted 8 seedling cypresses. When I last saw them, in 1844, the 7 which remained were about 35 feet in height. I added flowers as well. The ground I had purchased, I enclosed, and so ended my task.

(Edward Trelawny, *Records of Shelley, Byron, and the Author*)

⌁

When Lord Byron visited a cemetery in the Italian town of Bologna, a meeting with the custodian sparked some thoughts of Shakespeare's Hamlet *and also the reflection that the last thing he wanted on earth was to be buried in his native England. He is writing to his friend and publisher, John Murray.*

. . . I have been picture-gazing this morning at the famous Domenichino and Guido, both of which are superlative. I afterwards went to the beautiful cemetery of Bologna, beyond the walls, and found, besides the superb burial-ground, an original of a Custode, who reminded me of the grave-digger in *Hamlet*. He has a collection of capuchins' skulls, labelled on the forehead, and taking down one of them, said, "This was Brother Desiderio Berro, who died at 40 – one of my best friends. I begged his head of his brethren after his decease, and they gave it me. I put it in lime, and then boiled it. Here it is, teeth and all, in excellent preservation. He was the merriest cleverest fellow I ever knew. Wherever he went, he brought joy; and whenever any one was melancholy, the sight of him was enough to make him cheerful again. He walked so actively, you might have taken him for a dancer – he joked – he laughed – oh! he was such a Frate as I never saw before, nor ever shall again!"

He told me that he had himself planted all the cypresses in the cemetery, that he had the greatest attachment to them and to his dead people; that snce 1801 they had buried 53,000 persons. In showing some older monuments, there was that of a Roman girl of 20, with a bust by Bernini. She was a princess Bartorini, dead two centuries ago: he said that, on opening her grave, they had found her hair complete, and "as yellow as gold". Some of the epitaphs at Ferrara pleased me more than the more splendid monuments at Bologna; for instance:—

Martini Luigi
Implora pace.

Lucrezia Picini
Implora eterna quiete.

Can anything be more full of pathos? Those few words say all that can be said or sought: the dead had had enough of life; all they wanted was rest, and this they implore! There is all the helplessness, and humble hope, and deathlike prayer, that can arise from the grave – *implora pace.* I hope, whoever may survive me, and shall see me put in the foreigners' burying-ground at the Lido [in Venice], within the fortress by the Adriatic, will see those two words, and no more, put over me. I trust they won't think of "pickling, and bringing me home to Clod or Blunderbuss Hall". I am sure my bones would not rest in an English grave, or my clay mix with the earth of that country. I believe the thought would drive me mad on my deathbed, could I suppose that any of my friends would be base enough to convey my carcass back to your soil. I would not even feed your worms, if I could help it.

Despite the wishes that he'd expressed about never being buried in England (see above), that is exactly what happened after Byron's death. John Cam Hobhouse recorded in his diary a visit to the boat on which his friend had been returned home.

I went with Mr Hanson and proved Lord Byron's will at Doctor's Commons. Then I went to London Bridge and, getting into a boat, we rowed to London Dock Buoy, where the *Florida* was anchored. Messrs Woodeson, the undertakers, had been previously sent on board, and I found them employed in emptying the large cask enclosing the chest that contained the body. It was a long black box hooped with iron, something like a coffin – the best that could be made at Missolonghi [the town in Greece where Byron had died]. The leaden coffin brought by the undertakers was placed alongside of the chest, and a canvass covering having been drawn round them, everyone except the household withdrew. I retired to the cabin, and to distract my attention looked over the papers which Lord Byron had sealed up at Cephallonia and left there. Captain Hodgson of the *Florida*, his father, Fletcher, and myself minutely examined them. There was no testamentary document in them of any kind, and we signed a paper to that effect.

Mr Woodeson came to me and told me the body had been removed into the coffin, and asked me if I wished to see it. I believe I should have dropped down dead if I had looked at it. He told me, as also did Bruno the physician, that it had almost all the freshness and firmness of life. The chest, containing the vases in which the heart and brain and intestines were deposited, was not opened. I covered the coffin with a plane lid and the ship's flag, and watched by it whilst the Captain went on shore for the customs permit for its removal. Lord Byron's large Newfoundland dog was lying at my feet. A young man, whom I did not know, came on board and begged leave to see the body. He did this in terms so moving and was so much affected that I could not help promising him a sight of it before interment. He took up a bit of the cotton in which it had been wrapped and placed it carefully in his pocket-book.

At last the Custom House order arrived and the coffin was lowered into the undertakers' barge. There were a good many boats round the ship at the time, and the shore was crowded with spectators. I left the servants to take care of the effects, and carrying the papers with me went on board the barge. We passed quietly up the river, and landed at Palace Yard Stairs, at a quarter to five in the afternoon. A black cloth was strapped round the coffin, and it was removed on the shoulders of men to the house prepared for its reception, 20 George Street. The removal across Palace Yard was quite unobserved.

Byron was finally buried on Friday 16 July, 1824, in the family vault in the church near his estate of Newstead Abbey. For a description of his body as it appeared after death, and in particular of the lamed foot which Byron had suffered from throughout his life, see **Illness & Disability***.*

Jane Austen's brother Henry describes the final days of the author of Pride and Prejudice.

She supported, during two months, all the varying pain, irksomeness, and tedium, attendant on decaying nature, with more than resignation, with a truly elastic cheerfulness. She retained her faculties, her memory, her fancy, her temper, and her affections, warm, clear and unimpaired, to the last . . . She wrote whilst she could hold a pen, and with a pencil when a pen was become too laborious. The day preceding her death she composed some stanzas replete with fancy and vigour. Her last voluntary speech conveyed thanks to her medical attendant; and to the final question asked of her, purporting to know her wants, she replied, "I want nothing but death."

(Henry Austen, *Biographical Notice*)

Biographer John Gibson Lockhart recounts the last moments of Sir Walter Scott.

As I was dressing on the morning of Monday, the 17th of September, Nicolson came into my room, and told me that his master had awoke in a state of composure and consciousness, and wished to see me immediately. I found him entirely himself, though in the last extreme of feebleness. His eye was clear and calm – every trace of the wild fire of delirium extinguished. "Lockhart," he said, "I may have but a minute to speak to you. My dear, be a good man – be virtuous – be religious – be a good man. Nothing else will give you any comfort when you come to lie here." He paused, and I said, "Shall I send for Sophia and Anne?" "No," said he, "don't disturb them. Poor souls! I know they were up all night – God bless you all." With this he sunk into a very tranquil sleep, and, indeed, he scarcely afterwards gave any sign of consciousness, except for an instant on the arrival of his sons. They, on learning that the scene was about to close, obtained anew leave of absence from their posts, and both reached Abbotsford on the 19th. About half-past one p.m., on the 21st of September, Sir Walter breathed his last, in the presence of all his children.

It was a beautiful day – so warm that every window was wide open, and so perfectly still that the sound of all others most delicious to his ear, the gentle ripple of the Tweed over its pebbles, was distinctly audible as we knelt around the bed, and his eldest son kissed and closed his eyes.

(John Gibson Lockhart, *Life of Sir Walter Scott*)

Victorian writer Samuel Butler confided in his notebook how he had once offered some instruction to a dying woman. He told her: "Promise me solemnly, if you find in the world beyond the grave that you can communicate with me – that there is some way in which you can make me aware of your continued existence – promise me solemnly that you will never, never avail yourself of it." It seems that the woman recovered after all – but she never forgave Butler for these remarks.

In 1909, nine years after his death, the remains of Oscar Wilde were removed from Bagneux cemetery to the famous Père Lachaise cemetery in Paris, where his tomb still stands. Frank Harris describes a macabre discovery made by Wilde's friend and executor, Robbie Ross.

He [Ross] crossed to Paris with Oscar's son Vyvyan, to render the last service to his friend. When preparing the body for the grave years before Ross had taken medical advice as to what should be done to make his purpose possible. The doctors told him to put Wilde's body in quicklime, like the body of the man in [Wilde's poem] "The Ballad of Reading Gaol". The quicklime, they said, would consume the flesh and leave the white bones – the skeleton – intact, which could then be moved easily.

When the grave was opened, it was found that the quicklime, instead of destroying the flesh, had preserved it. Oscar's face was recognizable, only his hair and beard had grown long.

(Frank Harris, *Oscar Wilde*)

According to another report Ross then got into the grave and removed the remains into the new coffin, all the time handling Wilde's body with "loving reverence".

Disciples & Fans

Sir Walter Scott showed remarkable patience and generosity, to say nothing of a cool head, when a German friend and follower, who had acted as his occasional secretary for several years, turned violently against his protector.

Mention has been made in connection with an unlucky edition of [the Elizabethan playwrights] Beaumont and Fletcher, of Henry Weber, a German scholar, who, escaping to this country in 1804, from misfortunes in his own, excited Scott's compassion, and was thenceforth furnished, through his means, with literary employment of various sorts. Weber was a man of considerable learning; but Scott, as was his custom, appears to have formed an exaggerated notion of his capacity, and certainly countenanced him, to his own severe cost, in several most unhappy undertakings. When not engaged on things of a more ambitious character, he had acted for ten years as his protector's amanuensis, and when the family were in Edinburgh, he very often dined with them. There was something very interesting in his appearance and manners: he had a fair, open countenance, in which the honesty and the enthusiasm of his nation were alike visible; his demeanour was gentle and modest; and he had not only a stock of curious antiquarian knowledge, but the reminiscences, which he detailed with amusing simplicity, of an early life chequered with many strange-enough adventures. He was, in short, much a favourite with Scott and all the household; and was invited to dine with them so frequently, chiefly because his friend was aware that he had an unhappy propensity to drinking, and was anxious to keep him away from places where he might have been more likely to indulge it. This vice had been growing on him; and of late Scott had found it necessary to make some rather severe remonstrances about habits which were at once injuring his health and interrupting his literary industry.

They had, however, parted kindly when Scott left Edinburgh at Christmas; and the day after his return, Weber attended him as usual in his library – being employed in transcribing extracts during several hours, while his friend, seated over against him, continued working at the *Life of Swift*. The light beginning to fail, Scott threw himself back in his chair, and was about to ring for candles, when he observed the German's eyes fixed upon him with an unusual solemnity of expression. "Weber," said he, "what's the matter with you?" "Mr Scott," said Weber, rising, "you have long insulted me, and I can bear it no longer. I have brought a pair of pistols with me, and must insist on your taking one of them instantly." And with that he produced the weapons, which had been deposited under his chair, and laid one of them on Scott's manuscript. "You are mistaken, I think," said Scott, "in your way of setting about this affair – but no matter. It can, however, be no part of your object to annoy Mrs Scott and the children; therefore, if you please, we will put the pistols into the drawer till after dinner, and then arrange to go out together like gentlemen." Weber answered with equal coolness, "I believe that will be better," and laid the second pistol also on the table. Scott locked them both in his desk, and said, "I am glad you have felt the propriety of what I suggested – let me only request farther, that nothing may occur while we are at dinner to give my wife any suspicion of what has been passing." Weber again assented, and Scott withdrew to his dressing-room, from which he despatched a message to one of Weber's companions – and then dinner was served, and Weber joined the circle as usual. He conducted himself with composure, and everything seemed to go on in the ordinary way until, whisky and hot water being produced, Scott, instead of inviting his guest to help himself, mixed two moderate tumblers of toddy, and handed one of them to Weber, who, upon that, started up with a furious countenance, but instantly sat down again, and when Mrs Scott expressed her fear that he was ill, answered placidly that he was liable to spasms, but that the pain was gone. He then took the glass, eagerly gulped down its contents, and pushed it back to Scott. At this moment the friend who had been sent for made his appearance; and Weber, on seeing him enter the room, rushed past him and out of the house, without stopping to put on his hat. The friend, who pursued instantly, came up with him at the end of the street, and did all he could to soothe his agitation, but in vain. The same evening he was obliged to be put into a strait-waistcoat; and though in a few days he exhibited such symptoms of recovery that he was allowed to go by himself to pay a visit in the North of England, he there soon relapsed, and continued ever afterwards a hopeless lunatic, being supported to the end of his life, in June 1818, at Scott's expense, in an asylum at York.

(John Gibson Lockhart, *Life of Sir Walter Scott*)

The 19th-century American writer Rebecca Harding Davis remembers an encounter with the so-called "Sage of Concord", Ralph Waldo Emerson. Davis had a fairly robust view of the sometimes wishywashy mystical views of the group – known as Transcendentalists – which gathered round Emerson. Mr Alcott, who figures in this story, was the father of the famous author of Little Women, *Louisa M. Alcott.*

Early that morning when his lank, grey figure had first appeared at the gate, Mr [Nathaniel] Hawthorne said: "Here comes the Sage of Concord. He is anxious to know what kind of human beings come up from the back hills in Virginia. Now I will tell you," his eyes gleaming with fun, "what he will talk to you about. Pears. Yes. You may begin at Plato or the day's news, and he will come around to pears. He is now convinced that a vegetable diet affects both the body and soul, and that pears exercise a more direct and ennobling influence on us than any other vegetable or fruit. Wait. You'll hear presently."

When we went in to dinner, therefore, I was surprised to see the sage eat heartily of the fine sirloin of beef set before us. But with the dessert he began to advocate a vegetable diet and at last announced the spiritual influence of pears, to the great delight of his host, who laughed like a boy and was humored like one by the gentle old man.

Whether Alcott, Emerson, and their disciples discussed pears or the war, their views gave you the same sense of unreality, of having been taken, as Hawthorne said, at too long a range . . . Their theories were like beautiful bubbles blown from a child's pipe, floating overhead, with queer reflections on them of sky and earth and human beings, all in a glow of fairy colour and all a little distorted.

Mr Alcott once showed me an arbour which he had built with great pains and skill for Mr Emerson to "do his thinking in." It was made of unbarked saplings and boughs, a tiny round temple, two-storied, with chambers in which were seats, a desk, etc., all very artistic and complete, except that he had forgotten to make any door. You could look at it and admire it, but nobody could go in or use it. It seemed to me a fitting symbol for this guild of prophets and their scheme of life.

Mr Alcott at that time was their oracle, appointed and held in authority by Emerson alone. His faith in the old man was so sincere and simple that it was almost painful to see it.

He once told me, "I asked Alcott the other day what he would do when he came to the gate, and St Peter demanded his ticket. 'What have you to show to justify your right to live?' I said. 'Where is your book, your picture? You have done nothing in the world.' 'No,' he said, 'but somewhere on a hill up there will be Plato and Paul and Socrates talking, and they will say: 'Send Alcott over here, we want him with us.' " "And," said Emerson, gravely shaking his head, "he was right! Alcott was right."

(Rebecca Harding Davis, *Boston in the Sixties*)

William Dean Howells was an editor in Boston when he played host to the Californian writer Bret Harte. Harte had achieved enormous success with his Western short stories and his arrival was a daunting experience for the admiring Howells. This was as nothing, however, to the dangers of his departure.

The joyous visit of a week, which has been here so poorly recovered from the past, came to an end, and the host went with his guest to the station in as much vehicular magnificence as had marked his going to meet him there. Harte was no longer the alarming portent of the earlier time, but an experience of un-alloyed delight. You must love a person whose worst trouble-giving was made somehow a favour by his own unconsciousness of the trouble, and it was a most flattering triumph to have got him in time, or only a little late, to so many luncheons and dinners. If only now he could be got to the train in time the victory would be complete, the happiness of the visit without a flaw. Success seemed to crown the fondest hope in this respect. The train had not yet left the station; there stood the parlour-car which Harte had seats in; and he was followed aboard for those last words in which people try to linger out pleasures they have known together. In this case the sweetest of the pleasures had been sitting up late after those dinners, and talking them over, and then degenerating from that talk into the mere giggle and making giggle which Charles Lamb found the best thing in life. It had come to this as the host and guest sat together for those parting moments, when Harte suddenly started up in the discovery of having forgotten to get some cigars. They rushed out of the train together and, after a wild descent upon the cigar-counter of the restaurant, Harte rushed back to his car. But by this time the train was already moving with that deceitful slowness of the departing train, and Harte had to clamber up the steps of the rearmost platform. His host clambered after, to make sure that he was aboard, which done, he dropped to the ground, while Harte drew out of the station, blandly smiling, and waving his hand with a cigar in it, in picturesque farewell from the platform.

Then his host realized that he had dropped to the ground barely in time to escape being crushed against the side of the archway that sharply descended beside the steps of the train, and he went and sat down in that handsomest hack, and was for a moment deathly sick at the danger that had not realized itself to him in season. To be sure, he was able, long after, to adapt the incident to the exigencies of fiction, and to have a character, not otherwise to be conveniently disposed of, actually crushed to death between a moving train and such an archway.

(William Dean Howells, *Literary
Friends and Acquaintance*)

The now largely forgotten novelist Hall Caine struck up a friendship
with the poet and painter Dante Gabriel Rossetti in London in the
early 1880s. Caine was eager to get his foot on the literary ladder and
Rossetti obviously saw the young man as a breath of fresh air in his
large gloomy house in Cheyne Walk on the Thames embankment.
Another famous resident of Cheyne Walk was Thomas Carlyle, the
historian.

Down to the moment of my coming he [Rossetti] had for years
rarely been outside the doors of his great, gloomy house –
certainly never afoot, and only in closed carriages with his
friends; but on the second night of my stay I marched boldly
into the studio, announced my intention of taking a walk on the
Chelsea Embankment, and, without a qualm, asked Rossetti to
accompany me. To my amazement he consented, saying:
"Well, upon my word, really I think I will." Every night
for a week afterwards I induced him to repeat the unfamiliar
experiment.

But now I recall with emotion and some remorse the scene
and circumstance of those nightly walks; the Embankment
almost dark, with its gas-lamps far apart, and generally silent
at our late hour, except for an occasional footfall on the pavement under the tall houses opposite; the black river flowing
noiselessly behind the low wall and gurgling under the bridge;
and then Rossetti in his slouch hat, with its broad brim pulled
down low on his forehead as if to conceal his face, lurching along
with a heavy, uncertain step, breathing audibly, looking at
nothing, and hardly speaking at all. From these nightly per-
ambulations he would return home utterly exhausted, and
throwing himself on the couch, remain prostrate for nearly
an hour.

I seem to remember that on one of our walks along the
Embankment late at night we passed in the half-darkness
two figures which bore a certain resemblance to our own –
an old man in a Scotch plaid, accompanied by a slight young
woman in a sort of dolman [cloak]. The old man was forging
along sturdily with the help of a stick, and the young woman
appeared to be making some effort to keep pace with him. It was
Carlyle with his niece, and I caught but one glimpse of them as,

out on the same errand as ourselves, they went off in the other direction.

(Hall Caine, *Recollections of Rossetti*)

———✦———

Mark Twain (real name, Samuel Langhorne Clemens) was very gratified when he received a proposal for the setting up of a Mark Twain Club, dedicated to the serious study of his work. It took some years for the real story behind the Club to emerge.

One day he had received a communication from the north of England. The letter was written on heavily embossed and crested paper, and was to the effect that a club had been organized for the purpose of studying the works of the great American humorist. The writer delicately hinted that this had not yet been done in a scholarly and scientific manner, and that it was the intention of the Club to delve deeply into the stores of philosophic wisdom which were sometimes hidden from the casual reader by the super-fabric of wit and humour. The organization, with the permission of Mr Clemens, should be known as The Mark Twain Club, and would feel itself much honoured if it might send the record of its proceedings to Mr Clemens.

Mr Clemens was pleased, very much pleased. His works had not received the attention from scholars and from learned societies that he felt they deserved. Now justice would be done them.

With some pardonable degree of complacency he received and read the first papers of The Mark Twain Club. They were most satisfactory. The Club had printed not only the record of proceedings, but also the studies presented. From time to time Mr Clemens received these reports. The society was evidently flourishing. A letter came from the President saying that the Club had decided to have an emblem; that, after much thought and consideration, a suitable design had been chosen, and that they begged Mr Clemens to do them the honour of accepting one. A few days later a small box arrived containing a very beautiful and curiously wrought pin set with a number of precious stones. Mr Clemens took great pleasure in wearing the pin and in carelessly saying to inquiring friends: "Oh, yes! that's the pin of The Mark Twain Club, an English organization. – Yes, it's very interesting."

After some time the publications of The Mark Twain Club ceased to come, and the incident began to lose some of its vividness.

When Mr Clemens was making his lecture tour around the world, a fine-looking gentle man approached him at Sydney, Australia, after his lecture, and said: "Mr Clemens, I am Sir _____, the President of The Mark Twain Club. It would give me great pleasure if you would take supper with me. I could then give you some interesting details regarding the Club." Mr Clemens accepted, with pleasurable curiosity. When they were seated at table the Englishman leaned over and said, in a confidential tone, "I am The Mark Twain Club." He then went on to explain that some time before he had suffered from a nervous breakdown and, while in that condition, he was ordered by his physician to abstain entirely from all mental excitement. He had thereupon retired to his estate in the north of England and, while there, had conceived of the happy idea of the Club, as furnishing a mild distraction without any attendant mental strain. He was the charter member. There had never been any others. "But the pins?" queried Mr Clemens.

"You are wearing the only one that was ever made," replied the courteous founder of The Mark Twain Club.

(Elizabeth Wallace, *Memories of Mark Twain in Bermuda*)

Theodore Watts-Dunton has gone down in literary history, in a minor way, as the "saviour" of poet Algernon Charles Swinburne. Watts-Dunton, a solicitor by training, abandoned the law to become a literary groupie. In 1879 he took Swinburne to live with him at no. 11 The Pines on Putney Hill in south London, so preserving the poet from what would almost certainly have been an early alcoholic death. Swinburne lived for no less than 30 years in Watts-Dunton's house as a privileged lodger (£200 a year) in two rooms on the first floor. Watts-Dunton weaned the eccentric poet off drink (or at least kept the problem manageable) although he was regularly accused of having "tamed" the poet's free spirit. The two men inhabited a cosy domestic world, not at all disturbed by the marriage in 1905 of the 73-year-old Watts-Dunton to Clara Reich, a local girl less than a third his age. The writer and diarist A. C. Benson gives us a glimpse of the Swinburne-Watts-Dunton household shortly before the latter's marriage.

There stood before me a little, pale, rather don-like man, quite bald, with a huge head and dome-like forehead, a ragged red beard in odd whisks, a small aquiline red nose. He looked supremely shy, but received me with a distinguished courtesy, drumming on the ground with his foot, and uttering strange little whistling noises. He seemed very deaf. The room was crammed with books: bookcases all about – a great sofa entirely filled with stacked books – books on the table. He bowed me to a chair – "Will you sit?" On the fender was a pair of brown socks. Watts-Dunton said to me, "He has just come in from one of his long walks" – and took up the socks and put them behind the coal-scuttle. "Stay!" said Swinburne, and took them out carefully, holding them in his hand: "They are drying." Watts-Dunton murmured something about his fearing they would get scorched, and we sat down. Swinburne sat down, concealing his feet behind a chair, and proceeded with strange motions to put the socks on out of sight. "He seems to be changing them," said Watts-Dunton. Swinburne said nothing, but continued to whistle and drum. Then he rose and bowed me down to lunch, throwing the window open.

(A. C. Benson, *diary, April, 1903*)

The Irish writer James Joyce acquired an almost god-like reputation for his great experimental novel Ulysses, *first published in Paris in 1922. He was once approached by a young man in Zurich who asked if he could "kiss the hand that wrote* Ulysses?" *Joyce refused, saying,* "No, it did lots of other things too."

Forgeries & Frauds

Thomas Chatterton was born in Bristol in 1752. He was a strange, bookish child with a high estimate of his skills. While still in his early teens he created an imaginary medieval poet called Thomas Rowley, producing poems in an appropriate 15th-century style. He invented a family tree for a Bristol tradesman "proving" that he was of noble descent. Chatterton didn't merely imitate the style of old documents and poetry, he also created the materials they were written on, as the following story shows.

It was through a local event of some importance that the Bristol public in general was made familiar with Chatterton's story about the old parchments.

Seven years before, the old Gothic bridge which had crossed the Avon since the days of Henry II, and whose roadway was crowded with buildings overhanging the river, had been condemned as insufficient for the increasing traffic of the city, and the new one which supplanted it was now approaching completion. By the month of September, 1768, it was sufficiently advanced to allow of its being used by foot-passengers, and in the following November it was thrown open to general traffic. During this interval of two months the following letter appeared in the columns of Felix Farley's Bristol Journal.

> Mr Printer,
>   The following Description of the Mayor's first passing over the Old Bridge, taken from an old manuscript, may not at this time be unacceptable to the generality of your readers,
>   Yours, &c.,
>   Dunelmus Bristoliensis.

It was accompanied by the description referred to, giving an account, in antique diction and orthography [spelling], of the procession and public rejoicings which had signalized the opening of the old bridge.

This remarkable communication naturally excited considerable interest and curiosity, and many inquiries were made as to who was its sender. The printer, however, could only state that it had been left at his office by a stranger. But before long Chatterton again called there, and, of course, did not escape examination in respect to the manner in which he had acquired the document. He gave an evasive answer, and, when threatened, a haughty refusal to account for its possession; but milder arguments at length elicited the statement that he was employed to transcribe the contents of certain ancient manuscripts by a gentleman, who also had engaged him to furnish complimentary verses, inscribed to a lady with whom that gentleman was in love. This was probably an extempore invention . . . He further stated afterwards, that the description was transcribed from a parchment, which his father had taken from the muniment-room [place for storing documents] of St Mary's Church. This explanation, strange as it may seem, was accepted without further question, and with less scrutiny than Chatterton himself had anticipated. In this matter he seems to have had a confidant; as appears by the following account.

Mr John Rudhall, a native and inhabitant of Bristol, and formerly apprentice to Mr Francis Gresley, an apothecary in that city, was well acquainted with Chatterton . . . Chatterton frequently called upon him at his master's house and soon after he had printed this account of the bridge in the Bristol paper, told Mr Rudhall that he was the author of it, but it occurring to him afterwards that he might be called upon to produce the original, he brought to him one day a piece of parchment, about the size of a half-sheet of foolscap paper; Mr Rudhall does not think that anything was written on it, when produced by Chatterton, but he saw him write several words, if not lines, in a character which Mr Rudhall did not understand: which, he says, was totally unlike English, and, as he apprehended, was meant by Chatterton to imitate or represent the original, from which this account was printed. He cannot determine precisely, how much Chatterton wrote in this manner, but says, that the time he spent in that visit did not exceed three-quarters of an hour; the size of the parchment, however, (even supposing it to have been filled with writing), will in some measure ascertain the quantity which it contained. He says, also, that when Chatterton had written on the parchment, he held it over the candle, to give it the appearance of antiquity, which changed the colour of the ink, and made the parchment appear black and a little contracted; he never saw him make any similar attempt, nor was the parchment produced afterwards by Chatterton to him, or (as far as he knows) to any other person . . .

(Edward Bell, *Memoir of Thomas Chatterton*)

One of the strangest literary forgeries ever perpetrated was, like many frauds, connected to William Shakespeare and the tantalizing lack of information about the playwright's life. William-Henry Ireland (1777-1835) was the son of a fairly successful 18th-century engraver, Samuel Ireland. Samuel was obsessed with Shakespeare; he also had a low opinion of his son, considering that he'd never amount to much in life. To prove him wrong, William-Henry, who was influenced by the story of Chatterton (see above), decided to produce written "evidence" of his father's literary god. While he was working at a lawyer's office, he embarked on a daring and successful programme of forgery. When a non-Shakespearean forged signature was eagerly accepted by his father, he went on to produce more and more "documentary" proof, finally writing a complete undiscovered Shakespeare play, which he titled "Vortigern". Once William-Henry was eventually discovered, he wrote a kind of confession, partly to exonerate his father from blame. Below are some excerpts from it.

Frequently after dinner my father would read the different accounts of *Shakspear*, and say, it was wonderful, out of so many thousand lines which he must have wrote, that no vestige remained but his signature to the will in the *Commons*, and his name affixed to the mortgage deed presented by Mr *Wallis* to Mr *Garrick*; this was often repeated, and, with enthusiastick praises of *Shakspear*, my father would often say, that if there ever was a man inspired, Shakspear was that man. Curiosity led me to look at the signatures published in *Stevens' Shakspear*, and it occured to me, that if some old writing could be produced, and passed for Shakspear's, it might occasion a little mirth, and shew how far *credulity* would go in the search for antiquities.

Having one day purchased a thin quarto tract of the time of *Elizabeth*, illuminated and bound in vellum, with her arms on the cover, I determined on trying an experiment with it, and for the purpose wrote a letter (in imitation of the hand of that period) as from the author of the book, making it the presentation copy from himself to the queen. I wrote this epistle with common ink, weakened with water, but found its appearance too modern, notwithstanding I determined on shewing it; but before I went home from chambers, where it was contriv'd, I call'd on a book-binder in *New-Inn* passage, of the name of *Laurie*, and laughingly told him what I had contrived; then, producing the letter, I ask'd him his opinion? He told me it was well done, and might deceive many. A young man working in the shop then said, he could give me a composition which would have much more the appearance of old ink; I begg'd he would, upon which he mix'd a few drops of acid with some other liquid (used in marbling the covers of books) in a vial; then writing a few words on paper, held it to the fire to shew its effect, when the letters turn'd completely brown. Having procured this, I went back to chambers, and rewrote the letter, which I took home and shewed my father, who thought it genuine. This, and the book I exchanged with him for some other tract. It was the first thing of the kind I ever attempted, but after I had wrote a great quantity of the *Shakspear* manuscripts, I thought my first attempt, so badly executed, that I again got it from my father, and destroyed it, fearing a discovery.

Soon after my father went into the country, it being long vacation, I obtained permission of the gentleman with whom I was articled, to accompany him. The last place we visited before our return to town, was *Stratford* upon *Avon*, where we remained about ten days; during which time, my father made eager enquiries concerning *Shakspear*, but acquired little more knowledge than those who went before him. We visited *Clopton House*, about a mile from *Stratford*, the gentleman who occupied it, behaved with much civility. On my father saying, he wished to know any thing relative to our *Bard* the gentleman replied, that had he been there a few weeks sooner, he could have given him a great quantity of his, and his family's letters. My father, much astonished, begged to known what was become of them? The gentleman's answer was, that having some young partridges which he wished to bring up, he had, for the purpose, cleared out a small apartment wherein these papers lay, and burnt a large basketfull of them, he said they were all rotten as tinder, but to many of them, he could plainly perceive the signature of *William Shakspear*; and turning to his wife, said to her, "Don't you remember it, my Dear?" Her answer was, "Yes, perfectly well, and you know at the time, I blamed you for destroying them." My father exclaimed, "Good God, Sir! you do not know what an injury the world has sustained by the loss of them." He then begged permission to see the Room, which the gentleman acquiesced in, adding, "If there are any left, Sir, you may have them, for they are but rubbish, and litter up the place." Accordingly, we proceeded into the chamber, but found no trace of any papers; and in every other part of the house our search proved equally ineffectual . . .

My father would often lavish his usual praises on *Shakspear*, and frequently add, that he would give all his curious books to become possessed of a single line of his hand writing. An idea having struck me, that I might perhaps be fortunate enough to find a signature of his, that induced me to examine a number of deeds and other papers which I met with in the course of my researches: I also carefully looked over many useless deeds at chambers, but without success.

For mere frolick and diversion, I soon after formed the plan of attempting to imitate his hand[writing] . . . I wrote a deed in preference to any thing else, thinking it would more firmly stamp the signature as *Shakspear's*.

I took it home, and told my father, I had something curious to shew him, on which I wished to have his opinion. After looking over the deed, he assured me, that he thought it genuine. I then begged his acceptance of it, upon which he offered me any of his curious books, I told him, I would receive nothing. And here I must assure the world, that I had no attention whatever of attempting any thing further, my object was only to give my father pleasure, that wish accomplished, I was satisfied.

However, this deed was shewn, and was generally believed by those who saw it; several persons told me, that wherever it was found, there must undoubtedly be all the Manuscripts of *Shakspear* so long and vainly sought for; my father likewise said, he was certain that I knew of many more: thus urged, partly by the world, and more by my own vanity, I determined on attempting something further . . .

Inevitably, William-Henry Ireland had to face questions about the origin of these priceless documents. Some quick thinking was necessary.

I was much questioned as to where it came from? For some time I gave no particular answer, at length I found it necessary to say something, and for that purpose framed the following story.

That I had, by mere chance, formed an acquaintance with a gentleman, and being one day at dinner with him, expressing my partiality for old books, as well as the autographs of great personages, I said, the gentleman appointed me to meet him, and told me I might rummage over a large quantity of old deeds and papers which had descended to him from his father, who had practised the law, and acquired a great fortune; I added, that for some time I neglected calling according to my promise, alledging that as I was a young man, he had only meant perhaps to laugh at me; however, one day being near the place, curiosity prompted me to call; the gentleman, I said, was rather angry at my remissness and breach of promise, but having made an apology, he permitted me to go into the next room, where I saw a great quantity of papers tied up in bundles, having searched for some time, I at length found the deed before mentioned, which I took to the gentleman, who was much astonished, but said, since I promised you all you should find worthy your notice, I will not be worse than my word, then desiring me to make him a copy, he gave it me.

But when I had wrote more papers, the world wondered how any man could be weak enough to part with such a treasure; to reconcile them to a belief of this, I added the following story: that in searching among my friend's deeds, I had found one which ascertained to him some property, long a matter of litigation and dispute; upon this he promised me every thing I should find appertaining to *Shakspear*, and further, to stop all enquiries as to his name, *&c.* I added, that being a man of large fortune, he did not choose to undergo the impertinent questionings of the world, for which reason, he had bound me on oath, to secrecy, and the better to strengthen this, I hinted, that his father perhaps might have detained the papers illegally in the course of his practice, and should his name be known, it would undoubtedly lead to a discover, and throw a slur on the honour of his family; by such means, I for some time stopped all enquiries . . .

After this Ireland went wonderfully over the top in providing more and more documentary evidence of Shakespeare, forging communications from the playwright to a fellow-poet and to the Earl of Southampton as well as a love letter to Shakespeare's wife Anne Hathaway. Perhaps the peak of his achievement was to fake a letter from Queen Elizabeth. After that it must have been a simple step to write a whole "undiscovered" Shakespeare play. He did, and it was performed at Drury Lane. Ireland showed himself a real master at deception, enclosing a lock of hair at one point and even tampering with an old drawing at another.

I wrote the letter to *Cowley*, thereby wishing to prove *Shakspear* a perfect good natured man; nothing was meant by the pen and ink drawing, however, the world said it was certainly some witty *conundrum*, as to their not being able to explain it, there is nothing surprising in that, for I myself do not know its meaning. My reasons for writing *Heminge's* note and receipt I cannot at present recollect. The letter to *Anne Hatherwaye*, his wife, was to shew his love for her, and that was also meant by the lines addressed to her; as for the lock of hair, it was more a childish frolic than any ways done to strengthen the authenticity of the papers.

Having heard of the Lord *Southampton*'s bounty to *Shakspear*, I determined on writing the correspondence between them on that subject; but, on enquiry, could not learn that any signature of his Lordship's was in existence, I accordingly formed his mode of writing, merely from myself, and the better to disguise it from *Shakspear's*, I wrote the whole with my left hand; this was done to give more authenticity to the story . . .

I wrote Queen *Elizabeth*'s letter from her signature only, which I copied from an original in my father's possession, this letter was produced to make our *Bard* appear noticed by the greatest personage of his time, and thereby add, if possible, fresh lustre to his name . . .

To prove the papers still more genuine, I wrote the agreements between *Lowin* and *Condell* the players. I also produced the play house receipts, and other accounts, thereby to prove *Shakspear* correct in matters of the most trivial nature. Among these were the receipts for playing before Lord *Leicester*, the sum there mentioned was very high for that period: By this I meant to shew the esteem in which his company was held before all others, for I knew there were at that time several play houses in *London*. The strings with which I tied the bundles were unravelled from a piece of old tapestry, part of which I left in the hands of Mr *Wallis*, about the same time I entrusted him with the secret . . .

The play of *Vortigern* was then agreed for, and with much delay brought forward; the world condemned it, but that did not lessen the satisfaction I felt in having at so early an age wrote a piece which was not only acted, but brought forth as the work of the greatest of men . . .

After he was found out, William-Henry felt most guilty because of the general suspicion that his father was implicated in the deception. He wrote, "At length the world in general accused my father of being a party concerned in writing the papers, and then I first began to feel uneasy . . ." *His response was to issue this confession. Although he'd committed a literary "crime", the 19-year old couldn't help feeling a certain satisfaction that he'd fooled so many experts. He was surely conscious of the irony that he had embarked on this daring programme to impress his father, the very man who had earlier dismissed the idea of forgery because his son wasn't clever enough. This is how William-Henry Ireland finishes his confession, half boast, half apology.*

Before I conclude, I shall sum up this account, and am willing to make affidavit to the following declarations, as well as to the whole of this narration.

First, I solemnly declare that my father was perfectly un-acquainted with the whole affair, believing the papers most firmly the productions of *Shakspear*.

Secondly, That I am myself both the author and writer, and have had no aid or assistance from any soul living, and that I should never have gone so far, but that the world praised the papers so much, and thereby flattered my vanity.

Thirdly, That any publication which may appear tending to prove the manuscripts genuine, or contradict what is here *stated*, is false; this being the true account.

W. H. Ireland

Here then I conclude, most sincerely regretting any offence I may have given the world, or any particular individual, trusting at the same time, they will deem the whole the act of a boy, without any evil or bad intention, but hurried on thoughtless of any danger that awaited to ensnare him. Should I attempt another play, or any other stage performance, I shall hope the public will lay aside all prejudice my conduct may have deserved, and grant me that kind indulgence which is the certain inmate of every *Englishman*'s bosom.

Mark Twain has the following tale about a fake (though not exactly a literary one) in his autobiography. The witness was Bret Harte, writer of Western short stories and a friend of Twain. Harte was eating in a modest San Francisco restaurant with a sea-going friend. Harte liked to go to the restaurant to "observe mixed humanity". What follows must have seemed to Harte like a neat short story.

Captain Osborn and Bret Harte went there one day and took a meal, and in the course of it Osborn fished up an interesting reminiscence of a dozen years before and told about it. It was to this effect:

He was a midshipman in the navy when the Californian gold

craze burst upon the world and set it wild with excitement. His ship made the long journey around the Horn and was approaching her goal, the Golden Gate, when an accident happened.

"It happened to me," said Osborn. "I fell overboard. There was a heavy sea running, but no one was much alarmed about me, because we had on board a newly patented life-saving device which was believed to be competent to rescue anything that could fall overboard, from a midshipman to an anchor. Ours was the only ship that had this device; we were very proud of it, and had been anxious to give its powers a practical test. This thing was lashed to the garboard-strake of the main-to'gallant mizzen-yard amidships, and there was nothing to do but cut the lashings and heave it over; it would do the rest. One day the cry of 'Man overboard!' brought all hands on deck. Instantly the lashings were cut and the machine flung joyously over. Damnation, it went to the bottom like an anvil! By the time that the ship was brought to and a boat manned, I was become but a bobbing speck on the waves half a mile astern and losing my strength very fast; but by good luck there was a common seaman on board who had practical ideas in his head and hadn't waited to see what the patent machine was going to do, but had run aft and sprung over after me the moment the alarm was cried through the ship. I had a good deal of a start of him, and the seas made his progress slow and difficult, but he stuck to his work and fought his way to me, and just in the nick of time he put his saving arms about me when I was about to go down. He held me up until the boat reached us and rescued us. By that time I was unconscious, and I was still unconscious when we arrived at the ship. A dangerous fever followed, and I was delirious for three days; then I came to myself and at once inquired for my benefactor, of course. He was gone. We were lying at anchor in the Bay and every man had deserted to the gold-mines except the commissioned officers. I found out nothing about my benefactor but his name – Burton Sanders – a name which I have held in grateful memory ever since. Every time I have been on the Coast, these twelve or thirteen years, I have tried to get track of him, but have never succeeded. I wish I could find him and make him understand that his brave act has never been forgotten by me. Harte, I would rather see him and take him by the hand than any other man on the planet."

At this stage or a little later there was an interruption. A waiter near by said to another waiter, pointing, "Take a look at that tramp that's coming in. Ain't that the one that bilked the house, last week, out of ten cents?"

"I believe it is. Let him alone – don't pay any attention to him; wait till we can get a good look at him."

The tramp approached timidly and hesitatingly, with the air of one unsure and apprehensive. The waiters watched him furtively. When he was passing behind Harte's chair one of them said, "He's the one!" – and they pounced upon him and proposed to turn him over to the police as a bilk. He begged piteously. He confessed his guilt, but said he had been driven to his crime by necessity – that when he had eaten the plate of beans and slipped out without paying for it, it was because he was starving, and hadn't the ten cents to pay for it with. But the waiters would listen to no explanations, no palliations; he must be placed in custody. He brushed his hand across his eyes and said meekly that he would submit, being friendless. Each waiter took him by an arm and faced him about to conduct him away. Then his melancholy eyes fell upon Captain Osborn, and a light of glad and eager recognition flashed from them. He said,

"Weren't you a midshipman once, sir, in the old *Lancaster*?"

"Yes," said Osborn. "Why?"

"Didn't you fall overboard?"

"Yes, I did. How do you come to know about it?"

"Wasn't there a new patent machine aboard, and didn't they throw it over to save you?"

"Why, yes," said Osborn, laughing gently, "but it didn't do it."

"No, sir, it was a sailor that done it."

"It certainly was. Look here, my man, you are getting distinctly interesting. Were you of our crew?"

"Yes, sir, I was."

"I reckon you may be right. You do certainly know a good deal about that incident. What is your name?"

"Burton Sanders."

The Captain sprang up, excited, and said, "Give me your hand! Give me both your hands! I'd rather shake them than inherit a fortune!" – and then he cried to the waiters, "Let him go! – take your hands off! He is my guest, and can have anything and everything this house is able to furnish. I am responsible."

There was a love-feast, then. Captain Osborn ordered it regardless of expense, and he and Harte sat there and listened while the man told stirring adventures of his life and fed himself up to the eyebrows. Then Osborn wanted to be benefactor in his turn, and pay back some of his debt. The man said it could all be paid with ten dollars – that it had been so long since he had owned that amount of money that it would seem a fortune to him, and he should be grateful beyond words if the Captain could spare him that amount. The Captain spared him ten broad twenty-dollar gold pieces, and made him take them in spite of his modest protestations, and gave him his address and said he must never fail to give him notice when he needed grateful service.

Several months later Harte stumbled upon the man in the street. He was most comfortably drunk, and pleasant and chatty. Harte remarked upon the splendidly and movingly dramatic incident of the restaurant, and said, "How curious and fortunate and happy and interesting it was that you two should come together, after that long separation, and at exactly the right moment to save you from disaster and turn your defeat by the waiters into a victory. A preacher could make a great sermon out of that, for it does look as if the hand of Providence was in it."

The hero's face assumed a sweetly genial expression, and he said, "Well now, it wasn't Providence this time. I was running the arrangements myself."

"How do you mean?"

"Oh, I hadn't ever seen the gentleman before. I wus at the next table, with my back to you the whole time he was telling about it. I saw my chance, and slipped out and fetched the two waiters with me and offered to give them a commission out of what I could get out of the Captain if they would do a quarrel act with me and give me an opening. So, then, after a minute or two I straggled back, and you know the rest of it as well I do."

(Mark Twain, *Chapters from my Autobiography*)

In 1960 a graduate student of anthropology from the University of California was waiting for a Greyhound bus in Nogales, a small town on the border between Arizona and Mexico. He was on a field trip, accompanied by a friend and guide, and his aim was to collect information about the medicinal plants and drugs used by the native Americans of the Southwest USA. Suddenly the friend leaned towards the graduate student and whispered that, if he really wanted the low-down on native plants, then that old white-haired Indian sitting in front of the bus-station window was just the man to tap for information. The guide introduced his student friend to the elderly, dignified man and then made himself scarce. The UCLA graduate and the Indian – whose name was don Juan – started to talk. It seemed a perfect match. Here was an academic eager for knowledge and opposite him was a man who, it seemed, could give him some privileged insights into the use of drugs like peyote.

The meeting changed the life, and the fortunes, of Carlos Castaneda. From the obscurity of a researcher's life he sprang into the best-seller charts with books like *The Teachings of Don Juan* and *Journey to Ixtlan*. These books, which sold over eight million copies in the 1970s alone, chronicled Castaneda's apprenticeship to his "master" Don Juan and his attempt to become a "warrior" or "man of knowledge". Aided by psychedelic drugs (specifically, peyote, jimson weed and a mushroom called "humito"), a dash of sorcery and Don Juan's Zen-style utterances, Castaneda entered a world of "beauty and terror". The flavour of the relationship between master and apprentice is shown in the following snippet of dialogue from *The Teachings of Don Juan* – Carlos Castenada has just had the experience of imagining he's been turned into a crow:

Don Juan said: "It does not take much to become a crow. You did it and now you will always be one."

"What happened after I became a crow, Don Juan? Did I fly for three days?"

"No, you came back at nightfall as I had told you to."

"But how did I come back?"

"You were very tired and went to sleep. That is all."

"I mean, did I fly back?"

"I have already told you. You obeyed me and came back to the house. But don't concern yourself with that matter. It is of no importance."

The tone of the dialogue is well-managed: Castaneda's child-like wonder and his eager questioning of the master contrast with the cryptic assurances of Don Juan. No wonder the books did so well at the tail-end of the hippy era. They satisfied a counter-cultural search for a "spiritual" alternative to crass Western materialism. They chimed with the 60s belief that drugs weren't merely a way of getting high but a path to enlightenment. They had an exotic locale in the arid yet beautiful landscapes of the Southwest United States, and an enigmatic hero in the Yaqui Indian whom Castaneda had first encountered at an Arizona bus station.

The Teachings of Don Juan and its sequels achieved academic respectabilty too. *The Teachings* had a foreword by Walter Goldschmidt, then the anthropology professor at UCLA, who announced grandly that the book was both "ethnography and allegory". Castaneda gained his doctorate with the third book in the series, *Journey to Ixtlan*. But there were dissenting voices. Some people suggested he should have got an award for fiction rather than a doctorate. Others considered that the only magic performed by Castaneda (or Don Juan) had been to transform the University of California into an ass. Critics pointed out inconsistencies in the books and drew attention to the sheer lack of evidence. Castaneda never produced a single photograph or recording to support his narratives. No one else ever saw Don Juan.

For all the hostility, however, Castaneda continued (and continues) to attract fervent believers and admirers around the world. His ten books still sell, translated into seventeen languages. For some supporters, criticism only makes him a more authentic prophet. Perhaps wisely, Castaneda wrapped himself in the same cloak of mystery that he extended to his Yaqui Indian teacher. Biographical details about the one-time UCLA graduate are conflicting or altogether absent. He rarely gave interviews. Carlos Castaneda died of liver cancer in Westwood, California, in April 1998. It appears that his mentor predeceased him. In a very rare interview some years before his death Castaneda (or a man purporting to be Castaneda) revealed to the writer Keith Thompson that Don Juan had chosen to "displace his assemblage point from its fixation in the conventional human world." Just as the Indian's life had been exotic and alien by western standards, so too was his death – for the master had "combusted from within". By contrast, Carlos Castaneda's death was ordinary; he was described in at least one obituary as a Beverly Hills schoolteacher.

Perhaps the most notorious "literary" fraud of the later twentieth century was the discovery of Adolf Hitler's supposed diaries, a collection of the Führer's most private ruminations running to dozens of black-bound volumes. In the closing days of World War Two, so the story went, some German farmers near Dresden had found a cargo of crates from a crashed Junkers 352, crates which contained manuscripts flown out of a beseiged Berlin for safekeeping. Largely through the obsessive interest of Gerd Heinemann, who was an enthusiast for Nazi relics as well as being a journalist on the West German magazine *Stern*, the diaries were unearthed and an immensely profitable publishing scam set in motion. In fact, the "diaries", covering the period from Hitler's rise to power until shortly before his death, were the work of Konrad Kujau, a forger and compulsive liar. Kujau, working from his shop in Stuttgart, poured tea over the newly written pages and then battered each completed volume to give it an aged appearance.

In 1983 *Stern* magazine announced that it had come into possession of these diaries and a fierce bidding war broke out between foreign publishers and media proprietors. The diaries were of tremendous historical significance even though many of the Hitlerian entries sounded oddly flat and banal, along the lines of "I have violent flatulence and – says Eva – bad breath" and (even better) the homely reminder, "Must not forget tickets for the Olympic Games for Eva." Caution and common-sense went out the window, however, since the diary publication guaranteed a sales boom and a world-wide profile for any newspaper or magazine acquiring the rights. Rupert Murdoch, proprietor of *The Times* and *The Sunday Times*, decided to buy the diaries for publication in his newspapers and elsewhere. Through control of the company News International Murdoch, then an Australian citizen (he subsequently took out American citizenship), had – and still has – immense clout in the media world as well as financial muscle.

Inevitably, there was doubt about the authenticity of the diaries. One of the experts called in to give his opinion was the distinguished historian Hugh Trevor-Roper who had worked for British Intelligence during the war and written an early but definitive book on the death of the German dictator, *The Last Days of Hitler* (1947). Trevor-Roper, by then ennobled as Lord Dacre, was at first satisfied by the diaries but he later started to have suspicions about their genuineness. Unfortunately, these second thoughts surfaced on the eve of publication of the first episode in *The Sunday Times*. The paper was about to go to press when its senior editorial staff were informed of Dacre's doubts. The *Sunday Times* editor phoned Rupert Murdoch in New York to give him this latest and most unwelcome news. Murdoch's response was, in its way, a minor masterpiece of terseness: "Fuck Dacre. Publish."

The paper did not lose out by its publication of the diaries, retaining many of the readers it had attracted because of the serialization. Murdoch is reported to have commented later, "After all, we are in the entertainment business".

The whole story, with its mixture of greed, gullibility, self-delusion and tacky nostalgia for Nazidom, is entertainingly told by Robert Harris in *Selling Hitler* (1986). Harris went on to write the best-selling *Fatherland*, an "alternative history" novel which very plausibly imagines what would have happened if Germany had won World War Two.

Friendships & First Meetings

William Shakespeare and Ben Jonson were fellow playwrights and possibly rivals. This is a story about how they might have met, which throws a very favourable light on Shakespeare.

His [Shakespeare's] Acquaintance with *Ben Jonson* began with a remarkable piece of Humanity and good Nature; Mr *Jonson*, who was at that time altogether unknown to the World, had offer'd one of his Plays to the Players, in order to have it Acted; and the Persons into whose Hands it was put, after having turn'd it carelessly and superciliously over, were just upon returning it to him with an ill-natur'd Answer, that it would be of no service to their Company, when *Shakespear* luckily cast his Eye upon it, and found something so well in it as to engage him first to read it through, and afterwards to recommend Mr *Johnson* and his Writings to the Publick. After this they were profess'd Friends; tho' I don't know whether the other ever made him an equal return of Gentleness and Sincerity.

(Nicholas Rowe, *Some Account of the Life &c. of Mr William Shakespear*)

The Restoration playwright William Congreve, author of The Double Dealer *and* The Way of the World, *was a "close friend" of the Duchess of Marlborough. When he died he left her the then considerable sum of £10,000 although, according to Dr Johnson, for someone of her wealth "such a legacy was as a drop in the bucket".*

She showed devotion to his memory.

The great lady buried her friend with a pomp seldom seen at the funerals of poets . . . Her Grace laid out her friend's bequest in a superb diamond necklace, which she wore in honour of him, and, if report is to be believed, showed her regard for him in ways much more extraordinary. It is said that a statue of him in ivory, which moved by clockwork, was placed daily at her table, that she had a wax doll made in imitation of him, and that the feet of the doll were regularly blistered and anointed by doctors, as poor Congreve's feet had been when he suffered from the gout.

(Macauley, *Literary Essays*, quoted
in Ian Hamilton's *Keepers of the Flame*)

The 18th-century Irish playwright, novelist and poet Oliver Goldsmith writes a letter to his mother about a miserly friend. Goldsmith, in his early 20s, was on the point of emigrating to America but literally missed the boat.

My dear Mother,

If you will sit down and calmly listen to what I say, you shall be fully resolved in every one of those many questions you have asked me. I went to Cork, and converted my horse, which you prize so much higher than Fiddle-back, into cash, took my passage in a ship bound for America, and, at the same time paid the captain for my freight and all the other expenses of my voyage. But it so happened that the wind did not answer for three weeks; and you know, Mother, that I could not command the elements. My misfortune was, that, when the wind served, I happened to be with a party in the country, and my friend the captain never inquired after me, but set sail with as much indifference as if I had been on board. The remainder of my time I employed in the city and its environs, viewing everything curious, and you know no one can starve while he has money in his pocket.

Reduced, however, to my last two guineas, I began to think of my dear mother and friends whom I had left behind me, and so bought that generous beast Fiddle-back, and bade adieu to Cork with only five shillings in my pocket. This, to be sure, was but a scanty allowance for man and horse towards a journey of above a hundred miles; but I did not despair, for I knew I must find friends on the road.

I recollected particularly an old and faithful acquaintance I made at college, who had often and earnestly pressed me to spend a summer with him, and he lived but eight miles from Cork. This circumstance of vicinity he would expatiate on to me with peculiar emphasis. "We shall," says he, "enjoy the delights of both city and country, and you shall command my stable and my purse."

However, upon the way, I met a poor woman all in tears, who told me her husband had been arrested for a debt he was not able to pay, and that his eight children must now starve, bereaved as they were of his industry, which had been their only support. I thought myself at home, being not far from my good friend's house, and therefore parted with a moiety of all my store; and, pray, Mother, ought I not have given her the other half-crown, for what she got would be of little use to her? However, I soon arrived at the mansion of my affectionate friend, guarded by the vigilance of a huge mastiff, who flew at me, and would have torn me to pieces but for the assistance of a woman, whose countenance was not less grim than that of the dog; yet she with great humanity relieved me from the jaws of this Cerberus, and was prevailed on to carry up my name to her master.

Without suffering me to wait long, my old friend, who was then recovering from a severe fit of sickness, came down in his nightcap, nightgown and slippers, and embraced me with the most cordial welcome, showed me in, and, after giving me a history of his indisposition, assured me that he considered himself peculiarly fortunate in having under his roof the man he most loved on earth, and whose stay with him must, above all things, contribute to his perfect recovery. I now repented sorely I had not given the poor woman the other half-crown, as I thought all my bills of humanity would be punctually answered by this worthy man. I revealed to him all my distresses; and freely owned that I had but one half-crown in my pocket, but that now, like a ship after weathering out the storm, I considered myself secure in a safe and hospitable harbour. He made no answer, but walked about the room, rubbing his hands as one in deep study. This I imputed to the sympathetic feelings of a tender heart, which increased my esteem for him, and as that increased, I gave the most favourable interpretation to his silence. I construed it into delicacy of sentiment, as if he dreaded to wound my pride by expressing his commiseration in words, leaving his generous conduct to speak for itself.

It now approached six o'clock in the evening; and as I had eaten no breakfast, and as my spirits were raised, my appetite for dinner grew uncommonly keen. At length the old woman came into the room with two plates, one spoon, and a dirty cloth, which she laid upon the table. This appearance, without increasing my spirits, did not diminish my appetite. My protectress soon returned with a small bowl of sago, a small porringer of sour milk, a loaf of stale brown bread, and the heel of an old cheese all over crawling with mites. My friend apologized that his illness obliged him to live on slops, and that better fare was not in the house; observing, at the same time, that a milk diet was certainly the most healthful; and at eight o'clock he again recommended a regular life, declaring that for his part he would lie down with the lamb and rise with the lark. My hunger was at this time so exceedingly sharp that I wished for another slice of the loaf, but was obliged to go to bed without even that refreshment. This lenten entertainment I had received made me resolve to depart as soon as possible; accordingly, next morning, when I spoke of going, he did not oppose my resolution; he rather commended my design, adding some very sage counsel upon the occasion. "To be sure," said he, "the longer you stay away from your mother the more you will grieve her and your other friends; and possibly they are already afflicted at hearing of this foolish expedition you have made." Notwithstanding all this, and without any hope of softening such a sordid heart, I again renewed the tale of my distress, and asking "how he thought I could travel above a hundred miles upon one half-crown?" I begged to borrow a single guinea which I assured him should be repaid with thanks. "And you know, sir," said I, "it is no more than I have done for you." To which he firmly answered, "Why, look you, Mr Goldsmith, that is neither here nor there, I have paid you all you ever lent me, and this sickness of mine has left me bare of cash. But I have bethought myself of a conveyance for you; sell your horse, and I will furnish you a much better one to ride on." I readily grasped at his proposal, and begged to see the nag; on which he led me to his bed chamber, and from under the bed he pulled out a stout oak stick. "Here he is," said he; " take this in your hand, and it will carry you to your mother's with more safety than such a horse as you ride." I was in doubt when I got it into my hand, whether I should not, in the first place apply it to his pate; but a rap at the street door made the wretch fly to it, and when I returned to the parlour, he introduced me, as if nothing of the kind had happened, to the gentleman who entered, as Mr Goldsmith, his most ingenious and worthy friend, of whom he had so often heard him speak with rapture. I could scarcely compose myself; and must have betrayed indignation in my mien to the stranger, who was a counsellor-at-law in the neighbourhood, a man of engaging aspect and polite address.

After spending an hour, he asked my friend and me to dine with him at his house. This I declined at first, as I wished to have no further communication with my hospitable friend; but at the solicitation of both I at last consented, determined as I was by two motives; one, that I was prejudiced in favour of the looks and manner of the counsellor; and the other that I stood in need of a comfortable dinner. And there, indeed, I found everything that I could wish, abundance without profusion, and elegance without affectation. In the evening, when my old friend, who had eaten very plentifully at his neighbour's table, but talked again of lying down with the lamb, made a motion to me for retiring, our generous host requested I should take a bed with him, upon which I plainly told my old friend that he might go home and take care of the horse he had given me, but that I should never re-enter his doors. He went away with a laugh, leaving me to add this to the other little things the counsellor already knew of his plausible neighbour.

And now, my dear Mother, I found sufficient to reconcile me to all my follies; for here I spent three whole days. The counsellor had two sweet girls to his daughters, who played enchantingly on the harpsichord; and yet it was but a melancholy pleasure I felt the first time I heard them: for that being the first time also that either of them had touched the instrument since their mother's death, I saw the tears in silence trickle down their father's cheeks. I every day endeavoured to go away, but every day was pressed and obliged to stay. On my going, the counsellor offered me his purse, with a horse and servant to convey me home: but the latter I declined, and only took a guinea to bear my necessary expenses on the road.

Oliver Goldsmith

This famous account tells of the first meeting between Dr Samuel Johnson and his biographer James Boswell.

This is to me a memorable year [1763]; for in it I had the happiness to obtain the acquaintance of that extraordinary man whose memoirs I am now writing; an acquaintance which I shall ever esteem as one of the most fortunate circumstances in my life. Though then but two-and-twenty, I had for several years read his works with delight and instruction, and had the highest reverence for their author, which had grown up in my fancy into a kind of mysterious veneration, by figuring to myself a state of solemn elevated abstraction, in which I supposed him to live in the immense metropolis of London. Mr Gentleman, a native of Ireland, who passed some years in Scotland as a player and as an instructor in the English language, a man whose talents and worth were depressed by misfortunes, had given me a representation of the figure and manner of Dictionary Johnson, as he was then generally called; and during my first visit to London, which was for three months in 1760, Mr Derrick, the poet, who was Gentleman's friend and countryman, flattered me with hopes that he would introduce me to Johnson, an honour of which I was very ambitious. But he never found an opportunity; which made me doubt that he had promised to do what was not in his power; till Johnson some years afterwards told me, "Derrick, sir, might very well have introduced you. I had a kindness for Derrick, and am sorry he is dead . . ."

Mr Thomas Davies the actor, who then kept a bookseller's shop in Russell Street, Covent Garden, told me that Johnson was very much his friend, and came frequently to his house, where he more than once invited me to meet him; but by some unlucky accident or other he was prevented from coming to us.

Mr Thomas Davies was a man of good understanding and talents, with the advantage of a liberal education. Though somewhat pompous, he was an entertaining companion; and his literary performances have no inconsiderable share of merit. He was a friendly and very hospitable man. Both he and his wife (who has been celebrated for her beauty), though upon the stage for many years, maintained a uniform decency of character: and Johnson esteemed them, and lived in as easy an intimacy with them as with any family he used to visit. Mr Davies recollected several of Johnson's remarkable sayings, and was one of the best of the many imitators of his voice and manner, while relating them. He increased my impatience more and more to see the extraordinary man whose works I highly valued, and whose conversation was reported to be so peculiarly excellent.

At last, on Monday the 16th of May, when I was sitting in Mr Davies' back parlour after having drunk tea with him and Mrs Davies, Johnson unexpectedly came into the shop; and Mr Davies having perceived him through the glass-door in the room in which we were sitting, advancing towards us – he announced his awful approach to me, somewhat in the manner of an actor in the part of Horatio, when he addresses Hamlet on the appearance of his father's ghost, "Look, my lord, it comes." I found that I had a very perfect idea of Johnson's figure from the portrait of him painted by Sir Joshua Reynolds, soon after he had published his Dictionary, in the attitude of sitting in his easy chair in deep meditation; which was the first picture his friend did for him, which Sir Joshua very kindly presented to me (and from which an engraving has been made for this work). Mr Davies mentioned my name, and respectfully introduced me to him. I was much agitated; and recollecting his prejudice against the Scotch, of which I had heard much, I said to Davies, "Don't tell where I come from." – "From Scotland," cried Davies, roguishly. "Mr Johnson," said I, "I do indeed come from Scotland, but I cannot help it." I am willing to flatter myself that I meant this as light pleasantry to soothe and conciliate him, and not as a humiliating abasement at the expense of my country. But however that might be, this speech was somewhat unlucky; for with that quickness of wit for which he was so remarkable, he seized the expression "come from Scotland", which I used in the sense of being of that country; and, as if I had said that I had come away from it, or left it, retorted, "That, sir, I find, is what a very great many of your countrymen cannot help." This stroke stunned me a good deal; and when we had sat down, I felt myself not a little embarrassed, and apprehensive of what might come next. He then addressed himself to Davies: "What do you think of Garrick*? He has refused me an order for the play for Miss Williams, because he knows the house will be full, and that an order would be worth three shillings." Eager to take any opening to get into conversation with him, I ventured to say, "O sir, I cannot think Mr Garrick would grudge such a trifle to you." – "Sir," said he, with a stern look, "I have known David Garrick longer than you have done: and I know no right you have to talk to me on the subject." Perhaps I deserved this check; for it was rather presumptuous in me, an entire stranger, to express any doubt of the justice of his animadversion upon his old acquaintance and pupil. I now felt myself much mortified, and began to think that the hope which I had long indulged of obtaining his acquaintance was blasted and, in truth, had not my ardour been uncommonly strong, and my resolution uncommonly persevering, so rough a reception might have deterred me for ever from making any further attempts. Fortunately, however, I remained upon the field not wholly discomfited; and was soon rewarded by hearing some of his conversation . . .

I was highly pleased with the extraordinary vigour of his conversation, and regretted that I was drawn away from it by an engagement at another place. I had, for a part of the evening, been left alone with him, and had ventured to make an observation now and then, which he received very civilly; so that I was satisfied that though there was a roughness in his manner, there was no ill-nature in his disposition. Davies followed me to the door, and when I complained to him a little of the hard blows which the great man had given me, he kindly took upon him to console me by saying, "Don't be uneasy. I can see he likes you very well."

(James Boswell, *Life of Johnson*)

* Garrick – David Garrick (1717–79), the most famous actor of his time, had been a pupil of Johnson's at the private school which the latter had started near Lichfield. In 1737 they travelled to London together to try their fortunes there.

Dr Johnson wasn't always so alarming as he appeared at his first meeting with James Boswell (see above). Boswell again tells this story of a time when Johnson was invited to go for a late night walk by some friends.

When he was told their errand, he smiled, and with great good humour agreed to their proposal: "What, is it you, you dogs! I'll have a frisk with you." He was soon drest, and they sallied forth together into Covent Garden, where the greengrocers and fruiterers were beginning to arrange their hampers, just come in from the country. Johnson made some attempts to help them; but the honest gardeners stared so at his figure and manner, and odd interference, that he soon saw his services were not relished. They then repaired to one of the neighbouring taverns, and made a bowl of that liquor called *Bishop*, which Johnson had always liked; while in joyous contempt of sleep, from which he had been roused, he repeated the festive lines,

> Short, O short then be thy reign,
> And give us to the world again!

They did not stay long, but walked down to the Thames, took a boat, and rowed to Billingsgate. Beauclerk and Johnson were so well pleased with their amusement, that they resolved to persevere in dissipation for the rest of the day: but Langton deserted them, being engaged to breakfast with some young Ladies. Johnson scolded him for "leaving his social friends, to go and sit with a set of wretched un-idea'd girls." Garrick being told of this ramble, said to him smartly, "I heard of your frolick t'other night. You'll be in the Chronicle." Upon which Johnson afterwards observed, "He durst not do such a thing. His wife would not let him!"

(James Boswell, *Life of Johnson*)

William Hazlitt met Samuel Taylor Coleridge, author of "The Ancient Mariner" and "Kubla Khan", when the poet came to preach in the winter of 1798 in Shrewsbury. Coleridge was considering entering the Unitarian ministry and Hazlitt's father was a Dissenting

Minister in a nearby town. The 20-year-old Hazlitt was introduced to the brilliant talker.

On the Tuesday following, the half-inspired speaker came. I was called down into the room where he was, and went half-hoping, half-afraid. He received me very graciously, and I listened for a long time, without uttering a word. I did not suffer in his opinion by my silence. "For those two hours," he afterwards was pleased to say, "he was conversing with W. H.'s forehead!" His appearance was different from what I had anticipated from seeing him before. At a distance, and in the dim light of the chapel, there was to me a strange wildness in his aspect, a dusky obscurity, and I thought him pitted with the smallpox. His complexion was at that time clear, and even bright . . . His forehead was broad and high, light as if built of ivory, with large projecting eyebrows, and his eyes rolling beneath them like a sea with darkened lustre. "A certain tender bloom, his face overspread", a purple tinge as we see it in the pale thoughtful complexions of the Spanish portrait-painters, Murillo and Velasquez. His mouth was gross, voluptuous, open, eloquent; his chin good-humoured and round; but his nose, the rudder of the face, the index of the will, was small, feeble, nothing – like what he has done. It might seem that the genius of his face as from a height surveyed and projected him (with sufficient capacity and huge aspiration) into the world unknown of thought and imagination, with nothing to support or guide his veering purpose, as if Columbus had launched his adventurous course for the New World in a scallop, without oars or compass. So at least I comment on it after the event. Coleridge in his person was rather above the common size, inclining to the corpulent, or like Lord Hamlet, "somewhat fat and pursy". His hair (now, alas! grey) was then black and glossy as the raven's, and fell in smooth masses over his forehead. This long pendulous hair is peculiar to enthusiasts, to those whose minds tend heavenward; and is traditionally inseparable (though of a different colour) from the pictures of Christ. It ought to belong, as a character to all who preach Christ crucified, and Coleridge was at that time one of those!

Coleridge invited the young Hazlitt to visit him at his home in Nether Stowey in Somerset. William Wordsworth, who was collaborating with Coleridge on the landmark volume of poetry entitled Lyrical Ballads, *lived nearby.*

The next day Wordsworth arrived from Bristol at Coleridge's cottage. I think I see him now. He answered in some degree to his friend's description of him; but was more gaunt and Don Quixote-like. He was quaintly dressed (according to the *costume* of that unconstrained period) in a brown fustian jacket and striped pantaloons. There was something of a roll, a lounge in his gait, not unlike his own Peter Bell. There was a severe, worn pressure of thought about his temples, a fire in his eye (as if he saw something in objects more than the outward appearance), an intense high narrow forehead, a Roman nose, cheeks furrowed by strong purpose and feeling, and a convulsive inclination to laughter about the mouth, a good deal at variance with the solemn, stately expression of the rest of his face . . . He sat down and talked very naturally and freely, with a mixture of clear gushing accents in his voice, a deep guttural intonation, and a strong tincture of the northern burr, like the crust on wine. He instantly began to make havoc of the half of a Cheshire cheese on the table . . .

Wordsworth, looking out of the low, latticed window, said, "How beautifully the sun sets on that yellow bank!" I thought within myself, "With what eyes these poets see nature!" and ever after, when I saw the sunset stream upon the objects facing it, conceived I had made a discovery, or thanked Mr Wordsworth for having made one for me! . . .

Coleridge has told me that he himself liked to compose in walking over uneven ground, or breaking through the straggling branches of a copse wood; whereas Wordsworth always wrote (if he could) walking up and down a straight gravel-walk, or in some spot where the continuity of his verse met with no collateral interruption. Returning that same evening, I got into a metaphysical argument with Wordsworth, while Coleridge was explaining the different notes of the nightingale to his sister, in which we neither of us succeeded in making ourselves perfectly clear and intelligible. Thus I passed three weeks at

Nether Stowey and in the neighbourhood, generally devoting the afternoons to a delightful chat in an arbour made of bark by the poet's friend Tom Poole, sitting under two fine elm-trees, and listening to the bees humming round us, while we quaffed our *flip**. It was agreed, among other things, that we should make a jaunt down the Bristol Channel, as far as Lynton. We set off together on foot, Coleridge, John Chester, and I. This Chester was a native of Nether Stowey, one of those who were attracted to Coleridge's discourse as flies are to honey, or bees in swarming-time to the sound of a brass pan . . . He had on a brown cloth coat, boots, and corduroy breeches, was low in stature, bow-legged, had a drag in his walk like a drover, which he assisted by a hazel switch, and kept on a sort of trot by the side of Coleridge, like a running footman by a state coach; that he might not lose a syllable or sound, that fell from Coleridge's lips. He told me his private opinion, that Coleridge was a wonderful man. He scarcely opened his lips, much less offered an opinion the whole way: yet of the three, had I to choose during that journey, would be John Chester . . . We passed Dunster on our right, a small town between the brow of a hill and the sea. I remember eyeing it wistfully as it lay below us: contrasted with the woody scene around, it looked as clear, as pure, as *embrowned* and ideal as any landscape I have seen since, of Gaspar Poussin's or Domenichino's. We had a long day's march – (our feet kept time to the echoes of Coleridge's tongue) – through Minehead and by the Blue Anchor, and on to Lynton, which we did not reach till near midnight, and where we had some difficulty in making a lodgement. We, however, knocked the people of the house up at last, and we were repaid for our apprehensions and fatigue by some excellent rashers of fried bacon and eggs. The view in coming along had been splendid. We walked for miles and miles on dark brown heaths over-looking the channel, with the Welsh hills beyond, and at times descended into little sheltered valleys close by the sea-side, with a smuggler's face scowling by us, and then had to ascend conical hills with a path winding up through a coppice to a barren top, like a monk's shaven crown, from one of which I pointed out to

* Flip – hot drink of sweetened beer or spirits

Coleridge's notice the bare masts of a vessel on the very edge of the horizon, and within the red-orbed disk of the setting sun, like his own spectre-ship in the *Ancient Mariner*.

(William Hazlitt, *My First Acquaintance with Poets*)

Edward Trelawny meets the poet Percy Bysshe Shelley for the first time in Pisa.

After a long stop at that city [Genoa] of painted palaces, anxious to see the poet, I drove to Pisa alone. I arrived late, and after putting up my horse at the inn and dining, hastened to the Tre Palazzi, on the Lung' Arno, where the Shelleys and Williamses lived on different flats under the same roof, as is the custom on the Continent. The Williamses received me in their earnest cordial manner; we had a great deal to communicate to each other, and were in loud and animated conversation, when I was rather put out by observing in the passage near the open door, opposite to where I sat, a pair of glittering eyes steadily fixed on mine; it was too dark to make out whom they belonged to. With the acuteness of a woman, Mrs Williams' eyes followed the direction of mine, and going to the doorway, she laughingly said, "Come in, Shelley, it's only our friend Tre just arrived."

Swiftly gliding in, blushing like a girl, a tall thin stripling held out both his hands; and although I could hardly believe as I looked at his flushed, feminine, and artless face that it could be the Poet, I returned his warm pressure. After the ordinary greetings and courtesies he sat down and listened. I was silent from astonishment: was it possible this mild-looking beardless boy could be the veritable monster at war with all the world? – excommunicated by the Fathers of the Church, deprived of his civil rights by the fiat of a grim Lord Chancellor, discarded by every member of his family, and denounced by the rival sages of our literature as the founder of a Satanic school? I could not believe it; it must be a hoax.

(Edward Trelawny, *Records of Shelley, Byron, and the Author*)

In 1817 the painter and writer Benjamin Robert Haydon, a figure at the very centre of the Romantic movement in terms of his friendships, held a party. Among Haydon's guests at the so-called "immortal dinner" were the poets William Wordsworth and John Keats, the essayist Charles Lamb and an unexpected arrival in the shape of the Comptroller of the Stamp Office. Hanging above their heads was Haydon's half-finished picture titled "Christ's Entry into Jerusalem", into which the painter had incorporated as faces in the crowd the likenesses of Wordsworth, Keats and Isaac Newton among others.

In December Wordsworth was in town, and as Keats wished to know him I made up a party to dinner of Charles Lamb, Wordsworth, Keats and Monkhouse, his friend; and a very pleasant party we had.

I wrote to Lamb, and told him the address was "22 Lisson Grove, North, at Rossi's, halfway up, righthand corner". I received his characteristic reply.

> My dear Haydon,
>   I will come with pleasure to 22 Lisson Grove, North, at Rossi's, halfway up, righthand side, if I can find it.
>   C. LAMB.

> 20, Russel Court,
> Covent Garden East,
> halfway up, next the corner,
> lefthand side.

On 28 December the immortal dinner came off in my painting-room, with Jerusalem towering up behind us as a background. Wordsworth was in fine cue, and we had a glorious set-to – on Homer, Shakespeare, Milton and Virgil. Lamb got exceedingly merry and exquisitely witty; and his fun in the midst of Wordsworth's solemn intonations of oratory was like the sarcasm and wit of the Fool in the intervals of Lear's passion. He made a speech and voted me absent, and made them drink my health. "Now," said Lamb, "you old lake poet, you rascally poet, why do you call Voltaire dull?" We all defended Wordsworth, and affirmed there was a state of mind when Voltaire would be dull. "Well," said Lamb, "here's Voltaire – the Messiah of the French nation, and a very proper one too."

He then, in a strain of humour beyond description, abused me for putting Newton's head into my picture; "a fellow," said he, "who believed nothing unless it was as clear as the three sides of a triangle." And then he and Keats agreed he had destroyed all the poetry of the rainbow by reducing it to the prismatic colours. It was impossible to resist him, and we all drank "Newton's health, and confusion to mathematics." It was delightful to see the good humour of Wordsworth in giving in to all our frolics without affectation and laughing as heartily as the best of us.

By this time other friends joined, amongst them poor Ritchie who was going to penetrate by Fezzan to Timbuctoo. I introduced him to all as "a gentleman going to Africa." Lamb seemed to take no notice; but all of a sudden he roared out: "Which is the gentleman we are going to lose?" We then drank the victim's health, in which Ritchie joined.

In the morning of this delightful day, a gentleman, a perfect stranger, had called on me. He said he knew my friends, had an enthusiasm for Wordsworth, and begged I would procure him the happiness of an introduction. He told me he was a comptroller of stamps, and often had correspondence with the poet. I thought it a liberty; but still, as he seemed a gentleman, I told him he might come.

When we retired to tea we found the comptroller. In introducing him to Wordsworth I forgot to say who he was. After a little time the comptroller looked down, looked up and said to Wordsworth: "Don't you think, sir, Milton was a great genius?" Keats looked at me, Wordsworth looked at the comptroller. Lamb who was dozing by the fire turned round and said: "Pray, sir, did you say Milton was a great genius?" "No, sir; I asked Mr Wordsworth if he were not." "Oh," said Lamb, "then you are a silly fellow." "Charles! my dear Charles!" said Wordsworth; but Lamb, perfectly innocent of the confusion he had created, was off again by the fire.

After an awful pause the comptroller said: "Don't you think Newton a great genius?" I could not stand it any longer. Keats put his head into my books. Ritchie squeezed in a laugh. Wordsworth seemed asking himself: "Who is this?" Lamb got up, and taking a candle, said: "Sir, will you allow me to look at your phrenological development*?" He then turned his back on the poor man, and at every question of the comptroller he chaunted:

> Diddle diddle dumpling, my son John
> Went to bed with his breeches on.

The man in office, finding Wordsworth did not know who he was, said in a spasmodic and half-chuckling anticipation of assured victory: "I have had the honour of some correspondence with you, Mr Wordsworth." "With me, sir?" said Wordsworth, "not that I remember." "Don't you, sir? I am a comptroller of stamps." There was a dead silence, the comptroller evidently thinking that was enough. While we were waiting for Wordsworth's reply, Lamb sung out:

> Hey diddle diddle,
> The cat and the fiddle.

"My dear Charles!" said Wordsworth.

"Diddle diddle dumpling, my son John," chaunted Lamb, and then rising, exclaimed: "Do let me have another look at that gentleman's organs." Keats and I hurried Lamb into the painting-room, shut the door and gave way to inextinguishable laughter. Monkhouse followed and tried to get Lamb away. We went back, but the comptroller was irreconcilable. We soothed and smiled and asked him to supper. He stayed though his dignity was sorely affected. However, being a good-natured man, we parted all in good humour, and no ill effects followed.

All the while, until Monkhouse succeeded, we could hear Lamb struggling in the painting-room and calling at intervals:

"Who is that fellow? Allow me to see his organs once more."

---

* Phrenological development – Phrenology was a pseudo-science which acquired immense popularity in the nineteenth century. The various mental faculties sited in different parts of the brain could be assessed, it was thought, by feeling the bumps on the outside of the head.

It was indeed an immortal evening. Wordsworth's fine intonation as he quoted Milton and Virgil, Keats' eager inspired look, Lamb's quaint sparkle of lambent humour, so speeded the stream of conversation, that in my life I never passed a more delightful time. All our fun was within bounds. Not a word passed that an apostle might not have listened to. It was a night worthy of the Elizabethan age, and my solemn Jerusalem flashing up by the flame of the fire, with Christ hanging over us like a Vision, all made up a picture which will long glow upon

> that inward eye
> Which is the bliss of solitude.*

Keats made Ritchie promise he would carry his *Endymion* [a recently published poem by Keats] to the great desert of Sahara and fling it in the midst.

Poor Ritchie went to Africa, and died, as Lamb foresaw, in 1819. Keats died in 1821, at Rome. C. Lamb is gone, joking to the last. Monkhouse is dead, and Wordsworth and I are the only two now living (1841) of that glorious party.

(Benjamin Robert Haydon, *Autobiography*)

The diarist Tom Moore hears a story about the poet Samuel Taylor Coleridge's shabby appearance.

[Samuel] Rogers told of Coleridge riding about in a strange shabby dress, with I forget whom at Keswick, and on some company approaching them, Coleridge offered to fall behind and pass for his companion's servant. "No," said the other, "I am proud of you as a friend; but, I must say, I should be ashamed of you as a servant."

(Tom Moore, *Diaries, October 16th, 1833*)

---

* That inward eye – The lines are from Wordsworth's famous "daffodil" poem beginning "I wandered lonely as a cloud".

The Victorian painter W. P. Frith was a great enthusiast for Charles Dickens. He had already painted "Dolly Varden" (a character from Dickens's novel Barnaby Rudge*) and the success of this picture brought Frith to the attention of the great man himself.*

I had never seen the man, who in my estimation was, and is, one of the greatest geniuses that ever lived; my sensations therefore may be imagined when I received the following letter:

> 1, Devonshire Terrace,
> York Gate,
> Regent's Park,
> Nov. 15, 1842.

My dear sir,

I shall be very glad if you will do me the favour to paint me two little companion pictures; one, a Dolly Varden (whom you have so exquisitely done already), the other, a Kate Nickleby.

Faithfully yours always,

CHARLES DICKENS.

P.S. – I take it for granted that the original picture of Dolly with the bracelet is sold.

My mother and I cried over that letter, and the wonder is that anything is left of it, for I showed it to every friend I had, and was admired and envied by all.

And now came the fear that I might fail in again satisfying the author. Kate Nickleby, too! Impossible, perhaps, to please the author of her being with my presentment of her – but I must try. And many were the sketches I made, till I fixed upon a scene at Madame Mantalini's – where Kate figures as a workwoman – the point chosen being at the moment when her thoughts wander from her work, as she sits sewing a ball-dress spread upon her knees.

Dolly Varden was represented tripping through the woods, and looking back saucily at her lover.

The pictures were finished, and a letter was written to say so.

See me then in hourly and very trembling expectation of a visit from a man whom I thought superhuman. A knock at the door. "Come in." Enter a pale young man with long hair, a white hat, a formidable stick in his left hand, and his right extended to me with a frank cordiality, and a friendly clasp, that never relaxed till the day of his untimely death.

The pictures were on the easel. He sat down before them, and I stood waiting for the verdict in an agony of mind that was soon relieved by his cheery "All I can say is, they are exactly what I meant, and I am very much obliged to you for painting them for me."

I muttered something, and if I didn't look very foolish, my looks belied my sensations.

"Shall you be at home on Sunday afternoon? I should like to bring Mrs Dickens and my sister-in-law to see how well you have done your work. May I?"

"By all means. I shall be delighted."

Sunday came, and Dickens with it.

I was standing at the house-door, when a carriage driven by "Boz" drove up to it, the bright steel bar in front giving the "turn-out" a very striking appearance to one like myself not at all accustomed to curricles. 'Tis enough to say the ladies approved, and Dickens gave me a cheque for forty pounds for the two pictures.

(W. P. Frith, My Autobiography and Reminiscences)

⌇

Henriette Cockran was not impressed by her first sight, as a child, of the poets Robert and Elizabeth Barrett Browning, famous because they had eloped together.

During most of her visit Mrs Barrett Browning kept her right arm round her little son's neck, running her long, thin fingers through his golden curls . . . I had pictured to myself poets as being ethereal beings. It gave me a shock to see Mr Browning eat with avidity so much bread and butter and big slices of plum-cake. He never uttered a word that in any way suggested a poetical thought. His coat, trousers and gloves were according to the fashion of the time; his thick hair well brushed. Altogether, in my opinion, he looked like a prosperous man of business.

(Henriette Cockran, *Celebrities and I*)

First meetings with Robert Browning could be, literally, electrifying.

I have several times heard people state that a handshake from Browning was like an electric shock. Truly enough, it did seem as though his sterling nature rang in his genially dominant voice, and, again, as though his voice transmitted instantaneous waves of an electric current through every nerve of what, for want of a better phrase, I must perforce call his intensely alive hand. I remember once how a lady, afflicted with nerves, in the dubious enjoyment of her first experience of a "literary afternoon", rose hurriedly and, in reply to her hostess' inquiry as to her motive, explained that she could not sit any longer beside the elderly gentleman who was talking to Mrs So-and-so, as his near presence made her quiver all over, "like a mild attack of pins-and-needles," as she phrased it. She was chagrined to learn that she had been discomposed not by "a too exuberant financier", as she had surmised, but by . . . the "subtlest assertor of the Soul in song."

(William Sharp, *The Life of Robert Browning*)

Edmund Gosse tells the tale of how the Victorian poet Swinburne nearly drowned off the French coast. This was also the time when Swinburne met the French writer Guy de Maupassant. One of the versions that had obviously circulated about this encounter suggested that de Maupassant himself had rescued Swinburne. Gosse's investigations revealed a slightly different story.

The incident which led to his forming Swinburne's acquaintance must now be told with some minuteness, partly because, as an adventure, it was the most important in the poet's career, and partly because it has been made the subject of many vague and contradictory rumours. Swinburne, as we have already seen, was a daring bather, and one of the main attractions of

Etretat was the facility it gave for exercise in the sea. On a certain Friday in the late summer at about 10 a.m., the poet went down alone to a solitary point on the eastern side of the plage, the Porte d'Amont – for there is no real harbour at Etretat – divested himself of his clothes, and plunged in, as was his wont. The next thing that happened was that a man called Coquerel, who was on the outlook at the semaphore, being at the foot of the cliffs on the eastern side of the bay, heard continued cries for help and piercing screams. He climbed up on a sort of rock of chalk, called Le Banc à Cuve, and perceived that a swimmer, who had been caught by the tide, which runs very heavily at that place, was being hurried out to sea, in spite of the violent efforts which he was making to struggle for his life. As it was impossible for Coquerel to do anything else to help the drowning man, he was starting to race along the shore to Etretat, when he saw coming round the point one of the fishing-smacks of the village. Coquerel attracted the attention of this boat, and directed the captain to the point out at sea where Swinburne's cries were growing fainter and further. The captain of the smack very cleverly seized the situation, and followed the poet, who had now ceased to struggle, but who supported himself by floating on the surface of the tide. This was hurrying him along so swiftly that he was not picked up until at a point a mile to the east-north-east of the eastern point of Etretat. It is a great pleasure to me, after more than 40 years, to be able to give the name of the man who saved the life of one of the greatest poets of England. I hope that Captain Theodule Vallin may be remembered with gratitude by the lovers of literature.

The story hitherto is from Etretat sources. I now take it up as Swinburne told it to me, not very long after the event. His account did not differ in any essential degree from what has just been said. But he told me that soon after having left Porte d'Amont he felt the undercurrent of the tide take possession of him, and he was carried out to sea through a rocky archway. Now, when it was too late he recollected that the fishermen had warned him that he ought not to bathe without taking the tide into consideration. He tried to turn, to get out of the stream; but it was absolutely impossible, he was drawn on like a leaf. (What he did not say, of course, was that although he was absolutely untiring in the sea, and as familiar with it as a South Sea islander, the weakness of his arms prevented his being able to swim fast or far, so that he depended on frequent interludes of floating.) At first he fought to get out of the tide, and then, realizing the hopelessness of this, he set himself to shout and yell, and he told me that the sound of his own voice, in that stillness of racing water, struck him as very strange and dreadful. Then he ceased to scream, and floated as limply as possible, carried along, and then he was suddenly aware that in a few minutes he would be dead, for the possibility of his being saved did not occur to him.

I asked him what he thought about in that dreadful contingency, and he replied that he had no experience of what people often profess to witness, the concentrated panorama of past life hurrying across the memory. He did not reflect on the past at all. He was filled with annoyance that he had not finished his "Songs before Sunrise", and then with satisfaction that so much of it was ready for the press, and that Mazzini would be pleased with him. And then he continued: "I reflected with resignation that I was exactly the same age as Shelley was when he was drowned." (This, however, was not the case; Swinburne had reached that age in March, 1867; but this was part of a curious delusion of Swinburne's that he was younger by two or three years than his real age.) Then, when he began to be, I suppose, a little benumbed by the water, his thoughts fixed on the clothes he had left on the beach, and he worried his clouding brain about some unfinished verses in the pocket of his coat. I suppose that he then fainted, for he could not recollect being reached by the smack or lifted on board.

The fishermen, however, drew the poet successfully out of the water . . . He was given some food, and in the course of the morning the *Marie-Marthe*, with her singular lading, tacked into the harbour of Yport.

Meanwhile, Swinburne's English friend and host, who had been near him on the shore, but not himself bathing, had, with gathering anxiety, seen him rapidly and unresistingly hurried out to sea through the rocky archway until he passed entirely out of sight. He immediately recollected – what Swinburne had forgotten – the treacherous undercurrents so prevalent and so much dreaded on that dangerous coast. After Mr Powell had lost sight of the poet for what seemed to him at least ten minutes, his anxiety was turned to horror, for there were shouts heard on the cliffs above him to the effect that "a man was drowning." He gathered up Swinburne's clothes in his arms, and ran ankle-deep in the loose shingle to where some boats were lying on the beach. These immediately started to the rescue; in but a few minutes after their departure, however, a boat arriving at Etretat from the east brought the welcome news that no catastrophe had happened, but that the *Marie-Marthe* had been seen to pick the Englishman up out of the water, and to continue her course towards Yport. Mr Powell, therefore, took a carriage and galloped off at fullest speed, with Swinburne's clothes, and arrived at Yport just in time to see the *Marie-Marthe* enter the harbour, with Swinburne, in excellent spirits and wrapped in a sail, gesticulating on the deck.

What greatly astonished the Normans was that, after so alarming an adventure and so bitter an experience of the treachery of the sea, Swinburne was by no means willing to abandon it. The friends dismissed their carriage, and lunched at the pleasant little inn between the place and the sea; and having found that the *Marie-Marthe* was returning to Etretat in the afternoon, they took a walk along the cliffs until Captain Vallin had finished his business in Yport, when they returned with him by sea. This conduct was thought eccentric; it would have been natural to prefer a land journey at such a moment. But, as the captain approvingly said, "C'eut été trop peu anglais." Everybody who had helped in the salvage was generously rewarded, and Swinburne and his friend were, for at least twenty-four hours, the most popular of the residents of Etretat.

It is not till now, at the twelfth hour, that Guy de Maupassant comes into the story. It is only fair to say that he never asserted, nor acquiesced in the assertion made by others, that he himself, on his own yacht, rescued Swinburne. A collegian of nineteen, at home for the holidays, a yacht was the last thing he was likely to possess. But he jumped on board one of those fishing-smacks which Mr Powell sent out, and the boat he was on hurried back only on hearing that the *Marie-Marthe* had already saved the drowning man. Who the latter was Maupassant did not learn until the evening of the same day, when he discovered that it was the English poet who had arrived, not long before, to be the guest of a strange Englishman, accomplished and extravagant, who occasionally conversed with Maupassant, as he paced the shingle beach, and who had already excited his curiosity. "Ce Monsieur Powell," says Maupassant, "étonnait le pays par une vie extrêmement solitaire et bizarre aux yeux de bourgeois et de matelots peu accoutumés aux fantaisies et aux excentricités anglaises . . ."

Maupassant's obliging zeal in hurrying to Swinburne's help was rewarded on the following day by an invitation to lunch at the Chaumière de Dolmance. The two Englishmen were waiting for him in a pretty garden, verdurous and shady . . . The eyes of that visitor, by the way, if youthful, were exceedingly sharp and bright; although he had not yet learned the artifice of prose expression, the power of observing and noting character was already highly developed in him . . .

This, then, is how our poet struck the Norman boy who had never read a line of his verses. "M. Swinburne was small and thin, amazingly thin at first sight, a sort of fantastic apparition. When I looked at him for the first time, I thought of Edgar Poe. The forehead was very large under long hair, and the face went narrowing down to a tiny chin, shaded by a thin tuft of beard. A very slight moustache slipped over lips which were extraordinarily delicate and were pressed together, while what seemed an endless neck joined this head, which was alive only in its bright, penetrating, and fixed eyes, to a body without shoulders, since the upper part of Swinburne's chest seemed scarcely broader than his forehead. The whole of this almost supernatural personage was stirred by nervous shudders. He was very cordial, very easy of access; and the extraordinary charm of his intelligence bewitched me from the first moment." There may be a touch of emphasis in this, a slight effect of caricature; but no one who knew Swinburne in those days will dare to deny the general fidelity of the portrait.

(Edmund Gosse, *Swinburne*)

E. Gertrude Thomson was an artist who shared the very popular late Victorian interest in fairies. As she explains in an article written for The Gentlewoman *magazine in January 1898, it was her "fairy designs" that attracted the attention of Lewis Carroll, the pseudonym of Charles Dodgson, a lecturer in mathematics at Christ Church, Oxford, and, more famously, the creator of* Alice in Wonderland *and* Through the Looking Glass. *This is an account of their meeting.*

It was at the end of December, 1878, that a letter, written in a singularly legible and rather boyish-looking hand, came to me from Christ Church, Oxford, signed "C. L. Dodgson". The writer said that he had come across some fairy designs of mine, and he should like to see some more of my work. By the same post came a letter from my London publisher (who had supplied my address) telling me that the "Rev. C. L. Dodgson" was "Lewis Carroll".

"Alice in Wonderland" had long been one of my pet books, and as one regards a favourite author as almost a personal friend, I felt less restraint than one usually feels in writing to a stranger, though I carefully concealed my knowledge of his identity, as he had not chosen to reveal it.

This was the beginning of a frequent and delightful correspondence, and as I confessed to a great love for fairy lore of every description, he asked me if I would accept a child's fairytale book he had written, called "Alice in Wonderland". I replied that I knew it nearly all off by heart, but that I should greatly prize a copy given to me by himself. By return came "Alice", and "Through the Looking-Glass", bound most luxuriously in white calf and gold.

And this is the graceful and kindly note that came with them: "I am now sending you 'Alice,' and the 'Looking-Glass' as well. There is an incompleteness about giving only one, and besides, the one you bought was probably in red and would not match these. If you are at all in doubt as to what to do with the (now) superfluous copy, let me suggest your giving it to some poor sick child. I have been distributing copies to all the hospitals and convalescent homes I can hear of, where there are sick children capable of reading them, and though, of course, one takes some pleasure in the popularity of the books elsewhere, it is not nearly so pleasant a thought to me as that they may be a comfort and relief to children in hours of pain and weariness. Still, no recipient can be more appropriate than one who seems to have been in fairyland herself, and to have seen, like the "weary mariners" of old –

> Between the green brink and the running foam
> White limbs unrobed in a crystal air,
> Sweet faces, rounded arms, and bosoms prest
> To little harps of gold.

"Do you ever come to London?" he asked in another letter. "If so, will you allow me to call upon you?"

Early in the summer I came up to study, and I sent him word that I was in town. One night, coming into my room, after a long day spent at the British Museum, in the half-light I saw a card lying on the table. "Rev. C. L. Dodgson." Bitter, indeed, was my disappointment at having missed him, but just as I was laying it sadly down I spied a small T.O. in the corner. On the back I read that he couldn't get up to my rooms early or late enough to find me, so would I arrange to meet him at some museum or gallery the day but one following? I fixed on South Kensington Museum, by the "Schliemann" collection at twelve o'clock.

A little before twelve I was at the rendezvous, and then the humour of the situation suddenly struck me, that I had not the ghost of an idea what he was like, nor would he have any better chance of discovering *me*! The room was fairly full of all sorts and conditions, as usual, and I glanced at each masculine figure in turn, only to reject it as a possibility of the one I sought. Just as the big clock had clanged out twelve, I heard the high vivacious voices and laughter of children sounding down the corridor.

At that moment a gentleman entered, two little girls clinging to his hands, and as I caught sight of the tall slim figure with the clean-shaven, delicate, refined face, I said to myself, "*That's* Lewis Carroll." He stood for a moment, head erect, glancing swiftly over the room, then, bending down, whispered something to one of the children; she, after a moment's pause, pointed straight at me.

Dropping their hands he came forward, and with that winning smile of his that utterly banished the oppressive sense of the Oxford don, said simply, "I am Mr Dodgson; I was to meet you, I think?" To which I as frankly smiled, and said, "How did you know me so soon?"

"My little friend found you. I told her I had come to meet a young lady who knew fairies, and she fixed on you at once. But *I* knew you before she spoke."

(quoted in Stuart Didgson Collingwood,
The Life and Letters of Lewis Carroll)

The English essayist and critic Edmund Gosse tells of his first and only meeting with the revered American poet Walt Whitman.

In the early and middle years of his life, Whitman was obscure and rarely visited. When he grew old, pilgrims not unfrequently took scrip and staff, and set out to worship him. Several accounts of his appearance and mode of address on these occasions have been published, and if I add one more it must be my excuse that the visit to be described was not undertaken in the customary spirit. All other accounts, so far as I know, of interviews with Whitman have been written by disciples who approached the shrine adoring and ready to be dazzled. The visitor whose experience – and it was a very delightful one – is now to be chronicled, started under what was, perhaps, the disadvantage of being very unwilling to go; at least, it will be admitted that the tribute – for tribute it has to be – is all the more sincere.

When I was in Boston, in the winter of 1884, I received a note from Whitman asking me not to leave America without coming to see him. My first instinct was promptly to decline the invitation. Camden, New Jersey, was a very long way off. But better counsel prevailed; curiosity and civility combined to draw me, and I wrote to him that I would come. It would be fatuous to mention all this, if it were not that I particularly wish to bring out the peculiar magic of the old man, acting, not on a disciple, but on a stiff-necked and froward unbeliever.

To reach Camden, one must arrive at Philadelphia, where I put up on the 2nd of January, 1885, ready to pass over into New Jersey next morning. I took the hall-porter of the hotel into my confidence, and asked if he had ever heard of Mr Whitman. Oh, yes, they all knew "Walt", he said; on fine days he used to cross over on the ferry and take the tram into Philadelphia. He liked to stroll about in Chestnut Street and look at the people, and if you smiled at him he would smile back again; everybody knew "Walt". In the North, I had been told that he was almost bedridden, in consequence of an attack of paralysis. This seemed inconsistent with wandering round Philadelphia.

The distance being considerable, I started early on the 3rd, crossed the broad Delaware River, where blocks of ice bumped and crackled around us, and saw the flat shores of New Jersey expanding in front, raked by the broad morning light. I was put ashore in a crude and apparently uninhabited village, grim with that concentrated ugliness that only an American township in the depth of winter can display. Nobody to ask the way, or next to nobody. I wandered aimlessly about, and was just ready to give all I possessed to be back again in New York, when I discovered that I was opposite No. 328 Mickle Street, and that on a minute brass plate was engraved "W. Whitman". I knocked at this dreary little two-storey tenement house, and wondered what was going to happen. A melancholy woman opened the door; it was too late now to go away. But before I could speak, a large figure, hobbling down the stairs, called out in a cheery voice, "Is that my friend?" Suddenly, by I know not what magnetic charm, all wire-drawn literary reservations faded out of being, and one's only sensation was of gratified satisfaction at being the "friend" of this very nice old gentleman.

There was a good deal of greeting on the stairs, and then the host, moving actively, though clumsily, and with a stick, advanced to his own dwelling-room on the first storey. The opening impression was, as the closing one would be, of extreme simplicity. A large room without carpet on the scrubbed planks, a small bedstead, a little round stove with a stack-pipe in the middle of the room, one chair – that was all the furniture. On the walls and in the fireplace such a miserable wall-paper – tinted, with a spot – as one sees in the bedrooms of labourers' cottages; no pictures hung in the room, but pegs and shelves loaded with objects. Various boxes lay about, and one huge clamped trunk, and heaps, mountains of papers in a wild confusion, swept up here and there into stacks and peaks; but all the room, and the old man himself, clean in the highest degree, raised to the nth power of stainlessness, scoured and scrubbed to such a pitch that dirt seemed defied for all remaining time. Whitman, in particular, in his suit of hodden grey and shirt thrown wide open at the throat, his grey hair and whiter beard voluminously flowing, seemed positively blanched with cleanliness; the whole man sand-white with spotlessness, like a deal table that has grown old under the scrubbing-brush.

Whitman sat down in the one chair with a small poker in his hand and spent much of his leisure in feeding and irritating the stove. I cleared some papers away from off a box and sat opposite to him. When he was not actively engaged upon the stove his steady attention was fixed upon his visitor, and I had a perfect opportunity of forming a mental picture of him. He sat with a very curious pose of the head thrown backward, as if resting it one vertebra lower down the spinal column than other people do, and thus tilting his face a little upwards. With his head so poised and the whole man fixed in contemplation of the interlocutor, he seemed to pass into a state of absolute passivity, waiting for remarks or incidents, the glassy eyes half closed, the large knotted hands spread out before him. So he would remain, immovable for a quarter of an hour at a time, even the action of speech betraying no movement, the lips hidden under a cascade of beard. If it be true that all remarkable human beings resemble animals, then Walt Whitman was like a cat – a great old grey Angora tom, alert in repose, serenely blinking under his combed waves of hair, with eyes inscrutable dreaming.

His talk was elemental, like his writings. It had none of the usual ornaments or irritants of conversation. It welled out naturally, or stopped; it was innocent of every species of rhetoric or epigram. It was the perfectly simple utterance of unaffected urbanity. So, I imagine, an Oriental sage would talk, in a low uniform tone, without any excitement or haste, without emphasis, in a land where time and flurry were unknown. Whitman sat there with his great head tilted back, smiling serenely, and he talked about himself. He mentioned his poverty, which was patent, and his paralysis; those were the two burdens beneath which he crouched, like Issachar; he seemed to be quite at home with both of them, and scarcely heeded them. I think I asked leave to move my box, for the light began to pour in at the great uncurtained window; and then Whitman said that someone had promised him a gift of curtains, but he was not eager for them, he thought they "kept out some of the light". Light and air, that was all he wanted; and through the winter he sat there patiently waiting for the air and light of summer, when he would hobble out again and bask his body in a shallow creek he knew "back of Camden". Meanwhile he waited, waited with infinite patience, uncomplaining, thinking about the sand, and the thin hot layer of water over it, in that shy New Jersey creek. And he winked away in silence, while I thought of the Indian poet Valmiki, when, in a trance of voluptuous abstraction, he sat under the fig-tree and was slowly eaten of ants.

In the bareness of Whitman's great double room only two objects suggested art in any way, but each of these was appropriate. One was a print of a Red Indian, given him, he told me, by Catlin; it had inspired the passage about "the red aborigines" in "Starting from Paumanok". The other – positively the sole and only thing that redeemed the bareness of the back-room where Whitman's bound works were stored – was a photograph of a very handsome young man in a boat, sculling. I asked him about this portrait and he said several notable things in consequence. He explained, first of all, that this was one of his greatest friends, a professional oarsman from Canada, a well-known sporting character. He continued, that these were the people he liked best, athletes who had a business in the open air; that those were the plainest and most affectionate of men, those who lived in the light and air and had to study to keep their bodies clean and fresh and ruddy; that his soul went out to such people, and that they were strangely drawn to him, so that at the lowest ebb of his fortunes, when the world reviled him and ridiculed him most, fortunate men of this kind, highly prosperous as gymnasts or runners, had sought him out and had been friendly to him. "And now," he went on, "I only wait for the spring, to hobble out with my staff into the woods, and when I can sit all day long close to a set of woodmen at their work, I am perfectly happy, for something of their life mixes with the smell of the chopped timber, and it passes into my veins and I am old and ill no longer." I think these were his precise words, and they struck me more than anything else that he said throughout that long and pleasant day I spent with him.

It might be supposed, and I think that even admirers have said, that Whitman had no humour. But that seemed to me not quite correct. No boisterous humour, truly, but a gentle sort of sly fun, something like Tennyson's, he certainly showed. For example, he told me of some tribute from India, and added, with a twinkling smile, "You see, I 'sound my barbaric yawp over the roofs of the world.' " But this was rare: mostly he seemed dwelling in a vague pastoral past life, the lovely days when he was young, and went about with "the boys" in the sun. He read me many things; a new "poem" intoning the long irregular lines of it not very distinctly; and a preface to some new edition. All this had left, I confess, a dim impression, swallowed up in the serene self-unconsciousness, the sweet, dignified urbanity, the feline immobility.

As I passed from the little house and stood in dull, deserted Mickle Street once more, my heart was full of affection for this beautiful old man, who had just said in his calm accents, "Good-bye, my friend!" I felt that the experience of the day was embalmed by something that a great poet had written long ago, but I could not find what it was till we started once more to cross the frosty Delaware; then it came to me, and I knew that when Shelley spoke of

> Peace within and calm around,
> And that content, surpassing wealth,
> The sage in meditation found,
> And walk'd with inward glory crown'd,

he had been prophesying of Walt Whitman, nor shall I ever read those lines again without thinking of the old rhapsodist in his empty room glorified by patience and philosophy. And so an unbeliever went to see Walt Whitman, and was captivated without being converted.

(Edmund Gosse, *Walt Whitman*)

One of the more unlikely literary encounters of the 19th century was between Arthur Conan Doyle and Oscar Wilde. The two met at a dinner organized by Lippincott's Magazine at the Langham Hotel in London. On the face of it, neither of the authors would seem to have had much in common with each other. Wilde was about to embark on the last golden period of his career which saw the creation of masterpieces like The Importance of Being Earnest. *Conan Doyle was at an earlier stage in his prolific writing life, although he had already produced one Sherlock Holmes story and the historical novel* Micah Clarke, *which Wilde had read and liked. The biggest difference, though, was between their public images, the aesthete Wilde and the "hearty" Doyle, lover of adventure stories and historical romances. But Doyle, as he recounted the meeting afterwards, readily appreciated the enormous wit and charm of the older writer.*

His [Wilde's] conversation left an indelible impression upon my mind. He towered above us all, and yet had the art of seeming to be interested in all that we could say. He had delicacy of feeling and tact, for the monologue man, however clever, can never be a gentleman at heart. He took as well as gave, but what he gave was unique. He had a curious precision of statement, a delicate flavour of humour, and a trick of small gestures to illustrate his meaning, which were peculiar to himself. The effect cannot be reproduced, but I remember how in discussing the wars of the future he said: "A chemist on each side will approach the frontier with a bottle" – his upraised hand and precise face conjuring up a vivid and grotesque picture. His anecdotes, too, were happy and curious. We were discussing the cynical maxim that the good fortune of our friends made us discontented. "The devil," said Wilde, "was crossing the Libyan desert, and he came upon a spot where a number of small fiends were tormenting a holy hermit. The sainted man easily shook off their evil suggestions. The devil watched their failure, and then he stepped forward to give them a lesson. 'What you do is too crude,' said he. 'Permit me for one moment.' With that he whispered to the holy man, 'Your brother has just been made bishop of Alexandria.' A scowl of malignant jealousy at once clouded the serene face of the hermit. 'That,' said the devil to his imps, 'is the sort of thing which I should recommend.' "

Joseph Conrad remembers the impression that the American novelist Stephen Crane (author of the famous civil war novel Red Badge of Courage*) made on him when the two men met in London shortly before Crane's death in 1900.*

My acquaintance with Stephen Crane was brought about by Mr Pawling, partner in the publishing firm of Mr William Heinemann.

One day Mr Pawling said to me: "Stephen Crane has arrived in England. I asked him if there was anybody he wanted to meet and he mentioned two names. One of them was yours." I had then just been reading, like the rest of the world, Crane's *Red Badge of Courage*. The subject of that story was war, from the point of view of an individual soldier's emotions. That individual (he remains nameless throughout) was interesting enough in himself, but on turning over the pages of that little book which had for the moment secured such a noisy recognition I had been even more interested in the personality of the writer. The picture of a simple and untried youth becoming through the needs of his country part of a great fighting machine was presented with an earnestness of purpose, a sense of tragic issues, and an imaginative force of expression which struck me as quite uncommon and altogether worthy of admiration.

Apparently Stephen Crane had received a favourable impression from the reading of the *Nigger of the Narcissus*, a book of mine which had also been published lately. I was truly pleased to hear this.

On my next visit to town we met at a lunch. I saw a young man of medium stature and slender build, with very steady, penetrating blue eyes, the eyes of a being who not only sees visions but can brood over them to some purpose.

He had indeed a wonderful power of vision, which he applied to the things of this earth and of our mortal humanity with a penetrating force that seemed to reach, within life's appearances and forms, the very spirit of life's truth. His ignorance of the world at large – he had seen very little of it – did not stand in the way of his imaginative grasp of facts, events, and picturesque men.

His manner was very quiet, his personality at first sight interesting, and he talked slowly with an intonation which on some people, mainly Americans, had, I believe, a jarring effect. But not on me. Whatever he said had a personal note, and he expressed himself with a graphic simplicity which was extremely engaging. He knew little of literature, either of his own country or of any other, but he was himself a wonderful artist in words whenever he took a pen into his hand. Then his gift came out – and it was seen then to be much more than mere felicity of language. His impressionism of phrase went really deeper than the surface. In his writing he was very sure of his effects. I don't think he was ever in doubt about what he could do. Yet it often seemed to me that he was but half aware of the exceptional quality of his achievement.

This achievement was curtailed by his early death . . . My wife and I like best to remember him riding to meet us at the gate of the Park at Brede. Born master of his sincere impressions, he was also a born horseman. He never appeared so happy or so much to advantage as on the back of a horse. He had formed the project of teaching my eldest boy to ride, and meantime, when the child was about two years old, presented him with his first dog.

I saw Stephen Crane a few days after his arrival in London. I saw him for the last time on his last day in England. It was in Dover, in a big hotel, in a bedroom with a large window looking on to the sea. He had been very ill and Mrs Crane was taking him to some place in Germany, but one glance at that wasted face was enough to tell me that it was the most forlorn of all hopes. The last words he breathed out to me were: "I am tired. Give my love to your wife and child." When I stopped at the door for another look I saw that he had turned his head on the pillow and was staring wistfully out of the window at the sails of a cutter yacht that glided slowly across the frame, like a dim shadow against the grey sky.

(Joseph Conrad, *from an untitled note on Crane, 1919*)

At the start of the Second World War P. G. Wodehouse, the prolific and much-loved comic novelist, was living with his wife in northern France at Le Touquet. The advancing Germans captured the couple and interned them. Wodehouse was eventually released but not allowed to leave Germany. Perhaps naively he agreed to give a series of radio broadcasts from Berlin, mostly to reassure his fans in America that all was well. The five talks couldn't be described as propaganda for the Nazi cause – their tone is probably as light-hearted as it could be in the circumstances – but ever afterwards Wodehouse was regarded by some people in Britain as a traitor. Following the liberation of Paris in 1944, the writer and journalist Malcolm Muggeridge, who was working in Intelligence, found himself assigned to "keep an eye on P. G. Wodehouse". In his autobiography Muggeridge describes his first meeting with Wodehouse at the Hotel Bristol, and how he wanted to see the writer's reaction "to suddenly becoming a villain after having been for so many years a national hero, or class totem."

Nothing was working in the hotel, but the receptionist must have found some way of letting Wodehouse know that I was on my way up to his suite, because he seemed to be expecting me. "Oh, hullo!" he said when I opened the door and stepped inside. He was standing by the window; a large, bald, amiable-looking man, wearing grey flannel trousers, a loose sports jacket and what I imagine were golfing shoes, and smoking a pipe; a sort of schoolmaster's rig. He might, I suppose, easily have been a schoolmaster if he hadn't taken to writing – Wooders. Our meeting seemed so natural that it only occurred to me afterwards that he may have thought I had come to put him under arrest. If so, he showed no signs of anxiety, but seemed perfectly at ease. When I got to know him better I asked him what sort of person he had expected to come into his room. "Oh, I don't know," he said, "but not you." This, I must say, greatly pleased me.

I should, of course, before coming to see Wodehouse, have got hold of a dossier from somewhere – there always is a dossier – and studied the text of the offending broadcasts, generally familiarizing myself with the case. In fact, I had made no sort of preparation for my visit, and had no plan as to how I should approach Wodehouse. So I began with the banal observation that his books had given me great pleasure. Even this was not strictly true. In my Socialist home Bertie Wooster and Jeeves were as reprehensible figures as Sade and Casanova in a Methodist one. My feelings about him on first making his acquaintance, were, I should say, that he was a distinguished and original writer who had given a great deal of pleasure to a great many people, and that, as such, he was entitled to be kept clear of the monstrous buffooneries of war. Otherwise, I had no strong sense of partisanship one way or the other.

There was still a lot of rushing about and shouting in the street outside; even an occasional pistol shot. Wodehouse turned away from the window, and we both sat down. Then, after a short silence, I made a hesitant approach to the business in hand. I had no idea, I said, to what extent he had been able to follow what was going on in England, but there had been quite a public row about his broadcasts – a row which I personally considered to be unwarranted. All the same, in order to clear matters up, questions would have to be asked and the legal position gone into. I slipped in the reference to the legal position (about which, of course, I knew nothing) in order to stress the gravity of Wodehouse's plight – in the circumstances then prevailing, decidedly serious. Judges are as prone as anyone to swim with the tide – perhaps a bit more so – and the English, too, as the trial of William Joyce (Lord Haw-Haw) showed, were in a mood for sacrificial victims, though in their case, particular ones, rather than, as with the French, in bulk. Wodehouse might well have fared ill if he had come before a British court at that time.

From numerous talks I had with him, sometimes on walks that we took together through the streets of Paris, sometimes sitting and chatting, I was able to piece together what happened to him in the war years. When in the summer of 1940 the Germans arrived at Le Touquet, where Wodehouse and his wife Ethel had a villa in which they were living at the time, he was taken into custody as an enemy alien and transported to a prison camp at Tost in Poland. The building in which they were lodged, to his great satisfaction, turned out to have previously been a lunatic asylum. Here he lived relatively contentedly, though food was decidedly short; he found, he told me, that nourishment could be got out of match sticks if assiduously sucked. He had brought his typewriter with him, and, marvellous to relate, he continued to turn out his daily stint of words. When the war ended he had five novels, all up to his usual standard, ready for publication. I asked him whether the guards at Tost took any interest in his writing. Yes, he said, very markedly so; they would stand and watch him tapping with awe and fascination. I could quite believe it. Wodehouse has written an entertaining account of his life at Tost – what he calls his Camp Book – which he gave me to read. It must be unique in prison literature as minimizing the miseries of captivity, and stressing the pleasant relations he had even with the guards, as well as with his fellow-captives, and the solaces they found to alleviate their boredom and privation.

The normal procedure is to release civilian internees when they are 60; Wodehouse was released some months before his sixtieth birthday as a result of well-meant but ill-advised representation by American friends resident in Berlin, America not being then at war with Germany. He made for Berlin, where Ethel (who had not been interned) was awaiting him. Hearing of his presence there, the Berlin representative of the Columbia Broadcasting System, an American named Flaherty, asked him if he would like to broadcast to his American readers. For professional reasons, if for no others, the idea appealed to Wodehouse, who did not want to be forgotten in his most lucrative market. So he foolishly agreed to Flaherty's proposal, not realizing that the broadcasts would have to go over the German network, and therefore were bound to be exploited in the interest of Nazi propaganda. It has often been alleged that there was some sort of bargain whereby he agreed to broadcast in return for being released from Tost. This has been denied again and again, and is in fact totally untrue, but nonetheless continues to be widely believed. Lies seem to have much greater staying power than truth.

(Malcolm Muggeridge, *Chronicles of Wasted Time, Part 2*)

P. G. Wodehouse never returned to live in England but moved to the United States, taking American citizenship in 1953. A campaign continued for many years in England to "rehabilitate" him, led by friends and admirers like Macolm Muggeridge and Auberon Waugh. In a sign of his – eventual! – forgiveness by the British establishment, Wodehouse was given a knighthood shortly before his death in 1975.

Illness & Disability

The 17th-century minor poet Nathaniel Lee is totally forgotten now, but this story of how he was confined in the lunatic asylum of Bedlam deserves to be retold. The unfortunate Lee eventually died after a drinking bout.

When Lee the poet was confined in Bedlam, a friend went to visit him, and finding that he could converse reasonably, or at least reasonably for a poet, imagined that Lee was cured of his madness. The poet offered to show him Bedlam. They went over this melancholy medical prison, Lee moralizing philosophically enough all the time to keep his companion perfectly at ease. At length they ascended together to the top of the building, and as they were both looking down from the perilous height, Lee seized his friend by the arm, "Let us immortalize ourselves!" he exclaimed; "let us take this leap. We'll jump down together this instant." "Any man could jump down," said his friend, coolly; "we should not immortalize ourselves by that leap; but let us go down, and try if we can leap up again." The madman, struck with the idea of a more astonishing leap than that which he had himself proposed, yielded to this new impulse, and his friend rejoiced to see him run down stairs full of a new project for securing immortality.

(*Liber Facetarium*)

～～～

The progress of Jonathan Swift's various illnesses is recorded by Samuel Johnson in his Life of the author of Gulliver's Travels. *Swift eventually went mad and seems to have had forebodings of his final mental decay. There's a story that when he was out walking with friends near Dublin they passed an elm tree whose top was withered*

*and decayed. Swift was transfixed by the sight of the tree and,
pointing up to it, said, "I shall be like that tree, I shall die at the top."*

As his years increased, his fits of giddiness and deafness grew
more frequent, and his deafness made conversation difficult;
they grew likewise more severe, till in 1736, as he was writing a
poem called "The Legion Club", he was seized with a fit so
painful, and so long continued, that he never after thought it
proper to attempt any work of thought or labour.

He was always careful of his money, and was therefore no
liberal entertainer; but was less frugal of his wine than of his
meat. When his friends of either sex came to him, in expectation
of a dinner, his custom was to give every one a shilling, that they
might please themselves with their provision. At last his avarice
grew too powerful for his kindness; he would refuse a bottle of
wine, and in Ireland no man visits where he cannot drink.

Having thus excluded conversation, and desisted from study,
he had neither business nor amusement, for having, by some
ridiculous resolution or mad vow, determined never to wear
spectacles, he could make little use of books in his later years;
his ideas therefore, being neither renovated by discourse nor
increased by reading, wore gradually away, and left his mind
vacant to the vexations of the hour, till at last his anger was
heightened into madness . . .

He grew more violent; and his mental powers declined till
(1741) it was found necessary that legal guardians should be
appointed of his person and fortune. He now lost distinction.
His madness was compounded of rage and fatuity. The last face
that he knew was that of Mrs Whiteway, and her he ceased to
know in a little time. His meat was brought him cut into
mouthfuls; but he would never touch it while the servant staid,
and at last, after it had stood perhaps an hour, would eat it
walking; for he continued his old habit, and was on his feet ten
hours a day.

Next year (1742) he had an inflammation in his left eye,
which swelled it to the size of an egg, with boils in other parts;
he was kept long waking with the pain, and was not easily
restrained by five attendants from tearing out his eye.

The tumour at last subsided; and a short interval of reason

ensuing, in which he knew his physician and his family, gave hopes of his recovery; but in a few days he sunk into lethargick stupidity, motionless, heedless, and speechless. But it is said, that, after a year of total silence, when his housekeeper, on the 30th of November, told him that the usual bonfires and illuminations were preparing to celebrate his birthday, he answered, "It is all folly; they had better let it alone."

It is remembered that he afterwards spoke now and then, or gave some intimation of a meaning; but at last sunk into perfect silence, which continued till about the end of October 1744, when, in his 78th year, he expired without a struggle.

(Samuel Johnson, *Life of Swift*)

The poet Alexander Pope suffered from stunted growth and a deformed spine (probably the result of a tubercular infection in childhood). His difficult life and demanding personality are sketched out by Dr Johnson, one of his earliest biographers.

The person of Pope is well known not to have been formed by the nicest model. He has . . . compared himself to a spider, and by another is described as protuberant behind and before. He is said to have been beautiful in his infancy; but he was of a constitution originally feeble and weak; and as bodies of a tender frame are easily distorted, his deformity was probably in part the effect of application. His stature was so low, that, to bring him to a level with common tables, it was necessary to raise his seat. But his face was not displeasing, and his eyes were animated and vivid.

By natural deformity, or accidental distortion, his vital functions were so much disordered, that his life was a "long disease". His most frequent assailant was the headache, which he used to relieve by inhaling the steam of coffee, which he very frequently required.

Most of what can be told concerning his petty peculiarities was communicated by a female domestic of the Earl of Oxford who knew him perhaps after the middle of life. He was then so weak as to stand in perpetual need of female attendance, extremely sensible of cold, so that he wore a kind of fur doublet under a shirt of a very coarse warm linen with fine sleeves. When he rose, he was invested in bodice made of stiff canvas, being scarce able to hold himself erect till they were laced, and he then put on a flannel waistcoat. One side was contracted. His legs were so slender, that he enlarged their bulk with three pair of stockings, which were drawn on and off by the maid; for he was not able to dress or undress himself, and neither went to bed nor rose without help. His weakness made it very difficult for him to be clean.

His hair had fallen almost all away; and he used to dine sometimes with Lord Oxford, privately, in a velvet cap. His dress of ceremony was black, with a tye-wig and a little sword.

The indulgence and accommodation which his sickness required had taught him all the unpleasing and unsocial qualities of a valetudinary man. He expected that everything should give way to his ease or humour, as a child whose parents will not hear her cry, has an unresisted dominion in the nursery . . .

When he wanted to sleep, he "nodded in company"; and once slumbered at his own table while the Prince, of Wales was talking of poetry.

The reputation which his friendship gave procured him many invitations; but he was a very troublesome inmate. He brought no servant, and had so many wants that a numerous attendance was scarcely able to supply them. Wherever he was, he left no room for another, because he exacted the attention and employed the activity of the whole family. His errands were so frequent and frivolous that the footmen in time avoided and neglected him; and the Earl of Oxford discharged some of the servants for their resolute refusal of his messages . . . One of his constant demands was of coffee in the night . . .

He had another fault, easily incident to those who, suffering much pain, think themselves entitled to what pleasures they can snatch. He was too indulgent to his appetite; he loved meat highly seasoned and of strong taste; and, at the intervals of the table, amused himself with biscuits and dry conserves. If he sat down to a variety of dishes, he would oppress his stomach with repletion; and though he seemed angry when a dram was offered him, did not forbear to drink it. His friends, who knew the avenues to his heart, pampered him with presents of luxury, which he did not suffer to stand neglected. The death of great men is not always proportioned to the lustre of their lives . . . The death of Pope was imputed by some of his friends to a silver saucepan, in which it was his delight to heat potted lampreys.

That he loved too well to eat is certain; but that his sensuality shortened his life will not be hastily concluded, when it is remembered that a conformation so irregular lasted six and fifty years, notwithstanding such pertinacious diligence of study and meditation.

(Samuel Johnson, *Life of Pope*)

Dr Johnson was expert at analysing the weaknesses of others (see above) but he himself suffered from various morbid fears, particularly to do with his mental health. However, when it came to a real crisis he seems to have taken it quite calmly. This is Johnson's description of suffering a stroke.

On Monday the 16th [1783] I sat for my picture, and walked a considerable way with little inconvenience. In the afternoon and evening I felt myself light and easy, and began to plan schemes of life. Thus I went to bed, and in a short time waked and sat up, as has been long my custom, when I felt a confusion and indistinctness in my head, which lasted, I suppose, about half a minute. I was alarmed, and prayed God that however he might afflict my body, he would spare my understanding. This prayer, that I might try the integrity of my faculties, I made in Latin verse. The lines were not very good, but I knew them not to be very good: I made them easily, and concluded myself to be unimpaired in my faculties.

Soon after I perceived that I had suffered a paralytic stroke, and that my speech was taken from me. I had no pain, and so little dejection in this dreadful state, that I wondered at my own apathy, and considered that perhaps death itself when it should come would excite less horror than seems now to attend it.

In order to rouse the vocal organs I took two drams. Wine has been celebrated for the production of eloquence. I put myself into violent motion, and I think repeated it; but all was vain. I then went to bed, and, strange as it may seem, I think, slept.

When I saw light it was time to contrive what I should do. Though God stopped my speech he left me my hand; I enjoyed a mercy which was not granted to my dear friend Lawrence, who now perhaps overlooks me as I am writing, and rejoices that I have what he wanted [i.e.lacked]. My first note was necessarily to my servant, who came in talking, and could not immediately comprehend why he should read what I put into his hands.

I then wrote a card to Mr Allen, that I might have a discreet friend at hand, to act as occasion should require. In penning this note I had some difficulty; my hand, I know not how nor why, made wrong letters. I then wrote to Dr Taylor to come to me, and bring Dr Heberden, and I sent to Dr Brocklesby, who is my neighbour. My physicians are very friendly and very disinterested and give me great hopes; but you may imagine my situation. I have so far recovered my vocal powers, as to repeat the Lord's Prayer with no very imperfect articulation. My memory, I hope, yet remains as it was; but such an attack produces solicitude for the safety of every faculty . . .

(Samuel Johnson, *letter to Mrs Thrale, June, 1783*)

Mrs Thrale, who was the recipient of the letter quoted above (and who afterwards became Mrs Piozzi), writes about Johnson's mental health from a friend's point of view – but it's obvious that he tested the patience of some of those friends.

Mr Johnson's health had been always extremely bad since I first knew him, and his over-anxious care to retain without blemish the perfect sanity of his mind, contributed much to disturb it. He had studied medicine diligently in all its branches; but had given particular attention to the diseases of the imagination, which he watched in himself with a solicitude destructive of his own peace, and intolerable to those he trusted. Dr Lawrence told him one day, that if he would come and beat him once a week he would bear it, but to hear his complaints was more than *man* could support. 'Twas therefore that he tried, I suppose, and in eighteen years contrived to weary the patience of a *woman*. When Mr Johnson felt his fancy, or fancied he felt it, disordered, his constant recurrence was to the study of arithmetic, and one day that he was totally confined to his chamber, and I enquired what he had been doing to divert himself; he shewed me a calculation which I could scarce be made to understand, so vast was the plan of it, and so very intricate were the figures: no other indeed than that the national debt, computing it at one hundred and eighty millions sterling, would, if converted into silver, serve to make a meridian of that metal, I forget how broad, for the globe of the whole earth, the real *globe*.

(Hesther Lynch Piozzi, *Anecdotes of Samuel Johnson*)

Towards the end of his life the 18th-century novelist Henry Fielding suffered from dropsy (now usually known as oedema), a condition in which fluid builds up dangerously in parts of the body. Fielding's dropsy was a product of his cirrhosis of the liver, itself a product of hard drinking and high living. Fielding was more or less incapacitated by his advancing illness. His swollen body had to be drained, or "tapped", increasingly often.

It was no more than three weeks since my last tapping, and my belly and limbs were distended with water. This did not give me the worse opinion of tar-water*: for I never supposed there could be any such virtue in tar-water, as immediately to carry off a quantity of water already collected. For my delivery from this, I well knew I must be again obliged to the trochar†, and if the tar-water did me any good at all, it must be only by the slowest degrees; and that if it should ever get the better of my distemper, it must be the tedious operation of undermining; and not by a sudden attack and storm.

Some visible effects, however, and far beyond what my most sanguine hopes could with any modesty expect, I very soon experienced; the tar-water having, from the very first, lessened my illness, increased my appetite; and added, though in a very slow proportion, to my bodily strength.

But if my strength had increased a little, my water daily

* Tar-water – Cold infusion of tar in water, once used as medicine.
† Trochar – Device combining tube and perforator to draw off fluid from body.

increased much more. So that, by the end of May, my belly became again ripe for the trochar, and I was a third time tapped; upon which two very favourable symptoms appeared. I had three quarts of water taken from me less than had been taken the last time; and I bore the relaxation with much less (indeed with scarce any) faintness.

Those of my physical friends, on whose judgment I chiefly depended, seemed to think my only chance of life consisted in having the whole summer before me; in which I might hope to gather sufficient strength to encounter the inclemencies of the ensuing winter. But this chance began daily to lessen. I saw the summer mouldering away, or rather, indeed, the year passing away without intending to bring on any summer at all. In the whole month of May the sun scarce appeared three times. So that the early fruits came to the fulness of their growth, and to some appearance of ripeness, without acquiring any real maturity; having wanted the heat of the sun to soften and meliorate their juices. I saw the dropsy gaining rather than losing ground; the distance growing still shorter between the tappings. I saw the asthma likewise beginning again to become more troublesome. I saw the Midsummer quarter drawing towards a close. So that I conceived, if the Michaelmas quarter [period between July and September] should steal off in the same manner, as it was, in my opinion, very much to be apprehended it would, I should be delivered up to the attacks of winter, before I recruited my forces, so as to be any wise able to withstand them.

I now began to recall an intention, which from the first dawnings of my recovery I had conceiv'd, of removing to a warmer climate; and finding this to be approv'd of by a very eminent physician, I resolved to put it into immediate execution.

Fielding and his doctor decided on Lisbon. The mild air and shorter winter might do him good or at least slow down his deterioration. But while his ship was still in dock at Rotherhithe, the delay in leaving for Portugal brought on a fresh need for the novelist to be "tapped".

Now, as I saw myself in danger by the delays of the captain, who was in, reality, waiting for more freight, and as the wind had been long nested, as it were, in the south-west, where it constantly blew hurricanes, I began with great reason to apprehend that our voyage might be long, and that my belly, which began already to be much extended, would require the water to be let out at a time when no assistance was at hand; though, indeed, the captain comforted me with assurances, that he had a pretty young fellow on board, who acted as his surgeon, as I found he likewise did as steward, cook, butler, sailor. In short, he had as many offices as Scrub in the play, and went through them all with great dexterity; this of surgeon, was, perhaps, the only one in which his skill was somewhat deficient, at least that branch of tapping for the dropsy; for he very ingenuously and modestly confessed, he had never seen the operation performed, nor was possessed of that chirurgical [surgical] instrument with which it is performed.

Friday, June 28. By way of prevention, therefore, I this day sent for my friend Mr Hunter, the great surgeon and anatomist of Covent Garden; and though my belly was not yet very full and tight, let out ten quarts of water, the young sea-surgeon attended the operation, not as a performer, but as a student.

(Henry Fielding, *The Journal of a Voyage to Lisbon*)

Fielding reached Lisbon after a sea-voyage lasting about six weeks – there were frequent delays on the south coast of England because of contrary winds. But he survived for only two more months. The Journal of a Voyage to Lisbon, *his last book, was published posthumously. He was 47.*

～

The novelist Fanny Burney showed extraordinary fortitude when she was diagnosed with breast cancer and a mastectomy was performed. This was in 1811, before the discovery of anaesthetic. At the time she was living in Paris, and described the experience in a letter to her sister Esther. This description is not for the squeamish.

I mounted the bed stead. He placed me upon the mattress and spread a cambric handkerchief upon my face. It was transparent however and I saw through it, that the bed stead was instantly surrounded by seven men and my nurse. Through the cambric I saw the hand held up while his forefinger first described a straight line from top to bottom of the heart, secondly a cross and thirdly a circle; intimating that the whole was to be taken off. When the dreadful steel was plunged into the heart cutting through veins – arteries – nerves, I needed no injunctions not to restrain my cries. I began a scream that lasted during the whole time of the incision and marvel that it rings not in my ears still. When the wound was made and the instrument withdrawn the pain seemed undiminished, for the air that suddenly rushed into those delicate parts felt like sharp and forked poniards that were tearing the edges of the wound. Again I felt the instrument describing a curve cutting against the grain, while the flesh resisted in a manner so forcible to oppose and tire the hand of the operator. I concluded the operation over – Oh No! The terrible cutting was renewed and worse than ever. I felt the knife rackling against the breast bone – scraping it! To conclude, the evil was so profound that the operation lasted twenty minutes.

Fortunately the operation was a success. The cancer was arrested and Fanny Burney lived another 29 years after this terrible operation.

From an early stage of his life the poet Percy Bysshe Shelley suffered from mental delusions that he was being persecuted by his father. The elaborate detail of the stories required to support this mild paranoia is shown in the following account from Thomas Love Peacock's memoir of the poet.

In the early summer of 1816, the spirit of restlessness again came over him, and resulted in a second visit to the Continent. The change of scene was preceded, as more than once before, by a mysterious communication from a person seen only by himself, warning him of immediate personal perils to be incurred by him if he did not instantly depart.

I was alone at Bishopgate, with him and Mrs Shelley, when the visitation alluded to occurred. About the middle of the day, intending to take a walk, I went into the hall for my hat. His was there, and mine was not. I could not imagine what had become of it; but as I could not walk without it, I returned to the library. After some time had elapsed, Mrs Shelley came in, and gave me an account which she had just received from himself, of the visitor and his communication. I expressed some scepticism on the subject, on which she left me, and Shelley came in, with my hat in his hand. He said, "Mary tells me, you do not believe that I have had a visit from Williams." I said, "I told her there were some improbabilities in the narration." He said, "You know Williams of Tremadoc?" I said, "I do." He said, "It was he who was here today. He came to tell me of a plot laid by my father and my uncle to entrap me and lock me up. He was in great haste, and could not stop a minute, and I walked with him to Egham." I said, "What hat did you wear?" He said, "This, to be sure." I said, "I wish you would put it on." He put it on, and it went over his face. I said, "You could not have walked to Egham in that hat." He said, "I snatched it up hastily, and perhaps I kept it in my hand. I certainly walked with Williams to Egham, and he told me what I have said. You are very sceptical." I said, "If you are certain of what you say, my scepticism cannot affect your certainty." He said, "It is very hard on a man who has devoted his life to the pursuit of truth, who has made great sacrifices and incurred great sufferings for it, to be treated as a visionary. If I do not know that I saw Williams, how do I know that I see you?" I said, "An idea may have the force of a sensation; but the oftener a sensation is repeated, the greater is the probability of its origin in reality. You saw me yesterday, and will see me tomorrow." He said, "I can see Williams tomorrow if I please. He told me he was stopping at the Turk's Head Coffee-house, in the Strand, and should be there two days. I want to convince you that I am not under a delusion. Will you walk with me to London tomorrow, to see him?" I said, "I would most willingly do so." The next morning after an early breakfast we set off on our walk to London. We had got half way down Egham Hill, when he suddenly turned round, and said to me, "I do not think we shall find Williams at the Turk's Head." I said, "Neither do I." He said, "You say that, because you do not think he has been there; but he mentioned a contingency under which he might leave town yesterday, and he has probably done so." I said, "At any rate, we should know that he has been there." He said, "I will take other means of convincing you. I will write to him. Suppose we take a walk through the forest." We turned about on our new direction, and were out all day. Some days passed, and I heard no more of the matter. One morning he said to me, "I have some news of Williams; a letter and an enclosure." I said, "I shall be glad to see the letter." He said, "I cannot show you the letter; I will show you the enclosure. It is a diamond necklace. I think you know me well enough to be sure I would not throw away my own money on such a thing, and that if I have it, it must have been sent me by somebody else. It has been sent me by Williams." "For what purpose," I asked. He said, "To prove his identity and his sincerity." "Surely," I said, "your showing me a diamond necklace will prove nothing but that you have one to show." "Then," he said, "I will not show it you. If you will not believe me, I must submit to your incredulity." There the matter ended. I never heard another word of Williams, nor of any other mysterious visitor. I had on one or two previous occasions argued with him against similar semi-delusions, and I believe if they had always been received with similar scepticism, they would not have been often repeated; but they were encouraged by the ready credulity with which they were received by many who ought to have known better. I call them semi-delusions, because, for the most part, they had their basis in his firm belief that his father and uncle had designs on his liberty. On this basis, his imagination built a fabric of romance, and when he presented it as substantive fact, and it was found to contain more or less of inconsistency, he felt his self-esteem interested in maintaining it by accumulated circumstances, which severally vanished under the touch of investigation, like Williams' location at the Turk's Head Coffee-house.

(Thomas Love Peacock, *Memoirs of Shelley*)

This meeting of 1819 between the established poet Samuel Taylor Coleridge and the much younger John Keats shows Coleridge's intuitive powers.

A loose, slack, not well-dressed youth met Mr Green and myself in a lane near Highgate. Green knew him, and spoke. It was Keats. He was introduced to me, and stayed a minute or so. After he had left us a little way, he came back, and said, "Let me carry away the memory, Coleridge, of having pressed your hand!" "There is death in that hand," I said to Green, when Keats was gone; yet this was, I believe, before the consumption showed itself distinctly.

(S. T. Coleridge, *Table Talk*)

Coleridge was right. Keats died of tuberculosis in Rome in 1821 – see also **Death**.

Lord Byron was born with deformed feet which caused him to move awkwardly throughout his life. After Byron's death in Greece his friend Edward Trelawny took the opportunity to examine the poet's body. First he sent Byron's man-servant Fletcher out of the room on a pretext.

I asked Fletcher to bring me a glass of water. On his leaving the room, to confirm or remove my doubts as to the exact cause of his lameness, I uncovered the Pilgrim's feet, and was answered – it was caused by the contraction of the back sinews, which the doctors call "Tendon Achilles", that prevented his heels resting on the ground, and compelled him to walk on the fore part of his feet; except this defect, his feet were perfect. This was a curse, chaining a proud and soaring spirit like his to the dull earth. In the drama of "The Deformed Transformed", I knew that he had expressed all he could express of what a man of highly wrought mind might feel when brooding over a deformity of body; but when he said,

> I have done the best which spirit may to make
> Its way with all deformity's dull deadly
> Discouraging weight upon me,

I thought it exaggerated as applied to himself; now I saw it was not so. His deformity was always uppermost in his thoughts, and influenced every act of his life, spurred him on to poetry, as that was one of the few paths to fame open to him, – and as if to be revenged on Nature for sending him into the world "scarce half made up", he scoffed at her works and traditions with the pride of Lucifer; this morbid feeling ultimately goaded him on to his last Quixotic crusade in Greece . . .

Knowing and sympathizing with Byron's sensitiveness, his associates avoided prying into the cause of his lameness; so did strangers, from good breeding or common humanity. It was generally thought his halting gait originated in some defect of the right foot or ankle – the right foot was the most distorted, and it had been made worse in his boyhood by vain efforts to set it right. He told me that for several years he wore steel splints, which so wrenched the sinews and tendons of his leg, that they increased his lameness; the foot was twisted inwards, only the edge touched the ground, and that leg was shorter than the other. His shoes were peculiar – very high heeled, with the soles uncommonly thick on the inside and pared thin on the outside – the toes were stuffed with cotton-wool, and his trousers were very large below the knee and strapped down so as to cover his feet. The peculiarity of his gait was now accounted for; he entered a room with a sort of run, as if he could not stop, then planted his best leg well forward, throwing back his body to keep his balance. In early life whilst his frame was light and elastic, with the aid of a stick, he might have tottered along for a mile or two; but after he had waxed heavier, he seldom attempted to walk more than a few hundred yards, without squatting down or leaning against the first wall, bank, rock, or tree at hand, never sitting on the ground, as it would have been difficult for him to get up again. In the company of strangers, occasionally, he would make desperate efforts to conceal his infirmity, but the hectic flush on his face, his swelling veins, and quivering nerves betrayed him, and he suffered for many days after such exertions. Disposed to fatten, incapable of taking exercise to check the tendency, what could he do? If he added to his weight, his feet would not have supported him; in this dilemma he was compelled to exist in a state of semi-starvation; he was less than eleven stone when at Genoa, and said he had been fourteen at Venice. The pangs of hunger which travellers and shipwrecked mariners have described were nothing to what he suffered; their privations were temporary, his were for life, and more unendurable, as he was in the midst of abundance. I was exclaiming, "Poor fellow, if your errors were greater than those of ordinary men, so were your temptations and provocations," when Fletcher returned with a bottle and glass, saying, "There is nothing but slimy salt water in this horrid place, so I have been half over the town to beg this clear water," and answering my ejaculation of "Poor fellow," he said,

"You may well say so, sir – these savages are worse than any highwaymen; they have robbed my Lord of all his money and his life too, and those" – pointing to his feet – "were the cause of all my Lord's misfortunes."

> (Edward Trelawny *Records of Shelley, Byron, and the Author*)

The influential American poet and philosopher Ralph Waldo Emerson lost his reason in the last ten years of his life, becoming what has been called "a quiet blank". Shortly before Emerson died in 1882, he was visited in Concord by the teenage Edward Bok, even then in training for a distinguished journalistic career. (Bok went on to edit the Ladies' Home Journal and to win the Pulitzer Prize.) Many years later in his autobiography, in which he consistently refers to himself in the third person, Bok describes the poignant spectacle of Emerson's decline, with its moments of awareness. Louisa May Alcott, who figures in this story, was the author of Little Women *– her family had long been friendly with Emerson. To begin with, Bok is warned by Phillips Brooks, a preacher and also a friend of Emerson, that the great man is not as he once was.*

As he let the boy out of his house, at the end of that first meeting, he said to him: "And you're going from me now to see Emerson? I don't know," he added reflectively, "whether you will see him at his best. Still, you may. And even if you do not, to have seen him, even as you may see him, is better, in a way, than not to have seen him at all."

Edward did not know what Phillips Brooks meant. But he was, sadly, to find out the next day.

A boy of sixteen was pretty sure of a welcome from Louisa Alcott, and his greeting from her was spontaneous and sincere.

"Why, you good boy," she said, "to come all the way to Concord to see us," quite for all the world as if she were the one favoured. "Now take your coat off, and come right in by the fire."

"Do tell me all about your visit," she continued.

Before that cozy fire they chatted. It was pleasant to the boy to sit there with that sweet-faced woman with those kindly eyes! After a while she said: "Now I shall put on my coat and hat, and we shall walk over to Emerson's house. I am almost afraid to promise that you will see him. He sees scarcely any one now. He is feeble, and – " She did not finish the sentence. "But we'll walk over there, at any rate . . ."

Presently they reached Emerson's house, and Miss Emerson welcomed them at the door. After a brief chat Miss Alcott told of the boy's hope. Miss Emerson shook her head.

"Father sees no one now," she said, "and I fear it might not be a pleasure if you did see him."

Then Edward told her what Phillips Brooks had said.

"Well," she said, "I'll see."

She had scarcely left the room when Miss Alcott rose and followed her, saying to the boy: "You shall see Mr Emerson if it is at all possible."

In a few minutes Miss Alcott returned, her eyes moistened, and simply said: "Come."

The boy followed her through two rooms, and at the threshold of the third Miss Emerson stood, also with moistened eyes.

"Father," she said simply, and there, at his desk, sat Emerson – the man whose words had already won Edward Bok's boyish interest, and who was destined to impress himself upon his life more deeply than any other writer.

Slowly, at the daughter's spoken word, Emerson rose with a wonderful quiet dignity, extended his hand, and as the boy's hand rested in his, looked him full in the eyes.

No light of welcome came from those sad yet tender eyes. The boy closed upon the hand in his with a loving pressure, and for a single moment the eyelids rose, a different look came into those eyes, and Edward felt a slight, perceptible response of the hand. But that was all!

Quietly he motioned the boy to a chair beside the desk. Edward sat down and was about to say something, when, instead of seating himself, Emerson walked away to the window and stood there softly whistling and looking out as if there were no one in the room. Edward's eyes had followed Emerson's every footstep, when the boy was aroused by hearing a suppressed sob, and as he looked around he saw that it came from Miss Emerson. Slowly she walked out of the room. The boy looked at Miss Alcott, and she put her finger to her mouth, indicating silence. He was nonplussed.

Edward looked toward Emerson standing in that window, and wondered what it all meant. Presently Emerson left the window and, crossing the room, came to his desk, bowing to the boy as he passed, and seated himself, not speaking a word and ignoring the presence of the two persons in the room.

Suddenly the boy heard Miss Alcott say: "Have you read this new book by Ruskin yet?"

Slowly the great master of thought lifted his eyes from his desk, turned toward the speaker, rose with stately courtesy from his chair, and, bowing to Miss Alcott, said with great deliberation: "Did you speak to me, madam?"

The boy was dumbfounded! Louisa Alcott, his Louisa! And he did not know her! Suddenly the whole sad truth flashed upon the boy. Tears sprang into Miss Alcott's eyes, and she walked to the other side of the room. The boy did not know what to say or do, so he sat silent. With a deliberate movement Emerson resumed his seat, and slowly his eyes roamed over the boy sitting at the side of the desk. He felt he should say something.

"I thought, perhaps, Mr Emerson," he said, "that you might be able to favor me with a letter from Carlyle★."

At the mention of the name Carlyle his eyes lifted, and he asked: "Carlyle, did you say, sir, Carlyle?"

"Yes," said the boy, "Thomas Carlyle."

"Ye-es," Emerson answered slowly. "To be sure, Carlyle.

★ Carlyle – the English author Thomas Carlyle was a lifelong friend of Emerson.

Yes, he was here this morning. He will be here again tomorrow morning," he added gleefully, almost like a child.

Then suddenly: "You were saying – "

Edward repeated his request.

"Oh, I think so, I think so," said Emerson, to the boy's astonishment. "Let me see. Yes, here in this drawer I have many letters from Carlyle."

At these words Miss Alcott came from the other part of the room, her wet eyes dancing with pleasure and her face wreathed in smiles.

"I think we can help this young man; do you not think so, Louisa?" said Emerson, smiling toward Miss Alcott. The whole atmosphere of the room had changed. How different the expression of his eyes as now Emerson looked at the boy! "And you have come all the way from New York to ask me that!" he said smilingly as the boy told him of his trip. "Now, let us see," he said, as he delved in a drawer full of letters.

For a moment he groped among letters and papers, and then, softly closing the drawer, he began that ominous low whistle once more, looked inquiringly at each, and dropped his eyes straightway to the papers before him on his desk. It was to be only for a few moments, then Miss Alcott turned away.

The boy felt the interview could not last much longer. So, anxious to have some personal souvenir of the meeting, he said: "Mr Emerson, will you be so good as to write your name in this book for me?" and he brought out an album he had in his pocket.

"Name?" he asked vaguely.

"Yes, please," said the boy, "your name: Ralph Waldo Emerson."

But the sound of the name brought no response from the eyes.

"Please write out the name you want," he said finally, "and I will copy it for you if I can."

It was hard for the boy to believe his own senses. But picking up a pen he wrote: "Ralph Waldo Emerson, Concord; November 22, 1881."

Emerson looked at it, and said mournfully: "Thank you." Then he picked up the pen, and writing the single letter "R" stopped, followed his finger until it reached the "W" of Waldo, and studiously copied letter by letter! At the word "Concord" he seemed to hesitate, as if the task were too great, but finally copied again, letter by letter, until the second "c" was reached. "Another 'o'," he said, and interpolated an extra letter in the name of the town which he had done so much to make famous the world over. When he had finished he handed back the book . . .

The boy put the book into his pocket; and as he did so Emerson's eye caught the slip on his desk, in the boy's handwriting, and, with a smile of absolute enlightenment, he turned and said:

"You wish me to write my name? With pleasure. Have you a book with you?"

Overcome with astonishment, Edward mechanically handed him the album once more from his pocket. Quickly turning over the leaves, Emerson picked up the pen, and pushing aside the slip, wrote [his name] without a moment's hesitation.

The boy was almost dazed at the instantaneous transformation in the man!

Miss Alcott now grasped this moment to say: "Well, we must be going!"

"So soon?" said Emerson, rising and smiling. Then turning to Miss Alcott he said: "It was very kind of you, Louisa, to run over this morning and bring your young friend."

Then turning to the boy he said: "Thank you so much for coming to see me. You must come over again while you are with the Alcotts. Good morning! Isn't it a beautiful day out?" he said, and as he shook the boy's hand there was a warm grasp in it, the fingers closed around those of the boy, and as Edward looked into those deep eyes they twinkled and smiled back.

The going was all so different from the coming. The boy was grateful that his last impression was of a moment when the eye kindled and the hand pulsated.

The two walked back to the Alcott home in an almost unbroken silence. Once Edward ventured to remark:

"You can have no idea, Miss Alcott, how grateful I am to you."

"Well, my boy," she answered, "Phillips Brooks may be

right: that it is something to have seen him even so, than not to have seen him at all. But to us it is so *sad*, so very sad. The twilight is gently closing in."

And so it proved – just five months afterward.

(Edward Bok, *The Americanization of Edward Bok*)

*The Victorian poet and painter Dante Gabriel Rossetti was rather neurotic about his health. He was a long-time addict of the sleeping drug, chloral (see **Addiction**). On one occasion he took an overdose of strychnine – a deadly poison but also used at the time as a tonic and a stimulant in small doses.*

He [Rossetti] was not fond of telling stories against himself, being intensely sensitive to ridicule, but he could on occasion laugh at his own expense. One story he told was of his childish conduct with a dangerous medicine. It was a preparation of, I think, strychnine, and he had to take four doses a day: the first on rising, the second at noon, the third in the evening, and the last on going to bed. Having an engagement to lunch out of London one day, he was on the point of leaving the house when he remembered that he had not taken his medicine, and returning to the studio he took the dose that ought to have been taken in the morning. He was again on the point of leaving when he remembered that a second dose was due, so he went back and took that also. Once more he was on the point of going when he reflected that before he could return home a third dose might be overdue, so, to meet contingenicies, he took that as well. Fully satisfied that he had now discharged his duty, he sailed out of the house, but before he had gone far he found his hands twitching and his legs growing stiff, whereupon he remembered what his medicine had been, and becoming frightened, he looked out for a cab to take him to the doctor. No cab being anywhere in sight, he began to run in the direction of the nearest cab-rank, and from exercise and terror together he was soon in a flood of perspiration, which relieved his symptoms and carried off the mischief.

(Hall Caine, *Recollections of Rossetti*)

Inspiration

John Milton's great poem Paradise Lost – *the story of Satan's fall from heaven and the expulsion of Adam and Eve from Paradise – was followed some years later by* Paradise Found. *The idea for this "sequel" seems to have come from Milton's friend, Thomas Ellwood, who tells this story.*

After some common Discourses had passed between us, he called for a Manuscript of his; which being brought, he delivered to me; bidding me "Take it home with me, and read it at my Leisure; and, when I had so done, return it to him, with my Judgement thereupon." When I came home, and had set myself to read it, I found it was that Excellent POEM which he entitled PARADISE LOST. After I had, with the best Attention, read it through: I made him another Visit, and returned him his Book; with due Acknowledgment of the Favour he had done me in Communicating it to me. He asked me, how I liked it, and what I thought of it; which I modestly but freely told him. And, after some further Discourse about it, I pleasantly said to him, Thou has said much, here, of PARADISE LOST: but what hast thou to say of PARADISE FOUND? He made me no answer, but sate some time in a Muse: then brake off that Discourse, and fell upon another Subject . . .

Afterwards . . . he shewed me his Second Poem, called PARADISE REGAINED: and, in a pleasant tone, said to me, This is owing to you! For you put it into my head, by the question you put to me at Chalfont, which, before, I had not thought of.

(Thomas Ellwood, *History of his Life*)

Doctor Johnson told the painter Sir Joshua Reynolds that he had written his philosophical story *Rasselas, Prince of Abyssinia* in "the evenings of one week". There's a tradition that Johnson wrote the book at speed to pay for the cost of his mother's funeral and to settle some small debts which she had left. The story isn't quite as neat and straightforward as this but there is an element of truth in it. At the beginning of 1759 Johnson heard that his 89-year-old mother was seriously ill in Lichfield, the town where he had grown up. Johnson, in his house in Gough Square off Fleet Street, was almost without money himself. Nevertheless he managed to scrape together 12 guineas which he sent to pay the costs of her illness. In the meantime he negotiated with the publisher William Strahan over the purchase of an 'Eastern tale' which he had been planning for some time. A price of £100 was agreed. Johnson set to work but as he was finishing the book, ten days after the first news of his mother's illness, he learned that she had died. So, although the writer had not started with the intention of meeting Mrs Johnson's funeral expenses, that was the result of his week's labour. The news of her death may have prompted him to end *Rasselas* sooner than he'd planned in the beginning, and Johnson didn't look at the book again until he accidentally came across a copy years afterwards. *Rasselas, Prince of Abyssinia* was a tremendous success and is still in print in various languages two and a half centuries later.

The idea of writing a history of the Roman Empire came to the historian Edward Gibbon at a very precise moment as he recounted in his autobiography. The monumental work took him over 15 years to complete.

My temper is not very susceptible of enthusiasm, and the enthusiasm which I do not feel I have ever scorned to affect. But, at the distance of twenty-five years, I can neither forget nor express the strong emotions which agitated my mind as I first approached and entered the *eternal city* [of Rome]. After a sleepless night, I trod, with a lofty step, the ruins of the Forum; each memorable spot where Romulus stood, or Tully spoke, or

Caesar fell, was at once present to my eye; and several days of intoxication were lost or enjoyed before I could descend to a cool and minute investigation . . . It was at Rome, on the 15th of October, 1764, as I sat musing amidst the ruins of the Capitol, while the barefooted friars were singing vespers in the Temple of Jupiter, that the idea of writing the decline and fall of the city first started to my mind. But my original plan was circumscribed to the decay of the city rather than of the empire: and, though my reading and reflections began to point towards that object, some years elapsed, and several avocations intervened before I was seriously engaged in the execution of that laborious work.

(Edward Gibbon, *Autobiography*)

In Oliver Goldsmith's play She Stoops to Conquer *(1773) two of the characters are fooled into thinking that they're staying in an inn when they are actually in a private house. Apparently this was based on an incident in Goldsmith's own life.*

It has been said that Goldsmith's comedy of *She Stoops to Conquer*, originated in the following adventure of the author. Some friend had given the young poet a guinea, when he left his mother's residence at Ballymahon, for a school in Edgworth's Town, where, it appears, he finished his education. He had diverted himself by viewing the gentlemen's seats [houses] on the road, until nightfall, when he found himself a mile or two out of the direct road, in the middle of the streets of Ardagh. Here he inquired for the best house in the place, meaning an inn; but a fencing-master, named Kelly, wilfully misunderstanding him, directed him to the large, old-fashioned residence of Sir Ralph Featherstone, as the landlord of the town. There he was shown into the parlour, and found the hospitable master of the house sitting by a good fire. His mistake was immediately perceived by Sir Ralph, who being a man of humour, and well acquainted with the poet's family, encouraged him in the deception. Goldsmith ordered a good supper, invited his host and the family to partake of it, treated them to a bottle or two of wine, and, on going to bed, ordered a hot cake for his breakfast;

nor was it until his departure, when he called for his bill, that he discovered that, while he imagined he was at an inn, he had been hospitably entertained at a private family of the first respectability in the country.

(Leigh Hunt, *Readings for Railways*)

Horace Walpole describes in a letter to a friend how the idea for his Gothic fantasy-romance, The Castle of Otranto, *occurred to him.*

Shall I even confess to you what was the origin of this romance? I waked one morning in the beginning of last June from a dream, of which all I could recover was, that I had thought myself in an ancient castle (a very natural dream for a head filled like mine with Gothic story) and that on the uppermost bannister of a great staircase I saw a gigantic hand in armour. In the evening I sat down and began to write, without knowing in the least what I intended to say or relate. The work grew on my hands, and I grew fond of it – add that I was very glad to think of anything rather than politics – In short I was so engrossed with my tale, which I completed in less than two months, that one evening I wrote from the time I had drunk my tea, about six o'clock, till half an hour after one in the morning, when my hand and fingers were so weary, that I could not hold the pen to finish the sentence, but left Matilda and Isabella talking, in the middle of a paragraph. You will laugh at my earnestness, but if I have amused you by retracing with any fidelity the manners of ancient days, I am content, and give you leave to think me as idle as you please.

(Horace Walpole, *letter to the Rev.William Cole, March, 1765*)

Samuel Taylor Coleridge wrote the following account, almost an apology, for why he didn't complete his poem "Kubla Khan", perhaps the best-known unfinished work in literature. The poem was inspired by Coleridge's experimentation with opium or laudanum, a drug readily and legally available in a variety of "medicinal" forms in the 19th century. (See also **Addiction**.*) The person from Porlock,*

whatever his name, is one of the most famous visitors in English
Literature – not for what he did or said but because he supposedly
prevented Coleridge from finishing this dream-poem. Some people,
though, have doubted whether there ever was a visitor.

In the summer of the year 1797, the Author, then in ill health, had retired to a lonely farm-house between Porlock and Linton, on the Exmoor confines of Somerset and Devonshire. In consequence of a slight indisposition, an anodyne had been prescribed, from the effects of which he fell asleep in his chair at the moment that he was reading the following sentence, or words of the same substance, in "Purchas's Pilgrimage": "Here the Khan Kubla commanded a palace to be built, and a stately garden thereunto. And thus ten miles of fertile ground were inclosed with a wall." The Author continued for about three hours in a profound sleep at least of the external senses, during which time he has the most vivid confidence, that he could not have composed less than two to three hundred lines; if that indeed can be called composition in which all the images rose up before him as *things*, with a parallel production of the correspondent expressions, without any sensation or consciousness of effort. On awakening he appeared to himself to have a distinct recollection of the whole, and taking his pen, ink, and paper, instantly and eagerly wrote down the lines that are here preserved. At this moment he was unfortunately called out by a person on business from Porlock, and detained by him above an hour, and on his return to his room, found, to his no small surprise and mortification that though he still retained some vague and dim recollection of the general purport of the vision, yet, with the exception of some eight or ten scattered lines, and images, all the rest had passed away like the images on the surface of a stream into which a stone has been cast, but alas, without the after restoration of the latter.

❦

Mary Shelley wrote the novel Frankenstein when she was only 19.
She had earlier eloped with the poet Percy Bysshe Shelley to France
and, although they occasionally returned to England they preferred to
travel and live on the continent for the rest of their short time together

*(Shelley was drowned in Italy in 1822, see also **Death**). It was while they were staying at the Villa Diodati on the shores of Lake Geneva that Lord Byron issued the challenge to write a ghost story.*

In the summer of 1816 we visited Switzerland and became the neighbours of Lord Byron. At first we spent our pleasant hours on the lake or wandering on its shores; and Lord Byron, who was writing the third canto of *Childe Harold*, was the only one among us who put his thoughts upon paper. These, as he brought them successively to us, clothed in all the light and harmony of poetry, seemed to stamp as divine the glories of heaven and earth, whose influences we partook with him.

But it proved a wet, ungenial summer, and incessant rain often confined us for days to the house. Some volumes of ghost stories from the German into French fell into our hands . . . "We will each write a ghost story," said Lord Byron, and his proposition was acceded to. There were four of us. The noble author began a tale, a fragment of which he printed at the end of his poem of Mazeppa. Shelley, more apt to embody ideas and sentiments in the radiance of brilliant imagery and in the music of the most melodious verse that adorns our language than to invent the machinery of a story, commenced one founded on the experiences of his early life. Poor Polidori had some terrible idea about a skull-headed lady who was so punished for peeping through a key-hole – what to see I forget – something very shocking and wrong of course . . .

I busied myself to think of a story – a story to rival those which had excited us to this task. One which would speak to the mysterious fears of our nature and awaken thrilling horror – one to make the reader dread to look round, to curdle the blood, and quicken the beatings of the heart. If I did not accomplish these things, my ghost story would be unworthy of its name. I thought and pondered – vainly. I felt that blank incapability of invention which is the greatest misery of authorship, when dull Nothing replies to our anxious invocations. "Have you thought of a story?" I was asked each morning, and each morning I was forced to reply with a mortifying negative . . .

Many and long were the conversations between Lord Byron and Shelley, to which I was a devout but nearly silent listener.

During one of these, various philosophical doctrines were discussed, and among others the nature of the principle of life, and whether there was any probability of its ever being discovered and communicated. They talked of the experiments of Doctor Darwin [. . .] who preserved a piece of vermicelli in a glass case till by some extraordinary means it began to move with voluntary motion. Not thus, after all, would life be given. Perhaps a corpse would be reanimated; galvanism had given a token of such things: perhaps the component parts of a creature might be manufactured, brought together, and endued with vital warmth.

Night waned upon this talk, and even the witching hour had gone by before we retired to rest. When I placed my head on my pillow, I did not sleep, nor could I be said to think. My imagination, unbidden, possessed and guided me, gifting the successive images that arose in my mind with a vividness far beyond the usual bounds of reverie. I saw – with shut eyes, but acute mental vision – I saw the pale student of unhallowed arts kneeling beside the thing he had put together, I saw the hideous phantasm of a man stretched out, and then, on the working of some powerful engine, show signs of life, and stir with an uneasy, half-vital motion. Frightful must it be; for supremely frightful would be the effect of any human endeavour to mock the stupendous mechanism of the Creator of the world, his success would terrify the artist; he would rush away from his odious handiwork, horror-stricken. He would hope that, left to itself, the slight spark of life which he had communicated would fade; that this thing which had received such imperfect animation would subside into dead matter, and he might sleep in the belief that the silence of the grave would quench forever the transient existence of the hideous corpse which he had looked upon as the cradle of life. He sleeps; but he is awakened; he opens his eyes; behold, the horrid thing stands at his bedside, opening his curtains and looking on him with yellow, watery, but speculative eyes.

I opened mine in terror. The idea so possessed my mind that a thrill of fear ran through me, and I wished to exchange the ghastly image of my fancy for the realities around. I see them still: the very room, the dark parquet, the closed shutters with the moonlight struggling through, and the sense I had that the glassy lake and white high Alps were beyond. I could not so easily get rid of my hideous phantom; still it haunted me. I must try to think of something else. I recurred to my ghost story – my tiresome, unlucky ghost story! Oh! If I could only contrive one which would frighten my readers as I myself had been frightened that night!

Swift as light and as cheering was the idea that broke in upon me. "I have found it! What terrified me will terrify others; and I need only describe the spectre which had haunted my midnight pillow." On the morrow I announced that I had thought of a story. I began that day with the words, "It was on a dreary night of November . . ."

(Mary Shelley, *Introduction to Frankenstein, 1831*)

The poet John Keats visits the cottage that belonged to Scottish poet Robert Burns but fails to find inspiration.

We went to the cottage and took some Whisky. I wrote a sonnet for the mere sake of writing some lines under the roof – they are so bad I cannot transcribe them. The man at the cottage was a great bore with his anecdotes – I hate the rascal – his life consists in fuz, fuzzy, fuzziest. He drinks glasses five for the quarter and twelve for the hour – he is a mahogany-faced old Jackass who knew Burns. He ought to have been kicked for having spoken to him . . . Oh the flummery of a birthplace! Cant! Cant! Cant! It is enough to give a spirit the guts-ache. Many a true word they say, is spoken in jest – this may be because his gab hindered my sublimity: the Rat dog made me write a flat sonnet.

(John Keats, *letter to*
John Hamilton Reynolds, July 1818)

What follows is one of the strangest stories of inspiration and its aftermath in literary history. The Victorian poet and painter Dante Gabriel Rossetti was inspired to write by his model (later his wife) Elizabeth Siddall – she was also the model for the famous painting of the drowning Ophelia by Rossetti's fellow pre-Raphaelite artist, John

Millais. The Rosetti-Siddall marriage may have begun happily enough but things soon started to go wrong.

Friends who saw much of them in the earlier days of their married life spoke of their obvious happiness, and protested, in particular against evil rumours circulated later, that nothing could have been more marked than Rossetti's zealous attentions to his young wife. All the same, it is true that very soon her spirits drooped, her art was laid aside, and much of the cheerfulness of home was lost to both of them. Her health failed, she suffered from neuralgia, and began to be a victim of nervous ailments of other kinds.

To allay her sufferings she took laudanum, at first in small doses, but afterwards in excess. A child came, but it was stillborn; and then her mood, already sad, appears to have deepened to one of settled melancholy. I remember to have heard Madox Brown say that she would sit for long hours, with her feet inside the fender, looking fixedly into the fire. It is easy to believe that to a man so impressionable as Rossetti, so dependent on cheerful surroundings, so liable to dark moods of his own, this must have been a condition which made home hard to bear . . .

They were living in rooms in Chatham Place, by the old Blackfriars Bridge, and one evening, about half-past six, having been invited to dine with friends at a hotel in Leicester Square, they got into a carriage to go. It had been a bad day for the young wife, and they had hardly reached the Strand when her nervousness became distressing to Rossetti, and he wished her to return. She was unwilling to do so, and they went on to their appointment; but it may be assumed that her condition did not improve, for at eight o'clock they were back at home.

Soon after that Rossetti left his wife preparing to retire for the night, and went out again, apparently to walk. What happened to her during the hours in which she was alone, what impulse led her to the act she committed, whether it was due to an innocent accident common to persons in her low condition, or to dark if delusive broodings such as I may have occasion to indicate later, it is not needful to say now. When he returned at half-past eleven o'clock he found his rooms full of a strong odour of laudanum. His wife was breathing stertorously and lying unconscious on the bed. He called a doctor, who saw at once, what was only too obvious, that the lady had taken an overdose of her accustomed sleeping draught. Other doctors were summoned, and every effort was made to save the patient's life; but after lingering several hours without recovering consciousness for a moment – and therefore without offering a word of spoken explanation – towards seven o'clock in the morning she died.

Next day an inquest was held, at which Rossetti, though stunned and stupefied, had to give the evidence which is summarized in the foregoing statement. There had been no reason why his wife should wilfully take her own life – quite the contrary – and when he had left her about nine o'clock she seemed more at ease. The verdict was "accidental death". The proceedings of the coroner's court were reported in a short paragraph in one only of the London papers (I have a copy of it), and there the poet's name was wrongly spelled.

This was in 1862, no more than two years after the marriage that had been waited for so long. The blow to Rossetti was a terrible one. It was some days before he seemed to realize fully the loss that had befallen him; but after that his grief knew no bounds, and it first expressed itself in a way that was full of the tragic grace and beauty of a great renunciation.

Many of his poems had been inspired by and addressed to his wife, and at her request he [Rossetti] had copied them out, sometimes from memory, into a little book which she had given him for this purpose. With this book in his hand, on the day of her funeral, he walked into the room where her body lay, and quite unmindful of the presence of others, he spoke to his wife as though she could hear, saying the poems it contained had been written to her and for her and she must take them with her to the grave. With these words, or words to the same effect, he placed the volume in the coffin by the side of his wife's face and wrapped it round with her beautiful golden hair, and it was buried with her in Highgate Cemetery . . .

Thus seven years passed, and during that time Rossetti, who frequently immersed himself in the aims and achievements of his friends, and witnessed their rise to fame and honour, began to think with pain of the aspirations as a poet which he had himself renounced, and to cast backward glances at the book he had buried in his wife's coffin. That book contained the only perfect copy of his poems, other copies being either incomplete or unrevised; and it is hardly to be wondered at that he asked himself at length if it could not be regained. The impulse of grief or regret or even remorse, that had prompted him to the act of renunciation had been satisfied, and for seven years he had denied himself the reward of his best poetical effort – was not his penance at an end? It was doing no good to the dead to leave hidden in the grave the most beautiful works he been able to produce – was it not his duty to the living, to himself, perhaps even to God, to recover and publish them?

. . . at length the licence of the Home Secretary was obtained, the faculty of the Consistory Court was granted, and one night, seven and a half years after the burial, a fire was built by the side of the grave of Rossetti's wife in Highgate Cemetery, the grave was opened, the coffin was raised to the surface, and the buried book was removed.

I remember that I was told, with much else which it is unnecessary to repeat, that the body was apparently quite perfect on coming to the light of the fire on the surface, and that when the book was lifted, there came away some of the beautiful golden hair in which Rossetti had entwined it.

While the painful work was being done the unhappy author of it, now keenly alive to its gravity, and already torturing himself with the thought of it as a deed of sacrilege, was sitting alone, anxious and full of self-reproaches, at the house of the friend who had charge of the exhumation, until, later than midnight, he returned to say it was all over.

The volume was not much the worse for the years it had lain in the earth, but nevertheless it was found necessary to take it back to Rossetti, that illegible words might be deciphered and deficiencies filled in. This was done, with what results of fresh distress can easily be imagined; and then, with certain additions of subsequent sonnets, the manuscript was complete. Under the simple title of *Poems* it was published in 1870, 15 years after the greater part of it was produced, and when the author was 42.

The success of the book was immediate and immense, six or seven considerable editions being called for in rapid succession.

(Hall Caine, *Recollections of Rossetti*)

Boat trips down the Thames provided the inspiration for Charles Dodgson (Lewis Carroll) to produce Alice's Adventures in Wonderland. *Dodgson used to make up stories for the three daughters of Henry Liddell, a fellow academic at Christ Church, Oxford. Alice was the name of the middle one of the three. She gives her own account here.*

Most of Mr Dodgson's stories were told to us on river expeditions to Nuneham or Godstow, near Oxford. My eldest sister, now Mrs Skene, was "Prima", I was "Secunda", and "Tertia" was my sister Edith. I believe the beginning of "Alice" was told one summer afternoon when the sun was so burning that we had landed in the meadows down the river, deserting the boat to take refuge in the only bit of shade to be found, which was under a new-made hayrick. Here from all three came the old petition of "Tell us a story," and so began the ever-delightful tale. Sometimes to tease us – and perhaps being really tired – Mr Dodgson would stop suddenly and say, "And that's all till next time." "Ah, but it is next time," would be the exclamation from all three; and after some persuasion the story would start afresh. Another day, perhaps, the story would begin in the boat, and Mr Dodgson, in the middle of telling a thrilling adventure, would pretend to go fast asleep, to our great dismay.

Arthur Conan Doyle studied medicine at Edinburgh University between 1876 and 1881 where he encountered several academic mentors who would serve as models for his fictional creations. Doyle's own account of the lecturing and teaching methods of Dr Joseph Bell shows clearly that Bell was one of the principal sources of inspiration for Doyle's most famous character, Sherlock Holmes. There was more than a touch of theatricality about Bell, which Doyle later applied to Holmes. The author explains that Bell singled him out by making him his out-patient clerk. One of his duties was to show Bell's patients into the room where the doctor sat surrounded by his students.

Then I had ample chance of studying his methods and of noticing that he often learned more of the patient by a few quick glances than I had done by my questions. Occasionally the results were very dramatic, though there were times when he blundered. In one of his best cases he said to a civilian patient: "Well, my man, you've served in the army."

"Aye, sir."

"Not long discharged?"

"No, sir."

"A Highland regiment?"

"Aye, sir."

"A non-com officer?"

"Aye, sir."

"Stationed at Barbados?"

"Aye, sir."

"You see, gentlemen," he would explain, "the man was a respectful man but did not remove his hat. They do not in the army, but he would have learned civilian ways had he been long discharged. He has an air of authority and he is obviously Scottish. As to Barbados, his complaint is elephantiasis, which is West Indian and not British."

It is no wonder that after the study of such a character I used and amplified his methods when in later life I tried to build up a scientific detective who solved cases on his own merits and not through the folly of the criminal. Bell took a keen interest in these detective tales and even made suggestions which were not, I am bound to say, very practical.

(Arthur Conan Doyle, *Memories and Adventures*)

~~~~~~

Robert Louis Stevenson was in his early 30s when the idea of his most famous novel, Treasure Island, *came to him as a result of a painting. In* The Art of Writing *Stevenson describes how he got the idea and the difficulties of turning it into a full-length book. He also has some interesting comments to make to would-be novelists.*

Sooner or later, somehow, anyhow, I was bound to write a novel. It seems vain to ask why. Men are born with various manias: from my earliest childhood, it was mine to make a plaything of imaginary series of events; and as soon as I was able to write, I became a good friend to the paper-makers . . . By that time [Stevenson was 31], I had written little books and little essays and short stories; and had got patted on the back and paid for them – though not enough to live upon. I had quite a reputation, I was the successful man; I passed my days in toil, the futility of which would sometimes make my cheek to burn – that I should spend a man's energy upon this business, and yet could not earn a livelihood: and still there shone ahead of me an unattained ideal: although I had attempted the thing with vigour not less than 10 or 12 times, I had not yet written a novel. All – all my pretty ones – had gone for a little, and then stopped inexorably like a schoolboy's watch. I might be compared to a cricketer of many years' standing who should never have made a run. Anybody can write a short story – a bad one, I mean – who has industry and paper and time enough; but not every one may hope to write even a bad novel. It is the length that kills . . .

In the fated year I came to live with my father and mother at Kinnaird, above Pitlochry . . . There it blew a good deal and rained in a proportion; my native air was more unkind than man's ingratitude, and I must consent to pass a good deal of my time between four walls in a house lugubriously known as the Late Miss McGregor's Cottage. And now admire the finger of predestination. There was a schoolboy in the Late Miss McGregor's Cottage, home from the holidays, and much in want of "something craggy to break his mind upon." He had no thought of literature; it was the art of Raphael that received his fleeting suffrages; and with the aid of pen and ink and a shilling box of water colours, he had soon turned one of the rooms into a picture gallery. My more immediate duty towards the gallery was to be showman; but I would sometimes unbend a little, join the artist (so to speak) at the easel, and pass the afternoon with him in a generous emulation, making coloured drawings. On one of these occasions, I made the map of an island; it was elaborately and (I thought) beautifully coloured; the shape of it took my fancy beyond expression; it contained harbours that pleased me like sonnets; and with the unconsciousness of the predestined, I ticketed my performance "Treasure Island". I am told there are people who do not care for maps, and find it hard to believe. The names, the shapes of the woodlands, the courses of the roads and rivers, the prehistoric footsteps of man still distinctly traceable up hill and down dale, the mills and the ruins, the ponds and the ferries, perhaps the *standing stone* or the *druidic circle* on the heath; here is an inexhaustible fund of interest for any man with eyes to see or twopence-worth of imagination to understand with! No child but must remember laying his head in the grass, staring into the infinitesimal forest and seeing it grow populous with fairy armies.

Somewhat in this way, as I paused upon my map of "Treasure Island", the future character of the book began to appear there visibly among imaginary woods; and their brown faces and bright weapons peeped out upon me from unexpected quarters, as they passed to and fro, fighting and hunting treasure, on these few square inches of a flat projection. The next thing I knew I had some papers before me and was writing out a list of chapters. How often have I done so, and the thing gone no further! But there seemed elements of success about this enterprise. It was to be a story for boys; no need of psychology or fine writing; and I had a boy at hand to be a touchstone. Women were excluded. I was unable to handle a brig (which the *Hispaniola* should have been), but I thought I could make shift to sail her as a schooner without public shame . . .

On a chill September morning, by the cheek of a brisk fire, and the rain drumming on the window, I began *The Sea Cook*, for that was the original title. I have begun (and finished) a number of other books, but I cannot remember to have sat down to one of them with more complacency . . . It seemed to me original as sin; it seemed to belong to me like my right eye. I had counted on one boy, I found I had two in my audience. My father caught fire at once with all the romance and childishness of his original nature. His own stories, that every night of his life he put himself to sleep with, dealt perpetually with ships, roadside inns, robbers, old sailors, and commercial travellers before the era of steam. He never finished one of these romances; the lucky man did not require to! But in *Treasure Island* he recognized something kindred to his own imagination; it was *his* kind of picturesque; and he not only heard with delight the daily chapter, but set himself acting to collaborate. When the time came for Billy Bones' chest to be ransacked, he must have passed the better part of a day preparing, on the back of a legal envelope, an inventory of its contents, which I exactly followed; and the name of "Flint's old ship" – the *Walrus* – was given at his particular request. And now who should come dropping in, *ex machina*, but Dr Japp, like the disguised prince who is to bring down the curtain upon peace and happiness in the last act; for he carried in his pocket, not a horn or a talisman, but a publisher – had, in fact, been charged by my old friend, Mr Henderson, to unearth new writers for *young folks*. Even the ruthlessness of a united family recoiled before the extreme measure of inflicting on our guest the mutilated members of *The Sea Cook*; at the same time, we would by no means stop our readings; and accordingly the tale was begun again at the beginning, and solemnly redelivered for the benefit of Dr Japp. From that moment on, I have thought highly of his critical faculty; for when he left us, he carried away the manuscript in his portmanteau.

Here, then, was everything to keep me up, sympathy, help, and now a positive engagement. I had chosen besides a very easy style . . . It seems as though a full-grown experienced man of letters might engage to turn out *Treasure Island* at so many pages a day, and keep his pipe alight. But alas! this was not my case. Fifteen days I stuck to it, and turned out fifteen chapters; and then, in the early paragraphs of the sixteenth, ignominiously lost hold . . . I was 31; I was the head of a family; I had lost my health; I had never yet paid my way, never yet made 200 pounds a year; my father had quite recently bought back and cancelled a book that was judged a failure: was this to be another and last fiasco? I was indeed very close on despair; but I shut my mouth hard, and during the journey to Davos [in Switzerland], where I was to pass the winter, had the resolution to think of other things and bury myself in the novels of M. de Boisgobey. Arrived at my destination, down I sat one morning to the unfinished tale; and behold! it flowed from me like small talk; and in a second tide of delighted industry, and again at a rate of a chapter a day, I finished *Treasure Island* . . .

Treasure Island – it was Mr Henderson who deleted the first title, *The Sea Cook* – appeared duly in the story paper, where it figured in the ignoble midst, without woodcuts, and attracted not the least attention. I did not care. I liked the tale myself, for much the same reason as my father liked the beginning: it was my kind of picturesque. I was not a little proud of John Silver, also; and to this day rather admire that smooth and formidable adventurer. What was infinitely more exhilarating, I had passed a landmark; I had finished a tale, and written "The End" upon my manuscript, as I had not done since "The Pentland Rising", when I was a boy of sixteen not yet at college. In truth it was so by a set of lucky accidents; had not Dr Japp come on his visit, had not the tale flowed from me with singular ease, it must have been laid aside like its predecessors, and found a circuitous and unlamented way to the fire. Purists may suggest it would have been better so. I am not of that mind. The tale seems to have given much pleasure, and it brought (or, was the means of bringing) fire and food and wine to a deserving family in which I took an interest. I need scarcely say I mean my own.

(Robert Louis Stevenson, *The Art of Writing*)

Arnold Bennett remembers how the idea of writing his novel The Old Wives' Tale *came to him.*

Last night, when I went into the Duval for dinner, a middle-aged woman, inordinately stout and with pendent cheeks, had taken the seat opposite to my prescriptive seat. I hesitated, as there were plenty of empty places, but my waitress requested me to take my usual chair. I did so, and immediately thought: "With that thing opposite to me my dinner will be spoilt!" But the woman was evidently also cross at my filling up her table, and she went away, picking up all her belongings, to another part of the restaurant, breathing hard. Then she abandoned her second choice for a third one. My waitress was scornful and angry at this desertion, but laughing also. Soon all the waitresses were privately laughing at the goings-on of the fat woman, who was being served by the most beautiful waitress I have ever seen in any Duval. The fat woman was clearly a crotchet, a "maniaque", a woman who lived much alone. Her cloak (she displayed on taking it off a simply awful light puce flannel dress) and her parcels were continually the object of her attention and she was always arguing with her waitress. And the whole restaurant secretly made a butt of her. She was repulsive; no one could like or sympathize with her. But I thought – she has been young and slim once. And I immediately thought of a long ten- or fifteen-thousand word short story, "The History of Two Old Women". I gave this woman a sister, fat as herself. And the first chapter would be in the restaurant (both sisters) something like tonight – and written rather cruelly. Then I would go back to the infancy of these two, and sketch it all. One should have lived ordinarily, married prosaically, and become a widow. The other should have become a whore and all that; "guilty splendour". Both are overtaken by fat. And they live together again in old age, not too rich, a nuisance to themselves and to others. Neither has any imagination. For "tone" I thought of *Ivan Ilytch*, and for technical arrangement I thought of that and also of *Histoire d'une Fille de Ferme*. The two lines would have to intertwine. I saw the whole work quite clearly, and hoped to do it.

(Arnold Bennett, *Journals, 1903*)

The title of one of American novelist William Faulkner's best-known books was arrived at in the following way. Faulkner was using "Dark House" as a working title for a work in progress when he and his wife were having a drink on the veranda of their house in Oxford, Mississippi. Estelle Faulkner, looking at the way the sun fell on the grass and foliage, said, "Bill, does it ever seem to you that the light in August is different from any other time of the year?" Faulkner simply said, "That's it," entered the house and went straight to his study. He crossed out his working title and substituted "Light in August", explaining later that "in my country in August there's a peculiar quality to light and that's what that title means."

Writing to his mistress Catherine Walston, Graham Greene described how the idea for the story of The Third Man *first occurred to him.*

I believe I've got a book coming. I feel so excited . . . I walked
up Piccadilly and back and went into a Gent's in Brick Street,
and suddenly in the Gent's, I saw the three chunks, the
beginning, the middle and the end.

(Graham Greene, *letter to
Catherine Walston, September 1947*)

"The scent and smoke and sweat of a casino are nauseating at three in
the morning." So begins one of the most famous sequences of
twentieth century stories when Ian Fleming's James Bond burst
onto the scene in 1953. That first book, Casino Royale, was followed by 11 more full-length Bond novels and two collections of
short stories. Like Sherlock Holmes, Bond has floated free of his
creator and become an iconic figure, enduring yet curiously flexible
as – in his film incarnations at least – he adapts to the spirit of each
changing decade and is differently interpreted by a string of stars.

Ian Fleming always claimed that he started writing at the comparatively late age of 44 in order to take his mind off the "horrific
prospect" of marriage. For several years Fleming had been con-
ducting an intense, if on-off affair with Anne Rothermere, wife of
Esmond Rothermere, the newspaper proprietor. When Anne
decided to leave her husband she was already pregnant with Fleming's child, and the couple married in March, 1952. In the months
leading up to the wedding, while the couple were staying at Gold-
eneye, Fleming's house in Jamaica, the first-time author embarked
on *Casino Royale*. His biographer, Andrew Lycett, speculates that
his motives were more complex than the simple wish for distraction.
Fleming had long wanted to write a novel, and his background in
Naval Intelligence during World War Two as well as his own literary
tastes, made the thriller his preferred genre. In addition – with a
child on the way – there was a fairly pressing financial motive. Anne
Rothermere was used to being surrounded with smart "literary"
friends. So *Casino Royale* might have been a kind of wedding
present, designed to show that he could hold his own in her circle.
In the event, Fleming eclipsed everybody else, at least in popularity
and sales. By the time he died in 1964 he could be described as being
at "the centre of a large industry". And the Bond franchise,
adaptable, reliable, profitable, shows no signs of fading yet.

Jealousy, Rivalry & Malice

William Shakespeare and the playwright Ben Jonson were rivals, to an extent. One of the ways they competed was in battles of wit.

Many were the wit combats betwixt him [Shakespeare] and Ben Jonson, which two I behold like a Spanish great galleon, and an English man-of-war; Master Jonson (like the former) was built far higher in learning: solid but slow in his performance. Shakespeare, with the English man-of-war, lesser in bulk but lighter in sailing, could turn with all tides, tack about and take advantage of all winds, by the quickness of his wit and invention.

(Thomas Fuller, *Worthies*)

*There are several stories about William Davenant, the 17th-century poet and Poet Laureate, and they include one which he did nothing to discourage: that he was William Shakespeare's illegitimate son (see also **Shakespeariana**). He evidently appreciated a malicious joke, even if it was directed against him. The reference at the end is to Davenant's having lost his nose through catching syphilis (see also the brief story about him in **Love, Sex & Marriage**).*

Sir *William* walking by Temple Bar, a Fish-mongers Boy, in watering his Fish upon the Stall, sprinkled the *Laureat*: who snuffling loudly, complained of the abuse. The Master Begged the Knight's Pardon, and was for Chastising his Servant with some Expostulations, as well as a Cudgel. *Zounds, Sir*, cry'd the Boy, *its very hard I must be corrected for my Cleanliness, the Gentleman blew his Nose upon my Fish, and I was washing it off, that's all*. The Jest pleas'd Sir *William* so well, that he gave him a piece of Money. Since I have given you one old Jest upon the Nose of Sir *William*, I'll venture to throw in another. As he was walking along the Mews, an importunate Beggar-woman teiz'd him for Charity, with often repeating, *Heaven bless your Eye-sight! God preserve your Worship's Eye-sight – Why, what's the Matter with my Eye-sight, Woman?* reply'd Sir *William, I find no Defect there. Ah! good Sir! I wish you never may,* return'd the Beggar, *for should your sight ever fail you, you must borrow a Nose of your Neighbour to hang your Spectacles on.*

(W. R. Chetwood, *A General History of the Stage*)

~~~~~~~~~~~

James Boswell's relentless and shameless pursuit of any and all material for his biography of Dr Johnson is remembered, with a mixture of humour and resentment, by a man called Lowe.

Lowe (mentioned by him in his life of Johnson) once gave me a humorous picture of him [Boswell]. Lowe had requested Johnson to write him a letter, which Johnson did, and Boswell came in while it was writing. His attention was immediately fixed; Lowe took the letter, retired, and was followed by Boswell.

"Nothing," said Lowe, "could surprise me more. Till that moment he had so entirely overlooked me, that I did not imagine he knew there was such a creature in existence; and he now accosted me with the most overstrained and insinuating compliments possible:-

" 'How do you do, Mr Lowe? I hope you are very well, Mr Lowe? Pardon my freedom, Mr Lowe, but I think I saw my dear friend, Dr Johnson, writing a letter for you.'

" 'Yes, sir.'

" 'I hope you will not think me rude, but if it would not be too great a favour, you would infinitely oblige me, if you would just let me have a sight of it. Every thing from that hand, you know, is so inestimable.'

" 'Sir, it is on my own private affairs, but – '

" 'I would not pry into a person's affairs, my dear Mr Lowe, by any means. I am sure you would not accuse me of such a thing, only if it were no particular secret.'

" 'Sir, you are welcome to read the letter.'

" 'I thank you, my dear Mr Lowe, you are very obliging, I take it exceedingly kind. (Having read) It is nothing, I believe, Mr Lowe, that you would be ashamed of.'

" 'Certainly not.'

" 'Why then, my dear sir, if you would do me another favour, you would make the obligation eternal. If you would but step to Peele's coffee-house with me, and just suffer me to take a copy of it, I would do any thing in my power to oblige you.'

"I was overcome," said Lowe, "by this sudden familiarity and condescension, accompanied with bows and grimaces. I had no power to refuse; we went to the coffee-house, my letter was presently transcribed, and as soon as he had put his document in his pocket, Mr Boswell walked away, as erect and proud as he was half an hour before, and I ever afterward was unnoticed. Nay, I am not certain," added he sarcastically, "whether the Scotchman did not leave me, poor as he knew I was, to pay for my own dish of coffee."

(Thomas Holcroft, *Memoirs*)

Novelist and letter-writer Horace Walpole didn't like Dr Johnson as he makes clear in this description.

Often indeed Johnson made the most brutal speeches to living persons, for though he was good-natured at bottom, he was very ill-natured at top. He loved to dispute to show his superiority. If his opponents were weak, he told them they were fools; if they vanquished him, he was scurrilous – to nobody more than to Boswell himself who was contemptible for flattering him so grossly, and for enduring the coarse things he was continually vomiting on Boswell's own country, Scotland . . . I do not think I ever was in a room with him six times in my days. The first time I think was at the Royal Academy. Sir Joshua [Reynolds] said, "Let me present Dr Goldsmith to you"; he did. "Now I will present Dr Johnson to you." – "No," said I, "Sir Joshua, for Dr Goldsmith, pass – but you shall not present Dr Johnson to me."

Some time after, Boswell came to me, said Dr J. was writing the lives of the poets, and wished I would give him anecdotes of

[Walpole's friend, the poet] Mr Gray. I said very coldly, I had
given what I knew to Mr Mason. B. hummed and hawed and
then dropped, "I suppose you know Dr J. does not admire Mr
Gray" – Putting as much contempt as I could into my look and
tone, I said, "Dr Johnson don't! – humph!" – and with that
monosyllable ended our interview – After the Doctor's death,
Burke, Sir Joshua Reynolds and Boswell sent an ambling
circular letter to me begging subscriptions for a monument
for him – the two last, I think impertinently, as they could not
but know my opinion, and could not suppose I would contribute to a monument for one who had endeavoured, poor soul!
to degrade my friend's superlative poetry – I would not deign to
write an answer, but sent down word by my footman, as I would
have done to parish officers with a brief, that I would not
subscribe. In the two new volumes, Johnson says – and very
probably did, or is made to say, that Gray's poetry is dull, and
that he was a dull man! The same oracle dislikes Prior, Swift
and Fielding. If an elephant could write a book, perhaps one
that had read a great deal would say that an Arabian horse is a
very clumsy ungraceful animal – pass to a better chapter –

(Horace Walpole, *letter to Mary Berry, May, 1791*)

*Edward Trelawny, Byron's friend, recalls the competitive, sporting
streak in the poet.*

He bragged, too of his prowess in riding, boxing, fencing, and
even walking; but to excel in these things feet are as necessary as
hands. In the water a fin is better than a foot, and in that
element he did well; he was built for floating – with a flexible
body, open chest, broad beam, and round limbs. If the sea were
smooth and warm, he would stay in it for hours; but as he
seldom indulged in this sport, and when he did, over-exerted
himself, he suffered severely; which observing, and knowing
how deeply he would be mortified at being beaten, I had the
magnanimity when contending with him to give in.

He had a misgiving in his mind that I was trifling with him;
and one day as we were on the shore, and the *Bolivar* at anchor,
about three miles off, he insisted on our trying conclusions; we

were to swim to the yacht, dine in the sea alongside of her, treading water the while, and then to return to the shore. It was calm and hot, and seeing he would not be fobbed off, we started. I reached the boat a long time before he did; ordered the edibles to be ready, and floated until he arrived. We ate our fare leisurely, from off a grating that floated alongside, drank a bottle of ale and I smoked a cigar, which he tried to extinguish – as he never smoked. We then put about, and struck off towards the shore. We had not got a hundred yards on our passage, when he retched violently, and, as that is often followed by cramp, I urged him to put his hand on my shoulder that I might tow him back the schooner.

"Keep off, you villain, don't touch me. I'll drown ere I give in."

I answered as Iago did to Rodrigo [in Shakespeare's play *Othello*],

"'A fig for drowning. I drown cats and blind puppies.' I shall go on board and try the effects of a glass of grog to stay my stomach."

"Come on," he shouted, "I am always better after vomiting."

With difficulty I deluded him back; I went on board, and he sat on the steps of the accommodation-ladder, with his feet in the water. I handed him a wine-glass of brandy, and screened him from the burning sun. He was in a sullen mood, but after a time resumed his usual tone. Nothing could induce him to be landed in the schooner's boat, though I protested I had had enough of the water.

"You may do as you like," he called out, and plumped in, and we swam on shore.

He never afterwards alluded to this event, nor to his prowess in swimming, to me, except in the past tense. He was ill, and kept his bed for two days afterwards.

> (Edward Trelawny, *Records of
> Shelley, Byron, and the Author*)

If Byron could be jealous of others (see above) he also inspired jealousy. He was famously attractive to women and when he was living in Venice in 1816-17 found plenty of opportunities – or rather

they came looking for him. One of his mistresses was called Marianna.
He begins by describing her.

I have fallen in love with a very pretty Venetian of two and
twenty, with great black eyes. She is married – and so am I –
which is very much to the purpose. We have formed and sworn
an eternal attachment, which has already lasted a lunar month,
and I am more in love than ever, and so is the lady – at least she
says so. She does not plague me (which is a wonder) and I verily
believe we are one of the happiest – unlawful couples on this
side of the Alps. She is very handsome, very Italian or rather
Venetian, with something more of the Oriental cast of countenance; accomplished and musical after the manner of her
nation. Her spouse is a very good kind of man who occupies
himself elsewhere, and thus the world goes on here as
elsewhere . . .

Now for an adventure. A few days ago, a gondolier brought
me a billet without subscription, intimating a wish on the part
of the writer to meet me either in a gondola or at the island of
San Lazaro or at a third rendezvous indicated in the note. "I
know the country's disposition well" – in Venice "they do let
Heaven see those tricks they dare not show", etc. etc. So, for all
response, I said that neither of the three places suited me, but
that I would either be at home at ten at night *alone*, or at the
ridotto at midnight, where the writer might meet me masked.
At ten o'clock I was at home and alone, (Marianna was gone
with her husband to a conversazione), when the door of my
apartment opened and in walked a well-looking and (for an
Italian) *bionda* [fair-haired] girl of about 19, who informed me
that she was married to the brother of my *amorosa*, and wished
to have some conversation with me. I made a decent reply, and
we had some talk in Italian and Romaic (her mother being a
Greek of Corfu) when lo! in a very few minutes, in marches, to
my very great astonishment, Marianna, in *propria persona*, and
after making polite courtesy to her sister-in-law and to me,
without a single word seizes her sister-in-law by the hair and
bestows upon her some sixteen slaps, which would have made
your ear ache only to hear their echo. I need not describe the
screaming which ensued. The luckless visitor took flight. I

seized Marianna, who, after several vain efforts to get away in pursuit of the enemy, fairly went into fits in my arms; and in spite of reasoning, eau de Cologne, vinegar, half a pint of water, and God knows what other waters beside, continued so till past midnight.

After damning my servants for letting people in without apprising me, I found that Marianna in the morning had seen her sister-in-law's gondolier on the stairs, and, suspecting that this apparition boded her no good, had either returned of her own accord or been followed by her maids or some other spy of her people to the conversazione, from whence she returned to perpetrate this piece of pugilism. I had seen fits before, and also some small scenery of the same genus in and out of our island; but this was not all. After about an hour, in comes – who? why, Signor Segati, her lord and husband, and finds me with his wife fainting upon the sofa, and all the apparatus of confusion, dishevelled hair, hats, handkerchiefs, salts, smelling-bottles, and the lady as pale as ashes without sense or motion. His first question was "What is all this?" The lady could not reply – so I did. I told him the explanation was the easiest thing in the world; but in the meantime it would be as well to recover his wife – at least, her senses. This came about in due time of suspiration and respiration.

You need not be alarmed; jealousy is not the order of the day in Venice, and daggers are out of fashion, while duels, on love matters, are unknown – at least, with the husbands. But, for all this, it was an awkward affair, and though he must know that I made love to Marianna, yet I believe he was not, till that evening, aware of the extent to which it had gone. It is very well known that almost all the married women have a lover; but it is usual to keep up the form, as in other nations. I did not, therefore, know what the devil to say. I could not out with the truth, out of regard to her, and I did not choose to lie for my sake; besides, the thing told itself. I thought the best way would be to let her explain it as she would (a woman never being at a loss; the devil always sticks by them), only determining to protect and carry her off in case of any ferocity on the part of the Signor. I saw that he was quite calm. She went to bed, and next day – how they settled it, I know not, but settle it they

did. Well – then I had to explain to Marianna about this never to
be sufficiently confounded sister-in-law; which I did by swear-
ing innocence, eternal constancy, etc. etc. But the sister-in-law,
very much discomposed with being treated in such wise, has
(not having her own shame before her eyes) told the affair to
half Venice, and the servants (who were summoned by the fight
and the fainting) to the other half. But here, nobody minds such
trifles except to be amused by them.

(Byron, *letters to Augusta Leigh and*
Thomas Moore, December 1816, January 1817)

The American journalist and book-collector Eugene Field describes
the cool relationship between the ageing poet William Wordsworth and
the up-and-coming young novelist Charles Dickens.

Wordsworth and Dickens disliked each other cordially. Having
been asked his opinion of the young novelist, Wordsworth
answered: "Why, I'm not much given to turn critic on people
I meet; but, as you ask me, I will cordially avow that I thought
him a very talkative young person – but I dare say he may be
very clever. Mind, I don't want to say a word against him, for I
have never read a line he has written."

The same inquirer subsequently asked Dickens how he liked
Wordsworth.

"Like him!" roared Dickens. "Not at all; he is a dreadful Old
Ass!"

(Eugene Field, *Love Affairs of a Bibliomaniac*)

The American poet Walt Whitman was not highly regarded by many
of his literary contemporaries, who thought that he was a sham. This
criticism was particularly made about Whitman's first and most
famous volume Leaves of Grass.

Even so accomplished a man of letters as James Russell Lowell
saw in it nothing but commonplace tricked out with eccentricity. I remember walking with him once in Cambridge [Mas-
sachussetts], when he pointed out a doorway sign, "Groceries",

with the letters set zigzag, to produce a bizarre effect. "That," said he, "is Walt Whitman – with very common goods inside."

(John Townsend Trowbridge,
Reminiscences of Walt Whitman)

Perhaps the most notable literary feud of recent times has been that between the novelists and travel writers V. S. Naipaul and Paul Theroux. It's a little lop-sided with Theroux making most of the running but, even so, has been sustained for several years. Trinidad-born V. S. Naipaul – now Sir Vidia – acted as a kind of mentor to Theroux for some years after the two men first met in Uganda, where Theroux was teaching in the 1960s. There are similarities of subject matter and sometimes of attitude in their approach to a post-colonial world. The rift between American-born Theroux and Naipaul began when the former discovered one of his books, which he'd inscribed to Naipaul and his then wife, being offered for sale for $1,500. There was an exchange of faxes but no satisfaction. Theroux has written an entire book about their relationship, *Sir Vidia's Shadow*, in which he reports that they have met only once since hostilities began. During that chance encounter in a London street Naipaul reportedly said to Theroux, "Take it on the chin and move on." Theroux, however, returned to the fray when he wrote an extended review of Naipaul's novel *Half a Life* (2001) in the *Guardian* newspaper. There he claimed that without Naipaul's name on it the book would have been rejected. He added: "With his name on it, of course, its trajectory is certain: great reviews, poor sales, and a literary prize."

Kings, Queens & Presidents

Edward de Vere, the Earl of Oxford (1550-1604), has been put forward as the "real" author of Shakespeare's plays. The inconvenient fact that he died some years before a number of Shakespeare's later (and greater) dramas appeared has not deterred those who are desperate to prove that someone else apart from Shakespeare wrote Shakespeare. However, Oxford is here remembered for a more minor achievement.

This Earle of Oxford, making of his low obeisance to Queen Elizabeth, happened to let a Fart, at which he was so abashed and ashamed that he went to Travell, 7 yeares. On his returne the queen welcomed him home and sayd, My Lord, I had forgott the Fart.

(John Aubrey, *Brief Lives*)

Sir John Harington was a favourite at the court of Queen Elizabeth I; she was his godmother. He was a soldier, a translator of poetry – and an enthusiast for the introduction of water closets. Some claim he invented the flush lavatory. He also got on well with Elizabeth's successor, James I, as this report of a conversation between the two shows. James was a fierce campaigner against the "new weed" tobacco; one of the king's other interests was witchcraft.

Of late the King received Sir John Harington in audience, enquiring much of his learning and showing forth his own in such sort as put the knight in remembrance of his examiner at Cambridge, for his Majesty sought much to know his advances in philosophy, uttering profound sentences of Aristotle and such like writers. Then he pressed Sir John to read to him part of a canto in Ariosto, praising his utterance and saying that he had been informed of many as to his learning in the time of the Queen. Moreover he asked many questions, as what Sir John thought pure wit was made of; and whom it did best become? Whether a king should not be the best clerk [scholar] in his own country, and if this land did not entertain good opinion of his learning and good wisdom? He asked much concerning his opinion of the new weed tobacco, saying that it would by its use infuse ill qualities on the brain, and that no learned man ought to taste it, and wished it forbidden. He pressed Sir John much for his opinion touching the power of Satan in witchcraft, and asked with much gravity if he did truly understand why the devil did work more with ancient women than with others; to which Sir John replied with a scurvy jest that we were taught hereof in Scripture where it is told that the devil walketh in dry places.

(from *Harington's letters*)

The Restoration poet John Wilmot, Earl of Rochester was a member of Charles II's inner circle at court. The two men went horse-racing together at Newmarket, drank, joked and dined together, as well as sharing a mistress or two. This story of an attempt to cure Charles of his habit of visiting brothels in disguise should be treated with extreme caution. For one thing, it's more likely that Rochester would have been urging him on rather than trying to break him of the habit. However, the picture of the easy-going King that emerges is an accurate one.

The Earl of Rochester agreed to go out one night with him to visit a celebrated house of intrigue, where he told his Majesty the finest women in England were to be found. The King did not hesitate to assume his usual disguise and accompany him, and while he was engaged with one of the ladies of pleasure, being before instructed by Rochester how to behave, she pick'd his pocket of all his money and watch, which the king did not immediately miss. Neither she nor the people of the house were made acquainted with the quality of their visitor, nor had the least suspicion who he was.

When the intrigue was ended, the King enquired for Rochester but was told he had quitted the house, without taking leave. But into what embarrassment was he thrown when upon searching his pockets, in order to discharge the reckoning, he found his money gone; he was then reduced to ask the favour of the jezebel to give him credit till tomorrow, as the gentleman who came with him had not returned, who was to have pay'd for both. The consequence of this request was, he was abused, and laughed at; and the old woman told him, that she had often been served such dirty tricks, and would not permit him to stir till the reckoning was paid, and then called one of her bullies to take care of him.

In this ridiculous distress stood the British monarch, the prisoner of a bawd, and the life upon whom the nation's hopes were fixed, put in the power of a ruffian. After many altercations the King at last proposed that she should accept a ring which he took off his finger, in pledge for her money, which she likewise refused, and told him, that as she was no judge of the value of the ring, she did not choose to accept such a pledge. The King then desired that a jeweller might be called to give his opinion on the value of it but he was answered that the expedient was impracticable as no jeweller could then be supposed to be out of bed. After much entreaty, his Majesty at last prevailed upon the fellow to knock up a jeweller and show him the ring, which as soon as he had inspected, he stood amazed and enquired, with eyes fixed upon the fellow: who he had got in his house? To which the man answered, "A black-looking ugly son of a whore who had no money in his pocket and was obliged to pawn his ring."

"The ring," says the jeweller, "is so immensely rich that but one man in the nation could afford to wear it; and that one is the King."

The jeweller, being astonished at this incident, went out with the bully, in order to be fully satisfied of so extraordinary an affair; and as soon as he entered the room, he fell on his knees, and with the utmost respect presented the ring to his Majesty. The old jezebel and the bully finding the extraordinary quality of their guest were now confounded and asked pardon most submissively on their knees. The King in his best-natured manner forgave them, and laughing asked them whether the ring would bear another bottle.

Thus ended this adventure, in which the King learned how dangerous it was to risk his person in night frolics.

(Theophilus Cibber, *Lives of the Poets*)

Dr Johnson had an early encounter with royalty when taken to London to see the queen.

At the age of two years Mr Johnson was brought up to London by his mother, to be touched by Queen Anne for the scrophulous evil*, which terribly afflicted his childhood, and left such marks as greatly disfigured a countenance naturally harsh and rugged, besides doing irreparable damage to the auricular organs, which never could perform their functions since I knew him; and it was owing to that horrible disorder too, that one eye was perfectly useless to him; that defect, however, was not observable, the eyes looked both alike. As Mr Johnson had an astonishing memory, I asked him, if he could remember Queen Anne at all? He had (he said) a confused, but somehow a sort of solemn recollection of a lady in diamonds, and a long black hood.

(Hesther Lynch Piozzi, *Anecdotes of Samuel Johnson*)

Dr Johnson did eventually meet a monarch face to face. His biographer Boswell describes how Frederick Barnard, the librarian of George III, arranged a meeting between the two men.

His Majesty having been informed of his occasional visits, was pleased to signify a desire that he should be told when Dr Johnson came next to the library. Accordingly, the next time that Johnson did come, as soon as he was fairly engaged with a book, on which, while he sat by the fire, he seemed quite intent, Mr Barnard stole round to the apartment where the King was, and, in obedience to his Majesty's commands, mentioned that

* Scrophulous evil – form of tuberculosis affecting the lymph glands in the neck and sometimes known as the king's evil, because the touch of a monarch was supposed to cure it.

Dr Johnson was then in the library. His Majesty said he was at leisure, and would go to him; upon which Mr Barnard took one of the candles that stood on the King's table, and lighted his Majesty through a suite of rooms, till they came to a private door into the library, of which his Majesty had the key. Being entered, Mr Barnard stepped forward hastily to Dr Johnson, who was still in a profound study, and whispered him, "Sir, here is the King." Johnson started up, and stood still. His Majesty approached him, and at once was courteously easy.

His Majesty began by observing, that he understood he came sometimes to the library; and then mentioned his having heard that the Doctor had been lately at Oxford, and asked him if he was not fond of going thither. To which Johnson answered, that he was indeed fond of going to Oxford sometimes, but was likewise glad to come back again . . .

His Majesty inquired if he was then writing anything. He answered, he was not, for he had pretty well told the world what he knew, and must now read to acquire more knowledge. The King, as it should seem with a view to urge him to rely on his own stores as an original writer, and to continue his labours, then said, "I do not think you borrow much from any body." Johnson said, he thought he had already done his part as a writer. "I should have thought so too," said the King, "if you had not written so well." – Johnson observed to me, upon this, that "No man could have paid a handsomer compliment; and it was fit for a king to pay. It was decisive." When asked by another friend, at Sir Joshua Reynolds', whether he made any reply to this high compliment, he answered, "No, sir. When the King had said it, it was to be so. It was not for me to bandy civilities with my Sovereign." Perhaps no man who had spent his whole life in courts could have shown a more nice and dignified sense of true politeness, than Johnson did in this instance.

His Majesty having observed to him that he supposed he must have read a great deal; Johnson answered, that he thought more than he read; that he had read a great deal in the early part of his life, but having fallen into ill health, he had not been able to read much, compared with others: for instance, he said he had not read much, compared with Dr Warburton. Upon which the King said, that he heard Dr Warburton was a man of such general knowledge, that you could scarce talk with him on any subject on which he was not qualified to speak; and that his learning resembled Garrick's acting, in its universality . . .

During the whole of this interview, Johnson talked to his Majesty with profound respect, but still in his firm manly manner, with a sonorous voice, and never in that subdued tone which is commonly used at the levee and in the drawing-room. After the King withdrew, Johnson showed himself highly pleased with his Majesty's conversation, and gracious behaviour. He said to Mr Barnard, "Sir, they may talk of the King as they will; but he is the finest gentleman I have ever seen."

(James Boswell, *Life of Johnson*)

If Johnson's meeting with George III was a comparatively happy and coherent one, the same can't really be said of novelist Fanny Burney's encounter with the monarch in Kew Gardens. The King was suffering from one of his fits of mental disorder and his doctors were in close attendance. This is Fanny Burney's own account of what happened.

I had proceeded in my quick way, nearly half the round, when I suddenly perceived, through some trees, two or three figures. Relying on the instructions of Dr John [Willis], I concluded them to be workmen and gardeners; yet I tried to look sharp, and in so doing, as they were less shaded, I thought I saw the person of his Majesty!

Alarmed past all possible expression, I waited not to know more, but turning back, ran off with all my might. But what was my terror to hear myself pursued! – to hear the voice of the King himself loudly and hoarsely calling after me: "Miss Burney! Miss Burney!"

I protest I was ready to die. I knew not in what state he might be at the time; I only knew the orders to keep out of his way were universal; that the Queen would highly disapprove of any unauthorized meeting, and that the very action of my running away might deeply, in his present irritable state, offend him. Nevertheless, on I ran, too terrified to stop, and in search of some short passage, for the garden is full of little labyrinths, by which I might escape.

The steps still pursued me, and still the poor hoarse and altered voice rang in my ears – more and more footsteps resounded frightfully behind me – the attendants all running, to catch their eager master, and the voices of the two Doctor Willises loudly exhorting him not to heat himself so unmercifully.

Heavens, how I ran! . . .

Soon after, I heard other voices, shriller, though less nervous, call out: "Stop! Stop! Stop!"

I could by no means consent . . .

I knew not to what I might be exposed, should the malady be then high, and take the turn of resentment. Still, therefore, on I flew; and such was my speed, so almost incredible to relate or recollect, that I fairly believe no one of the whole party could have overtaken me, if these words, from one of the attendants, had not reached me: "Doctor Willis begs you to stop!" "I cannot! I cannot!" I answered, still flying on, when he called out: "You must, ma'am; it hurts the King to run." Then, indeed, I stopped – in a state of fear amounting to agony. I turned round, I saw the two Doctors had got the King between them, and three attendants of Dr Willis's were hovering about . . .

When they were within a few yards of me, the King called out: "Why did you run away?"

Shocked at a question impossible to answer, yet a little assured by the mild tone of his voice, I instantly forced myself forward, to meet him . . .

The effort answered: I looked up, and met all his wonted benignity of countenance, though something still of wildness in his eyes. Think, however, of my surprise, to feel him put both his hands round my two shoulders, and then kiss my cheek!

I wonder I did not really sink, so exquisite was my affright when I saw him spread out his arms! Involuntarily, I concluded he meant to crush me: but the Willises, who have never seen him till this fatal illness, not knowing how very extraordinary an action this was with him, simply smiled and looked pleased, supposing, perhaps, it was his customary salutation!

He now spoke in such terms of his pleasure in seeing me, that I soon lost the whole of my terror; astonishment to find him so nearly well, and gratification to see him so pleased, removed every uneasy feeling . . . What a conversation followed! When he saw me fearless, he grew more and more alive, and made me walk close by his side, away from the attendants, and even the Willises themselves, who, to indulge him, retreated. I own myself not completely composed, but alarm I could entertain no more.

Everything that came uppermost in his mind he mentioned; he seemed to have just such remains of his flightiness as heated his imagination without deranging his reason, and robbed him of all control over his speech, though nearly in his perfect state of mind as to his opinions.

What did he not say! He opened his whole heart to me – expounded all his sentiments, and acquainted me with all his intentions.

He assured me he was quite well – as well as he had ever been in his life; and then inquired how I did, and how I went on? and whether I was more comfortable? If these questions, in their implication, surprised me, imagine how that surprise must increase when he proceeded to explain them! He asked after the coadjutrix [i.e. Fanny Burney's associate – Burney was in the Queen's service, and did not get on with another of the ladies-in-waiting], laughing, and saying, "Never mind her – don't be oppressed – I am your friend! don't let her cast you down! I know you have a hard time of it – but don't mind her!"

Almost thunderstruck with astonishment, I merely curtsied to his kind "I am your friend", and said nothing.

Then presently he added: "Stick to your father – stick to your own family – let them be your objects."

How readily I assented !

Again he repeated all I have just written, nearly in the same words, but ended it more seriously: he suddenly stopped, and held me to stop too, and putting his hand on his breast, in the most solemn manner, he gravely and slowly said: "I will protect you! – I promise you that – and therefore depend upon me!"

I thanked him; and the Willises, thinking him rather too elevated, came to propose my walking on. "No, no, no!" he cried, a hundred times in a breath; and their good humour prevailed, and they let him again walk on with his new companion . . .

He next talked to me a great deal of my dear father, and made a thousand inquiries concerning his History of Music. This brought him to his favourite theme, Handel; and he told me innumerable anecdotes of him, and particularly that celebrated tale of Handel's saying of himself, when a boy: "While that boy lives, my music will never want a protector." And this, he said, I might relate to my father.

Then he ran over most of his oratorios, attempting to sing the subjects of several airs and choruses, but so dreadfully hoarse that the sound was terrible.

Dr Willis, quite alarmed at this exertion, feared he would do himself harm, and again proposed a separation. "No! No! No!" he exclaimed, "not yet; I have something I must just mention first."

Dr Willis, delighted to comply, even when uneasy at compliance, again gave way.

The good King then greatly affected me. He began upon my revered old friend, Mrs Delany; and he spoke of her with such warmth – such kindness! "She was my friend!" he cried, "and I loved her as a friend! I have made a memorandum when I lost her – I will shew it to you."

He pulled out a pocket-book, and rummaged some time, but to no purpose.

The tears stood in his eyes – he wiped them, and Dr Willis again became very anxious. "Come, sir," he cried, "now do come in and let the lady go on her walk – come, now, you have talked a long while – so we'll go in – if your Majesty pleases."

"No, no!" he cried, "I want to ask her a few questions; I have lived so long out of the world, I know nothing!" He then told me he was very much dissatisfied with several of his state officers, and meant to form an entire new establishment. He took a paper out of his pocket-book, and shewed me his new list.

This was the wildest thing that passed; and Dr John Willis now seriously urged our separating; but he would not consent;

he had only three more words to say, he declared, and again he conquered.

He now spoke of my father, with still more kindness, and told me he ought to have had the post of Master of the Band, and not that poor little musician Parsons, who was not fit for it: "But Lord Salisbury," he cried, "used your father very ill in that business, and so he did me! However, I have dashed out his name, and I shall put your father's in – as soon as I get loose again!"

This again – how affecting was this!

"And what," cried he, "has your father got at last? Nothing, but that poor thing at Chelsea? Oh, fie! fie! fie! But never mind! I will take care of him! I will do it myself!"

Then presently he added: "As to Lord Salisbury, he is out already, as this memorandum will shew you, and so are many more. I shall be much better served; and when once I get away, I shall rule with a rod of iron!" This was very unlike himself, and startled the two good doctors, who could not bear to cross him, and were exulting at my seeing his great amendment, but yet grew quite uneasy at his earnestness and volubility. Finding we now must part, he stopped to take leave, and renewed again his charges about the coadjutrix. "Never mind her!" he cried, "depend upon me! I will be your friend as long as I live! – I here pledge myself to be your friend!" And then he saluted me again just as at the meeting, and suffered me to go on.

(Fanny Burney, *Diary and Letters*)

Edward Gibbon's monumental work Decline and Fall *did not receive a very grateful recognition from its royal recipient, according to this well-known story.*

The Duke of Gloucester, brother of King George III, permitted Mr Gibbon to present him with the first volume of *The History of the Decline and Fall of the Roman Empire*. When the second volume of that work appeared, it was quite in order that it should be presented to His Royal Highness in like manner. The prince received the author with much good nature and affability, saying to him, as he laid the quarto on the table,

"Another damn'd thick, square book! Always scribble, scribble, scribble! Eh! Mr Gibbon?"

(Henry Digby Beste, *Personal and Literary Memorials*)

Not everybody was as concerned as Dr Johnson or Fanny Burney at the idea of meeting King George III. The playwright Richard Brinsley Sheridan, in particular, raised casualness to a kind of art form.

Another instance of his neglect for his own interest came (amongst many others) to my knowledge. He had a particular desire to have an audience of his late Majesty, who was then at Windsor; it was on some point which he wished to carry, for the good of the theatre. He mentioned it to his present Majesty [i.e. George IV], who, with the kindness which on every occasion he shewed him, did him the honour to say, that he would take him to Windsor himself; and appointed him to be at Carlton House, to set off with His Royal Highness precisely at eleven o'clock. He called upon me, and said, "My dear Mic, I am going to Windsor with the Prince the day after tomorrow; I must be with him at eleven o'clock in the morning, to a moment, and to be in readiness at that early hour, you must give me a bed at your house; I shall then only have to cross the way to Carlton House, and be punctual to the appointment of His Royal Highness."

I had no bed to offer him but my own, which I ordered to be got in readiness for him; and he, with his brother in-law, Charles Ward, came to dinner with me. Amongst other things at table, there was a roast neck of mutton, which was sent away untouched. As the servant was taking it out of the room, I observed, "There goes a dinner fit for a king," alluding to his late Majesty's known partiality for that particular dish.

The next morning I went out of town, to dine and sleep, purposely to accommodate Mr Sheridan with my bed; and got home again about four o'clock in the afternoon, when I was told by my servant, that Mr Sheridan was upstairs still, fast asleep – that he had been sent for, several times, from Carlton House, but nothing could prevail upon him to get up.

It appears that, in about an hour after I had quitted town, he called at the saloon, and told my servant-maid, that "he knew she had a dinner fit for a king in the house – a cold roast neck of mutton," and asked her if she had any wine. She told him there were, in a closet, five bottles of port, two of madeira, and one of brandy; the whole of which I found that he, Richardson, and Charles Ward, after eating the neck of mutton for dinner, had consumed: on hearing this, it was easy to account for his drowsiness in the morning. He was not able to raise his head from his pillow, nor did he get out of bed until seven o'clock, when he had some dinner.

(Michael Kelly, *Reminiscences*)

Jane Austen never met royalty but she discovered in a roundabout way that one of her fans was the Prince of Wales or Prince Regent (the future George IV).

It was not till towards the close of her life, when the last of the works that she saw published was in the press, that she received the only mark of distinction ever bestowed upon her; and that was remarkable for the high quarter whence it emanated rather than for any actual increase of fame that it conferred. It happened thus. In the autumn of 1815 she nursed her brother Henry through a dangerous fever and slow convalescence at his house in Hans Place. He was attended by one of the Prince Regent's physicians. All attempts to keep her name secret had at this time ceased, and though it had never appeared on a title-page, all who cared to know might easily learn it: and the friendly physician was aware that his patient's nurse was the author of "Pride and Prejudice". Accordingly he informed her one day that the Prince was a great admirer of her novels; that he read them often, and kept a set in every one of his residences; that he himself therefore had thought it right to inform his Royal Highness that Miss Austen was staying in London, and that the Prince had desired Mr Clarke, the librarian of Carlton House, to wait upon her. The next day Mr Clarke made his appearance, and invited her to Carlton House, saying that he had the Prince's instructions to show her the library and other apartments, and to pay her every possible attention. The invitation was of course accepted, and during the visit to Carlton House Mr Clarke declared himself commissioned to say that if Miss Austen had any other novel forthcoming she was at liberty to dedicate it to the Prince. Accordingly such a dedication was immediately prefixed to "Emma", which was at that time in the press.

(J. E. Austen-Leigh, *A Memoir of Jane Austen*)

In a magazine article American author Nathaniel Hawthorne recalled a meeting with Abraham Lincoln. Hawthorne's group was ushered in to see the President at the White House together with a delegation of whip-manufacturers. This was during the Civil War. The passages describing Lincoln's personal appearance were considered by the magazine editor to be not "wise or tasteful" and were omitted from the article when it was first published.

By and by there was a little stir on the staircase and in the passageway, and in lounged a tall, loose-jointed figure, of an exaggerated Yankee port and demeanor, whom (as being about the homeliest man I ever saw, yet by no means repulsive or disagreeable) it was impossible not to recognize as Uncle Abe . . .

There is no describing his lengthy awkwardness, nor the uncouthness of his movement; and yet it seemed as if I had been in the habit of seeing him daily, and had shaken hands with him a thousand times in some village street; so true was he to the aspect of the pattern American, though with a certain extravagance which, possibly, I exaggerated still further by the delighted eagerness with which I took it in. If put to guess his calling and livelihood, I should have taken him for a country schoolmaster as soon as anything else. He was dressed in a rusty black frock-coat and pantaloons, unbrushed, and worn so faithfully that the suit had adapted itself to the curves and angularities of his figure, and had grown to be an outer skin of the man. He had shabby slippers on his feet. His hair was black, still unmixed with gray, stiff, somewhat bushy, and had apparently been acquainted with neither brush nor comb that morning, after the disarrangement of the pillow; and as to a

nightcap, Uncle Abe probably knows nothing of such effemi-
nacies. His complexion is dark and sallow, betokening, I fear, an
insalubrious atmosphere around the White House; he has thick
black eyebrows and an impending brow; his nose is large, and
the lines about his mouth are very strongly defined.

The whole physiognomy is as coarse a one as you would meet
anywhere in the length and breadth of the States; but, withal, it
is redeemed, illuminated, softened, and brightened by a kindly
though serious look out of his eyes, and an expression of homely
sagacity, that seems weighted with rich results of village experience. A great deal of native sense; no bookish cultivation, no
refinement; honest at heart, and thoroughly so, and yet, in some
sort, sly . . . But, on the whole, I liked this sallow, queer,
sagacious visage, with the homely human sympathies that
warmed it; and, for my small share in the matter, would as lief
have Uncle Abe for a ruler as any man whom it would have been
practicable to put in his place.

Immediately on his entrance the President accosted our
member of Congress, who had us in charge, and, with a comical
twist of his face, made some jocular remark about the length of
his breakfast. He then greeted us all round, not waiting for an
introduction, but shaking and squeezing everybody's hand with
the utmost cordiality, whether the individual's name was announced to him or not. His manner towards us was wholly
without presence, but yet had a kind of natural dignity, quite
sufficient to keep the forwardest of us from clapping him on the
shoulder and asking for a story. A mutual acquaintance being
established, our leader took the whip out of its case, and began
to read the address of presentation. The whip was an exceedingly long one, its handle wrought in ivory (by some artist in the
Massachusetts State Prison, I believe), and ornamented with a
medallion of the President, and other equally beautiful devices;
and along its whole length there was a succession of golden
bands and ferrules. The address was shorter than the whip, but
equally well made, consisting chiefly of an explanatory description of these artistic designs, and closing with a hint that the gift
was a suggestive and emblematic one, and that the President
would recognize the use to which such an instrument should be
put.

This suggestion gave Uncle Abe rather a delicate task in his reply, because, slight as the matter seemed, it apparently called for some declaration, or intimation, or faint foreshadowing of policy in reference to the conduct of the war, and the final treatment of the Rebels. But the President's Yankee aptness and not-to-be-caughtness stood him in good stead, and he jerked or wiggled himself out of the dilemma with an uncouth dexterity that was entirely in character; although, without his gesticulation of eye and mouth – and especially the flourish of the whip, with which he imagined himself touching up a pair of fat horses – I doubt whether his words would be worth recording, even if I could remember them. The gist of the reply was, that he accepted the whip as an emblem of peace, not punishment; and, this great affair over, we retired out of the presence in high good humour, only regretting that we could not have seen the President sit down and fold up his legs (which is said to be a most extraordinary spectacle), or have heard him tell one of those delectable stories for which he is so celebrated.

(Nathaniel Hawthorne, *from
an article in Atlantic Monthly*)

*Mark Twain (Samuel Clemens) describes a meeting with President
Cleveland or rather with the First Lady. As usual with Twain, it's
hard to know whether to take the story at face value.*

When I was leaving Hartford for Washington, upon the occasion referred to, she [Livy, Twain's wife] said: "I have written a small warning and put it in a pocket of your dress-vest. When you are dressing to go to the Authors' Reception at the White House you will naturally put your fingers in your vest pockets, according to your custom, and you will find that little note there. Read it carefully, and do as it tells you. I cannot be with you, and so I delegate my sentry duties to this little note. If I should give you the warning by word of mouth, now, it would pass from your head and be forgotten in a few minutes."

It was President Cleveland's first term. I had never seen his wife – the young, the beautiful, the good-hearted, the sympathetic, the fascinating. Sure enough, just as I had finished dressing to go to the White House I found that little note, which I had long ago forgotten. It was a grave little note, a serious little note, like its writer, but it made me laugh. Livy's gentle gravities often produced that effect upon me, where the expert humorist's best joke would have failed, for I do not laugh easily.

When we reached the White House and I was shaking hands with the President, he started to say something, but I interrupted him and said:

"If your Excellency will excuse me, I will come back in a moment; but now I have a very important matter to attend to, and it must be attended to at once."

I turned to Mrs Cleveland, the young, the beautiful, the fascinating, and gave her my card, on the back of which I had written "He didn't" – and I asked her to sign her name below those words.

She said: "He didn't? He didn't what?"

"Oh," I said, "never mind. We cannot stop to discuss that now. This is urgent. Won't you please sign your name?" (I handed her a fountain-pen.)

"Why," she said, "I cannot commit myself in that way. Who is it that didn't? – and what is it that he didn't?"

"Oh," I said, "time is flying, flying, flying. Won't you take me out of my distress and sign your name to it? It's all right. I give you my word it's all right."

She looked nonplussed; but hesitatingly and mechanically she took the pen and said: "I will sign it. I will take the risk. But you must tell me all about it right afterward, so that you can be arrested before you get out of the house in case there should be anything criminal about this."

Then she signed; and I handed her Mrs Clemens' note, which was very brief, very simple, and to the point. It said: "*Don't wear your arctics* [a kind of boot] *in the White House.*' It made her shout; and at my request she summoned a messenger and we sent that card at once to the mail on its way to Mrs Clemens in Hartford.

(Mark Twain, *Chapters from my Autobiography*)

Last Words

The poet and rake John Wilmot, Earl of Rochester, died in 1680 in a penitent spirit after living a fairly wild life as "a debauched man and an atheist". Here his last hours and words are recounted by Gilbert Burnet.

I thought to have left him on Friday, but, not without some passion, he desired me to stay that day: there appeared no symptom of present death; and a worthy physician then with him told me that though he was so low that an accident might carry him away on a sudden, yet without that he thought he might live yet some weeks. So on Saturday at four of the clock in the morning I left him, being the 24th of July. But I durst not take leave of him, for he had expressed so great an unwillingness to part with me the day before that if I had not presently yielded to one day's stay it was likely to have given him some trouble, therefore I thought it better to leave him without any formality. Some hours after he asked for me, and when it was told him I was gone, he seemed to be troubled and said, *Has my friend left me, then I shall die shortly*. After that he spake but once or twice till he died: He lay much silent: Once they heard him praying very devoutly. And on Monday, about two of the clock in the morning, he died, without any convulsion or so much as a groan.

(Gilbert Burnet, *Some Passages of the Life and
Death of the Right Honourable John Earl of Rochester*)

Poet and playwright Oliver Goldsmith probably died of a kidney infection, aggravated by his own prescriptions (he'd received some medical training at Trinity College, Dublin).

The services of skilled doctors were not brought in until it was too late. A doctor called Turton was treating him and asked, "Your pulse is in greater disorder than it should be from the degree of fever you have. Is your mind at ease?" "No, it is not," was Goldsmith's answer, the last words he ever said.

The American writer Edgar Allan Poe, author of such classic horror stories as "The Fall of the House of Usher" and "Masque of the Red Death" died in Baltimore in 1849 at the age of 40. His chronic poor health was worsened by alcoholism – James Thurber described him as "the first great nonstop literary drinker of the 19th-century." Poe died in a delirium after a drinking bout. There is an unlikely story that his last word was "Nevermore" in response to the deathbed question "Would you like to see your friends?" ("Nevermore" is a repeated reply in Poe's poem "The Raven".) Better evidence suggests that he died calling out for someone called Reynolds – although no one knows exactly who "Reynolds" was – and that his very last words were "Lord help my poor soul".

Oscar Wilde descended into a kind of delirium in his last days in 1900 in a Paris hotel room. Among other things he talked about how "one steamboat was very like another". Fortunately Wilde left some more polished and typical observations among his last coherent remarks. Pointing to the gaudily decorated room he said, "My wallpaper and I are fighting a duel to the death. One or another of us has to go." He is also supposed to have remarked, after calling for champagne, "I am dying as I have lived, beyond my means."

Samuel Butler, the Victorian author of the satirical novels *Erewhon* and *The Way of All Flesh*, lived an isolated, rather friendless life. He had inherited enough money to follow up his enthusiasms, which included painting and music composition, as well as the attempt to prove that the author of the classical Greek poem *The Odyssey* was a woman. He died in 1902. His last words, to his manservant, were: "Have you brought the cheque book, Alfred?"

Novelist Henry James died in 1916 after a succession of three strokes. His long-time friend and fellow-novelist Edith Wharton described his death as "slow and harrowing". James had always been preoccupied with his health, and Wharton speculates that "the sense of disintegration must have been tragically intensified to a man like James". He suffered the first stroke as he was getting dressed and, according to a story told to another friend, as he was falling he heard a voice – not apparently his own – saying: "So here it is at last, the distinguished thing!"

Erskine Childers, author of the classic spy novel *Riddle of the Sands*, was executed in 1922 by the British for his involvement with the Irish Republican movement. His last words as he faced the firing-squad were: "Take a step forward, lads. It will be easier that way."

The American poet Hart Crane committed suicide in 1932 at the age of 33 by jumping overboard from a liner on its way from Vera Cruz to New York. Crane, an alcoholic and depressive, was returning from Mexico which he had visited on a Guggenheim Foundation fellowship to write a poem about the Spanish conquest of Central America. He is supposed to have leapt off the *Orizaba* after saying to his fellow-passengers, "Goodbye, everybody."

As American author Gertrude Stein lay dying of cancer in a Paris hospital in 1946 she made one last attempt to tackle the mystery of life. "What *is* the answer?" she asked her long-time companion Alice B. Toklas and the other people standing round the bedside. But no answer came. So Stein laughed and her dying words were, "In that case what is the question?"

American dramatist Eugene O'Neill was born in 1888 in a New York hotel room – his father was an actor, and the family travelled when he was at work. In the later years of his life O'Neill suffered from Parkinson's disease. When he died at the age of 65, he was being nursed by his wife Carlotta in a hotel in Boston. The playwright's last recorded comment was: "I knew it! Born in a hotel room – and God damn it – dying in a hotel room."

Law

The playwright Ben Jonson discovers a surprising cause of mourning.

B[en] Jonson, riding through Surrey, found the Women weep-
ing and wailing, lamenting the Death of a Lawyer, who lived
there: He enquired why so great Grief for the Losse of a
Lawyer? Oh, said they, we have the greatest Loss imaginable;
he kept us all in Peace and Quietness, and was a most charitable
good Man: Whereupon Ben made this Distich:

> *God works Wonders now and then,*
> *Behold a Miracle, deny't who can,*
> *Here lies a Lawyer and an* honest *man.*

'Tis Pity that good Man's Name should not be remember'd.
(John Aubrey, Brief Lives)

*The 18th-century novelist Henry Fielding was a London magistrate
who took the leading part in putting an end to a crime wave in the
capital, despite the fact that he was badly ill.*

Within a few days after this, whilst I was preparing for my
journey [to Bath], and when I was almost fatigued to death
with several long examinations, relating to five different
murders, all committed within the space of a week, by different gangs of street robbers, I received a message from his
Grace the Duke of Newcastle, by Mr Carrington, the King's
messenger, to attend his Grace the next morning, in Lincoln's-inn-fields, upon some business of importance; but I
excused myself from complying with the message, as besides

being lame, I was very ill with the great fatigues I had lately
undergone, added to my distemper.

His Grace, however, sent Mr Carrington, the very next
morning, with another summons; with which, tho' in the utmost distress, I immediately complied; but the Duke happen-
ing, unfortunately for me, to be then particularly engaged, after
I had waited some time, sent a gentleman to discourse with me
on the best plan which could be invented for putting an
immediate end to those murders and robberies which were
every day committed in the streets: upon which, I promised
to transmit my opinion, in writing, to his Grace, who, as the
gentleman informed me, intended to lay it before the privy
council.

Tho' this visit cost me a severe cold, I, notwithstanding, set
myself down to work, and in about four days sent the Duke as
regular a plan as I could form, with all the reasons and arguments I could bring to support it, drawn out in several sheets of
paper; and soon received a message from the Duke by Mr
Carrington, acquainting me that my plan was highly approved
of, and that all the terms of it would be complied with.

The principal and most material of those terms was the
immediately depositing 600 l. [pounds] in my hands; at which
small charge I undertook to demolish the then reigning gangs,
and to put the civil policy into such order, that no such gangs
should ever be able, for the future, to form themselves into
bodies, or at least to remain any time formidable to the public.

I had delayed my Bath-journey for some time, contrary to the
repeated advice of my physical acquaintance, and to the ardent
desire of my warmest friends, tho' my distemper was now
turned to a deep jaundice; in which case the Bath-waters are
generally reputed to be almost infallible. But I had the most
eager desire of demolishing this gang of villains and cut-throats,
which I was sure of accomplishing the moment I was enabled to
pay a fellow who had undertaken, for a small sum, to betray
them into the hands of a set of thief-takers whom I had enlisted
into the service, all men of known and approved fidelity and
intrepidity.

After some weeks the money was paid at the Treasury, and
within a few days after 200 l. of it had come to my hands the

whole gang of cut-throats was entirely dispersed, seven of them were in actual custody, and the rest driven, some out of the town, and others out of the kingdom.

Tho' my health was now reduced to the last extremity, I continued to act with the utmost vigour against these villains; in examining whom, and in taking the depositions against them, I have often spent whole days, nay sometimes whole nights, especially when there was any difficulty in procuring sufficient evidence to convict them; which is a very common case in street-robberies, even when the guilt of the party is sufficiently apparent to satisfy the most tender conscience. But courts of justice know nothing of a cause more than what is told them on oath by a witness; and the most flagitious villain upon earth is tried in the same manner as a man of the best character, who is accused of the same crime.

Mean while, amidst all my fatigues and distresses, I had the satisfaction to find my endeavours had been attended with such success, that this hellish society were almost utterly extirpated, and that, instead of reading of murders and street-robberies in the news, almost every morning, there was, in the remaining part of the month of November, and in all December, not only no such thing as a murder, but not even a street-robbery committed. Some such, indeed, were mentioned in the public papers; but they were all found, on the strictest enquiry, to be false.

In this entire freedom from street-robberies, during the dark months, no man will, I believe, scruple to acknowledge, that the winter of 1753 stands unrival'd, during a course of many years; and this may possibly appear the more extraordinary to those who recollect the outrages with which it began.

(Henry Fielding, *Introduction to The Journal of a Voyage to Lisbon*)

Playwright and wit Oscar Wilde endured three trials in 1895. In the first he unwisely brought a libel suit against the Marquess of Queensbury, the father of Lord Alfred Douglas (see **Mistakes**). *But the evidence which surfaced at that trial concerning Wilde's association with various young men resulted in Queensbury's acquittal. Within*

*weeks Wilde found himself in the dock on charges of gross indecency.
The second trial was abandoned because the jury couldn't agree. A
third followed, and Wilde was sentenced to two years' hard labour. If
there was a single moment when things went wrong for Oscar Wilde in
his encounter with the law, it was during his cross-examination at the
first trial, the one in which Queensbury was the defendant. Wilde was
being questioned by Edward Carson, Q.C. By chance these two
Irishmen had known each other as students at Trinity College, Dublin.
Carson didn't care for Wilde and that probably added an edge to his
cross-examination. On the first day the case had gone quite well for the
playwright but the atmosphere changed on the second as Carson
started to ask about Alfred Taylor, who, detectives had discovered,
seemed to be at the centre of a homosexual circle.*

The second day of the trial was very different from the first.
There seemed to be a gloom over the Court. Oscar went into the
box as if it had been the dock; he had lost all his spring. Mr
Carson settled down to the cross-examination with apparent
zest. It was evident from his mere manner that he was coming to
what he regarded as the strong part of the case. He began by
examining Oscar as to his intimacy with a person named Taylor.

"Has Taylor been to your house and to your chambers?"
"Yes."
"Have you been to Taylor's rooms to afternoon tea parties?"
"Yes."
"Did Taylor's rooms strike you as peculiar?"
"They were pretty rooms."
"Have you ever seen them lit by anything else but candles
even in the day time?"
"I think so. I'm not sure."
"Have you ever met there a young man called Wood?"
"On one occasion."
"Have you ever met Sidney Mavor there at tea ?"
"It is possible."
"What was your connection with Taylor?"
"Taylor was a friend, a young man of intelligence and
education: he had been to a good English school."
"Did you know Taylor was being watched by the police?"
"No."

"Did you know that Taylor was arrested with a man named Parker in a raid made last year on a house in Fitzroy Square?"

"I read of it in the newspaper."

"Did that cause you to drop your acquaintance with Taylor?"

"No; Taylor explained to me that he had gone there to a dance, and that the magistrate had dismissed the case against him."

"Did you get Taylor to arrange dinners for you to meet young men?"

"No; I have dined with Taylor at a restaurant."

"How many young men has Taylor introduced to you?"

"Five in all."

"Did you give money or presents to these five?"

"I may have done."

"Did they give you anything?"

"Nothing."

"Among the five men Taylor introduced you to, was one named Parker?"

"Yes."

"Did you get on friendly terms with him?"

"Yes."

"Did you call him 'Charlie' and allow him to call you 'Oscar'?"

"Yes."

"How old was Parker?"

"I don't keep a census of people's ages. It would be vulgar to ask people their age."

"Where did you first meet Parker?"

"I invited Taylor to Kettner's [restaurant] on the occasion of my birthday, and told him to bring what friends he liked. He brought Parker and his brother."

"Did you know Parker was a gentleman's servant out of work and his brother a groom?"

"No; I did not."

"But you did know that Parker was not a literary character or an artist, and that culture was not his strong point?"

"I did."

"What was there in common between you and Charlie Parker?"

"I like people who are young, bright, happy, careless and original. I do not like them sensible, and I do not like them old; I don't like social distinctions of any kind, and the mere fact of youth is so wonderful to me that I would sooner talk to a young man for half an hour than be cross-examined by an elderly Q.C."

Everyone smiled at this retort.

"Had you chambers in St James' Place?"

"Yes, from October 93 to April 94."

"Did Charlie Parker go and have tea with you there?"

"Yes."

"Did you give him money?"

"I gave him three or four pounds because he said he was hard up."

"What did he give you in return?"

"Nothing."

"Did you give Charlie Parker a silver cigarette case at Christmas?"

"I did."

"Did you visit him one night at 12:30 at Park Walk, Chelsea?"

"I did not."

"Did you write him any beautiful prose-poems?"

"I don't think so."

"Did you know that Charlie Parker had enlisted in the Army?"

"I have heard so."

"When you heard that Taylor was arrested what did you do?"

"I was greatly distressed and wrote to tell him so."

"When did you first meet Fred Atkins?"

"In October or November 92."

"Did he tell you that he was employed by a firm of bookmakers?"

"He may have done."

"Not a literary man or an artist, was he?"

"No."

"What age was he?"

"Nineteen or twenty."

"Did you ask him to dinner at Kettner's?"

"I think I met him at a dinner at Kettner's."

"Was Taylor at the dinner?"

"He may have been."

"Did you meet him afterwards?"

"I did."

"Did you call him 'Fred' and let him call you 'Oscar?'"

"Yes."

"Did you go to Paris with him?"

"Yes."

"Did you give him money?"

"Yes."

"Was there ever any impropriety between you?"

"No."

"When did you first meet Ernest Scarfe?"

"In December 1893."

"Who introduced him to you?"

"Taylor."

"Scarfe was out of work, was he not?"

"He may have been."

"Did Taylor bring Scarfe to you at St James' Place ?"

"Yes."

"Did you give Scarfe a cigarette case ?"

"Yes: it was my custom to give cigarette cases to people I liked."

"When did you first meet Mavor?"

"In 93."

"Did you give him money or a cigarette case?"

"A cigarette case."

"Did you know Walter — ?" . . . and so on till the very air in the court seemed peopled with spectres.

On the whole Oscar bore the cross-examination very well; but he made one appalling slip.

Mr Carson was pressing him as to his relations with the boy Walter, who had been employed in Lord Alfred Douglas' rooms in Oxford.

"Did you ever kiss him?" he asked.

Oscar answered carelessly, "Oh, dear, no. He was a peculiarly plain boy. He was, unfortunately, extremely ugly. I pitied him for it."

"Was that the reason why you did not kiss him?"

"Oh, Mr Carson, you are pertinently insolent."

"Did you say that in support of your statement that you never kissed him?"

"It is a childish question."

But Carson was not to be warded off; like a terrier he sprang again and again:

"Why, sir, did you mention that this boy was extremely ugly?"

"For this reason. If I were asked why I did not kiss a door-mat, I should say because I do not like to kiss door-mats."

"Why did you mention his ugliness?"

"It is ridiculous to imagine that any such thing could have occurred under any circumstances."

"Then why did you mention his ugliness, I ask you?"

"Because you insulted me by an insulting question."

"Was that a reason why you should say the boy was ugly?"

(Here the witness began several answers almost inarticulately and finished none of them. His efforts to collect his ideas were not aided by Mr Carson's sharp staccato repetition: "Why? why? why did you add that?"). At last the witness answered:

"You sting me and insult me and at times one says things flippantly."

(Frank Harris, *Oscar Wilde*)

The most important legal intervention in 20th century British literature took place in October, 1960. This was the month when Penguin Books were prosecuted for their publication of *Lady Chatterley's Lover* by D. H. Lawrence. It was more than thirty years since Lawrence had written the novel but the jury took just three hours to decide that *Lady Chatterley* was not an obscene book and that the publishers were free to distribute a relatively cheap paperback edition of this long-banned volume. The trial is generally seen as a defining moment in the history of censorship in Britain and as the beginning of the "permissive" 1960s. Other prosecutions were to follow – the attempt to ban Hubert Selby's *Last Exit to Brooklyn* in 1967, the *Schoolkids Oz* magazine trial in 1971 – but it was the *Chatterley* case which (depending on your point of view) either raised the floodgates of pornography or opened a window so that "fresh air [was] blown right through England".

The United States was ahead of Britain so far as *Lady Chatterley* was concerned. In 1959 a Federal Court Judge had argued that the book had literary merit and that Lawrence's sexual explicitness and frequent use of four-letter words were relevant to plot and character development. The judge's decision was upheld by the New York Court of Appeals. Penguin Books were undoubtedly influenced by the US court decision and by recent changes in the United Kingdom Obscene Publications Act which stated that a book could still be published, even if it had "a tendency to deprave and corrupt", as long as there was the defence of literary merit, scientific interest, etc. In any case, Penguin were in the process of publishing Lawrence's complete works and, however problematic, *Chatterley* was a necessary part of his output.

D. H. Lawrence wrote *Lady Chatterley's Lover* in the almost certain knowledge that it wouldn't be published in his own country in his lifetime. He'd had brushes with the law before. Some of his paintings had been confiscated from a London gallery in 1929 because the naked figures in them showed glimpses of pubic hair. The publishers of an earlier novel, *The Rainbow* (1915), had been raided by the police because of that book's supposed obscenity and its anti-war stance. So when Lawrence set out in *Lady Chatterley* to deal with sex in a way that was – even for him – unprecedently frank and uncompromised, he knew that he would meet opposition and outright censorship.

Lady Chatterley was privately printed in Florence in 1928 and then sent out to subscribers in Britain. When the novel was inevitably confiscated by the Customs and by postal officials, its value as a "dirty book" rose, just as inevitably. This made it worthwhile for unscrupulous publishers to produce pirate copies, as Lawrence himself described with a mixture of humour and irritation:

"Owing to the existence of various pirated editions ... I brought out in 1929 a cheap popular edition, produced in

France and offered to the public at sixty francs, hoping at least
to meet the European demand. The pirates, in the United States
certainly, were prompt and busy. The first stolen edition was
being sold in New York almost within a month of the arrival in
America of the first genuine copies from Florence. It was a
facsimile of the original, produced by the photographic method,
and was sold, even by reliable booksellers, to the unsuspecting
public as if it were the original first edition. The price was
usually fifteen dollars, whereas the price of the original was ten
dollars: and the purchaser was left in fond ignorance of the
fraud.

"This gallant attempt was followed by others. I am told there
was still another facsimile edition produced in New York or
Philadelphia: and I myself possess a filthy-looking book bound
in a dull orange cloth, with green label, smearily produced by
photography, and containing my signature forged by the little
boy of the piratical family. It was when this edition appeared in
London, from New York, towards the end of 1928, and was
offered to the public at thirty shillings, that I put out from
Florence my little second edition of two hundred copies, which
I offered at a guinea. I had wanted to save it for a year or more,
but had to launch it against the dirty orange pirate. But the
number was too small. The orange pirate persisted."

Lady Chatterley lived an underground existence for several
decades. Like many other suspect books it was unavailable in
Britain but could be purchased by the persistent literary traveller – or dirty-book seeker – in France. Lawrence's elevation
to the status of a great author, even a genius, made the continued banning of one of his most significant works increasingly
questionable, and the court decisions produced by the slightly
more liberal atmosphere of the United States encouraged Penguin to bring what has been called a "test case by arrangement".
The publishers knew they would be prosecuted and may even
have given copies directly to the Director of Public Prosecutions to speed things along. Everyone wanted the status of the
book cleared up once and for all.

What was it about *Lady Chatterley* that brought down the full
weight of the English law on the creation of a man who'd been

dead thirty years? By current standards the book looks pretty tame. But the England of the late 1950s was still a deferential, class-bound place. *Lady Chatterley* describes a passionate affair between an upper class woman and her social inferior, a game-keeper; this sexual crossing of class boundaries was part of the book's shock value. But the greater part lay in Lawrence's description of "thirteen episodes of sexual intercourse" and his taboo-breaking use of four-letter words. During the trial, the prosecuting counsel Mervyn Griffith-Jones itemized these. He told the jury of the number of times the words "fuck" or "fucking" appeared in the book (30 times); similarly for "cunt" (14) and "cock" (rather under-represented at 4), etc.

The publishers had arranged for an impressive array of the literary great and the good to give evidence about the book's merits. Thirty-five experts – novelists, poets, critics – were called by the defence, including Dame Rebecca West, E. M. Forster and C. Day Lewis. Thirty-five more were lined up to appear. In the event they weren't required. The prosecution called only one witness: a detective inspector who testified to the fact that the book had actually been published. It almost seemed as though the prosecution had conceded the case in advance.

The most famous remark in the trial came during the prosecution's very first appeal to the jury, and it served to show the gap – the abyss – between the legal establishment and the "ordinary" men and women who made up the jury. Referring to *Lady Chatterley's Lover*, Mervyn Griffith-Jones asked them two questions which wouldn't have raised an eyebrow in the 19th century: "Is it a book that you would wish to have lying around the house? Is it a book you would even wish your wife or servants to read?"

The jury included a furniture-maker, a dock worker and a teacher. The *Chatterley* trial was a nail, perhaps the last nail, in the coffin of an already-dead England in which a husband might "permit" his wife to read something or in which the average household included servants and a male employer who could be concerned for their moral welfare.

Within a year of its official publication in Britain *Lady Chatterley's Lover* had sold more than two million copies.

Love, Sex & Marriage

Sir Thomas More, the Lord Chancellor of England executed by Henry VIII, was also an author. His most famous work is Utopia, *a description of an imaginary kingdom. In that book it is the law of the land that young people should see each other 'stark naked' before marriage. This was evidently based on the reality of the More household. William Roper was More's prospective son-in-law.*

Sir [William] Roper, of Eltham in Kent, came one morning, pretty early, to my lord, with a proposall to marry one of his daughters. My lord's daughters were then both together a bed in a truckle-bed in their father's chamber asleep. He carries Sir William into the chamber and takes the sheet by the corner and suddenly whippes it off. They lay on their Backs, and their smocks up as high as their armpitts. This awakened them, and immediately they turned on their Bellies. Quoth Roper, I have seen both sides, and so gave a patt on her Buttock he made choice of, sayeing, Thou art mine. Here was all the trouble of the wooing.

(John Aubrey, Brief Lives)

Mary Herbert, Countess of Pembroke, was the sister of Sir Philip Sidney, one of the most charismatic literary and court figures of the Elizabethan age. She was also a poet in her own right and a patron of other writers. John Aubrey, in his Brief Lives, *comments on her beauty and her sexual appetite.*

Mary, Countesse of Pembroke, was sister to Sir Philip Sydney: maried to Henry, the eldest son of William Earle of Pembroke but this subtile old Earle did see that his faire and witty daughter-in-lawe would horne* his sonne, and told him so, and advise him to keepe her in the Countrey and not to let her frequent the Court.

She was a beautifull Ladie and had an excellent witt, and had the best breeding that that age could afford. Shee had a pritty sharpe-ovall face. Her haire was of a reddish yellowe.

She was very salacious, and she had a Contrivance that in the Spring of the yeare, when the Stallions were to leape the Mares, they were to be brought before such a part of the house, where she had a vidette (a hole to peepe out at) to looke on them and please herselfe with their Sport; and then she would act the like sport herselfe with her stallions. One of her great Gallants was Crooke-back't Cecill, Earl of Salisbury.

(John Aubrey *Brief Lives*)

Sir Walter Raleigh, the famous adventurer, explorer, poet and historian, was – in his spare moments – a noted seducer.

He [Sir Walter Raleigh] loved a wench well; and one time getting up one of the Mayds of Honour up against a tree in a Wood ('twas his first Lady) who seemed at first boarding to be something fearfull of her Honour, and modest, she cryed, sweet Sir Walter, what doe you me ask; Will you undoe me? Nay, sweet Sir Walter! Sweet Sir Walter! Sir Walter! At last, as the danger and the pleasure at the same time grew higher, she cryed in the extasey, Swisser Swatter Swisser Swatter. She proved with child, and I doubt not but this Hero tooke care of them both, as also that the Product was more than an ordinary mortal.

(John Aubrey, *Brief Lives*)

When the playwright Ben Jonson visited the Scots writer William Drummond, the talk turned to all sorts of subjects including Jonson's sex life. Drummond later made notes on their conversations.

* Horne – cuckold, i.e. commit adultery.

In his youth [Jonson was] given to Venerie. He thought the use of a maide, nothing in comparison to ye wantoness of a wife & would never have ane other Mistress. He said two accidents strange befell him, one that a man made his owne wyfe to court him, whom he enjoyed two yeares ere he knew of it, & one day finding them by chance was passingly delighted with it, one other lay diverse tymes with a woman, who shew him all that he wished except the last act, which she would never agree unto.

(William Drummond, *Conversations
with William Drummond of Hawthornden*)

❧

*Sir William Davenant, 17th-century Poet Laureate and just possibly
illegitimate son of William Shakespeare (see **Shakespeariana**),
paid a noticeable penalty when he contracted syphilis.*

He gott a terrible clap of a Black handsome wench that lay in Axe-yard, Westminster . . . which cost him his Nose, with which unlucky mischance many witts were too cruelly bold.

(John Aubrey, *Brief Lives*)

❧

Samuel Johnson in his life of the poet John Milton, author of Paradise
Lost, *deals fairly briskly with Milton's wives. His first wife, Mary
Powell, came from a royalist family. Perhaps the outbreak of the Civil
War was responsible for her failure to return to him after a visit home,
but Johnson suggests it may also have been to do with the poet's austere
way of life.*

At Whitsuntide, in his thirty-fifth year, he married Mary, the daughter of Mr Powell, a justice of the Peace in Oxfordshire. He brought her to town with him, and expected all the advantages of a conjugal life. The lady, however, seems not much to have delighted in the pleasures of spare diet and hard study; for, as Philips [Milton's nephew] relates, "having for a month led a philosophical life, after having been used at home to a great house, and much company and joviality, her friends, possibly by her own desire, made earnest suit to have her company the remaining part of the summer; which was granted, upon a promise of her return at Michaelmas."

Milton was too busy to much miss his wife: he pursued his studies; and now and then visited the Lady Margaret Leigh, whom he has mentioned in one of his sonnets. At last Michaelmas arrived; but the lady had no inclination to return to the sullen gloom of her husband's habitation, and therefore very willingly forgot her promise. He sent her in a letter, but had no answer; he sent more with the same success [outcome]. It could be alleged that letters miscarry; he therefore dispatched a messenger, being by this time too angry to go himself. His messenger was sent back with some contempt. The family of the lady were Cavaliers.

Milton's first wife eventually returned to him; she died ten years later.

About this time [1652] his first wife died in childbed, having left him three daughters. As he probably did not much love her, he did not long continue the appearance of lamenting her; but after a short time married Catherine, the daughter of one Captain Woodcock of Hackney; a woman doubtless educated in opinions like his own. She died, within a year, of childbirth, or some distemper that followed it; and her husband honoured her memory with a poor sonnet.

John Milton waited another ten years before marrying for the third and last time.

He then removed to Jewin-street, near Aldersgate-street; and being blind, and by no means wealthy, wanted a domestick companion and attendant; and therefore, by the recommendation of Dr Paget, married Elizabeth Minshul, of a gentleman's family in Cheshire, probably without a fortune. All his wives were virgins; for he has declared that he thought it gross and indelicate to be a second husband: upon what other principles his choice was made, cannot now be known; but marriage afforded not much of his happiness. The first wife left him in disgust, and was brought back only by terror; the second, indeed, seems to have been more a favourite, but her life was short. The third, as Philips relates, oppressed his children in his life-time, and cheated them at his death.

(Samuel Johnson, *Life of John Milton*)

The Restoration poet Charles Sedley was famous for his unbuttoned behaviour. On one occasion at least it got him into trouble with the law. "Oxford Kate's" was presumably a brothel.

Mr Batten telling us of a late triall of Sir Charles Sydly the other day before my Lord Chief Justice Foster and the whole Bench – for his debauchery a little while since at Oxford Kate's; coming in open day into the Balcone and showed his nakedness – acting all the postures of lust and buggery that could be imagined, and abusing of scripture, and as it were, from thence preaching a Mountebanke sermon from that pulpitt, saying that there he hath to sell such a pouder as should make all the cunts in town run after him – a thousand people standing underneath to see and hear him.

And that being done, he took a glass of wine and washed his prick in it and then drank it off; and then took another and drank the King's health . . . Upon this discourse, Sir J. Mennes and Mr Batten both say that buggery is now almost grown as common among our gallants as in Italy, and that the very pages of the town begin to complain of their masters for it. But blessed be God, I do not to this day know what is the meaning of this sin, nor which is the agent nor which the patient.

(Samuel Pepys, *Diary, July 1663*)

17th-century diarist Samuel Pepys may have seemed surprised at other men's public behaviour (see above). When he got up to something it was usually in private. Pepys's relations with his wife Elizabeth were often strained because of his habit of chasing other women (see below). Here he describes how he narrowly avoided bodily harm.

Jan. 12, 1668. This evening I observed my wife mighty dull, and I myself was not mighty fond, because of some hard words she did give me at noon, out of a jealousy at my being abroad this morning, which, God knows, it was upon the business of the Office* unexpectedly; but I to bed, not thinking but she would come after me. But waking by and by, out of a slumber, which I usually fall into presently after my coming into the bed, I found she did not prepare to come to bed, but got fresh candles, and more wood for her fire, it being mighty cold, too. At this being troubled, I after a while prayed her to come to bed; so, after an hour or two, she silent, and I now and then praying her to come to bed, she fell into a fury, that I was a rogue, and false to her. I did, as I might truly, deny it, and was mightily troubled, but all would not serve. At last, about one o'clock, she came to my side of the bed, and drew my curtain open, and with the tongs red hot at the ends made as if she did design to pinch me with them, at which, in dismay, I rose up, and with a few words she laid them down; and did by little and little, very sillily, let all the discourse fall; and about two, but with much seeming difficulty, come to bed, and there lay well all night, and long in bed talking together, with much pleasure, it being, I know, nothing but her doubt of my going out yesterday, without telling her of my going, which did vex her, poor wretch! last night, and I cannot blame her jealousy, though it do vex me to the heart.

(Samuel Pepys, *Diary*)

The reason why Elizabeth Pepys was often in a bad temper with her husband is suggested by another excerpt from his Diary. Deb Willett was a servant girl who Pepys eventually got rid of, at his wife's insistence. Pepys used a code in writing his diary, though not a particularly difficult one: "main" in the following extract means "hand" while "cunny" is pretty obvious.

Oct. 25. And at night W. Batelier comes and sups with us; and after supper, to have my head combed by Deb, which occasioned the greatest sorrow to me that ever I knew in this world; for my wife, coming up suddenly, did find me embracing the girl con my hand sub su coats; and indeed, I was with my main

* The Office – Pepys worked at the Admiralty.

in her cunny. I was at a wonderful loss upon it, and the girl also; and I endeavoured to put it off, but my wife was struck mute and grew angry, and as her voice came to her, grew quite out of order; and I do say little, but to bed; and my wife said little also, but could not sleep all night; but about 2 in the morning waked me and cried, and fell to tell me as a great secret that she was a Roman Catholique and had received the Holy Sacrament; which troubled me but I took no notice of it, but she went on from one thing to another, till at last it appeared plainly her trouble was at what she saw; but yet I did not know how much she saw and therefore said nothing to her. But after her much crying and reproaching me with inconstancy and preferring a sorry girl before her, I did give her no provocations but did promise all fair usage to her, and love, and forswore any hurt I did with her – till at last she seemed to be at ease again; and so toward morning, a little sleep; and so I, with some little repose and rest, rose, and up by water to Whitehall, but with my mind mightily troubled for the poor girl, whom I fear I have undone by this, my wife telling me that she would turn her out of door.

(Samuel Pepys, *Diary*)

John Wilmot, Earl of Rochester, poet and rake, was famous for his pursuit of pleasure.

This Lord (who died at the High Lodge in Woodstock, 26 July, 1680) used sometimes, with others of his companions, to run naked, and particularly they did so once in Woodstock Park, upon a Sunday in the afternoon, expecting that several of the female sex would have been spectators, but not one appeared. The man that stripped them, & pulled off their shirts, kept the shirts, & did not deliver them any more, going off with them before they finished the race . . . Once the wild Earl of Rochester and some of his companions, a little way from Woodstock, meeting in a morning with a fine young maid going with butter to market, they bought all the butter of her, and paid her for it, & afterwards stuck it up against a tree, which the maid perceiving after they were gone, she went & took it off, thinking it pity that it should be quite spoiled. They observed her, &, riding after her, soon overtook her &, as a punishment, set her upon her head & clapped the butter upon her breech . . .

The said Earl of Rochester . . . (among other girls) used the body of one Nell Browne of Woodstock, who, though she looked pretty well when clean, yet she was a very nasty, ordinary, silly creature, which made people much admire.

(Thomas Hearne, *Remarks and Collections*)

The 17th-century playwright William Wycherley met his mistress, the Duchess of Cleveland, through the first of his plays, St James' Park. *She demonstrated that she knew his work, and the dialogue that followed reads like an excerpt from one of Wycherley's own dramas, sharp, sexy, knowing.*

Upon the writing his first Play, which was *St James' Park*, he became acquainted with several of the most celebrated Wits both of the Court and Town. The writing of that Play was likewise the Occasion of his becoming acquainted with one of King Charles' Mistresses after a very particular manner. As Mr Wycherley was going thro' Pall-mall towards St James' in his Chariot, he met the foresaid Lady in hers, who, thrusting half her Body out of the Chariot, cry'd out aloud to him, You, Wycherley, *you are a Son of a Whore*, at the same time laughing aloud and heartily. Perhaps, Sir, if you never heard of this Passage before, you may be surpris'd at so strange a Greeting from one of the most beautiful and best bred Ladies in the World. Mr Wycherley was certainly very much surpris'd at it, yet not so much but he soon apprehended it was spoke with Allusion to the latter End of a Song in the foremention'd Play.

> When Parents are Slaves
> Their Brats cannot be any other,
> Great Wits and great Braves
> Have always a Punk★ to their Mother.

★ Punk – prostitute.

As, during Mr Wycherley's Surprise, the Chariots drove different ways, they were soon at a considerable Distance from each other, when Mr Wycherley, recovering from his Surprise, ordered his Coachman to drive back, and to overtake the Lady. As soon as he got over-against her, he said to her, *Madam, you have been pleased to bestow a Title on me which generally belongs to the Fortunate. Will your Ladyship be at the Play to Night? Well,* she reply'd, *what if I am there? Why then I will be there to wait on your Ladyship, tho' I disappoint a very fine Woman who has made me an Assignation. So,* said she, *you are sure to disappoint a Woman who has favour'd you for one who has not. Yes,* he reply'd, *if she who has not favour'd me is the finer Woman of the two. But he who will be constant to your Ladyship, till he can find a finer Woman, is sure to die your Captive.* The Lady blush'd, and bade her Coachman drive away. As she was then in all her Bloom, and the most celebrated Beauty that was then in England, or perhaps that has been in England since, she was touch'd with the Gallantry of that Compliment. In short, she was that Night in the first Row of the King's Box in Drury Lane and Mr Wycherley in the Pit under her, where he entertained her during the whole Play. And this, Sir, was the beginning of a Correspondence between these two Persons, which afterwards made a great Noise in the Town.

(John Dennis, *letter, September 1720*)

Having succeeded with the beautiful Duchess of Cleveland, Wycherley then found a wife through literature, specifically through her interest in yet another of his own plays, The Plain Dealer. .

Wycherley was in a bookseller's shop at Bath or Tunbridge when Lady Drogheda came in and happened to inquire for the *Plain Dealer*. A friend of Wycherley's who stood by him pushed him toward her and said, "There's the plain dealer, Madam, if you want him." Wycherley made his excuses, and Lady Drogheda said that "she loved plain dealing best." He afterwards visited that lady, and in some time married her. This proved a great blow to his fortunes. Just before the time of his courting he was designed for governor to the late Duke of Richmond*, and was to have been allowed £1,500 a year from the government. His absence from court in the progress of this amour, and his being yet more absent after his marriage (for Lady Drogheda was very jealous of him), disgusted his friends there so much that he lost all his interest [influence] with them. His lady died; he got but little by her, and his misfortunes were such that he was thrown into the Fleet [prison] and lay there seven years.

(Joseph Spence, *Anecdotes*)

The following dialogue is supposed to have taken place between the 17th-century poet John Dryden and his wife:

Mrs Dryden: Lord, Mr Dryden, how can you always be poring over those musty books? I wish I were a book then I should have more of your company.

Mr Dryden: If you do become a book, let it be an almanac, for then I shall change you every year.

When Sir Richard Steele, the 17th-century essayist, playwright and politician, married Mary Scurlock, he called her "Prue", half in affection, half in mockery.

The most striking incident in the life of this man of volition, was his sudden marriage with a young lady who attended his first wife's funeral – struck by her angelical beauty, if we trust to his raptures. Yet this sage, who would have written so well on the choice of a wife, united himself to a character the most uncongenial to his own; cold, reserved, and most anxiously prudent in her attention to money, she was of a temper which every day grew worse by the perpetual imprudence and thoughtlessness of his own. He calls her "Prue" in fondness and reproach; she was Prudery itself! His adoration was permanent, and so were his complaints; and they never parted but with bickerings

* Duke of Richmond – Wycherley fell out of favour with Charles II through his marriage to the widowed Lady Drogheda and so lost the lucrative opportunity of being tutor to Charles' son, the duke of Richmond.

– yet he could not suffer her absence, for he was writing to her three or four passionate notes in a day, which are dated from his office, or his bookseller's, or from some friend's house – he has risen in the midst of dinner to despatch a line to "Prue," to assure her of his affection since noon. Her presence or her absence was equally painful to him.

(Isaac Disraeli, *Calamities and Quarrels of Authors*)

Radical journalist and campaigning writer William Cobbett had no doubts about his choice of wife. He was serving in the army in Canada at the time.

I first saw my wife [in New Brunswick]. She was thirteen years old, and I was within a month of 21. She was the daughter of a sergeant of artillery. I sat in the same room with her for about an hour, in company with others, and I made up my mind that she was the very girl for me. That I thought her beautiful was certain, for that I had always said should be an indispensable qualification; but I saw in her what I deemed marks of that sobriety of conduct, which has been by far the greatest blessing of my life. It was dead of winter, and, of course, the snow several feet deep on the ground, and the weather piercing cold. In about three mornings after I had first seen her, I had got two young men to join me in my walk; and our road lay by the house of her father and mother. It was hardly light, but she was out on the snow, scrubbing out a washing-tub. "That's the girl for me", I said, when we had got out of her hearing.

(William Cobbett, *Autobiography*)

William Cobbett (see above) was obviously a devoted husband. When his young wife was ill he went to extreme lengths to make sure she wouldn't be disturbed. The Cobbetts were living in Philadelphia at the time.

My wife having been brought to bed of a stillborn child a short time before, I was greatly afraid of fatal consequences, she not having, after all was over, had any sleep for 48 hours. All great cities, in hot countries, are, I believe, full of dogs; and they, in the very hot weather, keep up during the night, a horrible barking and fighting and howling. Upon the particular occasion to which I am adverting, they made a noise so terrible and so unremitted, that it was next to impossible that even a person in full health should obtain a minute's sleep. I was, about nine in the evening, sitting by the bed: "I do think", said she, "that I could go to sleep now, if it were not for the dogs." Downstairs I went, and out I sallied, in my shirt and trousers, and without shoes and stockings; and, going to a heap of stones lying beside the road, set to work upon the dogs, going backward and forward, and keeping them at two or three hundred yards distance from the house. I walked thus the whole night, bare-footed, lest the noise of my shoes might possibly reach her ears; and I remember that the bricks of the causeway were, even in the night, so hot as to be disagreeable to my feet. My exertions produced the desired effect: a sleep of several hours was the consequence; and, at eight o'clock in the morning, off I went to a day's business which was to end at six in the evening. Women are all patriots of the soil; and when her neighbours used to ask my wife whether all English husbands were like hers, she boldly answered in the affirmative.

(William Cobbett, *Autobiography*)

Thomas Butts was a patron of the poet William Blake. One day he called at the Lambeth house of the poet and his wife, and was surprised to find the couple sitting naked in the summer-house at the bottom of the garden. Mr and Mrs Blake were reciting passages from Milton's *Paradise Lost* to each other. The poem was an appropriate choice since it describes the Fall of mankind and the expulsion from the Garden of Eden. "Come in!" cried Blake cheerfully to his patron. "It is only Adam and Eve, you know!"

This is the story of Percy Bysshe Shelley's first elopement and honeymoon – as odd as anything else in the poet's life.

Harriet Westbrook, he said, was a schoolfellow of one of his sisters; and when, after his expulsion from Oxford, he was in London, without money, his father having refused him all assistance, this sister had requested her fair schoolfellow to be the medium of conveying to him such small sums as she and her sisters could afford to send, and other little presents which they thought would be acceptable. Under these circumstances the ministry of the young and beautiful girl presented itself like that of a guardian angel, and there was a charm about their intercourse which he readily persuaded himself could not be exhausted in the duration of life. The result was that in August, 1811, they eloped to Scotland, and were married in Edinburgh. Their journey had absorbed their stock of money. They took a lodging, and Shelley immediately told the landlord who they were, what they had come for, and the exhaustion of their resources, and asked him if he would take them in, and advance them money to get married and to carry them on till they could get a remittance. This the man agreed to do, on condition that Shelley would treat him and his friends to a supper in honour of the occasion. It was arranged accordingly; but the man was more obtrusive and officious than Shelley was disposed to tolerate. The marriage was concluded, and in the evening Shelley and his bride were alone together, when the man tapped at their door. Shelley opened it, and the landlord said to him – "It is customary here at weddings for the guests to come in, in the middle of the night, and wash the bride with whisky." "I immediately," said Shelley, "caught up my brace of pistols, and pointing them both at him, said to him, I have had enough of your impertinence; if you give me any more of it I will blow your brains out; on which he ran or rather tumbled down stairs, and I bolted the doors."

The custom of washing the bride with whisky is more likely to have been so made known to him than to have been imagined by him.

(Thomas Love Peacock, *Memoirs of Shelley*)

Shelley's marriage to Harriet Westbrook (see above) faltered when he met Mary Wollstonecraft Godwin. Mary came from an intellectual

family – her father was the writer and philosopher William Godwin –
and this was part of her attraction for Shelley. His separation from his
first wife, however, was not happy.

The separation did not take place by mutual consent. I cannot
think that Shelley ever so represented it. He never did so to me:
and the account which Harriet herself gave me of the entire
proceeding was decidely contradictory of any such supposition.

He might well have said, after first seeing Mary Wollstonecraft Godwin, "*Ut vidi! ut perii!*" Nothing that I ever read in
tale or history could present a more striking image of a sudden,
violent, irresistible, uncontrollable passion, than that under
which I found him labouring when, at his request, I went up
from the country to call on him in London. Between his old
feelings towards Harriet, from whom he was not then separated,
and his new passion for Mary, he showed in his looks, in his
gestures, in his speech, the state of a mind "suffering, like a little
kingdom, the nature of an insurrection". His eyes were bloodshot, his hair and dress disordered. He caught up a bottle of
laudanum, and said: "I never part from this." He added: "I am
always repeating to myself your lines from Sophocles:

> Man's happiest lot is not to be:
> And when we tread life's thorny steep,
> Most blest are they, who earliest free
> Descend to death's eternal sleep.

Again, he said more calmly: "Every one who knows me must
know that the partner of my life should be one who can feel
poetry and understand philosophy. Harriet is a noble animal,
but she can do neither." I said, "It always appeared to me that
you were very fond of Harriet." Without affirming or denying
this, he answered: "But you did not know how I hated her
sister."

The term "noble animal" he applied to his wife, in conversation with another friend now living, intimating that the noble-
ness which he thus ascribed to her would induce her to
acquiesce in the inevitable transfer of his affections to their
new shrine. She did not so acquiesce, and he cut the Gordian

knot of the difficulty by leaving England with Miss Godwin on the 28th of July, 1814.

Shortly after this I received a letter from Harriet, wishing to see me. I called on her at her father's house in Chapel Street, Grosvenor Square. She then gave me her own account of the transaction, which, as I have said, decidedly contradicted the supposition of anything like separation by mutual consent.

She at the same time gave me a description, by no means flattering, of Shelley's new love, whom I had not then seen. I said, "If you have described her correctly, what could he see in her?" "Nothing," she said, "but that her name was Mary, and not only Mary, but Mary Wollstonecraft."

The lady had nevertheless great personal and intellectual attractions, though it is not to be wondered at that Harriet could not see them.

(Thomas Love Peacock, *Memoirs of Shelley*)

Lord Byron's marriage was short-lived. Some indication of the reason for this can be gathered from this brief description of the relationship by one of Byron's friends who was also unsympathetic to his wife, Annabella.

Women, when young, are usually pliant, and readily adapt themselves to any changes. Lady Byron was not of this flexible type: she had made up her mind on all subjects, and reversed the saying of Socrates, that "all he had learned was, he knew nothing." She thought she knew everything. She was exacting, capricious, resentful, excessively jealous, suspicious, and credulous. She only lived with him one year out of her long life. Byron was not demonstrative of things appertaining to himself, especially to women, and Lady Byron judged men by her father and the country neighbours, and Byron was so dissimilar to them in all his ways as to bewilder her. She would come into his study when he was in the throes of composition, and finding he took no notice of her, say,

"Am I interrupting you?"

"Yes, most damnably."

This was to her a dreadful shock; he thought nothing of it; he had received his greater shock in being interrupted.

(Edward Trelawny, *Records of Shelley, Byron, and the Author*)

⟍⟍⟍⟍⟋

Lord Byron's separation from his wife after only a few months of marriage sparked a dynamite trail of rumours as to its cause. She had left the famous poet, taking with her their daughter Allegra. Byron had, it was rumoured by his wife and her supporters, committed some dreadful offence. Anything from homosexuality to some form of Satanism was grist for the rumour-mill. Years later, after the death of Byron's wife, the American author Harriet Beecher Stowe claimed to have been the recipient of the secret from none other than Lady Byron herself: it was that Byron had been guilty of incest with his half-sister Augusta Leigh. This was reportedly the way Byron defended himself, according to his wife (warning: this story needs to be treated with caution).

. . . he said that it was no sin; that it was the way the world was first peopled; the Scriptures taught that all the world descended from one pair; and how could that be unless brothers married their sisters? that, if not a sin then, it could not be a sin now.

I immediately said, "Why, Lady Byron, those are the very arguments given in the drama of 'Cain'."

"The very same," was her reply. "He could reason very speciously on this subject." She went on to say that when she pressed him hard with the universal sentiment of mankind as to the horror and the crime, he took another turn, and said that the horror and crime were the very attraction; that he had worn out all ordinary forms of sin, and that he *"longed for the stimulus of a new kind of vice"*.

(Harriet Beecher Stowe, *Lady Byron Vindicated*, quoted in Ian Hamilton's *Keepers of the Flame*)

⟍⟍⟍⟍⟋

Byron's easy-going sexual prowess is shown in the following extract from a long letter which he wrote in Ravenna to his publisher John Murray. He describes an affair with Margarita Cogni, a baker's wife.

At the same time he was involved with a woman called Marianna
*Segati (see also **Jealousy, Rivalry & Malice**).*

. . . since you desire the story of Margarita Cogni, you shall be
told it, though it may be lengthy.

Her face is of the fine Venetian cast of the old Time, and her
figure, though perhaps too tall, not less fine – taken altogether
in the national dress.

In the summer of 1817, [Byron's friend, John Cam] Hobhouse and myself were sauntering on horseback along the
Brenta one evening, when amongst a group of peasants we
remarked two girls as the prettiest we had seen for some time.
About this period there had been great distress in the country,
and I had a little relieved some of the people. Generosity makes
a great figure at very little cost in Venetian lives, and mine had
probably been exaggerated as an Englishman's. Whether they
remarked us looking at them or no I know not, but one of them
called out to me in Venetian, "Why do not you, who relieve
others, think of us?" I turned round and answered her, "*Cara,
tu sei troppo bella e giovane per aver' bisogno del soccorso mio.*"
["Darling, you're too young and beautiful to need my help."]
She answered, "If you saw my hut and my food, you would not
say so." All this passed half jestingly, and I saw no more of her
for some days.

A few evenings after, we met with these two girls again, and
they addressed us more seriously, assuring us of the truth of
their statement. They were cousins, Margarita married, the
other single. As I doubted still of the circumstances, I took the
business up in a different light, and made an appointment with
them for the next evening. Hobhouse had taken a fancy to the
single lady, who was much shorter in stature, but a very pretty
girl also. They came attended by a third woman, who was
cursedly in the way, and Hobhouse's charmer took fright (I
don't mean at Hobhouse but at not being married, for here no
woman will do anything under adultery) and flew off, and mine
made some bother at the propositions and wished to consider
them. I told her, "If you really are in want I will relieve you
without any conditions whatever, and you may make love with
me or no just as you please, that shall make no difference; but if

you are not in absolute necessity, this is naturally a rendezvous, and I presumed you understood this when you made the appointment." She said that she had no objection to make love with me, as she was married, and all married women did it, but that her husband (a Baker) was somewhat ferocious and would do her a mischief. In short, in a few evenings we arranged our affairs, and for two years, in the course of which I had more women than I can count or recount, she was the only one who preserved over me an ascendancy which was often disputed and never impaired. As she herself used to say publicly, "It don't matter; he may have five hundred, but he will always come back to me."

The reasons for this were firstly her person, very dark, tall, the Venetian face, very fine black eyes and certain other qualities which need not be mentioned. She was two and twenty years old, and never having had children had not spoiled her figure [nor *anything else*], which is I assure you a great desideration in a hot climate where they grow relaxed and doughy and *flumpity* in a short time after breeding. She was besides a thorough Venetian in her dialect, in her thoughts, in her countenance, in every thing, with all their naivete and Pantaloon humour. Besides, she could neither read nor write, and could not plague me with letters, except twice she paid sixpence to a public scribe under the Piazza to make a letter for her upon some occasion when I was ill and could not see her. In other respects she was somewhat fierce and *prepotente* – that is, overbearing – and used to walk in whenever it suited her, with no very great regard to time, place nor persons, and if she found any woman in her way she knocked them down.

When I first knew her I was in *relazione* (liaison) with la Signora Segati, who was silly enough one evening at Dolo, accompanied by some of her female friends, to threaten her – for the Gossips of the Villeggiatura had already found out by the neighing of my horse one evening that I used to "ride late in the night" to meet the Fornarina [baker's wife]. Margarita threw back her veil (*fazziolo*) and replied in very explicit Italian, "*You* are *not* his *wife*: *I* am *not* his *wife*. *You* are his *donna*, and *I* am his *donna, your* husband is a cuckold and mine is another. For the rest, what *right* have you to reproach me? If he prefers what is mine to what is yours, is it my fault? If you wish to secure him, tie him to your petticoat-string, but do not think to speak to me without a reply because you happen to be richer than I am." Having delivered this pretty piece of eloquence (which I translate as it was related to me by a bystander) she went on her way, leaving a numerous audience with Madame Segati to ponder at their leisure on the dialogue between them.

When I came to Venice for the winter she followed. I never had any regular liaison with her, but whenever she came I never allowed any other connection to interfere with her, and as she found herself out to be a favourite she came pretty often. But she had inordinate self-love, and was not tolerant of other women, except of the Segati, who was as she said my regular "Amica"; so that I being at that time somewhat promiscuous there was great confusion and demolition of headdresses and handkerchiefs, and sometime my servants in "redding the fray" between her and other feminine persons, received more knocks than acknowledgments for their peaceful endeavours. At the "Cavalchina", the masqued ball on the last night of the Carnival, where all the world goes, she snatched off the mask of Madame Contarini, a lady noble by birth and decent in conduct, for no other reason than because she happened to be leaning on my arm. You may suppose what a cursed noise this made; but this is only one of her pranks.

At last she quarrelled with her husband and one evening ran away to my house. I told her this would not do; she said she would lie in the street but not go back to him; that he beat her (the gentle tigress), spent her money and scandalously neglected his Oven. As it was midnight, I let her stay, and next day there was no moving her at all. Her husband came roaring and crying and entreating her to come back – not she! He then applied to the police, and they applied to me. I told them and her husband to take her, I did not want her, she had come and I could not fling her out of the window, but they might conduct her through that or the door if they chose it. She went before the Commissary, but was obliged to return with that "*becco Ettico*" (consumptive cuckold), as she called the poor man . . .

She was always in extremes, either crying or laughing, and so fierce when angered that she was the terror of men, women and children, for she had the strength of an Amazon with the temper of Medea. She was a fine animal, but quite untameable. *I* was the only person that could at all keep her in order, and when she saw me really angry (which they tell me is rather a savage sight) she subsided . . .

That she had a sufficient regard for me in her wild way I had many occasions to believe. I will mention one. In the autumn one day going to the Lido with my gondoliers we were over-taken by a heavy squall and the gondola put in peril – hats blown away, boat filling, oar lost, tumbling sea, thunder, rain in torrents, night coming and wind increasing. On our return, after a tight struggle, I found her on the steps of the Mocenigo Palace on the Grand Canal with her great black eyes flashing through her tears and the long dark hair which was streaming drenched with rain over her brows and breast; she was perfectly exposed to the storm, and the wind blowing her hair and dress about her tall, thin figure, and the lightning flashing round her with the waves rolling at her feet made her look like Medea alighted from her chariot, or the Sibyl or the tempest that was rolling around her – the only living thing within hail at that moment except ourselves. On seeing me safe, she did not wait to greet me as might be expected, but calling out to me *"Ah! Can' della Madonna xe esto il tempo per andar' al Lido?"* ("Ah! Dog of the Virgin, is this the time to go to the Lido?") ran into the house and solaced herself with scolding the boatmen for not foreseeing the "temporale". I was told by the servants that she had only been prevented from coming in a boat to look for me by the refusal of all the gondoliers of the canal to put out into the harbour in such a moment, and that then she sat down on the steps in all the thickest of the squall, and would neither be removed nor comforted. Her joy at seeing me again was mod-erately mixed with ferocity, and gave me the idea of a tigress over her recovered cubs.

(Byron, *letter to John Murray. August, 1818*)

The relationship between Victorian novelist Bulwer Lytton, author of The Last Days of Pompeii, *and his wife was a strained one from the very beginning, according to the first story here. And when they*

became Lord and Lady Lytton things went from bad to worse, as the
second anecdote proves. (The couple were separated in 1836.)

Not long after their marriage Mr and Mrs Bulwer Lytton, as they
then were, were travelling in an open carriage along the Riviera,
between Genoa and Spezzia; Lord Lytton was dressed in the
somewhat fantastic costume which at that period he affected. The
vetturino [driver] drove. Mrs Bulwer's maid was sitting beside
him: the happy couple were in an open carriage. Passing through
one of the many villages close to the sea, they observed a
singularly handsome girl standing at a cottage door. Mr Bulwer,
with somewhat ill-advised complacency, turning to his wife, said,
"Did you notice how that girl looked at me?" The lady, with an
acidity which developed itself later in life, replied, "The girl was
not looking at you in admiration: if you wear that ridiculous dress
no wonder people stare at you." The bridegroom thereupon with
an admirable sense of Logic said: "You think that people stare at
my dress; and not at me: I will give you the most absolute and
convincing proof that your theory has no foundation." He then
proceeded to divest himself of every particle of clothing except
his hat and boots: and taking the place of the lady's maid drove for
ten miles in this normal condition.

(William Fraser, *Hic et Ubique*)

Immediately after the production of *The Woman in White**, when all
England was admiring the arch-villainy of "Fosco", the author
received a letter from a lady who has since figured very largely in the
public view. She congratulated him upon his success with somewhat
icy cheer, and then said, "But, Mr Collins, the great failure of your
book is your villain. Excuse me if I say, you really do not know a
villain. Your Count Fosco is a very poor one, and when next you
want a character of that description I trust you will not disdain to
come to me. I know a villain, and have one in my eye at this moment
that would far eclipse anything that I have read of in books. Don't
think that I am drawing upon my imagination. The man is alive and

---

* *The Woman in White* – mystery story by Wilkie Collins, featuring
melodramatic villain Count Fosco.

constantly under my gaze. In fact he is my own husband." The lady was the wife of Edward Bulwer Lytton.

(Hall Caine, *My Story*)

Charles Dickens had a robust, even threatening sense of humour which didn't always meet with his wife's approval. Eleanor Christian remembered a summer holiday spent with Dickens' family in Broadstairs.

Dickens seemed suddenly to be possessed with the demon of mischief; he threw his arm around me and ran me down the inclined plane to the end of the jetty till we reached the tall post. He put his other arm round this, and exclaimed in theatrical tones that he intended to hold me there till "the sad sea waves" should submerge us . . . I implored him to let me go, and struggled hard to release myself.

"Let your mind dwell on the column in *The Times* wherein will be vividly described the pathetic fate of the lovely E. P., drowned by Dickens in a fit of dementia! Don't struggle, poor little bird; you are powerless in the claws of such a kite as this child!"

By this time the gleam of light had faded out, and the water close to us looked uncomfortably black. The tide was coming up rapidly and surged over my feet. I gave a loud shriek and tried to bring him back to common sense by reminding him that "My dress, my best dress, my only silk dress, would be ruined." Even this climax did not soften him; he still went on with his serio-comic nonsense, shaking with laughter all the time, and panting with his struggles to hold me.

"Mrs Dickens!" a frantic shriek this time, for now the waves rushed up to my knees; "help me! make Mr Dickens let me go – the waves are up to my knees!"

"Charles!" cried Mrs Dickens, echoing my wild scream, "how can you be so silly? You will both be carried off by the tide" (tragically, but immediately sinking from pathos to bathos) "and you'll spoil the poor girl's silk dress!"

(Eleanor Christian, quoted in
Michael Slater, *Dickens and Women*)

The Victorian artist and art historian John Ruskin endured a traumatic wedding night from which he never recovered. His marriage to the teenage Effie (she was 18, he was 34) was annulled six years afterwards because of his impotence. The story was told by James McNeill Whistler – admittedly, an enemy of Ruskin.

On their wedding night he [Ruskin] made an alarming discovery: pubic hair. He explained to his bride, after he got his breath back, that he had never seen a female body before (he was over 30, mark you) and hers was not what he had been led to expect. He had formed his expectations of a woman's body, he said, from his observations of Greek and Roman statuary, Aphrodites and Venuses, and they hadn't this curious disfigurement. It was clear, therefore, that this pubic hair must represent a deformity peculiar to his bride. The sight so staggered and repelled Ruskin that he spent the next six years in a solitary bedroom.

The poet Alfred Tennyson tries to impress his wife. There is no record of whether he succeeded.

During an evening spent at Tent Lodge Tennyson remarked, on the similarity of the monkey's skull to the human, that a young monkey's skull is quite human in shape, and gradually alters – the analogy being borne out by the human skull being at first more like the statues of the gods, and gradually degenerating into human; and then, turning to Mrs Tennyson, "There, that's the second original remark I've made this evening!"

(S. Dodgson Collingford, *Life of Lewis Carroll*)

The Victorian poet Algernon Charles Swinburne developed his taste for being beaten when he was a boy at Eton. Flagellation – so popular in 19th-century England that it was known in France as *le vice anglais* – was rife in the English public school system of the period. Eton had its own "Eton Block Club", membership being open to those who'd been birched over the block on at least three occasions. Swinburne's masochistic tendencies were instilled or confirmed by his boyhood experiences. He wrote of one such beating that "before giving me a swishing that I had the marks of for more than a month, the tutor let me saturate my face with eau-de-cologne . . . He meant to stimulate and excite the senses by that preliminary pleasure so as to inflict the acuter pain afterwards on their awakened and intensified sensibility . . ." In later life Swinburne frequented a house in St John's Wood, an area of London known at the time for its brothels and also as the place where upper-class married men kept their mistresses. Here, at no. 7 Circus Road, "two golden-haired and rouge-cheeked ladies received, in luxuriously furnished rooms, gentlemen whom they consented to chastise for large sums." But there was – according to a private account written by Swinburne's friend, Edmund Gosse – a therapeutic aspect to this rough treatment: "these scourgings were in some extraordinary way a mode by which the excessive tension of Swinburne's nerves was relieved."

The interest that the creator of Alice in Wonderland *Charles Dodgson (Lewis Carroll) took in little girls has long been seen as a shadowy area of his character. There was certainly something child-like about him but also child-loving. His feelings were strong but generally suppressed, as this memory by Isa Bowman shows.*

I had an idle trick of drawing caricatures when I was a child, and one day when he was writing some letters I began to make a picture of him on the back of an envelope. I quite forget what the drawing was like – probably it was an abominable libel – but suddenly he turned round and saw what I was doing. He got up from his seat and turned very red, frightening me very much. Then he took my poor little drawing, and tearing it into small pieces threw it into the fire without a word. Afterwards he came suddenly to me, and saying nothing, caught me up in his arms and kissed me passionately. I was only ten or eleven years of age at the time but now the incident comes back to me very clearly, and I can see it as if it happened but yesterday – the sudden snatching of my picture, the hurried striding across the room, and then the tender light in his face as he caught me up to him and kissed me.

The sexual orientation of the highly distinguished novelist Henry James has never been entirely clear. Suppression and reticence are its hallmarks, as the following story perhaps suggests.

In 1891 . . . [James] had a dachshund bitch with a beautiful countenance. He sat with the dachshund in his lap much of the time. We were speaking on the subject of sex in women and were comparing European women with American women in this regard. I had a notion that American women had less of this quality than European women, that in many American women it was negative, and in European women positive, and that many American girls looked like effeminate boys . . . James said, stroking the head of the dachshund: "She's got sex, if you like, and she's quite intelligent enough to be shocked by this conversation."

(E. S. Nadal, *Personal Recollections of Henry James*)

When Oscar Wilde was released from gaol he went into a self-imposed exile in Europe from which he never returned. One of his earliest stopping-points was the French port of Dieppe. Wilde was accompanied by the poet Ernest Dowson, who suggested to his friend that, sexually, he should acquire "a more wholesome taste" – Wilde had been sentenced to gaol for homosexual offences. The two men pooled their money and set off for the nearest brothel. The news had spread and they were were followed by an excited crowd. Once at the brothel the crowd and Dowson remained outside while Wilde entered the establishment. When he reappeared, he whispered to Dowson, "The first these ten years, and it will be the last. It was like cold mutton." In a louder tone so that the assembled company might hear, he said: "But tell it in England, for it will entirely restore my character."

The relationship between poet and novelist Thomas Hardy and his first wife Emma had for many years been strained and distant before her death from heart failure. Emma, who had married the novelist in the early days before his international fame, felt that Hardy ignored her. She had long suffered from poor health. On the morning of 27 November, 1912, at the couple's house in Dorchester, Emma's maid Dolly Gale found her mistress moaning in pain, and was alarmed enough to summon Hardy from the study where he was already at work. Hardy was not particularly sympathetic to his wife's ailments and did not at first respond to the maid's pleas. In fact what he said to her was: "Your collar is crooked." When he eventually went to see Emma, she had only minutes left to live. Although Hardy later married the much younger Florence Dugdale, the death of Emma sparked in him a flame of posthumous love and regret for his first wife and produced some of his greatest poetry.

Novelist H. G. Wells was the lover of Rebecca West for ten years. They met when he was 46, a famous literary celebrity, and she was 19. West, whose real name was Cecily Isabel Fairchild, took her pseudonym from a play by Ibsen when she started her journalistic career on a feminist weekly magazine. She was invited to Wells' house after reviewing his novel aptly (or ironically) titled Marriage. *Wells led an exuberant sexual life, delighting in pursuing and being pursued, apparently claiming at one point that the women who chased him made him feel that he "was wearing glass trousers". Early on in the affair Rebecca West got pregnant.*

The baby had been conceived only the second time they were together, in Wells' new flat at St James' Court, Westminster. According to Wells, there was a danger of interruption, and he failed to take his usual precaution.

However much they were to diverge in their accounts of their life together, Rebecca and Wells were at one on the point that the pregnancy was inadvertent and unwanted by Rebecca. "Nothing of the sort was our intention . . . It should not have happened, and since I was the experienced person, the blame was wholly mine," wrote Wells. Once, later, Rebecca suggested that the child had been forced on her by Wells "in an angry moment"; sometimes she said that he had wanted to make her pregnant in order to bind her to him, which was unlikely, considering the obloquy that he had suffered as a result of Amber Reeves' pregnancy only a few years before. In 1976, goaded into candour by a television interviewer, Rebecca declared brusquely and simply: "The child was not intended."

She and Wells, in the early months, were happy lovers. He called her Panther, she called him Jaguar, and they quickly evolved a private mythology in which Panther and Jaguar played in a secret erotic world. "There is NO Panfer but Panfer," wrote Wells in one of the notes which he embellished with comic illustrations or "picshuas", "and she is the Prophet of the most High Jaguar which is Bliss and Perfect Being." She was "the sweetest of company, the best of friends, the most wonderful of lovers."

Wells's whimsical love-letters show that he had no intention of letting her down. With the help of his solicitor and friend E. S. P. Haynes, he made and remade plans about where and how she would live after the baby was born. She was to be Mrs West, and he would visit her as Mr West. "Panther, I love you as I have never loved anyone. I love you like a first love. I give myself to you. I am glad beyond any gladness that we are to have a child."

But as he wrote much later, they were "linked by this living tie" before they had had time to get to know one another properly and, as things turned out, "we never achieved any adjustment of any sort." It was harder for Rebecca, without marriage or the support of her family, to be "glad beyond any gladness" about the baby.

Rebecca West was fully aware of the shame, even disgrace, that went with illegitimacy in those days. The baby would have to be born, if not in secret, then well away from London. H. G. Wells found lodgings for his pregnant lover in Hunstanton on the Norfolk coast. Rebeccca spent six months there. In the meantime, Wells kept his wife informed of everything that was going on.

The house in which she [West] was marooned was called Brig-y-don, on Victoria Avenue, a straight street of newish red-brick, bow-windowed semi-detached villas of a severe kind, set back and at right angles from the esplanade and the wide, windy beach below. Her landlords were a postman and his wife, who needed the money. On 4 August 1914, the day on which Britain declared war on Germany, her baby was born in the house, with the help of the local doctor, an Irish midwife, and chloroform. He was named Anthony Panther. Wells, hurrying to Hunstanton from London, conveyed to his wife that it had been a difficult birth; she told him to give her dear love to Rebecca "if you can". Sixty years later Anthony Panther, visiting Hunstanton, sent his mother a picture postcard: "What a surprising place to have been born in. It doesn't appear to be aware of its important place in history. Bless you."

(Victoria Glendinning, *Rebecca West: A Life*)

The historical biographer Lytton Strachey, author of *Elizabeth and Essex* and *Eminent Victorians*, was a Conscientious Objector during World War One. He was also gay. During his examination by a tribunal to decide his case, he was asked a question that was obviously intended to rouse the blood-lust of even the most pacifist and principled objector. "What would you do," they said, "if you saw a German soldier attempting to rape your sister?" Strachey's reply has acquired an almost legendary status: "I should try and interpose my own body."

Another story has Lytton Strachey attending a party where guests were asked which historical figure they would most have liked to go to bed with. Responses were conventional, along the lines of "Cleopatra". When it was Strachey's turn he did not give the expected answer – Queen Victoria, whose biography he was writing – but instead proclaimed in his squeaky voice, "Julius Caesar!"

Poet T. S. Eliot had an unhappy marriage with his first wife, Vivienne, and they separated in 1932. Neurotic and unstable, Vivienne turned into a shadowy figure haunting her husband. She sent an advertisement to the *The Times* which read "Will T. S. Eliot please return to his home, 68 Clarence Gate Gardens, which he abandoned Sept. 17th, 1932", and also carried a sandwich board outside the offices of publishers Faber & Faber (of which Eliot was a director) proclaiming "I am the wife that T. S. Eliot abandoned." She was eventually committed to an asylum and died in 1947. Though Eliot's literary friends tended to see her as a persecutor she was also regarded by some as a victim. The poet Edith Sitwell said, "At some point in their marriage Tom went mad, and promptly certified his wife."

In 1935 the poet W. H. Auden married Erika Mann, the daughter of the German writer Thomas Mann. It was a marriage of convenience – not particularly for Auden, despite his homosexuality, but for Erika, who required a British passport to get out of Nazi Germany. Later Auden persuaded John Hampson, a gay friend, to marry Therese Giehse, a friend of Erika Mann and an actress who was running an anti-Nazi cabaret in Zurich. The clinching line as he urged Hampson to go through with the ceremony was, "What are buggers for?"

Cyril Connolly was a distinguished critic and reviewer. Ever since his time at Eton he had been part of a glamorous, well-connected literary and social circle. One of his earliest friends was W. H. Auden (see above). Many years later, Connolly recounted a comically erotic dream involving Auden.

My feelings towards him were entirely platonic . . . but my subconscious demanded more and I was put out by a dream (based on his ballad) in which, stripped to the waist beside a basin ("O plunge your hands in water") he indicated to me two small firm breasts: "Well, Cyril, how do you like my lemons?"

(Cyril Connolly, *article in* Encounter *magazine, March 1975*)

Perhaps the most famous "literary" affair of the 20th century was that between Henry Miller and Anaïs Nin. Miller was born in

Brooklyn and spent his early years in the USA. But the really formative years of his literary life began with his first trip to Paris in 1928, and out of this experience of Europe emerged autobiographical works like Tropic of Cancer *and* Tropic of Capricorn. *Their combination of sexual explicitness and literary experimentalism made Miller unpublishable in his own country for many years. Anais Nin's background was more exotic than Miller's. Daughter of a Spanish composer and a Danish singer, she had an unsatisfactory marriage to a wealthy young banker Hugh Guiler. The couple lived on the outskirts of Paris in Louveciennes. Nin's sexual and artistic restlessness and aspirations made Henry Miller an attractive prospect to her. Unfortunately, Miller was living with his (second) wife June. In some ways this merely sharpened Nin's determination.*

What Nin needed was someone worth being unfaithful for, and Henry [Miller] fitted the bill on several counts. A part he could play most successfully in Paris, since it was only partly acting, was that of the noble savage, or, as far as nice ladies were concerned, "a bit of rough". His boast in *Americans Abroad* of having "no education" was a part of this act, like the representation of himself as a rambling hobo and ex-gravedigger rather than someone who had lived, largely on his wife's earnings, in a succession of occasionally small but usually quite comfortable Brooklyn apartments. Nin was excited by the violence and the primitivism of the extracts from *Tropic of Cancer* which Osborn had shown her, and even before Henry arrived for that first meal together she was looking forward to an encounter between "delicacy and violence".

When Henry returned to [his wife] June from Louveciennes that evening, she found his mood disturbing. Instead of joining her in the mockery of another rich sucker with artistic pretensions he was unnaturally quiet. June asked him how the evening had gone and he shrugged and said: "Oh, so-so." What was Nin like? She was like a bird. June asked him what kind of bird, but he declined to elaborate. She knew him sufficiently well to recognize that Anais had made a strong personal impact, and that evening they had the first in the short series of explosive rows that would mark the route to the end of their marriage. She would not give in without a fight, however, and made sure she accompanied him for the next meeting at Louveciennes on New Year's Eve.

She was determined to out-weird Nin that night, and dressed for the occasion in her red velvet dress with a hole in one sleeve and her velvet cape; she covered her hair, now shoulder-length and a colour described by Bald as "a gold-kissed rust, almost red", with a battered slouch hat and wore, as usual, no stockings and a single cat's eye earring. Henry annoyed her by asking her, as they left the hotel, to be sure to watch her language at the Guilers. He was usually the one whose language was unpredictable; with prudes or with what June called holier-than-thou people he was liable to use the most shocking vocabulary, while he was propriety itself in the company of whores. As far as she knew, Nin did not seem to fit into either category.

The maid Emilia served up a souffle of carrots, and Nin enjoyed the disorientated discomfiture of her working-class guests:

> They were already hypnotized by the oddness of Louveciennes, the coloring, the strangeness of my dressing, my foreignness [. . .] Henry, who is thoroughly bourgeois, began to feel uncomfortable, as if he had not been properly fed. His steak was real and juicy, but cut neatly round, and I am sure he did not recognize it. June was in ecstasy.

June's enjoyment of the meal was spoiled by Anais's pet chow, Ruby, which sat beneath the table masturbating against her leg as she ate. June's powerful erotic signals were also picked up by Ruby's mistress, who developed in the course of the evening a quite fantastic infatuation with June. Nin invited her to visit again the following week on her own, and between New Year and June's departure in late January the two women spent a great deal of time together. On Nin's side at least these hours were a sort of tormented ecstasy, minutely recorded in her diary at the close of day. Yet despite the fervour in her account of her emotional turmoil, she never quite manages to convince us that the experience was part of an important and heroic search for her real self rather than merely another leg in the flight from the banality of everyday life.

June was partly to blame for the situation in wishing to be thought of as unusual, though one suspects that, of the three of them, she was the most clearly aware of the real extent to which they were all playing emotional games. As Henry had done, she allowed Anaïs' innocence to encourage her in her promotion of a weird image, hinting strongly to her of a life of unorthodox sexual practices with Mara Andrews, and of orgies of drug-taking in [Greenwich] Village vice dens. Anaïs refused to play the bourgeois wet and countered with an aggressive intimacy, asking June point blank if she were a lesbian and getting an evasive answer which was actually a "no", followed by a swift attempt to steer the conversation round to the subject of clothes.

Yet June continued for a few days to go along with the flirtation, almost as though sensing Nin's desire to play at Real People by taking over the position left vacant in the original New York triangle by the departure of Mara. Nin dreamed about June at night, and June revealed that she was so fond of Nin that, under other circumstances, she would like to have taken opium with her. They dressed for each other. June came to their meetings carrying the battle-scarred Count Bruga [a doll] at Anaïs's special request. They flirted intensely with one another, went shopping hand in hand, and in general carried on like adolescent schoolgirls discovering sexuality for the first time. At one point June walked along with Anaïs's hand on her bare breast. They even exchanged a mouth kiss. "Henry is uneasy. Hugo is sad," Nin confided to her diary; yet in essence it was self-delusion, disguising a fierce skirmish between the two to see who was going to win the battle for Henry.

Miller continued with his pursuit of Nin, using his own writing to excite her and win her over. At the same time Nin was paying attention to June Miller.

Nin spent the first week in March posing for an artist friend of hers in Montparnasse, and on Friday the fourth she and Henry met at the *Rotonde*. Nin again forced herself into a triangular love situation with the Millers, puzzling and fascinating Henry with talk of her "torment" at hearing about the influence of Mara Andrews on her beloved June. Henry's letters had done their work well, and her fascination with him was becoming increasingly erotic. She relished the contrast between the violence of his writing and the softness of his person, the "soft voice, trailing off, soft gestures, soft, fine white hands". Yet the courtship insistently hid behind literature, as though both needed constantly to remind themselves and each other of the fact that they were writers in order to justify and excuse the infidelities they contemplated. At one point during their meeting at the *Rotonde*, as Anais sat reading aloud to Henry from her notes on the effect his notes had had on her, he reached out and tried to take hold of her hand. She withdrew it. The following day she wrote to him in purple ink on silver paper: "I will be the one woman you will never have." On 5 March they met at the *Vikings*, on rue Vavin, where Henry made a declaration of love to her. Anais was still not quite ready to give in. Her resistance precipitated a sudden swoop into complete humility in which he berated himself for his presumptions: "I'm a peasant, Anais. Only whores can appreciate me." . . .

His sincerity and extraordinary truthfulness about his own weakness finally persuaded her to capitulate, and on the night of 8 March [1932] they climbed the stairs to his room at Hotel Central and became lovers. June's photograph observed them from the mantelpiece. Miller cried out how swift and unreal it all was. Afterwards he covered Nin's legs with her coat and asked her whether she had expected him to be more brutal.

Once begun, the affair between the literary lovers Nin and Miller continued easily – and passionately.

On a practical level, Miller's affair with Anais Nin was conducted with remarkable ease. He was a frequent and welcome visitor to the Guilers' house at Louveciennes, and his overnight stays and extended visits of four or five days excited little suspicion from Anais' husband. Though not yet recognized by the world at large as such, both lovers thought of themselves as writers, and their common pursuit of the craft seemed to them an excuse to justify any behaviour. On one occasion when Anais, her mother, her husband and Henry were all together at the house Henry got up and said to Anais: "I must talk to you a few minutes. I have corrected your manuscript." Moments later, in Anais' bedroom downstairs, they were making passionate love. She had to bite her finger to prevent herself screaming. Afterwards she went upstairs, "still throbbing," and resumed her conversation with her mother. Henry reappeared a little later, "looking like a saint, creamy voiced".

(Robert Ferguson, *Henry Miller: A Life*)

William Burroughs, the American author of *Junkie* and *The Naked Lunch*, was once the object of fear and incomprehension. Censored, banned and condemned, he was a target because of his homosexuality, his unapologetic treatment of drug addiction – and his experimental literary technique. Burroughs ended his life as one of the grand old men of American literature but it had been a long drug-fuelled road for him and others. In 1951, Burroughs and his wife, Joan Vollmer, were living in Mexico City. One evening they went to an apartment above a bar on Calle Monterey. Burroughs was carrying a bag containing a gun which he wanted to sell. There were a least two witnesses to the scene that followed, including a young man he was interested in. At some point in what Burroughs later described as a "very hazy" evening, he took out the automatic pistol and said to his wife, "I guess it's about time for our William Tell act." Joan Vollmer put a glass on her head, and Burroughs tried to shoot it off. He missed the glass but put a bullet through his wife's forehead. Lewis Marker, the young man Burroughs was pursuing, said, "Bill, I think you've killed her."

There was some confusion over exactly what had happened. Burroughs' words to his wife might suggest that "William Tell" was a "game" they'd played before but in fact there was no evidence of this. The object that Joan balanced on her head has been variously decribed as a champagne glass, a water glass, a glass of gin, even as an apricot or orange. First newspaper reports indicated that the whole thing was an accident, with Burroughs claiming that the gun had gone off when he dropped it by mistake. He served a very short time in jail (less than a fortnight) before being released on bail. Burroughs came from a prosperous family – his grandfather had patented a type of adding machine in the 1890s – and their money may have oiled the wheels of justice. Ballistics experts were bribed and Burroughs eventually jumped bail. In his absence he was given a two year suspended sentence.

While he may have escaped the law over his wife's death, Burroughs continued to examine himself and his motives. He was aware that what looked like a reckless accident could conceal what he termed "unconscious intent". And he was very definite about the way Joan's death had set him on a particular course.

"I am forced to the appalling conclusion that I would never have become a writer but for Joan's death and to the realization of the extent to which this event has motivated and formulated my writing."

The English novelist Simon Raven led a rather rackety early life. Thrown out of one instution after another – public school, university, army – either for unabashed homosexual activity or for his tendency to get into debt, he eventually put his experiences to good use in the 12-volume sequence *Alms for Oblivion* and other fiction which, in the more hidebound 1950s and 60s, was usually described as scandalous, louche, etc. Raven did once get married and father a child. Serving in the army at the time, he received an allowance as a married officer which he neglected to pass over to his wife Susan. In response to her melodramatic telegram, WIFE AND BABY STARVING SEND MONEY SOONEST, Raven replied just as telegraphically: SORRY NO MONEY SUGGEST EAT BABY.

Manuscripts

Thomas Cooper was a 16th-century clergyman and a scholar who compiled chronicles and dictionaries, one of which so impressed Queen Elizabeth I that she determined to promote Cooper's career in the church as far as she could. His wife, though, was not such a fan of his work.

Dr Edward Davenant told me that this learned man had a shrew to his wife: who was irreconcileably angrie with him for sitting-up late at night so, compileing his Dictionarie.

When he had halfe donne it, she had the opportunity to gett into his studie, tooke all his paines out in her lap, and threw it into the fire, and burnt it. Well, for all that, the good man had so great a zeale for the advancement of learning, that he began it again, and went through with it to that Perfection that he hath left it to us, a most usefull Worke. He was afterwards made Bishop of Winton.

(John Aubrey, *Brief Lives*)

Sometimes the author can be relied on to destroy his own books in a fit of temper.

His Booke [Sir Walter Raleigh's *History of the World*] sold very slowly at first, and the Booke-seller complayned of it, and told him that he should be a looser by it, which put Sir W into a passion, and sayd that since the world did not understand it, they should not have his second part, which he tooke and threw into the fire, and burnt before his face.

(John Aubrey, *Brief Lives*)

Sir Walter Raleigh was easily provoked into destroying the manuscripts of his *History of the World* if another story is to be believed. George Orwell recounts in one of his essays how Raleigh, at the time imprisoned in the Tower of London, was working on the first volume of the *History* when a fight broke out among some workmen beneath the window of his cell. One of the men was killed. Raleigh looked into the incident carefully but, despite his having been a witness to the killing, he was never able to establish by his inquiries what the workmen's quarrel had been about in the first place. So, no doubt reflecting on the impossibility of the historian's task of finding the truth even when the evidence is right under his nose, Raleigh burned what he'd written and gave up his plan to produce a history of the world. As Orwell says, this is one of those stories that, even if it isn't true, ought to be. In fact, Raleigh did go on to complete his *History of the World.*

The hectic pace of play composition in the Elizabethan and Jacobean period is suggested in the following little story about the dramatist Thomas Heywood. Manuscripts were not highly prized in those days.

'Tis said, that he [Thomas Heywood] not only acted himself almost every day, but also wrote each day a Sheet: and that he might lose no time, many of his Plays were composed in the Tavern, on the backside of Tavern bills, which may be the occasion so many of them be lost.

(William Winstanley, *Lives of the Most Famous English Poets*)

Like many authors, Dr Johnson was less than enthusiastic when friends asked him to read their work in manuscript.

Mr Johnson did not like that his friends should bring their manuscripts for him to read, and he liked still less to read them when they were brought: sometimes however when he could not refuse he would take the play or poem, or whatever it was, and give the people his opinion from some one page that he had peeped into. A gentleman carried him his tragedy, which, because he loved the author, Johnson took, and it lay about our rooms some time. What answer did you give your friend, Sir? said I, after the book had been called for. "I told him (replied he), that there was too much *Tig* and *Tirry* in it." Seeing me laugh most violently, "Why what would'st have, child?" (said he). "I looked at nothing but the dramatis [list of characters], and there was *Tigranes* and *Tiridates*, or Teribazus, or such stuff. A man can tell but what he knows, and I never got any further than the first page. Alas, Madam! (continued he) how few books are there of which one ever can possibly arrive at the last page! Was there ever yet any thing written by mere man that was wished longer by its readers, excepting Don Quixote, Robinson Crusoe, and the Pilgrim's Progress?" After Homer's Iliad, Mr Johnson confessed that the work of Cervantes was the greatest in the world . . .

(Hesther Lynch Piozzi, *Anecdotes of Samuel Johnson*)

Like many authors, Sir Walter Scott received manuscripts from other would-be writers.

Last February a person named Lake sent a MS copy of a Comedy to Sir Walter desiring his opinion: it came at the time of his distresses and was thought no more of: since he came to town he received a letter complaining of his not having restored the Comedy of which the Author had no copy: the horror of Sir Walter was not to be described: however he took heart of grace, and replied by every possible excuse, stating the unhappy time in which the MS arrived, and promising a thorough search on his return to Scotland: he received to his great relief a reply, begging him to take no further trouble for the author had relinquished all commerce with the Muses, and having resumed his trade of a Taylor solicited his custom: "Guess ye how I was relieved to find that an order for a pair of Pantaloons would make amends for the loss of a MS of which the author had no copy."

(*Letters & Recollections of Sir Walter Scott*)

One of the great lost manuscripts of literary history is that of Lord Byron's Memoirs. Had they survived, their supposedly scandalous contents would have made for a best-seller. Byron's friend, Tom Moore, was the intended beneficiary of this hot potato and describes how he obtained the Memoirs when he was staying with Byron in Venice.

A short time after dinner Byron left the room, and returned carrying in his hand a white leather bag. "Look here," he said, holding it up; "this would be worth something to Murray [Byron's publisher], though *you*, I dare say, would not give sixpence for it." "What is it?" I asked. "My life and adventures," he answered. "It is not a thing," he answered, "that can be published during my lifetime, but you may have it if you like. There, do whatever you please with it." In taking the bag, and thanking him most warmly, I added, "This will make a nice legacy for my little Tom, who shall astonish the latter days of the 19th century with it."

*Because the Memoirs were seen by very few people, the gossip about what they contained was even more excited and scandalized. They certainly included material about the bitter separation between Byron and his wife (see also **Love, Sex & Marriage**). Another of Byron's friends – although one who hadn't actually seen the manuscript – wrote in his journal that he had been told "that the first part of the Memoirs contained nothing objectionable except one anecdote – namely that Lord B. had Lady B. on the sofa before dinner on the day of their marriage . . . The second part contained all sorts of erotic adventures and Gifford of the Quarterly who read it at Murray's request said that the whole Memoirs were fit only for a brothel and would damn Lord B. to everlasting infamy if published." After the poet's death, there were legal complications about who had a claim to the manuscript, and a nervous publisher together with others concerned to protect Lady Byron ensured that the Memoirs were torn up and burned.*

Losing the first draft of a manuscript may not be that much of a disaster if you've stored it on disk or made a hard copy, automatic precautions for the wise author, actual or would-be. But to lose your only manuscript in the days when first drafts were laboriously com-posed by hand must have been profoundly depressing. The writer and historian Thomas Carlyle showed remarkable patience and restraint when he described in this letter to his brother how the sole copy of his manuscript of The French Revolution *was casually thrown away. "Mill" is John Stuart Mill, the philosopher. Jane was Carlyle's wife.*

Cheyne Row, Chelsea, London, 23 March, 1835.
My dear brother,

Your letter came in this morning (after sixteen days from Rome); and, tomorrow being post-day, I have shoved my writing-table into the corner, and sit (with my back to the fire and Jane, who is busy sewing at my old jupe of a dressing-gown), forthwith making answer. It was somewhat longed for; yet I felt, in other respects, that it was better you had not written sooner; for I had a thing to dilate upon, of a most ravelled character, that was better to be knit up a little first. You shall hear . . .

Mill had borrowed that first volume of my poor *French Revolution* (pieces of it more than *once*) that he might have it all before him, and write down some observations on it, which perhaps I might print as notes. I was busy meanwhile with Volume Second . . . indeed, I know not how it was, I had not felt so dear and independent, sure of myself and of my task for many long years.

Well, one night about three weeks ago, we sat at tea, and Mill's short rap was heard at the door: Jane rose to welcome him; but he stood there unresponsive, pale, the very picture of despair; said, half articulately gasping, that she must go down and speak to "Mrs Taylor". After some considerable additional gasping, I learned from Mill this fact: that my poor Manuscript, all except some four tattered leaves, was annihilated. He had left it out (too carelessly); it had been taken for waste-paper; and so five months of as tough labour as I could remember of, were as good as vanished, gone like a whiff of smoke.

There never in my life had come upon me any other accident of much moment; but this I could not but feel to be a sore one. The thing was lost, and perhaps worse; for I had not only forgotten all the structure of it, but the spirit it was written with was past; only the general impression seemed to remain, and the recollection that I was on the whole well satisfied with that, and could now hardly hope to equal it. Mill, whom I had to comfort and speak peace to, remained injudiciously enough till almost midnight, and my poor Dame and I had to sit talking of indifferent matters; and could not till then get our lament freely uttered. *She* was very good to me; and the thing did not beat us. I felt in general that I was as a little schoolboy, who had laboriously written out his *Copy* as he could, and was showing it not without satisfaction to the Master: but lo! the Master had suddenly torn it, saying: "No, boy, thou must go and write it *better*." What could I do but sorrowing go and try to obey.

That night was a hard one; something from time to time tying me tight as it were all round the region of the heart, and strange dreams haunting me; however, I was not without good thoughts too that came like healing life into me. Next morning accordingly I wrote to Fraser (who had *advertised* the book as "preparing for publication") that it was all gone back; that he must not *speak of it* to any one (till it was made good again); finally that he must send me some *better paper*, and also a *Biographie Universelle*, for I was determined to risk ten pounds more upon it.

Poor Fraser was very assiduous; I got bookshelves put up (for the whole house was flowing with books) where the *Biographie* (not Fraser's, however, which was countermanded, but Mill's), with much else stands all ready, much readier than before: and so, having first finished out the Piece I was actually upon, I began again at the beginning. Early the day after tomorrow (after a hard and quite novel kind of battle) I count on having the First Chapter on paper a second time, no worse than it was, though considerably different. The bitterness of the business is past therefore; and you must conceive me toiling along in that new way for many weeks to come. This is my ravelled concern, dear Jack; which you see is in the way to knit itself up again – I have not been fortunate in my pen tonight: indeed for the last page I have been writing with back of it. This and my speed will account for the confusion. Porridge has just come in. I will to bed without writing more. Good night, dear Brother.

　　Ever yours!

The poet and publisher James T. Fields had to use gentle persuasion to get the American novelist Nathanel Hawthorne to show him the manuscript of what turned out to be his most famous book.

In the winter of 1849, after he had been ejected from the customhouse, I went down to Salem to see him and inquire after his health, for we heard he had been suffering from illness. He was then living in a modest wooden house in Mall Street, if I remember rightly the location. I found him alone in a chamber over the sitting-room of the dwelling; and as the day was cold, he was hovering near a stove. We fell into talk about his future prospects, and he was, as I feared I should find him, in a very desponding mood. "Now," said I, "is the time for you to publish, for I know during these years in Salem you must have got something ready for the press." "Nonsense," said he; "what heart had I to write anything, when my publishers (M. and Company) have been so many years trying to sell a small edition of the 'Twice-Told Tales'?" I still pressed upon him the good chances he would have now with something new. "Who would risk publishing a book for me, the most unpopular writer in America?" "I would," said I, "and would start with an edition of two thousand copies of anything you write." "What madness!" he exclaimed; "your friendship for me gets the better of your judgment. No, no," he continued; "I have no money to indemnify a publisher's losses on my account." I looked at my watch and found that the train would soon be starting for Boston, and I knew there was not much time to lose in trying to discover what had been his literary work during these last few years in Salem. I remember that I pressed him to reveal to me what he had been writing. He shook his head and gave me to understand he had produced nothing. At that moment I caught sight of a bureau or set of drawers near where we were sitting; and immediately it occurred to me that hidden away somewhere in that article of furniture was a story or stories by the author of the "Twice-Told Tales", and I became so positive of it that I charged him vehemently with the fact. He seemed surprised, I thought, but shook his head again; and I rose to take my leave, begging him not to come into the cold entry, saying I would come back and see him again in a few days. I was hurrying down the stairs when he called after me from the chamber, asking me to stop a moment. Then quickly stepping into the entry with a roll of manuscript in his hands, he said: "How in Heaven's name did you know this thing was there? As you have found me out, take what I have written, and tell me, after you get home and have time to read it, if it is good for anything. It is either very good or very bad, I don't know which." On my way up to Boston I read the germ of "The Scarlet Letter"; before I slept that night I wrote him a note all aglow with admiration of the marvellous story he had put into my hands, and told him that I would come again to Salem the next day and arrange for its publication.

(James T. Fields, *Yesterdays With Authors*)

The first manuscript version of Robert Louis Stevenson's famous horror story Dr Jekyll and Mr Hyde *was destroyed in unusual circumstances.*

A subject much in his [Stevenson's] thoughts at this time was the duality of man's nature and the alternation of good and evil; and he was for a long while casting about for a story to embody this central idea . . . The true case still delayed till suddenly one night he had a dream. He awoke, and found himself in possession of two, or rather three, of the scenes in the *Strange Case of Dr Jekyll and Mr Hyde*.

Its waking existence, however, was by no means without incident. He dreamed these scenes in considerable detail, including the circumstance of the transforming powders, and so vivid was the impression that he wrote the story off at a red heat, just as it had presented itself him in his sleep.

"In the small hours of one morning," says Mrs Stevenson, "I was awakened by cries of horror from Louis. Thinking he had a nightmare, I awakened him. He said angrily: 'Why did you wake me? I was dreaming a fine bogey tale.' I had awakened him at the first transformation scene."

Mr Osbourne [Stevenson's stepson] writes: "I don't believe that there was ever such a literary feat before as the writing of *Dr Jekyll*. I remember the first reading as though it were yesterday. Louis came downstairs in a fever; read nearly half the book aloud; and then, while we were still gasping, he was away again, and busy writing. I doubt if the first draft took so long as three days."

He had lately had a haemorrhage, and was strictly forbidden all discussion or excitement. No doubt the reading aloud was contrary to the doctor's orders; at any rate Mrs Stevenson, according to the custom then in force, wrote her detailed criticism of the story as it then stood, pointing out her chief objection – that it was really an allegory, whereas he had treated it purely as if it were a story. In the first draft Jekyll's nature was bad all through, and the Hyde change was worked only for the sake of a disguise. She gave the paper to her husband and left the room. After a while his bell rang; on her return she found him sitting up in bed (the clinical thermometer in his mouth), pointing with a long denunciatory finger to a pile of ashes. He had burned the entire draft. Having realized that he had taken the wrong point of view, that the tale was an allegory and not another "Markheim", he at once destroyed his manuscript, acting not out of pique, but from a fear that he might be tempted to make too much use of it, and not rewrite the whole from a new standpoint.

It was written again in three days ("I drive on with Jekyll: bankruptcy at my heels"); but the fear of losing the story altogether prevented much further criticism. The powder was condemned as too material an agency but this he could not eliminate, because in the dream it had made so strong an impression upon him.

"The mere physical feat," Mr Osbourne continues, "was tremendous; and instead of harming him, it roused and cheered him inexpressibly." Of course it must not be supposed that these three days represent all the time Stevenson spent upon the story, for after this he was working hard for a month or six weeks in bringing it into its present form.

(Graham Balfour, The Life of
Robert Louis Stevenson)

William Allingham describes two small losses suffered by the poet Alfred Tennyson.

Looking at the chimney-piece, Tennyson said, "When I began to read Italian, I wrote down every word that puzzled me on the sides and front of the chimney-piece where I lodged – painted white – and made a kind of dictionary for myself. I went away for two or three days and when I came back it was all washed off. 'Thought it was dirt,' the woman said.

"Worse than that – when I was 22 I wrote a beautiful poem on Poland, hundreds of lines long, and the housemaid lit the fire with it. I never could recover it."

(William Allingham, *diary entry, October 1880*)

The 19th-century poet Algernon Charles Swinburne had a lifelong method of dealing with written material he didn't want, including his own manuscripts.

All around Swinburne's sitting-room there were discovered after his death unsightly rolls of parcels tied up in old newspaper, some of them looking as if they had not been opened for half a century. These parcels were found to contain proofs, bills, letters, prospectuses and every species of rubbish, together with occasional MSS in prose and verse. . . For many years Swinburne was in the habit of allowing miscellaneous material to gather on his table, until a moment came when he could bear the pressure of it no longer. He would then gather everything up, tie the whole in the current newspaper of the day, and then delicately place it on a shelf, where it never was again disturbed. A fresh heap would then begin to grow, till the day when the poet suddenly pounced upon it, and doomed it to the recesses of another newspaper. Through a great part of his life, Swinburne seems to have carried out this curious plan, and in earlier days, when he wandered from lodging-house to lodging-house, he must always have carried with him his carpet-bag of newspaper parcels.

(Edmund Gosse and Thomas Wise, *from the introduction to Swinburne's Posthumous Poems*)

The life of Richard Burton, 19th-century adventurer, anthropologist and author, could have come out of the pages of a novel by John

Buchan or Rider Haggard. Burton visited the forbidden city of Mecca in Arabic disguise, spoke 25 languages and wrote dozens of travel books. He also translated the Arabian Nights *and the* Kama Sutra. *During the fourteen years before his death in 1890 he had been working on the translation of another Arabic erotic text,* The Scented Garden. *After Burton's death, his wife Isabel burnt his papers and diaries. This is how and why she decided to destroy* The Scented Garden.

Her mind was still uneasy about *The Scented Garden,* and she took out the manuscript to examine it . . . When she opened it, she was perfectly bewildered and horrified . . . Calming herself, she reflected that the book was written only for scholars and mainly for Oriental students, and that her husband "never wrote a thing from the impure point of view . . ." Then she looked up, and there before her stood her husband, just as he had stood in the flesh. He pointed to the manuscript, and said, "Burn it!" Then he disappeared. As she had for years been a believer in spirits, the apparition did not surprise her, and yet she was tremendously excited. "Burn it!" she echoed. "This valuable manuscript? At which he laboured for so many weary hours? Yet, doubtless, it would be wrong to preserve it . . . What a gentleman, a scholar, and a man of the world, may write when living, he would see very differently as a poor soul standing naked before its God . . . What would he care for the applause of fifteen hundred men now – for the whole world's praise, and God offended? And yet the book is for students only . . ."

At this moment the apparition again stood before her, and in a sterner and more authoritative voice said, "Burn it!" and then again disappeared. In her excitement she scarcely knew where she was, or what she did . . .

Then for the third time Sir Richard stood before her. Again he sternly bade her burn the manuscript, and, having added threatenings to his command, he again disappeared. By this time her excitement had passed away, and a holy joy irradiated her soul. She took up the manuscript and . . . burnt it, sheet after sheet, until the whole was consumed. As each leaf was licked up by the fire, it seemed to her that "a

fresh ray of light and peace" transfused the soul of her
beloved husband.

(Thomas Wright, Life of Sir Richard Burton)

⌒⌒⌒⌒⌒⌒➤

Joseph Conrad's first novel, Almayer's Folly, *was many years in the
making. Conrad spent the early part of life as a sailor and he carried
the chapters of the growing manuscript around with him, at one point
nearly losing it when his boat capsized in the Congo river. Finally, on
a voyage to Australia, he plucked up the confidence to show his writing
to a passenger.*

Providence which saved my MS from the Congo rapids brought
it to the knowledge of a helpful soul far out on the open sea. It
would be on my part the greatest ingratitude ever to forget the
sallow, sunken face and the deepset, dark eyes of the young
Cambridge man (he was a "passenger for his health" on board
the good ship *Torrens* outward bound to Australia) who was the
first reader of *Almeyer's Folly* – the very first reader I ever had.
"Would it bore you very much reading a MS in a handwriting
like mine?" I asked him one evening on a sudden impulse at the
end of a longish conversation whose subject was Gibbon's
History. Jacques (that was his name) was sitting in my cabin
one stormy dog-watch below, after bringing me a book to read
from his own travelling store.

"Not at all," he answered with his courteous intonation and a
faint smile. As I pulled a drawer open his suddenly aroused
curiosity gave him a watchful expression. I wonder what he
expected to see. A poem, maybe. All that's beyond guessing
now. He was not a cold, but a calm man, still more subdued by
disease – a man of few words and of an unassuming modesty in
general intercourse, but with something uncommon in the
whole of his person which set him apart from the undistin-
guished lot of our sixty passengers. His eyes had a thoughtful
introspective look. In his attractive, reserved manner, and in a
veiled, sympathetic voice, he asked:

"What is this?" "It is a sort of tale," I answered with an
effort. "It is not even finished yet. Nevertheless, I would like to
know what you think of it."

He put the MS in the breast-pocket of his jacket; I remember perfectly his thin brown fingers folding it lengthwise. "I will read it tomorrow," he remarked, seizing the door-handle, and then, watching the roll of the ship for a propitious moment, he opened the door and was gone. In the moment of his exit I heard the sustained booming of the wind, the swish of the water on the decks of the *Torrens*, and the subdued, as if distant, roar of the rising sea. I noted the growing disquiet in the great restlessness of the ocean, and responded professionally to it with the thought that at eight o'clock, in another half-hour or so at the furthest, the top-gallant sails would have to come off the ship.

Next day, but this time in the first dog-watch, Jacques entered my cabin. He had a thick, woollen muffler round his throat and the MS was in his hand. He tendered it to me with a steady look but without a word. I took it in silence. He sat down on the couch and still said nothing. I opened and shut a drawer under my desk, on which a filled-up log-slate lay wide open in its wooden frame waiting to be copied neatly into the sort of book I was accustomed to write with care, the ship's log-book. I turned my back squarely on the desk. And even then Jacques never offered a word. "Well, what do you say?" I asked at last. "Is it worth finishing?" This question expressed exactly the whole of my thoughts.

"Distinctly," he answered in his sedate veiled voice, and then coughed a little.

"Were you interested?" I inquired further, almost in a whisper.

"Very much!"

In a pause I went on meeting instinctively the heavy rolling of the ship, and Jacques put his feet upon the couch. The curtain of my bed-place swung to and fro as it were a punkah, the bulkhead lamp circled in its gimbals, and now and then the cabin door rattled slightly in the gusts of wind. It was in the latitude 40 south, and nearly in the longitude of Greenwich, as far as I can remember . . . I heard on deck the whistle of the officer of the watch and remained on the alert to catch the order that was to follow this call to attention. It reached me as a faint, fierce shout to "Square the yards." "Aha!" I thought to myself, "a westerly blow coming on." Then I turned to my very first reader, who, alas! was not to live long enough to know the end of the tale.

"Now let me ask you one more thing: Is the story quite clear to you as it stands?"

He raised his dark, gentle eyes to my face and seemed surprised.

"Yes! Perfectly."

This was all I was to hear from his lips concerning the merits of *Almayer's Folly*. We never spoke together of the book again. A long period of bad weather set in and I had no thoughts left but for my duties, whilst poor Jacques caught a fatal cold and had to keep close in his cabin. When we arrived at Adelaide the first reader of my prose went at once up-country, and died rather suddenly in the end, either in Australia or it may be on the passage while going home through the Suez Canal. I am not sure which it was now, and I do not think I ever heard precisely; though I made inquiries about him from some of our return passengers who, wandering about to "see the country" during the ship's stay in port, had come upon him here and there. At last we sailed, homeward bound, and still not one line was added to the careless scrawl of the many pages which poor Jacques had had the patience to read with the very shadows of Eternity gathering already in the hollows of his kind, steadfast eyes.

(Joseph Conrad, *A Personal Record*)

If Joseph Conrad was lucky with his first manuscript and first reader, he wasn't so fortunate with another manuscript, that of his story End of the Tether.

Last night the lamp exploded here and before I could run back into the room the whole round table was in a blaze, books, cigarettes, MS – alas. The whole second part of *End of the Tether* . . . This morning looking at the pile of charred paper – MS and typed copy – my head swam; it seemed to me the earth was turning backwards.

(Joseph Conrad, *letter to Ford Madox Ford, June 1902*)

T. E. Lawrence (of Arabia) claimed to have lost the manuscript of *Seven Pillars of Wisdom*, the famous account of the Arab Revolt and his role in it, while on a railway journey. Travelling to Oxford in December, 1919, he changed trains at Reading. He left the case containing a major part of the manuscript under a table in the station buffet, and did not realize the loss – or theft – until later. According to his own account, only the Introduction and the two final sections remained, and the notes which were the basis for the book had already been destroyed. Nevertheless, in the space of three months Lawrence produced another draft manuscript of over 400,000 words, the equivalent of three or four full-length novels. Doubt has been cast on his version of the event. Lawrence was a highly complex man and may have had last-minute anxieties about how much of himself would be revealed by the autobiography. Perhaps it's revealing that he reported "joyously" to one friend, "I've lost the damn thing."

Railway stations are dangerous places for manuscripts. Ernest Hemingway was in the early stages of his career as an author during his stay in Europe in the early 1920s. He had written a number of (unpublished) short stories and other pieces and, while he was staying in Lausanne, his first wife Hadley brought down some manuscripts so that he could work on them "on our holiday in the mountains". She left her suitcase, which contained all her husband's material in manila folders, in a train compartment at the Gare de Lyon in Paris, having asked a porter to keep an eye on them. She got back to discover that the case had been stolen. Hemingway had no choice but to begin again. His pessimism about being published wasn't justified, for his first volume, *Three Stories and Ten Poems*, appeared soon after in 1923.

Mistakes

Here is a passage which suggests that for, for some authors, mistakes come naturally – and, for an easy-going author like Oliver Goldsmith, don't matter very much.

Macaulay, in his life of Goldsmith in the Encyclopaedia Britannica, relates that that author, in the *History of England*, tells us that Naseby is in Yorkshire, and that the mistake was not corrected when the book was reprinted. He further affirms that Goldsmith was nearly hoaxed into putting into the *History of Greece* an account of a battle between Alexander the Great and Montezuma. This, however, is scarcely a fair charge, for the backs of most of us need to be broad enough to bear the actual blunders we have made throughout life without having to bear those which we almost made.

Goldsmith was a very remarkable instance of a man who undertook to write books on subjects of which he knew nothing. Thus, Johnson said that if he could tell a horse from a cow that was the extent of his knowledge of zoology; and yet the *History of Animated Nature* can still be read with pleasure from the charm of the author's style.

(Henry Wheatley, *Literary Blunders*)

The poet Samuel Taylor Coleridge seems to have attracted odd incidents and misunderstandings wherever he went. At the time of this story he'd just written Remorse, *a play about the Spanish Inquisition. The play, put on at the Drury Lane theatre in 1813, had been quite successful.*

A few days after the appearance of his piece he was sitting in the coffee-room of a hotel, and heard his name coupled with a coroner's inquest, by a gentleman who was reading a newspaper to a friend. He asked to see the paper, which was handed to him with the remark that it was very extraordinary that Coleridge, the poet, should have hanged himself just after the success of his play; but he was always a strange mad fellow. "Indeed, sir," said Coleridge, "it is a most extraordinary thing that he should have hanged himself, be the subject of an inquest, and yet that he should at this moment be speaking to you." The astonished stranger hoped he had said nothing to hurt his feelings, and was made easy on that point. The newspaper related that a gentleman in black had been cut down from a tree in Hyde Park, without money or papers in his pocket, his shirt being marked "S. T. Coleridge"; and Coleridge was at no loss to understand how this might have happened, since he seldom travelled without losing a shirt or two.

(Charles Robert Leslie, *Autobiographical Recollections*)

Visting American poet Henry Longfellow mistook the Victorian poet and painter Dante Gabriel Rossetti for two separate people.

Then he [Rossetti] told a story of Longfellow, "the good old bard"; how the poet had called on him during his visit to England, and been courteous and kind in the last degree, but having fallen into the error of thinking that Rossetti the painter and Rossetti the poet were different men, he had said, on leaving the house:

"I have been very glad to meet you, Mr Rossetti, and should like to have met your brother, also. Pray tell him how much I admire his beautiful poem, 'The Blessed Damozel'."

"I'll tell him," Rossetti had said.

(Hall Caine, *Recollections of Rossetti*)

Mark Twain (real name, Samuel Clemens) had a deserved reputation as a wit and humorist. On one occasion at least, however, he made a bad misjudgement when he gave an after-dinner talk in which he imagined three tramps passing themselves off in a California mining camp as three very famous "senior" American writers, Ralph Waldo

Emerson, Henry Wadsworth Longfellow, and Oliver Wendell Holmes. Unfortunately, Emerson, Longfellow and Holmes were guests at the dinner. William Dean Howells, who was a close friend of Twain and his editor at the Atlantic Monthly, *tells the story of what he called the "awful speech".*

I suppose the year was about 1879, but here the almanac is unimportant, and I can only say that it was after Clemens had become a very valued contributor of the magazine, where he found himself to his own great explicit satisfaction. He had jubilantly accepted our invitation, and had promised a speech, which it appeared afterwards he had prepared with unusual care and confidence. It was his custom always to think out his speeches, mentally wording them, and then memorizing them by a peculiar system of mnemonics which he had invented. On the dinner-table a certain succession of knife, spoon, salt-cellar, and butter-plate symbolized a train of ideas, and on the billiard-table a ball, a cue, and a piece of chalk served the same purpose. With a diagram of these printed on the brain he had full command of the phrases which his excogitation had attached to them, and which embodied the ideas in perfect form. He believed he had been particularly fortunate in his notion for the speech of that evening, and he had worked it out in joyous self-reliance. It was the notion of three tramps, three dead-beats, visiting a California mining-camp, and imposing themselves upon the innocent miners as respectively Ralph Waldo Emerson, Henry Wadsworth Longfellow, and Oliver Wendell Holmes. The humour of the conception must prosper or must fail according to the mood of the hearer, but Clemens felt sure of compelling this to sympathy, and he looked forward to an unparalleled triumph.

But there were two things that he had not taken into account. One was the species of religious veneration in which these men were held by those nearest them, a thing that I should not be able to realize to people remote from them in time and place. They were men of extraordinary dignity, of the thing called *presence*, for want of some clearer word, so that no one could well approach them in a personally light or trifling spirit. I do not suppose that anybody more truly valued them or more piously loved them than Clemens himself, but the intoxication of his fancy carried him beyond the bounds of that regard, and emboldened him to the other thing which he had not taken into account – namely, the immense hazard of working his fancy out before their faces, and expecting them to enter into the delight of it. If neither Emerson, nor Longfellow, nor Holmes had been there, the scheme might possibly have carried, but even this is doubtful, for those who so devoutly honoured them would have overcome their horror with difficulty, and perhaps would not have overcome it at all.

The publisher, with a modesty very ungrateful to me, had abdicated his office of host, and I was the hapless president, fulfilling the abhorred function of calling people to their feet and making them speak. When I came to Clemens I intro-duced him with the cordial admiring I had for him as one of my greatest contributors and dearest friends. Here, I said, in sum, was a humorist who never left you hanging your head for having enjoyed his joke; and then the amazing mistake, the bewildering blunder, the cruel catastrophe was upon us. I believe that after the scope of the burlesque made itself clear, there was no one there, including the burlesquer himself, who was not smitten with a desolating dismay. There fell a silence, weighing many tons to the square inch, which deepened from moment to moment, and was broken only by the hysterical and blood-curdling laughter of a single guest, whose name shall not be handed down to infamy. Nobody knew whether to look at the speaker or down at his plate. I chose my plate as the least affliction, and so I do not know how Clemens looked, except when I stole a glance at him, and saw him standing solitary amid his appalled and appalling listeners, with his joke dead on his hands. From a first glance at the great three whom his jest had made its theme, I was aware of Longfellow sitting upright, and regarding the humorist with an air of pensive puzzle, of Holmes busily writing on his menu, with a well-feigned effect of preoccupation, and of Emerson, holding his elbows, and listening with a sort of Jovian oblivion of this nether world in that lapse of memory which saved him in those later years from so much bother. Clemens must have dragged his joke to the climax and left it there, but I cannot

say this from any sense of the fact. Of what happened afterwards at the table where the immense, the wholly innocent,
the truly unimagined affront was offered, I have no longer the
least remembrance. I next remember being in a room of the
hotel, where Clemens was not to sleep, but to toss in despair,
and Charles Dudley Warner's saying, in the gloom "Well,
Mark, you're a funny fellow." It was as well as anything else
he could have said, but Clemens seemed unable to accept the
tribute.

I stayed the night with him, and the next morning after a
haggard breakfast, we drove about and he made some pur-
chases of bric-à-brac for his house in Hartford, with a soul as
far away from bric-à-brac as ever the soul of man was. He went
home by an early train and he lost no time in writing back to
the three divine personalities which he had so involuntarily
seemed to flout. They all wrote back to him, making it as light
for him as they could. I have heard that Emerson was a good
deal mystified, and in his sublime forgetfulness asked, Who
was this gentleman who appeared to think he had offered him
some sort of annoyance? But I am not sure that this is accurate.
What I am sure of is that Longfellow, a few days after, in my
study, stopped before a photograph of Clemens and said, "Ah,
he is a wag!" and nothing more. Holmes told me, with deep
emotion, such as a brother humorist might well feel, that he
had not lost an instant in replying to Clemens' letter, and
assuring him that there had not been the least offence, and
entreating him never to think of the matter again. "He said that
he was a fool, but he was God's fool," Holmes quoted from the
letter, with a true sense of the pathos and the humour of the
self-abasement.

(William Dean Howells, My Mark Twain)

*The Victorian artist and writer of nonsense verse Edward Lear was
once told on a train journey that he didn't exist.*

A few days ago in a railway as I went to my sister's a gentleman
explained to two ladies (whose children had my *Book of Nonsense*) that thousands of families were grateful to the author

(which in silence I agreed to) who was not generally known – but was really Lord Derby: and now came a showing forth, which cleared up at once to my mind why that statement has already appeared in several papers. Edward Earl of Derby (said the Gentleman) did not choose to publish the book openly, but dedicated it as you see to his relations, and now if you will transpose the letters LEAR you will read simply EDWARD EARL. – Says I, joining spontanious in the conversation – "That is quite a mistake: I have reason to know that Edward Lear the painter and author wrote and illustrated the whole book." "And I," says the Gentleman, says he – "have good reason to know Sir, that you are wholly mistaken. There is no such a person as Edward Lear." "But," says I, "there is – and I am the man – and I wrote the book!" Whereon all the party burst out laughing and evidently thought me mad or telling fibs. So I took off my hat and showed it all round, with Edward Lear and the address in large letters – also one of my cards, and a marked handkerchief: on which amazement devoured those benighted individuals and I left them to gnash their teeth in trouble and tumult.

(Edward Lear, *letter to
Lady Waldegrave, October 1866*)

Oscar Wilde said once, "A poet can survive anything but a misprint." It wasn't exactly a misprint but a misspelling which has gone down in the history of the fall of Oscar Wilde. In 1891 Wilde met Lord Alfred Douglas ("Bosie") and the affair began which would ultimately ruin the great playwright as well as overshadow the rest of Douglas's life. The Marquess of Queensbury, the enraged father of Douglas, was scandalized by their relationship and conducted a long campaign against Wilde. At the opening night in February 1895 of what would be Wilde's last play, *The Importance of Being Earnest*, Queensbury planned to harangue the audience. Denied admission to the theatre, he left at the stage door a "grotesque bouquet of vegetables" as a mark of his contempt for Wilde. Four days later the still furious Marquess called at the Albermarle Club in Piccadilly, of which Wilde was a member, and wrote a message on the back of a visiting card, telling the hall porter to give it to Oscar Wilde when he next appeared.

Almost a fortnight went by before Wilde visited the club. As he walked into the building, the porter handed him an open envelope containing the card. What Queensbury had scribbled was "For Oscar Wilde posing as a somdomite". In his fury Douglas's father had misspelled "sodomite". Wilde rose to the bait even though at that stage no one had seen the card apart from Douglas and the so-called "somdomite" – and the porter, who anyway hadn't understood what was written on the card. Wilde returned to the hotel where Douglas had recently been staying with him and wrote to his friend Robbie Ross: "Bosie's father has left a card at my club with hideous words on it. I don't see anything now but a criminal prosecution. My whole life seems ruined by this man. The tower of ivory is assailed by the foul thing."

Wilde would have been wiser to have done what at least one of his legal advisers suggested later – tear up the card with its incriminating message and throw it on the fire. But his anger and despair at Queensbury's unrelenting persecution, together with Bosie's own hatred of his father, decided him to launch a prosecution against the Marquess. Queensbury was arrested and bailed to appear at the Old Bailey on a charge of libel. At the trial Wilde and Douglas's association with various young men was revealed (see also *Law*), while Wilde's own responses under cross-examination showed that it was all too likely that the accusation of sodomy – whether "posing" or not – was justified. A "not guilty" verdict was returned for Queensbury. Wilde left the court, knowing that the information which had surfaced during the trial meant that he would almost certainly find himself taking his persecutor's place in the dock. He was arrested later that afternoon at the Cadogan Hotel, taken to Scotland Yard and charged with gross indecency.

The Marquess of Queensbury was delighted. Afterwards he claimed that the message on the card was a deliberate attempt to bring matters to a head but the angry scrawl, and the misspelled "somdomite", perhaps suggest that it was intended to be no more than a pinprick in his anti-Wilde campaign. The tragic error was Wilde's, and he later described the trivial chain of circumstances which had caused him to walk into his club and accept the fatal card. He had been intending to travel to France that very day but stayed behind in London to settle a hotel bill – the hotel where he had been staying with Douglas.

Money

Andrew Marvell, the 17th-century poet, is best remembered now for his seduction poem "To His Coy Mistress". He was also Member of Parliament for Hull. Although the government of the day tried to "buy" him, this (anonymous) story shows that he wasn't easily corrupted by bribes.

The borough of Hull, in the reign of Charles II, chose Andrew Marvell, a young gentleman of little or no fortune, and maintained him in London for the service of the public. His understanding, integrity, and spirit, were dreadful to the then administration. Persuaded that he would be theirs for properly asking, they sent his old school-fellow, the Lord Treasurer Danby, to renew acquaintance with him in his garret. At parting, the Lord Treasurer, out of *pure affection*, slipped into his hand an order upon the treasury for £1000, and then went to his chariot. Marvell, looking at the paper, calls after the Treasurer, "My Lord, I request another moment." They went up again to the garret, and Jack, the servant boy, was called. "Jack, child, what had I for dinner yesterday?" "Don't you remember, sir? you had the little shoulder of mutton that you ordered me to bring from a woman in the market?" "Very right, child. What have I for dinner today?" "Don't you know, sir, that you bid me lay by the blade-bone to broil?" "'Tis so, very right, child, go away." "My Lord, do you hear that? Andrew Marvell's dinner is provided; there's your piece of paper. I want it not. I know the sort of business you intended. I live here to serve my constituents: the ministry may seek men for their purpose: *I am not one.*"

Sir Richard Steele was a dramatist and essayist. Like many 18th-century writers, he added politics and propaganda to his more artistic endeavours. Also, like other writers of the time – and of any time – he ran into money problems. In his life of the poet Richard Savage, Samuel Johnson tells these anecdotes.

[Richard Savage] was once desired by Sir Richard [Steele], with an air of the utmost importance, to come very early to his house the next morning. Mr Savage came as he had promised, found the chariot at the door, and Sir Richard waiting for him and ready to go out. What was intended, and whither they were to go, Savage could not conjecture, and was not willing to inquire; but immediately seated himself with Sir Richard. The coachman was ordered to drive, and they hurried with the utmost expedition to Hyde Park Corner, where they stopped at a petty tavern and retired to a private room. Sir Richard then informed him that he intended to publish a pamphlet, and that he had desired him to come thither that he might write for him. He soon sat down to the work. Sir Richard dictated, and Savage wrote, till the dinner that had been ordered was put upon the table. Savage was surprised at the meanness of the entertainment, and after some hesitation ventured to ask for wine, which Sir Richard, not without reluctance, ordered to be brought. They then finished their dinner, and proceeded in their pamphlet, which they concluded in the afternoon.

Mr Savage then imagined his task over, and expected that Sir Richard would call for the reckoning and return home; but his expectations deceived him, for Sir Richard told him that he was without money, and that the pamphlet must be sold before the dinner could be paid for; and Savage was therefore obliged to go and offer their new production to sale for two guineas, which with some difficulty he obtained. Sir Richard then returned home, having retired that day only to avoid his creditors, and composed the pamphlet only to discharge his reckoning.

Mr Savage related another fact equally uncommon, which, though it has no relation to his life, ought to be preserved. Sir Richard Steele having one day invited to his house a great number of persons of the first quality, they were surprised at the number of liveries [servants in uniform] which surrounded the table; and, after dinner, when wine and mirth had set them free from the observation of a rigid ceremony, one of them inquired of Sir Richard how such an expensive train of domestics could be consistent with his fortune. Sir Richard very frankly confessed that they were fellows of whom he would very willingly be rid. And being then asked why he did not discharge them, declared that they were bailiffs, who had introduced themselves with an execution, and whom, since he could not send them away, he had thought it convenient to embellish with liveries, that they might do him credit while they stayed.

His friends were diverted with the expedient, and by paying the debt discharged their attendants, having obliged Sir Richard to promise that they should never again find him graced with a retinue of the same kind.

(Samuel Johnson, *Life of Savage*)

Oliver Goldsmith struggled to make a living as a writer. James Boswell tells the story of how their mutual friend Dr Johnson saved Goldsmith from arrest for debt.

He [Goldsmith] boasted to me at this time of the power of his pen in commanding money, which I believe was true in a certain degree, though in the instance he gave he was by no means correct. He told me that he had sold a novel for four hundred pounds. This was his *Vicar of Wakefield*. But Johnson informed me, that he had made the bargain for Goldsmith and the price was sixty pounds. "And, sir," said he, "a sufficient price too, when it was sold; for then the fame of Goldsmith had not been elevated, as it afterwards was, by his [poem] *Traveller*; and the bookseller had such faint hopes of profit by his bargain, that he kept the manuscript by him a long time, and did not publish it till after the *Traveller* had appeared. Then, to be sure, it was accidentally worth more money."

Mrs Piozzi and Sir John Hawkins have strangely misstated the history of Goldsmith's situation and Johnson's friendly interference, when this novel was sold. I shall give it authentically from Johnson's own exact narration:

"I received one morning a message from poor Goldsmith that he was in great distress, and, as it was not in his power to come to me, begging that I would come to him as soon as possible. I sent him a guinea, and promised to come to him directly. I accordingly went as soon as I was drest, and found that his landlady had arrested him for his rent, at which he was in a violent passion. I perceived that he had already changed my guinea, and had got a bottle of Madeira and a glass before him. I put the cork into the bottle, desired he would be calm, and began to talk to him of the means by which he might be extricated. He then told me that he had a novel ready for the press, which he produced to me. I looked into it, and saw its merit; told the landlady I should soon return, and having gone to a bookseller, sold it for sixty pounds. I brought Goldsmith the money, and he discharged his rent, not without rating his landlady in a high tone for having used him so ill."

(James Boswell, *Life Of Dr Johnson*)

On the other hand, when he did actually get hold of any money, Oliver Goldsmith showed a sense of fairness (which made him a profit in the long run). The book-seller here was Goldsmith's publisher.

Previous to the publication of his [poem] *Deserted Village*, the book-seller had given him a note for one hundred guineas for the copy, which the Doctor [Goldsmith] mentioned, a few hours after, to one of his friends, who observed it was a very great sum for so short a performance. "In truth," replied Goldsmith, "I think so too; I have not been easy since I received it; therefore, I will go back, and return him his note;" which he absolutely did, and left it entirely to the book-seller to pay him according to the profits produced by the sale of the piece which turned out to be very considerable.

(from *The Annual Register of the year 1774*)

The 18th-century novelist Tobias Smollett is asked for money by a beggar.

A beggar asking Dr Smollett for alms, he gave him, through mistake, a guinea. The poor fellow, on perceiving it, hobbled after him to return it; upon which, Smollett returned it to him, with another guinea as a reward for his honesty, exclaiming at the same time, "What a lodging has honesty taken up with."

(Anon, *Anecdotes of Books and Authors*)

The Victorian novelist Anthony Trollope worked for most of his writing life in the Post Office (see also **Day Jobs**). *During his junior years in the office he was haunted by a money-lender who seems to have stepped straight out of the pages of one of Dickens' novels.*

I rarely at this time had any money wherewith to pay my bills. In this state of things a certain tailor had taken from me an acceptance for, I think £12, which found its way into the hands of a money-lender. With that man, who lived in a little street near Mecklenburgh Square, I formed a most heart-rending but a most intimate acquaintance. In cash I once received from him £4. For that and for the original amount of the tailor's bill, which grew monstrously under repeated renewals, I paid ultimately something over £200. That is so common a story as to be hardly worth the telling; but the peculiarity of this man was that he became so attached to me as to visit me every day at my office. For a long period he found it to be worth his while to walk up those stone steps daily, and come and stand behind my chair, whispering to me always the same words: "Now I wish you would be punctual. If you only would be punctual, I should like you to have anything you want." He was a little, clean, old man, who always wore a high starched white cravat, inside which he had a habit of twisting his chin as he uttered his caution. When I remember the constant persistency of his visits, I cannot but feel that he was paid very badly for his time and trouble. Those visits were very terrible, and can have hardly been of service to me in the office.

(Anthony Trollope, *An Autobiography*)

Jane Welsh Carlyle kept a journal from 1855-6. When it came to dealing with the Tax Commissioners she was reluctant to leave things to her husband, the historian Thomas Carlyle.

20 November, 1855. I have been fretting inwardly all this day at the prospect of having to go and appeal before the Tax Commissioners at Kensington tomorrow morning. Still, it must be done. If Mr C. should go himself he would run his head against some post in impatience; and besides for me, when it is over it will be over, whereas he would not get the better of it for twelve months – if ever at all . . .

21 November. Mr. C. said "the voice of honour seemed to call on him to go himself". But either it did not call loud enough, or he would not listen to that charmer. I went in a cab, to save all my breath for appealing. Set down at 30 Hornton Street, I found a dirty private-like house, only with Tax Office painted on the door. A dirty woman-servant opened the door, and told me the Commissioners would not be there for half an hour, but I might walk up. There were already some half-score of men assembled in the waiting-room, among whom I saw the man who cleans our clocks, and a young apothecary of Cheyne Walk. All the others, to look at them, could not have been suspected for an instant, I should have said, of making a hundred a year . . .

"First-come lady," called the clerk, opening a small sidedoor, and I stept forward into a *grand peut-être* [the great unknown]. There was an instant of darkness while the one door was shut behind and the other opened in front; and there I stood in a dim room where three men sat round a large table spread with papers. One held a pen ready over an open ledger; another was taking snuff, and had taken still worse in his time, to judge by his shaky, clayed appearance. The third, who was plainly the cock of that dung-heap, was sitting for Rhadamanthus★ – a Rhadamanthus without the justice.

"Name," said the horned-owl-looking individual holding the pen.

"Carlyle."

"What?"

★ Rhadamanthus – A severe judge in the classical underworld.

"Carlyle."

Seeing he still looked dubious, I spelt it for him.

"Ha!" cried Rhadamanthus, a big, bloodless-faced, insolent-looking fellow, "What is this? Why is Mr Carlyle not come himself? Didn't he get a letter ordering him to appear? Mr Carlyle wrote some nonsense about being exempted from coming, and I desired an answer to be sent that he must come, must do as other people."

"Then, sir," I said, "your desire has been neglected, it would seem, my husband having received no such letter; and I was told by one of your fellow Commissioners that Mr Carlyle's personal appearance was not indispensable."

"Huffgh! Huffgh! what does Mr Carlyle mean by saying he has no income from his writings, when he himself fixed it in the beginning at a hundred and fifty?"

"It means, sir, that, in ceasing to write, one ceases to be paid for writing, and Mr Carlyle has published nothing for several years."

"Huffgh! Huffgh! I understand nothing about that."

"I do," whispered the snuff-taking Commissioner at my ear. "I can quite understand a literary man does not always make money. I would take it off, for my share, but (sinking his voice still lower) I am only one voice here, and not the most important."

"There," said I, handing to Rhadamanthus Chapman and Hall's account; "that will prove Mr Carlyle's statement."

"What am I to make of that? Huffgh! We should have Mr Carlyle here to swear to this before we believe it."

"If a gentleman's word of honour written at the bottom of that paper is not enough, you can put me on my oath: I am ready to swear to it."

"You! You, indeed! No, no! we can do nothing with *your* oath."

"But, sir, I understand my husband's affairs fully, better than he does himself."

"That I can well believe; but we can make nothing of this" – flinging my document contemptuously on the table. The horned owl picked it up, glanced over it while Rhadamanthus was tossing papers about, and grumbling about "people that wouldn't conform to rules"; then handed it back to him, saying deprecatingly: "But, sir, this is a very plain statement."

"Then what has Mr Carlyle to live upon? You don't mean to tell me he lives on that?" – pointing to the document.

"Heaven forbid, sir! but I am not here to explain what Mr Carlyle has to live on, only to declare his income from literature during the last three years."

"True! True!" mumbled the not-most-important voice at my elbow.

"Mr Carlyle, I believe, has landed income."

"Of which," said I haughtily, for my spirit was up, "I have fortunately no account to render in this kingdom and to this board."

"Take off fifty pounds, say a hundred – take off a hundred pounds," said Rhadamanthus to the horned owl. "If we write Mr Carlyle down a hundred and fifty he has no reason to complain, I think. There, you may go. Mr Carlyle has no reason to complain."

Second-come woman was already introduced, and I was motioned to the door; but I could not depart without saying that "at all events there was no use in complaining since they had the power to enforce their decision". On stepping out, my first thought was, what a mercy Carlyle didn't come himself! For the rest, though it might have gone better, I was thankful it had not gone worse.

William Dean Howells remembers how Samuel Clemens (Mark Twain) responded to a telling-off from a railroad employee.

Another time, some years afterward, we sat down together in places near the end of a [rail]car, and a brakeman came in looking for his official notebook. Clemens found that he had sat down upon it, and handed it to him; the man scolded him very abusively, and came back again and again, still scolding him for having no more sense than to sit down on a notebook. The patience of Clemens in bearing it was so angelic that I saw fit to comment, "I suppose you will report this fellow." "Yes," he answered, slowly and sadly. "That's what I should have done

once. But now I remember that he gets twenty dollars a
month."

(William Dean Howells, My Mark Twain)

D. H. Lawrence came from a working-class Nottinghamshire
family. His autobiographical novel *Sons and Lovers* tells of the
tension between his ambitious mother and his father, who was a
miner with little time or patience for "art". When his first novel,
The White Peacock, was published in 1911 his mother was dying.
After her funeral, Lawrence's father struggled through half a page
of the book. He didn't understand it and the following dialogue
took place.

"And what dun they gie thee for that, lad?"
"Fifty pounds, father."
"Fifty pounds! Fifty pounds! An' tha's niver done a day's hard
work in thy life."

The American mystery writer Erle Stanley Gardner is best
known for his creation of the lawyer Perry Mason, who had a
habit of revealing the identity of the real murderer at the last
moment, in the court-room itself. Mason, memorably played by
Raymond Burr in a long-running TV series, never lost any of
the 82 cases he contested against District Attorney Hamilton
Burger. Gardner had himself been a lawyer before he started
writing crime stories for pulp magazines in the 1920s. He was
ferociously productive, turning out 200,000 words a *month* – the
equivalent of two full-length novels. He was paid by the word, a
fact not unconnected with the way in which his fictional villains
survived until the final bullet. When Gardner's editor asked
him why the heroes always missed with the other five shots,
Gardner answered, "At three cents a word, every time I say
bang in the story I get three cents. If you think I'm going to
finish the gun battle while my hero has got fifteen cents' worth
of unexploded ammunition in his gun, you're nuts."

Obsessions & Eccentricities

The biographer James Boswell gives a candid picture of Dr Johnson's habits and peculiarities.

He had another particularity of which none of his friends even ventured to ask an explanation. It appeared to me some superstitious habit, which he had contracted early, and from which he had never called upon his reason to disentangle him. This was his anxious care to go out or in at a door or passage, by a certain number of steps from a certain point, or at least so as that either his right or his left foot (I am not certain which), should constantly make the first actual movement when he came close to the door or passage. Thus I conjecture: for I have, upon innumerable occasions, observed him suddenly stop, and then seem to count his steps with a deep earnestness; and when he had neglected or gone wrong in this sort of magical movement, I have seen him go back again, put himself in a proper posture to begin the ceremony, and, having gone through it, break from his abstraction, walk briskly on, and join his companion. A strange instance of something of this nature, even when on horseback, happened when he was in the Isle of Skye. Sir Joshua Reynolds has observed him to go a good way about, rather than cross a particular alley in Leicester Fields; but this Sir Joshua imputed to his having had some disagreeable recollection associated with it.

That the most minute singularities which belonged to him, and made very observable parts of his appearance and manner, may not be omitted, it is requisite to mention, that while talking or even musing as he sat in his chair, he commonly held his head to one side towards his right shoulder, and shook it in a tremulous manner, moving his body backwards and forwards, and rubbing his left knee in the same direction, with the palm of his hand. In the intervals of articulating he made various sounds with his mouth, sometimes as if ruminating, or what is called chewing the cud, sometimes giving half a whistle, sometimes making his tongue play backwards from the roof of his mouth, as if clucking like a hen, and sometimes protruding it against his upper gums in front, as if pronouncing quickly under his breath, *too, too, too*: all this accompanied sometimes with a thoughtful look, but more frequently with a smile. Generally when he had concluded a period, in the course of a dispute, by which time he was a good deal exhausted by violence and vociferation, he used to blow out his breath like a whale. This I suppose was a relief to his lungs; and seemed in him to be a contemptuous mode of expression, as if he had made the arguments of his opponent fly like chaff before the wind.

I am fully aware how very obvious an occasion I here give for the sneering jocularity of such as have no relish of an exact likeness; which to render complete, he who draws it must not disdain the slightest strokes. But if witlings should be inclined to attack this account, let them have the candour to quote what I have offered in my defence.

(James Boswell, *Life of Johnson*)

The poet Alexander Pope describes the idiosyncratic behaviour of his friend Jonathan Swift, the author of Gulliver's Travels. *Pope and John Gay, author of* The Beggar's Opera, *went to visit Swift one evening.*

Dr Swift has an odd blunt way that is mistaken by strangers for ill-nature. 'Tis so odd that there's no describing it but by facts. I'll tell you one that just comes into my head. One evening Gay and I went to see him: you know how intimately we all were acquainted. On our coming in, "Hey-day, gentlemen," says the Doctor, "what's the meaning of this visit? How come you to leave all the great lords that you are so fond of, to come hither to see a poor Dean?"

"Because we would rather see you than any of them."

"Ay, any one that did not know you as well as I do might

believe you. But since you are come, I must get some supper for you, I suppose?"

"No, Doctor, we have supped already."

"Supped already! that's impossible: why, 'tis not eight o'clock yet."

"Indeed, we have."

"That's very strange: but if you had not supped I must have got something for you. Let me see, what should I have had? a couple of lobsters? Ay, that would have done very well – two shillings: tarts – a shilling. But you will drink a glass of wine with me, though you have supped so much before your usual time, only to spare my pocket?"

"No, we had rather talk with you than drink with you."

"But if you had supped with me, as in all reason you ought to have done, you must have drank with me. A bottle of wine – two shillings. Two and two is four; and one is five: just two and sixpence a piece. – There, Pope, there's half-a-crown for you; and there's another for you, sir: for I won't save any thing by you I am determined."

That was all said and done with his usual seriousness on such occasions; and in spite of everything we could say to the contrary, he actually obliged us to take the money.

(quoted in Joseph Spence, *Anecdotes*)

The poet Samuel Taylor Coleridge was renowned for his forgetfulness and general oddness. Here Charles Lamb recalls a meeting which sounds almost too good to be true.

Brimful of some new idea, and in spite of my assuring him [Coleridge] that time was precious, he drew me within the door of an unoccupied garden by the roadside, and there, sheltered from observation by a hedge of evergreens, he took me by the button of my coat, and closing his eyes commenced an eloquent discourse, waving his right hand gently, as the musical words flowed in an unbroken stream from his lips. I listened entranced; but the striking of a church clock recalled me to a sense of duty. I saw it was of no use to attempt to break away so, taking advantage of his absorption in his subject, I, with my penknife, quietly severed the button from my coat, and de-camped. Five hours afterwards, in passing the same garden on my way home, I heard Coleridge's voice, and on looking in, there he was, with closed eyes – the button in his fingers – and his right hand gracefully waving, just as when I left him. He had never missed me!

(Charles Lamb, *quoted in English Wits*)

Like Coleridge (see above), the poet Percy Bysshe Shelley was a rich source of stories which stressed his eccentricities and obsessions, as these three memories of him show.

About the end of 1813, Shelley was troubled by one of his most extraordinary delusions. He fancied that a fat old woman who sat opposite to him in a mail coach was afflicted with elephantiasis, that the disease was infectious and incurable, and that he had caught it from her. He was continually on the watch for its symptoms; his legs were to swell to the size of an elephant's, and his skin was to be crumpled over like goose-skin. He would draw the skin of his own hands, arms, and neck very tight, and if he discovered any deviation from smoothness, he would seize the person next to him, and endeavour by a corresponding pressure to see if any corresponding deviation existed. He often startled young ladies in an evening party by this singular process, which was as instantaneous as a flash of lightning . . . When he found that, as the days rolled on, his legs retained their proportion, and his skin its smoothness, the delusion died away.

(Thomas Love Peacock, *Memoirs of Shelley*)

*Shelley drowned during a storm off the Italian coast (see also **Death**). All his life he was obsessed with water and boats, although he never learned to swim.*

He [Shelley] was a devoted worshipper of the water-nymphs; for whenever he found a pool, or even a small puddle, he would loiter near it, and it was no easy task to get him to quit it. He had not yet learned that art, from which he afterwards derived so much pleasure – the construction of paper boats. He twisted a morsel of paper into a form that a lively fancy might consider a likeness of a boat and, committing it to the water, he anxiously watched the fortunes of the frail bark, which, if it was not soon swamped by the faint winds and miniature waves, gradually imbibed water through its porous sides, and sank. Sometimes, however, the fairy vessel performed its little voyage and reached the opposite shore of the puny ocean in safety. It is astonishing with what keen delight he engaged in this singular pursuit. It was not easy for an uninitiated spectator to bear with tolerable patience the vast delay, on the brink of a wretched pond upon a bleak common, and in the face of a cutting north-east wind, on returning to dinner from a long walk at sunset on a cold winter's day; nor was it easy to be so harsh as to interfere with a harmless gratification, that was evidently exquisite. It was not easy, at least, to induce the ship-builder to desist from launching his tiny fleets, so long as any timber remained in the dockyard. I prevailed once, and once only; it was one of those bitter Sundays that commonly receive the new year; the sun had set, and it had almost begun to snow. I had exhorted him long in vain, with the eloquence of a frozen and famished man, to proceed; at last, I said in despair – alluding to his never-ending creations, for a paper-navy that was to be set afloat simultaneously lay at his feet, and he was busily constructing more, with blue and swollen hands, "Shelley, there is no use in talking to you – you are the Demiurgus of Plato!" He instantly caught up the whole flotilla, and bounding homeward with mighty strides, laughed aloud laughed like a giant, as he used to say. So long as his paper lasted, he remained riveted to the spot, fascinated by this peculiar amusement; all waste paper was rapidly consumed, then the covers of letters, next letters of little value: the most precious contributions of the most esteemed correspondent, although eyed wistfully many times, and often returned to the pocket, were sure to be sent at last in pursuit of the former squadrons. Of the portable volumes which were the companions of his rambles, and he seldom went out without a book, the flyleaves were commonly wanting – he had applied them as our ancestor Noah applied Gopher wood; but learning was so sacred in his eyes, that he never trespassed farther upon the integrity of the copy; the work itself was always respected. It has been said, that he once found himself on the north bank of the Serpentine river without the materials for indulging those inclinations, which the sight of water invariably inspired, for he had exhausted his supplies on the Round Pond in Kensington Gardens. Not a single scrap of paper could be found, save only a bank-post bill for fifty pounds; he hesitated long, but yielded at last; he twisted it into a boat with the extreme refinement of his skill, and committed it with the utmost dexterity to fortune, watching its progress, if possible, with a still more intense anxiety than usual. Fortune often favours those who frankly and fully trust her; the north-east wind gently wafted the costly skiff to the south bank, where, during the latter part of the voyage, the venturous owner had waited its arrival with patient solicitude. The story, of course, is a Mythic fable, but it aptly portrays the dominion of a singular and most unaccountable passion over the mind of an enthusiast.

(Thomas Jefferson Hogg, *Life of Shelley*)

This third story recounts a supper-party at the Italian house on the bay of Spezzia where the Shelleys were living. An unnamed visitor has arrived.

The visitor came, and he was most anxious to see the Poet, with whose works he was enchanted, and of whose great knowledge and simple habits he had heard so much from me and others; however, they knew how uncertain the Poet was, and never waited for him. The dinner was served with more precision than was usual, and, as sailors have it, "Compliments pass when gentlefolks meet."

The stranger told them the news of the outer world from which they were isolated, for newspapers at that period were a mere farrago of Austrian lies [Italy was under Austrian rule at the time]. From German humbug they got into literature. The visitor said the German students of English literature considered Shelley as a metaphysical and moral philosopher, a writer of transcendent imagination; that he awakened all the dormant faculties of his readers, was the Poet of the inner mind, that he surpassed our popular poets in depth of thought and refinement. One of the party remarked that genius purifies: the naked statues of the Greeks are modest, the draped ones of the moderns are not. The talk was here interrupted by a concussion of glass and crockery, and a vehement exclamation, "Oh my gracious!" from one of the trio of ladies, drew all eyes her way. Appalled by the sight, the ladies instantly averted their gaze and held up their hands, not having fans, in mute despair. Had it been a ghoul, he would have been scoffed at, as they prey on the dead; if it had been a spectre or phantom he would have been robed, and therefore welcome, for they are shadowy and refined spirits; but the company were confronted by an apparition not tolerated in our chaste and refined age even in marble – by our poet, washed, indeed, for he was just out of the sea, not in an evening costume, nor was his hair dressed, as his wife had promised it should be; but, like Adam before the fall –

> Such of late
> Columbus found the Americans, so girt
> With feathered cincture; naked else, and wild.

The brine from his shock of hair trickling down his innocent nose; if he were girt with a feathered cincture or anything else, it was not visible; small fragments of seaweed clung to his hair, and he was odorous of the salt brine – he scorned encumbering himself with combs or towels. He was gliding noiselessly round the two sides of the saloon to his room, and might possibly have succeeded unnoticed, or certainly unchallenged – as the Italian maid, with accustomed tact, had walked by his side, carefully screening him from the company – but for the refined and excitable lady calling attention to such an unprecedented licence even in a poet.

The simple and innocent bard, grieved at having given pain by his alleged breach of etiquette, felt bound to explain his case so, stopping beside the complainant, and drawing himself up (as the novelists have it) to his full height, with the air and accent of a boy wrongfully accused, said,

"How can I help it? I must go to my room to get my clothes;

there is no way to get to it but through this. At this hour I have always found this place vacant. I have not altered my hour of bathing, but you have changed yours for dining. The skittish skiff has played me one of her usual tricks by upsetting all my clothes in the water; the land breeze is getting up, and they will be drifting out to sea again, if I don't make haste to recover them."

His blushing wife could not bandy words with a sea monster. Having thus refuted to his own satisfaction the implied censure on his manners, he, without noticing any one else, glided from out the puddle he had made on the floor into his dormitory. The dinner circle were thus indebted to the sensitive lady, not only for a full view of our poet in his character of a merman, but for an oration.

In a few minutes he reappeared, rushing down to secure his former attire. Speedily coming back, he held up a book, saying, "I have recovered this priceless gem from the wreck." (Aeschylus).

He then took his place, unconscious of having done anything that could offend any one.

(Edward Trelawny, *Records of
Shelley, Byron, and the Author*)

George Dyer was a minor poet and full-time eccentric. His friend, the essayist Charles Lamb, describes how Dyer visited one day.

What I now tell you is literally true. Yesterday week George Dyer called upon us, at one o'clock (*bright noonday*) on his way to dine with Mrs Barbauld at Newington. He sat with Mary about half an hour, and took leave. The maid saw him go out, from her kitchen window, but suddenly losing sight of him, ran up in a fright to Mary. G. D., instead of keeping the slip that leads to the gate, had deliberately, staff in hand, in broad open day, marched into the New River. He had not his spectacles on, and you know his absence. Who helped him out, they can hardly tell; but between 'em they got him out, drenched thro' and thro'. A mob collected by that time and accompanied him in. "Send for the Doctor!" they said: and a one-eyed fellow, dirty and drunk, was fetched from the Public House at the end, where it seems he lurks, for the sake of picking up water practice, having formerly had a medal from the Humane Society for some rescue. By his advice, the patient was put between blankets; and when I came home at four to dinner, I found G. D. a-bed and raving, light-headed with the brandy-and-water which the doctor had administered. He sung, laughed, whimpered, screamed, babbled of guardian angels, would get up and go home; but we kept him there by force; and by next morning he departed sobered, and seems to have received no injury. All my friends are open-mouthed about having paling before the river, but I cannot see that, because a . . . lunatic chooses to walk into a river with his eyes open at midday, I am any the more likely to be drowned in it, coming home at midnight.

(Charles Lamb, *letter to Sarah Hazlitt*)

Thomas de Quincey describes the poet William Wordsworth's legs and his individual style of walking.

Wordsworth was, upon the whole, not a well-made man. His legs were pointedly condemned by all the female connoisseurs in legs that ever I heard lecture upon that topic; not that they were bad in any way which would force itself upon your notice – there was no absolute deformity about them; and undoubtedly they had been serviceable legs beyond the average standard of human requisition; for I calculate, upon good data, that with these identical legs Wordsworth must have traversed a distance of 175 to 180,000 English miles – a mode of exertion which, to him, stood in the stead of wine, spirits, and all other stimulants whatsoever to the animal spirits; to which he has been indebted for a life of unclouded happiness, and we for much of what is most excellent in his writings. But, useful as they have proved themselves, the Wordsworthian legs were certainly not ornamental; and it was really a pity, as I agreed with a lady in thinking, that he had not another pair for evening dress parties – when no boots lend their friendly aid to masque our imperfections from the eyes of female rigorists . . . the total effect of Wordsworth's person was always worst in a state of motion; for, according to the remark I have heard from many country people, "he walked like a cade" – a cade being some sort of insect which advances by an oblique motion. This was not always perceptible, and in part depended (I believe) upon the position of his arms; when either of these happened (as was very customary) to be inserted into the unbuttoned waistcoat, his walk had a wry or twisted appearance; and not appearance only – for I have known it, by slow degrees, gradually to edge off his companion from the middle to the side of the highroad.

(Thomas de Quincey, *Recollections of the Lake Poets*)

Thomas Lovell Beddoes was a poet and dramatist who lived in the first half of the nineteenth century. Now largely forgotten, he led an odd life, divided between medicine and writing. In 1835 he moved to Switzerland. His last years are described by Lytton Strachey in his essay "The Last Elizabethan". The "Gothic-styled tragedy" which Beddoes had worked on for years and which was incomplete at the time of his death was called – appropriately enough in view of his interest in the subject – Death's Jest Book.

During the following years we catch glimpses of him [Beddoes], flitting mysteriously over Germany and Switzerland, at Berlin, at Baden, at Giessen, a strange solitary figure, with tangled hair and meerschaum pipe, scribbling lampoons upon the King of Prussia, translating Grainger's *Spinal Cord* into German, and Schoenlein's *Diseases of Europeans* into English . . . or brooding over the scenes of his "Gothic-styled tragedy", wondering if it were worthless or inspired, and giving it – as had been his wont for the last twenty years – just one more touch before he sent it to the press. He appeared in England once or twice, and in 1846 made a stay of several months, visiting the Procters in London, and going down to Southampton to be with Kelsall once again. Eccentricity had grown on him; he would shut himself for days in his bedroom, smoking furiously; he would fall into fits of long and deep depression. He shocked some of his relatives by arriving at their country house astride a donkey; and he amazed the Procters by starting out one evening to set fire to Drury Lane Theatre with a lighted five-pound note.

After this last visit to England, his history becomes even more obscure than before. It is known that in 1847 he was in Frankfurt, where he lived for six months in close companionship with a young baker called Degen – "a nice-looking young man, nineteen years of age," we are told, "dressed in a blue blouse, fine in expression, and of a natural dignity of manner"; and that, in the spring of the following year, the two friends went off to Zurich, where Beddoes hired the theatre for a night in order that Degen might appear on the stage in the part of Hotspur [in Shakespeare's *Henry IV*]. At Basle, however, for some unexplained reason, the friends parted, and Beddoes fell immediately into the profoundest gloom. "Il a été miserable," ["he has been depressed"] said the waiter at the Cigogne Hotel, where he was staying, "il a voulu se tuer." ["he has wanted to kill himself"]. It was true. He inflicted a deep wound in his leg with a razor, in the hope, apparently, of bleeding to death. He was taken to the hospital, where he constantly tore off the bandages, until at last it was necessary to amputate the leg below the knee. The operation was successful, Beddoes began to recover, and, in the autumn, Degen came back to Basle. It seemed as if all were going well; for the poet, with his books around him, and the blue-bloused Degen by his bedside, talked happily of politics and literature, and of an Italian journey in the spring. He walked out twice; was he still happy? Who can tell? Was it happiness, or misery, or what strange impulse, that drove him, on his third walk, to go to a chemist's shop in the town, and to obtain there a phial of deadly poison? On the evening of that day – the 26th of January, 1849 – Dr Ecklin, his physician, was hastily summoned, to find Beddoes lying insensible upon the bed.

He never recovered consciousness, and died that night. Upon his breast was found a pencil note, addressed to one of his English friends. "My dear Philips," it began, "I am food for what I am good for – worms." A few testamentary wishes followed. Kelsall was to have the manuscripts; and – "W. Beddoes must have a case (50 bottles) of Champagne Moet, 1847 growth, to drink my death in . . . I ought to have been, among other things," the gruesome document concluded, "a good poet. Life was too great a bore on one peg, and that a bad one. Buy for Dr Ecklin one of Reade's best stomach-pumps." It was the last of his additions to Death's Jest Book, and the most macabre of all.

(Lytton Strachey, *Books and Characters*)

When the author Nathaniel Hawthorne was living in England in the mid-1850s (he was the American consul in Liverpool) he visited Lord Byron's home at Newstead Abbey. Byron was long dead but the housekeeper showed Hawthorne the poet's unusual drinking vessel.

Here, I think, the house-keeper unlocked a beautiful cabinet, and took out the famous skull which Lord Byron transformed into a drinking-goblet. It has a silver rim and stand, but still the ugly skull is bare and evident, and the naked inner bone receives the wine. I should think it would hold at least a quart – enough to overpower any living head into which this death's-head should transfer its contents; and a man must be either very drunk or very thirsty, before he would taste wine out of such a goblet. I think Byron's freak was outdone by that of a cousin of my own, who once solemnly assured me that he had a spittoon made out of the skull of his enemy. The ancient coffin in which the goblet-skull was found was shown us in the basement of the Abbey.

Charles Dodgson, who used the pen-name Lewis Carroll to write the Alice books, was a genuine eccentric.

An old bachelor is generally very precise and exact in his habits. He has no one but himself to look after, nothing to distract his attention from his own affairs; and Mr Dodgson was the most precise and exact of old bachelors. He made a precis of every letter he wrote or received from the 1st of January, 1861, to the 8th of the same month, 1898. These precis were all numbered and entered in reference books, and by an ingenious system of cross-numbering he was able to trace a whole correspondence, which might extend through several volumes. The last number entered in his book is 98,721.

He had scores of green cardboard boxes, all neatly labelled, in which he kept his various papers. These boxes formed quite a feature of his study at Oxford, a large number of them being arranged upon a revolving bookstand. The lists, of various sorts, which he kept were innumerable; one of them, that of unanswered correspondents, generally held seventy or eighty names at a time, exclusive of autograph-hunters, whom he did not answer on principle. He seemed to delight in being arithmetically accurate about every detail of life.

He always rose at the same early hour, and, if he was in residence at Christ Church [Oxford], attended College Service. He spent the day according to a prescribed routine, which usually included a long walk into the country, very often alone, but sometimes with another Don, or perhaps, if the walk was not to be as long as usual, with some little girlfriend at his side. When he had a companion with him, he would talk the whole time, telling delightful stories, or explaining some new logical problem; if he was alone, he used to think out his books, as probably many another author has done and will do, in the course of a lonely walk. The only irregularity noticeable in his mode of life was the hour of retiring, which varied from 11 p.m. to four o'clock in the morning, according to the amount of work which he felt himself in the mood for.

He had a wonderfully good memory, except for faces and dates. The former were always a stumbling-block to him, and people used to say (most unjustly) that he was intentionally short-sighted. One night he went up to London to dine with a friend, whom he had only recently met. The next morning a gentleman greeted him as he was walking. "I beg your pardon," said Mr Dodgson, "but you have the advantage of me. I have no remembrance of having ever seen you before this moment." "That is very strange," the other replied, "for I was your host last night!" Such little incidents as this happened more than once . . .

That he was, in some respects, eccentric cannot be denied; for instance he hardly ever wore an overcoat, and always wore a tall hat, whatever might be the climatic conditions. At dinner in his rooms small pieces of cardboard took the place of table-mats; they answered the purpose perfectly well, he said, and to buy anything else would be a mere waste of money. On the other hand, when purchasing books for himself, or giving treats to the children he loved, he never seemed to consider expense at all.

He very seldom sat down to write, preferring to stand while thus engaged. When making tea for his friends, he used, in order, I suppose, to expedite the process, to walk up and down the room waving the teapot about, and telling meanwhile those delightful anecdotes of which he had an inexhaustible supply.

Great were his preparations before going a journey; each separate article used to be carefully wrapped up in a piece of paper all to itself, so that his trunks contained nearly as much paper as of the more useful things. The bulk of the luggage was sent on a day or two before by goods train, while he himself followed on the appointed day, laden only with his well-known little black bag, which he always insisted on carrying himself.

He had a strong objection to startling colours in dress, his favourite combination being pink and grey. One little girl who came to stay with him was absolutely forbidden to wear a red frock, of a somewhat pronounced hue, while out in his company.

At meals he was very abstemious always, while he took nothing in the middle of the day except a glass of wine and a biscuit. Under these circumstances it is not very surprising that the healthy appetites of his little friends filled him with wonder, and even with alarm. When he took a certain one of them out with him to a friend's house to dinner, he used to give the host or hostess a gentle warning, to the mixed amazement and indignation of the child, "Please be careful, because she eats a good deal too much."

Another peculiarity, which I have already referred to, was his objection to being invited to dinners or any other social gatherings; he made a rule of never accepting invitations. "Because you have invited me, therefore I cannot come," was the usual form of his refusal. I suppose the reason of this was his hatred of the interference with work which engagements of this sort occasion.

(Stuart Dodgson Collingwood, *Life of Lewis Carroll*)

Novelist Henry James didn't exactly possess the common touch. His style of speaking was so elaborate that it sometimes left people confused – or amused. His fellow-American and author Edith Wharton recounted the story of how she and James were once being driven to Windsor. It was dark, and their driver didn't know the route. James spotted a doddery old man and, after summoning him to the car, began to explain things: "My friend, to put it to you in two words, this lady and I have just arrived here from Slough; that is to say, to be more strictly accurate, we have recently *passed through* Slough on our way here, having actually motored to Windsor from Rye, which was our point of departure; and the darkness having overtaken us, we should be much obliged if you would tell us where we now are in relation, say, to the High Street, which, as you of course know, leads to the Castle, after leaving on the left hand the turn down to the railway station."

The old man said nothing. Instead he looked dazed. James ploughed on:

"In short, my good man, what I want to put to you in a word is this: supposing we have already (as I have reason to think we have) driven past the turn down to the railway station (which in that case, by the way, would probably not have been on our left hand, but on our right), where are we now in relation to . . ."

At this point, James' companion Edith Wharton cut in impatiently: "Oh, please, do ask him where the King's Road is."

"Ah – ? The King's Road? Just so! Quite right! Can you, as a matter of fact, my good man, tell us where, in relation to our present position, the King's Road exactly is?"

The doddery old man's reply was as short and simple as it could be. All he said was: "Ye're in it."

Parents & Children

Sir Thomas More, the Lord Chancellor of England executed by Henry VIII, was the author of Utopia. *Beheaded in 1535, his head was exhibited (like the heads of others convicted of treason) on London Bridge.*

After he was beheaded, his trunke was interred in Chelsey church, neer the middle of the South wall, where was some slight Monument erected. His head was upon London bridge. There goes this story in the family, viz. that one day as one of his daughters was passing under the Bridge, looking on her father's head, sayd she, That head haz layn many a time in my Lapp, would to God it would fall into my Lap as I passe under. She had her wish, and it did fall into her Lappe, and is now preserved in a vault in the Cathedral Church at Canterbury.

(John Aubrey, *Brief Lives*)

In fact, More's daughter Margaret did somehow get possession of her father's severed head, although probably not in the way described here. She put it in a leaden box and guarded it with devotion.

The son of Sir Walter Raleigh was too similar to his father for comfort.

My old friend James Harrington, Esq. was well acquainted with Sir Benjamin Ruddyer, who was an acquaintance of Walter Raleigh's. He told Mr J. H. that Sir Walter Raleigh being invited to dinner with some great person, where his son was to goe with him: He sayd to his Son, Thou art such a quarrelsome, affronting creature that I am ashamed to have such a Beare in my Company. Mr Walt humbled himselfe to his Father, and promised he would behave himselfe mightily mannerly. So away they went, and Sir Benjamin, I thinke, with them. He sate next to his Father and was very demure at least halfe dinner time. Then sayd he, I this morning, not having the feare of God before my eies, but by the instigation of the devill, went to a Whore. I was very eager of her, kissed and embraced her, and went to enjoy her, but she thrust me from her, and vowed I should not, *For your father lay with me but an hower ago*. Sir Walt, being so strangely supprized and putt out of his countenance at so great a Table, gives his son a damned blow over the face; his son, as rude as he was, would not strike his father; but strikes over the face of the Gentleman that sate next to him, and sayed, *Box about, 'twill come to my Father anon*. 'Tis now a common used Proverb.

(John Aubrey, *Brief Lives*)

The playwright and poet Ben Jonson heard of the death of his son in September 1603.

Ben Jonson's eldest son, a boy of seven years old, is dead of the plague, Ben himself being in the country at Sir Robert Cotton's house with Master Camden. He declareth that he saw in a vision his son with the mark of a bloody cross on his forehead, and in the morning he told Master Camden who would persuade him that it was but an apprehension of his fantasy; but anon came letters from his wife of the death of that boy. Upon whom Ben hath written an epigram wherein he calls him "Ben Jonson, his best piece of poetry."

(Ben Jonson, *Conversations with Drummond of Hawthornden*)

The poet and clergyman John Donne has a disturbing dream on a diplomatic mission in Paris in the early 1600s.

At this time of Mr Donne's and his wife's living in Sir Robert's house, the Lord Hay was, by King James, sent upon a glorious embassy to the then French King, Henry the Fourth; and Sir Robert put on a sudden resolution to accompany him to the French court, and to be present at his audience there. And Sir Robert put on a sudden resolution, to solicit Mr Donne to be his companion in that journey and this desire was suddenly made known to his wife, who was then with child, and otherwise under so dangerous a habit of body as to her health, that she professed an unwillingness to allow him any absence from her; saying, "Her divining soul boded her some ill in his absence"; and therefore desired him not to leave her. This made Mr Donne lay aside all thoughts of the journey and really to resolve against it. But Sir Robert became restless in his persuasions for it, and Mr Donne was so generous as to think he had sold his liberty, when he received so many charitable kindnesses from him; and told his wife so; who did therefore, with an unwilling-willingness, give a faint consent to the journey, which was proposed to be but for two months; for about that time they determined their return. Within a few days after this resolve, the Ambassador, Sir Robert, and Mr Donne, left London; and were the twelfth day got all safe to Paris. Two days after their arrival there, Mr Donne was left alone in that room, in which Sir Robert, and he, and some other friends had dined together. To this place Sir Robert returned within half an hour; and as he left, so he found, Mr Donne alone; but in such an ecstasy, and so altered as to his looks, as amazed Sir Robert to behold him; insomuch that he earnestly desired Mr Donne to declare what had befallen him in the short time of his absence. To which Mr Donne was not able to make a present answer: but, after a long and perplexed pause, did at last say, "I have seen a dreadful vision since I saw you: I have seen my dear wife pass twice by me through this room, with her hair hanging about her shoulders, and a dead child in her arms: this I have seen since I saw you." To which Sir Robert replied, "Sure, Sir, you have slept since I saw you; and this the result of some melancholy dream, which I desire you to forget, for you are now awake." To which Mr Donne's reply was: "I cannot be surer that I now live, than that I have not slept since I saw you: and am as sure, that her second appearing, she stopped, and looked me in the face, and vanished." – Rest and sleep had not altered Mr Donne's opinion the next day: for he then affirmed this vision with a more deliberate, and so confirmed a confidence, that he inclined Sir Robert to a faint belief that the vision was true. – It is truly said, that desire and doubt have no rest; and it proved so with Sir Robert; for he immediately sent a servant to Drewry-House, with a charge to hasten back, and bring him word, whether Mrs Donne were alive: and, if alive, in what condition she was as to her health. The twelfth day the messenger returned with this account – That he found and left Mrs Donne very sad, and sick in her bed; and that, after a long and dangerous labour, she had been delivered of a dead child. And, upon examination, the abortion proved to be the same day, and about the very hour, that Mr Donne affirmed he saw her pass by in his chamber.

This is a relation that will beget some wonder, and it well may; for most of our world are at present possessed with opinion, that Visions and Miracles are ceased. And, though it is most certain, the two lutes being both strung and tuned to an equal pitch, and then one played upon, the other, that is not touched, being laid upon a table at a fit distance, will – like an echo to a trumpet – warble a faint audible harmony in answer to the same tune; yet many will not believe there is any such thing as a sympathy of souls; and I am well pleased, that every Reader do enjoy his own opinion.

(Izaak Walton, *Life Of Donne*)

The poet John Milton went blind in his middle age and before he had composed his most famous work, Paradise Lost. *He had three daughters by his first wife and one of their duties was to read aloud to their scholarly father, even though they had no understanding of the foreign works he demanded.*

Mr Philips [Milton's nephew] tells us, "that though our author had daily about him one or other to read, some persons of man's estate, who, of their own accord, greedily catched at the opportunity of being his readers, that they might as well reap the benefit of what they read to him, as oblige him by the benefit of their reading; and others of younger years were sent by their parents to the same end: yet excusing only the eldest daughter,

by reason of her bodily infirmity, and difficult utterance of
speech; (which, to say truth, I doubt was the principal cause of
excusing her), the other two were condemned to the performance of reading, and exactly pronouncing of all the languages
of whatever book he should, at one time or other, think fit to
peruse, viz. the Hebrew (and I think the Syriac), the Greek, the
Latin, the Italian, Spanish, and French. All which sorts of
books to be confined to read, without understanding one word,
must needs be a trial of patience almost beyond endurance. Yet
it was endured by both for a long time, though the irksomeness
of this employment could not be always concealed, but broke
out more and more into expressions of uneasiness; so that at
length they were all, even the eldest also, sent out to learn some
curious and ingenious sorts of manufacture, that are proper for
women to learn; particularly embroideries in gold or silver."

                    (Samuel Johnson, *Life of Milton*)

*Tom Sheridan was the son of the late 18th-century playwright
Richard Brinsley Sheridan.*

Tom Sheridan did not "ape his sire" in all things; for whenever
he made an appointment, he was punctuality personified. In
every transaction I had with him, I always found him uniformly
correct; nor did he unfrequently lament his father's indolence
and want of regularity, although he had (indeed naturally) a
high veneration for his talents.

Tom Sheridan had a good voice, and true taste for music,
which, added to his intellectual qualities and superior accom-
plishments, caused his society to be sought with the greatest
avidity.

The two Sheridans were supping with me one night after the
opera, at a period when Tom expected to get into Parliament.

"I think, Father," said he, "that many men, who are called great
patriots in the House of Commons are great humbugs. For my
own part, if I get into Parliament, I will pledge myself to no party
but write upon my forehead, in legible characters 'To be let'."

"And under that, Tom," said his father, "write – 'Unfurn-
ished'."

Tom took the joke, but was even with him on another occasion.

Mr Sheridan had a cottage about half a mile from Hounslow Heath. Tom, being very short of cash, asked his father to let him have some.

"Money I have none," was the reply.

"Be the consequence what it may, money I must have," said Tom.

"If that is the case, my dear Tom," said the affectionate parent, "you will find a case of loaded pistols upstairs, and a horse ready saddled in the stables – the night is dark, and you are within half a mile of Hounslow Heath."

"I understand what you mean," said Tom, "but I tried that last night. I unluckily stopped Peake, your treasurer, who told me that you had been beforehand with him, and had robbed him of every sixpence he had in the world."

(Michael Kelly, *Reminiscences*)

Money was obviously a touchy subject in relations between Richard Sheridan and his son, as this short anecdote shows.

3 October 1818. Sheridan, the first time he met Tom, after the marriage of the latter, seriously angry with him; told him he had made his will, and had cut him off with a shilling. Tom said he was, indeed, very sorry, and immediately added, "You don't happen to have the shilling about you now, sir, do you?" Old S. burst out laughing, and they became friends again.

(Tom Moore, *Diary*)

The sparring relationship between Sheridan and his son, and the quick wit of the latter, is shown by another story told by Tom after his father's death. Recalling that his father had once told him that, since their family was descended from a line of Irish kings, they really should be known as the O'Sheridans, Tom responded, "Yes, that's because we owe everybody money."

Walter Scott had some odd memories of his early life. The second passage refers to his lameness – the result of polio which he contracted when he was less than two years old.

An odd incident is worth recording. It seems, my mother had sent a maid to take charge of me, at this farm of Sandy-Knowe, that I might be no inconvenience to the family. But the damsel sent on that important mission had left her heart behind her, in the keeping of some wild fellow, it is likely, who had done and said more to her than he was like to make good. She became extremely desirous to return to Edinburgh; and, as my mother made a point of her remaining where she was, she contracted a sort of hatred at poor me, as the cause of her being detained at Sandy-Knowe. This rose, I suppose, to a sort of delirious affection; for she confessed to old Alison Wilson, the house-keeper, that she had carried me up to the craigs under a strong temptation of the Devil to cut my throat with her scissors, and bury me in the moss. Alison instantly took possession of my person, and took care that her confidant should not be subject to any farther temptation, at least so far as I was concerned. She was dismissed of course, and I have heard afterwards became a lunatic . . .

It is here, at Sandy-Knowe, in the residence of my paternal grandfather, already mentioned, that I have the first conscious-ness of existence; and I recollect distinctly that my situation and appearance were a little whimsical. Among the odd remedies recurred to, to aid my lameness, some one had recommended that so often as a sheep was killed for the use of the family, I should be stripped, and swathed-up in the skin warm as it was flayed from the carcass of the animal. In this Tartar-like habiliment I well remember lying upon the floor of the little parlour in the farmhouse, while my grandfather, a venerable old man with white hair, used every excitement to make me try to crawl. I also distinctly remember the late Sir George M'Dougal of Mackerstown, father of the present Sir Henry Hay M'Dou-gal, joining in the attempt. He was, God knows how, a relation of ours; and I still recollect him, in his old-fashioned military habit (he had been Colonel of the Greys), with a small cocked-hat deeply laced, an embroidered scarlet waistcoat, and a light-coloured coat, with milk-white locks tied in a military fashion, kneeling on the ground before me, and dragging his watch along the carpet to induce me to follow it. The benevolent old soldier, and the infant wrapped in his sheepskin, would have afforded an odd group to uninterested spectators. This must have happened about my third year (1774), for Sir George M'Dougal and my grandfather both died shortly after that period.

(Sir Walter Scott, *from an autobiographical fragment*)

Edward Trelawny has the following account of Percy Bysshe Shelley's casual attitude towards children. Shelley's son was named after his father.

[Shelley] sprang down the stairs, and striding adroitly over a fair fat child squatting on the doorstep beside its nurse, stepped into my chaise at the door. The child cried.
SHELLEY: "When we are born, we cry that we are come
    To this great stage of fools."*
TRELAWNY: Whose child is it?
POET: (looking at it): Don't know.
MRS SHELLEY (from open casement): That's too bad, not to know your own child. Why, you goose, it is Percy!
TRELAWNY: You are not the wise man who knows his own child.
SHELLEY: The wise men have none.
TRELAWNY: Those wise men must be in the moon; there are few such on the earth.

(Edward Trelawny, *Records of Shelley, Byron, and the Author*)

The Bronte sisters, Emily, Charlotte and Anne, were very secretive about their first literary efforts. They wrote under the pseudonyms of Ellis, Currer and Acton Bell. So secretive were they that even their clergyman father didn't know what they were doing.

* When we are born . . . . – Lines from Shakespeare's *King Lear*.

The sisters had kept the knowledge of their literary ventures from their father, fearing to increase their own anxieties and disappointment by witnessing his; for he took an acute interest in all that befell his children, and his own tendency had been towards literature in the days when he was young and hopeful. It was true he did not much manifest his feelings in words; he would have thought that he was prepared for disappointment as the lot of man, and that he could have met it with stoicism; but words are poor and tardy interpreters of feelings to those who love one another, and his daughters knew how he would have borne ill-success worse for them than for himself. So they did not tell him what they were undertaking. He says now that he suspected it all along, but his suspicions could take no exact form, as all he was certain of was, that his children were perpetually writing – and not writing letters. We have seen how the communications from their publishers were received "under cover to Miss Bronte". Once, Charlotte told me, they overheard the postman meeting Mr Bronte, as the latter was leaving the house, and inquiring from the parson where one Currer Bell could be living, to which Mr Bronte replied that there was no such person in the parish. This must have been the misadventure to which Miss Bronte alludes in the beginning of her correspondence with Mr Aylott.

Now, however, when the demand for the work had assured success to *Jane Eyre*, her sisters urged Charlotte to tell their father of its publication. She accordingly went into his study one afternoon after his early dinner, carrying with her a copy of the book, and one or two reviews, taking care to include a notice adverse to it.

She informed me that something like the following conversation took place between her and him. (I wrote down her words the day after I heard them; and I am pretty sure they are quite accurate.)

"Papa, I've been writing a book."

"Have you, my dear?"

"Yes, and I want you to read it."

"I am afraid it will try my eyes too much."

"But it is not in manuscript: it is printed."

"My dear! you've never thought of the expense it will be. It will be almost sure to be a loss, for how can you get a book sold? No one knows you or your name."

"But, papa, I don't think it will be a loss; no more will you, if you will just let me read you a review or two, and tell you more about it."

So she sate down and read some of the reviews to her father; and then, giving him the copy of *Jane Eyre* that she intended for him, she left him to read it. When he came in to tea, he said, "Girls, do you know Charlotte has been writing a book, and it is much better than likely?"

(Elizabeth Gaskell, *Life of Charlotte Bronte*)

Charles Dickens' favourite daughter, Katey, remembers visiting her father very shortly before his death. He was at his house in Gad's Hill near Rochester.

There was a matter of some little importance to myself that I wished to consult him upon. This I told him, and he said that later in the evening, when my aunt and sister went to bed, we would talk of it together. My sister then played and sang, and her voice, which was very sweet and thrilling, reached us from the drawing-room, where she sat alone. My father enjoyed her music, as he always did, and was quite happy, although silent now, and looking very pale, I thought. At about eleven o'clock my sister and aunt retired; the servants were dismissed, and my father and I remained seated at the table: the lamps which had been placed in the conservatory were now turned down, but the windows that led into it were still open. It was a very warm, quiet night, and there was not a breath of air: the sweet scent of the flowers came in through the open door, and my father and I might have been the only creatures alive in the place, so still it was.

I told him of what was on my mind, and for a long time he gave his close attention to it, helping and advising me to come to a decision. It was very late when I at last rose from my seat and said that I thought it was time for him to rest, as he looked so tired; but he bade me stay with him for a little, as he had much to say. He was silent, however, for some minutes after this, resting his head upon his hand, and then he began talking of his own affairs, telling me exactly how he stood in the world, and speaking, among other things, of "Edwin Drood", and how he hoped that it might prove a success – "if, please God, I live to finish it."

I must have turned to him, startled by his grave voice, for he put his hand upon my arm and repeated, "I say if, because you know, my dear child, I have not been strong lately." Again he was silent, gazing wistfully through the darkened windows; and then in a low voice spoke of his own life, and many things that he had scarcely ever mentioned to me before. I was not surprised, nor did it seem strange at the time, that he should be speaking thus; but what greatly troubled me was the manner in which he dwelt upon those years that were gone by, and never, beyond the one mention of "Edwin Drood", looked to the future. He spoke as though his life were over and there was nothing left. And so we sat on, he talking, and I only interrupting him now and then to give him a word of sympathy and love. The early summer dawn was creeping into the conservatory before we went upstairs together, and I left him at his bedroom door.

(from an article in the *Pall Mall Magazine*, quoted by Michael Slater in *Dickens and Women*)

Edmund Gosse described in Father and Son *his upbringing in a strict religious household. Here he comments on the way in which his father, a famous zoologist, noted down the fact of his birth.*

In this strange household the advent of a child was not welcomed, but was borne with resignation. The event was thus recorded in my father's diary:

E. delivered of a son. Received green swallow from Jamaica.

This entry has caused amusement, as showing that he was as much interested in the bird as in the boy. But this does not follow; what the wording exemplifies is my father's punctilio. The green swallow arrived later in the day than the son, and the earlier visitor was therefore recorded first; my Father was scrupulous in every species of arrangement.

(Edmund Gosse, *Father and Son*)

Lockwood Kipling was an author and illustrator as well as being the father of Rudyard Kipling. The son had a high regard for his father while Lockwood had a matter-of-fact view of things, as the American journalist Edward Bok discovered when he travelled with the Kipling family from America to England on a transatlantic liner in 1899. Bok refers to himself in the third person.

Bok derived special pleasure on this trip from his acquaintance with Father Kipling, as the party called him. Rudyard Kipling's respect for his father was the tribute of a loyal son to a wonderful father.

"What annoys me," said Kipling, speaking of his father one day, "is when the pater comes to America to have him referred to in the newspapers as 'the father of Rudyard Kipling'. It is in India where they get the relation correct: there I am always 'the son of Lockwood Kipling'."

Father Kipling was, in every sense, a choice spirit: gentle, kindly, and of a most remarkably even temperament. His knowledge of art, his wide reading, his extensive travel, and an interest in every phase of the world's doings, made him a rare conversationalist, when inclined to talk, and an encyclopædia of knowledge as extensive as it was accurate. It was very easy to grow fond of Father Kipling, and he won Bok's affection as few men ever did.

Father Kipling's conversation was remarkable in that he was exceedingly careful of language and wasted few words . . .

Bok tried on one occasion to ascertain how the father regarded the son's work.

"You should feel pretty proud of your son," remarked Bok.

"A good sort," was the simple reply.

"I mean, rather, of his work. How does that strike you?" asked Bok.

"Which work?"

"His work as a whole," explained Bok.

"Creditable," was the succinct answer.

"No more than that?" asked Bok.

"Can there be more?" came from the father.

"Well," said Bok, "the judgment seems a little tame as applied to one who is generally regarded as a genius."

"By whom?"

"The critics, for instance," replied Bok.

"There are no such," came the answer.

"No such what, Mr Kipling?" asked Bok.

"Critics."

"No critics?"

"No," and for the first time the pipe was removed for a moment. "A critic is one who only exists as such in his own imagination."

"But surely you must consider that Rud has done some great work?" persisted Bok.

"Creditable," came once more.

"You think him capable of great work, do you not?" asked Bok. For a moment there was silence. Then:

"He has a certain grasp of the human instinct. That, some day, I think, will lead him to write a great work."

There was the secret: the constant holding up to the son, apparently, of something still to be accomplished; of a goal to be reached; of a higher standard to be attained. Rudyard Kipling was never in danger of unintelligent laudation from his safest and most intelligent reader.

(Edward Bok, *The Americanization of Edward Bok*)

Graham Greene famously remarked that there was a splinter of ice in the heart of every writer, and the comment is borne out by Arnold Bennett. A realist writer, Bennett took trouble to get the details right. He claimed that the description of the death of an old character in one of his novels could not be improved on. "I took infinite pains over it," he said. "All the time my father was dying I was at the bedside making copious notes."

Auberon Waugh had an often awkward relationship with his famous father, the novelist Evelyn Waugh. The latter usually

wanted nothing to do with his offspring and the height of praise
was a comment like the following in a letter to Nancy Mitford:
"The more I see of other people's children the less I dislike my
own." In his autobiography, *Will This Do?*, Auberon Waugh
recounts the occasion when, just after the end of World War
Two, his mother managed to get hold of three bananas. Under
the strict food-rationing then in force, neither Auberon nor his
two sisters had ever eaten this exotic fruit. The bananas – which
his mother had exchanged for "banana coupons", issued by the
state for the benefit of children – were piled on Evelyn Waugh's
plate. The great satirical novelist proceeded to load the plate
with cream and sugar (also strictly rationed) and, under the
distraught gaze of his children, finished off the three bananas.
The episode had its comic side, but the effect on Auberon
Waugh was long-lasting. He comments that it "would be
absurd to say that I never forgave him, but he was permanently
marked down in my estimation from that moment . . ."

Pastoral

The diarist Samuel Pepys goes for a ride in the country with some friends. They don't travel far from London but, even so, get lost in a wood.

At last got out of the wood again; and I, by leaping down the little bank, coming out of the wood, did sprain my right foot, which brought me great present pain, but presently, with walking, it went away for the present, and so the women and W. Hewer and I walked upon the Downes, where a flock of sheep was; and the most pleasant and innocent sight that ever I saw in my life. We found a shepherd and his little boy reading, far from any houses or sight of people, the Bible to him; so I made the boy read to me, which he did, with the forced tone that children do usually read, that was mighty pretty, and then I did give him something, and went to the father, and talked with him; and I find he had been a servant in my cozen Pepys' house, and told me what was become of their old servants. He did content himself mightily in my liking his boy's reading, and did bless God for him, the most like one of the old patriarchs that ever I saw in my life, and it brought those thoughts of the old age of the world in my mind for two or three days after . . . I did give the poor man something, for which he was mighty thankful, and I tried to cast stones with his horne crooke. He values his dog mightily, that would turn a sheep any way which he would have him when he goes to fold them: told me there was about eighteen score sheep in his flock, and that he hath four shillings a week the year round for keeping of them: and Mrs Turner, in the common fields here, did gather one of the prettiest nosegays that ever I saw in my life. So to our coach, and through Mr Minnes' wood, and looked upon Mr Evelyn's house; and so over the common, and through Epsom towne to our inne in the way stopping a poor woman with her milk-pail, and in one of my gilt tumblers, did drink our bellyfulls of milk, better than any creame; and so to our inne, and there had a dish of creame, but it was sour, and so had no pleasure in it; and so paid our reckoning, and took coach, it being about seven at night, and passed and saw the people walking with their wives and children to take the ayre, and we set out for home, the sun by and by going down, and we in the cool of the evening all the way with much pleasure home, talking and pleasing ourselves with the pleasures of this day's work. Mrs Turner mightily pleased with my resolution, which, I tell her, is never to keep a country-house, but to keep a coach, and with my wife on the Saturday to go sometimes for a day to this place, and then quit to another place; and there is more variety and as little charge, and no trouble, as there is in a country house. Anon it grew dark, and we had the pleasure to see several glow-wormes, which was mighty pretty, but my foot begins more and more to pain me, which Mrs Turner, by keeping her warm hand upon it, did much ease; but so that when we come home, which was just at eleven at night, I was not able to walk from the lane's end to my house without being helped. So to bed, and there had a cere-cloth laid to my foot, but in great pain all night long.

(Samuel Pepys, *Diary, July, 1667*)

The poet Alexander Pope discovered a touching story of rural romance and tragedy when he was staying in the country.

I have a mind to fill the rest of this paper with an accident that happened just under my eyes, and has made a great impression upon me. I have just passed part of this summer at an old romantic seat of my Lord Harcourt's, which he lent me. It overlooks a common-field, where, under the shade of a haycock, sat two lovers, as constant as ever were found in romance, beneath a spreading beech. The name of the one (let it sound as it will) was John Hewet; of the other, Sarah Drew. John was a well-set man about five and twenty, Sarah a brown [i.e. with a dark complexion] woman of eighteen. John had for several months borne the labour of the day in the same field with Sarah; when she milked, it was his morning and evening charge to bring the cows to her pail. Their love was the talk, but not the scandal, of the whole neighbourhood; for all they aimed at was the blameless possession of each other in marriage. It was but this very morning that he had obtained her parents' consent, and it was but till the next week that they were to wait to be happy. Perhaps this very day, in the intervals of their work, they were talking of their wedding clothes; and John was now matching several kinds of poppies and field-flowers to her complexion, to make her a present of knots for the day. While they were thus employed (it was on the last of July), a terrible storm of thunder and lightning arose, that drove the labourers to what shelter the trees or hedges afforded. Sarah, frighted and out of breath, sunk on a haycock, and John (who never separated from her) sate by her side, having raked two or three heaps together to secure her. Immediately there was heard so loud a crack as if heaven had burst asunder. The labourers, all solicitous for each other's safety, called to one another: those that were nearest our lovers, hearing no answer, stepped to the place where they lay: they first saw a little smoke, and after, this faithful pair – John with one arm about his Sarah's neck, and the other held over her face, as if to screen her from the lightning. They were struck dead, and already grown stiff and cold in this tender posture. There was no mark or discolouring on their bodies, only that Sarah's eyebrow was a little singed, and a small spot between her breasts. They were buried the next day in one grave, in the parish of Stanton Harcourt in Oxfordshire; where my Lord Harcourt, at my request, has erected a monument over them.

(Alexander Pope, *letter to
Lady Mary Montagu, September, 1718*)

~~~~~~~~~~

In 1882 the Reverend Hardwicke Drummond Rawnsley produced for the Wordsworth Society a collection of reminscences of the great poet, drawn from his own interviews with the "peasantry of Westmoreland" who had known Wordsworth in his later years. Rawnsley (who later went on to be one of the founding members of the National Trust) adopted a slightly patronizing attitude towards the farm-workers and domestic servants whose dialect words he noted down. The picture that emerges of Wordsworth isn't particularly flattering. Here, in a conversation with a local builder, Rawnsley discovers how Wordsworth, like many middle-class inhabitants of the countryside, didn't like the idea of change.

Onward we trudged, entered the pastures leading to the Grasmere Common that stretches up to the Grisedale Pass, there sat, and had a talk as follows, the Tongue Ghyll Beck murmuring among the budding trees at our feet:

"Why, why, Wudsworth nevver said much to t' fowk, quite different fra lile Hartley, as knawed t' inside o' t' cottages for miles round, and was welcome i' them a'. He was distant, ye may saay, verra distant. He wasn't made much count on nayther i' these parts, but efter a time fwoaks began to tak his advice, ye kna, aboot trees, and plantin', and cuttin', and buildin' chimleys, and that mak o' things. He hed his say at t'maist o' t' houses i' these parts, and was verra particler fond of round chimleys."

It was delicious this description of the path to fame among his countrymen the poet had taken, but my friend explained himself as he went on:

"He was yan as keppit his head doon and eyes upo' t' ground, and mumbling to hissel; but why, why, he 'ud never pass folks draining, or ditching, or walling a cottage, but what he'd stop and say, 'Eh dear, but it's a pity to move that stean, and doant ya think ya might leave that tree?' I mind there was a walling chap just going to shoot a girt stean to bits wi' powder i' t' grounds at Rydal, and he came up and saaved it, and wreat summat on it."

"But what was his reason," I asked, "for stopping the wallers or ditchers, or tree-cutters, at their work?"

"Well, well, he couldn't bide to see t' faace o' things altered, ye kna. It was all along of him that Grasmere folks have their Common open. Ye may ga now reet up t' sky ower Grizedale, wi'out liggin' leg to t' fence, and all through him. He said it was a pity to enclose it and run walls over it, and the quality backed him, and he won. Fwoaks was angry eneuf, and wreat rhymes aboot it; but why, why, it's a deal pleasanter for them as walks up Grisedale, ye kna, let alean reets o' foddering and goosage for freemen i' Gersmer."

(Hardwicke Drummond Rawnsley, *Reminiscences of Wordsworth among the Peasantry of Westmoreland*)

William Allingham describes a pleasant day out in the country with poet Alfred Tennyson.

Breakfast at 9.30. A. T. [Alfred Tennyson] out at 12. Swan Green forest path, Haliday's Hall, we *swim* through tall bracken. T. pauses midway, turns to me, and says solemnly, "I believe *this* place is quite full of vipers!" After going a little further, he stopped again and said, "I am told that a viper-bite may make a woman silly for life, or deprive a man of his virility."

We entered Mark Ash, a wood of huge solemn Beech trees, the floor thick-matted with dead leaves; a few trees were broken or fallen; some towered to a great height before branching. We sat on the roots of a mighty Beech. T. smoked. We shared sandwiches and brandy. Then he produced a little pocket *As You Like It*, and read some parts aloud.

(William Allingham, *diary entry for July, 1866*)

*The novelist Henry James, born in New York, became a British citizen in 1915 shortly before his death. For many years before that he had lived in Rye, Sussex. His rather courtly, elaborate manner of speaking could easily frighten the locals, as novelist Hugh Walpole recollected (see also **Obsessions & Eccentricities**).*

I remember once walking with him in the fields beyond Rye, and two very small and grubby children opened the gate for us. He smiled beneficently, felt in his deep pocket for coppers, found some and then began an elaborate explanation of what the children were to buy. They were to go to a certain sweet shop because there the sweets were better than at any other; they were to see that they were not deceived and offered an inferior brand, for those particular sweets had a peculiar taste of nuts and honey with, he fancied, an especial flavour that was almost the molasses of his own country. If the children took care to visit the right shop and insisted that they should have only that particular sweet called, he fancied, "Honey-nut" – or was it something with "delight" in it? "Rye's Delight" or "Honey Delights" or – But at this moment the children, who had been listening open-mouthed, their eyes fixed on the pennies, of a sudden took fright and turned, running and roaring with terror across the fields.

He stood, bewildered, the pennies in his hand. What had he done? What had he said? He had meant nothing but kindness. Why had they run from him crying and screaming? He was greatly distressed, going over every possible corner of it in his mind. He alluded to it for days afterwards.

———

Another memory of Henry James – by his friend, the American author, Edith Wharton – describes his profound love for the rolling quiet of the Sussex countryside. One day the two writers went to Bodiam Castle, a moated ruin, secluded and unvisited. "Tranquil white clouds hung above it in a windless sky, and the silence and solitude were complete as we sat looking across at the crumbling towers, and at their reflection in a moat starred with water-lilies and danced over by great blue dragon-flies. For a long time no one spoke; then James turned to me and said solemnly: 'Summer afternoon – summer afternoon; to me those have always been the two most beautiful words in the English language.' "

Publishers, Patrons & Booksellers

The Elizabethan poet Edmund Spenser found the kind of patron that most authors can only dream of. His great (and now largely unread) poem the Faerie Queene *was shown section by section to Philip Sidney. Sidney was himself a poet; more important for Spenser's purposes, he was glamorous, aristocratic – and rich.*

It is said he was a Stranger to Mr *Sidney* (afterwards Sir *Philip*) when he had begun to write his Faerie Queene, and that he took occasion to go to Leicester House, and to introduce himself by sending in to Mr *Sidney* a Copy of the Ninth Canto of the First Book of that Poem. Mr Sidney was much surpriz'd with the Description of *Despair* in that Canto, and is said to have shewn an unusual kind of Transport on the Discovery of so new and uncommon a Genius. After he had read some Stanza's, he turn'd to his Steward, and bid him give the Person that brought those verse Fifty Pounds; but upon reading the next Stanza, he order'd the Sum to be doubled. The Steward was no less surpriz'd than his Master, and thought it his Duty to make some Delay in executing so sudden and lavish a Bounty; but upon reading one Stanza more, Mr *Sidney* rais'd his Gratuity to Two Hundred Pounds, and commanded the Steward to give it immediately, lest as he read further, he might be tempted to give away his whole Estate. From this time he admitted the Author to his Aquaintance and Conversation, and prepar'd the way of his being known and receiv'd at Court.

(J. Hughes, *The Life of Mr Edmund Spenser*)

❧

The American writer and book-collector Eugene Field recalls some anecdotes of London writers and booksellers during the 18th-century.

Samuel Johnson once rolled into a London bookseller's shop to ask for literary employment. The bookseller scrutinized his burly frame, enormous hands, coarse face, and humble apparel. "You would make a better porter," said he.

This was too much for the young lexicographer's patience. He picked up a folio and incontinently let fly at the bookseller's head, and then stepping over the prostrate victim he made his exit, saying: "Lie there, thou lump of lead!"

This bookseller was Osborne, who had a shop at Gray's Inn Gate. To Boswell Johnson subsequently explained: "Sir, he was impertinent to me, and I beat him."

Jacob Tonson was Dryden's bookseller; in the earlier times a seller was also a publisher of books. Dryden was not always on amiable terms with Tonson, presumably because Dryden invariably was in debt to Tonson. On one occasion Dryden asked for an advance of money, but Tonson refused upon the grounds that the poet's overdraft already exceeded the limits of reasonableness. Thereupon Dryden penned the following lines and sent them to Tonson with the message that he who wrote these lines could write more:

> With leering looks, bull-faced and freckled fair,
> With two left legs, with Judas-colored hair,
> And frowzy pores that taint the ambient air.

These lines wrought the desired effect: Tonson sent the money which Dryden had asked for. When Dryden died Tonson made overtures to Pope, but the latter soon went over to Tonson's most formidable rival, Bernard Lintot. On one occasion Pope happened to be writing to both publishers, and by a curious blunder he inclosed to each the letter intended for the other. In the letter meant for Tonson, he said that Lintot was a scoundrel, and in the letter meant for Lintot he declared that Tonson was an old rascal. We can fancy how little satisfaction Messrs Lintot and Tonson derived from the perusal of these missent epistles.

(Eugene Field, *Love Affairs of a Bibliomaniac*)

John Murray, Byron's publisher, regrets that he was pressured into turning down the poet's later "immoral" works.

In after years I called on Mr Murray, his late publisher whom I met coming from his sanctum, accompanied by a sallow-visaged young man. As soon as the young man had left the shop, Murray said,

"He asked me to read a poem he had with him, and, if I approved, to publish it; said that it was highly commended, &c., &c. I declined, saying I was no judge; that I had refused several popular writers. I had made up my mind, on losing the great poet [i.e. Lord Byron], not to publish another line of verse."

"Have you," I asked, "found poetry unprofitable?"

He replied, "This morning I looked over my ledger, and I find £75,000 has passed over that counter from Lord Byron's pen alone. Can any one in the trade say as much? And then look at the time it was done in – ten years. I think that proves he was a great poet."

I said, "And yet you declined publishing what he wrote in the last year of his life, intimating that his popularity was declining and that his writings were becoming immoral, which offended him. Shelley said his 'Vision of Judgment' and the last cantos of 'Don Juan' were excellent."

Murray replied, "His friends were at me from morning till night. They said that the people in good society were shocked at the low tone he had fallen into. They attributed this to the vicious set he had got about him at Pisa (looking knowingly at me, as I was one of them); and they bothered me into remonstrating with him, and I was fool enough to do so in haste, and have repented at leisure of my folly, for Mr Gifford, the ablest scholar of them all, and one who did not throw his words away, as well as a few men of the same stamp, occasionally dropped remarks which satisfied me I had done wrong in alluding to the subject, for it was after reading the latter cantos of 'Don Juan' that Mr Gifford said – 'Upon my soul, I do not know where to place Byron. I think we can't find a niche for him unless we go back and place him after Shakespeare and Milton' – after a pause – 'there is no other place for him.'

"When I advertised a new poem from his pen, this quiet street was as thronged with carriages and people as Regent Street, and this shop was crowded with lords and ladies and footmen, so that the trade could not get near the counter to be served. That was something like business. That great man with his pen could alone have supported a publishing establishment, and I was bereft of my senses to throw it away. They talked of his immoral writings: there is a whole row from the greatest writers – including sermons – why don't they buy them? I am sick of the sight of them, they have remained there so long they seem glued to the shelf."

I said, "That is what Byron tells you is the cant of the age."

(Edward Trelawny, *Records of Shelley, Byron, and the Author*)

Another story involving Byron and his publisher has the poet presenting to John Murray a fine Bible. This gift, inscribed by Byron, was left about where it might be seen by visitors. One of them, however, drew Murray's attention to a change that Byron had made to one of the verses in John's gospel. In the verse reading "Now Barabbas was a robber" Byron had deleted "robber" and substituted "publisher". The Bible was quickly removed from public display.

This entry from Tom Moore's diaries passes on an anecdote from the poet Samuel Taylor Coleridge.

Coleridge told some tolerable things. One of a poor author, who, on receiving from his publisher an account of the proceeds (as he expected it to be) of a work he had published, saw among the items, "Cellarage, £3.10s. 6d." and thought it was a charge for the trouble of selling the 700 copies, which he did not consider unreasonable; but on inquiry he found it was the cellar-room occupied by his work, not a copy of which had stirred from thence.

(Tom Moore, *Diaries, April 4th 1823*)

The 19th-century poet John Clare, who took the countryside as his subject, had a tough life. He eventually went mad and spent his last thirty years in Northampton Asylum. On one occasion in earlier life he was compelled to go round selling his own poetry.

Market Deeping [in Lincolnshire] was the scene of perhaps his happiest day as author. He had gone there hawking his own book. The Rector had refused to buy a copy, telling him into the bargain that hawking was unbecoming. It rained, and the hawker took shelter in the covered yard of an inn among horse-dealers. One of them, a jolly-looking man with red hair and a red nose, after scanning Clare for a while, engaged him in conversation. "You have got something to sell there; what is it?" The answer was, "Books." "Whose books?" "My own." "Yes, I know they are your own, or, at least, I suppose so. But what kind of books, and by what author?" "Poems, written by myself." The horse-dealer stared. He looked fixedly at Clare, who was sitting on a stone, utterly dejected and scarcely noticing his interlocutor. The latter seemed to feel stirred by sympathy, and in a more respectful tone than before exclaimed, "May I ask your name?" "My name is John Clare," was the reply, pronounced in a faint voice. But the words were no sooner uttered when the jolly man with the red nose seized Clare by both hands. "Well, I am really glad to meet you," he cried. "I often heard of you, and many a time thought of calling at Helpston, but couldn't manage it." Then, shouting at the top of his voice to some friends at the farther end of the yard, he ejaculated, "Here's John Clare! I've got John Clare!" The appeal brought a score of horse-jobbers up in a moment. They took hold of the poet without ceremony, dragged him off his stone, and round the yard into the back entrance of the inn. "Brandy hot or cold?" inquired the eldest of Clare's friends. There was a refusal under both heads, coupled with the remark that a cup of tea would be acceptable. An order for it was given at once, and after a good breakfast, and a long conversation with his new acquaintances, Clare left the inn, delighted with the reception he had met with. He had sold all his books, and received for them more than the full price, several of his customers refusing to take change.

(Edward Thomas, *A Literary Pilgrim in England*)

~~~~~

Thackeray thought little of any publishers if the following story is to be believed.

I believe that sixteen publishers refused him the pittance required to print his immortal work, "Vanity Fair". Not one of them was capable intellectually of appreciating it . . . Calling on a publisher, Thackeray waited with a friend, who told me the story: the carpet of the drawing-room was of a gaudy design of red and white: on the host appearing, the Author of "Vanity Fair" said, "We have been admiring your carpet: it is most appropriate! You wade in the blood and brains of Authors!"

(William Fraser, *Hic et Ubique*)

~~~~~

As Anthony Trollope's reputation and sales as a novelist started to rise, he considered that he had a stronger bargaining position with his publisher, Longman's.

When I went to Mr Longman with my next novel, *The Three Clerks*, in my hand, I could not induce him to understand that a lump sum down was more pleasant than a deferred annuity. I wished him to buy it from me at a price which he might think to be a fair value, and I argued with him that as soon as an author has put himself into a position which ensures a sufficient sale of his works to give a profit, the publisher is not entitled to expect the half of such proceeds. While there is a pecuniary risk, the whole of which must be borne by the publisher, such division is fair enough; but such a demand on the part of the publisher is monstrous as soon as the article produced is known to be a marketable commodity. I thought that I had now reached that point, but Mr Longman did not agree with me. And he endeavoured to convince me that I might lose more than I gained, even though I should get more money by going else-where. "It is for you," said he, "to think whether our names on your title-page are not worth more to you than the increased payment." This seemed to me to savour of that high-flown doctrine of the contempt of money which I have never admired. I did think much of Messrs Longman's name, but I liked it best at the bottom of a cheque.

(Anthony Trollope, *An Autobiography*)

Reading & Readers

The following story sounds as though it might – just about – be true.

Shakespeare seeing Ben Johnson in a necessary-house [lavatory], with a book in his hand reading it very attentively, said he was sorry his memory was so bad, that he could not *sh-te without a book*.

> (Anonymous, *Shakespeare's Jests, or the Jubilee Jester*)

The 17th-century diarist Samuel Pepys wonders whether to buy an erotic novel, L'Ecole des Filles *(loosely translated as "Girls' School"). It's a toss-up between shame and the itch for a bit of pornography.*

13 Jan., 1668. Stopped at Martin's, my bookseller, where I saw the French book which I did think to have had for my wife to translate, called "L'escholle des filles", but when I come to look in it, it is the most bawdy lewdy book I ever saw ... so that I was ashamed of reading it, and so away home.

8 Feb. To my bookseller's, and there staid an hour, and bought the idle rogueish book, "L'escholle des filles"; which I have bought in plain binding, avoiding the buying of it better bound, because I resolve, as soon as I have read it, to burn it, that it may not stand in the list of books, nor among them, to disgrace them if it should be found.

9 Feb. (Lord's Day) I to my chamber, where I did read through "L'escholle des filles", a lewd book, but what do no wrong once to read it for information sake ... And after I had done it I burned it, that it might not be among

my books to my shame, and so at night to supper and to
bed.

(Samuel Pepys, *Diary*)

*William Cobbett, the radical journalist, ran away from home at the
age of 11. An ambitious reader even then, he made a choice between a
book and his supper.*

At 11 years of age my employment was clipping of box-edgings
and weeding beds of flowers in the garden of the Bishop of
Winchester, at the Castle of Farnham. I had always been fond of
beautiful gardens; and, a gardener, who had just come from the
King's gardens at Kew, gave such a description of them as made
me instantly resolve to work in these gardens. The next morning, without saying a word to anybody, off I set, with no clothes,
except those upon my back, and thirteen halfpence in my
pocket. I found that I must go to Richmond, and I, accordingly,
went on, from place to place, inquiring my way thither. A long
day (it was in June) brought me to Richmond in the afternoon.
Two pennyworth of bread and cheese and a pennyworth of
small beer, which I had on the road, and one halfpenny that I
had lost somehow or other, left three pence in my pocket. With
this for my whole fortune, I was trudging through Richmond in
my blue smock-frock and my red garters tied under my knees,
when, staring about me, my eye fell upon a little book, in a
bookseller's window: *Tale of a Tub* [by Jonathan Swift]; price
3d. The title was so odd, that my curiosity was excited. I had the
3d., but, then, I could have no supper. In I went and got the
little book, which I was so impatient to read, that I got over into
a field, at the upper corner of Kew Gardens, where there stood a
haystack. On the shady side of this, I sat down to read. The
book was so different from anything that I had ever read before:
it was something so new to my mind, that, though I could not at
all understand some of it, it delighted me beyond description;
and it produced what I have always considered a sort of birth of
intellect. I read on till it was dark, without any thought about
supper or bed. When I could see no longer, I put my little book
in my pocket, and tumbled down by the side of the stack, where

I slept till the birds in Kew Garden awaked me in the morning; when off I started to Kew, reading my little book.

(William Cobbett, *Autobiography*)

William Cobbett (see above) showed just as much determination to educate himself when he enlisted in the army. Paid no more than 6d (2½ p) a day, out of which he had to buy food and clothing, he found little left to buy books.

My leisure time was spent, not in the dissipations common to such a way of life, but in reading and study. In the course of this year I learned more than I had ever done before. I subscribed to a circulating library at Brompton, the greatest part of the books in which I read more than once over. The library was not very considerable, it is true, nor in my reading was I directed by any degree of taste or choice. Novels, plays, history, poetry, all were read, and nearly with equal avidity.

Such a course of reading could be attended with but little profit: it was skimming over the surface of everything. One branch of learning, however, I went to the bottom with, and that the most essential too, the grammar of my mother tongue. I had experienced the want of knowledge of grammar during my stay with Mr Holland; but it is very probable that I never should have thought of encountering the study of it, had not accident placed me under a man whose friendship extended beyond his interest. Writing a fair hand procured me the honour of being copyist to Colonel Debieg, the commandant of the garrison. I transcribed the famous correspondence between him and the Duke of Richmond. The Colonel saw my deficiency, and strongly recommended study. He enforced his advice with a sort of injunction, and with a promise of reward in case of success. I procured me a Lowth's grammar, and applied myself to the study of it with unceasing assiduity.

The edge of my berth, or that of the guard-bed, was my seat to study in; my knapsack was my bookcase; a bit of board lying on my lap was my writing desk; and the task did not demand anything like a year of my life. I had no money to purchase candle or oil; in winter time it was rarely that I could get any evening light but that of the fire, and only my turn even of that. To buy a pen or a sheet of paper I was compelled to forgo some portion of food, though in a state of half-starvation; I had no moment of time that I could call my own; and I had to read and to write amidst the talking, laughing, singing, whistling, and brawling of at least half a score of the most thoughtless of men, and that, too, in the hours of their freedom from all control. Think not lightly of the farthing that I had to give, now and then, for ink, pen, or paper. That farthing was, alas! a great sum to me! I was as tall as I am now; I had great health and great exercise. I remember, and well I may! that, upon one occasion, I, after all absolutely necessary expenses, had, on a Friday, made shift to have a halfpenny in reserve, which I had destined for the purchase of a red herring in the morning; but, when I pulled off my clothes at night, so hungry then as to be hardly able to endure life, I found that I had lost my halfpenny! I buried my head under the miserable sheet and rag, and cried like a child.

(William Cobbett, *Autobiography*)

Edward Trelawny remembers Percy Bysshe Shelley's voracious and eccentric reading habits.

Shelley's thirst for knowledge was unquenchable. He set to work on a book, or a pyramid of books; his eyes glistening with an energy as fierce as that of the most sordid gold-digger who works at a rock of quartz, crushing his way through all impediments, no grain of the pure ore escaping his eager scrutiny. I called on him one morning at ten, he was in his study with a German folio open, resting on the broad marble mantelpiece, over an old-fashioned fire-place, and with a dictionary in his hand. He always read standing if possible. He had promised over night to go with me, but now begged me to let him off. I then rode to Leghorn [Livorno], eleven or twelve miles distant, and passed the day there; on returning at six in the evening to dine with Mrs Shelley and the Williamses, as I had engaged to do, I went into the Poet's room and found him exactly in the position in which I had left him in the morning, but looking pale and exhausted.

"Well," I said, "have you found it?"

Shutting the book and going to the window, he replied, "No, I have lost it": with a deep sigh: "I have lost a day."

"Cheer up, my lad, and come to dinner."

Putting his long fingers through his masses of wild tangled hair, he answered faintly, "You go, I have dined – late eating don't do for me."

"What is this?" I asked, as I was going out of the room, pointing to one of his bookshelves with a plate containing bread and cold meat on it.

"That," – colouring – "why, that must be my dinner. It's very foolish; I thought I had eaten it."

(Edward Trelawny, *Records, of Shelley, Byron, and the Author*)

Thomas de Quincey describes how the poet William Wordsworth picked up a volume of writings by Edmund Burke, the political philosopher, from de Quincey's bookshelf. In those days, books were issued with uncut pages. Wordsworth was so eager to read that he started to cut the pages of the unread volume with the nearest knife to hand.

On a level with the eye, when sitting at the tea-table in my little cottage at Grasmere, stood the collective works of Edmund Burke. The book was to me an eye-sore and an ear-sore for many a year in consequence of the cacophanous title lettered by the bookseller upon the back – "Burke's Works" . . . Wordsworth took down the volume; unfortunately it was uncut; fortunately, and by a special Providence as to him, it seemed, tea was proceeding at the time. Dry toast required butter; butter required knives; and knives then lay on the table; but sad it was for the virgin purity of Mr Burke's as yet unsunned pages, that every knife bore upon its blade testimonies of the service it had rendered. Did that stop Wordsworth? Did that cause him to call for another knife ? Not at all; he

> Look'd at the knife that caus'd his pain:
> And look'd and sigh'd, and look'd and sigh'd again;

and then, after this momentary tribute to regret, he tore his way into the heart of the volume with this knife, that left its greasy honours behind it upon every page: and are they not there to this day? This personal experience first brought me acquainted with Wordsworth's habits in that particular especially, with his intense impatience for one minute's delay which would have brought a remedy . . .

(Thomas de Quincey, *Recollections of the Lake Poets*)

The American journalist and author Edward Bok listened to the wife of the preacher Henry Ward Beecher as she described how reading the famous anti-slavery novel Uncle Tom's Cabin *affected her husband. Harriet Beecher Stowe, the author of the famous best-seller, was Henry Beecher's sister.*

"When the story was first published in *The National Era*, in chapters, all our family, excepting Mr Beecher, looked impatiently for its appearance each week. But, try as we might, we could not persuade Mr Beecher to read it, or let us tell him anything about it.

" 'It's folly for you to be kept in constant excitement week after week,' he would say. 'I shall wait till the work is completed, and take it all at one dose.'

"After the serial ended, the book came to Mr Beecher on the morning of a day when he had a meeting on hand for the afternoon and a speech to make in the evening. The book was quietly laid one side, for he always scrupulously avoided everything that could interfere with work he was expected to do. But the next day was a free day. Mr Beecher rose even earlier than usual, and as soon as he was dressed he began to read *Uncle Tom's Cabin*. When breakfast was ready he took his book with him to the table, where reading and eating went on together; but he spoke never a word. After morning prayers, he threw himself on the sofa, forgot everything but his book, and read uninterruptedly till dinner-time. Though evidently intensely interested, for a long time he controlled any marked indication of it. Before noon I knew the storm was gathering that would conquer his self-control, as it had done with us all. He frequently 'gave way to his pocket-handkerchief', to use one of his old humorous remarks, in a most vigorous manner. In return for his teasing me for reading the work weekly, I could not refrain from saying demurely, as I passed him once: 'You seem to have a severe cold, Henry. How could you have taken it?' But what did I gain? Not even a half-annoyed shake of the head, or the semblance of a smile. I might as well have spoken to the Sphinx.

"When reminded that the dinner-bell had rung, he rose and went to the table, still with his book in his hand. He asked the blessing with a tremor in his voice, which showed the intense excitement under which he was laboring. We were alone at the table, and there was nothing to distract his thoughts. He drank his coffee, ate but little, and returned to his reading, with no thought of indulging in his usual nap. His almost uncontrollable excitement revealed itself in frequent half-suppressed sobs.

"Mr Beecher was a very slow reader. I was getting uneasy over the marks of strong feeling and excitement, and longed to have him finish the book. I could see that he entered into the whole story, every scene, as if it were being acted right before him, and he himself were the sufferer. He had always been a pronounced Abolitionist, and the story he was reading roused intensely all he had felt on that subject.

"The night came on. It was growing late, and I felt impelled to urge him to retire. Without raising his eyes from the book, he replied:

" 'Soon; soon; you go; I'll come soon.'

"Closing the house, I went to our room; but not to sleep. The clock struck twelve, one, two, three; and then, to my great relief, I heard Mr Beecher coming upstairs. As he entered, he threw *Uncle Tom's Cabin* on the table, exclaiming: 'There; I've done it! But if Hattie Stowe ever writes anything more like that I'll – well! She has nearly killed me.'

"And he never picked up the book from that day."

(Edward Bok, *The Americanization of Edward Bok*)

When Charles Dickens moved into Tavistock House in the Bloomsbury area of London, he disguised the door to his study so that it looked like part of an unbroken wall of books, complete with fake shelving and imaginary titles. Dickens' humour emerges in his choice of titles, ranging from the absurd – *Five Minutes in China*, in three volumes, and *Heaviside's Conversations with Nobody* – to straight puns, such as *The Gunpowder Magazine*. Also on the novelist's imagined shelves were *Cat's Lives* (in nine volumes, naturally) and *The Wisdom of Our Ancestors*, which consisted of volumes on ignorance, superstition, the block, the stake, the rack, dirt, and disease. The companion volume, titled *The Virtues of Our Ancestors*, was so narrow the title had to be printed sideways.

Charles Dickens drew large audiences in Britain and America when he gave public readings from his novels. All Dickens' acting flair was poured into these dramatized recitations. The painter W. P. Frith, however, thought that the writer could make a better job of at least one of his characters. At the time Dickens was sitting for his portrait.

It was at this time that Dickens commenced the public readings of his works, and they became immediately very popular as well as profitable. I availed myself of his offer of tickets of admission to Hanover Square Rooms, and heard him read the trial from "Pickwick", and from some other novel, the name of which I forget. It seems a bold thing for me to say, but I felt very strongly that the author had totally misconceived the true character of one of his own creations. In reading the humorous repartees and quaint sayings of Sam Weller [in *Pickwick Papers*], Dickens lowered his voice to the tones of one who was rather ashamed of what he was saying, and afraid of being reproved for the freedom of his utterances. I failed in being able to reconcile myself to such a rendering of a character that of all others seemed to me to call for an exactly opposite treatment. Sam is self-possessed, quick, and never-failing in his illustrations and rejoinders, even to the point of impudence.

When I determined to tell the great author that he had mistaken his own work, I knew I should be treading on dangerous ground. But on the occasion of a sitting, when my victim was more than ever good-tempered, I unburthened my mind, giving reasons for my objections. Dickens listened, smiled faintly, and said not a word. A few days after this my friend Elmore asked my opinion of the readings, telling me he was going to hear them, and I frankly warned him that he would be disappointed with the character of Sam Weller. A few days more brought a call from Elmore, who roundly abused me for giving him an utterly false account of the Weller episode.

"Why," he said, "the sayings come from Dickens like pistol-shots; there was no 'sneaking' way of talking, as you described it."

"Can it be possible," thought I, "that this man, who, as it is told of the great Duke of Wellington, never took anybody's opinion but his own, has adopted from my suggestion a rendering of one of the children of his brain diametrically opposed to his own conception of it?"

At the next sitting all was explained, for on my telling Dickens what Elmore had said, with a twinkle in his eye which those who knew him must so well remember, he replied:

"I altered it a little – made it smarter."

"You can't think how proud I feel," said I, "and surprised, too; for from my knowledge of you, and from what I have heard from other people, you are about the last man to take advice about anything, least of all about the way of reading your own books."

"On the contrary," was the reply, "whenever I am wrong I am obliged to anyone who will tell me of it; but up to the present I have never been wrong."

(W. P. Frith, *My Autobiography and Reminiscences*)

Charles Dickens was not only a fine reader and amateur actor but also a great story-teller and mimic. The anecdote Dickens tells here was passed to him by a friend, the poet Samuel Rogers.

He [Dickens] told stories with real dramatic effect; he gave one at my table, as related by Rogers (who made story-telling a fine art), of the English and French duelists who agreed to fight with pistols, the candles being extinguished, in a small room. The brave but humane Englishman, unwilling to shed blood, gropes his way to the fire-place, and discharges his weapon up the chimney; when, lo and behold! whom should he bring down but the dastardly Frenchman, who had crept thither for safety! Dickens said that Roger's postscript was not the worst part of the story – "When I tell that in Paris, I always put the Englishman up the chimney!" Dickens mimicked Rogers's calm, low-pitched, drawling voice and dry biting manner very comically.

(Frederick Locker-Lampson, *My Confidences*)

Another story from the painter W. P. Frith (see the anecdote about Pickwick Papers *above) shows how Charles Dickens was constantly being sent books by new writers.*

With Dickens' permission I used to read the early sheets of the new novel as they lay upon his desk. On one of the few occasions on which I got to work before him, I saw upon the table a paper parcel with a letter on the top of it. From the shape I guessed that it contained books, as the event proved. Presently Dickens came in, read the letter, and handed it to me, saying:

"Here you are again! This is the kind of thing I am subject to; people send me their books, and what is more, they require me to read them; and what is almost as bad, demand my opinion of them. Read that."

I obeyed, and read what appeared to me a very well-written appeal to the great master in the art, of which the writer was a very humble disciple, etc., begging for his perusal of the accompanying work, and his judgment upon it, and so on. The work was "Adam Bede", and the writer's name was George Eliot. Dickens took up one of the volumes, looked into it, and said: "Seems clever – a good style; suppose I must read it."

And read it he did that very day, for the next morning he said: "That's a very good book, indeed, by George Eliot. But unless I am mistaken, G. Eliot is a woman*."

(W. P. Frith, *My Autobiography and Reminiscences*)

---

* G. Eliot is a woman – Dickens' intuition was right of course. George Eliot's real name was Marian Evans.

Edmund Gosse was brought up by parents who were members of the Plymouth Brethren, a strict religious sect. He got into difficulties when he started to read the Elizabethan love poets.

There was occasionally some trouble about my reading, but now not much nor often. I was rather adroit, and careful not to bring prominently into sight anything of a literary kind which could become a stone of stumbling. But, when I was nearly sixteen, I made a purchase which brought me into sad trouble, and was the cause of a permanent wound to my self-respect. I had long coveted in the bookshop window a volume in which the poetical works of Ben Jonson and Christopher Marlowe were said to be combined. This I bought at length, and I carried it with me to devour as I trod the desolate road that brought me along the edge of the cliff on Saturday afternoons. Of Ben Jonson I could make nothing, but when I turned to "Hero and Leander", I was lifted to a heaven of passion and music. It was a marvellous revelation of romantic beauty to me, and as I paced along that lonely and exquisite highway, with its immense command of the sea, and its peeps every now and then, through slanting thickets, far down to the snow-white shingle, I lifted up my voice, singing the verses, as I strolled along:

> Buskins of shells, all silver'd, used she,
> And branch'd with blushing coral to the knee,
> Where sparrows perched, of hollow pearl and gold,
> Such as the world would wonder to behold—

so it went on, and I thought I had never read anything so lovely—

> Amorous Leander, beautiful and young,
> Whose tragedy divine Musaeus sung –

it all seemed to my fancy intoxicating beyond anything I had ever even dreamed of, since I had not yet become acquainted with any of the modern romanticists.

When I reached home, tired out with enthusiasm and exercise, I must needs, so soon as I had eaten, search out my stepmother that she might be a partner in my joys. It is remarkable to me now, and a disconcerting proof of my still almost infantile innocence, that, having induced her to settle to her knitting, I began, without hesitation, to read Marlowe's voluptuous poem aloud to that blameless Christian gentlewoman. We got on very well in the opening, but at the episode of Cupid's pining, my stepmother's needles began nervously to clash, and when we launched on the description of Leander's person, she interrupted me by saying, rather sharply, "Give me that book, please, I should like to read the rest to myself." I resigned the reading in amazement, and was stupefied to see her take the volume, shut it with a snap and hide it under her needlework. Nor could I extract from her another word on the subject.

The matter passed from my mind, and I was therefore extremely alarmed when, soon after my going to bed that night, my Father came into my room with a pale face and burning eyes, the prey of violent perturbation. He set down the candle and stood by the bed, and it was some time before he could resolve on a form of speech. Then he denounced me, in unmeasured terms, for bringing into the house, for possessing at all or reading, so abominable a book. He explained that my stepmother had shown it to him, and that he had looked through it, and had burned it.

The sentence in his tirade which principally affected me was this. He said, "You will soon be leaving us, and going up to lodgings in London, and if your landlady should come into your room, and find such a book lying about, she would immediately set you down as a profligate." I did not understand this at all, and it seems to me now that the fact that I had so very simply and childishly volunteered to read the verses to my stepmother should have proved to my Father that I connected it with no ideas of an immoral nature.

(Edmund Gosse, *Father and Son*)

The Victorian novelist Anthony Trollope tells the story in his autobiography of how an overheard conversation persuaded him to kill off one of his principal characters, Mrs Proudie, the strictly evangelical wife of the Bishop of Barsetshire in Trollope's Barsetshire sequence.

It was with many misgivings that I killed my old friend Mrs Proudie. I could not, I think, have done it, but for a resolution taken and declared under circumstances of great momentary pressure.

It was thus that it came about. I was sitting one morning at work upon the novel at the end of the long drawing-room of the Athenaeum Club – as was then my wont when I had slept the previous night in London. As I was there, two clergymen, each with a magazine in his hand, seated themselves, one on one side of the fire and one on the other, close to me. They soon began to abuse what they were reading, and each was reading some part of some novel of mine. The gravamen of their complaint lay in the fact that I reintroduced the same characters so often! "Here," said one, "is that archdeacon whom we have had in every novel he has ever written." "And here," said the other, "is the old duke whom he has talked about till everybody is tired of him. If I could not invent new characters, I would not write novels at all." Then one of them fell foul of Mrs Proudie. It was impossible for me not to hear their words, and almost impossible to hear them and be quiet. I got up, and standing between them, I acknowledged myself to be the culprit. "As to Mrs Proudie," I said, "I will go home and kill her before the week is over." And so I did. The two gentlemen were utterly confounded, and one of them begged me to forget his frivolous observations.

I have sometimes regretted the deed, so great was my delight in writing about Mrs Proudie, so thorough was my knowledge of all the little shades of her character. It was not only that she was a tyrant, a bully, a would-be priestess, a very vulgar woman, and one who would send headlong to the nethermost pit all who disagreed with her; but that at the same time she was conscientious, by no means a hypocrite, really believing in the brimstone which she threatened, and anxious to save the souls around her from its horrors. And as her tyranny increased so did the bitterness of the moments of her repentance increase, in that she knew herself to be a tyrant – till that bitterness killed

her. Since her time others have grown up equally dear to me –
Lady Glencora and her husband, for instance; but I have never
dissevered myself from Mrs Proudie, and still live much in
company with her.

(Anthony Trollope, *Autobiography*)

Rejection

The poet Alexander Pope produced a very successful translation of the classical Greek poem about the Trojan war, the Iliad, *in 1715. Before it was published Lord Halifax asked to hear Pope reading some of this new version. Though Halifax was himself a poet and "a patron of poetry", as Pope tells the story, he was also easy to fool.*

The famous Lord Halifax was rather a pretender to taste than really possessed of it. When I had finished the two or three first books of my translation of the Iliad, that Lord desired to have the pleasure of hearing them read at his house. Addison, Congreve, and Garth were there at the reading. In four or five places Lord Halifax stopt me very civilly, and with a speech each time much of the same kind, "I beg your pardon, Mr. Pope, but there is something in that passage that does not quite please me. Be so good as to mark the place, and consider it a little at your leisure. I am sure you can give it a better turn." I returned from Lord Halifax's with Dr Garth, in his chariot; and, as we were going along, was saying to the Doctor, that my Lord had laid me under a good deal of difficulty by such loose and general observations; that I had been thinking over the passages almost ever since, and could not guess at what it was that offended his Lordship in either of them. Garth laughed heartily at my embarrassment; said I had not been long enough acquainted with Lord Halifax to know his way yet; that I need not puzzle myself about looking those places over and over when I got home. "All you need do (said he) is to leave them just as they are; call on Lord Halifax two or three months hence, thank him for his kind observations on those passages, and then read them to him as altered. I have known him much longer than you have, and will be answerable for the event." I followed his advice; waited on Lord Halifax some time after; said, I hoped he would find his objections to those passages removed; read them to him exactly as they were at first: and his Lordship was extremely pleased with them, and cried out, "Ay, now, Mr Pope, they are perfectly right; nothing can be better."

(quoted in Samuel Johnson's *Life of Pope*)

It took a long time for Jane Austen's name to become familiar to the public.

Her reward was not to be the quick return of the cornfield, but the slow growth of the tree which is to endure to another generation. Her first attempts at publication were very discouraging. In November, 1797, her father wrote the following letter to Mr Cadell :

> Sir, – I have in my possession a manuscript novel, comprising 3 vols., about the length of Miss Burney's "Evelina." As I am well aware of what consequence it is that a work of this sort shd make its first appearance under a respectable name, I apply to you. I shall be much obliged therefore if you will inform me whether you choose to be concerned in it, what will be the expense of publishing it at the author's risk, and what you will venture to advance for the property of it, if on perusal it is approved of. Should you give any encouragement, I will send you the work.

> I am, Sir, your humble Servant, George Austen.

This proposal was declined by return of post! The work thus summarily rejected must have been "Pride and Prejudice".

The fate of "Northanger Abbey" was still more humiliating. It was sold, in 1803, to a publisher in Bath, for ten pounds, but it found so little favour in his eyes, that he chose to abide by his first loss rather than risk further expense by publishing such a work. It seems to have lain for many years unnoticed in his drawers; somewhat as the first chapters of "Waverley" lurked forgotten amongst the old fishing-tackle in Scott's cabinet. Tilneys, Thorpes, and Morlands [characters in *Northanger Abbey*] consigned apparently to eternal oblivion! But when four novels of steadily increasing success had given the writer some confidence in herself, she wished to recover the copyright of this early work. One of her brothers undertook the negotiation. He found the purchaser very willing to receive back his money, and to resign all claim to the copyright. When the bargain was concluded and the money paid, but not till then, the negotiator had the satisfaction of informing him that the work which had been so lightly esteemed was by the author of "Pride and Prejudice." I do not think that she was herself much mortified by the want of early success. She wrote for her own amusement. Money, though acceptable, was not necessary for the moderate expenses of her quiet home. Above all, she was blessed with a cheerful contented disposition, and an humble mind; and so lowly did she esteem her own claims, that when she received 150l. [pounds] from the sale of "Sense and Sensibility", she considered it a prodigious recompense for that which had cost her nothing.

(J. E. Austen-Leigh, *A Memoir of Jane Austen*)

The poet Robert Browning was often found to be obscure by his 19th-century readers, even by fellow poets. An early biographer, William Sharp, tells these stories of incomprehension and angry rejection. ("Sordello", "Fifine at the Fair" and "Red Cotton Nightcap Country" are all works by Browning.)

Who can fail to sympathise with Douglas Jerrold when, slowly convalescent from a serious illness, he found among some new books sent him by a friend a copy of "Sordello". Thomas Powell, writing in 1849, has chronicled the episode. A few lines, he says, put Jerrold in a state of alarm. Sentence after sentence brought no consecutive thought to his brain. At last the idea occurred to him that in his illness his mental faculties had been wrecked. The perspiration rolled from his forehead, and smiting his head he sank back on the sofa, crying, "O God, I AM an idiot!" A little later, adds Powell, when Jerrold's wife and sister entered, he thrust "Sordello" into their hands, demanding what they thought of it. He watched them intently while they read. When at last Mrs Jerrold remarked, "I don't understand what this man means; it is gibberish," her delighted husband gave a sigh of relief and exclaimed, "Thank God, I am NOT an idiot!"

Many friends of Browning will remember his recounting this incident almost in these very words, and his enjoyment therein: though he would never admit justification for such puzzlement.

But more illustrious personages than Douglas Jerrold were puzzled by the poem. Lord Tennyson manfully tackled it, but he is reported to have admitted in bitterness of spirit: "There were only two lines in it that I understood, and they were both lies; they were the opening and closing lines, 'Who will may hear Sordello's story told', and 'Who would has heard Sordello's story told!'" Carlyle was equally candid: "My wife," he writes, "has read through 'Sordello' without being able to make out whether 'Sordello' was a man, or a city, or a book . . ."

And who does not remember the sad experience of generous and delightful Gilead P. Beck, in [the novel] *The Golden Butterfly*: how, after "Fifine at the Fair", frightful symptoms set in, till in despair he took up "Red Cotton Nightcap Country", and fell for hours into a dull comatose misery. "His eyes were bloodshot, his hair was pushed in disorder about his head, his cheeks were flushed, his hands were trembling, the nerves in his face were twitching. Then he arose, and solemnly cursed Robert Browning. And then he took all his volumes, and, disposing them carefully in the fireplace, set light to them. 'I wish,' he said, "that I could put the poet there too.'" One other anecdote of the kind was often, with evident humorous appreciation, recounted by the poet. On his introduction to the Chinese Ambassador, as a "brother-poet", he asked that dignitary what kind of poetic expression he particularly affected. The great man deliberated, and then replied that his poetry might be defined as "enigmatic". Browning at once admitted his fraternal kinship.

(William Sharp, *The Life of Robert Browning*)

The American novelist Edith Wharton had her first great literary success with *The House of Mirth* (1905), a tragic novel which she later adapted for the stage. It flopped on Broadway but, as they left the theatre together, her fellow-novelist and critic William Dean Howells attempted some ironic consolation when he told her: "What the American public always wants is a tragedy with a happy ending."

James Joyce wrote in a letter that his collection of short stories titled *The Dubliners* had been read by 22 publishers before being accepted. "When at last it was printed," he said, "some very kind person brought out the entire edition and had it burnt in Dublin." The facts aren't quite as dramatic, but it did take Joyce nine years to find someone willing to publish the book, partly because of the "immoral" realism of the stories and the unflattering picture which they painted of his native city. Almost a year after *The Dubliners* first appeared in June 1914, only 379 out of a total of 1250 copies had been sold – and of those Joyce had bought 120 himself. The publisher assured him that the war was affecting book sales.

The two books which won George Orwell international fame – *Animal Farm* and *1984* – were written in the last few years of the novelist's life. *Animal Farm* has since sold in its millions but it nearly didn't get published at all. Orwell wrote the book during World War Two, at a time (1944) when Russia was an ally of Britain and America in the fight against the Nazis. The book, a fable about animals expelling human beings from a farm and running it themselves, describes how the farm pigs quickly establish themselves as the natural leaders of the other animals. The ideals of brotherhood and equality with which the animal revolution began are abandoned as the pigs grow to enjoy power and to abuse it. Eventually the pigs turn out to be worse taskmasters than the humans ever were. *Animal Farm* was a thinly disguised satire on the Russian Revolution of 1917 and its aftermath. Some of the animal characters were based on recognizable figures – the ruthless boar Napoleon was Joseph Stalin while the more intellectual Snowball represented Leon Trotsky, who was assassinated in Mexico on Stalin's orders and who, in his character as a pig, is driven from the farm by a pack of guard dogs (the Russian secret police). As a whole the book offered a deeply unflattering portrait of Communist Russia at a time when that country was fighting alongside the Allied forces.

English publishers were nervous about the political trouble which the satire was likely to stir up. The war-time government was worried too. The manuscript went to publisher Jonathan Cape. Pressure was put on Cape by the Ministry of Information, which was fearful of upsetting the Russians and generally damaging the war effort. Particular offence was taken at the casting of *pigs* as the villains of the piece and the way they would be identified with the Russian ruling class. George Orwell then sent *Animal Farm* to Faber & Faber. This distinguished publishing firm had an equally distinguished director in the shape of the poet, T. S. Eliot. Eliot wasn't happy with the book either. He wrote to Orwell and praised him for writing a skilful fable but declared that it wasn't the right moment to criticize "the political situation". He also added a comment which somehow by-passed the central concerns of the satire. For Eliot there was nothing much wrong with the pigs being in charge: ". . . your pigs are far more intelligent than the other animals, and therefore best qualified to run the farm – in fact, there couldn't have been an Animal Farm at all without them: so that what was needed (someone might argue) was not more communism but more public-spirited pigs."

In the end, the manuscript of *Animal Farm* went to the firm of Secker & Warburg, who published it in August 1945. By that time the war was over and Soviet Russia, the target of Orwell's satire, was about to become the new enemy in a Cold War which lasted over forty years.

In one of her diary entries for 1950 the poet Sylvia Plath described how a rainy August day made her think of writing a poem. But the recollection of the words on a rejection slip she'd once received caused her to think again: "After a heavy rainfall, poems titled 'Rain' pour in from across the nation."

The novelist Barbara Pym (1913–80) was often regarded as a kind of 20th-century Jane Austen. She wrote several novels in the genteel 1950s but fell out of favour in the trendier 60s. Her literary career was resurrected almost two decades later when the poet Philip Larkin, among others, drew attention to her in *The Times Literary Supplement*. As an unjustly "neglected" author she enjoyed a revival in the years before her death. Writing to Larkin in 1974, she commented on the ultimate in rejection: "The letter I wrote to *The Author* [magazine] about not getting published was never published, which seems to be the final accolade of failure."

Religion

George Herbert was one of the finest poets of the 17th-century. A devout Christian, he became rector of Bemerton, near Salisbury, in 1630. The following story shows Herbert's reputation for charity and mildness. He was also well-known for his love of music.

His chiefest recreation was Musick, in which heavenly Art he was a most excellent Master, and composed many *divine Hymns and Anthems*, which he set and sung to his *Lute* or *Viol* and though he was a lover of retiredness, yet his love of Musick was such, that he went usually twice every week, on certain appointed, days, to the Cathedral Church in *Salisbury*; and at his return would say, That his time spent in prayer, and Cathedral Music, elevated his soul, and was his Heaven upon Earth. But before his return thence to Bemerton, he would usually sing and play his part at an appointed private Musick meeting; and, to justify this practice, he would often say, Religion does not banish mirth, but only moderates and sets rules to it.

And, as his desire to enjoy his Heaven upon Earth drew him twice every week to *Salisbury*, so, his walks thither were the occasion of many accidents to others; of which I will mention some few.

In one of his walks to *Salisbury* he overtook a Gentleman, that is still living in that City; and in their walk together, Mr *Herbert* took a fair occasion to talk with him, and humbly begged to be excused, if he asked him some account of his faith; and said, I do this the rather, because though you are not of my parish, yet I receive tithe from you by the hand of your Tenant; and, Sir, I am the bolder to do it, because I know there be some Sermon-hearers that be like those fishes, that always live in salt water, and yet are always fresh.

After which expression, Mr *Herbert* asked him some needful Questions, and having received his answer, gave him such rules for the trial of his sincerity, and for a practical piety, and in so loving and meek a manner, that the Gentleman did so fall in love with him, and his discourse, that he would often contrive to meet him in his walk to *Salisbury*, or to attend him back to *Bemerton*; and still mentions the name of Mr *Herbert* with veneration, and still praiseth God that he knew him.

In another walk to *Salisbury*, he saw a poor man with a poorer horse, that was fallen under his load: they were both in distress and needed present help; which Mr *Herbert* perceiving, put off his canonical coat, and helped the poor man to unload, and after to load his horse. The poor man blessed him for it, and he blessed the poor man; and was so like the *good Samaritan*, that he gave him money to refresh both himself and his horse; and told him, That if he loved himself, he should be merciful to his beast. Thus he left the poor man and at his coming to his musical friends at *Salisbury*, they began to wonder that Mr *George Herbert*, which used to be so trim and clean, came into that company so soiled and discomposed; but he told them the occasion. And when one of the company told him, He had disparaged himself by so dirty an employment, his answer was, That the thought of what he had done, would prove Musick to him at midnight; and that the omission of it would have upbraided and made discord in his conscience, whensoever he should pass by that place: for if I be bound to pray for all that be in distress, I am sure that I am bound, so far as it is in my power to practise what I pray for. And though I do not wish for the like occasion every day, yet let me tell you, I would not willingly pass one day of my life, without comforting a sad soul, or showing mercy; and I praise God for this occasion. And now let us tune our Instruments.

(Izaak Walton, *Life of George Herbert*)

John Bunyan, 17th-century author of Pilgrim's Progress, *was a preacher. Perhaps he was as tough on his congregations as he was on himself.*

He may be supposed to have been always vehement and vigorous in delivery, as he frequently is in his language. One day when he had preached "with peculiar warmth and enlargement", some of his friends came to shake hands with him after the service, and observed what "a sweet sermon" he had delivered. "Aye," he replied, "you need not remind me of that; for the Devil told me of it before I was out of the pulpit."

(Robert Southey, *Life of John Bunyan*)

The poet Percy Bysshe Shelley considers (but only for a moment) the advantages of becoming a clergyman. One of the problems might have been his unbelief – he'd been sent down from Oxford for writing an atheist tract (see also **School & University**).

He had many schemes of life. Amongst them all, the most singular that ever crossed his mind was that of entering the church. Whether he had ever thought of it before, or whether it only arose on the moment, I cannot say: the latter is most probable; but I well remember the occasion. We were walking in the early summer through a village where there was a good vicarage house, with a nice garden, and the front wall of the vicarage was covered with corchorus in full flower, a plant less common then than it has since become. He stood some time admiring the vicarage wall. The extreme quietness of the scene, the pleasant pathway through the village churchyard, and the brightness of the summer morning, apparently concurred to produce the impression under which he suddenly said to me, – "I feel strongly inclined to enter the church." "What," I said, "to become a clergyman, with your ideas of the faith?" "Assent to the supernatural part of it," he said, "is merely technical. Of the moral doctrines of Christianity I am a more decided disciple than many of its more ostentatious professors. And consider for a moment how much good a good clergyman may do. In his teaching as a scholar and a moralist; in his example as a gentleman and a man of regular life; in the consolation of his personal intercourse and of his charity among the poor, to whom he may often prove a most beneficent friend when they have no other to comfort them. It is an admirable institution that admits the possibility of diffusing such men over the surface of the land. And am I to deprive myself of the advantages of this admirable institution because there are certain technicalities to which I cannot give my adhesion, but which I need not bring prominently forward?" I told him I thought he would find more restraint in the office than would suit his aspirations. He walked on some time thoughtfully, then started another subject, and never returned to that of entering the church.

(Thomas Love Peacock, *Memoirs of Shelley*)

When Lord Byron visited a monastery on the Greek island of Ithaca he was treated as an honoured guest. In Edward Trelawny's account it is doubtful whether the monks were praying to him or to God. Byron, however, was in a volatile – not to say volcanic – mood.

In the morning we rode through the pleasant little island to Vathy, the capital. The Resident, Captain Knox, his lady, and everyone else who had a house, opened their doors to welcome us and the Pilgrim [Trelawny's half-joking name for Byron] was received as if he had been a prince. On the summit of a high mountain in the island there is an ancient monastery, from which there is a magnificent view of the Ionian Sea, Greece, and many islands. The day after our arrival we ascended it, our party amounting to ten or twelve, including servants and muleteers. As usual, it was late when we started; there was not a breath of air, and the heat was intense. Following a narrow zigzag path between rocks and precipices in single file, as our mules crept upwards our difficulty increased, until the path became merely stone steps, worn by time and travel in the solid limestone. We all dismounted but Byron; he was jaded and irritable, as he generally was when deprived of his accustomed midday siesta: it was dusk before we reached the summit of the mountain. The Abbot had been apprized by the Resident of our visit; and when we neared the monastery, files of men stood each side of our path, bearing pine torches. On coming up to the walls we saw the monks in their grey gowns, ranged along terrace; they chanted a hymn of glorification and welcome to the great lord, saying, "Christ has risen to elevate the cross and trample on the crescent* in our beloved Greece." The Abbot, clad in his sacerdotal robes, received Byron in the porch, and conducted him into the great hall, illuminated for the occasion; monks and others clustered round the honoured guest; boys swung censers with frankincense under the Poet's nose. The Abbot, after performing a variety of ceremonies in a very dignified manner, took from the folds of his ample garments a roll of paper, and commenced intoning through his nasal organ a turgid and interminable eulogium on my "Lordo Inglese", in a polyglot of divers tongues; while the eyes of the silent monks, anxious to observe the effect of the holy father's eloquence, glanced from the Abbot to the Lord.

Byron had not spoken a word from the time we entered the monkery; I thought he was resolved to set us an example of proper behaviour. No one was more surprised than I was, when suddenly he burst into a paroxysm of rage, and vented his ire in a torrent of Italian execrations on the holy Abbot and all his brotherhood. Then, turning to us with flashing eyes, he vehemently exclaimed,

"Will no one release me from the presence of these pestilential idiots? They drive me mad!" Seizing a lamp, he left the room.

The consternation of the monks at this explosion of wrath may be imagined. The amazed Abbot remained for some time motionless, his eyes and mouth wide open; holding the paper he had been reading in the same position, he looked at the vacant place left by Byron, and then at the door through which he had disappeared. At last he thought he had solved the mystery, and in a low tremulous voice said – significantly putting his finger to his forehead: –

"Eccolo, é matto poveretto!" (Poor fellow, he is mad.)

Leaving Hamilton Browne to pacify the monks, I followed Byron. He was still fretting and fuming, cursing the "whining dotard", as he called the Abbot, who had tormented him. Byron's servant brought him bread, wine, and olives. I left him and joined the mess of the monks in their refectory. We had

---

* Trample on the crescent – at the time Greece was under Turkish rule.

the best of everything the island produced for supper. Our host broached several flasks of his choicest vintages: but although he partook largely of these good things, they failed to cheer him. We were glad to retire early to our cells.

In the morning, Byron came forth refreshed, and acted as if he had forgotten the occurrences of the evening. The Abbot had not, and he took care not to remind him of them. A handsome donation was deposited in the alms-box, and we mounted our mules and departed, without any other ceremony than a hasty benediction from the holy father and his monks. However we might have doubted the sincerity of their ovation on receiving us, we did not question the relief they felt and expressed by their looks on our departure.

(Edward Trelawny, *Records of Shelley, Byron, and the Author*)

Sydney Smith was a 19th-century clergyman and author, noted for his wit and provocative opinions. (Sometimes he sounds like an early version of Oscar Wilde – "I never read a book before reviewing it; it prejudices a man so.") As a clergyman Smith had various livings and in 1831 was made a canon of St Paul's. Among his "religious" observations are: "How can a bishop marry? How can he flirt? The most he can say, 'I will see you in the vestry after the service.'" and "My idea of heaven is eating pâté de foie gras to the sound of trumpets." Smith once said of his own sermons that they were "long and vigorous, like the penis of a jackass."

The Victorian writer, Edmund Gosse, brought up in a very strict religious household, began early on to experiment with his sense of doubt.

All these matters drew my thoughts to the subject of idolatry, which was severely censured at the missionary meeting. I cross-examined my Father very closely as to the nature of this sin, and pinned him down to the categorical statement that idolatry consisted in praying to any one or anything but God himself. Wood and stone, in the words of the hymn, were peculiarly liable to be bowed down to by the heathen in their blindness. I pressed my Father further on this subject, and he assured me that God would be very angry, and would signify His anger, if any one, in a Christian country, bowed down to wood and stone. I cannot recall why I was so pertinacious on this subject, but I remember that my Father became a little restive under my cross-examination. I determined, however, to test the matter for myself, and one morning, when both my parents were safely out of the house, I prepared for the great act of heresy. I was in the morning-room on the ground floor, where, with much labour, I hoisted a small chair on to the table close to the window. My heart was now beating as if it would leap out of my side, but I pursued my experiment. I knelt down on the carpet in front of the table and looking up I said my daily prayer in a loud voice, only substituting the address "O Chair!" for the habitual one.

Having carried this act of idolatry safely through, I waited to see what would happen. It was a fine day, and I gazed up at the slip of white sky above the houses opposite, and expected something to appear in it. God would certainly exhibit his anger in some terrible form, and would chastise my impious and wilful action. I was very much alarmed, but still more excited; I breathed the high, sharp air of defiance. But nothing happened; there was not a cloud in the sky, not an unusual sound in the street. Presently I was quite sure that nothing would happen. I had committed idolatry, flagrantly and deliberately, and God did not care.

The result of this ridiculous act was not to make me question the existence and power of God; those were forces which I did not dream of ignoring. But what it did was to lessen still further my confidence in my Father's knowledge of the Divine mind. My Father had said, positively, that if I worshipped a thing made of wood, God would manifest his anger. I had then worshipped a chair, made (or partly made) of wood, and God had made no sign whatever. My Father, therefore, was not really acquainted with the Divine practice in cases of idolatry. And with that, dismissing the subject, I dived again into the unplumbed depths of the "Penny Cyclopaedia".

When he was older, Gosse became more subtle when he wanted to get round his father.

I remember, on one occasion – when the Browns, a family of Baptists who kept a large haberdashery shop in the neighbouring town, asked for the pleasure of my company "to tea and games", and carried complacency so far as to offer to send that local vehicle, "the midge", to fetch me and bring me back – my Father's conscience was so painfully perplexed, that he desired me to come up with him to the now-deserted "boudoir" of the departed Marks, that we might "lay the matter before the Lord." We did so, kneeling side by side, with our backs to the window and our foreheads pressed upon the horsehair cover of the small, coffin-like sofa. My Father prayed aloud, with great fervour, that it might be revealed to me, by the voice of God, whether it was or was not the Lord's will that I should attend the Browns' party. My Father's attitude seemed to me to be hardly fair, since he did not scruple to remind the Deity of various objections to a life of pleasure and of the snakes that lie hidden in the grass of evening parties. It would have been more scrupulous, I thought, to give no sort of hint of the kind of answer he desired and expected.

It will be justly said that my life was made up of very trifling things, since I have to confess that this incident of the Browns' invitation was one of its landmarks. As I knelt, feeling very small, by the immense bulk of my Father, there gushed through my veins like a wine the determination to rebel. Never before, in all these years of my vocation, had I felt my resistance take precisely this definite form. We rose presently from the sofa, my forehead and the backs of my hands still chafed by the texture of the horsehair, and we faced one another in the dreary light. My Father, perfectly confident in the success of what had really been a sort of incantation, asked me in a loud wheedling voice, "Well, and what is the answer which our Lord vouchsafes?" I said nothing, and so my Father, more sharply, continued, "We have asked Him to direct you to a true knowledge of His will. We have desired Him to let you know whether it is, or is not, in accordance with His wishes that you should accept this invitation from the Browns." He positively beamed down at me; he had no doubt of the reply. He was already, I believe, planning some little treat to make up to me for the material deprivation. But my answer came, in the high-piping accents of despair: "The Lord says I may go to the Browns." My Father gazed at me in speechless horror. He was caught in his own trap, and though he was certain that the Lord had said nothing of the kind, there was no road open for him but just sheer retreat. Yet surely it was an error in tactics to slam the door.

(Edmund Gosse, *Father and Son*)

When Evelyn Waugh was told off by his friend and fellow-novelist Nancy Mitford for his indifference to other people's feelings and his occasional cruelty, she asked him how he could square his behaviour with being a practising Catholic. "You have no idea how much nastier I would be if I was not a Catholic," Waugh replied. "Without supernatural aid I would hardly be a human being."

Reputation

Elizabethan poet, translator and all-round wit John Harington, knew how to get good service in a tavern ("ordinary").

It happened that while the said Sir John repaired often to an ordinary in Bath, a female attendress at the table, neglecting other gentlemen which sat higher, and were of greater estates, applied herself wholly to him, accommodating him with all necessaries, and preventing his asking anything with her officiousness. She, being demanded by him the reason of her so careful waiting on him, "I understand," said she, "you are a very witty man, and if I should displease you in anything, I fear you would make an epigram of me."

(Thomas Fuller's *Worthies*)

The poet Alexander Pope resorted to very roundabout methods to let everyone know he was on terms of friendship with members of the English aristocracy. He wanted to bring out a volume of letters from his noble friends but didn't want to look immodest so he tricked a rogue publisher into producing a pirated copy.

One of the passages of Pope's life which seems to deserve some inquiry was a publication of Letters between him and many of his friends, which falling into the hands of Curll, a rapacious bookseller of no good fame, were by him [May 1735] printed and sold. This volume containing some letters from noblemen, Pope incited a prosecution against him in the House of Lords for breach of privilege, and attended himself to stimulate the resentment of his friends. Curll appeared at the bar, and, knowing himself in no great danger, spoke of Pope with very little reverence. "He has," said Curll, "a knack at versifying, but in prose I think myself a match for him." When the orders of the House were examined, none of them appeared to have been infringed; Curll went away triumphant; and Pope was left to seek some other remedy.

Curll's account was, that one evening a man in a clergyman's gown, but with a lawyer's band, brought and offered for sale a number of printed volumes, which he found to be Pope's epistolary correspondence; that he asked no name, and was told none, but gave the price demanded, and thought himself authorized to use his purchase to his own advantage.

That Curll gave a true account of the transaction, it is reasonable to believe, because no falsehood was ever detected; and when some years afterwards I mentioned it to Lintot [a bookseller/publisher] . . . he declared his opinion to be, that Pope knew better than anybody else how Curll obtained the copies, because another parcel was at the same time sent to himself, for which no price had ever been demanded, and he made known his resolution not to pay a porter, and consequently not to deal with a nameless agent.

Such care had been taken to make them public, that they were sent at once to two booksellers: to Curll, who was likely to seize them as prey; and to Lintot, who might be expected to give Pope information of the seeming injury. Lintot, I believe, did nothing, and Curll did what was expected. That to make them public was the only purpose may be reasonably supposed, because the numbers offered to sale by the private messengers showed that hope of gain could not have been the motive of the impression.

It seems that Pope, being desirous of printing his letters, and not knowing how to do, without imputation of vanity, what has in this country been done very rarely, contrived an appearance of compulsion; that when he could complain that his letters were surreptitiously published, he might decently and defensively publish them himself.

Pope's private correspondence, thus promulgated, filled the nation with praises of his candour, tenderness, and benevolence, the purity of his purposes, and the fidelity of his friendship. There were some letters which a very good or a very wise man would wish suppressed, but, as they had been already exposed, it was impracticable now to retract them.

(Samuel Johnson, *Life of Pope*)

The graves and relics of famous people often turn into shrines – witness the tombs of Oscar Wilde and Jim Morrison in the Père Lachaise cemetery in Paris.

*When the coffin of the poet John Milton (d.1674) was discovered more than a century after his death, it led to an unholy and grisly scramble to get bodily bits and pieces as souvenirs. This account comes from Philip Neve who wrote "*A Narrative of the Disinterment of Milton's Coffin, in the Parish-Church of St Giles, Cripplegate, on Wednesday, August 4, 1779; and the Treatment of the Corpse during that and the following day"*. Neve seems to been both fascinated and disgusted by what happened, and to have gathered up the scattered remains only in order to return them to the grave.*

On Tuesday evening the 3rd, Mr Cole, Messrs Laming & Taylor, Holmes, &c., had a merry meeting, as Mr Cole expresses himself, at Fountain's house; the conversation there turned upon Milton's coffin having been discovered; and, in the course of the evening, several of those present expressing a desire to see it, Mr Cole assented that, if the ground was not already closed, the closing of it should be deferred until they should have satisfied their curiosity. Between eight and nine on Wednesday morning, the 4th, the two overseers (Laming and Fountain) and Mr Taylor, went to the house of Ascough, the clerk, which leads into the church-yard, and asked for Holmes; they then went with Holmes into the church, and pulled the coffin, which lay deep in the ground, from its original station to the edge of the excavation, into daylight. Mr Laming told me that, to assist in thus removing it, he put his hand into a corroded hole, which he saw in the lead, at the coffin foot. When they had thus removed it, the overseers asked Holmes if he could open it, that they might see the body. Holmes immediately fetched a mallet and a chisel, and cut open the top of the coffin, slantwise from the head, as low as the breast; so that the top, being doubled backwards, they could see the corpse; he cut it open also at the foot.

Upon first view of the body, it appeared perfect, and completely enveloped in the shroud, which was of many folds; the ribs standing up regularly. When they disturbed the shroud, the ribs fell. Mr Fountain told me that he pulled hard at the teeth, which resisted, until some one hit them a knock with a stone, when they easily came out. There were but five in the upper jaw, which were all perfectly sound and white, and all taken by Mr Fountain; he gave one of them to Mr Laming; Mr Laming also took one from the lower jaw; and Mr Taylor took two from it. Mr Laming told me that he had, at one time, a mind to bring away the whole underjaw, with the teeth in it; he had it in his hand, but tossed it back again. Also that he lifted up the head, and saw a great quantity of hair, which lay straight and even behind the head, and in the state of hair which had been combed and tied together before interment; but it was wet, the coffin having considerable corroded holes, both at the head and foot, and a great part of the water with which it had been washed on the Tuesday afternoon having run into it. The overseers and Mr Taylor went away soon afterwards, and Messrs Laming and Taylor went home to get scissors to cut off some of the hair: they returned about ten, when Mr Laming poked his stick against the head, and brought some of the hair over the forehead; but, as they saw the scissors were not necessary, Mr Taylor took up the hair, as it lay on the forehead, and carried it home. The water, which had got into the coffin on the Tuesday afternoon, had made a sludge at the bottom of it, emitting a nauseous smell, which occasioned Mr Laming to use his stick to procure the hair, and not to lift up the head a second time. Mr Laming also took out one of the leg-bones, but threw it in again . . .

The coffin was removed from the edge of the excavation back to its original station; but was no otherwise closed than by the lid, where it had been cut and reversed, being bent down again. Mr Ascough, the clerk, was from home the greater part of that day, and Mrs Hoppey, the sexton, was from home the whole day. Elizabeth Grant, the grave-digger, who is servant to Mrs Hoppey, therefore now took possession of the coffin; and, as its situation under the common-councilmen's pew would not admit of its being seen without the help of a candle, she kept a tinder-box in the excavation, and, when any persons came, struck a light, and conducted them under the pew, where, by reversing the part of the lid which had been cut, she exhibited the body, at first for sixpence, and afterwards for threepence and twopence each person. The workers in the church kept the doors locked to all those who would not pay the price of a pot of beer for entrance, and many, to avoid that payment, got in at a window at the west end of the church, near to Mr Ascough's counting-house.

I went on Saturday, the 7th, to Mr Laming's house, to request a lock of the hair; but, not meeting with Mr Taylor at home, went again on Monday, the 9th, when Mr Taylor gave me part of what hair he had reserved for himself. Hawkesworth having informed me, on the Saturday, that Mr Ellis, the player, had taken some hair, and that he had seen him take a rib-bone, and carry it away in paper under his coat, I went from Mr Laming's on Monday to Mr Ellis, who told me that he had paid 6d. to Elizabeth Grant for seeing the body; and that he had lifted up the head, and taken from the sludge under it a small quantity of hair, with which was a piece of the shroud, and, adhering to the hair, a bit of the skin of the skull, of about the size of a shilling. He then put them all into my hands, with the rib-bone, which appeared to be one of the upper ribs. The piece of the shroud was of coarse linen. The hair which he had taken was short; a small part of it he had washed, and the remainder was in the clotted state in which he had taken it. He told me that he had tried to reach down as low as the hands of the corpse, but had not been able to effect it. The washed hair corresponded exactly with that in my possession, and which I had just received from Mr Taylor. Ellis is a very ingenious worker in hair, and he said that, thinking it would be of great advantage to him to possess a quantity of Milton's hair, he had returned to the church on Thursday, and had made his endeavours to get access a second time to the body; but had been refused admittance. Hawkesworth took a tooth, and broke a bit off the coffin; of which I was informed by Mr Ascough. I purchased them both

of Hawkesworth, on Saturday the 7th for 2/-; and he told me
that, when he took the tooth out, there were but two more
remaining; one of which was afterwards taken by another of
Mr Ascough's men. And Ellis informed me that, at the time
when he was there, on Wednesday, the teeth were all gone;
but the overseers say they think that all the teeth were not
taken out of the coffin, though displaced from the jaws, but
that some of them must have fallen among the other bones as
they very readily came out, after the first were drawn. Haslib,
son of William Haslib, of Jewin Street, undertaker, took one
of the small bones, which I purchased of him, on Monday the
9th, for 2/- . . .

In recording a transaction which will strike every liberal
mind with horror and disgust, I cannot omit to declare that
I have procured those relics which I possess, only in hope of
bearing part in a pious and honourable restitution of all that has
been taken; the sole atonement which can now be made to the
violated rights of the dead, to the insulted parishioners at large,
and to the feelings of all good men.

*Jane Austen's reputation took time to grow. She was more famous
after death.*

A few years ago, a gentleman visiting Winchester Cathedral
desired to be shown Miss Austen's grave. The verger, as he
pointed it out, asked, "Pray, sir, can you tell me whether there
was anything particular about that lady; so many people want to
know where she was buried?" During her life the ignorance of
the verger was shared by most people; few knew that "there was
anything particular about that lady."

(J. E. Austen-Leigh *A Memoir of Jane Austen*)

*William Beckford was the rich and eccentric author of the Oriental
fantasy* Vathek. *Really an 18th-century figure, he lived well into the
19th, for much of the time at Fonthill, a Wiltshire estate which he
inherited from his father. At Fonthill he built a Gothic-style "abbey"
which was distinguished by a 276-foot tower. Beckford's reputation as*

an eccentric, reclusive figure was well deserved if these stories by the painter W. P. Frith are accurate.

The late Mr Phillips, the well-known Bond Street auctioneer, was an intimate friend of my uncle Scaife's, at whose house I frequently met him; and though I was a very young student fifty years ago, and quite incapable of properly appreciating fine works of art, I often, at Mr Phillips's suggestion, visited his rooms whenever great collections were dispersed there. Hearing that a Holy Family by Raphael was to be sold, I went to see it, and though it was of doubtful authenticity, I thought it was a very fine picture. I was discussing its merits – with all the ignorant assurance of youth – with Mr Phillips in his office, when an elderly gentleman walked briskly past the door on his way to the gallery. He was a short man, dressed in a green coat with brass buttons, leather breeches, and top-boots, and his hair was powdered. "That is Mr Beckford," said Phillips. I had just read "Vathek", and was very curious to see the author of it; so I rushed upstairs to the auction-rooms, and found the great little man studying the so-called Raphael. I stood close to the picture, and studied Mr Beckford, who proceeded to criticize the work in language of which my respectable pen can give my readers but a faint idea. It must not be thought that the remarks were addressed to me or to anybody but the speaker himself. "That d—d thing a Raphael! Great heavens! Think of that now! Can there be such d—d fools as to believe that a Raphael! What a d—d fool I was to come here!" and without a glance at other pictures, the critic departed.

It was many years after this that a distant connection of mine, who, I must premise, was a person of an inquiring mind, found himself involved in a curious adventure. My relative had been in business, from which he retired at an unusually early time of life, having acquired a handsome competence. He was married, but childless, and having bought a house in the salubrious city of Bath, he retired there, and passed his time in reading and in finding out everything he could about all the people in the place. There was one house, and that the most interesting of all, that shut its door against my inquisitive friend and everybody else. Fonthill Abbey, or Fonthill Splendour, as it was sometimes called, situated a few miles from Bath, was a treasure-house of beauty. Every picture was said to be a gem, and the gardens were unequalled by any in England, the whole being guarded by a dragon in the form of Mr Beckford. "Not only," says an authority, "had the art-treasures of that princely place been sealed against the public, but the park itself – known by rumour as a beautiful spot – had for several years been inclosed by a most formidable wall, about seven miles in circuit, twelve feet high, and crowned by a *chevaux-de-frise* [iron spikes]." These formidable obstacles my distant cousin undertook to surmount, and he laid a wager of a considerable sum that he would walk in the gardens, and even penetrate into the house itself.

Having nothing better to do, he spent many an anxious hour in watching the great gate in the wall, in the hope that by some inadvertence it might be left open and unguarded; and one day that happy moment arrived. The porter was ill, and his wife opened the gate to a tradesman, who, after depositing his goods at the lodge (no butcher or baker was permitted to go to the Abbey itself), retired, leaving the gate open, relying probably upon the woman's shutting it. Quick as thought my relative passed the awful portals, and made his way across the park. Guided by the high tower – called "Beckford's Folly" – my inquisitive friend made his way to the gardens and, not being able immediately to find the entrance, was leaning on a low wall that shut the gardens from the park, and taking his fill of delight at the gorgeous display – the gardens being in full beauty – when a man with a spud [trowel] in his hand – perhaps the head gardener – approached, and asked the intruder how he came there, and what he wanted.

"The fact is, I found the gate in the wall open, and having heard a great deal about this beautiful place, I thought I should like to see it."

"Ah !" said the gardener, "you would, would you ? Well, you can't see much where you are. Do you think you could manage to jump over the wall? If you can, I will show you the gardens."

My cousin looked over the wall, and found such a palpable obstacle – in the shape of a deep ditch – on the other side of it, that he wondered at the proposal.

"Oh, I forgot the ditch! Well, go to the door; you will find it about a couple of hundred yards to your right, and I will admit you."

In a very short time, to his great delight, my cousin found himself listening to the learned names of rare plants, and inhaling the perfume of lovely flowers. Then the fruit-gardens and hot-houses – "acres of them," as he afterwards declared – were submitted to his inspection. After the beauties of the gardens and grounds had been thoroughly explored, and the wager half won, the inquisitive one's pleasure may be imagined when his guide said:

"Now, would you like to see the house and its contents? There are some rare things in it – fine pictures and so on. Do you know anything about pictures?"

"I think I do, and should, above all things, like to see those of which I have heard so much; but are you sure that you will not get yourself into a scrape with Mr Beckford? I've heard he is so very particular."

"Oh, no!" said the gardener. "I don't think Mr Beckford will mind what I do. You see, I have known him all my life, and he lets me do pretty well as I like here."

"Then I shall only be too much obliged."

"Follow me, then," said the guide.

My distant cousin was really a man of considerable taste and culture, a great lover of art, with some knowledge of the old masters and the different schools; and he often surprised his guide, who, catalogue in hand, named the different pictures and their authors, by his acute and often correct criticisms. So intimate was his acquaintance with the styles of some of the different painters, that he was frequently able to anticipate his guide's information. When the pictures had been thoroughly examined, there remained bric-à-brac of all kinds – costly suits of armour, jewellery of all ages, bridal coffers beautifully painted by Italian artists, numbers of ancient and modern musical instruments, with other treasures, all to be carefully and delightedly examined, till, the day nearing fast towards evening, the visitor prepared to depart, and was commencing a speech of thanks in his best manner, when the gardener said, looking at his watch:

"Why, bless me, it's five o'clock! Ain't you hungry? You must stop and have some dinner."

"No, really, I couldn't think of taking such a liberty. I am sure Mr Beckford would be offended."

"No, he wouldn't. You must stop and dine with me; I am Mr Beckford."

My far-off cousin's state of mind may be imagined. He had won his wager, and he was asked, actually asked, to dine with the man whose name was a terror to the tourist, whose walks abroad were so rare that his personal appearance was unknown to his neighbours. What a thing to relate to his circle at Bath! How Mr Beckford had been belied, to be sure! The dinner was magnificent, served on massive plate – the wines of the rarest vintage. Rarer still was Mr Beckford's conversation. He entertained his guest with stories of Italian travel, with anecdotes of the great in whose society he had mixed, till he found the shallowness of it; in short, with the outpouring of a mind of great power and thorough cultivation. My cousin was well read enough to be able to appreciate the conversation and contribute to it, and thus the evening passed delightfully away. Candles were lighted, and host and guest talked till a fine Louis Quatorze clock struck eleven. Mr Beckford rose and left the room. The guest drew his chair to the fire, and waited the return of his host. He thought he must have dozed, for he started to find the room in semi-darkness, and one of the solemn powdered footmen putting out the lights.

"Where is Mr Beckford?" said my cousin.

"Mr Beckford has gone to bed," said the man, as he extinguished the last candle.

The dining-room door was open, and there was a dim light in the hall.

"This is very strange," said my cousin; "I expected Mr Beckford back again. I wished to thank him for his hospitality."

This was said as the guest followed the footman to the front door. That functionary opened it wide and said:

"Mr Beckford ordered me to present his compliments to you, sir, and I am to say that as you found your way into Fonthill Abbey without assistance, you may find your way out again as best you can; and he hopes you will take care to avoid the bloodhounds that are let loose in the gardens every night. I wish you good evening. No, thank you, sir; Mr Beckford never allows vails [tips]."

My cousin climbed into the branches of the first tree that promised a safe shelter from the dogs, and there waited for daylight; and it was not till the sun showed himself that he made his way, terror attending each step, through the gardens into the park, and so to Bath. "The wager was won," said my relative; "but not for fifty million times the amount would I again pass such a night as I did in Fonthill Abbey."

I am in a position to assure my reader that this story of Fonthill Abbey is absolutely true.

> (W. P. Frith, *My Autobiography and Reminiscences*)

The remarkable Bronte sisters published a volume of poems in 1846 under the names of Currer, Acton and Ellis Bell. The next year saw the publication of Charlotte Bronte's Jane Eyre, *Anne Bronte's* Agnes Grey, *and the acceptance for publication of Emily's* Wuthering Heights. *Since the sisters kept the Bell pen-names, there was great curiosity about their identity (see also* **Parents & Children**). *The general assumption was that they were male or that their books were co-authored. In November 1848, Charlotte writes to her publisher in some amusement at the frightening reputation which they've made for themselves. Charlotte Bronte refers to Emily's "pale and wasted" looks: her sister was dying of consumption.*

I put your most friendly letter into Emily's hands as soon as I had myself perused it. The *North American Review* is worth reading; there is no mincing the matter here. What a bad set the Bells must be. What appalling books they write. To-day, as Emily appeared a little easier, I thought the *Review* would amuse her, so I read it aloud to her and Anne.

As I sat between them at our quiet but now somewhat melancholy fireside, I studied the two ferocious authors. Ellis [Emily Bronte], the "man of uncommon talents, but dogged, brutal and morose", sat leaning back in his easy chair drawing his impeded breath as best he could, and looking alas, piteously pale and wasted; but it is not his wont to laugh, but he smiled half-amused and half in scorn as he listened. Acton [Anne Bronte] was sewing, no emotion ever stirs him to loquacity, so he only smiled too, dropping at the same time a single word of calm amazement to hear his character so darkly portrayed. I wonder what the reviewer would have thought of his own sagacity could he have beheld the pair as I did. Vainly, too, might he have looked round for the masculine partner in the firm of "Bell & Co." How I laugh in my sleeve when I read the solemn assertions that *Jane Eyre* was written in partnership, and that it "bears the marks of more than one mind and one sex."

The wise critics would certainly sink a degree in their own estimation if they knew that yours or Mr Smith's was the first masculine hand that touched the MS. of *Jane Eyre*, and that till you or he read it, no masculine eye had scanned a line of its contents, no masculine ear heard a phrase from its pages. However, the view they take of the matter rather pleases me than otherwise. If they like, I am not unwilling they should think a dozen ladies and gentlemen aided at the compilation of the book. Strange patchwork it must seem to them – this chapter being penned by Mr, and that by Miss or Mrs Bell; that character or scene being delineated by the husband, that other by the wife. The gentleman, of course, doing the rough work, the lady getting up the finer parts. I admire the idea vastly.

Walt Whitman offended many of his fellow Americans with the outspokenness of his work, in particular his volume of poetry Leaves of Grass. *Whitman's friend John Townsend Trowbridge tried to use his influence with Salmon P. Chase, Secretary of the Treasury in Abraham Lincoln's administration, to get Whitman a government job. Conveniently, he was staying with Chase at the time. As extra ammunition, Trowbridge brought along two letters from the highly respected man of letters and all-round sage, Ralph Waldo Emerson. But Whitman's "notoriety" was more powerful than Trowbridge's friendship or Emerson's recommendation.*

I thought no man more than Whitman merited recognition and assistance from the government, and I once asked him if he would accept a position in one of the departments. He answered frankly that he would. But he believed it improbable that he could get an appointment, although (as he mentioned casually) he had letters of recommendation from Emerson.

There were two of these, and they were especially interesting to me, as I knew something of the disturbed relations existing between the two men, on account of Whitman's indiscreet use of Emerson's famous letter to him, acknowledging the gift copy of the first *Leaves of Grass*. Whitman not only published that letter without the writer's authority, but printed an extract from it, in conspicuous gold, on the back of his second edition – "I greet you at the beginning of a great career"; thus making Emerson in some sense an endorser not only of the first poems, but of others he had never seen, and which he would have preferred never to see in print. This was an instance of bad taste, but not of intentional bad faith, on the part of Whitman . . .

With these things in mind, I read eagerly the two letters from Emerson recommending Whitman for a government appointment. One was addressed to Senator Sumner; the other, I was surprised and pleased to find, to Secretary [of the Treasury] Chase. I had but a slight acquaintance with Sumner, and the letter to him I handed back. The one written to Chase I wished to retain, in order to deliver it to the Secretary with my own hands, and with such furthering words as I could summon in so good a cause. Whitman expressed small hope in the venture, and stipulated that in case of the failure he anticipated I should bring back the letter.

As we left the breakfast table, the next morning, I followed the Secretary into his private office, where, after some pleasant talk, I remarked that I was about to overstep a rule I had laid down for myself on entering his house. He said, "What rule?" I replied, "Never to repay your hospitality by asking of you any official favour." He said I needn't have thought it necessary to make that rule, for he was always glad to do for his friends such things as he was constantly called upon to do for strangers. Then I laid before him the Whitman business. He was evidently impressed by Emerson's letter, and he listened with interest to what I had to say of the man and his patriotic work. But he was troubled. "I am placed," he said, "in a very embarrassing position. It would give me great pleasure to grant this request, out of my regard to Mr Emerson"; and he was gracious enough to extend the courtesy of this "regard" to me, also. But then he went on to speak of *Leaves of Grass* as a book that had made the author notorious; and I found that he judged it, as all but a very few persons then did, not independently, on its own epoch-making merits, but by conventional standards of taste and propriety. He had understood that the writer was a rowdy – "one of the roughs" – according to his descriptions of himself.

I said, "He is as quiet a gentleman in his manners and conversation as any guest who enters your door." He replied: "I am bound to believe what you say; but his writings have given him a bad repute, and I should not know what sort of a place to give to such a man," – with more to the same purpose.

I respected his decision, much as I regretted it; and, per-suaded that nothing I could urge would induce him to change it, I said I would relieve him of all embarrassment in the business by withdrawing the letter. He glanced again at the signature, hesitated, and made this surprising response: "I have nothing of Emerson's in his handwriting, and I shall be glad to keep this."

I thought it hardly fair, but as the letter was addressed to him, and had passed into his hands, I couldn't well reclaim it against his wishes.

Whitman seemed really to have formed some hopes of the success of my mission, after I had undertaken it, as he showed when I went to give him an account of my interview with the Secretary. He took the disappointment philosophically, but indulged in some sardonic remarks regarding Chase and his department. "He is right," he said, "in preserving his saints from contamination by a man like me!" But I stood up for the Secretary, as, with the Secretary, I had stood up for Whitman. Could any one be blamed for taking the writer of *Leaves of Grass* at his word when, in his defiance of conventionality, he had described himself as "rowdyish", "disorderly," and worse? " 'I cock my hat as I please, indoors and out,' " I quoted. Walt laughed, and said, "I don't blame him; it's about what I expected." He asked for the letter, and showed his amused disgust when I explained how it had been pocketed by the Secretary.

I should probably have had no difficulty in securing the appointment if I had withheld Emerson's letter, and called my friend simply Mr Whitman, or Mr Walter Whitman, without mentioning *Leaves of Grass*. But I felt that the Secretary, if he was to appoint him, should know just whom he was appointing; and Whitman was the last person in the world to shirk the responsibility of having written an audacious book.

(John Townsend Trowbridge,
Reminiscences of Walt Whitman)

The Victorian poet Alfred Lord Tennyson was more interested in being recognized than he pretended to be, as these two stories show.

Tennyson, while affecting to dread observation, was none the less no little vain, a weakness of which Meredith gave me this amusing illustration. Tennyson and William Morris were once walking together on a road in the Isle of Wight. Suddenly in the distance appeared two cyclists wheeling towards them. Tennyson immediately took alarm, and, turning to Morris, growled out, "Oh, Morris, what shall I do? Those fellows are sure to bother me!" Thereupon Morris drew him protectively to his side. "Keep close to me," he said, "I'll see that they don't bother you." The cyclists came on, sped by without a sign, and presently disappeared on the horizon. There was a moment or two of silence, and then Tennyson, evidently huffed that he had attracted no attention once more growled out, "They never even looked at me!"

(Richard Le Gallienne, *The Romantic '90s*)

In his later years his [Tennyson's] appearance was eccentric. He wore his hair long, flowing over his shoulders. He had a big black sombrero hat with a soft wide brim; a large, loose, soft Byronic collar; a big, floppy tie and a cloak, flung over one shoulder *à la mousquetaire*. He complained to a lady that it was one of the penalties of celebrity that he was stared at and even sometimes followed. Her little girl of eight, hoping to be helpful, suggested: "Perhaps, sir, if you cut your hair and dressed like other people, they wouldn't stare so much." He was not pleased.

(George Gower, *Mixed Grill*)

The late Victorian writer Samuel Butler didn't share the general enthusiasm for Charles Dickens.

On one of our Sunday walks Jones and my Cousin and I were at Gad's Hill [near Rochester in Kent]. An American tourist came up and asked if that was Charles Dickens' house, pointing to it. I looked grave, and said, "Yes, I am afraid it was," and left him.

(Samuel Butler, *Notebooks*)

The reputation of Arthur Conan Doyle, creator of Sherlock Holmes, was so widespread by the time he made a lecture tour of the USA in 1894 that he came across a cab-driver who was able to do a convincing imitation of Holmes' own methods of deduction.

A cab-driver in Boston refused payment from Conan Doyle, asking instead for a ticket to that evening's lecture.

"How on earth did you recognize me?" queried Conan Doyle.

Taking a deep breath, the cab-driver said, "If you will excuse me, your coat lapels are badly twisted downwards where they have been grasped by the pertinacious New York reporters. Your hair has the Quakerish cut of a Philadelphia barber, and your hat, battered at the brim in front, shows where you have tightly grasped it, in the struggle to stand your ground at a Chicago literary luncheon. Your right shoe has a large block of Buffalo mud just under the instep; the odor of a Utica cigar hangs about your clothing and the overcoat itself shows the slovenly brushing of the porters of the through sleepers from Albany. The crumbs of the doughnut on the top of your waistcoat could only have come there in Springfield."

Conan Doyle looked dumbfounded. The cabman let out a roar of laughter before adding, "And stenciled on the very end of your walking stick in perfectly plain lettering is the name Conan Doyle."

In the early 1990s the novelist and biographer, Justin Wintle, set off in pursuit of the Welsh poet R. S. Thomas. Thomas had a reputation for being "difficult" and repelling attempts to write about him: "I don't want fingers poked into my life," he said in an interview. A clergyman and a distinguished poet, Thomas had early on allied himself with the cause of Welsh nationalism. In north Wales, however, Wintle, travelling with his friend Owens, heard some recollections that were rather more down-to-earth than anything to do with church or country – or poetry, for that matter.

Beyond the bridge was a little piazza with a shop and the old post office and two hotels: the Ship Inn and the obviously more expensive Ty Newydd. We tried the Ship first, but they had no rooms available, so we checked in across the street. The receptionist there, an American girl called Caitlin who was studying at Bangor, told me, when I enquired, that Thomas was famous in Pen Llyn for annoying everybody by driving his white mini as slowly as he could and refusing to let anyone overtake him.

"He is quite old, you know. Old people drive like that."

"Not him. He does it intentionally. He thinks people shouldn't have cars."

My room at the Ty Newydd was on the top floor and had an unobstructed view of the bay: a great bowl of water, with its two Seagull islands arranged like boulders in a Japanese rock garden and thin, unbroken waves, a mile or more long, lapping the shore metronomically.

It was late afternoon. "This is heaven," I said when Owens knocked at my door.

"I won't know about that until I've had a drink. You coming for a pint?"

"Is the bar open?"

"Not here. It's too respectable. At the Ship. I've made some enquiries and there's no pub, but the Ship is where the locals hang out. If you want to find out about R. S. that's your best bet."

I'd been thinking about poking my nose into St Hywyn's, but Owens as usual was irresistible.

"Just watch what you say, boy, that's all. I don't know these people yet."

We repaired to the Ship. The long bar there was already filling up. Probably this had something to do with the barmaid, an especially fine-looking woman called Sue.

"Where are you from?" I asked.

"Manchester. I'm one of the dreaded lergies around here. But then a lot of us are. I came with my husband a few years ago. We bought a croft."

"Problems?"

"Not really. The people are mainly very nice as it happens."

"Does the name R. S. Thomas mean anything to you?"

"Oh, *him!*"

"You know him?"

"Who doesn't? Mainly from the rear, though. The rear of his car, that is. Blocking up the lane. Why do you ask?"

I explained to Sue my mission in life. She said:

"The good thing is he moved away a year or two ago. Gone off to Holyhead, I think. He had a genius for making himself unpopular round here, at least among us English-speakers. He used to be vicar but was retired by the time we came. He had a reputation for being keen on birds, though. You can't imagine what happened. One afternoon I found a gannet on the beach. Poor thing's wing was broken. Well, I knew where Mr Thomas was living, up in Rhiw. So I put the gannet in a box and took it to him. Was he interested? As soon as I opened my mouth he asked me where I was from and how long had I lived here and when was I leaving? I told him I'd only come because of the bird. Oh, there's nothing I can do about that, he said. I thought it was all very offensive of him and said so to his face. Not that it made the slightest difference."

"And the gannet?"

"The gannet I ended up taking to a sanctuary in Anglesey. It was well cared for and survived."

"I like this place," Owens broke in, "I like this place very much. Shall we have another?"

We had another, then we had supper. When we returned to

the bar at the Ship, Sue had gone, replaced by an older barmaid called Ivy. Ivy was also from Manchester, and was even more outspoken in her opinions about Thomas. When I mentioned his name she cackled.

"I could never make that one out," she said. "I was here when he first moved in. I'd heard there was a new vicar coming, and I'm a churchgoer myself. Or I was until then. The first time I saw him was outside on the bridge. 'Morning, Vicar!' I said to him, wanting him to feel at home in his new parish. But he just turned his head and looked the other way, like so. I was very upset at the time, although afterwards people told me he usually did that when people greeted him in English. But was that the proper way for a man of God to treat his flock?"

"Perhaps he was busy thinking up some poetry."

"I dare say he was. But it's no way to treat people. That was his attitude, you see. There's also the thing about his car. Where he lives in Rhiw is a cottage off the main road. What he used to do was go to the shops, then stop his car in the middle of the road and take his bags out one by one. Nobody could get past, but bugger everyone was his notion."

"What else?"

"Oh, loads and loads. Like the time he went to Pwllheli and took part in a march wearing a balaclava, just like the IRA. And him a priest! It's not right. I tell you, there's a black spot in that man's head, a very black spot indeed."

(Justin Wintle, *Furious Interiors: Wales, R. S. Thomas and God*)

School & University

Playwright Ben Jonson prided himself on his learning, particularly in "the antients" (classical Latin and Greek authors). Though generally admiring of Shakespeare, he saw this as one area in which he could claim to be ahead of his more famous contemporary, of whom Jonson said he had "small Latin and less Greek". This difference between the two playwrights was discussed among their admirers.

Jonson was certainly a very good Scholar, and in that had the advantage of Shakespear; tho' at the same time I believe it must be allow'd, that what Nature gave the latter, was more than a Ballance for what Books had given the former; and the Judgment of a Great Man upon this occasion was, I think, very just and proper. In a Conversation between Sir John Suckling, Sir William D'Avenant, Endymion Porter, Mr Hales of Eaton, and Ben Jonson; Sir John Suckling, who was a profess'd Admirer of Shakespear, had undertaken his Defence against Ben Jonson with some warmth; Mr Hales, who had sat still for some time, hearing Ben frequently reproaching him with the want of Learning and Ignorance of the Antients, told him at last, *That if Mr Shakespear had not read the Antients, he had likewise not stollen any Thing from 'em;* (a Fault the other made no Conscience of) *and that if he would produce any one Topick finely treated by any of them, he would undertake to shew something upon the same Subject at least as well written by Shakespear.*

(Nicholas Rowe, *The Works of Mr William Shakespear*)

Ben Jonson didn't always present such a dignified front as in the above story. He knew Sir Walter Raleigh, who made him "governor" *(tutor) to his son Wat when the pair travelled to France. Wat was obviously a more than lively copy of his father (see also **Parents & Children**).*

Sir Walter Ralegh sent him governor with his son, anno 1613, to France. This youth being knavishly inclined, among other pastimes (as the setting of the favour of damosells on a codpiece), caused him to be drunken, and dead drunk, so that he knew not where he was; thereafter laid him on a car, which he made to be drawn by pioners [workmen] through the streets, at every corner showing his governor stretched out, and telling them that was a more lively image of the crucifix than any they had. At which sport young Ralegh's mother delighted much (saying his father young was so inclined), though the father abhorred it.

(William Drummond, *Conversations with William Drummond of Hawthornden*)

~

The tutor to 17th-century poet John Wilmot, Earl of Rochester, seems to have had a different attitude towards his charge than Ben Jonson did to young Wat Raleigh (see above). But Rochester led a life that was both doomed and charmed. He also suffered from some bodily disorder ("distemper") which apparently caused terrible constipation.

Mr Giffard tells me that he was tutor to the Earl of Rochester (mad Rochester) before he came to Wadham College, which was in the eleventh year of his age, and that he was then a very hopeful youth, very virtuous and good natured (as he was always) and willing & ready to follow good advice. He was to have come to Oxford with his Lordship, but was supplanted. His Lordship had always a very good opinion of Mr Giffard. Mr Giffard used to lie with him in the family, on purpose that he might prevent any ill accidents . . . Mr Giffard says that my Lord understood very little or no Greek, and that he had but little Latin, & that therefore 'tis a great mistake in making him (as Burnet & Wood have done) so great a master of classic learning. He said my Lord had a natural distemper upon him which was extraordinary, & he thinks might be one occasion of shortening his days, which was that sometimes he could not have a stool for three weeks or a month together. Which distemper his Lordship told him was a very great occasion of that warmth and heat he always expressed, his brain being heated by the fumes and humours that ascended and evacuated themselves that way.

(Remarks and Collections of Thomas Hearne)

The poet Percy Bysshe Shelley was thrown out of Oxford for writing a pamphlet titled "The Necessity of Atheism".

It was a fine spring morning, on Lady-day, in the year 1811, when I went to Shelley's rooms. He was absent; but before I had collected our books he rushed in. He was terribly agitated. I anxiously enquired what had happened.

"I am expelled," he said, as soon as he had recovered himself a little. "I am expelled! I was sent for suddenly a few minutes ago; I went to the common room, where I found our master, and two or three of the fellows. The master produced a copy of the little syllabus, and asked me if I were the author of it. He spoke in a rude, abrupt, and insolent tone. I begged to be informed for what purpose he put the question. No answer was given; but the master loudly and angrily repeated, 'Are you the author of this book?' 'If I can judge from your manner,' I said, 'you are resolved to punish me if I should acknowledge that it is my work. If you can prove that it is, produce your evidence; it is neither just nor lawful to interrogate me in such a case and for such a purpose. Such proceedings would become a court of inquisitors, but not free men in a free country.' 'Do you choose to deny that this is your composition?' the master reiterated in the same rude and angry voice."

Shelley complained much of his violent and ungentlemanlike deportment, saying, "I have experienced tyranny and injustice before, and I well know what vulgar violence is, but I never met with such unworthy treatment. I told him calmly but firmly that I was determined not to answer any questions respecting the publication on the table.

"He immediately repeated his demand; I persisted in my refusal. And he said furiously, 'Then you are expelled; and I desire you will quit the college early tomorrow morning at the latest.'

"One of the fellows took up two papers, and handed one of them to me; here it is." He produced a regular sentence of expulsion, drawn up in due form, under the seal of the college. Shelley was full of spirit and courage, frank and fearless; but he was likewise shy, unpresuming, and eminently sensitive. I have been with him in many trying situations of his after-life, but I never saw him so deeply shocked and so cruelly agitated as on this occasion. A nice sense of honour shrinks from the most distant touch of disgrace – even from the insults of those men whose contumely can bring no shame. He sat on the sofa, repeating with convulsive vehemence the words, "Expelled, expelled!" his head shaking with emotion, and his whole frame quivering.

(Thomas Jefferson Hogg, *Life of Shelley*)

Novelist Walter Scott, a man of great integrity, confessed to his friend Samuel Rogers that he'd once resorted to trickery to get to the top of the class in school.

"There was a boy in my class at school who always stood at the top, nor could I with all my efforts supplant him. Day came after day, and still he kept his place, do what I would; till at length I observed that when a question was asked him he always fumbled with his fingers at a particular button on the lower part of his waistcoat. To remove it, therefore, became expedient in my eyes; and in an evil moment it was removed with a knife. Great was my anxiety to know the success of my measure, and it succeeded too well. When the boy was again questioned, his fingers sought at once for the button, but it was not to be found. In his distress he looked down for it; it was to be seen no more than to be felt. He stood confounded, and I took possession of his place; nor did he ever recover it, or ever, I believe, suspect who was the author of his wrong. Often in after life has the sight of him smote me as I passed by him; and often have I resolved to make some reparation, but it ended simply in good resolutions as usual, accompanied by nothing else."

Nineteenth-century public schools were unpleasant places to attend but novelist Anthony Trollope's experience as a 7-year-old at Harrow seems to have been worse than most.

My two elder brothers had been sent as day-boarders to Harrow School from the bigger house, and may probably have been received among the aristocratic crowd, not on equal terms, because a day-boarder at Harrow in those days was never so received, but at any rate as other day-boarders. I do not suppose that they were well treated, but I doubt whether they were subjected to the ignominy which I endured. I was only seven, and I think that boys at seven are now spared among their more considerate seniors. I was never spared; and was not even allowed to run to and fro between our house and the school without a daily purgatory. No doubt my appearance was against me. I remember well, when I was still the junior boy in the school, Dr Butler, the headmaster, stopping me in the street, and asking me, with all the clouds of Jove upon his brow and all the thunder in his voice, whether it was possible that Harrow School was disgraced by so disreputably dirty a little boy as I! Oh, what I felt at that moment! But I could not look my feelings. I do not doubt that I was dirty; but I think that he was cruel. He must have known me had he seen me as he was wont to see me, for he was in the habit of flogging me constantly. Perhaps he did not recognize me by my face.

(Anthony Trollope, *An Autobiography*)

Shakespeariana

There are many tales in circulation about what Shakespeare did between leaving Stratford-on-Avon and becoming an established playwright in London. This one could be true.

Concerning Shakespear's first appearance in the playhouse. When he came to London, he was without money and friends, and being a stranger he knew not to whom to apply, nor by what means to support himself. At that time coaches not being in use, and as gentlemen were accustomed to ride to the playhouse, Shakespear, driven to the last necessity, went to the playhouse door, and pick'd up a little money by taking care of the gentlemen's horses who came to the play; he became eminent even in that profession, and was taken notice of for his diligence and skill in it; he had soon more business than he himself could manage, and at last hired boys under him, who were known by the name of Shakespear's boys: Some of the players accidentally conversing with him, found him so acute, and master of so fine a conversation, that struck therewith, they recommended him to the house, in which he was first admitted in a very low station, but he did not long remain so, for he soon distinguished himself, if not as an extraordinary actor, at least as a fine writer. His name is printed, as the custom was in those times, amongst those of the other players, before some old plays, but without any particular account of what sort of parts he used to play: and as Mr Rowe says, "that tho' he very carefully enquired, he found the top of his performance was the ghost in Hamlet."

(Theophilus Cibber, *The Lives of the Poets*)

Nothing is known for certain about the parts that Shakespeare played on stage but there's a tradition that, as well as the ghost of Hamlet's father, he played the fairly undemanding part of "old" Adam in As You Like It. *There is also a tradition that he "was a much better poet than Player".*

This is one version of another very popular, long established story about Shakespeare. Richard Burbage was a leading player in the Company.

One evening when Richard III was to be performed, Shakespeare observed a young woman delivering a message to Burbage in so cautious a manner as excited his curiosity to listen to. It imported, that her master was gone out of town that morning, and her mistress would be glad of his company after Play; and to know what signal he would appoint for admittance. Burbage replied, "Three taps at the door, and 'It is I, Richard the Third.'" She immediately withdrew, and Shakespeare followed till he observed her to go into a house in the city; and enquiring in the neighbourhood, he was informed that a young lady lived there, the favourite of a rich old merchant. Near the appointed time of meeting, Shakespeare thought proper to anticipate Mr Burbage, and was introduced by the concerted signal. The lady was very much surprised at Shakespeare's presuming to act Mr Burbage's part; but as he (who had written Romeo and Juliet), we may be certain, did not want wit or eloquence to apologize for the intrusion, she was soon pacified, and they were mutually happy till Burbage came to the door, and repeated the same signal; but Shakespeare popping his head out of the window, bid him be gone: for that William the Conqueror had reigned before Richard III.

The poet and dramatist Sir William Davenant (1606–1668) was accustomed to making some very flattering claims about his parentage.

Sir William Davenant, Knight, Poet Laureate, was borne in the City of Oxford at the Crowne Taverne. He went to schoole at

Oxon to Mr Sylvester, but I feare he was drawne from schoole before he was ripe enough.

His father was John Davenant, a Vintner there, a very grave and discreet Citizen; his mother was a very beautifull woman and of a very good witt, and of conversation extremely agreable.

Mr William Shakespeare was wont to goe into Warwickshire once a yeare, and did commonly in his journey lye at this house in Oxon, where he was exceedingly respected. (I have heard Parson Robert say that Mr William Shakespeare haz given him a hundred kisses.) Now Sir William would sometimes, when he was pleasant over a glasse of wine with his most intimate friends – e.g. Sam Butler, author of *Hudibras*, etc, say, that it seemed to him that he writt with the very spirit that did Shakespeare, and seemed contented enough to be thought his Son. He would tell them the story as above, in which way his mother had a very light report, whereby she was called a Whore.

(John Aubrey, *Brief Lives*)

In 1773 James Boswell, Dr Johnson's devoted friend and disciple, persuaded the great man away from London to accompany him on a tour of Scotland. Here Boswell writes to their mutual friend David Garrick, the most famous actor of his day, about a place that was heavy with literary and dramatic significance.

Inverness
29 August, 1773

My dear Sir,

Here I am, and Mr Samuel Johnson actually with me. We were a night at Forres, in coming to which, in the dusk of the evening, we passed over the bleak and blasted heath where Macbeth met the Witches. Your old preceptor repeated, with much solemnity, the speech "How far is't to Forres? What are these, so withered and so wild in their attire?"

This day we visited the ruins of Macbeth's castle at Inverness. I have had great romantic satisfaction in seeing Johnson upon the classical scenes of Shakespeare in Scotland; which I really looked upon as almost as improbable as that "Birnam Wood should come to Dunsinane". Indeed, as I have always been accustomed to view him as a permanent London object, it would not be much more wonderful to me to see St. Paul's church moving along where we now are . . .

Hitherto we have had a very prosperous expedition. He is in excellent spirits, and I have a rich journal of his conversation. Look back, Davy, to Lichfield; run up through the time that has elapsed since you first knew Mr Johnson, and enjoy with me his present extraordinary tour. I could not resist the impulse of writing to you from this place. The situation of the old castle corresponds exactly to Shakespeare's description. While we were there today, it happened oddly that a raven perched upon one of the chimney-tops and croaked. Then I in my turn repeated –

> The raven himself is hoarse
> That croaks the fatal entrance of Duncan
> Under my battlements.*

I wish you had been with us.

In December 1785 the author Fanny Burney met King George III at Windsor. He questioned her about her novel Evelina and then began to talk about the theatre.

From players he went on to plays, and complained of the great want of good modern comedies, and of the extreme immorality of most of the old ones.

"And they pretend," cried he, "to mend them; but it is not possible. Do you think it is? – what?"

"No, sir, not often, I believe; the fault, commonly, lies in the very foundation."

"Yes, or they might mend the mere speeches; – but the characters are all bad from the beginning to the end."

* The raven himself . . . – Lady Macbeth's words when she learns that King Duncan, whom she and her husband plan to murder, is coming to stay at their castle that night.

Then he specified several; but I had read none of them and consequently could say nothing about the matter; – till, at last, he came to Shakespeare.

"Was there ever," cried he, "such stuff as great part of Shakespeare? Only one must not say so! But what think you? – what? – what?"

"Yes, indeed, I think so, sir, though mixed with such excellencies, that –"

"O!" cried he, laughing good-humouredly, "I know it is not to be said, but it's true. Only it's Shakespeare, and nobody dare abuse him."

Then he enumerated many of the characters and parts of plays that he objected to; and when he had run them over, finished with again laughing, and exclaiming, "But one should be stoned for saying so!"

(Fanny Burney, *Diaries and Letters*)

The line of Shakespeare's direct descendants died out relatively soon after his own death. None of his granchildren had any issue. His nephew William Hart, by contrast, originated a line whose descendants survive to the present day. In the early 19th century a magazine editor went in search of one member of this branch of the family. He didn't take much pride in the connection with the playwright.

In answer to inquiries about the great bard, Hart said his father and grandfather often talked of the subject, and buoyed themselves with hopes that the family might sometime be remembered; but, for his part, the name had hitherto proved of no other use to him than as furnishing jokes among his companions, by whom he was often annoyed on this account. On the writer presenting him with a guinea, he declared that it was the first benefit which had arisen from his being a Shakespeare.

(Sir Richard Philips, *The Monthly Magazine*)

In 1828 the painter and diary-writer Benjamin Robert Haydon visited Shakespeare's birthplace of Stratford-upon-Avon. By this

*time Shakespeare was idolized, and the town was waking up to the
tourist potential of its most famous inhabitant. Even so there was a
comic aspect to Haydon's visit as he encountered some of the contemporary Stratford citizens.*

I left Oxford next morning outside, and got to Stratford at two.
I ordered dinner, and hurried away to Henley Street. The first
thing I saw was a regular sign, projecting from a low house:
"The immortal Shakespeare was born in this house." I darted
across, and cursed the door for keeping me out a moment when
a very decent and neat widow-looking woman came from a door
that entered from the other house and let me in. I marched
through, mounted an ancient staircase and in a moment was in
the immortal room where Shakespeare gave the first puling cry,
which announced he was living and healthy.

It is low and long, and has every appearance of having been in
existence long before Shakespeare's time. The large old chimney has a cross-beamed front. There is a document to the effect
that his father bought the house when Shakespeare was ten
years old, and a tradition he occupied it before: so that there is
perhaps little doubt he was born in it, and as people generally
are born in bedrooms, why this upstairs room probably gave
birth to the poet.

The present possessor complains bitterly of the previous
tenant, who after promising not to injure the names of all
the illustrious visitors for the last eighty years, in mere spite
because she was obliged to leave, whitewashed the whole room.
His Majesty's name, as Prince of Wales, can't be found; Garrick's, and the whole host of the famous of the last century, are
for ever obliterated; and hundreds on hundreds of immortal
obscure who hoped to cut out a little freehold of fame are again
and for ever sunk to their natural oblivion . . .

A squinting Cockney came in while I was there; so left and
walked to the sequestered and beautiful spot where the dust of
this great genius lies at rest. A more delightful place could not
have been found. It is Shakespeare in every leaf. It must have
been chosen by himself as he stood in the chancel musing on the
fate of the dead about him, and listening to the humming
murmur and breezy rustle of the river and trees by which it

stands. The most poetical imagination could not have imagined a burial-place more worthy, more suitable, more English, more native for a poet than this – above all, for Shakespeare. As I stood over his grave and read his pathetic entreaty and blessing on the reader who revered his remains, and curses on him who dared to touch [see next item]; as I looked up at his simple unaffected bust, executed while his favourite daughter was living and put up by her husband; as I listened to the waving trees and murmuring Avon, saw the dim light of the large windows and thought I was hearing what Shakespeare had often heard, and was standing where he had stood many times, I was deeply touched . . .

Haydon continued his exploration of Stratford and its surroundings the next morning. He ended up by going into a pub.

Wet to the knees, I passed, as I approached the old bridge, a humble sign of the Plough and Harrow. In I walked, and found an old dame blowing a wood fire; the room and chimney of the same age as Shakespeare; on a form with a back sat a country-man smoking, and by the window a decent girl making a gown; on the table by the door was a bundle of pipes, enclosed rings, the two end rings resting on two feet; a clock made by Sharp (who bought Shakespeare's mulberry tree), a chest of drawers on three legs. The old furniture and the whole room looked clean, humble and honest. I ordered ale, which was excellent, and giving the smoker a pint asked him if he ever heard of Shakespeare. "To be sure," said he, "but he was not born in Henley Street." "Where was he born?" "By the water-side, to be sure." "Why," said I, "how do you know that?" "Why, John Cooper, in the almshouses." "Who's he?" said I. "What does he know about it?" said the old hostess. "Nonsense," said the young girl. My pot companion, giving a furious smoke at being thus floored at his first attempt to put forth a new theory of Shakespeare's birthplace, looked at me very grave and prepared to overwhelm me at once. He puffed away, and after taking a sip said, "Ah, sir, there's another wonderful fellow." "Who?" said I, imagining some genius of Stratford who might contest the palm. "Why," said he, with more gravity than ever "why, John

Cooper." "John Cooper!" said I: "Why, what has he done?" "Why, zur, I'll tell 'ee "; and then laying his pipe down, and leaning on his elbow, and looking right into my eyes under his old weather-beaten, embrowned hat, "I'll tell 'ee. He's lived ninety years in this here town, man and boy, and has never had the toothache, and never lost *wan*." He then took up his pipe, letting the smoke ooze from the sides of his mouth instead of puffing it out horizontally, till it ascended in curls of conscious victory to the ceiling of the apartment; while my companion leaned back his head and crossed his legs with an air of superior intelligence as if this conversation must now conclude. We were no longer on a level.

I spoke not another word: retired to my inn, the Red House; took another sequestered sigh at the grave, another peep at the house; got into the garden where the mulberry tree grew; heard the clock strike which Shakespeare had often heard, and getting into a Shrewsbury stage at nine the next morning was buried in London smoke and London anxieties before nine at night.

(Benjamin Haydon, *Autobiography and Memoirs*)

There is a superstition hanging round Shakespeare's burial place in Holy Trinity Church in Stratford. A curse apparently lies in wait for anyone who dared to dig up his bones. But the well-known inscription on Shakespeare's tomb is probably not by the playwright. Anonymous or not, it reads:

GOOD FREND FOR IESVS SAKE FORBEARE,
TO DIGG THE DVST ENCLOASED HEARE.
BLESTE BE YE MAN YT SPARES THES STONES,
AND CVRST BE HE YT MOVES MY BONES.

Not everyone has been so struck by the playwright's stone image as Benjamin Haydon was (see above). Writing 150 years later Anthony Burgess said that the "bust was a travesty, but the sculptor must have believed that Shakespeare looked plump, complacent and faintly imbecilic."

There's something about the Shakespeare story that drives people crazy. This was especially true in the 19th century when "scholars" and fanatics grew desperate to prove that someone else – anyone else – wrote the plays. Delia Bacon is a representative example, and a slightly poignant one. She was born in Ohio in 1811 and raised in Connecticut. From a poor background, she was determined to make something of herself. Prompted by her own surname and by her wide reading among Elizabethan writers, she became convinced that the "real" author of Shakespeare's plays was the aristocratic Francis Bacon. A great fraud had been perpetrated on the world. She had a very low opinion of Shakepeare ("this old actor . . . this old tradesman") and a very elevated view of Bacon. She gained the backing of some prominent Americans, including Ralph Waldo Emerson, and sailed for England in 1853. After three years, when her attempts at publication were going badly, she wrote in desperation to Nathaniel Hawthorne, the American consul in Liverpool. Hawthorne couldn't agree with Miss Bacon's fantasies but he admired her single-mindedness and pitied her lonely struggle to convince the world that she had uncovered the secret of the "stupid, ignorant, third-rate play-actor". In particular, Delia Bacon was gripped by the belief that Shakespeare's tomb held the solution. Hawthorne describes his one and only meeting with Miss Bacon and what happened when she visited the Stratford church containing the tomb and memorial.

The only time I ever saw Miss Bacon was in London, where she had lodgings in Spring Street, Sussex Gardens, at the house of a grocer, a portly, middle-aged, civil, and friendly man, who, as well as his wife, appeared to feel a personal kindness towards their lodger. I was ushered up two (and I rather believe three) pair of stairs into a parlour somewhat humbly furnished, and told that Miss Bacon would come soon . . .

I had expected (the more shame for me, having no other ground of such expectation than that she was a literary woman) to see a very homely, uncouth, elderly personage, and was quite agreeably disappointed by her aspect. She was rather uncommonly tall, and had a striking and expressive face, dark hair, dark eyes, which shone with an inward light as soon as she began to speak, and by and by a colour came into her cheeks and made her look almost young. Not that she really was so; she must have been beyond middle age: and there was no unkindness in coming to that conclusion, because, making allowance for years and ill-health, I could suppose her to have been handsome and exceedingly attractive once. Though wholly estranged from society, there was little or no restraint or embarrassment in her manner: lonely people are generally glad to give utterance to their pent-up ideas, and often bubble over with them as freely as children with their new-found syllables. I cannot tell how it came about, but we immediately found ourselves taking a friendly and familiar tone together, and began to talk as if we had known one another a very long while. A little preliminary correspondence had indeed smoothed the way, and we had a definite topic in the contemplated publication of her book . . .

I had heard, long ago, that she believed that the material evidences of her dogma as to the authorship, together with the key of the new philosophy, would be found buried in Shakespeare's grave. Recently, as I understood her, this notion had been somewhat modified, and was now accurately defined and fully developed in her mind, with a result of perfect certainty. In Lord Bacon's Letters, on which she laid her finger as she spoke, she had discovered the key and clew to the whole mystery. There were definite and minute instructions how to find a will and other documents relating to the conclave of Elizabethan philosophers, which were concealed (when and by whom she did not inform me) in a hollow space in the under surface of Shakespeare's gravestone. Thus the terrible prohibition [the curse on anyone who "disturbs" Shakespeare's grave] to remove the stone was accounted for. The directions, she intimated, went completely and precisely to the point, obviating all difficulties in the way of coming at the treasure, and even, if I remember right, were so contrived as to ward off any troublesome consequences likely to ensue from the interference of the parish-officers. All that Miss Bacon now remained in England for – indeed, the object for which she had come hither, and which had kept her here for three years past – was to obtain possession of these material and unquestionable proofs of the authenticity of her theory . . .

Her book, as I could see by turning it over, was a very remarkable one, and worthy of being offered to the public, which, if wise enough to appreciate it, would be thankful for what was good in it and merciful to its faults. It was founded on a prodigious error, but was built up from that foundation with a good many prodigious truths . . .

Months before that [the publication of the book] happened, however, Miss Bacon had taken up her residence at Stratford-on-Avon, drawn thither by the magnetism of those rich secrets which she supposed to have been hidden by Raleigh, - or Bacon, or I know not whom, in Shakespeare's grave, and protected there by a curse, as pirates used to bury their gold in the guardianship of a fiend. She took a humble lodging and began to haunt the church like a ghost. But she did not condescend to any stratagem or underhand attempt to violate the grave, which, had she been capable of admitting such an idea, might possibly have been accomplished by the aid of a resurrection-man [body snatcher]. As her first step, she made acquaintance with the clerk, and began to sound him as to the feasibility of her enterprise and his own willingness to engage in it. The clerk apparently listened with not unfavourable ears; but as his situation (which the fees of pilgrims, more numerous than at any Catholic shrine, render lucrative) would have been forfeited by any malfeasance in office, he stipulated for liberty to consult the vicar. Miss Bacon requested to tell her own story to the reverend gentleman, and seems to have been received by him with the utmost kindness, and even to have succeeded in making a certain impression on his mind as to the desirability of the search. As their interview had been under the seal of secrecy, he asked permission to consult a friend, who, as Miss Bacon either found out or surmised, was a practitioner of the law. What the legal friend advised she did not learn; but the negotiation continued, and certainly was never broken off by an absolute refusal on the vicar's part . . .

The affair certainly looked very hopeful. However erroneously, Miss Bacon had understood from the vicar that no obstacles would be interposed to the investigation, and that he himself would sanction it with his presence. It was to take place after nightfall; and all preliminary arrangements being made, the vicar and clerk professed to wait only her word in order to set about lifting the awful stone from the sepulchre. So, at least, Miss Bacon believed; and as her bewilderment was entirely in her own thoughts, and never disturbed her perception or accurate remembrance of external things, I see no reason to doubt it, except it be the tinge of absurdity in the fact. But, in this apparently prosperous state of things, her own convictions began to falter. A doubt stole into her mind whether she might not have mistaken the depository and mode of concealment of those historic treasures; and, after once admitting the doubt, she was afraid to hazard the shock of uplifting the stone and finding nothing. She examined the surface of the gravestone, and endeavoured, without stirring it, to estimate whether it were of such thickness as to be capable of containing the archives of the Elizabethan club. She went over anew the proofs, the clews, the enigmas, the pregnant sentences, which she had discovered in Bacon's Letters and elsewhere, and now was frightened to perceive that they did not point so definitely to Shakespeare's tomb as she had heretofore supposed . . . this now became strong enough to restrain her from a decisive step.

But she continued to hover around the church, and seems to have had full freedom of entrance in the daytime, and special licence, on one occasion at least, at a late hour of the night. She went thither with a dark-lantern, which could but twinkle like a glow-worm through the volume of obscurity that filled the great dusky edifice. Groping her way up the aisle and towards the chancel, she sat down on the elevated part of the pavement above Shakespeare's grave. If the divine poet really wrote the inscription there, and cared as much about the quiet of his bones as its deprecatory earnestness would imply, it was time for those crumbling relics to bestir themselves under her sacrilegious feet. But they were safe. She made no attempt to disturb them; though, I believe, she looked narrowly into the crevices between Shakespeare's and the two adjacent stones, and in some way satisfied herself that her single strength would suffice to lift the former, in case of need. She threw the feeble ray of her lantern up towards the bust, but could not make it visible beneath the darkness of the vaulted roof. Had she been subject to superstitious terrors, it is impossible to conceive of a situation that could better entitle her to feel them, for, if Shakespeare's ghost would rise at any provocation, it must have shown itself then; but it is my sincere belief, that, if his figure had appeared within the scope of her dark-lantern, in his slashed doublet and gown, and with his eyes bent on her beneath the high, bald forehead, just as we see him in the bust, she would have met him fearlessly, and controverted his claims to the authorship of the plays, to his very face. She had taught herself to contemn "Lord Leicester's groom" (it was one of her disdainful epithets for the world's incomparable poet) so thoroughly, that even his disembodied spirit would hardly have found civil treatment at Miss Bacon's hands.

Her vigil, though it appears to have had no definite object, continued far into the night. Several times she heard a low movement in the aisles: a stealthy, dubious footfall prowling about in the darkness, now here, now there, among the pillars and ancient tombs, as if some restless inhabitant of the latter had crept forth to peep at the intruder. By and by the clerk made his appearance, and confessed that he had been watching her ever since she entered the church.

At some point after this Nathaniel Hawthorne fell out with Delia Bacon, and the two Americans didn't speak again.

At that time her book was passing through the press. Without prejudice to her literary ability, it must be allowed that Miss Bacon was wholly unfit to prepare her own work for publication, because, among many other reasons, she was too thoroughly in earnest to know what to leave out . . . there tumbled out a ponderous octave volume, which fell with a dead thump at the feet of the public, and has never been picked up . . .

The next intelligence that I had of Miss Bacon was by a letter from the mayor of Stratford-on-Avon. He was a medical man, and wrote both in his official and professional character, telling me that an American lady, who had recently published what the mayor called a "Shakespeare book", was afflicted with insanity. In a lucid interval she had referred to me, as a person who had some knowledge of her family and affairs. What she may have suffered before her intellect gave way, we had better not try to imagine. No author had ever hoped so confidently as she; none ever failed more utterly. A superstitious fancy might suggest that the anathema on Shakespeare's tombstone had fallen heavily on her head, in requital of even the unaccomplished purpose of disturbing the dust beneath, and that the "Old Player" had kept so quietly in his grave, on the night of her vigil, because he foresaw how soon and terribly he would be avenged. But if that benign spirit takes any care or cognizance of such things now, he has surely requited the injustice that she sought to do him – the high justice that she really did – by a tenderness of love and pity of which only he could he capable.

(Nathaniel Hawthorne, *Our Old Home*)

Edmund Gosse was the son of a famous 19th-century zoologist, Philip Gosse. His parents were members of the Plymouth Brethren, a fundamentalist religious sect that believed in the Bible with a fierce literalness and that condemned most pleasures as sinful (see also **Reading** and **Religion**). In Father and Son, an autobiography of his early life, Gosse tells of the clash between his father and himself. This almost extended to whether Shakespeare should be rejected because he was not one of the "saved".

It was in my fifteenth year that I became again, this time intelligently, acquainted with Shakespeare. I got hold of a single play, "The Tempest", in a school edition, prepared, I suppose, for one of the university examinations which were then being instituted in the provinces. This I read through and through, not disdaining the help of the notes, and revelling in the glossary. I studied "The Tempest" as I had hitherto studied no classic work, and it filled my whole being with music and romance. This book was my own hoarded possession; the rest of Shakespeare's works were beyond my hopes.

But gradually I contrived to borrow a volume here and a volume there. I completed "The Merchant of Venice", read "Cymbeline", "Julius Caesar" and "Much Ado" ; most of the others, I think, remained closed to me for a long time. But these were enough to steep my horizon with all the colours of sunrise. It was due, no doubt, to my bringing up, that the plays never appealed to me as bounded by the exigencies of a stage or played by actors. The images they raised in my mind were of real people moving in the open air, and uttering, in the natural play of life, sentiments that were clothed in the most lovely, and yet, as it seemed to me, the most obvious and the most inevitable language.

It was while I was thus under the full spell of the Shake-spearean necromancy that a significant event occurred. My Father took me up to London for the first time since my infancy. Our visit was one of a few days only, and its purpose was that we might take part in some enormous Evangelical conference. We stayed in a dark hotel off the Strand, where I found the noise by day and night very afflicting. When we were not at the conference, I spent long hours, among crumbs and blue-bottle flies, in the coffee-room of this hotel, my Father being busy at the British Museum and the Royal Society. The conference was held in an immense hall, some-where in the north of London. I remember my short-sighted sense of the terrible vastness of the crowd, with rings on rings of dim white faces fading in the fog. My Father, as a privileged visitor, was obliged with seats on the platform, and we were in the heart of the first really large assemblage of persons that I had ever seen.

The interminable ritual of prayers, hymns and addresses left no impression on my memory, but my attention was suddenly stung into life by a remark. An elderly man, fat and greasy, with a voice like a bassoon, and an imperturbable assurance, was denouncing the spread of infidelity, and the lukewarmness of professing Christians, who refrained from battling the wicked-ness at their doors. They were like the Laodiceans, whom the angel of the Apocalypse spewed out of his mouth. For instance, who, the orator asked, is now rising to check the outburst of idolatry in our midst? "At this very moment," he went on, "there is proceeding, unreproved, a blasphemous celebration of the birth of Shakespeare, a lost soul now suffering for his sins in hell!" My sensation was that of one who has suddenly been struck on the head; stars and sparks beat round me. If some person I loved had been grossly insulted in my presence, I could not have felt more powerless in anguish. No one in that vast audience raised a word of protest, and my spirits fell to their nadir. This, be it remarked, was the earliest intimation that had reached me of the tercentenary of the Birth at Stratford, and I had not the least idea what could have provoked the outburst of outraged godliness.

But Shakespeare was certainly in the air. When we returned to the hotel that noon, my Father of his own accord reverted to the subject. I held my breath, prepared to endure fresh torment. What he said, however, surprised and relieved me. "Brother So-and-so," he remarked, "was not, in my judgment, justified in saying what he did. The uncovenanted mercies of God are not revealed to us. Before so rashly speaking of Shakespeare as 'a lost soul in hell', he should have remembered how little we know of the poet's history. The light of salvation was widely disseminated in the land during the reign of Queen Elizabeth, and we cannot know that Shakespeare did not accept the atonement of Christ in simple faith before he came to die." The concession will today seem meagre to gay and worldly spirits, but words cannot express how comfortable it was to me. I gazed at my Father with loving eyes across the cheese and celery, and if the waiter had not been present I believe I might have hugged him in my arms.

(Edmund Gosse, *Father and Son*)

Arnold Bennett visits the Italian city of Verona, the setting for Romeo and Juliet.

Juliet's home town, I suppose some would call it. The phrase takes the edge off romance, and I designed it to do so, determined as I am somehow to vent my rage at being shown Juliet's house, a picturesque and untidy tenement, with balconies certainly too high for love, unless Juliet was a trapeze artist, accustomed to hanging downwards by her toes.

This was not Juliet's house, for the sufficient reason that so far as authentic history knows, there never was any Juliet.

(Arnold Bennett, *Journals*)

Theatre & Film

The most famous play by Christopher Marlowe, Shakespeare's contemporary, is Dr Faustus. This drama of a man who sells his soul to the devil was immensely popular at the time but gave the actors some sleepless nights. During the course of Dr Faustus devils appear on the stage and at several performances it seemed to the players that their numbers were swelled by "real" demons. There's a legend that Edward Alleyn, who played the part of Faustus, was so alarmed at one such apparition during a performance in Dulwich that he vowed to found a college in that town, to be called the College of God's Gift (he did – and the school has existed in Dulwich for the last 400 years). The play was obviously a risky piece of theatre. Below is another contemporary account of a production of Dr Faustus, this time in Exeter.

Certaine Players at Exeter acting upon the stage the tragicall storie of Dr Faustus the Conjurer; as a certain number of Devels kept everie one his circle there, and as Faustus was busie in his magicall invocations, on a sudden they wer all dasht, every one harkning other in the eare, for they were all perswaded there was one devell too many amongst them; and so after a little pause desired the people to pardon them, they could go no further with this matter: the people also understanding the thing as it was, every man hastened to be first out of dores. The players (as I heard it) contrarye to their custome spending the night in reading and in prayer got them out of the towne the next morning.

~

Colley Cibber was a playwright and poet laureate in the early 18th century. Like many laureates he is almost forgotten, and any fame he *has now rests on the fact that he was one of Pope's targets in the satirical poem* The Dunciad. *Cibber started out on stage with a walk-on part in which he displeased the ageing actor Thomas Betterton.*

He was known only for some years, by the name of Master Colley. After waiting impatiently for some time for the Prompter's Notice, by good fortune he obtained the honour of carrying a message on the stage, in some play, to Betterton. Whatever was the cause, Master Colley was so terrified, that the scene was disconcerted by him. Betterton asked, in some anger, who the young fellow was that had committed the blunder. Downes replied, "Master Colley!" – "Master Colley! Then forfeit [fine] him!" – "Why Sir," said the prompter, "he has no salary." "No!" said the old man; "why then put him down 10s. a week, and forfeit him 5s."

(Thomas Davies, *Dramatic Miscellanies*)

John Dennis was another early 18th-century poet and dramatist. He doesn't seem to have been very successful on the stage, although he did invent a device for producing the sound of thunder by rattling a sheet of tin.

The actors refused to perform one of his tragedies to empty houses, but they retained some excellent thunder which Dennis had invented; it rolled one night when Dennis was in the pit, and it was applauded! Suddenly starting up, he cried to the audience, "By G—, they won't act my tragedy, but they steal my thunder!"

(Isaac Disraeli, *Calamaties and Quarrels of Authors*)

The 18th-century novelist Henry Fielding, best known as the author of Joseph Andrews *and* Tom Jones, *was also a playwright.*

After the publication of *Joseph Andrews*, Fielding had again recourse to the stage, and brought out *The Wedding-Day*, which, though on the whole unsuccessful, produced him some small profit. This was the last of his theatrical efforts which appeared during his life . . . An anecdote respecting the carelessness with which Fielding regarded his theatrical fame, is thus given by former biographers:

"On one of the days of its rehearsal (i.e. the rehearsal of *The Wedding-Day*) Garrick, who performed a principal part, and who was even then a favourite with the public told Fielding he was apprehensive that the audience would make free with him in a particular passage, and remarked that, as a repulse might disconcert him during the remainder of the night, the passage should be omitted: – 'No, d— 'em,' replied he, 'if the scene is not a good one, let them find *that* out.' Accordingly the play was brought out without alteration, and, as had been foreseen, marks of disapprobation appeared. Garrick, alarmed at the hisses he had met with, retired into the green-room, where the author was solacing himself with a bottle of champagne. He had by this time drunk pretty freely – and glancing his eye at the actor, while clouds of tobacco issued from his mouth, cried out, 'What's the matter, Garrick? What are they hissing now?' 'Why, the scene that I begged you to retrench,' replied the actor; 'I knew it would not do; and they have so frightened me that I shall not be able to collect myself again the whole night.' – 'Oh ! d— 'em,' rejoined he with great coolness, 'they *have* found it out, have they?' "

(Walter Scott, *Lives of the Novelists*)

The critic and essayist Charles Lamb also tried his hand at writing for the stage. In 1806 his farce *Mr H* was badly received at the Drury Lane Theatre. In the theatre pit Lamb joined in the general hissing which greeted his own effort. Afterwards he explained that he had done this because he was "so damnably afraid of being taken for the author".

The Theatre Royal in Drury Lane burned down in 1672 and was rebuilt by Christopher Wren. Over a century later the playwright Richard Brinsley Sheridan took a share in the place and staged some of his own works, such as The Rivals. *Sheridan was also a Member of*

Parliament and displayed tremendous style and grace when the Theatre burned down for a second time.

On the night of the 24th of February 1809, when the House of Commons was occupied with Mr Ponsonby's motion on the Conduct of the War in Spain, and Mr Sheridan was in attendance, with the intention, no doubt, of speaking, the House was suddenly illuminated by a blaze of light; and, the Debate being interrupted, it was ascertained that the Theatre of Drury Lane was on fire. A motion was made to adjourn; but Mr. Sheridan said, with much calmness, that "whatsoever might be the extent of the private calamity, he hoped it would not interfere with the public business of the country". He then left the House; and, proceeding to Drury Lane, witnessed, with a fortitude which strongly interested all who observed him, the entire destruction of his property. It is said that, as he sat at the Piazza Coffee-house during the fire, taking some refreshment, a friend of his having remarked on the philosophic calmness with which he bore his misfortune, Sheridan answered, "A man may surely be allowed to take a glass of wine by his own fireside."

(Thomas Moore, *Memoirs of Sheridan*)

An early biographer records Shelley's views on some popular entertainment.

He had a prejudice against theatres which I took some pains to overcome. I induced him one evening to accompany me to a representation of the *School for Scandal*. When, after the scenes which exhibit Charles Surface in his jollity, the scene returned in the fourth act, to Joseph's library, Shelley said to me – "I see the purpose of this comedy. It is to associate virtue with bottles and glasses, and villainy with books." I had great difficulty to make him stay to the end. He often talked of "the withering and perverted spirit of comedy" . . .

In the season of 1817, I persuaded him to accompany me to the opera. The performance was *Don Giovanni*. Before it commenced he asked me if the opera was comic or tragic. I said it was composite – more comedy than tragedy. After the killing of the Commendatore, he said, "Do you call this comedy?"

(Thomas Love Peacock, *Memoirs of Shelley*)

In 1877 Mark Twain and Bret Harte, the writer of Western short stories, worked together on a play.

The new play, "Ah Sin", by Mark Twain and Bret Harte, was put on at Washington, at the National Theater, on the evening of 7 May, 1877. It had been widely exploited in the newspapers, and the fame of the authors insured a crowded opening. Clemens was unable to go over on account of a sudden attack of bronchitis. Parsloe [the principal actor] was nervous accordingly, and the presence of Harte does not seem to have added to his happiness.

"I am not very well myself," he wrote to Clemens [Twain's real name]. "The excitement of the first night is bad enough, but to have the annoyance with Harte that I have is too much for a new beginner."

Nevertheless, the play seems to have gone well, with Parsloe as Ah Sin – a Chinese laundryman who was also a great number of other diverting things – with a fair support and a happy-go-lucky presentation of frontier life, which included a supposed murder, a false accusation and a general clearing-up of mystery by the pleasant and wily and useful and entertaining Ah Sin. It was not a great play. It was neither very coherent nor convincing, but it had a lot of good fun in it, with character parts which, if not faithful to life, were faithful enough to the public conception of it to be amusing and exciting. At the end of each act not only Parsloe, but also the principal members of the company, were called before the curtain for special acknowledgments. When it was over there was a general call for Ah Sin, who came before the curtain and read a telegram.

Charles T. Parsloe, – I am on the sick-list, and therefore cannot come to Washington; but I have prepared two speeches – one to deliver in event of failure of the play,

and the other if successful. Please tell me which I shall send. Maybe better to put it to vote.
Mark Twain.

The house cheered the letter, and when it was put to vote decided unanimously that the play had been a success – a verdict more kindly than true.

(Albert Bigelow Paine, *Mark Twain: A Biography*)

Wee Willie Winkie, a 1937 US film featuring the child star Shirley Temple, is pretty much forgotten now, although it played a significant, if unintended, part in the career of a great writer as well as helping in the demise of a magazine. *Wee Willie Winkie* – a tale of the British Raj loosely adapted from a story by Rudyard Kipling – had a distinguished director in John Ford, who would go on to make classic pictures like *Stagecoach* and *My Darling Clementine*. Producers Twentieth Century Fox also had, in nine-year-old Shirley Temple, their most highly paid star and their most profitable asset. When the film opened in Britain, it was reviewed by Graham Greene in Night and Day, a new weekly magazine of which Greene was the literary editor. *Night and Day* was modelled on the US magazine, *The New Yorker*, with the same mixture of witty comment and cartoons, all delivered with a metropolitan gloss.

Greene went too far in presuming on the sophistication of his readership – or a small section of it. He didn't like the film much although he conceded that, as directed by Ford, it was "horrifyingly competent". But the remarks which caused a storm were to do with Shirley Temple and her appeal to "her admirers – middle-aged men and clergymen". Greene was explicit when he talked about her "dubious coquetry" and suggested that her allure wasn't much to do with childhood. The review still makes for slightly uncomfortable reading, as Greene probably intended since he was exposing what he saw as a hypocritical, unspoken link between film-makers and audience.

The response was immediate. Newsagents and distributors W. H. Smith's refused to handle that issue of Night and Day. The magazine took legal advice, which was reassuring at first: Greene's review wasn't defamatory, counsel claimed, and could be published without risk. Counsel were wrong. Twentieth Century Fox sued magazine and author for libel and won, the Lord Chief Justice describing the article as "a gross outrage" and leaving the way open for a prosecution for criminal libel. The case was heard at the High Court in March 1938. The cost to the publishers of Night and Day was £3,500. The more serious charge of criminal libel was averted but the magazine was already in severe financial difficulties quite apart from the costs of the action and, by the time the case was settled, it had already ceased publication.

Shirley Temple Black, as she became after marriage, retired from films in 1949 and, unlike many child stars, went on to have a respected and successful career. She became a diplomat, first as a US delegate to the United Nations and then as ambassador to Ghana and, in 1989, to the Czech Republic. *Wee Willie Winkie* is apparently her favourite film role. Graham Greene's involvement with the cinema continued, but as a screen-writer rather than a reviewer. Most of Greene's stories have been filmed but the best – and the most critically acclaimed – is one which was conceived as a film rather than a novel, *The Third Man* (1949), directed by Carol Reed. Greene himself appeared at least once in a film, when he was living in the south of France in the later part of his life. In Francois Truffaut's *Day for Night* (1973), he appears on the credits as "Henry Graham" and has a cameo role as an insurance representative. His patent awkwardness in the part suggests that it's as well he never took up acting in a serious way.

The screenplay for Raymond Chandler's private-eye novel *The Big Sleep* was written by the distinguished US novelist William Faulkner and two other screenwriters. A 1946 classic of the *noir* genre – it was the film that first brought together Humphrey Bogart and Lauren Bacall on celluloid and in real life – it is famously complicated, if not completely incomprehensible, in plot terms. The director Howard Hawks adopted a fairly free-wheeling approach on set which indicated that the "story" was just about the least important part of the process. While *The Big Sleep* was being shot, there was some doubt about who'd killed one of the characters. Hawks or Bogart suggested they ask

William Faulkner, who had written the screenplay. But Faulkner couldn't help and told them to talk to Raymond Chandler, who had after all written the original novel. But Chandler never had much concern with pure plot either and his response was a spoof on those old-style "golden age" detective stories which he hated: "The butler did it." To this Howard Hawks is supposed to have replied, "Like hell he did; he was down at the beach house at the time."

Raymond Chandler (see above) got more directly involved with films shortly before the release of *The Big Sleep*. The first film Chandler worked on was the classic film noir *Double Indemnity* (1944). Director Billy Wilder didn't find it easy working with Chandler – the writer was "kind of acid, sour" – but he admired Chandler's talent, in particular his ability to capture the atmosphere of California in his prose. When they first met to discuss *Double Indemnity*, Chandler was unhappy at the idea of collaborating on the script with Wilder. He was used to working by himself. "Then he repeated that he wanted a thousand dollars," said Wilder in an interview with Ivan Moffat. "We said, 'None of that thousand dollar shit. You are going to get 750.' And he said, '750, I will not work for 750.' We said, 'No, relax, 750 a week. Just relax, you are going to get 750 a week.' And he said, 'Oh, really? Then it only goes two or three weeks?' And we said, 'No, fourteen weeks. You don't know how scripts are written.' "

Chandler had a sometimes difficult relationship with producers and directors (see also **Addiction**) and seemed resistant to the whole Hollywood process. As he wrote to a friend, "If my books had been any worse, I should not have been invited to Hollywood, and if they had been any better, I should not have come." He worked with Alfred Hitchcock on *Strangers on a Train* (1951), adapted from a story by Patricia Highsmith. Hitchcock said in an interview with French director Francois Truffaut: "Our association didn't work out at all. We'd sit together and I would say, 'Why not do it this way?', and he'd answer, "Well, if you can puzzle it out, what do you need me for?' "

Ernest Hemingway didn't like the 1957 film version of his classic novel *A Farewell to Arms*, which starred Jennifer Jones and Rock Hudson. In *Papa Hemingway*, his memoir of the author, A. E. Hotchner tells the story of how Hemingway spent three days explaining why he was going to give the film a miss. Eventually he and Hotchner did go to see it. "Afterwards we walked along Forty-ninth Street and up Fifth Avenue in silence. Finally Ernest said, 'You know, Hotch, you write a book like that that you're fond of over the years, then you see that happen to it, it's like pissing in your father's beer.' "

Wars & Fights

Sir Philip Sidney, poet and courtier, was a model of chivalry. He died after being wounded at the battle of Zutphen in the Netherlands in 1586. His reputation was amply justified, according to this story told by friend and fellow-poet Fulke Greville.

Howsoever, by this stand, an unfortunate hand out of those forespoken trenches, brake the bone of Sir Philip's thighs with a musket-shot. The horse he rode upon was rather furiously choleric than bravely proud, and so forced him to forsake the field, but not on his back, as the noblest and fittest bier to carry a martial commander to his grave. In which sad progress, passing along by the rest of the army, where his uncle the general was, and being thirsty with excess of bleeding, he called for drink, which was presently brought him: but as he was putting the bottle to his mouth, he saw a poor soldier carried along, who had eaten his last at the same feast, ghastly casting up his eyes at the bottle. Which Sir Philip perceiving, took the bottle from his head, before he drank, and delivered it to the poor man, with these words *Thy necessity is yet greater mine.* And when he had pledged this poor soldier, he was presently carried to Arnheim.

Elizabethan playwright Ben Jonson was used to a fight. Before beginning his writing career he served in the army in the Netherlands (see the story about Sir Philip Sidney above) and talked of how he had once killed an enemy soldier "in the face of both the camps". But the nearest Jonson came to losing his life was not on the battlefield but back in London. In 1598 he fought a duel against the actor Gabriel Spencer at Hoxton Fields in north London. The reasons for the duel are obscure, although Spencer seems to have had a reputation for a hot temper – a couple of years earlier he had killed the son of a goldsmith in a violent quarrel. Despite the difference in their ages (Jonson was several years older than Spencer) and the fact that the actor's rapier was ten inches longer than the playwright's weapon, Jonson managed to see off his opponent, giving him a fatal thrust in the side. He was arrested and charged with murder, for which the penalty was death.

But there was a loophole in the law for first-time offenders. A man who was in danger of execution could plead "benefit of clergy" – by showing that he was able to read, the defendant put himself out of reach of the noose and put himself within a bishop's jurisdiction. This peculiar law went back to the Middle Ages when, by and large, literacy was confined to churchmen. Taking for its authority a Biblical verse ("Touch not mine anointed, and do my prophets no harm"), the church maintained that priests should be exempt from civil punishment. To read meant that you were a priest; to be a priest meant that the law couldn't hang you. The moment the guilty verdict came in, Jonson pleaded benefit of clergy and was handed a book of psalms from which to choose the so-called "neck verse". He satisfied the court that he could indeed read, and escaped the gallows at Tyburn.

Ben Jonson didn't escape altogether, however. Benefit of clergy worked for first-time offenders only. To ensure that he would be identifiable again – if there was a second time – a letter was branded on the base of his left thumb with a hot iron. The stories vary about the mark which Jonson carried around for the rest of his life: it was either an M (for murderer) or a T (for Tyburn). In the circumstances, Jonson must have considered himself lucky, something perhaps confirmed by the fact that he converted to Catholicism when he was awaiting trial in Newgate Prison. It would be over two hundred years before the "benefit of clergy" law was finally abolished, in 1827.

~

The 17th-century poet and rake John Wilmot, Earl of Rochester, went while still in his teens to fight against the Dutch fleet which was lying in the Norwegian port of Bergen.

When he went to sea in the year 1665, there happened to be in the same ship with him Mr Mountague and another gentleman of quality; these two, the former especially, seemed persuaded that they should never return into England. Mr Mountague said he was sure of it: the other was not so positive. The Earl of Rochester and the last of these entered into a formal engagement, not without ceremonies of religion, that if either of them died, he should appear and give the other notice of the future state, if there was any. But Mr Mountague would not enter into the bond.

When the day came that they thought to have taken the Dutch fleet in the port of Bergen, Mr Mountague, though he had such a strong presage in his mind of his approaching death, yet he generously stayed all the while in the place of greatest danger: The other gentleman signalized his courage in a most undaunted manner till near the end of the action, when he fell on a sudden into such a trembling that he could scarce stand: and Mr Mountague going to him to hold him up, as they were in each other's arms, a cannon ball killed him outright and carried away Mr Mountague's belly, so that he died within an hour after. The Earl of Rochester told me that these presages they had in their minds made some impressions on him, that there were separated beings: and that the soul, either by a natural sagacity or some secret notice communicated to it, had a sort of divination: But that gentleman's never appearing was a great snare to him during the rest of his life. Though when he told me this, he could not but acknowledge it was an unreasonable thing, for him to think that beings in another state were not under such laws and limits that they could not command their own motions but as the Supreme Power should order them: and that one who had so corrupted the natural principles of Truth, as he had, had no reason to expect that such an extraordinary thing should be done for his conviction.

(Gilbert Burnet, *Some Passages of the Life and Death of the Right Honourable John Earl of Rochester*)

～

On another occasion Rochester narrowly avoided being involved in a duel. The story is told by his would-be opponent, the Duke of Buckingham, who subtly paints Rochester in a bad light. As in the story about Ben Jonson (see above), duelling was against the law.

During this time and heat of temper I had the good fortune not to be engaged in more than one quarrel; but that had somewhat in it singular enough to be related. I was informed that the Earl of Rochester had said something of me which, according to his custom was very malicious; I therefore sent Colonel Aston, a very mettled friend of mine, to call him to account for it. He denied the words and indeed I was soon convinced that he had never said them; but the mere report, though I found it to be false, obliged me (as I then foolishly thought) to go on with the quarrel; and the next day was appointed for us to fight on horseback, a way in England a little unusual, but it was his part to choose. Accordingly, I and my second lay the night before at Knightsbridge privately, to avoid the being secured at London upon any suspicion; which yet we found ourselves more in danger of there, because we had all the appearance of high-waymen that had a mind to lie skulking in an odd inn for one night; but this I suppose the people of that house were used to, and so took no notice of us, but liked us the better. In the morning we met the Lord Rochester at the place appointed, who, instead of James Porter, whom he had assured Aston he would make his second, brought an errant lifeguardman whom nobody knew. To this Mr Aston took exception, upon the account of his being no suitable adversary; especially consider-ing how extremely well he was mounted, whereas we had only a couple of pads [inferior horses]: Upon which we all agreed to fight on foot. But as my Lord Rochester and I were riding into the next field in order to it, he told me that he had at first chosen to fight on horseback because he was so weak with a certain distemper, that he found himself unfit to fight at all any way, much less afoot. I was extremely surprised, because at that time no man had a better reputation for courage; and (my anger against him being quite over, because I was satisfied that he never spoke those words I resented) I took the liberty of representing what a ridiculous story it would make if we returned without fighting; and therefore advised him for both our sakes, especially for his own, to consider better of it; since I must be obliged in my own defence to lay the fault on him by telling the truth of the matter. His answer was, that he sub-mitted to it and hoped that I would not desire the advantage of having to do with any man in so weak a condition. I replied that by such an argument he had sufficiently tied my hands, upon condition I might call our seconds to be witnesses of the whole business; which he consented to, and so we parted. When we returned to London, we found it full of this quarrel, upon our being absent so long; and therefore Mr Aston thought himself obliged to write down every word and circumstance of the whole matter, in order to spread everywhere the true reason of our returning without having fought; which, being never in the least either contradicted or resented by the Lord Rochester, entirely ruined his reputation as to courage (of which I was really sorry to be the occasion) though nobody had still a greater as to wit; which supported him pretty well in the world notwithstanding some more accidents of the same kind, that never fail to succeed one another when once people know a man's weakness.

(*Memoirs of His Grace John Duke of Buckingham, written by himself*)

Richard Sheridan, author of The School for Scandal, *had a turbulent time before he was able to marry Eliza Linley, a beautiful singer from Bath. Not only did Sheridan have to deal with her father's opposition, but he had other rivals to fight off – in one case literally (and twice over).*

When Mr Sheridan became the avowed suitor of Miss Linley, the celebrated vocal performer, her father, the late composer, did not at first encourage his suit, and he had many rivals to overcome in his attempts to gain the lady's affections. His perseverance, however, increased with the difficulties that presented themselves; and his courage and resolution in vindicating Miss Linley's reputation from a calumnious report, which had been basely thrown out against her, obtained for him the fair prize for which he twice exposed his life.

Mr Matthews, a gentleman, then well known in the fashionable circles at Bath, had caused a paragraph to be inserted in a public paper at that place, which tended to prejudice the character of this young lady, and Mr Sheridan immediately applied for redress to the publisher, who gave up the writer's name.

Mr Matthews had, in the meantime, set out for London, and was closely followed by Mr Sheridan. They met, and fought a duel with swords, at a tavern in Henrietta Street, Covent Garden. Mr Sheridan's second on the occasion was his brother, Charles Francis, afterwards Secretary at War in Ireland.

Great courage and skill were displayed on both sides; but Mr Sheridan having succeeded in disarming his adversary, compelled him to sign a formal retractation of the paragraph which had been published.

Sheridan instantly returned to Bath; and thinking, very properly, that as the insult had been publicly given, the apology should have equal notoriety, caused it to be inserted in the same paper. Mr Matthews soon heard of the circumstance; and irritated at his defeat, as well as at the use which his antagonist had made of his apology, determined to call upon Mr Sheridan for satisfaction. A message was accordingly sent, and a meeting agreed upon.

Mr Sheridan would have been fully justified, according to the most delicate punctilios of honour, in declining the call; but he silenced all the objections that were started by his friends, and the parties met on Kingsdown.

The victory was desperately contested, and after a discharge of pistols, they fought with swords. They were both wounded and, closing with each other, fell on the ground, where they continued to fight until they were separated. They received several cuts and contusions in this arduous struggle for life and honour, and a part of Matthews' sword was actually broken off in Sheridan's ear.

Miss Linley did not suffer the prowess of her champion to remain long unrewarded, and accompanied him on a matrimonial trip to the Continent. The ceremony was again performed on their return to England, with the consent of the lady's parents.

(anonymous account in *The History of Duelling*)

The aftermath of an unhappy love affair caused the poet Samuel Taylor Coleridge to enlist in the army in his early 20s. He joined the 15th Light Dragoons under the assumed name of Comerbache. He was not a great success as a soldier.

He fell off his horse on several occasions, but, perhaps, not more than raw recruits are apt to do when first put under the riding master. But Coleridge was naturally ill-framed for a good horseman. He is also represented . . . as having found peculiar difficulty or annoyance in grooming his horse. But the most romantic incident in that scene of his life was in the circumstances of his discharge. It is said (but I vouch for no part of the story) that Coleridge, as a private, mounted guard at the door of a room in which his officers happened to give a ball. Two of them had a dispute upon some Greek word or passage when close to Coleridge's station. He interposed his authentic decision of the case. The offficers stared as though one of their own horses had sung "Rule Britannia"; questioned him; heard his story; pitied his misfortune; and, finally, subscribed to purchase his discharge.

(Thomas de Quincey, *Recollections of the Lake Poets*)

*The radical journalist and writer William Cobbett joined the army in 1784, when he was 21. He served for a period in Canada after the end of the American War of Independence before leaving in order to expose the corruption of the officer class (see **Crime, Punishment & Mystery**). Cobbett doesn't appear to have done any fighting when he was actually in the army but this fearless, pugnacious man was certainly ready to fight for his rights in England when, many years later, he was standing for Parliament. The behaviour of his opponents – the "savages" – makes present day politics look tame by comparison.*

On Wednesday morning, the election began; and the poll closed in the afternoon, leaving me at the head of it! On Thursday, the savages came well fed and well supplied, all the day long, with gin and brandy, brought out to them in glass bottles, and handed about from one to another. I, that day, saw about twenty of my voters actually torn away from the polling-place, and ripped up behind, and stripped of their coats. During the afternoon, several fresh bands of savages arrived from the country; so that, by the hours of closing the poll, an immense multitude of these wretches roaring like wolves, and foaming with rage and drink, were collected round the Booth.

As I went out of the Booth, I had to pass through bands of savages; and I was scarcely among them, when they began an endeavour to press me down. I got many blows in the sides, and, if I had been either a short or a weak man, I would have been pressed under foot, and inevitably killed. However, the crowd took a sway toward a row of houses, standing on a pavement above the level of the area of the open street. With a good deal of difficulty I reached the pavement keeping my feet. I had to fight with my right hand. I had to strike back-handed. One of the sharp corners of my snuff-box, which stuck out beyond the bottom of my little finger, did good service. It cut noses and eyes at a famous rate, and assisted mainly in securing my safe arrival, on the raised pavement. Just at this time, one of the savages exclaimed: "Damn him, I'll rip him up." He was running his hand into his breeches pocket, apparently to take out his knife, but I drew up my right leg, armed with a new and sharp gallashe over my boot, and dealt the ripping savage so delightful a blow, just between his two eyes, that he fell back upon his followers. For this I should certainly have been killed in a few moments, had not Mr Frank Serjeant made shift to get along, by the side of the houses, to the spot where I was. Getting to me, he turned round, saying, *follow me, Sir*, and, beating back three or four so as to make them press upon others behind them, the whole body turned about, while he with thumps on some, with kicks bestowed on others, set the body on a sway toward the house, at which we arrived safely . . .

The savages finally conceived the idea of driving me out of the city [of Coventry]. They made a regular attack upon Mr Serjeant's house. They first dashed in the upper-room windows; next they pulled down the shutters of the ground-floor room. Then they broke into the house passage by forcing the door; and while the main body were entering in front, others were (as we could see from the window of our room) scaling a wall to get into the house in the rear. I, who was very ill with a cold, was sitting in my bedroom with my daughter Nancy. Some gentlemen came running up for our poker and tongs. One or two took station at the top of the stairs; while I fixed the bedstead in a way to let the door open no wider than to admit one man only at a time, and stood with a sword. I had pulled off my coat, and was prepared to give with a clear conscience, as hearty a thrust as was ever given by man.

However, their cowardice soon put an end to the siege. They entered the passage, stabbed one man twice in his arm and did some other mischief: retreated hastily into the street. The thing went off without bodily hurt to any but our friends! And the natural consequence was, that the poor men who wished to vote for me dared no longer even talk of it! We got some firearms, and were quite secure in the house; but as to the election, there remained nothing belonging to it worthy of the name. I stood at the bottom of the poll.

(William Cobbett, *An Autobiography*)

Cobbett was eventually elected Member of Parliament for Oldham in Lancashire.

The early 19th-century poet George Crabbe had a cool head, as shown in this story by his son about his father's attitude towards a possible French landing in East Anglia.

We happened to be on a visit at Aldborough [in Suffolk], when the dread of a French invasion was at its height. The old artillery of the fort had been replaced by cannon of a large calibre; and one, the most weighty I remember to have seen, was constantly primed, as an alarm gun. About one o'clock one dark morning, I heard a distant gun at sea; in about ten minutes another, and at an equal interval a third; and then at last, the tremendous roar of the great gun on the fort, which shook every house in the town. After inquiring into the state of affairs, I went to my father's room, and, knocking at the door, with difficulty waked the inmates, and said, "Do not be alarmed, but the French are landing." I then mentioned that the alarm gun had been fired, that horsemen had been despatched for the troops at Ipswich, and that the drum on the quay was then beating to arms. He replied, "Well, my old fellow, you and I can do no good, or we would be among them; we must wait the event." I returned to his door in about three quarters of an hour, to tell him that the agitation was subsiding, and found him fast asleep. Whether the affair was a mere blunder, or there had been a concerted manoeuvre to try the fencibles [volunteer defence], we never could learn with certainty; but I remember that my father's coolness on the occasion, when we mentioned it next day, caused some suspicious shakings of the head among the ultra-loyalists of Aldborough.

(from *The life of George Crabbe by his son*)

Samuel Clemens (Mark Twain) tells the story of how, in his early writing days, he got involved in a duel. At the time he was standing in as a newspaper editor in Virginia City, Nevada, and wrote an editorial against a Mr Laird, the proprietor of another Virginia City paper. In Nevada at that time, Twain explains, duelling had become a fashion.

I woke up Mr Laird with some courtesies of the kind that were fashionable among newspaper editors in that region, and he came back at me the next day in the most vitriolic way. He was hurt by something I had said about him – some little thing – I don't remember what it was now – probably called him a horse-thief, or one of those little phrases customarily used to describe another editor. They were no doubt just, and accurate, but Laird was a very sensitive creature and he didn't like it. So we expected a challenge from Mr Laird, because according to the rules – according to the etiquette of duelling as reconstructed and reorganized and improved by the duellists of that region – whenever you said a thing about another person that he didn't like, it wasn't sufficient for him to talk back in the same offensive spirit: etiquette required him to send a challenge; so we waited for a challenge – waited all day. It didn't come. And as the day wore along, hour after hour, and no challenge came, the boys grew depressed. They lost heart. But I was cheerful; I felt better and better all the time. They couldn't understand it, but I could understand it. It was my *make* that enabled me to be cheerful when other people were despondent. So then it became necessary for us to waive etiquette and challenge Mr Laird. When we reached that decision, they began to cheer up, but I began to lose some of my animation. However, in enterprises of this kind you are in the hands of your friends; there is nothing for you to do but to abide by what they consider to be the best course. Daggett wrote a challenge for me, for Daggett had the language – the right language – the convincing language – and I lacked it. Daggett poured out a stream of unsavory epithets upon Mr Laird, charged with a vigour and venom of a strength calculated to persuade him; and Steve Gillis, my second, carried the challenge and came back to wait for the return. It didn't come. The boys were exasperated, but I kept my temper. Steve carried another challenge, hotter than the other, and we waited again. Nothing came of it. I began to feel quite comfortable. I began to take an interest in the challenges myself. I had not felt any before; but it seemed to me that I was accumulating a great and valuable reputation at no expense, and my delight in this grew and grew, as challenge after challenge was declined, until by midnight I was beginning to think that there was nothing in the world so much to be desired as a chance to fight a duel. So I hurried Daggett up; made him keep on sending challenge after challenge. Oh, well, I overdid it; Laird accepted. I might have known that that would happen – Laird was a man you couldn't depend on.

The boys were jubilant beyond expression. They helped me make my will, which was another discomfort – and I already had enough. Then they took me home. I didn't sleep any – didn't want to sleep. I had plenty of things to think about, and less than four hours to do it in – because five o'clock was the hour appointed for the tragedy, and I should have to use up one hour – beginning at four – in practising with the revolver and finding out which end of it to level at the adversary. At four we went down into a little gorge, about a mile from town, and borrowed a barn door for a mark – borrowed it of a man who was over in California on a visit – and we set the barn door up and stood a fence-rail up against the middle of it, to represent Mr Laird. But the rail was no proper representative of him, for he was longer than a rail and thinner. Nothing would ever fetch him but a line shot, and then as like as not he would split the bullet – the worst material for duelling purposes that could be imagined. I began on the rail. I couldn't hit the rail; then I tried the barn door; but I couldn't hit the barn door. There was nobody in danger except stragglers around on the flanks of that mark. I was thoroughly discouraged, and I didn't cheer up any when we presently heard pistol-shots over in the next little ravine. I knew what that was – that was Laird's gang out practising him. They would hear my shots, and of course they would come up over the ridge to see what kind of a record I was making – see what their chances were against me. Well, I hadn't any record; and I knew that if Laird came over that ridge and saw my barn door without a scratch on it, he would be as anxious to fight as I was – or as I had been at midnight, before that disastrous acceptance came.

Now just at this moment, a little bird, no bigger than a sparrow, flew along by and lit on a sage-bush about thirty yards away. Steve whipped out his revolver and shot its head off. Oh, he was a marksman – much better than I was. We ran down there to pick up the bird, and just then, sure enough, Mr Laird and his people came over the ridge, and they joined us. And when Laird's second saw that bird, with its head shot off, he lost color, he faded, and you could see that he was interested.

He said: "Who did that?"

Before I could answer, Steve spoke up and said quite calmly, and in a matter-of-fact way, "Clemens did it."

The second said, "Why, that is wonderful. How far off was that bird?"

Steve said, "Oh, not far – about thirty yards."

The second said, "Well, that is astonishing shooting. How often can he do that?"

Steve said languidly, "Oh, about four times out of five."

I knew the little rascal was lying, but I didn't say anything. The second said, "Why, that is *amazing* shooting; I supposed he couldn't hit a church."

He was supposing very sagaciously, but I didn't say anything. Well, they said good morning. The second took Mr Laird home, a little tottery on his legs, and Laird sent back a note in his own hand declining to fight a duel with me on any terms whatever.

Well, my life was saved – saved by that accident. I don't know what the bird thought about that interposition of Providence, but I felt very, very comfortable over it – satisfied and content. Now, we found out, later, that Laird had *hit* his mark four times out of six, right along. If the duel had come off, he would have so filled my skin with bullet-holes that it wouldn't have held my principles . . .

I have never had anything to do with duels since. I thoroughly disapprove of duels. I consider them unwise, and I know they are dangerous. Also, sinful. If a man should challenge me now, I would go to that man and take him kindly and forgivingly by the hand and lead him to a quiet retired spot, and *kill* him.

(Mark Twain, *Chapters from my Autobiography*)

The encounter between W. E. Johns, the creator of flying ace Biggles, and T. E. Lawrence (of Arabia), rates as one of the most bizarre meetings on the fringes of literary history. Johns, who had been an airforce pilot during World War One, subsequently joined the RAF Inspectorate of Recruiting based in London's Covent Garden. One day in August 1922, a thin palefaced man entered the recruiting office. "There was something so off-hand about his manner, almost amounting to insolence," Johns wrote afterwards, "that I took an instinctive dislike to him. I had got to know the type. He was 'different' from the other recruits and he was letting me know."

The would-be recruit announced himself as John Hume Ross but Johns was suspicious – individuals sometimes tried to join the RAF to escape from the law – and told him to produce a birth certificate and references. Ross gave his birth details, which Johns soon discovered were false, and references, also fake. Then "Ross" started to pull strings by returning to the Recruitment Office with an emissary from the Air Ministry carrying an order demanding that he be enlisted. During the medical examination which followed, Lawrence/Ross was asked about the scars on his back. He claimed they were the result of an accident (a barbed-wire tear) but they were actually the marks of Lawrence's masochistic taste for flagellation.

W. E. Johns was deeply unhappy about this latest recruit but, when he protested to his senior officer, was told that they had no choice but to accept "Ross", for the man they were dealing with was the famous Lawrence of Arabia. Lawrence was immensely well-connected, and his recruitment scheme was known to the Chief of the Air Staff. It was actually the latter's deputy, Air Vice-Marshal Sir Oliver Swann, who had come up with the "Ross" identity and the forged references. With high-placed friends like these, Lawrence couldn't fail in his eccentric intention to enlist in the RAF while the honest objections of a mere recruitment officer carried no weight at all.

George Orwell and the novelist Anthony Powell both had a liking for uniform. In the 1920s Orwell had served in the Indian Imperial Police in Burma (the setting for his first novel, *Burmese Days*) while Powell's wartime service provides to the background to three novels in his great narrative sequence *A Dance to the Music of Time*. Meeting Orwell during the Second World War in the Café Royal in London, the uniformed Powell was asked: "Do your trousers strap under the foot?" When Powell confirmed that they did, Orwell replied, "Those straps under the foot give you a feeling like nothing else in life."

The best and most famous anti-war book of all time is *Catch-22* by Joseph Heller. The title phrase has entered the language to describe a no-win situation. The novel, a surreal satire, centres on an American airfield on a small Mediterranean island during World War Two, like the one in Corsica where Heller himself served as a bombardier in 1944. Yossarian, the central character, is determined to survive or escape intact from the war zone. But his efforts are constantly frustrated by the crazy logic applied by higher command, particularly in upping the number of bombing missions required before any airman is allowed to finish his tour of duty and go home. One way out would be to plead insanity. But there's a catch. In Joseph Heller's own words:

> There was only one catch and that was Catch-22, which specified that a concern for one's own safety in the face of dangers that were real and immediate was the process of a rational mind. Orr [a pilot] was crazy and could be grounded. All he had to do was ask; and as soon as he did, he would no longer be crazy and would have to fly more missions. Orr would be crazy to fly more missions and sane if he didn't, but if he was sane he had to fly them. If he flew them he was crazy and didn't have to; but if he didn't want to he was sane and had to. Yossarian was moved very deeply by the absolute simplicity of this clause of Catch-22 and let out a respectful whistle.

"That's some catch, that Catch-22," he observed.

Heller was a slow, methodical writer. He began *Catch-22*, his first novel, when he was working as an advertising copywriter in New York in 1953 but it was not published until eight years later in 1961. The book's reception was mixed but it soon picked up increasingly enthusiastic – and eventually ecstatic – reviews, and went on to sell more than two million copies in paperback in 1963 alone. The Vietnam war, and the protests against it in the late 1960s, gave *Catch-22* an even greater popularity as its anti-war message chimed with the spirit of the time.

The novel, however, almost emerged with a different number in the title: *Catch-18*. This was in fact the title which Heller had used for a chapter from the work in progress and which had first seen the light of day in the quarterly magazine *New World Writing* back in 1955. But by the time Heller's book was finished and ready for publication in 1961 another novel had already appeared in that year using the same number. *Mila* 18, by Leon Uris, centres on the Jewish uprising in the Warsaw Ghetto in 1942 (there was a bunker in no. 18 Mila Street where the Jewish resistance held out against the Nazis). Accordingly, the title of Heller's book was changed to avoid conflict or confusion with Uris'. It's hard not to conclude that the enforced change of number/title was to the ultimate benefit of *Catch-22*, perhaps contributing substantially to its world-wide success. *Catch-22* has more of a ring to it than *Catch-18* and the novel's trapped logic is better reflected in the repeated digits of 22.

Heller's writing life was overshadowed by *Catch-22*, with critics and readers praising his other half dozen novels but also finding fault with them because they didn't quite live up to his first – although his second novel *Something Happened* (1974) deserves, in its sombre way, to be considered as great a book. Heller always had an answer for those who told him that he'd never written a novel as fine as *Catch-22*. It was straightforward enough: "Who has?"

Writing

The 18th-century poet and dramatist Richard Savage led a very up-and-down existence (see also **Crime, Punishment & Mystery***). When he was writing his play* The Tragedy of Thomas Overbury *he was without anywhere to live and lacked even the basic materials of a writer's existence.*

During a considerable part of the time in which he was engaged upon this performance [writing the play] he was without lodging, and often without meat; nor had he any other conveniences for study than the fields or the streets allowed him; there he used to walk and form his speeches, and afterwards step into a shop, beg for a few moments the use of the pen and ink, and write down what he had composed upon paper which he had picked up by accident.

(Samuel Johnson, Life of Savage)

The dramatist Richard Brinsley Sheridan, best remembered for School for Scandal *and* The Rivals, *sometimes left writing until the last moment. On one occasion he was translating a drama by a German dramatist minutes before it was actually being presented on stage in his English version. The following story is by Michael Kelly, a singer and composer who was both friend and artistic collaborator to Sheridan.*

On the 24th of May, in the same year [1799], Mr Sheridan's celebrated play of "Pizarro", from Kotzebue, was produced; it was admirably acted, and I had the proud distinction of having my name joined with that of Mr Sheridan, in its production, having been selected by him to compose the whole of the music.

Expectation was on tip-toe: and strange as it may appear, "Pizarro" was advertised, and every box in the house taken, before the fourth act of the play was begun; nor had I one single word of the poetry for which I was to compose the music. Day after day was I attending on Mr Sheridan, representing that time was flying, and that nothing was done for me. His answer uniformly was, "Depend upon it, my dear Mic, you shall have plenty of matter to go on with tomorrow"; but day after day, that morrow came not, which, as my name was advertised as the composer of the the music, drove me half crazy . . .

But if this were a puzzling situation for a composer, what will my readers think of that, in which the actors were left, when I state the fact, that, at the time the house was over-flowing on the first night's performance, all that was written of the play was actually rehearsing, and that incredible as it may appear, until the end of the fourth act, neither Mrs Siddons, nor Charles Kemble, nor Barrymore, had all their speeches for the fifth? Mr Sheridan was upstairs in the prompter's room, where he was writing the last part of the play, while the earlier parts were acting; and every ten minutes he brought down as much of the dialogue as he had done, piece-meal, into the green room, abusing himself and his negligence, and making a thousand winning and soothing apologies, for having kept the performers so long in such painful suspense.

One remarkable trait in Sheridan's character was, his penetrating knowledge of the human mind; for no man was more careful in his carelessness; he was quite aware of his power over his performers, and of the veneration in which they held his great talents; had he not been so, he would not have ventured to keep them (Mrs Siddons particularly) in the dreadful anxiety which they were suffering through the whole of the evening. Mrs Siddons told me that she was in an agony of fright; but Sheridan perfectly knew, that Mrs Siddons, C. Kemble, and Barrymore, were quicker in study than any other performers concerned; and that he could trust them to be perfect in what they had to say, even at half an hour's notice. And the event proved that he was right: the play was received with the greatest approbation, and though brought out so late in the season, was played thirty-one nights; and for years afterwards proved a mine of wealth to the Drury Lane Treasury, and, indeed, to all the theatres in the United Kingdom.

Such, however, were the delays during the first night's performance, that the play did not end until within five minutes of midnight! The farce of "My Grandmother" was to follow, but the exhaustion of the audience was so complete, that, when the afterpiece commenced, only 17 persons remained in the whole dress circle, and 22 in the pit.

This was obviously the kind of working pattern which Sheridan preferred, to judge by another story from the same author.

His quickness in writing may be judged of by the circumstances I have already mentioned, relative to the state in which his "Pizarro" was produced and he made a similar exertion at the time he brought out "The Critic". Two days previous to the performance, the last scene was not written; Dr Ford and Mr Linley, the joint proprietors, began to get nervous and fidgetty, and the actors were absolutely *au désespoir*, especially King, who was not only stage-manager, but had to play Puff; to him was assigned the duty of hunting down and worrying Sheridan about the last scene; day after day passed, until, as I have just said, the last day but two arrived, and it made not its appearance.

At last, Mr Linley, who being his father-in-law, was pretty well aware of his habits, hit upon a stratagem. A night rehearsal of "The Critic" was ordered, and Sheridan, having dined with Linley, was prevailed upon to go; while they were on the stage, King whispered Sheridan that he had something particular to communicate, and begged he would step into the second green-room.

Accordingly, Sheridan went, and there found a table, with pens, ink, and paper, a good fire, an armed chair at the table, and two bottles of claret, with a dish of anchovy sandwiches. The moment he got into the room, King stepped out, and locked the door; immediately after which, Linley and Ford came up and told the author that, until he had written the scene, he would be kept where he was.

Sheridan took this decided measure in good part; he ate the anchovies, finished the claret, wrote the scene, and laughed heartily at the ingenuity of the contrivance.

(Michael Kelly, *Reminiscences*)

Jane Austen's nephew, J. E. Austen-Leigh, remembers the modest and secretive methods of his aunt at Chawton, the house in Hampshire where she spent her last years.

. . . as soon as she was fixed in her second home, she resumed the habits of composition which had been formed in her first, and continued them to the end of her life. The first year of her residence at Chawton seems to have been devoted to revising and preparing for the press "Sense and Sensibility", and "Pride and Prejudice"; but between February 1811 and August 1816, she began and completed "Mansfield Park", "Emma", and "Persuasion", so that the last five years of her life produced the same number of novels with those which had been written in her early youth. How she was able to effect all this is surprising, for she had no separate study to retire to, and most of the work must have been done in the general sitting-room, subject to all kinds of casual interruptions. She was careful that her occupation should not be suspected by servants, or visitors, or any persons beyond her own family party. She wrote upon small sheets of paper which could easily be put away, or covered with a piece of blotting paper. There was, between the front door and the offices, a swing door which creaked when it was opened; but she objected to having this little inconvenience remedied, because it gave her notice when anyone was coming . . . In that well-occupied female party there must have been many precious hours of silence during which the pen was busy at the little mahogany writing-desk, while Fanny Price, or Emma Woodhouse, or Anne Elliot was growing into beauty and interest. I have no doubt that I and my sisters and cousins, in our visits to Chawton, frequently disturbed this mystic process, without having any idea of the mischief that we were doing; certainly we never should have guessed it by any signs of impatience or irritability in the writer.

(J. E. Austen-Leigh, *A Memoir of Jane Austen*)

❧

If the Irish-born writer Charles Maturin is remembered at all now it is for his Gothic novel Melmoth the Wanderer *— and, in turn, that is remembered in part because Oscar Wilde adopted the name Sebastian Melmoth after his release from prison. Charles Maturin had an odd method of telling people he was at work.*

The late Mr Maturin was profligate in expence and mean in his applications for pecuniary and literary aid: as soon as he obtained a sum of money either by his writings or by borrowing, he gave great balls and fetes, indulged in eating quantities of Pine Apples, and as soon as possible exhausted his resources. Once when he gave a breakfast, he entered to the company with a red wafer stuck in the middle of his forehead: he made signs that he was not to be spoken to and soon returned with the wafer taken off, and ready to converse: he said when he was in the act of composition he put on this signal to denote that he was not to be interrupted.

(anecdote told by Sir Walter Scott, *Letters and Recollections of Sir Walter Scott*)

❧

Anthony Trollope, the prolific Victorian novelist, was highly disciplined in his writing habits, which he describes in these excerpts from his autobiography, taken from different stages of his life. His "day job" was as a surveyor for the Post Office.

As I journeyed across France to Marseilles, and made thence a terribly rough voyage to Alexandria, I wrote my allotted number of pages every day. On this occasion more than once I left my paper on the cabin table, rushing away to be sick in the privacy of my state-room. It was February, and the weather was miserable; but still I did my work . . . I do not say that to all men has been given physical strength sufficient for such exertion as this, but I do believe that real exertion will enable most men to work at almost any season. I had previously to this arranged a system of task-work for myself, which I would strongly recommend to those who feel as I have felt, that labour, when not made absolutely obligatory by the circumstances of the hour, should never be allowed to become spasmodic. There was no day on which it was my positive duty to write for the publishers, as it was my duty to write reports for the Post Office. I was free to be idle if I pleased. But as I had made up my mind to undertake this second profession, I found it to be expedient to bind myself by certain self-imposed laws. When I have commenced a new book, I have always prepared a diary, divided into weeks, and carried it on for the period which I have allowed myself for the completion of the work. In this I have entered, day by day, the number of pages I have written, so that if at any time I have slipped into idleness for a day or two, the record of that idleness has been there, staring me in the face, and demanding of me increased labour, so that the deficiency might be supplied. According to the circumstances of the time – whether my other business might be then heavy or light, or whether the book which I was writing was or was not wanted with speed – I have allotted myself so many pages a week. The average number has been about forty. It has been placed as low as twenty, and has risen to one hundred and twelve. And as a page is an ambiguous term, my page has been made to contain two hundred and fifty words, and as words, if not watched, will have a tendency to straggle, I have had every word counted as I went. In the bargains I have made with publishers I have – not, of course, with their knowledge, but in my own mind – under-taken always to supply them with so many words, and I have never put a book out of hand short of the number by a single word. I may also say that the excess has been very small. I have prided myself on completing it within the proposed time – and I have always done so. There has ever been the record before me, and a week passed with an insufficient number of pages has been a blister to my eye, and a month so disgraced would have been a sorrow to my heart . . .

The work I did during the twelve years that I remained there [Waltham Cross near London], from 1859 to 1871, was certainly very great. I feel confident that in amount no other writer contributed so much during that time to English literature. Over and above my novels, I wrote political articles, critical, social, and sporting articles, for periodicals, without number. I did the work of a surveyor of the General Post Office, and so did it as to give the authorities of the department no slightest pretext for fault-finding. I hunted always at least twice a week. I was frequent in the whist-room at the Garrick. I lived much in society in London, and was made happy by the presence of many friends at Waltham Cross. In addition to this we always spent six weeks at least out of England. Few men, I think, ever lived a fuller life. And I attribute the power of doing this altogether to the virtue of early hours. It was my practice to be at my table every morning at 5.30 a.m.; and it was also my practice to allow myself no mercy. An old groom, whose business it was to call me, and to whom I paid £5 a year extra for the duty, allowed himself no mercy. During all those years at Waltham Cross he was never once late with the coffee which it was his duty to bring me. I do not know that I ought not to feel that I owe more to him than to any one else for the success I have had. By beginning at that hour I could complete my literary work before I dressed for breakfast.

All those I think who have lived as literary men – working daily as literary labourers – will agree with me that three hours a day will produce as much as a man ought to write. But then he should so have trained himself that he shall be able to work continuously during those three hours – so have tutored his mind that it shall not be necessary for him to sit nibbling his pen, and gazing at the wall before him till he shall have found the words with which he wants to express his ideas. It had at this time become my custom – and it still is my custom, though of late I have become a little lenient to myself – to write with my watch before me, and to require from myself two hundred and fifty words every quarter of an hour. I have found that the two hundred and fifty words have been forthcoming as regularly as my watch went. But my three hours were not devoted entirely to writing. I always began my task by reading the work of the day before, an operation which would take me half an hour, and which consisted chiefly in weighing with my ear the sound of the words and phrases. I would strongly recommend this practice to all tyros in writing. That their work should be read after it has been written is a matter of course – that it should be read twice at least before it goes to the printers, I take to be a matter of course. But by reading what he has last written, just before he recommences his task, the writer will catch the tone and spirit of what he is then saying, and will avoid the fault of seeming to be unlike himself. This division of time allowed me to produce over ten pages of an ordinary novel volume a day, and if kept up through ten months, would have given as its results three novels of three volumes each in the year – the precise amount which so greatly acerbated [irritated] the publisher in Paternoster Row, and which must at any rate be felt to be quite as much as the novel-readers of the world can want from the hands of one man.

(Anthony Trollope, *Autobiography*)

During the early 1850s Herman Melville was farming in Berkshire County, Massachusetts. He was also writing his greatest work, Moby Dick.

Do you want to know how I pass my time? – I rise at eight – thereabouts – & go to my barn – say good-morning to the horse, & give him his breakfast. (it goes to my heart to give him a cold one, but it can't be helped) Then, pay a visit to my cow – cut up a pumpkin or two for her, & stand by to see her eat it – for it's a pleasant sight to see a cow move her jaws – she does it so mildly and with such a sanctity. – My own breakfast over, I go to my work-room & light my fire – then spread my M.S.S. [*Moby Dick*] on the table – take one business squint at it, & fall to with a will. At 2 1/2 p.m. I hear a preconcerted knock at my door, which (by request) continues till I rise & go to the door, which serves to wean me effectively from my writing, however interested I may be. My friends the horse & cow now demand their dinner – & I go & give it to them. My own dinner over, I rig my sleigh & with my mother or sisters start off for the village – & if it be a Literary World day, great is the satisfaction thereof. – My evenings I spend in a sort of mesmeric state in my room – not being able to read – only now & then skimming over some large-printed book.

(Herman Melville, *letter to Evert Duyckinck, December, 1850*)

The life of the American short story writer O. Henry (whose real name was William Sydney Porter) resembled one of his own twist-in-the-tail stories. Facing a charge of embezzlement, he fled from his job in a bank to Honduras. When he was imprisoned after his return to America he began to write and eventually became so prolific that he was turning out a story a week. O. Henry's creativity was fuelled by a strenuous consumption of alcohol, sometimes reaching two quarts of whisky a day. Productive as he was, he was also careless over deadlines. That well-known and sentimentally effective Christmas story "The Gift of the Magi" was a victim – or perhaps a beneficiary – of O. Henry's delaying tactics. As the date for the Christmas copy drew nearer and with no manuscript yet in sight, the frantic editor despatched his illustrator to look for O. Henry. There was no copy to collect because O. Henry hadn't yet thought of anything he could write. He reputedly told the illustrator: "I'll tell you what to do . . . Just draw a picture of a poorly furnished room . . . On the bed, a man and a girl are sitting side by side. They are talking about Christmas. The man has a watch fob in his hand . . . The girl's principal feature is the long beautiful hair that is hanging down her back. That's all I can think of now, but the story is coming." Although the picture came first, O. Henry's creative unconscious had suggested two key elements in the story: the man's fob chain and the girl's long hair. When he did eventually write the story – whisky in hand, as well as editor in waiting – it took him three hours to complete it.

Novelist Henry James dictated his books for the last twenty or so years of his life. One of his most effective stories is *The Turn of the Screw*, an ambiguous narrative of the ghostly possession of two children. However, in James' account of how it was

written, it failed to achieve the desired reaction: "I wrote the
story with the intention of terrifying every reader, and in the
course of its composition I thought it would be a total failure. I
dictated every word of it to a Scot, who never from first to last
betrayed the slightest emotion, nor did he ever make any
comment. I might have been dictating statistics. I would dictate
some phrase that I thought was blood-curdling; he would
quietly take this down, look up at me and in a dry voice say,
'What next?' "

In his memoir of Ernest Hemingway, *Papa Hemingway*, A. E.
Hotchner asked the novelist about his working methods. Hemingway explained that he liked to start early ("I've seen every
sunrise of my life") and that his first task was to re-read and edit
everything he'd written up to that point. In this way he went
through a book "several hundred times". He set great store by
editing, "honing [the stuff] and honing it until it gets an edge
like the bullfighter's *estoque*, the killing sword. One time my
son, Patrick brought me a story and asked me to edit it for him. I
went over it carefully and changed one word. 'But, Papa,'
Mousy said, 'you've only changed one word.' I said, 'If it's
the right word, that's a lot.' "

Index of Writers

Dates and very brief biographical details of most of the writers mentioned in this anthology are given below, together with the titles of some of their principal works.

Alcott, Louisa May (1832–88) US author, friend of Emerson and Thoreau and campaigner for women's suffrage; best known for her autobiographical novel *Little Women*.

Aubrey, John (1626–97) Early biographical writer and anti-quarian/archaeologist; *Aubrey's Brief Lives* is the source of many anecdotes about writers and other public figures of the 16th–17th centuries.

Auden, W(ystan) H(ugh) (1907–73) British-born, US-nat-uralized poet; key post-war writer and essayist, very influ-ential on his own and later generations of poets; works include plays and librettos; *Letters from Iceland; The Shield of Achilles; About the House; The Age of Anxiety*.

Austen, Jane (1775–1817) Satirical and comic novelist; still remarkably popular (partly because of film and TV adapta-tions of her work) as well as being the subject of constant critical reappraisal; *Pride and Prejudice; Emma; Mansfield Park; Persuasion*.

Bacon, Francis (1561–1626) Elizabethan/Jacobean lawyer; statesman and writer on philosophy and science; *Essays, The New Atlantis*.

Beckett, Samuel (1906–89) Dublin-born novelist and playwright; achieved worldwide recognition with bleakly absurdist play *Waiting for Godot*; awarded Nobel Prize for Literature in 1969; *Molloy; Krapp's Last Tape; Breath*.

Beckford, William (1759-1844) Eccentric and very wealthy art collector and creator of grandiose architectural constructions; author of several travel books and of one significant fantasy novel, *Vathek*.

Bennett, (Enoch) Arnold (1867–1931) Dramatist and novelist; highly successful and acclaimed "realist" writer of early 20th century; *The Old Wives' Tale, Clayhanger; Riceyman Steps*.

Bok, Edward (1863–1930) Dutch-born US writer, journalist and editor; his autobiography *The Americanization of Edward Bok*, describing his association with many famous literary figures, was awarded the Pulitzer Prize (1920).

Boswell, James (1740-95) Scots-born diarist, best known as the tireless friend and first biographer of Dr Johnson; *The Life of Samuel Johnson*.

Bronte, Charlotte (1816–55) Oldest of the three Bronte sisters, daughters of Patrick Bronte, curate of Haworth, Yorkshire; achieved immediate success with her second novel *Jane Eyre*; other novels include *Villette* and *Shirley*.

Bronte, Emily (1818-48) Sister to Charlotte and Anne Bronte; Emily was also a poet but is remembered for her one novel, *Wuthering Heights*.

Browning, Elizabeth Barrett (1806–61) Poet; most famous for her part in the Victorian literary romance, her elopement with Robert Browning; *Sonnets from the Portuguese; Aurora Leigh*.

Browning, Robert (1812–89) Poet and husband of Elizabeth Barrett Browning with whom he famously eloped after her father wouldn't let them marry; *Men and Women; The Ring and the Book*.

Burney, Fanny (1752–1840) Novelist and journal and letter writer, spanning late 18th-century and pre-Victorian literary periods; admired by Jane Austen; *Camilla; Evelina*.

Burns, Robert (1759–96) Scottish writer acclaimed as the national poet; known for his use of dialect in verse; *Poems, chiefly in the Scottish Dialect*.

Burroughs, William (1914–97) US writer, once banned and reviled for his experimental writing, which was influenced by his drug addiction and homosexuality; later regarded as one of the grand old men of American literature; *Junkie; The Naked Lunch*.

Byron, George Gordon (Lord) (1788–1824) Wildly glamorous and charismatic figure who achieved mythic status across Europe in his lifetime; poet and hectic letter writer; died at Missolonghi in Greece before he could participate in Greek War of Independence; *Childe Harold's Pilgrimage; The Corsair; Don Juan.*

Caine, (Thomas Henry) Hall (1853–1931) Novelist and friend of Victorian poet Dante Gabriel Rossetti; his *Recollections of D. G Rossetti* is an entertaining source of anecdotes about the period.

Carlyle, Thomas (1795–1881) Scots-born historian and social theorist; *The French Revolution; Sartor Resartus.*

Carroll, Lewis (1832–98) Real name Charles Lutwidge Dodgson; lecturer in mathematics at Christ Church, Oxford, famous eccentric and creator of *Alice's Adventures in Wonderland* and *Through the Looking-Glass*; these two "children's" novels reflect Carroll's interest in games, riddles and skewed logic.

Chandler, Raymond (1888–1959) US crime writer and screen writer; creator of Philip Marlowe, private detective of battered integrity; *The Big Sleep; The Lady in the Lake; The Long Goodbye; Farewell, My Lovely.*

Chatterton, Thomas (1752–70) Bristol-born poet, famous for his imitations/forgeries of medieval verse; committed suicide by taking arsenic at age of 18; iconic figure seen by later Romantic poets as archetypal doomed writer, unappreciated in his lifetime.

Christie, Agatha (1891–1976) Prolific and enormously successful whodunnit writer and creator of super-sleuths Miss Marple and Hercule Poirot; *The Mysterious Affair at Styles; Who Killed Roger Ackroyd?; Murder on the Orient Express.*

Clare, John (1793–1864) Poet noted for his rural subject-matter; Clare went mad and spent large part of his life in Northampton General Asylum; *The Shepherd's Calendar.*

Cobbett, William (1763–1835) Radical campaigning journalist and writer; *Rural Rides.*

Coleridge, S(amuel) T(aylor) (1772–1834) Poet and literary critic; almost legendary figure in Romantic movement of early 19th century, and friend and literary collaborator of William Wordsworth with whom he co-wrote *Lyrical Bal-*

lads; opium addict; famous for individual poems like *The Rime of the Ancient Mariner, Christabel,* the abandoned *Kubla Khan.*

Collins, (William) Wilkie (1824–89) Mid-19th-century author of mystery and psychological romance; friend and literary collaborator of Charles Dickens; *The Moonstone; The Woman in White.*

Congreve, William (1670–1729) Playwright; one of circle of political/literary figures like Jonathan Swift and Richard Steele; *Love for Love; The Way of the World.*

Conrad, Joseph (1857–1924) Polish-born, British-naturalized novelist; spent early life as sailor and the sea forms background for much of his writing; influential writer whose work anticipates 20th-century political/colonial troubles; *Heart of Darkness; Nostromo; The Secret Agent.*

Coryate, Thomas (?1577–1617) Early English traveller who visited Europe (mostly on foot) and Far East; wrote story of his travels titled *Coryats Crudities, Hastily Gobbled up in Five Moneths Travells.*

Crabbe, George (1754–1832) Poet and clergyman; noted for realistic treatment of rural subjects; *The Village; The Borough.*

Crane, Stephen (1871–1900) US writer best known for his novel of the Civil War *The Red Badge of Courage*; Crane had no experience of war when he wrote it but later became war correspondent; died prematurely of tuberculosis.

Cumberland, Richard (1732–1811) Now forgotten 18th-century dramatist but source or target of some good stories.

D'Avenant, William (1606–68) Poet and playwright; encouraged the rumour that he was Shakespeare's illegitimate son; prominent Royalist supporter in Civil War; *The Wits.*

De Quincey, Thomas (1785–1859) Prolific essayist and biographical writer; friend of Romantic poets like William Wordsworth and S. T. Coleridge; best known for his account of his own drug addiction, *Confessions of an English Opium Eater*; *Recollections of the Lake Poets.*

Dickens, Charles (1812–70) Dominant 19th-century novelist but also journalist, campaigner and amateur actor; *Pickwick Papers; Nicholas Nickleby; Great Expectations; Tale of Two Cities; David Copperfield.*

Donne, John (1572–1631) Poet and priest, eventually Dean of St Paul's; noted for split in his verse between secular, often sexually charged poetry and later religious poems; *Satires; Songs and Sonets.*

Doyle, Arthur Conan (1859–1930) Edinburgh-born novelist and short story writer; trained and practised as doctor; Doyle wanted to make his name writing historical romances but achieved worldwide fame as creator of Sherlock Holmes and Dr Watson; *A Study in Scarlet; The Hound of the Baskervilles; The Lost World.*

Dryden, John (1631–1700) Prolific poet, dramatist and critic; appointed Poet Laureate in 1668; *All for Love; Absalom and Achitophel.*

Eliot, T(homas) S(tearns) (1888–1965) US-born, British-naturalized poet, dramatist and literary critic/theorist; major figure in 20th-century writing, highly influential in his ideas, style and subject-matter; awarded Nobel Prize for Literature in 1948; *The Waste Land; Murder in the Cathedral; The Cocktail Party; Four Quartets; Old Possum's Book of Practical Cats* (basis of Andrew Lloyd Webber's musical *Cats*).

Emerson, Ralph Waldo (1803–82) US poet, essayist and philosopher; sage or guru figure for his Wordsworth-like mystical beliefs and writings; *Nature and Representative Men.*

Evelyn, John (1620–1706) Diary writer and traveller; Evelyn's *Diaries* are valuable source of information about 17th-century events and characters.

Faulkner, William (1897–1962) US novelist who used his Mississippi roots as the basis for a sequence of novels exploring the clash between the old and new South; *As I Lay Dying; Light in August; Intruder in the Dust.*

Fielding, Henry (1707–54) Comic novelist and dramatist; London magistrate responsible for tackling early 18th-century crime wave; *Joseph Andrews; Tom Jones; Journal of a Voyage to Lisbon.*

Fleming, Ian (1908–1964) Wartime Naval Intelligence officer and later journalist; creator of the world's most famous fictional spy, James Bond; *Casino Royale; Dr No; From Russia With Love.*

Gardner, Erle Stanley (1889–1970) One-time US lawyer and pulp-magazine writer; later the prolific creator of 82 "Perry Mason" legal mysteries.

Gibbon, Edward (1737–94) Historian; *Decline and Fall of the Roman Empire.*

Goldsmith, Oliver (?1730–74) Poet, playwright and novelist; one of Dr Johnson's circle; *The Deserted Village; The Vicar of Wakefield; She Stoops to Conquer.*

Gosse, Edmund (1849–1928) Biographer and literary critic; friend of late Victorian, early 20th-century writers like Swinburne, Stevenson, Henry James; his fundamentalist Christian upbringing produced classic autobiography describing struggle against his father, *Father and Son.*

Gray, Thomas (1716–71) Poet and letter writer; *Elegy Written in a Country Churchyard.*

Greene, (Henry) Graham (1904–91) Leading 20th-century English novelist, travel writer and occasional playwright; *Stamboul Train; The Power and the Glory; Our Man in Havana; The Honorary Consul.*

Hardy, Thomas (1840–1928) Late 19th-century novelist and poet, who created "Wessex" as the setting for his work; *Far from the Madding Crowd; Tess of the D'Urbervilles; Jude the Obscure.*

Harington, Sir John (c1561–1612) Courtier, translator and wit; one story credits him with the invention of the flush toilet.

Harte, (Francis) Bret (1836–1902) US short story writer; early journalistic experience in San Francisco produced his best-known work; later settled in England after his reputation declined in America; *The Luck of Roaring Camp and Other Sketches.*

Hawthorne, Nathaniel (1804–64) US novelist and short story writer; resident in England while US consul in Liverpool; *The Scarlet Letter; The House of the Seven Gables.*

Haydon, Benjamin Robert (1786–1846) Painter but best known for his journals; at centre of literary circle which included Wordsworth and Keats; committed suicide in 1846.

Hazlitt, William (1778–1830) Essayist and critic; friend and disciple of older Romantic writers like S. T. Coleridge.

Heller, Joseph (1923–99) US novelist noted for his satirical, often savage books; *Catch-22; Something Happened; Good as Gold*.

Hemingway, Ernest (1899–1961) US novelist; war reporter; famous for macho pursuits like bull-fighting and deep-sea fishing; awarded Nobel Prize for Literature in 1954; *A Farewell to Arms; For Whom the Bell Tolls; The Old Man and the Sea*.

Henry, O. (1862–1910) US short story writer (real name William Sydney Porter), highly successful for his "twist-in-the-tail" pieces.

Herbert, George (1593–1633) Poet and clergyman; *The Temple*.

Howells, William Dean (1837–1920) US novelist and journalist; friend of Mark Twain and Henry James; *Literary Friends and Acquaintances*.

Hunt, (James Henry) Leigh (1784–1859) Poet, essayist and journalist; imprisoned for libelling Prince Regent; member of literary circles from Byron's time to Dickens'; "Jenny Kissed Me".

Ireland, William-Henry (1777–1835) Forger of Shakespeare documents and of complete "unknown" play, *Vortigern*, all produced while he was a teenager.

James, Henry (1843–1916) US-born, novelist, short story writer, dramatist and travel writer; British-naturalized just before his death; "difficult" but very highly regarded writer, made slightly more accessible by recent film adaptations; *Washington Square; Portrait of a Lady; The Golden Bowl; The Turn of the Screw*.

Johnson, Samuel (1709–84) The dominant figure in 18th-century literary London; poet, critic, editor, dictionary compiler, biographer, wit and conversationalist, and subject of many anecdotes; at centre of artistic/cultural/political circle which included writer Oliver Goldsmith, actor David Garrick, painter Joshua Reynolds; subject of first great biography, Boswell's *Life of Johnson*; Johnson's own writings include *Lives of the Poets, Rasselas, The Vanity of Human Wishes*.

Jonson, Ben (1572–1637) Elizabethan/Jacobean playwright and actor, contemporary of Shakespeare; wrote mostly realistic and satirical London-based comedy; *Volpone; The Alchemist; Bartholomew Fayre*.

Joyce, James (1882–1941) Dublin-born novelist and short story writer who spent most of creative life in Europe; highly influential figure in "modernist" movement who pioneered radical changes in narrative form; *The Dubliners; Ulysses; Finnegans Wake; A Portrait of the Artist as a Young Man.*

Keats, John (1795–1821) Archetypal Romantic poet with a key place in literary history despite his short life; London-born, Keats was apprenticed as a surgeon but turned to poetry in his early 20s; he wrote intensively, haunted by the tubercular history of his family; died of the disease in Rome; *The Eve of St Agnes; Lamia; Ode to a Nightingale; Ode to Autumn.*

Kelly, Michael (1762–1826) Dublin-born singer and stage manager; associate of Mozart (who wrote roles in *The Marriage of Figaro* for him) and of playwright Richard Sheridan; Kelly's *Reminiscences* is a good source of anecdotes about the period.

Kipling, Rudyard (1865–1936) Novelist, poet and short story writer; born in India and later worked as journalist there; awarded Nobel Prize for literature in 1907; *Plain Tales from the Hills; Kim; The Jungle Book.*

Lamb, Charles (1775–1834) Essayist and critic; co-author with sister Mary of *Tales from Shakespeare*; popular figure in literary circles; *Essays of Elia.*

Lawrence, D(avid) H(erbert) (1885–1930) Nottinghamshire-born novelist and short story writer; caused outrage in his day with frank treatment of sex, culminating in ban on his most explicit book *Lady Chatterley's Lover* (not openly published in UK until 1960); deeply serious writer and unorthodox thinker; *Sons and Lovers; The Rainbow; Women in Love.*

Lawrence, T(homas) E(dward) (1888–1935) Almost mythical figure who, as Lawrence of Arabia, participated in Arab struggle against Turkish rule during World War One; his account of it became his best-known book, *The Seven Pillars of Wisdom.*

Marlowe, Christopher (1564–93) Elizabethan playwright, killed in mysterious circumstances; *Edward II; Jew of Malta; Dr Faustus.*

Melville, Herman (1819–91) US novelist and poet; early experience at sea gave him background for several works; best-known work *Moby-Dick* has some claim (along with Twain's *Huckleberry Finn*) to be the "Great American Novel"; Melville's other works include *Typee, Billy Budd.*

Miller, Henry (1891–1980) US author, widely banned in his early days but later admired and imitated; noted for the experimentalism and sexual explicitness of his autobiographical writing; lover of Anais Nin; *Tropic of Cancer*; *Tropic of Capricorn; The Rosy Crucifixion.*

Milton, John (1608–74) Poet, pamphlet writer and (during Cromwell's time) politician/civil servant; author of perhaps most influential single poem in English literature, *Paradise Lost*, 12,000-line account of fall of mankind and expulsion from Garden of Eden; other works include *Comus, Paradise Regained, Samson Agonistes.*

More, Thomas (?1477–1535) Lawyer and author; created the imaginary country of *Utopia* in book of same name; became Lord Chancellor of England under Henry VIII; executed at king's orders in 1535.

Nin, Anais (1903–77) US writer and diarist, lover of Henry Miller, author of experimental novels and erotica; *Spy in the House of Love; Delta of Venus.*

Orton, Joe (1933–67) Leicester-born playwright; satirical and surreal writer who embodied subversive spirit of 1960s; *Entertaining Mr Sloane; Loot; What the Butler Saw.*

Pepys, Samuel (1633–1703) Famous for his *Diary*, written (in cipher) between 1660 and 1669; became secretary to the Admiralty and naval specialist.

Pope, Alexander (1688–1744) Satirical and philosophical poet; at centre of early 18th-century literary circle that included Jonathan Swift and John Gay; *The Rape of the Lock; The Dunciad.*

Raleigh, Walter (?1554–1618) Dynamic explorer, poet, historian of the Elizabethan/Jacobean age, eventually executed on the orders of James I.

Rochester, John Wilmot (Earl of) (1647–80) Satirical poet; member of the court circle surrounding Charles II; famous for rakish life and sexual explicitness of his poetry.

Rolfe, Frederick (1860–1913) Bizarre figure who took pseudonym "Baron Corvo" and whose best-known book, *Hadrian the Seventh*, describes how unknown Englishman is elected pope; inspired good literary "detective" story, A. J. A. Symons's *The Quest for Corvo*.

Rossetti, D(ante) G(abriel) (1828–82) Poet and painter of the mid-Victorian Pre-Raphaelite school; had body of his wife disinterred to recover poems buried with her; addicted to medical drug chloral; *Ballads and Sonnets*.

Savage, Richard (c.1697–1743) Playwright and poet, mostly remembered now for his unfortunate life (including being tried on charge of murder); subject of Samuel Johnson's *Life of Savage; The Wanderer*.

Scott, Walter (1771–1832) Edinburgh-born novelist and poet; immensely successful, influential and prolific "historical" novelist; took on debt created by publisher's bankruptcy and shortened own life by working strenuously to clear it; *Rob Roy; Ivanhoe; Redgauntlet; Marmion; Waverley*.

Shakespeare, William (1564–1616) Elizabethan/Jacobean playwright and shareholder in Globe playhouse (and the most famous author in the world); *Romeo and Juliet; Midsummer Night's Dream; Hamlet; Macbeth; The Tempest*.

Shelley, Mary (1797–1851) Author of *Frankenstein* and second wife of poet Percy Bysshe Shelley, to whose memory she devoted herself after his death by drowning; other novels include *The Last Man* and *Lodore*.

Shelley, Percy Bysshe (1792–1822) Archetypal poet of Romantic period; famously eccentric and source of many anecdotes; eloped with both first and second wives (see above); drowned in storm off north Italian coast in 1822; *The Mask of Anarchy; Adonais*.

Sheridan, Richard Brinsley (1751–1816) Playwright, theatre-manager, wit and politician; chronically short of money for most of his life, despite his success, he died in poverty; *The Rivals; The School for Scandal*.

Smollett, Tobias (1721–71) Comic novelist and travel writer; *The Adventures of Roderick Random; The Expedition of Humphrey Clinker*.

Southey, Robert (1774–1843) Poet and essayist; part of "Lake

Poets" circle, including William Wordsworth and S. T. Coleridge; became Poet Laureate in 1813; *The Vision of Judgement*.

Steele, Richard (1672–1729) Playwright, editor, essayist and politician; member of influential literary circle that included Jonathan Swift and Joseph Addison.

Sterne, Laurence (1713–68) Writer and clergyman; achieved overnight success with comic, almost experimental "novel" *Tristram Shandy*; also wrote *A Sentimental Journey*.

Stevenson, Robert Louis (1850–94) Edinburgh-born writer of novels, short stories and travel pieces; suffered from lifelong poor health and died at 44 on Pacific island of Samoa; *Treasure Island; Kidnapped; The Strange Case of Dr Jekyll and Mr Hyde*.

Stowe, Harriet Beecher (1811–96) US novelist and anti-slavery campaigner; best-known for *Uncle Tom's Cabin*.

Strachey, (Giles) Lytton (1880–1932) Biographer/historian; significant member of literary/cultural Bloomsbury Group, which included economist Maynard Keynes and writer Virginia Woolf; author of *Eminent Victorians; Elizabeth and Essex*.

Suckling, Sir John (1609–41) Poet, playwright and wit of pre-Civil war period; according to one story he invented the game of cribbage.

Swift, Jonathan (1667–1745) Dublin-born writer and clergyman; associate of Alexander Pope, John Gay and other early 18th-century literary figures; poet, pamphleteer and satirical writer; received payment (£200) for only one of his works, the most famous, *Gulliver's Travels*.

Swinburne, Algernon Charles (1837–1909) Poet and critic; eccentric, self-destructive figure eventually saved from early alcoholic death by living in suburban seclusion in Putney for last 30 years of his life; *Atalanta in Calydon; Poems and Ballads*.

Tennyson, Alfred (1809–92) The "national" poet of the Victorian era for works like "The Charge of the Light Brigade"; made Poet Laureate in 1850 after death of William Wordsworth; immensely popular, eventually given peerage; *In Memoriam; Idylls of the King*.

Thackeray, William Makepeace (1811–63) Novelist and journalist; received artistic training and contributed caricatures to comic magazine *Punch*; best known for humorous, satirical novel *Vanity Fair*; other novels include *Barry Lyndon; Henry Esmond.*

Thomas, R(onald) S(tuart) (1913–2000) Cardiff-born poet and clergyman; identified with "nationalist" movement in Wales.

Thrale, Hester (1741–1821) Friend of Dr Johnson; after death of her husband, wealthy brewer Henry Thrale, she re-married (to Johnson's distress); as Mrs Hester Lynch Piozzi she produced *Anecdotes of Samuel Johnson.*

Trelawny, Edward John (1792–1881) Adventurer and biographer of the Romantic poets; author of *Records of Shelley, Byron, and the Author.*

Trollope, Anthony (1815–82) Extraordinarily prolific and popular writer who also achieved success as senior civil servant in Post Office (he introduced the pillar box for letters); "realist" novelist who chronicled life in cathedral city (the Barchester sequence) and Victorian politics (the Palliser novels); *The Warden; Barchester Towers; Doctor Thorne; The Eustace Diamonds.*

Twain, Mark (Samuel Clemens) (1835–1910) US novelist, short story writer, journalist and travel writer (real name Samuel Langhorne Clemens); humorous and sometimes bitter satirist; creator of what some regard as the "Great American Novel" in *Huckleberry Finn*; other novels include *Tom Sawyer; A Connecticut Yankee in King Arthur's Court; Pudd'nhead Wilson.*

Walpole, Horace (1717–97) Son of Prime Minister Robert Walpole and prolific letter and memoir writer; author of one of the earliest Gothic fantasy novels, *The Castle of Otranto.*

Waugh, Evelyn (1903–66) English comic and satirical novelist; *Decline and Fall; Vile Bodies; Brideshead Revisited; The Loved One.*

Wells, H(erbert) G(eorge) (1866–1946) Prolific English novelist and controversial thinker; pioneer of science-fiction writing; *The Time Machine; War of the Worlds; The History of Mr Polly.*

West, Rebecca (1892–1983) Anglo-Irish novelist, essayist and travel writer (real name Cecily Isobel Fairfield); lover of H.

G. Wells; *The Return of the Soldier; The Meaning of Treason; The Birds Fall Down*.

Wharton, Edith (1862–1937) US novelist and short story writer; friend of Henry James with whom she shares some similarities of style and subject-matter; *The House of Mirth; Ethan Frome; A Backward Glance*.

Whitman, Walt (1819–92) Influential, iconic US poet who pioneered free, rhapsodic verse style; *Leaves of Grass; Drum Taps*.

Wilde, Oscar (1854–1900) Dublin-born dandy, wit, essayist and supreme comic playwright, eventually imprisoned for homosexual offences; *Lady Windermere's Fan; The Importance of Being Earnest*.

Wodehouse, P(elham) G(renville) (1881–1975) English-born, US-naturalized comic writer; creator of manservant Jeeves and his dim employer Bertie Wooster; *The Inimitable Jeeves; Carry on, Jeeves; The Heart of a Goof*.

Wordsworth, William (1770–1850) Key poet of Romantic period, who drew for much of his work on his upbringing in Lake District as described in autobiographical poem *The Prelude*; friend and literary collaborator of S. T. Coleridge with whom he co-wrote *Lyrical Ballads*; Poet Laureate for last 7 years of his life.

Wycherley, William (1641–1715) Restoration playwright and wit; *The Country Wife; The Plain-Dealer*.